Praise for *Always the Bridesmaid*

'Lively dialogue, strong female characters
with whom readers can happily identify'
Irish Times

'A real girlie page-turner that keeps you amused,
entertained and guessing until the final page'
Belfast Telegraph

'A realistic take on life, love and friendship'
Company Magazine

Praise for *Something to Talk About*

'Wickedly romantic comedy'
Sunday World

'An Irish version of *Friends*, well worth reading'
U Magazine

Praise for *Some Kind of Wonderful*

'A modern day fairy tale with the frogs
(and even the odd Prince Charming) included!'
U Magazine

'With two best-sellers already under her belt,
Webb's ta⬚⬚⬚⬚⬚⬚⬚⬚⬚⬚⬚⬚⬚⬚⬚⬚⬚⬚⬚⬚⬚⬚⬚⬚⬚⬚⬚

D0993451

Three Times a Lady
and
It Had To Be You

Sarah Webb worked in bookselling for over ten years, and is currently a children's book consultant. She lives in Dun Laoghaire, Co. Dublin, with her partner and young family. She reviews books for many Irish magazines and newspapers, and is featured regularly on Irish television's *The Den*. Her previous novels, *Always the Bridesmaid* and *Something to Talk About*, were number-one bestsellers in Ireland and she is currently working on her sixth novel, *Take a Chance*.

Find out more on her website www.sarahwebb.info.

Also by Sarah Webb

Always the Bridesmaid

Something to Talk About

Some Kind of Wonderful

Kids Can Cook

Kids Can Cook Around the World

Children's Parties

The Eason Guide to Children's Books

Sarah Webb

Three Times a Lady
and
It Had To Be You

PAN BOOKS

Three Times a Lady first published 2000 by Poolbeg Press, Ireland
This edition published 2004 by Pan Books
It Had To Be You first published 2005 by Macmillan
This edition published 2005 by Pan Books

This omnibus first published 2008 by Pan Books
an imprint of Pan Macmillan Ltd
Pan Macmillan, 20 New Wharf Road, London N1 9RR
Basingstoke and Oxford
Associated companies throughout the world
www.panmacmillan.com

ISBN 978-0-330-50805-6

1 3 5 7 9 8 6 4 2

A CIP catalogue record for this book is available from
the British Library.

Printed in the UK by CPI Mackays, Chatham ME5 8TD

Three Times a Lady

Dedicated to Sam, now and forever

It is not because things are difficult that we do not dare; it is because we do not dare that they are difficult.

Seneca

My thanks as always to my wonderful family, Mum, Dad, Kate, Emma, Peter, Richard, Luan and Charlie. And to my own mini family, Ben, Sam and Amy-Rose.

To Tanya Delargy, Nicky Cullen and Andrew Algeo who have been there for me from the very beginning.

To Ali Gunn, my agent for all her encouragement and enthusiasm. And also to Stephanie Thwaites.

To Gaye Shortland, my first fiction editor, who rang me after reading three chapters of *Three Times a Lady* and told me just how much she liked it – a phone call I'll never forget. And to Imogen Taylor, Trish Jackson, David North, Dave Adamson, Emma Bravo and everyone in Pan Macmillan for all their hard work and for believing in me.

To all the booksellers who have helped me along the way, especially the gang in Eason.

And last, but certainly not least, to my son, Sam, who let me write this one when I should have been playing with him. This one's for you, Sam.

To the Class of 1990
TEN-YEAR REUNION DINNER
AND DANCE

*Remember Peig, the life cycle of the Fasciola Hepatica
(otherwise known as the Liver Fluke), the 'Stony grey soil
of Monaghan', crop rotation in the 17th century . . .*

*Remember Mark 'The Man' Mulhearne, Mad Maxie,
Ice Eve, Monty, Minnow, Lucy the Lips, Nicely Nicky
or Mustang Sally?*

*Relive those classic memories, dine and dance to
the music of the '80's in the 'Ballroom of Romance'
(the sports hall!).*

*GUEST SPEAKERS:
Gerry O'Reilly of 2FM and Mark Mulhearne, class of 1990
barrister and best-selling author.*

*Be there or be somewhere else and missing
out on all the fun . . .*

OCTOBER 31   BLACK TIE RSVP

Chapter 1

Sally Hunter slowly opened her eyes. Bright Caribbean sunlight in golden shafts was piercing through the round portholes and reflecting off the shining white chart table and polished metal surfaces. Even the dark varnished interior wood seemed to funnel light into her pupils. Sally winced and narrowed her eyes. She turned her head slowly and carefully and surveyed the floor of the yacht's cabin. It was littered with cigarette butts and empty beer-cans. An empty Mount Gay Rum bottle was lodged against the chart table held in place by a large, man-sized brown Timberland docksider. The unpleasant odour of stale drink and smoke filled the 'living-room' of the luxury 60 foot Swan yacht.

"Sal!" a voice yelled from the deck above. A tousled, blonde-headed girl appeared at the hatch.

"Not so loud, Ginny," Sally muttered.

Ginny smiled and padded down the wooden steps into the cabin. Small, brown as a berry, with the mad energy of a three-year-old, Ginny was the crazy

Corkwoman who worked with Sally on *Queen of the Sea*. Wearing a plain white T-shirt, an indecently tiny pair of cut-off jeans masquerading as shorts and an ancient pair of docksiders, Ginny still managed to look stunning. With long white-blonde hair cascading down her back, shockingly clear, tanned skin, striking green eyes and a smile to stop the traffic, Ginny was a natural beauty. Sally found it sickening, but forgave her because to top it all she was the nicest and kindest girl you could meet and more fun than a basket full of puppies. She even drank Mel, the middle-aged playboy owner of *Queen*, under the table.

"Oh, Sal," Ginny whispered, as her eyes roamed around the cabin, settling finally on the makeshift 'bed' on the floor. "You didn't."

For a split second Sally was reminded of her mother.

* * *

"Oh, Sally, you haven't," spluttered Mrs Hunter, one summer's morning in the vicarage kitchen four years ago. "Is it the exam pressure? You know, darling, I'm sure you'll get them this year."

Sally tried to silence her shocked mother and explain why she had dropped out of her Teacher Training Diploma at UCD. She had failed the exams last June, badly enough to necessitate her repeating the whole year. But exam stress wasn't the reason and if her mother would stop blustering and fussing for one minute she would try to explain.

"Oh my, what will I tell your father?" Mrs Hunter

continued. "Oh Sally, he'll be so disappointed, he so wanted you to succeed this time."

"But, Mum . . ." Sally tried to interrupt her mother's flow, but she had as much chance as stopping lava flowing from a newly erupted volcano.

"Sally, it's just so . . ."

Sally tried again. "I know it's hard to understand, Mum, but if you'll just let me . . ." But it was no use.

"What will we tell the parishioners? They were so proud of you, Mrs Bailey in the choir and Mrs O'Reilly who does the flowers and . . . oh dear, oh dear, whatever to do, what a thing, what a thing . . ."

"Mum," said Sally firmly, "it's not the end of the world, please be reasonable."

But by now April Hunter was pacing up and down the kitchen, wringing her hands and talking to the ceiling above the central light fitting.

When Sally and her younger brother and sister, Jamie and Emma, were small they thought that God lived in that very same light fitting. Mrs Hunter had a habit of addressing 'The Lord' through her kitchen ceiling.

"What to do? Oh Lord, please help me."

"Ah, Mum," Sally sighed, completely exasperated at the overwrought woman, "it's not that bad, I have a great contingency plan . . ."

Just then the Reverend Hunter came striding into the kitchen from his study, where he was trying to write next Sunday's sermon on 'Family Values in a Modern World'.

"Commotion, commotion! How is a body supposed to work around here?"

The tall, silver-haired man looked enquiringly at his fraught wife. James Hunter, was a good husband and father. Endowed with endless reserves of patience, he was quite used to his dear wife's histrionics.

"Now what's all this about, April?" he asked firmly.

April Hunter took a deep breath and began. "Sally has dropped out of college and as if that isn't bad enough, she's decided to join a convent . . ."

Sally looked at her mother in amazement and began to laugh.

"Ah, Mum," she giggled. "I didn't say convent, I said contingency."

James held his hands up in a gesture of peace. He calmly addressed his wife and daughter.

"Now, April, knowing our daughter I think a convent is possibly the worst place in the world for her. Let's just listen to Sally about all this and see what she has to say."

They sat down at the kitchen table and Sally unfolded her plan. She explained why she had made this unusual decision. Her mother was less than enthused with what she was hearing. The prospect of telling the neighbours about her 'drifter' daughter did not amuse her. But Mr Hunter was practical and realistic to the last.

"Sally has to find her own way in this world, April. We may not like it but she has to make her own decisions – she's a big girl now."

Relations with her mother since Sally had left Ireland for Antigua had been decidedly frosty, thawing a little from time to time – at Christmas and birthdays. Of course she never failed to write if there was what she considered 'news', which always meant the engagement of someone who had been in school with Sally, or a neighbour's child's promotion in the bank or, lately, which local Protestant boy was single! All of which made Sally less and less keen to return home. Until the news of Mark and the reunion of course.

* * *

Sally removed the large bronzed hand from her left breast. She twisted away from the heavily sleeping body beside her and sat up gingerly. Spying her crumpled T-shirt on the cabin floor near her she reached over and scooped it up. Naked torso covered, she carefully stood up. The man beneath her groaned in his sleep and rolled towards the middle of the opened-out sofa which was masquerading as a bed. His dark-skinned back was smooth and muscular and moved gently with the steady rhythm of his breathing. Sal glanced down at her jeans in disgust. They were covered with beer stains, dried sea salt, old rust and paint marks. The sleeping prince's dark blue 501's were still immaculate. "Typical," she thought to herself. Ginny was sitting on the navigation table, gazing in amazement at the sleeping shape.

"Sal, do you know who that is?" she whispered.

"Of course I do – that's Jay, Mel's accountant," Sally replied triumphantly, delighted that she'd remembered his name.

"Like hell it is," muttered Ginny darkly. "Sal, he's

7

darling daughter's fiancé!"

A small smile came to Sally's lips, widening slowly into a deliciously wicked grin.

"I don't believe you, Ginny,' she whispered. "Are you serious?"

The two Irish girls hated their boss Mel's only daughter Iona with a passion. An arrogant little madam of twenty-one, she loved to lord it over the two friends, bossing them about and packing her rich and stupid girlie 'friends' onto 'Daddy's yacht' to sunbathe. Iona in turn hated her father's boathands as she didn't have a clue how to hoist a sail, let alone how to sail the yacht. So if Iona wanted to leave the marina she had to ask Sally and Ginny for assistance. And how she hated asking them for anything! It didn't help that Sally had once forced the spoilt girl to break two precious long, red talons by making her winch in a rope. Or that Ginny had refused to tack the boat because Iona complained that the sun was hidden behind the sail.

"Iona," the Corkwoman had yelled, "we're on a set course and I'm not turning *Queen* unless it's important.'

Iona, in the shadow of the large mainsail for what seemed to her an age, had missed valuable sunbathing time, not to mention losing face in front of her giggling friends.

To add insult to injury Sally had quipped, "Hey, Iona, this is a sailing machine not a tanning parlour."

The girls climbed up the wooden steps from the cabin.

The sun's rays hit their faces as they stepped onto the immaculately varnished wooden deck. Ginny closed over the hatch to the cabin.

"Let Prince Charming sleep," she said laughing. "Anyway, where did you find him?"

The two girls settled themselves comfortably, Sally sitting with her back against the thick wooden mast and her friend lying on her stomach facing her with her head resting on her hands.

"On the marina yesterday evening around seven, I guess," Sally replied, grinning widely. "He came by to have a look at *Queen* with Mel and we chatted briefly. I was washing down the deck after Princess Iona spilt sun-cream all over it in the afternoon. She knows that greasy muck she uses is hard to clean off, little cow."

Ginny murmured in agreement.

"Anyway Mel and Iona were meeting Mel's ex-wife up in the hotel, the second one I think, not the first one – wife I mean, not hotel!"

Ginny laughed.

"So Jay hung around a bit and one thing led to another. After all he had a rather nice smile, and ass for that matter. I thought it would have been a shame to waste it, you know."

Ginny knew all right. She knew only too well. Sally liked men and they liked her. Feeling something digging into her hip, through her shorts, she suddenly remembered why she had been looking for her friend. She rolled over and wriggled a folded white envelope from her tight, cut-off jean's pocket.

"Post for you," she said. "Sorry, I almost forgot. It's from home." She flattened the envelope with the palm of her hand and passed it to Sally.

Sally glanced at the writing and grimaced. "It's from Mum," she muttered, ripping open the envelope. As she pulled out the letter a bright white rectangular card fell onto the brown deck. It seemed to glisten and glow against the dark wood. Sally picked up the card and read it, her face a picture of growing astonishment.

"Well?" asked Ginny, gagging to hear the news, "What's up?" She gazed at the animated girl questioningly.

"You remember the guy I once told you about – Mark Mulhearne?"

Ginny nodded eagerly.

"He's only the guest speaker at my ten-year school reunion!"

"OK, let me get this right – Mark is the guy you were in love with in sixth year? The one you've never forgotten?" Ginny asked. "The one who lives in Boston and writes those amazing crime books?"

"Yes, yes," Sally answered impatiently as she began to read her mother's accompanying letter. As usual it was written in purple ink on lilac paper – as Sally described it 'an insult to the discerning eye and a horror to decipher'.

Suddenly Sally exclaimed. "Mum's an angel!"

Ginny snorted. "Only last week you wrote her off as an annoying snob and a gossip, if I remember correctly."

Sally's smile lit up her face. Her eyes danced with excitement and she could hardly contain herself. "That's before she used her jungle drums usefully. For once she is telling me news I want to hear."

"Go on," Ginny goaded her dizzy friend. "I'm waiting, what is it? This amazingly interesting news?"

Sally took a deep breath and exhaled slowly. "It's Mark. He's back in Ireland. Mum met his sister, Susan, on Grafton Street." Sally continued breathlessly. "And guess what? He's staying with her and her family on their farm in Wicklow. And get this – best of all, God bless her cotton socks for asking Susan, he's broken up with that 'Park ma car in Haavard yard' Boston creature. Mum reckons Mark's coming home to find an Irish wife! Good old Mum, always on the ball!" Sally really was impressed. Usually her Mum's insatiable curiosity and matchmaking tendencies drove her up the wall but this time it was different. Hell, Mark was the future Mr Hunter and that's all there was to it!

Sally's mind began to drift. She imagined herself in a cream sheath Sharon Hoey wedding dress, with a tasteful bouquet of white roses. Walking up the aisle, with Mark by her side. He would be wearing a grey morning suit, with a waistcoat, perhaps in red or maybe gold . . .

"Earth calling Sally, come in Sally!" Ginny interrupted her friend's reverie. "I asked you if you're going to the school thing, the reunion?"

"Are you joking? Of course I'm bloody going, you thick culchie."

Ginny thumped the smiling girl's leg.

"Ah, there's no need for violence now," Sally continued. "It's my big chance, Ginny, damn right I'm going! Mrs Mulhearne, here I come."

Her eyes flickered and danced as a wild and bold plan began to concoct in her mind. "It just might work," she said. "He won't know what's hit him, poor man."

"God help the guy," Ginny said, trying to keep a straight face. "He won't stand a chance with Mustang Sally."

Chapter 2

Eve Arnold removed her Calvin Klein reading glasses and placed them on the green leather-covered mahogany desk in front of her. She leaned back in her plush black leather chair and rubbed her tired eyes with her knuckles. Glancing at the brass ship's clock on the wall she realised with a start that it was nearly eleven o'clock. She had been in the office since seven that morning – sixteen hours. But as far as Eve was concerned that was nothing new.

The petite woman was immaculately dressed in a sharply cut Louise Kennedy on-the-knee skirt in efficient 'New York' grey. Her dark brown hair was tightly cut to her head in an elfin, yet smart style. She pushed herself up from the large, curved desk and straightened up her papers. She looked triumphantly at the empty 'in' tray to her left and pressed off the power buttons on her black computer and screen. Striding over to the door, she slid her size twelve Louise Kennedy jacket off its wooden hanger and shimmied it over her cream silk shirt.

The fax machine under her window whirred into action and spat out a new document. Eve sighed and walked over to receive it.

Giving it a cursory glance, she scrunched it up into a tight ball and dropped it into the wicker bin. The Financial Services Centre were having a Masked Ball in the Burlington for all its 'residents'. Eve didn't have the time for such frivolities, or so she liked to tell herself. In reality Eve, the successful, cool and confident accountant for Viva Notre, the Italian bank, a woman in a man's world, giving as good as she got, was above all lonely.

Eve's town house was an immaculately decorated, two-bedroom professional 'home'. If you could call it a home. The walls were painted in tasteful shades of white and varying degrees of off-white. The hall was terracotta and the generous upstairs bathroom was a delicate shade of eggshell blue. Eve had chosen the colours herself, something she had approached in a businesslike manner, but at times a definite artistic streak had come peeking out, inherited from her mother. The furniture was modern yet functional. The living-room boasted generous sofas in cream brocade. Dramatic original oil paintings and silk-screen prints in striking colours from the Solomon Gallery adorned her walls. And in her bedroom the French-designed wicker King-sized bed, topped with a sky blue duvet and piles of blue and white covered cushions, dominated the room. The second bedroom functioned as an office.

Eve had two bedrooms because she could afford them, not because she had anyone to share the space with. She lived on her own, using her house more like a hotel than her own special retreat from the world. From Monday to Saturday she worked and on Saturday evening she packed a small overnight bag and ordered a taxi. Because every weekend, unless she was away on business or at a business dinner, she went to stay with her mother.

Mrs Betty Arnold was a widow and had a close relationship with her daughter. She lived comfortably in a small cottage in Sandymount, on the coast road. She owned a beautiful golden retriever called Sam, who she walked on the strand religiously every morning. The remainder of her day was spent doing what she loved best – decorating houses, giving classes in interior design, rescuing old furniture and renovating it with loving care.

* * *

Tom Arnold had died when Eve was six, leaving a vibrant widow in her late twenties – a tall, willowy blonde with a striking face – strong, square cheekbones, full, rose-red lips, dark blue eyes and olive skin. Betty had married straight out of school and was devoted to her older husband, who treated her with love and respect. She had been distraught when he had died of a heart attack when he was only forty. But with the help of close friends and the distraction of a child to love and comfort she pulled herself through the ordeal, day by day.

Luckily Tom had been an organised and practical man and had ensured his loved ones would live comfortably in the event of his death. Not needing to work, Betty threw herself into rearing her child. She ironed everything from dusters to knickers, polished any metal, glass or wooden surface in their large Georgian house in Rathgar until it sparkled. The garden was immaculate, the shrubs were trimmed into perfectly symmetrical shapes and the flower beds were filled with the correct seasonal flowers and plants. And Eve was the smartest turned-out child in Ireland, with gleaming shoes and the whitest starched shirts. After a year the house was a veritable showcase, but Betty was bored.

One Sunday morning when Eve was nine, Betty looked around the cleanest kitchen in Ireland and made a decision. The next week she put her 'elegant and tastefully decorated family home, convenient to the city centre' up for sale. Then, to the astonishment of her friends, she bought a run-down cottage in need of well . . . everything. The optimistic estate agents had described it as a 'challenge' in their brochure. The small property in Sandymount needed re-wiring, re-plumbing, re-plastering, re-flooring. In fact nothing was in any way salvageable except the four walls and miraculously, under the green moss covering, the original dark grey slates and tall Victorian terracotta chimney pots.

But the widow had taken one long look at the

ramshackle cottage and had smiled, much to the astonishment of the young man from Wilson's Estate Agents who was showing her the house.

"What character," the tall woman stated, on first gazing at the exterior of 3 Sandymount Villas. "Lead on."

The young man turned the key in the rusting lock and pushed the door open with his right shoulder.

"Sorry, the door's a bit stiff . . ." he muttered anxiously.

Inside the house was in a shambles. There was no carpet in the hall and the bare floorboards seemed decidedly dangerous.

"Watch your step, Mrs Arnold," warned the estate agent.

But Betty had noticed the original stained glass in the fan light over the door, the delicate egg and dart mouldings at the top of the walls and the heavy, old pine doors with stained glass panels. Here was a house which needed tender loving care. It would provide her with something that her daughter, as she grew older and became more and more self-sufficient, could no longer provide. A reason for getting up in the morning. Betty Arnold was sold!

The newly energised woman threw herself into renovating the cottage from top to tail. She engaged the services of an enthusiastic young local carpenter and builder, Sean Connolly, who specialised in renovations. Together they spent many happy mornings, while Eve was schoolbound, trawling architectural salvage shops for original Victorian features.

Betty sanded and varnished the replaced floorboards, supervised the stripping, plastering and re-painting of the walls. She chose rich, glowing colours – deep red in the hall, sunflower yellow in the kitchen and a bold turquoise blue in the bathroom. She designed the bedroom wallpaper herself and had it exclusively printed for her in London: an elegant yet vibrant pattern of abstract flowers in blues, yellows, reds and purples. Eve had enjoyed helping her mother decorate the cottage at the weekends. Surprisingly Eve, an earnest young girl, found living in an unfinished house, 'a work in progress' as her Mum described it, fun and marvelled at her mother's gradual transition from a 'take your shoes off before you come in' type of Mum to a ' watch the sawdust on the floor, love, I stepped in it earlier' type. Eve, a hard-working and dedicated pupil, admired her mother's energy and dedication to her task.

A year after the Arnolds had first moved into their new home, Betty was finally satisfied. She held a drinks party to show off her stunning work. Some of Betty's 'friends' were less than impressed with the light, airy, liveable-in house. The smart set, Brown-Thomas-suited women, were used to rich brocade fabrics, velvet curtains, dark green walls and Laura Ashley or imitation William Morris wallpaper. This house was more *Cosmopolitan* than *Country House* or *House and Home*. Where were the gold light fittings, the brass taps, where was the glamour, the old-world elegance?

The women at the party sighed, clucked and whispered among themselves. But some guests were full of admiration.

"Betty," a tall, well-built man with dark hair peppered with grey and a wide, firm smile approached her. "My son was right, quite a place you have here. I'm Jack Connolly, Sean's father. I hope you don't mind, I came to have a look."

Betty smiled shyly at him, and thought to herself, "Mumm, must be early fifties I guess, and what a nice smile." It was the first time since her husband had died that she had felt any interest in any man and she was caught off guard. Sean had mentioned his father, a respected architect, but she had thought nothing of it at the time. Mr Arnold was happily married – what was she thinking?

"Oh no, not at all," she replied, blushing and feeling decidedly flustered. "I'm afraid I must open some more bottles of red . . ."

Jack Connolly followed Betty into the kitchen. He lifted one of the bottles of Bordeaux off the pine kitchen table and opened it for her.

"You've really captured a fresh, modern look, Betty. It's contemporary yet homely. Have you ever thought of interior design as a career?"

Betty stammered, "That's very flattering, Jack, but I'm sure you're just being kind."

"Not at all Betty," he continued. He lifted two wine bottles out of Betty's hands, set them on the table and pulled out a kitchen chair, newly upholstered in red corduroy.

"Sit and listen for one second," he commanded firmly.

Betty sat and looked up at him expectantly.

"I mean it, you have a real eye for design. Quite frankly your ideas are exciting and at times daring." He looked around him. "The wall colours for example – clean, crisp and modern. The way you have integrated contemporary features with traditional materials. Sorry, I'm beginning to talk like an architect," he laughed. "And these chairs, they're great, where did that idea come from?" He gestured towards the kitchen chairs, jauntily covered in a rainbow of colours – poppy red, golden yellow and jewel-like green and purple. Before she had a chance to answer he powered ahead. "Betty, please tell me you will do something with your gift."

"Jack, I did it for the sheer enjoyment. Getting paid for decorating . . . well, that's another matter. To be honest, I'm not looking for a career or even a job," she stated hesitantly, a little overwhelmed by his enthusiasm. "Anyway, I've never had a job, I wouldn't know where to start."

"Well," Jack replied thoughtfully. "Start small, with commissions for friends. Maybe try an ad in the local supermarket." He paused for a moment, rubbing his strong, square chin. "In fact I think I have just the right job to get you started . . . yes, I think it would definitely work."

Three days later Betty had started work on an

apartment beside the Four Courts which Jack had recently purchased. Nessa Connolly, Jack's wife, was delighted with her husband's choice of interior designer. A small, bubbly redhead in her late thirties, originally from Northern Ireland, Nessa soon became firm friends with Betty.

Number 44, Four Courts Square, was a joy to decorate. A large, newly built modern penthouse, it was ideally suited to Betty's clean, airy colours. Nessa helped choose the furniture and together the two women gave the apartment a distinctive and striking look.

* * *

Eve opened the door of her townhouse and flicked on the uplights. She stepped out of her Italian leather court shoes and allowed the natural coir flooring to massage her weary feet. She picked up her shoes and placed them at the end of the stairs. There was post on the floor, the usual brown windowed bills and glossy, loud junk mail and one large rectangular, hand-written envelope. Eve walked into the kitchen, placed her black Chesneau brief-case and the envelopes on the sand-blasted glass kitchen table and made herself a cup of instant coffee. The kitchen, designed by her mother, was wasted on someone who didn't cook. It was perfectly laid out for ease of use, from the sea-green storage cupboards to the top of the range American silver fridge and gleaming silver gas cooker. The walls were cream, tiled above the granite counters in hand-made matt blue tiles. The lighting was mellow and relaxing when dimmed and Eve loved the sculptured, curving Habitat kitchen chairs in pastel shades.

Sitting down, Eve reached for the letters. She glanced at her Visa and American Express bills and set them aside. The hand-written envelope looked a little more interesting.

"Dear class of 1990," she read. *"Remember Peig, the life cycle of the Fasciola Hepatica . . ."*

Eve read on until her eyes focused on that one name: Mark Mulhearne. A rush of blood shot to her head and she felt dizzy and slightly sick. Old memories came flooding back, of that strong face with navy blue eyes, of the blonde hair and that smile. Of the smile to make you smile back and really mean it, no matter how bad you were feeling. And of the way he used to look at her, Eve Arnold. It seemed like a whole lifetime ago.

Eve pressed the small of her back into her chair and closed her eyes, blinking back the tears that threatened to tumble down her cheeks.

"Oh, Mark," she whispered to herself. "What was I thinking of?"

She sat still, allowing the memories of a former, happier time to flood into her head and assault her senses. It was almost as if she was a spectator, watching her own past from the sidelines.

She winced as she heard those brutal, sharp and hurtful words which had sealed both their fates.

"I'm sorry, Mark, but it's over and that's final."

Eve's head pounded. But at the back of her mind the tiny seed that the reunion invitation had planted had begun to grow. The whisper of a smile began to form on her tightly pursed lips.

"Mark Mulhearne," she thought. 'Well, stranger things have happened . . ."

Chapter 3

"Daniel, please stop that jumping, I'm trying to write." Ashling smiled up at her bouncing six-year-old who was using the bed as a trampoline. "I'm sorry, pet, but I have to get this finished before I go to sleep and I still have to type it up, do you understand?"

The small blonde boy stopped suddenly halfway through a jump, landed on his back and scrunched up his bright blue eyes tightly. The bed shook with the impact and Ashling looked over at her young son.

"I'm pretending to be asleep, Mummy, and I'll be asleep for sixteen hundred seconds, OK?"

Ashling laughed to herself – he was a panic. "OK, Dan, I'll tell you what. You stay asleep and I'll wake you when the time is up."

She scribbled frantically for a few minutes before glancing over at her strangely silent son. He was fast asleep, his little face the picture of innocence, rosy red cheeks framed by a shock of messy golden hair. She folded the white antique lace-covered duvet over his small body, right up to his chin. She breathed a long sigh of relief. Ashling loved her son with all her heart but he always left her completely exhausted by the end of the day.

It wasn't easy being a single Mum. As a busy journalist she spent her life juggling work and Daniel. Sometimes it felt as if she had too many balls suspended in the air at once and it was only a matter of time before they all came crashing down on top of her head, giving her major concussion.

Daniel was the centre of her universe but sometimes Ashling felt guilty. Guilty for working, guilty for not providing Dan with a Dad, guilty that she snapped at him sometimes because she was tired or fed up. One night Ashling had fallen asleep on her bed fully clothed, shoes and all. Daniel had removed her shoes, pulled the duvet over her, put on his pyjamas, leaving his top unfastened as he couldn't get his fingers around small buttons yet, and put himself to bed. The next morning Ashling woke up. Daniel was standing beside her bed watching her.

"I don't think you should work so hard, Mummy," he had said in a serious little voice, "You get knackered."

Tears came to Ashling's eyes when she realised what had happened and she hadn't the heart to chastise him for using a 'bad word'.

Ashling stopped writing and read over her news piece for the following day's *Courier*. It had been a hectic morning and a manic afternoon and now she was dog tired. The County Council meeting to discuss the building of a new hotel in Dun Laoghaire had dragged on and on. When she was satisfied with her piece she climbed up the narrow stairs to her desk in the living-room and sat down in front of the computer.

Ashling and Daniel had lived in a converted stables in the gentle south Dublin 'village' of Dalkey for seven years. She had been lucky to find somewhere in such a nice area at such a reasonable rent, whose owner didn't balk at the sight of a small child. Her previous flat in Rathmines was totally unsuitable for a child. The other residents were all students and didn't understand how difficult it was to put a woken-up baby back to sleep at three in the morning. Ashling's Dalkey pad was ideal; she knew she was very lucky. The Stables was on the grounds of a larger house, Dalkey Manor. The owner was an eccentric widow called Mrs O'Connor or Tizzy as she insisted on being called, no one knew why. It was said that she and her husband had worked as secret agents or spies for the British in Russia during the Second World War. Tizzy certainly had fluent Russian and was one of the most astute and intellectual of people when she wanted to be. Ashling had never met the late Mr O'Connor, but she had spotted old photographs of a handsome young man in Army uniform on Tizzy's grand piano. Perhaps the rumours weren't that far-fetched after all.

The woman had taken a shine to the shy but determined blonde and her lively son. The O'Connor boys were both married and lived abroad, one in America and one in Australia, but neither had children.

The handsome widow longed for some company and underneath her crusty exterior and abrupt manner, lay one fascinating, loyal and ultimately kind lady. She had grown fond of Ashling over the years and had seen Daniel grow from a fractious toddler to a beaming six-year-old. And she had watched Ashling grow in confidence and blossom into an ambitious and spirited young woman. In many ways Tizzy thought that having a baby had been the making of the formerly timid girl. Daniel had focused the budding journalist's thoughts and made her hunger to succeed, for her beloved son.

* * *

Ashling was all alone in the world, with no family to fall back on, when she found herself a pregnant student at the age of twenty-one. She had been seeing Owen, a fellow Arts student from Galway, for several months. He was an attractive and charismatic young man of twenty, with long chestnut-brown hair and an intense and almost religious fervour for left-wing politics.

Ashling had been mildly concerned at the first missed period, convincing herself it was stress, exam worries, that kind of thing. By the third skipped month she had became more than anxious. She furtively bought a pregnancy-testing kit in the chemists opposite Trinity. She climbed the concrete stairs to the very top of the Arts Block and chose a cubicle in the deserted ladies' toilet. Hands shaking, she ripped the foil covering off the white plastic wand and positioned it in her urine stream.

"Shit," she muttered to herself as she sprinkled her hand.

Placing the wand on the floor in front of her, she dried her hand and watched the long piece of plastic which determined her fate.

The minutes crawled by agonisingly. Her eyes were glued to the small, clear window on the wand. Slowly a thin, blue line began to appear in the window. Ashling began to shake. Her eyes filled with tears and she felt physically sick.

Pregnant, she was definitely pregnant.

The next day she visited the college doctor. Perhaps the test had been wrong. There was always a chance, she hoped. But in her heart of hearts she knew it was highly unlikely.

"Well, young lady," the grey-haired doctor had said gently. "The test is positive." The doctor had then outlined her options. Ashling hadn't taken in one word; she was in complete shock. Leaving the surgery she had staggered to the nearest wooden bench in New Square and had sat for nearly three hours, her mind racing.

That evening Owen met her in the Buttery.

"Owen, we need to talk," she had whispered.

They had walked to Owen's bedsit on the quays in total silence. Owen had asked his pale and anxious girlfriend several general, conversation-opening questions but she either hadn't heard or had chosen not to reply. In reality Ashling was going over and over what she was going to say to him in her head.

"You're what?" Owen exclaimed when Ashling had

broken the news. "Jesus, Ash. You're joking, love. Ah, Ash, come here."

He reached over and put his arms around the now crying Ashling. They sat in silence on Owen's old, bumpy sofa for what seemed like an age.

"Ash, it's going to be fine, we'll work it out. I'll help you, you know that. We both know what has to be done."

Ashling lifted her head off Owen's Aran-sweatered chest and looked at him. "Owen, I don't want you to feel like you have to . . . you know marriage is a big step and . . ."

The young man seemed confused.

"Ash, love, I don't mean we have to get married. I mean . . . well, you know."

"No, Owen, I don't know," said Ashling quietly. "Why don't you tell me?"

"Ah, Ash. You've been on all the marches with me, the Pro-Choice ones. I thought, well, I thought that's what you'd do, you know."

Ash stared at him in genuine astonishment.

"Owen, damn right I went on the marches. And I am pro-choice. But choice means exactly that, choice. And abortion, which I presume you are referring to, would never, ever be my choice. I can't believe you've never listened to me."

They sat and stared into space. Ashling was distraught but also angry.

How dare he presume like that, she thought to herself, fuming.

29

Owen broke the silence.

"Ash, you know I love you. But I'm too young to be tied down with a kid. Jesus, I'm only a kid myself. And I've been thinking of taking a few years off. Maybe go to Oz or San Fran for a while. I could finish my degree later . . . I've been meaning to say it to you but . . ."

"But what, Owen?" Ashling spluttered. "I can't believe you. When were you going to tell me? From the airport. From where normal people call Australia or San Francisco?" Ashling suddenly stood up and faced her boyfriend. "I'm keeping this baby. With or without you."

Owen laughed. "Shit, love, you sound like a U2 song . . ." He stopped laughing as soon as he noticed the grim, stony face in front of him. "Sorry," he mumbled.

Ashling walked towards the door. "Good-bye, Owen," she said firmly, retaining her composure until she left the building, expecting him to be right behind her, apologising for his selfish and immature comments and behaviour. But he wasn't.

She then ran down the street in floods of tears, still hoping in her heart of hearts that Owen would come after her. But he didn't.

"That's it," she stated firmly to herself. She put her right hand under her jumper and rested it on her flat, smooth stomach. "It's just you and me now, baby," she whispered into the air. "Just you and me . . ."

Ashling had managed to pull herself through the living nightmare with the help of two special friends, Annie and Mark. Annie now worked with her in the *Courier* where she was Fashion Editor, and Mark . . . well, a strange thing had happened this morning which had made her think of that eventful day that seemed a lifetime ago when she had first met the student union Welfare Officer, Mark Mulhearne . . .

"Well, how can I help you? Ashling isn't it?" the Welfare Officer smiled at her kindly and clasped his hands on the battered old desk. His 'office' was nothing more than a glorified cupboard, with open shelves overflowing with thick files and legal books. The walls were covered with old Student Union election posters; the eager young candidates' faces had been embellished with huge curling moustaches, freckles and in one case a set of Dracula fangs.

The welfare officer, Mark Mulhearne, was considered very attractive although he liked to think he had been elected on talent alone. He had tousled dark-blonde hair, dark blue eyes, a beatific smile that lit up his whole face and a small diagonal scar on his upper lip. Mark loved his sabbatical job. He enjoyed helping students and it was excellent training for his chosen future career in law. A typical day involved anything from talking to college officials about the working order of the Arts Block lift for disabled students, to dealing with an irate and difficult landlord who was threatening to evict his 'hooligan' tenants for throwing an 'all night orgy' otherwise known as a Boat Club party!

Mark sensed that Ashling's problem was serious.

Her face was pale and drawn and there were dark, purple-tinted shadows under her eyes. She seemed very nervous and on the brink of tears. He had often noticed Ashling in the Buttery Bar in the evenings; they had been in the same year at school but in different classes. She had been a quiet, studious girl in school, shy perhaps now thinking back. But she had seemed more confident and happier in Trinity, Mark mused. He admired her style – silver-sprayed Doc Martin boots, colourful dark red tights teamed with short denim skirt and a soft, fitted red knitted top. A smile flickered over his lips – unusual-looking girl but definitely cute.

"I . . . I . . . need help," whispered Ashling. Her eyes were fixed on her hands which were clasped tightly on her knee. Mark gave her a few seconds to collect her thoughts.

"Tell me, what is it?" he asked gently.

"I'm pregnant and I . . . I don't know what . . . oh shit, I'm sorry," Ashling started to cry, in great heaving shudders. In seconds a torrent of tears was flooding down her face. "I'm sorry, I'm sorry," she sobbed.

Mark stood up and squeezed past the desk. He knelt down at Ashling's side, putting one arm around her shoulders and holding her now wringing hands in his large, strong clasp. "It'll be OK," he murmured. "Ashling, everything will be fine." He stayed by her side until her breathing had slowed and finally she had stopped crying. He then offered her a tissue from a box in his drawer.

She dried her face and screwed the sodden mass into a ball in her shaking hands. Her face was red and blotchy.

She finally looked up at Mark's compassionate and thoughtful face. It was as if he understood.

"It's going to be all right," he smiled. "Whatever you decide I'll help you. Ashling, you're going to be fine, trust me."

And she did trust him. And he was right. She was fine – with the help of her old friend Annie and her new friend, Mark. Ashling and Mark had become good friends after the initial meeting. He had given her a lot of practical support along the way plus emotional support and she had been very grateful for the help. As time went on they began to spend more and more time together. They spent happy days and nights, the three of them – herself , Mark and Daniel – feeding the ducks in Herbert Park, carrying Daniel up the Sugar Loaf and bumping the buggy over the potholes along Bray head. It was difficult for Ashling as her friends were all out most evenings, in the pub or at parties. She felt very isolated and alone. Mark seemed to recognise this and went out of his way to spend time with the young mother and her wonderful son. They had even kissed one strange, summer's night. But the next day he had left for the States. He had promised to write and Ashling had waited for a letter. And waited, and waited. She had tried writing to the address he had given her, but still she had received no reply. Eventually, she had resigned herself to the fact that he was not going to write . . . ever. So she had pushed Mark Mulhearne from her mind and got on with her life.

* * *

When Ashling had opened her invitation to the Class of 1990 Reunion and saw Mark's name his kindness and warmth had come flooding back to her. It all seemed like a lifetime ago and he had helped her in more ways than he could ever imagine. Ashling sighed. Why was the world so complicated? If only . . . still, there was no point in mulling over the past.

This article had to be finished tonight. Tomorrow morning she was interviewing the cantankerous male author of a controversial new travel guide to Ireland. John Maguire had condemned Dun Laoghaire as 'dirty, unfriendly and badly planned' much to the dismay and outcry of local councillors. Leary was a well-known old begrudger, with no time for 'young whippersnappers' or 'these new dolly-bird reporters' as he liked to call any young female journalist much to their collective disgust. Ashling knew she had her work cut out. As her slim fingers danced over the keys, her article began to take shape on the screen before her. Finally she was finished. With an aching neck and stinging, flickering eyes she was tired to the bone but content. It was a good, solid piece of writing. She saved the document, printed out a hard copy, popped the disk into her bag and shut down the computer for the night.

She tossed the last pieces of Daniel's train set into his wooden toy box. She straightened the rug on the wooden floor, winced as she spied a pool of pink strawberry yoghurt under the coffee table and after scooping it up with kitchen roll and plopping the whole lot in the bin, she made her weary way to bed.

She crawled between the bedcovers beside her sleeping son, too tired to lift him into his own bed, and quickly followed him to dreamland. And that night she dreamed she was waltzing around the old school gym hall in a shimmering red dress with a smiling Mark Mulhearne.

Chapter 4

Sally stared out the window of the Boeing 737. She gazed at the azure sky, the heat shimmering off the sticky black tarmacadam of the runway and the colourful uniforms of the Caribbean airport staff. Wistfully she let out a deep sigh. "Back to sunny, warm Ireland, I don't think!" she muttered to herself.

The stern businessman to her right glanced briefly at the bronzed girl. He then pulled his thin lips into a stiff smile for a split second and immersed himself in a newspaper. Sally was relieved in a way. She wasn't in the humour for polite chat.

Sally would miss the Carribbean weather terribly. She would miss the outdoor lifestyle, the daily sailing on clear blue seas, the evening walks, eating and drinking *al fresco* . . . she tried to prevent her agitated mind from going over and over the cons.

Right, concentrate on the good things about the old green sod, she said to herself.

Number one – green sods, excellent Sally. Now number two – a long cool pint of Guinness. Number three – um number three. Got it – Marky Mark the Man himself. Sally's musings were interrupted by the pilot's voice.

"Ladies and Gentlemen, we are now leaving Antigua for Dublin. It should be a pleasant flight, conditions are good. Dublin is a stable sixteen degrees with light rain."

A groan was emitted from her fellow passengers. Sally smiled. At least she wasn't alone in her thoughts!

Life in Dublin would be a million miles away from what she had become used to over the past few years. And in a way, although the madcap girl would never have admitted it to anyone, sometimes, only sometimes mind, she longed for a 'normal', regular life. What was happening? Maybe it was old age creeping up on her. But she wanted somewhere solid to call her own. Sally was, in her heart of hearts, ready to go home.

An attractive blonde air hostess began her safety talk. Sally watched with a vague, detached air. The hostess was pretty in a Barbie sort of way. Lots of hair piled on top of her head, bright pink lipstick and highly defined cheeks, blushered into shape. Her eyebrows were carefully plucked into thin, high arcs. Sally ran a finger critically along her own natural eyebrows.

A few moments later the plane was hurtling down the runway. Sally gasped as the G force pushed her back into her seat. She always hated this bit. She would never forget the first time she had flown, over ten years ago. She leaned back in her window seat and closed her eyes.

* * *

"Come on Sal, the others are already in the bar."

Sally followed her fellow team-mate, Jean, towards The Dubliner airport pub. Large stripy McWilliam sailing bags were slung over their shoulders, two each. The two girls also carried a long, blue canvas 'sausage' between them, containing a crisp new McWilliam sail. St John's sailing team had won the Irish school's final and were on their way to La Rochelle on the west coast of France, to the World School Championships.

Sally and Jean, a tall Howth girl with long dark hair which cascaded down her strong back, were the two girls on the six-'man' team. The duo wore their bright yellow sailing jackets complete with eagle symbols on the right sleeve (their school's crest) with pride. Although Sally's jacket had a dark splodge just over her eagle, where the team captain Mark Mulhearne had spilt a pint of Guinness. It had been the evening after the team had won the Irish championships and to be honest Sally hadn't even realised until Mark had apologised the following day.

Jean's legs were resplendent in garish Pucci leggings, in psychedelic shades of acid green, yellow, orange and pink. On her feet were yellow sailing boots – a necessity rather than a fashion statement as the rubber articles wouldn't fit into either of her large red-striped bags, no matter how she tried. Sally wore her favourite faded Levi's and the obligatory Timberland docksiders in light brown.

Both friends were hyper with excitement at the thought of being let loose for a whole week under the 'watchful' eye of their coach, Miss Murphy, or 'the Murphs' as the team called her affectionately.

"Just imagine it," Sally had positively purred. "Two guys for every girl, heaven Jean, heaven!"

Jean had nodded enthusiastically in agreement.

The noise from the St John's team in the bar was already reaching danger level.

"Hi ladies, looking good," yelled Mark, their good-humoured captain, as he spied Sally and Jean making their way towards the rowdy group. The bags and sail were unceremoniously dumped at the foot of the high, dark-wood bar table.

"Where's the Murph?" asked Jean.

"Out getting the tickets sorted out," replied Peter, the tall, slim bow or front-of-the-boat man. Peter was more than a little fond of Jean. A shy and quiet seventeen-year-old, he was the fastest and most agile young bowman in the country. He had a lopsided grin and a mop of sandy brown hair. He was hoping that perhaps Jean would notice him this week. He admired and respected her but he was also a little terrified of her outgoing nature and easy confidence.

The table in front of the boys was littered with a rake of beer glasses, both empty and full.

"Guys," laughed Sally. "It's not even lunch-time yet!"

"We know," grinned Jimbo. "Start as you mean to go on, that's what I say!"

Jimbo was fourteen stone and built like a truck. A sweet and gentle ginger-haired giant.

"What are you having, girls?" he asked.

They just had time for a swift pint of Heineken before Miss Murphy reappeared.

"Right, gang," she bellowed in her rounded, plummy voice, ignoring the glass-crammed table. "Check the bags in together. And girls, tag the sail, won't you? It's our secret weapon."

The animated group hurriedly downed the dregs of their pints, swung their bags over their shoulders and headed towards the Aer Lingus check in-desk.

After a minor incident which involved Shane, the blonde, blue-eyed Romeo of the team, flustering the young ground hostess by flirting outrageously and shamelessly while she attempted to keep a professional distance, and after a slight delay while the same unfortunate hostess received authorisation for the 'long sausage' bag, they all passed through the departure gates. They were called to board the plane straight away, much to their collective dismay at missing out on another pint stop.

"Not to worry, lads," Jimbo stated reassuringly. "There'll be loads of wine on the plane. Sure aren't we off to France?"

"Right, St John's," Miss Murphy began once they were all seated. "Quiet for one second."

Mark stopped thumping Peter on the arm for stealing the window seat. Sally and Jean stopped checking out the talent on the plane, and Shane stopped winking at the bemused air hostesses. The team looked at the Murphs expectantly.

Sheila Murphy was the games teacher in St John's. Originally from Dublin, she had been educated in England at an exclusive boarding-school called Raleigh Ladies. She had only qualified from PE teacher training in Thormond College a year ago and St John's was her first posting. A single, attractive brunette of twenty-four, she was popular with the other teachers and pupils alike. Sheila loved sailing and was delighted with the success of her team. She too intended to enjoy herself in La Rochelle. Within reason, as she kept telling herself firmly.

"A few rules, team, listen up," Sheila continued in her loud, clear voice. "Number one –" She looked around her at the other passengers and lowered her voice a few notches. "Number one, if you're going to drink, and I presume you are . . ." Sally, Jean and the boys laughed. "Guys, guys, quiet for a second. All I ask is that you take it easy. And take care of each other. Enjoy yourselves by all means, but remember you are representing your school not to mention your country. And I don't want to have to report any missing persons in the mornings either. Hangovers or no hangovers, I want you all on the boat in good time for the races."

Shane interrupted. "If I'm missing, it won't be a hangover you have to worry about, miss. It'll be a hanger-oner, if you know what I mean."

She had to laugh. Shane was something else. He had overtly flirted with his games teacher so many times that she was well used to him. There had been rumours of Shane and one of the student teachers, Lucy, and a few stolen kisses in the changing rooms last year. But Sheila was sure that it had all been highly exaggerated and blown out of all proportion.

The teacher threw a disapproving look at Shane and continued. "As I was saying, we are here to sail, guys, not to party. And another thing, if I catch even one of you calling me Murphs when we get back to Ireland, there'll be trouble."

"Right you are, Murphs," Mark agreed, smiling.

"Careful," she warned, "we're not on French soil yet." She smiled at Mark. Sheila Murphy had a bit of a soft spot for the team's handsome and charming captain. "Right. Rule number two: the Lambay rule. What happens over here is to be kept strictly between the team. I'll promise to overlook a little partying and certain other aspects of the proceedings," she fixed her eyes on Shane, a dedicated smoker, pointedly. Shane grinned, sheepishly. "But I don't want any mad stories, true or not, reaching the eager ears of the headmaster or any of the parents, OK?" The team all nodded in agreement. "Last thing . . ."

Jean stifled a yawn.

"Jean, try to stay awake. As I was saying, last thing and most importantly, I'll expect you all to sail hard and win. You know you can do it, St John's."

Mark and his crew cheered loudly which sent an irritated air hostess scuttling down the aisle towards them. At that moment the plane's engines revved and the huge bird began to make its lumbering way towards the runway. The red-faced hostess retreated, clucking her tongue in disapproval, and began to demonstrate the safety features of the aircraft. She glared at Shane who was making lewd comments as she simulated inflating the bright orange life-jacket by blowing into the attached yellow tube.

"Go on, ya good thing!" Shane yelled at her, before he was hushed by Sheila and thumped on the arm by Jimbo.

"I'm John O'Mara and I'll be your captain on this flight," a voice stated over the intercom. "The weather conditions today are favourable and we should arrive at La Rochelle Airport at sixteen hundred hours local time. Cabin crew, please take your seats."

Jean, who knew it was Sally's first flight, turned to her friend in concern.

"How are you coping, Sal?" she asked.

Sally was clenching her hands on her knees and gazing out the small window at the soon-to-be-departing hard ground. "I'm OK, thanks, Jean," she replied.

"Hey, girls," Shane leered. He was sitting behind the two friends with Jimbo beside him. "Either of you want to join the Mile High Club?"

Sally and Jean groaned. It was going to be some week!

Arriving in La Rochelle was an event in itself. School sailing teams from all over the world were meeting in the large marquee beside the yacht club where the busy registration desk was located. The lively sailors were then congregating in the yacht-club bar. The Australian team, resplendent in gold and green jackets, with matching cotton rugby-type shirts, had been holding court at the bar counter since mid-morning. Allegedly they had also become evening residents in the dodgy local 'disco bar', Pierre's, since their arrival two days ago.

On walking into the yacht club bar, Mark and his team were greeted with huge cheers from the Aussies. "G'day, Paddies, we've been waiting for you," shouted a large, toothy blonde boy. "Saved a place for you at the bar, mates, sit down, sit down," he continued. "I'm Greg, and this lovely lot is my crew. Cracking sailors, every one of them." Greg gestured towards the five other bodies who were gazing with interest at the Irish students.

Within the space of a few minutes the two teams were sharing sailing stories like old friends. Sally and Jean struck up a conversation with the two tall, blonde Australian girls. Jo and Lara were seasoned sailors, like themselves, and well able to stand up for themselves. The Irish girls warmed to them immediately. Especially after Jo put Shane in his place.

"Hey, babe," he had crooned. "Ever had an Irish tongue sandwich?"

"No," Jo had retorted coolly. "But I bet you've shagged your fair share of Aussie sheep – you have that desperate look about you."

The collective sailors had laughed into their pints. Shane had been dumbstruck. He was used to girls at the very least smiling at his jokes, usually while batting their eyelashes. But this one, well . . . he hadn't expected that. But for the first time in an age Shane was truly interested.

Later, all the teams returned to the La Perla apartment complex, where they were staying for the week. A busy holiday-resort complex in the high season, the rooms were big and bright, with balconies overlooking the sea. The St John's group had been given three rooms between the Australian and the American teams' rooms, one for the two girls, one for the Murphs and one for the 'lads'.

"I like it!" Shane had exclaimed on hearing the news. "A blonde Aussie on top and a leggy American babe below and lucky old Shane in the middle!"

Sally and Jean had both thumped him hard on the arm, laughing.

"In your dreams, Shane," Jean had said. "I wouldn't let Jo hear you say that. She'd eat you for breakfast."

That evening had been spent in Pierre's with the Australian team, the French team and organisers. Pierre's was definitely on the dingy side. It reminded Sally of a Leeson Street club, with grease-streaked mirrors on the walls and stained red velvet 'lounge' seats. Tinny Lambada and Salsa music filled the muggy air, interspersed bizzarely with early U2 songs. Several middle-aged women in tight black figure-hugging skirts, lacy or leopard-skin tops and vertigo-inducing high heels danced with their mirror reflections.

"There you go, Shane," Jo had nodded towards a particularly 'interesting' woman. "I'm sure she'd dance with you, mate, for the right price!"

Behind the bar was a dark-skinned woman, weighed down with heavy gold jewellery. A small Frenchman with a thin sparse moustache, Pierre apparently, greeted the students with rapture at the door. "Welcome, my friends. *Bonne chance* with the boats. My bar is your bar."

Most of the other teams had retired early, with the British and Germans the first to leave. The Murphs was talking animatedly in the corner to the dark and dashing French coach, Jean. When all the other competitors had left, Greg turned to Mark.

"They may get more shut-eye, but we'll still win. You guys can come second."

"Thanks, 'mate'," Mark had laughed. "But you wait till you see us on the water. We'll blow your mind!"

Chapter 5

The next morning Sheila Murphy dragged her hungover crew out of their beds, starting with the two girls, then moving into the sweaty stench of the boys' room.

"Boys, is there a dead mouse in this room?" Sheila exclaimed, holding her nose at the unsavoury, decaying smell.

"It's Jimbo's shoes," Mark explained. Jimbo blushed to the roots of his ginger hair.

The bright Mediterranean sun poured through the apartment windows. The sky outside was a clear, azure blue. There was a strong breeze rippling over the bay, creating regular chains of choppy white-topped waves. Mark, dressed in a white tee shirt and light blue striped boxer shorts, joined his teacher at the window.

"Perfect," he pronounced. At that moment Sally and Jean just walked in the door. Sally noticed that Mark's legs were . . . well, perfect too. Firm, lightly tanned and muscular, with just the right amount of hair.

The captain turned and looked at his team with a wickedly wide grin on his face. "It's our weather, guys. We're going to win today, I can feel it in my sailing bones!"

Two hours later, after a rushed continental breakfast in the marquee and a perfunctory briefing in the La Rochelle yacht club, the St John's team were on their 38-foot Beneteau yacht, the *Madeline*, and heading out towards the centre of the bay.

The day's racing was a straight run from a fixed starting line, around a lighthouse seven nautical miles offshore, and back again. The Irish team were psyched. Professionally kitted up in pale yellow oilskins with a large black eagle design on the back of the jackets, they had all the appearance of winners. As they sailed smoothly towards the starting line they surveyed the other yachts.

"Sexy oilys or what?" Sal asked loudly as the French team glided past them, dressed in sparkling white team oilskins, which emphasised their dark Mediterranean colouring. The US team had opted for a 'subtle' American stars-and-stripes design on their waterproof outfits. But best of all were the Australians, in gold and green, each head proudly topped with brown caps on which large, stuffed toy kangaroos sat in splendour.

After much jostling and shouting on the starting line, the gun fired. *Madeline* moved smoothly and swiftly over the line.

"Way to go, Ireland! Great start!" Mark yelled encouragingly.

"Mark, clear wind to the right," Peter shouted from the bow of the yacht.

"Tack, guys, tack," cried Mark, the tactician or decision-maker on the boat.

Shane, the 'helm' or driver, steered *Madeline* to the right. The crew leapt into action, moving the sails to the other side of the boat. Jimbo turned the winch with all his might. Sally pulled the ropes on the large mainsail, repositioning it on the correct side with practised skill. The sleek white yacht pulled away from the other competitors and was soon ahead by a significant margin. With a strong breeze and an attentive and talented crew, *Madeline* led the fleet out of the bay and towards the lighthouse.

Jean navigated, using detailed charts of the local waters and the yacht's digital compass. "Right Mark," Jean stated, "the lighthouse is at 44 degrees north-west, about seven nautical miles."

"Thanks, Jean," Mark said. "Right, gang. With the tide pushing us towards the coast and this strong wind, I think we should head further north and we'll be carried north-west. How does that sound?"

The crew nodded and murmured assent.

"Two tight reaches, right, Mark?" Sally asked.

"Yes, exactly," Mark agreed. "Are you ready for the spinny, Jimbo, Jean, Peter?"

"Ready," the eager threesome answered.

Jimbo pulled up the brightly coloured spinnaker sail, Peter attached the long metal support pole to the mast and pulled down the heavier front-sail or 'jenny'. Jean had the new, lighter front sail flying within seconds.

"Well done, guys," Mark exclaimed.

The yacht was now powering along at speed. Each crew member concentrated on his or her task with full attention. They were still ahead but the Australian team had steered their boat closer to the shore. Sally wondered if they would catch up.

After nearly two hours, Peter spotted the lighthouse on the horizon. Mark had been right. *Madeline* would reach the tall building with the jagged surrounding rocks streets in front of the Aussies.

Mark smiled. "There it is, guys. We'll gybe around it Shane, leaving plenty of room between us and those scary-looking yacht grounders."

The yacht soon approached the lighthouse and executed a perfect turn, quickly and ultra-professionally. The spinnaker flapped in the strong, sharp breeze for a nanosecond before Jean had it flying again.

"Brilliant guys, fucking brilliant," Mark exclaimed. They headed in towards the coast.

"Shane, head right in to avoid the tide. Guys, drop the spinny and reef the sails full in," Mark commanded firmly. His crew responded quickly and efficiently. "This race isn't in the bag yet," he stated. The Australian boat had tacked out to sea and was moving through the choppy waves smartly.

Sally, Jean and the four boys concentrated on their tasks. Sally watched the telltales or wind-indicators on her mainsail and pulled the large sail in or let it out, to extract the optimum boat speed. Jean similarly watched the jenny. Peter watched the sea fixedly, calling out big waves to Shane, so that he could steer into them and lessen their blow to the yacht. Mark kept a close eye on every small detail, the speedometer, the sails and the other yachts. The only other contender at this late stage was the Australian boat. Mark hoped he had made the correct tactical decision.

After a gruelling further three hours of sailing, the La Rochelle bay came into sight. The St John's team had been on the water for nearly seven hours, with only sandwiches and bottled Evian to sustain them. Shane had been allowed a total of three cigarettes and he wasn't a happy camper.

"Come on, Mark, we're nearly there – can I have just a few drags, pal, please?"

Mark had been insistent. "Shane, you can smoke your poor old lungs black once we pass through that damn finishing line."

The *Madeline* sailed towards the line, powering through the waves. The Irish team could see the officials on the finishing boat getting ready to fire the gun to mark their win. They moved closer and closer until *bang*, they sailed through the line.

"Bullet, guys! Bullet!" yelled Mark excitedly.

Shane steered the boat into the wind and *Madeline* came to a shuddering halt.

Jean hugged Peter, much to his shocked delight. Each member of the team grinned from ear to ear. Shane lit up a celebratory cigarette, Jimbo lay on his back, exhausted but happy. Sally felt amazing. She loved winning, but winning a world championship race – well, that was something else. Sally smiled over at Mark, pushing her salt-matted, windswept hair off her face. He smiled back.

"We did it, Sal," he said. "Come here and give me a hug, you little darling."

One strong, warm and firm hug later, Sally was hooked.

That evening the Irish and the Australians decided to celebrate the day's sailing success. Greg's team had finished second, followed closely in third and fourth places by the Brits and the Germans. The winners and runners-up chose to leave the remaining teams to their civilised dinner in the marquee at the yacht club, complete with speeches from the Lord Mayor of La Rochelle, local Councillors and fawning politicians. Instead the intrepid twelve descended on a small traditional restaurant, L'Escargot Rouge, which Jo and Lara had spotted in a guide book.

"There's no way I'm eating snails," muttered Shane, as Jean translated the menu for the group.

They had been seated outside, on a raised wooden balcony overlooking the bay. The area was surrounded on two sides by white wooden trellising, on which dark green vine-leaves meandered giving an Italian, *trattoria* atmosphere. Overhead white wooden beams were festooned with more freely growing vines, the musty green leaves and curling tendrils hanging over the trestle table which was covered with a cheerful red and white checked tablecloth. Tall red candles stood, some in a slightly haphazard manner, in pot-bellied green wine bottles. The melted red wax of candles past ran down the bottles, like cooled volcanic lava. A gentle, warm breeze played over the physically weary but animated sailors.

Sally played with the warm, dripping wax from the candle in front of her. She rolled the smooth, greasy ball between her thumb and forefinger rhythmically. She noticed Mark, sitting opposite her, watching her long, brown fingers with interest.

"Right, guys," Greg pronounced. "We need a serious wake-up call." He caught the eye of the young, dark-haired waitress. "Six large jugs of wine, mercy buckets . . . I mean *merci beaucoups*. Three white, three red."

The amiable waitress smiled at the good-looking Australian, her eyes twinkling. *"Oui, monsieur."*

A few minutes later their glasses were full and the two teams were talking at a rapid rate and tucking into baskets of warm, crusty bread.

Soon the food was served, with the Australian team's choices proving to be the more adventurous. Jo's choice was a glistening plate of snails with garlic butter. She took great delight in licking off the sweet shiny surface juices with the tip of her tongue, before popping the small molluscs into her mouth.

Shane, sitting opposite her, was disgusted. "That is revolting, Jo," he exclaimed, shovelling huge forkfuls of his chicken-tasting starter into his wide open mouth. His table manners, among other things, left a lot to be desired. "I can't believe you are eating snails."

Jean leaned over towards him. "Shane," she smiled.

"You know I translated *Cuisses de Grenouille* as chicken pieces, well, I lied."

Shane looked over at her expectantly, his strong white teeth munching on the tasty, herby dish.

"I hate to break it to you," continued Jean, stifling a giggle. "But you are eating what we in English-speaking countries would call frogs' legs."

The whole table convulsed into rowdy laughter, jeers and catcalls.

Shane's face turned pale. His jaw stopped moving and he felt instantly nauseous. The finely chewed 'chicken' lingering in his mouth tasted suddenly sickening. He attempted to swallow but his shocked throat wouldn't allow him. He spat the contents of his mouth onto the plate in front of him, and gasped for breath.

"Shane, that's revolting," Jo exclaimed. "Wait till those American babes hear about this, not to mention the cute French girls."

Shane's face turned even paler. He gulped down a large mouthful of red wine and glared dangerously at Jo. "You wouldn't dare," he growled.

Jo smiled, angelically.

After the meal was finished and a further seven large terracotta jugs of wine had been consumed, things began to get a little out of hand. Shane started throwing lumps of bread at Jo, who was more than a match for him. She retaliated by returning the same bread, this time soaked in red wine.

Soon the whole table had joined in. Bread, sodden

paper napkins, uneaten pastry crusts and wilting vegetables filled the air over the table. When Greg emptied the dregs of a jug of red wine over Mark's head the Irish captain gave a rousing roar.

The young waitress rushed outside and, on surveying the mayhem, skuttled inside to fetch the L'Escargot Rouge's 'heavies', two large rotund chefs and the tall, wiry owner.

"*Arête!*" bellowed one of the chefs. "*Maintenant!*"

The twleve sailors stopped in their tracks. The place was a bombsite. Lumps of food clung to the table top, there were French beans hanging from the rafters and debris all over the scrubbed wooden floor.

"Shit," whispered Sally under her breath.

Chapter 6

The French owner of L'Escargot had been suprisingly
reasonable, after a rambling, hand-wringing apology
from Jean, accompanied by embarassed grins from the
remainder of the crew.

"*Ah, Irlandais,*" the owner had nodded. "*Je
comprends.* On 'olidays, oui? Football fans, non? Tony
Cascarino, *il est très bien, non?*"

Jean smiled and nodded enthuastically.

The Frenchman shrugged. "*Pas de probleme.* You are
jeune, young and having the fun. It is 'ow you say, ah –
no worry!"

The relieved bunch left the restaurant and headed
towards the yacht club for the evening's prizegiving.
They arrived just in time. Staggering through the glass-
paned wooden doors of the marquee, arms linked,
chatting at a rapid pace and singing snippets of
remembered songs, they heard the commodore of the
club announce the results of the first race in perfect
English.

"In third place, the British team."

A tall young man with closely cut hair and small, round wire-framed glasses walked confidently up to the podium to collect the prize, a cut-glass tankard. He received a polite round of applause from the audience.

"In second place," the commodore continued, as the tall sailor returned to his seat. "The Australian team."

Mark and Greg's teams cheered loudly. Greg strode up to the podium and clasped the commodore's hand firmly. "Thanks, mate," he said. "I'll be back tomorrow for the next prize."

The commodore was slightly taken aback with the Australian boy's antipodean sense of humour, or was it cocky confidence? He battled on. "And in first place – the Irish team!"

Again Mark and Greg's teams cheered, this time jumping up and down and hugging and kissing each other, soccer-style. As Mark approached the podium Sally felt her heart skip a beat. She was so proud of her team and so pleased for Mark. Sheila Murphy beamed up at Mark from a table in front of the podium. She wondered why he had what looked like red wine and tomato sauce all over his white T-shirt. And what on earth was the mushy, white stuff in his hair? Sitting beside her was the French coach, Jules, who she was beginning to like more than a little.

Mark accepted his prize and leaned towards the microphone. "I'd just like to say thanks to all my great crew and to the Murphs . . . I mean Miss Murphy, our coach."

"Watch out Paddies, we'll get you tomorrow," yelled Greg from the back of the marquee.

After the prizegiving Sheila Murphy made her way to the back of the tent. The other teams had started to leave in droves, through the doors at the side. Sheila was anxious to hustle her own sailors back to the apartments, avoiding Pierre's or any other bar en route.

She took one look at her crew and stifled a laugh. "What have you lot been playing at?"

Sally hiccupped.

"Right, gang," the coach commanded. "We are all going to walk back to the apartments along the beach, OK?"

Jimbo and Shane were slumped against each other, attempting to stay upright. The motley Irish crew, together with Greg, Jo and Lara from the Aussie team, reluctantly followed the Irish coach.

"Ah, Miss," complained Sally. "It's dead early. Can we just pop in to Pierre's?"

"No way, Sally," the Murphs stated firmly. "Don't even think about it."

Jo and Lara had miraclously found a donkey cart trundling along the road parallel to the beach, pulled by an ancient moth-eaten donkey and an even more ancient local man, with no teeth and not a word of English. They persuaded the kindly man to transport the lumbering and brain-dead Jimbo and Shane back to the apartments, for a small fee. The two girls walked behind the cart, laughing and singing.

Sheila Murphy led the way along the beach, with

Jules for company. Peter and Jean sauntered behind them barefoot, skipping in and out of the gentle, swirling wash at the edge of the beach. Sally and Mark brought up the rear, chatting amicably about the day, bumping shoulders from time to time. The moon was full, illuminating the beach and giving the flat calm sea an eerie glow. The air was warm and tangy with salty promise.

Sally felt Mark slide his cool, firm hand into hers and she turned her face towards his and smiled. They walked towards the apartments in companionable silence, listening to the gentle clink of the metal yacht's halyards against the masts and the faint hum of talk and music from nearby bars and restraurants.

"This is heaven," murmured Mark as he pulled Sally towards him and planted a firm but soft kiss on her warm mouth. Sally had to agree.

Later, as she lay on her top bunk in the La Perla apartments, covered only by a crisp white linen sheet, she touched her lips with her right index finger and smiled to herself. Happy and content, she fell fast asleep.

Sally was woken some hours later by a strange, melodic noise coming from outside. She sat up slowly and popped her head over the side of the bunk. Jean's eyes were open, pupils wide and glistening like a cat's in the faint light.

"Can you hear that?" Sally asked quietly.

Jean nodded. "It sounds like someone singing, but it can't be."

The girls were intrigued. They slipped out of their

beds and made their way over to the French door onto the balcony. Jean pulled open the glass door slowly and carefully, making no sound. The now wide-awake pair then stuck their heads out into the warm night air. To their amazement they saw Sheila Murphy on the adjoining balcony, dressed in a pair of silk pyjamas. Their young teacher was leaning over the balcony enraptured. Because beneath her, on the grass, stood Jules. He was gently strumming a guitar and serenading her in the moonlight with a wonderfully slow and emotive version of 'Wonderful Tonight'.

Sally and Jean were dumbstruck. The two girls looked at each other. Jean raised her eyebrows and put her finger to her lips. Sally nodded. They slid the glass door closed noiselessly and returned to their bunks, where they both fell into deep, romance-filled Cinderella slumbers.

Chapter 7

Luckily there was no racing until the following evening so Sally and Jean slept until mid-morning, when they were woken by a loud thwack on the plate glass of the balcony patio door.

Sally groaned and opened her eyes. The room was filled with bright sunlight. She heard the loud thud against the window again. "Jean, are you awake?" She heard a low moan from the bed below hers.

"What was that?"

Jean pushed herself up in the bunk gingerly. Her head was throbbing and the inside of her mouth felt like she had eaten a rat. "I'll go and investigate, Sal," she muttered.

As Jean padded towards the window she saw a large round object coming towards her at speed. It hit the window with a jolt and bounced back towards the ground. Jean leapt back in fright. She peered carefully out the window. Mark, Jimbo, Peter and Shane were gathered on the grass beneath her, all dressed in shorts,

T-shirts and shades and holding what looked like a football.

Jean opened the patio doors and waved at the boys. "What are you lot doing?" she asked, laughing. "What are you throwing at our window? You could have broken it."

"Sorry, Jean," Mark yelled. "We had to wake you two somehow. We're going to play volleyball on the beach with the Aussies. Are you coming?"

"I don't suppose it crossed your tiny minds to knock on our door?" Jean asked, grinning.

"Ah no, that would have been too easy," Mark replied. "And anyway, I wanted to practise my long shots."

Twenty minutes later Sally and Jean walked towards the beach in shorts and bikini tops to meet the others. The sun was splitting the heavens and the sky was a bright, cloudless blue. The girls had bolted down some French bread and coffee, trying to ignore their cloudy heads and light-sensitive eyes. There were shouts coming from the beach. Sally recognised Shane's voice, doing a passable John McEnroe impression.

"You cannot be serious, man, the ball was in."

The volley-ball 'net' consisted of a length of rope suspended between two spinnaker sail poles. The 'court' was scored out in the damp sand near the water. A heated game was in progress between the four Irish lads on one team and Greg, Lara, Jo and the Murphs on the other. It looked like the Aussies, with the Murphs' expert assistance, were winning.

"Hi, guys," Sally shouted. "Need some help?"

"You're with us, Sal," Mark insisted. "In fact I think we need the both of you – we're seriously behind here!"

Within seconds the game had started again. It was fast and furious with very few recognisable rules, although the Murphs was attempting to keep some sort of order. The ball hurtled over the net, served with great power by Lara. Mark returned it, feeling the ball impact solidly on his clenched hands. The Murphs returned his shot with deadly accuracy – it landed just inside the left-side line.

"Good one, Murphs," Greg shouted. "Way to go, team!"

Half an hour later the exhausted sailors collapsed onto the sand. The Aussie team under the control of Sheila Murphy had won by miles.

"I'm starving," Jimbo stated. "It's definitely lunch-time."

"Dead right, mate," Shane added. "I could eat a small pony."

Sheila went off in search of provisions with Jean and Peter, leaving everyone else resting on the beach.

"This is the life," said Lara, passing around the P20 sunblock. "Sand, sun and loads of sailing. Not to mention the great company." The charming Aussie girl was really warming to the Irish team, Jimbo in particular. He was different to the boys she usually met – he was more gentle and thoughtful. And she was hugely attracted to the ginger hair.

Sheila Murphy returned laden down with provisions for the hungry troops. They spread the French bread, cold meats, cheese, fruit and blissfully cool bottled water on the sand and tucked in. Mark cut the cheese into thick slices with his sailing knife. Jo broke the bread up and shared it out, while Lara took control of the much-in-demand bottles of water.

"You forgot the wine, Murphs," Sally joked.

Sheila Murphy looked at her carefully before she realised her ward wasn't serious.

"The race this evening will be demanding enough without alcohol in your poor old systems," she said. "You all need to be in top mental form for this race, no exceptions. So I advise a rest after lunch and we'll meet up for a team talk on the *Madeline* at six-ish, OK?"

"No problem, Murphs," Mark agreed good-naturedly. "And hey, did anyone hear a weird noise last night? It sounded like a bad imitation of Barry Manilow singing Eric Clapton songs or something."

Sally and Jean couldn't help themselves. Sally, who was taking a slug of carbonated mineral water at the time, spat it all over herself and Jean had to slap her on the back, stifling her own laughs. Sheila Murphy was turning a delicate shade of lobster.

"That was just a car stereo I think, Mark," Jean said, glancing over at her mortified teacher, who smiled at her gratefully. Jules would have to be kept in check!

Just after six, the Irish team gathered on their yacht. The sun was still shining brightly and warmly but soon the light would begin to fade and the demanding night race would begin.

"Right, gang, one or two things," the Murphs instructed. "Jean, have you studied the charts?" Jean nodded confidently. "Jimbo, have you checked the instruments, especially the compass?"

"Everything's working grand," Jimbo assured her.

"And Mark, you're satisfied with all the safety equipment?" Mark nodded assent.

"This race is about teamwork and decision-making. I expect you all to pull together and help each other. Jean and Mark will plot your course, but I want everyone to be alert and awake throughout the race. No slacking off, guys, OK?"

"Is that it, Murphs?" Shane asked.

"Yes, Shane," she replied. "Good luck, team, see you later."

The *Madeline* made its way smoothly towards the starting line a little before seven. Some of the other teams were already hovering around.

"See you in the bar, Paddies," Greg yelled over from his boat. "Jo's a crack navigator, we'll be miles ahead of you."

"We'll see," yelled Shane in reply. "Last one in buys the drinks."

"You're on," shouted Jo, her head popping up from the cabin of their yacht. "Prepare your wallet, Shane, you're going down."

"I wish I was," Shane retorted, smiling wickedly.

The Irish team started well. Shane steered the yacht gently up into the wind and over the starting line, cruising past the other competitors. Within minutes the

Irish team were heading towards the open sea, to a mark 18 nautical miles offshore. After rounding that mark the sailors had to head down the coast, around another mark and back to the marina. They wouldn't reach La Rochelle until the early hours of the morning. The light was fading rapidly; soon they would have to rely on Jean's navigational skills to bring them safely to the first mark.

"What are the bearings, Jean?" Mark yelled down into the *Madeline*'s cabin.

Jean stuck her head up into the night air. "Eight degrees north-east to the mark, then twelve degrees south-east to the next mark and twelve degrees south-west back home. Allowing for a strong tide and varying wind conditions. And watch the depth metre around the second mark – there are sandbanks and it would be easy to run aground."

"Thanks, Jean," Mark said. "Let's get this tub moving. Sally, get the top telltales flying on the mainsail; Jimbo, weight over the rail please and Shane, keep us slightly off the wind until we build up some speed."

Shane steered the *Madeline* carefully to the left, allowing more wind into the sails. Within seconds the yacht had picked up speed and was powering into the open sea.

After almost two hours of solid sailing, the Irish team were almost at the second mark. They had rounded the first mark successfully, making good time and in first place. It was a beautiful evening, warm with a light but steady breeze. Clouds covered the moon, making the night sky as black as pitch.

"Look at the water, guys," Sally exclaimed suddenly, breaking the silence. "Turn off the deck lights for a sec', it's amazing."

Jimbo flicked off the deck light switch, plunging the *Madeline* into eerie darkness.

"God, that's beautiful," Jean said in wonderment, gazing down at the water. "The water is dancing with light, it's . . . I can't find words for it."

The surface of the water was illuminated with tiny, flickering lights as the water lapped the sides of the boat.

"Phosphorescence," Peter stated confidently. "I've never seen it quite so bright though. It's the salts in the seawater reflecting the light. Amazing, isn't it?"

"Wow, man, that's cool," Shane agreed.

"Right, team, enough David Attenborough stuff. Back to the sailing. Jean, how far are we from . . ."

The *Madeline* came to a shuddering and unexpected halt. The crew were flung forwards, and there was a loud splash from the water beside the yacht.

"Shit," Mark shouted. "Bloody sandbank. Sally, main out now. Jean, dump the jenny. Jimbo, deck lights on. And what the hell was that splash?"

From the back of the boat came Jimbo's booming voice.

"It was me, Mark, I went for a swim."

Jimbo had swum to the back of the boat and was clinging onto the guard-rail for dear life. The crew pulled him in, struggling to cope with his new, seawater-soaked dead weight. They dumped him unceremoniously into the bottom of the boat.

"Now where the hell is Jean?" Mark said irritably. He was worried. How the hell were they going to get the *Madeline* off the sandbank? This was serious.

"I sent her downstairs to check the tides," Sally replied firmly. "If I'm right it's turning and we'll float off the sand in less than an hour."

Mark breathed a huge sigh of relief. Sally really knew her stuff. "Right," he said. "Drop the anchor so at least we'll stay where we are for the moment. Jimbo, as you're already wet how about ditching the oilies and joining me for a real swim. We may as well make the most of things. Any other takers?"

Jean popped her head out of the cabin. "Good news. Sally was right, we'll be floating again in no time, and the mark is only a short distance away."

After a quick swim, Mark and Jimbo climbed back into the yacht. "'According to the depth metre we should be OK in a few more minutes," Sally said confidently.

"Right crew, back on track. Up anchor, Pete. And this time no nature observations, thank you!"

Sally turned a delicate shade of lobster, unnoticed in the darkness. She regretted pointing out the phosphorescence to the crew. Mark was right – she should have had her mind on the race. She had to concentrate.

Soon they were sailing again. They rounded the mark professionally and began the sail back to La Rochelle bay.

"We're nearly there, gang," Mark encouraged his team. "Great trimming, Sally."

"Thanks," she replied gratefully.

"Is that a light ahead of us?" Peter asked, scanning the horizon.

"I think it's someone's deck lights," Mark said. "I'm sure the grounding set us back at least one or two places."

The crew were silent for a few minutes. They hated losing.

"Hey, it's the ladies' race tomorrow. With Jean helming and Sally on tactics, not to mention the Murphs on bow, we're bound to win," Mark laughed. "What a team!"

"And I'll try to avoid any sandbanks," Sally joked.

"I'll get you later," Mark laughed. "And who was it waxing lyrical about the bloody sparkling sea, may I ask?"

The crew laughed and Mark was relieved. He needed them all in good humour tomorrow and for the crucial last match race on Thursday between the top two teams. If they made it that far. The girls knew the pressure was on. Mark hoped they were up to it.

As Mark had predicted, St John's were beaten home by two teams, the Australians and the Germans. The weary team were met on the marina by a worried Miss Murphy.

"What happened, guys? Greg said he thought you were ahead of them until the second mark and then he lost track of you."

Mark grimaced. "Murphs, we'll tell you about it later. Right now I think we all could do with a stiff drink."

"And a cigarette," Shane added, searching his oilies for his Marlboro Lights.

Sheila Murphy recognised a despondent team when she saw one.

"Right so, Pierre's it is. But only for a short time, mind. It's almost two o'clock and we have an important race in the morning – right, girls?"

"You bet, Miss," Sally agreed.

"And don't forget about the talent show in the evening. I hope you have something prepared, Mark?"

The captain smiled broadly. "We certainly do, Murphs."

Sally and Jean giggled.

He continued unabashed. "We'll just have to leave you in suspense until tomorrow night."

"Sounds ominous," Sheila said smiling. "I hope it's – how will I put this . . . respectable."

"Miss, how could you doubt us?" Shane asked, pretending to be hurt.

"Shane, with you on team, quite easily I'm afraid."

Chapter 8

The next morning was sunny again. Sally had found it difficult to sleep the previous night. She knew exactly how important the ladies' race was. If they didn't win they had little or no chance of making the cut for the final match racing. The pressure was certainly on.

The sun was splitting the heavens and a gentle breeze was rippling over the bay when the St John's team made their way along the seafront towards the yacht club.

"OK, Sal?" Mark asked gently.

Sally was miles away, thinking about the race that afternoon.

"Oh, yeah. I'm fine, thanks, Mark."

She would have liked to talk to him alone last night, but Pierre's was noisy and packed. Sally wondered if the other night was just that . . . the other night, and not to be repeated. Although he did seem to be attentive and he was walking to the yacht club by her side.

Sally sighed to herself. I'm being paranoid. I'm sure

Mark likes me, so what if he's not holding my hand. Grow up, Sal, she said to herself.

The team wanted to be on the water early to practise. Sally was calling the shots today, with Jean helming and Sheila, as she was allowed call her on the boat, taking Peter's position at the front of the boat. The boys filled in the other slots.

"You're going to find it hard not being in charge," Sheila Murphy said to Mark as they pulled up the jenny together.

"I know, you're right, it will be strange. But Sally's really good, so I'm not worried. I'll probably learn a thing or two." Mark glanced over at Sally. She looked calm and collected.

A few minutes later, the *Madeline* was under sail and practising some manoeuvres.

"Good tack," encouraged Sally. "Mark, watch the top of the main, it may need to come in a little. Jean, point her up into the wind a little – yes, perfect."

"We're ready, St John's," shouted Sheila from the front of the boat. "Let's go down to the start."

After a blinding start, timed perfectly by Sally, the *Madeline* was heading towards the first mark at an even pace. In front of them were the Australians, with Jo at the helm.

"Right, after we round this mark, pull the sails right in and head up inside the Australian boat," Sally said firmly. "Then we'll head down with the spinnaker flying and hopefully pass them out around the mark."

"OK, Sal," Jean agreed.

The team were working perfectly together like a well-oiled engine. They had absolute confidence in Sally – even Shane. Mr Male Chauvinist himself had to hand it to her – she knew her stuff. Mark was especially impressed. He knew exactly how difficult keeping the team together could be, both physically and mentally.

They rounded the mark closely, with only inches to spare. And Sally was right. As they headed towards the second mark, the Australians were now behind them.

"That's it, St John's," Sheila smiled. "Great rounding, Jean. Keep it going." The finishing line was now in sight and the *Madeline* was darting through the waves at a lively pace. The crew concentrated on squeezing every little ounce of speed out of the boat. They held their collective breath as they reached the line. Crossing it, Sally let out a huge sigh of relief. Sheila danced a jig at the front of the boat. Jimbo and Shane cheered. Jean let out a huge squeak and hugged Sally who was in front of her.

"You did it, girl," she laughed. "Finals, here we come!"

"No," Sally said, beaming from ear to ear. "We did it."

"Did you see Greg's face after the race?" Mark asked as they all walked back to the apartments munching on huge crusty hunks of French bread, filled with cheese and ham. Sally took a swig of the bottle of cheap white wine.

73

"He was disgusted," Jean said smiling. "He hates losing almost as much as you do, Mark."

Mark thumped her good-naturedly on the arm.

"Ow, you big bully," Jean said, rubbing her arm and pretending to be hurt.

Shane smiled. "Don't be hurting, Jean you big idiot, we need her for tonight. We don't want any bruises showing."

Sheila pricked up her ears. "I hope the girls are going to have clothes on, Shane," she said with a slight edge to her voice. "I know we're in France and everything but . . ."

"Ah, Miss," Sally laughed. "Give us some credit. We won today and we're going to win the talent show too. Guaranteed."

"I just wish I knew what you lot had planned," Sheila muttered.

"Welcome to the World Sailing Championship's Talent Show," Jules began. The French coach was compere for the night. He looked particularly dapper in a crisp white shirt and black trousers. Sheila gazed up at the stage in admiration. She was sitting in the judging panel in the front row, large cards with scores on them by her feet. The other judges included the local Mayor and his wife, a local journalist and two other coaches. The marquee was filled with people: locals, tourists, cameramen and journalists.

"First this evening, for your entertainment, we have the American team with their medley of traditional American folk-songs."

Mark and his team stifled the laughs backstage.

"They're taking the piss," Shane said succinctly. "No way. Bloody folk-songs!"

"Shut up," Jean chided. "They're in the middle of some sort of Bruce Springsteen song."

Shane snorted. 'Born in the USA' is hardly an American folk-song, is it?"

Sally laughed, pulling at her short green dress. "Stop, would you, at least they can sing."

Shane decided to turn his attention to Sally and Jean instead. "Those costumes really suit you, girls," he leered openly. "You should show your knickers more often."

Jean squealed. "I'll kill you, Shane McCarthy," she said, grabbing him by his clerical collar.

"Guys, calm down," Mark said.

Jules' voice came wafting from the stage. "Well, um, that was very . . . nice, America. As we can see from the judging panel, a respectable seven out of sixty. Are you voting, Ireland? Oh, I see, no points. Yes, well, moving swiftly on. And now for something completely different, the French team with their version of the cancan."

"Right," Shane said instantly. "We'll have to watch this one, rude not to."

The team jostled their way to the side of the stage, bumping arms with Greg and his team in Bush hats complete with hanging corks.

"G'day, mate," Mark said smiling.

"How's it going, Father?" Greg countered. "Give us a blessing there, mate."

The cancan music started up. The entire French team were dressed in flowing flounced skirts, black fishnet stockings and suspenders.

"Where did they get the tights?" Sally asked giggling. "I love the tall, hairy guy. His legs look the business in them."

The French contestants started their high leg-kicks, twirling their skirts and yelping and cheering. One of the girls turned cartwheels and the other pulled off a perfectly executed splits.

"She's mine," Shane shouted excitedly. "The one with the legs spread!"

"Shane!" said Jean and Sally in unison.

Wild clapping followed the French team's finale.

"Bravo, France," Jules clapped enthusiastically along with the crowd. "And I can see the judges were impressed. Ten out of ten from the mayor. Thank you, sir. A total of fifty-two out of sixty, a hard score to beat. And next the Aussies. I'll leave the Australian captain, Greg, to introduce his team himself."

Greg strode onto the stage, followed closely behind by Lara, Jo and the others.

"G'day, we'd like to present real life in Summer Bay and Ramsey Street, leaving in the good bits."

The Australian team were in their element, running around the stage, acting out various scenes with the help of the audience.

"Right, Donald and the sheep are getting on down when in comes Marilyn," Jo narrated. The audience laughed loudly and clapped as a curly blonde-wigged Lara walked onto the stage. Greg, as Donald, was a natural.

As the Australians took a bow Mark was looking anxious. They had scored an almost perfect fifty-eight points. "They were great, they're definitely going to win."

"Think positive, Mark," Jean said. "They haven't had the Irish experience yet."

There were no real contenders in the remaining teams. Finally Jules introduced the Irish gang.

"And now, last but certainly not least. The act we've all been waiting for – Ireland. A tribute to Irish Dancing and priests?"

Shane, Jimbo, Mark and Peter walked slowly and solemnly onto the stage with their heads bowed, dressed in black suits complete with dog collars. The audience clapped and whistled. The traditional Irish music started playing softly, slowly becoming louder. From either side of the stage Jean and Sally danced onto the stage, in bright green Irish dancing costumes, borrowed from Jean's little sister Aoife. The dresses were on the tight side and indecently short, but as Aoife was eleven it was a miracle they fitted at all. From the appreciative wolf-whistles and cheers from the crowd, no one seemed to mind the shortness of the skirts.

Aoife had trained Sally and Jean for weeks in the finer points of Irish dancing and the girls were high-kicking to beat the band. The 'priests' looked on in amazement. They knew Sally and Jean had been practising but they hadn't realised just how good they'd become! The boys removed their black jackets, put their arms around each other's shoulders and began their dancing, a strange and solemn type of Greek dancing, legs in the air, trying hard not to laugh.

Sally and Jean then moved in front of the boys, looked at the audience and whipped the 'priest's' shirts off! They had spent hours one evening in Dublin cutting the seams and sewing velcro tabs onto the boy's shirts. Sally had seen it on a documentary about male strippers and decided that automatic release shirts were just the thing for their act. The hours had been worth it though. The audience went wild. Mark, Shane and Jimbo's torsos had been covered with baby oil and glistened in the stage lights. The whole team lined up and began to dance in unison, faster and faster. As the music reached its climax they were having a ball, grins plastered all over their faces. Sweat glistened on Jimbo's flushed skin, Shane was showing unusual skill and lightness of foot for a novice and Sally longed to be in the audience watching Mark's naked six-pack as he danced.

As their act drew to a close the team were exhausted but elated. The audience were on their feet clapping and stamping their feet.

Jules stepped onto the stage from the wings, clapping. "The wonderful Irish team! Can I have the scores, please? Ah I see, fifty-seven points. Australia wins! Congratulations!"

As Greg and his team took the stage for an encore, a

disappointed Shane and Mark watched from the wings.

"Bloody Italians, they gave us one point," Shane muttered darkly.

"As long as we win tomorrow, that's the most important thing," Mark whispered back.

Later that evening Mark, Sally, Jean and Peter were sitting at a large round table to the side of the marquee dance floor with Greg, Jo and some of the French team. Shane was spinning the mayor's wife around the floor.

"Where's Jimbo?" Sally asked.

"He's outside showing Lara the stars," Jo laughed. "At least that's what they claimed they were doing!"

"I can't get over your hidden talent," Mark said, turning towards Sally. "You and Jean must have put some serious time into dance practice. Or else you're naturals."

"And you guys were brilliant, the shirts worked perfectly. What a night," Sally smiled.

"It's been fun all right. Would you like to go for a walk, Sal?"

"To look at the stars?" Sally asked mischievously.

"Something like that," Mark grinned.

Sally woke up the next morning with a smile plastered on her face. Mark, she thought to herself as she lay in her bed. Mark Mulhearne. Sally Mulhearne, Mr and Mrs Mulhearne . . .

"Are you awake, Sal?" Jean's voice cut into her thoughts of white weddings.

"Hi, Jean," Sally said. "Beautiful morning, isn't it?"

"You're in a good mood. I want to hear all about last night, every last detail."

"My pleasure," Sally said, dying to divulge the finer details of the previous evening's encounter with Mark. She lowered herself carefully onto the floor and sat down on the end of Jeans' bunk. "Oh, Jean. I'm in love. He's just so perfect."

Jean smiled to herself. She'd heard that one before.

Sally continued. "We went for a walk on the marina and then sat on the deck of the *Madeline* for ages talking."

"Just talking?" Jean asked with a wry smile on her lips.

"Well . . ." Sally grinned. "He has the most amazing lips, Jean. Firm but soft and gentle. And he kisses like an angel." She sighed deeply. "What a guy!"

"Sally, Jean, are you girls ready?" Miss Murphy's voice came booming through the door.

"You can tell me more about Prince Charming later," Jean laughed. "Right now we have a race to win."

St John's had made it into the final, thanks to Sally, Jean and the Murph's Trojan work the previous day. Today they were match racing, one on one, against Greg and his team. Mark and Peter were already on the marina when the rest of the Irish gang arrived.

"Hi, crew," the captain yelled when he saw them walking down the wooden planks towards him. "Beautiful morning."

"You're here early," Shane said, shielding his eyes from the bright morning sun. "We brought you some breakfast." He handed Mark and Peter two huge filled rolls and a bottle of mineral water each.

"Thanks," Peter smiled. "Just the ticket."

The team sat on the deck of the *Madeline* and munched on their breakfast rolls. It was already warm, with a lively sea breeze playing over the water.

"Where did you and Lara disappear off to last night?" Shane asked Jimbo.

The large teenager blushed to the roots of his ginger hair. "We, um, we went for a walk by the sea. We were looking at the stars."

Shane sniggered. "Yeah, right. Is that what they call it these days?"

Mark interrupted his team mate's taunts. Shane could be cruel sometimes and Jimbo wasn't able for it, especially when it came to girls. "And what about yourself, Shane? Any luck with the mayor's wife?"

"Ha, bloody ha," Shane replied. "She was old enough to be my mother." He stopped for a second. "Although to be honest that wouldn't bother me, but her husband was there so that put a stop to anything."

"She'd be mad into an Irish teenager, of course," Jean said sarcastically.

Shane glared at her sourly. "I've had plenty of older women in my time, thank you. Remember that teacher, Lucy, well . . ."

The whole team began to cough loudly, looking over at

Sheila Murphy who was looking a little uncomfortable. She was dying to hear the story about Shane and the student teacher, but didn't want to appear too interested.

"Oh, sorry, Miss," Shane smiled. "I forgot you were a teacher for a second. But if you're ever feeling a bit lonely at home, without Jules and all . . ."

"Shane!" Sally and Jean yelled.

"Girls," Shane said. "Would you stop doing that?"

"What?" Sally asked.

"The 'Shane' thing."

"Shane," Jean replied quickly. "We can't help it, you're just so . . . well . . . impossible."

Sheila smiled. She was used to Shane by this stage. He was sort of cute, in a young Turk kind of way. Sheila Murphy, she scolded herself. The sun must be getting to you. What are you thinking of? She tried to settle her mind on the job at hand.

"Right, St John's, once you're all finished we'll start thinking about the race. Shane, try to get older women out of your head for the duration, please."

"I'll try, Miss, but it'll be hard with you around, know what I mean," he gave the teacher a saucy wink.

"I know, I know," he muttered, noticing the expression on Jean and Sally's face. "But I can't help it. It's in me jeans." He placed his hand suggestively on his crotch.

"Shane!" spluttered Sally and Jean joined this time by the whole team. Shane simply smiled. It was hard work being the Tom Jones of the team but someone had to do it.

"It's dog eat dog time," Greg shouted over from the Australian yacht as both teams headed out towards the starting line.

"May the best team win," Mark shouted back. "And I don't mean you!"

"Same to you, mate," Greg yelled back, smiling. "Loser buys the drinks tonight."

"You're on. It's going to cost you."

The two boats sailed backwards and forwards in front of the line, waiting for the starting gun. Crowds of people were watching from spectator boats dotted around the race area. The course was small, consisting of three buoys placed in a triangular pattern in the water. The two boats had to race each other around the buoys, trying to out-manoeuvre each other in a match of quick thinking and tight sailing skills.

"All clear ahead, two minutes to the gun," Peter shouted from the front of the boat.

"Sally, ease the main. Jimbo, ready on the winch. We're going for a start at the pin end of the line."

The Australian team were approaching the starting line at the same end, the opposite end to the starting-boat.

"Thirty seconds," Peter shouted.

"Sal, main hard in," Mark yelled, as they moved up towards the line. "Let's get her motoring. Right up on the line, Shane."

"Mark, we're going to be early, I'm easing the main," Sally shouted.

"Leave it, Sal. We're fine," Mark countered.

Sally looked at him, sparks flying in her grey-blue eyes. What was he playing at? The *Madeline* was moving too damn fast.

"Ten seconds," Peter shouted.

The Australian yacht was now beneath them, only metres away from the side of the *Madeline*. They could hear Greg shouting at them to keep clear.

"Keep up, *Madeline*. Windward boat!" he was screaming. "Don't you read your rules, Paddies? Get up now!"

"We're going to hit them," Peter yelled.

Shane looked at Mark.

"We'll go over and tack around the end of the line," Mark decided. "We have no choice." Damn, he thought to himself, Sally was right. They were far too early and now they would start well behind the Australians. "Tack now," Mark commanded, trying to rescue the situation. "Now, Shane, around the starting-boat and back over the line. Let's move it, team!"

The starting gun fired and the Australians powered over the line. Shane brought the *Madeline* around and over the line again, more than a minute behind the other yacht.

"We have to work our butts off now," Mark shouted to his crew, angry with himself. He should have listened to Sally but he was being stubborn. He'd have to try and make up for it now. "Peter, watch the water for gusts of wind. Jimbo and Jean, keep trimming that sail. Sal . . . um, well, do your stuff!"

Sally glared at Mark. He tried smiling at her contritely but she was having none of it. Bloody typical testosterone behaviour, she thought to herself. He's no better than the rest of them. Mark mouthed a 'sorry' at her but she gave him one more icy stare before turning her attention to the mainsail.

"Wind to the right," Peter yelled. Mark decided to trust his team-mate's judgement this time.

"Tack over," Mark told Shane. The crew, all aware that their mistake at the start had set them back considerably, executed a perfect tack. "Nice work, gang," Mark encouraged.

The wind was shifting in their favour, helping them reach the mark swiftly. As they approached the first buoy the Australians rounded the mark and were heading towards the second.

"See you in the bar!" Greg yelled over the stern of the yacht, grinning.

"It's not over yet," Mark replied determinedly.

After rounding the mark, Peter attached the spinnaker pole to the mast and carefully lowered the large Jenny onto the deck. Jimbo and Jean hoisted and set the light front-sail perfectly.

"Head up, Shane, on a tight reach," Mark commanded. The *Madeline* cut through the waves like a warm knife through butter, leaving a wash of white foam trailing behind her. They were getting closer and closer to the Australian yacht. As they reached the gybe mark their competitors were only a few boat-lengths ahead. "Be very afraid, Greggy boy!" Mark yelled confidently.

The St John's crew gybed the *Madeline* like professionals, keeping the spinnaker filling and the yacht sailing smoothly and fast. They could hear spectators cheering and clapping but they couldn't let it break their concentration.

"Keep the heads together, gang. We're doing great. Don't lose it," Mark encouraged.

As the third mark loomed closer the Australian boat was only a few metres ahead. Greg's team whipped down the spinnaker seconds before rounding the mark faultlessly.

"We'll tack straight after rounding the mark," Mark stated. "We don't want to lose the Aussies."

Sally bit her lip. The wind was filling in from the right. They needed to forget Greg's team and concentrate on sailing a perfect second beat. Mark watched Sally's face. He knew she had something to say. He swallowed his pride. After all he was wrong before and he could be again. "Sal?" he asked. "What do you think?"

Sally looked carefully at Mark's sincere face. Feck it, she said to herself, and took a deep breath. He'd asked her so she was going to tell him what she thought. She took a deep breath. "We should be going right, Mark. We need to get ahead of the Australians, not just follow them. There's wind filling in from the right. We need to sail our own beat."

Mark thought quickly, checking the compass readings and the clouds to the far right of the course.

"She's right, gang. We're going with Sal."

St John's sailed the second beat as if their lives depended on it. The finishing line was between the mark and the committee boat and spectator boats of all shapes and sizes littered the water nearby. Once again the crew, with Sally's impeccable judgement, had chosen the favoured side of the beat. They inched closer and closer to the mark, lifted all the time by the oscillating wind-shifts. The Australian boat was approaching the line from the far side.

"Get ready to tack for the line," Mark told his crew, looking at Sally with one eyebrow raised. She nodded curtly. Mark checked their position and the position of Greg's team. "They'll have to approach the line on port," Mark stated. "We have the advantage as they'll have to give way to us." He waited almost half a second before galvanising the Irish team into action. "Right, go, go, go!" Mark yelled. Shane tacked the boat and the crew tacked in record time, without a hitch. "OK, this is it, St John's," Mark stated. "Start praying!"

The Australians tacked. The two boats were now heading for the line, which was ten or twelve boat-lengths away. The two teams grew closer and closer.

"Starboard," Mark boomed at the Australian boat. "Do you not read your rules, Aussies? Tack now!"

There was a deathly silence for a split second before Greg's voice rang out. "Shit . . . they've got us. Tack," he yelled frantically. The Australian boat turned, away from the *Madeline*. It was a sloppy, makeshift tack. The

Madeline powered towards the line, speeding across it with the Australians behind them by a mere four boat lengths. The gun acknowledged the Irish triumph. The St John's team went wild.

"We did it," Mark screamed. "We fucking did it!"

Shane and Jimbo hooted and cheered. Peter hugged and kissed an astonished Jean. Mark grabbed Sally by the hands and pulled her towards him. "Sal, I couldn't have done it without you. You're the best."

Sally's heart melted. She decided to overlook his previous bad judgement and gazed at him in open admiration. "It was you who kept us all together, Mark. You were the glue."

The *Madeline* was now head to wind, sails flapping wildly in the breeze. Jimbo and Peter lowered the sails, helped by Jean. Sally started up the engine. Spectator boats buzzed around the yacht, like bees around a honey-pot, cheering the Irish team.

Sheila and Jules came alongside in the French coach's rescue boat.

"How are my world champions?" she asked, grinning ecstatically at Mark and his crew. She climbed onto the *Madeline* with Jules following close behind her. Shane admired the way the Frenchman was having a good grope of her firm buttocks as he 'helped' her up. A guy after his own heart!

"What a race!" Jules said. "You sailed two of ze best beats I ever see. And the mark roundings!" He kissed his fingers loudly with Gallic flair.

The St John's team beamed from ear to ear. Sally started to cry, huge, heavy tears falling from her eyes onto the deck of the yacht.

"Ah, Sal, what's the matter?" Mark asked with concern.

Sally gulped and smiled through her tears. "Nothing's the matter. Everything's perfect. I'm just so happy."

That evening at the packed prize-giving dinner the Irish team partied like they'd never partied before. Greg and the rest of the Australian team was disappointed but were taking it well. True to their word, they filled the St John's table with drink and kept it coming all night. After the meal, lubricated with lots of French wine, Mark's team were called to the stage to collect their prizes. The mayor's wife presented each of the crew with a cut-glass vase. She winked at Shane and gave him two smacking kisses, precariously near his lips.

"And now," the mayor announced. "I'd like to present the captain of the Irish team, Mark Mulhearne, with the World Sailing Championship Trophy. Mark, would you like to say a few words?"

Mark grinned and took his place in front of the microphone, holding the large silver trophy in front of him. "Unaccustomed as I am to public speaking . . ." he grinned. "Only joking, guys, this is going to be short and sweet. Thanks to Sheila Murphy, our coach, for all her hard work and encouragement." Sheila beamed up at him from her seat in front of him. "I'd like to thank the host club, all the organisers and all the competitors, especially the Aussies for making this an event we'll never forget." Greg and his team cheered and clapped. "And finally I'd like to thank my team – Jean, Jimbo, Peter, Shane and Sally for all their talent, charm, enthusiasm and hard work. It was an honour to sail with you all." Mark's speech was greeted with a rousing response of claps, whistles and cheers. He held the silver trophy high above his head. Sally smiled at him, tears in her eyes once again, and he smiled back, blowing her a kiss and nearly crowning himself with the trophy in the process.

"What a night!" Sally said to herself, as she listened to the applause and watched the smiling faces looking up at her on the stage. "What an amazing night!"

Later that evening Sally rested her head on Mark's shoulder. They had been strutting their stuff on the dance floor for hours and now they were taking a well-deserved break. Shane was dancing with Jo, Peter and Jean, blatantly eyeing up girls on the dance floor. Lara and Jimbo were dancing their own slow set to the strains of 'Great Balls of Fire', belted out energetically in pidgin English by the local band. Jules and Sheila had disappeared, ostensibly to 'look at the stars'.

"Ah, Miss," Jimbo had cried earlier when she had smilingly stated her intention. "That's my line!"

Sally closed her eyes. It didn't get much better than this . . .

* * *

Sally woke with a jolt.

"We are experiencing some turbulence, please fasten

your seat belts."

Her head was resting on the shoulder of the businessman beside her.

Sally lifted her head and smiled sheepishly. "Sorry," she murmured.

The man smiled back.

"Don't worry, my wife does it all the time. Who's Mark by the way?"

Sally's cheeks tingled. She must have been talking in her sleep. She smiled. "It's a long story."

"Ah," said the businessman kindly. "I see." He nodded his head wisely before picking up his paper and recommencing his reading.

Chapter 9

"Well, Eve, what can I do for you today?"

The seated figure, whose dark-haired head was buried in the latest copy of *Hello* looked up.

About time, she thought to herself. The incessant drone of bland pop music had begun to annoy her. The noise had rendered her unable to concentrate on the morning's stock-market figures, leaving her to the mercy of the glossies. Eve would never have admitted it, but she had actually quite enjoyed flicking through the pages of fashion, make-up and advice on men and relationships.

Eve was a loyal customer of Blue's hair salon. She appreciated their professional, no-nonsense attitude and, as she liked to be perfectly groomed at all times, Michael or 'Mick' as everyone called him, was an excellent choice. An award-winning stylist with a refreshingly male down-to-earth manner, firm, cool hands and none of the inane 'Going anywhere nice on your holidays? Anything nice planned for the weekend?' patter.

Mick knew this customer's hair intimately, right down to the follicles, and he also knew that she liked to keep her private life just that – private.

Eve stared intently at her austere reflection in the mirror for a few lingering seconds.

"I'd like something softer," she stated firmly to the waiting stylist. "With a more gentle effect around my face, and maybe a colour."

Mick nodded, showing no emotion on his handsome face. This client always asked for the same style, businesslike and rather severe. He wondered what had instigated this change. He lifted the fringe of her short, black hair in his fingers and began twisting the ends in towards her face.

"Perhaps a feathered effect to the fringe," he suggested. "With low lights to give the style movement and shine. In chestnut, I think, with a touch of honey." Mick looked at his client in the mirror.

"Sounds fine, Mick," she assented.

Mick gestured to a waiting junior who draped a black cape over Eve's perfectly cut dark navy suit and tucked a dark red towel around her neck. The young girl who introduced herself as 'Jewel' led Eve over to the stainless-steel sinks, tottering on painfully high plastic leopardskin wedge sandals. Jewel was wearing combats and a belly top, revealing a startling spiral belly-ring. She carefully shampooed Eve's hair, massaging her scalp rhythmically with her fingertips.

Eve began to relax, under the pressure of the firm and obviously experienced fingers and her mind began to wander. She thought of the school reunion and of Mark, for whom, if the truth be known, she was changing her hair. A scene from many years ago drifted into her head . . .

* * *

"Eve, you look different, what is it?"

Eve walked into the snug of the Stag's Head where her boyfriend, Mark Mulhearne, was waiting.

She frowned slightly before smiling. "Can you not tell, Mark?"

"Hang on, give me a minute." Mark looked carefully at Eve, concentrating. "I know, new glasses, that's it, isn't it?"

Eve sighed in exasperation. "I'll give you one more chance," she said, running her fingers obviously through her newly shorn locks.

"Oh, sorry, of course, your hair. Eve, it's great, turn around."

Eve pirouetted obediently, smiling.

"Hey, it's great, but it's kind of short, isn't it?"

Eve sat down slowly. "Yes, it is Mark, but I needed a change and what with these interviews coming up soon I want to look, well you know, professional and smart. Appearances are very important, you know, in interviews. Professor Marr says that the Milk Round is an excellent starting point for any young professional and . . ."

"Eve," Mark interrupted. "I know all this interview stuff is important to you, love, but can we just drop it for one evening, do you think? Please? We are here to enjoy ourselves after all."

The young woman stared straight in front of her at the stuffed animal to the left of the bar. She took a deep breath before turning to face her boyfriend. "Mark, you know, I don't like your attitude. These interviews may be the turning point of my life. It's different for you Law students – you know exactly what's in store for you next, bar exams or the like. But for us Business students it's a tough old world out there, and no-one is going to tell me that these interviews are not important." Eve's voice had lifted an octave and she began to talk more quickly. "It's a tough world, Mark. I want to be successful in my career and it's even harder for a woman. International finance is a man's world, you know. I'll have accountacy exams in the first few years while working full-time and I'll have to out-perform everyone to get what I want . . ."

Mark placed his hands on her agitated shoulders. "Eve, calm down," he said gently. "There is more to life than work. You need to get things in perspective. You're becoming obsessed with all this. I'm worried about you."

Eve's eyes glinted with anger. "I'm sick of you being so patronising, Mark Mulhearne. It's my life and I'll be 'obsessed', as you call it, with whatever I like. Don't you tell me what I can or cannot do. How dare you!"

The young man sighed deeply. "I wasn't trying to tell you what to do," he stated evenly. "I'm just worried about you, that's all. You are studying so hard and we never seem to spend any time together anymore. Whenever I suggest a night out you always seem to be studying."

Eve looked intently at her boyfriend. He was really starting to annoy her and she failed to understand his easy-going *laissez-faire* attitude to his exams and his future. And as for him giving her advice on how to live her life, well, that was just plain ridiculous. In fact, she decided suddenly, she had had enough. She would be much better off on her own – she could study all the time and she wouldn't have Mark annoying her about going out.

"I don't want to see you anymore," she blurted out to her astonished boyfriend. "I'm sorry but that's what I want. I need to concentrate on my studies and you . . . well, you're just getting in the way. I'm sorry."

Mark was dumbstruck. He loved this intense, serious girl with all his heart. How could she do this? Was her study and her future career more important to her than their relationship? Obviously it was.

"Eve, I don't know what to say," he whispered in shock. "Are you sure? I mean, can we have a break, maybe just see each other at weekends until after the exams? I don't want to lose you."

She shook her head solemnly. "I'm sorry, Mark, but it's over, and that's final." Final and brutal.

* * *

"Miss Arnold, excuse me, Miss Arnold. Would you like conditioner?"

Eve's thoughts fell abruptly down to earth and landed with a bump.

"Oh, yes, thank you," she replied.

A few minutes later she was seated in the black leather and stainless-steel studio chair in front of a large, ornate steel-framed mirror. Eve watched with interest as Mick divided her hair into sections, brushed one of two different strong-smelling purple mixtures on the strands and wrapped them in tin-foil-like rectangles. Soon her entire head was silver and Eve felt like a Christmas turkey waiting to be cooked. As if on cue, a space-age heating contraption, divided into three modules, was placed over and around her head, sending warm currents wafting around her. The sultry air made her feel quite sleepy and once again she thought about the past, about earlier days when herself and Mark were happy and content.

* * *

"What are you thinking about?" Mark ran his fingertips over Eve's left arm, slowly and delicately, catching each hair on her warm flesh. They were in Mark's single bed, lying closely together under the duvet. Mark's back was touching the wall and his left arm was draped around Eve's shoulders. They were both pleasantly tired and sated after an afternoon's lovemaking. Eve had never known sex like this before. Mark was a highly considerate lover, gentle and kind, yet with the right amount of passion and strength. He made her feel hugely desirable and sexy, and she responded to his caresses with warmth and excitement.

Mark had been nervous with Eve at first. She was a serious girl and he hadn't known quite how to approach the whole sex thing. But he had been surprised and at times emotionally overwhelmed at her passion – not to mention her stamina.

Eve turned her head, focusing her eyes on the face next to hers on the white pillow. She smiled. "I'm supposed to be asking you that," she said. "It's definitely a girl's question."

"Seems like a logical enough question to me," Mark replied thoughtfully.

"If you really want to know," Eve replied, "I was thinking about the debate this evening in the Hist. I should really be going over my notes."

Mark sighed inwardly. He knew Eve wasn't one for declarations of undying love, but she could at least give him some encouragement every now and again. He may have asked a 'girl's question', but no guy in their right mind would answer in the way Eve had, unless they wanted to be ignored for the following hours or hit where it hurt. It wouldn't kill Eve to embellish the truth once in a while. He was disappointed.

"Eve, I love you, you know I do. But sometimes I wonder if you feel the same way I do, you know."

"Oh, Mark, you know I love you. It's just that there are other things going on in my life right now and I have to give them some thought too."

Mark leaned over and clicked the play button on the tape recorder resting on the bedside table. The gentle strains of Van Morrison's 'Brown Eyed Girl' filled the tense air.

"Eve, I need you to talk to me. Sometimes I have no

idea what is going on in your head. You shut me out so much and it really gets to me."

She bristled with irritation. Not this again. Mark was always telling her to 'talk to' him, but she thought she did. It just wasn't in her nature to divulge her deepest thoughts. In fact, she tried not to navel-gaze if she could help it. Keeping on a calm and even keel suited her; she knew where she was going, career-wise, and her emotional life had to follow on behind. If she needed to talk to someone, her mother was always there in the background. Betty was the only person in the world she trusted with her personal worries and stresses.

Mark was startled by Eve's lack of response.

"Eve, I just want to be close to you."

She smiled through gritted teeth and tried to placate him.

"I know, Mark, and I understand. We'll talk about it some other time. But right now I have to get back to the library. I'm sorry." She rolled over, planted a fleeting kiss on his cheek, and jumped out of bed. Mark gazed at her perfectly formed buttocks and sighed, this time openly.

* * *

A sharp, metallic ping resounded from Eve's heater and Mick strode over. Eve's cheeks were flushed, a gentle natural pink.

She could be a good-looking bird, he thought to himself, if she smiled and loosened up a bit.

After Jewel removed the tin-foil rectangles from Eve's hair and washed it, Mick cut her newly coloured head.

He then blow-dried it personally, taking especial care. Eve was one of his best clients and he valued her custom. And strangely, he recognised that the woman was different this visit, more anxious somehow, eager to look her best. Mick wondered if there was a new man in her life and before he could stop himself he asked –

"Have you anything special coming up, Eve?"

"Well, actually, my class ten-year reunion is coming up in a few weeks. I'm looking forward to meeting some old friends."

Mick smiled gently. "Well, you'll knock them dead, Eve. I hope you have a brilliant time."

"Thank you," she replied gratefully. She gazed at the face looking out from the soft, new fringe. The expertly applied colours and the clever cut gave her hair movement and depth and she was very pleased with the whole effect.

Eve walked out of Blue's with her head held high and a renewed vigour and jaunty confidence in her step. Next stop, dress, she decided.

Chapter 10

The following Saturday, Eve and her mother went shopping. They travelled into Dublin city on the Dart, chatting easily about Betty's business and the forthcoming reunion. Mrs Arnold was in flying form and she looked great. Dressed in a pair of boot-legged black trousers with stylish black high-heeled boots, a chunky black cotton polo-neck jumper and a padded sleeveless cream fleece, she would have passed for a woman in her twenties, not in her early fifties. In fact, Eve felt positively dowdy beside her in a grey fleece jacket, indigo denims and Nike runners.

"Is the reunion dressy?" Betty asked.

"It's black tie," Eve replied. "I want to find something classy but sexy, maybe a slinky long slip dress in BT's."

Betty stared at her daughter with interest. She wasn't usually all that concerned with clothes, except business suits. What had brought this on? And was Eve blushing, under the expertly applied make-up?

After a few seconds of silence, both women gazing out the window, Eve ventured –

"Did I tell you Mark Mulhearne will be there – he's one of the speakers?"

Suddenly Betty understood. She knew her only child better than she knew herself at times. Eve had never been one to volunteer her thoughts, but she opened up to people, if given space and a little time. Betty hoped that someday a special man would understand this too. She remembered Mark Mulhearne well and she had been disappointed when the two students had broken up. She had hoped that he might be the one.

"It's fine, Mum," her daughter had reassured her at the time. "It was a mutual thing. We are both young and we have to think of our studies. It was getting too serious."

Betty had liked Mark, he had been good for Eve, kind but strong. In the last few years Eve had had several dates, always with work-related men, but nothing solid had come out of it. Betty worried sometimes that her stubborn daughter worked too hard and didn't take enough time out for herself. Eve didn't seem to have any close friends. She met female colleagues for lunch from time to time, and attended dinners with clients at the weekends. But there didn't seem to be anyone there that Eve could talk to. Perhaps she was too close to her daughter; she had always been more of a friend than a mother. Betty wanted Eve to find the same kind of happiness that she had found with Tom and now with Sean. Maybe Mark and Eve would get together again.

She could sense that this is what her daughter was mulling over. Maybe now that Eve had this to think about, breaking the news about Sean would be easier.

Betty dreaded telling Eve about Sean, but today was the day.

Last night Sean had spoken firmly and reproachfully to her. "Betty, you have to tell Eve – it's only right. She deserves to know and to be honest I'm not prepared to sneak around like some sort of criminal any more. And I want to see you all the time, not just when Eve isn't around."

"I know, Sean," Betty had replied, sighing. "I'll tell her this weekend, I promise. It's difficult, I know you hate me mentioning it but with the age gap and everything, I don't know how Eve will take it."

"Betty, your daughter loves you and I'm sure she just wants you to be happy. I understand how you feel but please, for us, you have to be honest with her. Because I want to marry you."

Sean was almost ten years younger than the vibrant, attractive widow. She had become a firm friend of the family over the last few years, working with Sean's mum Nessa. The Connolly family had practically adopted Eve as their own, and Betty and her daughter had enjoyed years of Sunday lunches, Christmas dinners and summer barbecues at their friends' house in Donnybrook.

Sean had been married briefly in his thirties to a stunning French girl, who he had met on holidays in Galway of all places. But Chantal had missed her homeland dreadfully and Sean, in the end, didn't love her enough to follow her over to Paris. In the back of his mind he knew that it would break his heart to leave Betty Arnold, the calm, beautiful, talented woman who he knew he shouldn't love.

After the break-up of his marriage, Sean had talked to Betty about his true feelings for her, one balmy August evening. They were sitting in her garden in Sandymount, drinking cool glasses of Chardonnay. The air around them held the tangy smell of sea, mixed with the heady fragrance of Betty's blooming flower garden. They were sitting in companionable silence when Sean reached over and placed his hand on Betty's.

"Betty, much as I miss Chantal, I realise now that without you my life means nothing." He placed a finger on Betty's lips as she opened them to speak. "Betty, before you say anything, I have to tell you. The age thing, it doesn't matter to me – and Mum and Dad, well, they'll get used to it. I just love you, Betty."

Betty, confused and scared yet strangely ecstatic, started to cry. She knew then that she loved this intelligent, hard-working and considerate man. She looked at him through bleary, wet eyes.

Sean took Betty's head in his hands and held it to his chest. He stroked her hair lovingly, whispering to her gently, "I love you, Betty. I love you so much."

The Connollys had reacted surprisingly to the news. Nessa had cried when Betty told her and Jack had given her a huge bear hug.

"We always hoped that some day this would

happen," Jack had stated. "We could see how close the two of you were but with Chantal and everything . . . well, that's all in the past now. Betty, Sean, what can I say? It's brilliant news. Let's open a bottle of bubbly and celebrate."

That had been almost two years ago, and Betty had been reluctant to tell Eve then. She wasn't sure how she felt about Sean or if it would last and she didn't want to worry Eve. But most of all she was worried that it might change her close relationship with her daughter. The years had drifted by and she still hadn't told Eve. And last night they had talked about getting married. She really had to tell Eve and fast!

The train approached Pearse Street station and the two women were soon striding up Nassau Street.

"Sean was asking for you," Betty began gingerly.

"Oh, how is he?" Eve asked.

"He's great. Eve, there's something . . ."

Eve stopped suddenly and looked in the window of a clothes shop. "What do you think of that red dress, Mum?"

Betty sighed. This was going to be more difficult than she thought. Maybe she would leave the revelation until later. She smiled and ran her practised eye over the dress.

"Eve, that's a pregnancy dress," Betty laughed. "Are you trying to tell me something?"

Eve blushed and shook her head. "Of course not, how stupid. Let's go on."

She was embarrassed at her mistake. Was her mother

making fun of her? Betty Arnold was in annoyingly good form and it made Eve envious.

As they made their way towards Grafton Street Betty suggested that they have a look in Oasis.

"Mum, we're too old for the clothes there. It's all teeny-bopper stuff, you know – rave and club wear."

Betty smiled. At times she wondered about her daughter. She was definitely getting old before her time. "But Eve, that's where I got this fleece. And they have some nice shift dresses."

But Eve was having none of it. In her opinion, unless you spent at least two hundred pounds on a dress, it wasn't worth wearing.

The two women took the escalator to the first floor of Brown Thomas, after treating themselves to two lipsticks each, 'winning' a complimentary Clinique Bonus Pack with their purchases, packed with baby versions of lipsticks, various luxury creams and washes and rather snazzy pink and orange satin make-up bags. Eve had chosen long-lasting lipsticks in 'Plum Jam' and 'Creamy Nude', perfect for work. Betty had gone for a luscious pink lipstick, with the provocative name of 'Naughty Naughty' and a funky dark red lip gloss called 'Mambo Kisses'.

"Right, let's try DKNY and Miu Miu," pronounced Betty.

Eve looked doubtful. "I was thinking more along the lines of Versace or Paul Costello," she said. "You know, classic and understated."

"Eve, you want to knock his . . . I mean their socks off, don't you? I don't think classic and understated will have that effect, do you? Anyway, I thought you said in the train that you wanted something sexy."

Her daughter was staring at her with a strange look on her face.

"What?" Betty asked.

"You know, don't you?"

"Know what?"

"Oh, don't play games with me, Mum, I know you know."

Betty considered replying with "I know you know I know what?", but she thought better of it. Her daughter had a rather serious expression on her pale face.

"Yes, love, I think I understand. It was the way you mentioned Mark on the train. Now I'm sure you don't want to talk about it, but I'm here if you do, OK?"

Betty perused her anxious child's features. Eve may be a grown woman, she thought to herself, but she's still my little baby, and if I could live her life for her I would.

"Maybe later, Mum," Eve said quietly. "Right now I want to find the right dress."

Eve tried on several classic long evening dresses. Her mother was right, they were all too safe, she wanted something dramatic and different. They left the department store and walked up to the Powerscourt Centre where Betty had noticed an interesting shop called Karen Millen.

On walking through the doors of the boutique, Eve stopped in her tracks.

"I don't think this is the right kind of shop for me, Mum. Let's go."

"Wait a second, Eve." Betty Arnold walked over to a rack of long silver dresses in a heavy, satin-look material. "These are amazing. Come on, try one on."

"Mum, this shop is full of teenagers. I'm not trying on a dress in front of a gang of giggling size eights."

"What size are you in dresses again, Eve?" Betty asked, ignoring her.

"I'm a twelve."

Betty picked a dress off the rail and pulled her sullen daughter over to the changing rooms. Eve is as bad as any teenager, she thought as she peered into the stylish curtained area, which was divided into private compartments.

"You see, there are proper changing rooms," she hissed. "Just humour me, love, it will look great."

Eve took the dress from her mother without saying a word and closed the heavy black curtain in her face. She would have to try the bloody dress on now to get her mother off her back. Who did she think she was – Cher? She was fifty-one for God's sake, not twenty-one. Eve removed her clothes, fuming with the injustice of it all and wriggled the silver sheath over her slim hips.

She stepped out of the cubicle and Betty whistled under her breath. Was this incredible woman before her really her daughter? The dress had looked good on the hanger, but on Eve it was Oscar-Award-winning.

"Eve, you look just beautiful. It really suits you. I'd forgotten you have such an amazing figure."

Eve surveyed herself critically in the large mirror. "It's a bit on the long side. And do you not think it's a bit tight?"

The heavy silver material clung in all the right places, and shimmered in the subdued lighting of the changing room. It had shoestring straps, embellished with silver embroidery and tiny silver beads. The front of the dress was cut straight across, dipping dramatically at the back, and hanging miraculously, skimming Eve's hips and sweeping to the ground. It was simply perfect.

A small red-haired woman trying on a tight, strappy green dress gazed at Eve enviously. "You have to buy that dress, love. If I had your figure I know I would. You look like a movie star."

Betty smiled at her.

Eve was still doubtful but her mother was adamant.

"Eve, I want to buy it for you. Please let me. I won't take no for an answer."

Chapter 11

Eve and Betty Arnold were now sipping frothy cappuccinos in Café en Seine. At their feet were stylish paper and plastic shopping bags in all colours of the rainbow.

Betty had spent a happy hour browsing in the Popular Psychology section of Waterstone's, perfectly at home in the 'New Age' room at the back of the ground floor. She liked the atmosphere in this bookshop, studious and intellectual, yet in some strange way homely and comforting. The black shelves were rather severe, from an interior design point of view, she thought to herself, but they worked. And she had recently begun to notice the attentive young staff, the cute males in particular.

Betty Arnold, she reprimanded herself, would you ever stop, you're fifty-one now.

Sean Connolly definitely had a bad effect on her. But life was just so much fun with Sean around, and the sex . . . A warm feeling swept over her, from head to toe.

It was just getting better and better. Sean was an incredible lover and he made her feel so young and full of life.

He was working on an old Church Hall today, replacing the rotting floorboards with original pine ones he had salvaged from another job. He adored his work, which enabled him to use both his head and his hands. Coming from a middle-class family, it had been a brave move to leave school straight after his Leaving and take a carpentry apprenticeship. Jack and Nessa Connolly had been dead set against it at first, but when they realised how determined their son was, they slowly relented.

Jack had hoped his only son would follow him into architecture – as a boy Sean had loved accompanying him to sites. But he had always been more interested in old buildings than bright and shiny new buildings. The active and energetic young man could never see himself sitting in front of a desk or a drawing-board all day. In time Jack realised that his stubborn son had made the right decision.

"Eve, there is something I need to tell you." Betty started tentatively, raising her voice to be heard in the buzzing coffee bar.

Her daughter seemed in better form, now that she had a dress for the reunion and a pair of silver strappy sandals from Carl Scarpa to accompany it.

Eve looked up from the *Irish Times Weekender* 'On the Town' column which she was scanning. "What's up, Mum?"

"I'm not sure how to start really."

Eve raised her eyebrows quizzically. Her mother seemed nervous. Was it something serious, her health perhaps?

"Well, Sean and I are – well, we are . . ."

"You and Sean what, Mum?" Eve asked slowly. What had Sean got to do with anything?

"Well, there is no easy way to say this love. Sean and I are in love and we are planning to get married."

Eve stared at her mother in shock.

"What are you on about, Mum? This is a joke, right? Sean Connolly is years younger than you, he's more my age."

"Eve, Sean isn't your age, and he's only a few years younger than me. Are you not pleased for me, love?"

Eve glared at her mother. "What do you mean pleased? Of course I'm not bloody pleased for you, I think it's crazy." Eve started to inhale quickly and the words came out of her mouth faster and faster. "What do you think people will think, Mum? You getting married again. It's an insult to Dad and . . ."

"Eve, that's enough." Betty stated firmly. "Stop it, you're getting yourself into a state. Your father would want me to be happy. I thought that's what you would want too. I know it's hard for you, but maybe yourself and Mark . . ."

"You leave Mark out of it," Eve spat angrily. How dare her mother bring him into this?

"Eve, I'm just saying that when you have someone you will understand."

"Understand what, Mum?" Eve asked. "What are you saying?"

Betty really didn't want to continue. She loved her daughter with all her heart and she didn't want to hurt her in any way.

"Forget it, Eve," she said.

"No, Mum, go on. What do you mean?"

Betty sighed. "Well, I just think you need someone, Eve. We all do. I just think you put too much of your time and energy into your work. I'd love to see you settled. You deserve to be happy and maybe Mark is the right man for you."

Eve's face turned purple with anger. How dare her mother make presumptions about her life. She was perfectly happy, she had a great job and – and a house. She was doing just fine thank you very much. She didn't need anyone feeling sorry for her, especially her own mother. A thought flickered through her mind. How long had this 'affair' between Sean and her mother been going on?

"When, Mum?"

Betty was confused and a little disturbed. She had worried that her daughter wouldn't take this too well but Eve seemed more than just a little upset.

"When what, Eve?" she asked gently.

"When did things with Sean start?"

Shit, thought Betty. She was hoping her daughter wouldn't ask that question, but in a way it was inevitable. "Well, a year or so ago, but it only got serious recently."

Eve's face was stony. "How many years ago?" she asked quietly.

"Ah, Eve, it's not important. Over a year, OK?"

"No, Mum, that's not OK. How many years have you kept this from me? Tell me."

Her daughter's intensity scared her. Eve's pale face showed no emotion. Betty felt decidedly uncomfortable but she had to tell the truth.

"About two years," she whispered.

"Sorry, I can't hear you," Eve sneered nastily. "Louder please."

"Two years."

Eve looked her mother straight in the eye.

"I will never forgive you for this, never."

She stood up abruptly, looking straight in front of her, and strode purposefully towards the door, leaving her mother sobbing, still surrounded by both their shopping bags.

Betty spent Sunday curled up on the sofa, with Sean beside her, attempting to comfort her. He found it hard to believe that Eve had been so cold and brutal towards her own mother. They were so close and Betty loved her only daughter so much. In fact, if it wasn't for Eve, things would have been a lot easier, but Betty was so concerned for her daughter's happiness that she had often sacrificed her own.

"It'll be all right," Sean soothed her. "Eve didn't mean what she said, she was upset, it all came as a bit of a shock to her."

Betty was unconvinced. "You don't know Eve like I do, Sean. You think you're stubborn – well – you're a pushover compared to Eve. She's the proudest and most immovable person in the whole world. Once she's made her mind up over something, that's it, there's no budging her."

Sean sighed. "But this is different, Betty. You're her mum for God's sake. The pair of you are really close, it will be fine. You'll see."

Betty started crying again. "Why do I feel like I've lost my baby? Oh Sean . . ."

Sean put his arms around her. It wasn't like Betty to get so upset, she was normally so rational and together. He could kill Eve Arnold for being so cruel.

On Monday morning Betty dropped into the IFSC in the hope of meeting Eve for lunch. She was greeted by Julie, the young blonde receptionist.

"Sorry, Mrs Arnold, Eve asked to be left undisturbed all morning," Julie said when Betty asked to see her daughter.

"Would you mind just telling her that I'm here?" Betty asked. "See what she says." She hoped that Eve had cooled off overnight.

Julie picked up her phone and talked briefly into it.

"Sorry, Mrs Arnold, she won't be able to see you," Julie said, feeling decidedly uncomfortable. Eve had been brisk and short on the phone. Wierd, not wanting to see your own mam. She lowered her voice. "Do you think she's sick, Mrs Arnold?" she asked in a whisper. "She looks terrible, like she's been up all night and she's in – well, I shouldn't say this but you're her mother – she's in really bad humour – you know, kind of snappy."

Betty smiled despite herself. Eve was always complaining about Julie and her busy-body nature. Her daughter would be horrified if she thought that she had been gossiping with the receptionist. Betty was half tempted to tell Julie everything to get at Eve but she dismissed this thought as childish. But surely Eve was being childish by refusing to talk to her? She had tried ringing several times last night but Eve had left the phone off the hook.

"Thanks anyway," she said to the over-friendly girl. "Would you mind giving these to Eve?" Betty handed over several shopping bags.

As soon as Betty had left the office, Julie had a good root through the bags. She fingered the heavy silver fabric of the Karen Millen dress enviously. Strange, she thought. I can't imagine the prim and proper Ms Arnold in this dress – it's so sexy. I wonder what's going on?

Eve stayed ensconced in her office all day, eating a gourmet chicken and salad sandwich at lunch and not tasting one crumb. She felt physically sick but she was trying to block out the previous weekend's events. Eve knew that she was behaving irrationally and hurting her mother, but she couldn't help herself. She felt so betrayed and so bloody alone. If she couldn't trust her own mother, then who could she trust? How could Betty have done this to her? And with that Sean Connolly. And she'd always secretly thought that Sean had fancied her, Eve, not her ancient mother.

And worst of all, now her mother had someone she wouldn't need Eve anymore. She would become completely redundant. Well, that was just fine by her! She was damned if she would let it bother her.

As she left her office at six, after an annoyingly unproductive day, Julie handed her the shopping bags.

"Your Mam left these in for you, Ms Arnold."

Eve snatched the bags from the receptionist and gave her an angry glare. "Thank you, Julie," she muttered through tight lips. "And Julie, next time if I say no interruptions I mean no interruptions, do you understand?"

"Yes, Ms Arnold," the cowering girl replied.

Bitch, Julie spat under her breath, after Eve had left. What's her problem?

Eve walked home at a brisk pace. She had left the office much earlier than usual – but she couldn't concentrate. She felt like punching someone or something. On reaching her front door she fumbled with the key in the lock, her eyes filling with sharp, stinging tears. I'm damned if I'm going to cry, she told herself. Stepping into her house she felt a little better. It was easier to deal with things when there was no one watching you. The red light on her answering machine was flashing. She pressed the play button.

"Eve, love, it's Mum. I called into your office earlier, I'm sure Julie told you. Are you OK? I'm worried about you. Please ring me when you get in. Eve . . ." her mother's voice broke slightly. "Eve, I'm sorry I didn't tell you earlier, I really am. I love you, I'm sorry."

Eve stared at the white answering machine, her eyes filling with tears. She knew in her heart of hearts that she should just ring her Mum and say it was OK and that she loved her too. But she couldn't. She stubbornly took several deep breaths, flicked the tears away with a beautifully manicured and French-polished finger and walked into her immaculate kitchen. She made a cup of coffee and sat at the kitchen table until the light began to fade. Several hours later she swallowed three sleeping pills and fell into a dull, senseless sleep.

Chapter 12

Ashling was woken by the incessant ring of the telephone beside her bed. She grabbed the receiver, pushed her wild morning hair out of the way and answered groggily.

"Hello?"

"Ashling, I know it's your day off but I need you to cover a story."

"Morning, Jim," Ashling said, smiling at the hectic voice of her news editor. "And how are you this morning?"

"Ash, it's a great story. Paul from *Lads Unlimited* has just had twins in the Rotunda. And he's agreed to give us an exclusive interview. And having a youngster and all I thought of you."

Ashling laughed. Typical man.

"Jim, are you sure it was Paul who had the baby? That wouldn't just be a good story, that would be a bloody miracle!"

"OK, so it was his girlfriend Jackie who did all the

hard work. I know, I know. But listen, Ash, will you do it or not?"

Ashling sighed. Due to their long and erratic hours, staffers in the *Courier* worked a four-day week and Friday was her day off, but Daniel was in school today. Tizzy had kindly dropped him in, giving her a extra stint of much needed-shut eye.

"Yes, yes, what time do I need to be there and who's taking the pictures?"

"Thanks, Ash, I owe you one," Jim replied. "Eleven-thirty, ask at the reception for the room number, there's heavy security but they are expecting you. And the snapper is Chris Doyle, I'm not sure if you've met him yet, he's the new staffer."

Ashling grabbed a banana on her way out the door. She had had just enough time to have a quick shower. Her brown leather back-pack was always full of the necessary notebook, pens, and address book, bottle of Evian, make-up, and hairbrush. She removed her yellow Nokia mobile phone from its recharger and thrust into the already bulging bag.

In less than ten minutes from the time Jim called, Ashling was in her old red Volkswagen Golf on the way to the Rotunda hospital. She sang along to a David Gray tune on Phantom FM as she whizzed along the coast road towards town. It was a lovely summer's day, warm and bright. The sun was peeping its way around fluffy white clouds, and the sea to her right at Dun Laoghaire was sparkling blue. She noticed some brightly coloured blue sails bobbing about in the harbour. Lucky things, she said to herself.

Soon she was driving up O'Connell Street. Turning left she approached the Rotunda entrance and spotted a parking space right beside the door.

"Excellent," she exclaimed manoeuvring her car deftly into the space.

There were several photographers standing outside the door, smoking.

"Hi, Ash," bellowed a rotund man with a red face. It was Eric, one of the photographers from a rival newspaper. "Have you got an interview with the *Lads* lad?" he asked, grinning.

"I might have," retorted Ashling. "You'll just have to read this evening's *Courier* to see, won't you."

The good-natured man laughed. "Good on you, Ash." He liked the smiley, bright young journalist. Some of the other women could be right stuck-up madams, but Ashling McKenna was different. She had a real spark and she was bloody good at her job too. Jim at the *Courier* was always singing her praises.

Ashling walked past the other curious photographers and journalists, straight to the reception desk. She smiled at the woman behind the desk.

"Hi, I'm Ashling McKenna from the *Evening Courier*. I'm here to see Paul and Jackie, please."

The receptionist looked at Ashling carefully. She seemed a little young to be an *Evening Courier* journalist. She had been warned to be vigilant. Sensing the woman's scepticism and well used to it, Ashling handed her a laminated press card. The receptionist peered at it carefully and handed it back to Ashling.

"That's fine, Miss McKenna, I'll get one of the porters to bring you up. Mr Doyle is already up there."

A chatty young porter in a navy uniform showed her through a maze of corridors and gestured her into the lift. "I'm not into *Lads Unlimited* myself, mind, but the girlfriend Millie loves Paul, so she does. He's a real star, nice too. Gave me an autograph for Millie. His kids are only gorgeous, got their mammy's looks so they do. Crystal and Juniper they're calling them. Born at three in the morning so they were. Difficult birth . . . although don't quote me on that."

Ashling couldn't get a word in edgeways and was glad when they reached the private room. There were two well-built men in jeans and black leather jackets loitering outside the door. One of them held a filofax open in his hand and was talking animatedly into a flashy silver mobile. He stopped as he noticed Ashling approaching.

He looked at her suspiciously, taking in her dungarees and what looked like a school-bag on her back.

"Ashling McKenna, *Courier,*" she stated calmly, smiling.

The man's face softened slightly. "Right, we were expecting you. The photographer is in there talking to Paul, it seems they met before in a club or somefink . . . Anyway, go on in."

"Thank you," Ashling said smiling again.

Cute girl, the *Lads Unlimited* manager thought to himself as Ashling disappeared through the door.

The room was unbearably hot. Ashling felt a rush of humid air brush past her face as she walked in the door. It reminded her of when Daniel was born, in St Paul's, another maternity hospital on the other side of town. She hadn't been in a private room, however, far from it. And she hadn't had many visitors. It had been a quiet and in some ways solemn affair.

Ashling could hardly see Jackie. The bed was surrounded by huge bouquets of exotic flowers, in all colours of the rainbow. Cards of all sizes stood, hung or were propped in every possible location. Giant stuffed animals sat on the counter behind the bed and there were boxes of smaller cuddly toys just inside the door. The young journalist had never seen anything like it. Paul O'Dee was certainly popular!

The new mum, Jackie Power, was lying in the large steel hospital bed, her eyes closed. At her side were two plastic cribs in which two tiny pink and wrinkly babies were sleeping soundly, swaddled in pink and blue hospital-issue cotton blankets. She looked exhausted; the skin around her eyes was grey from lack of sleep and she was deathly pale. Her natural blonde hair was scraped severely back off her face and she hadn't a scrap of make-up on. But despite all this, Jackie still managed to look beautiful. With high cheekbones, perfect skin and full, generous lips she was one of nature's success stories.

Paul O'Dee was sitting by the window, dressed casually yet carefully in a whiter than white shirt (Ashling decided it had just been taken out of its designer shopping bag as the iron creases were so sharply defined), black jeans and black boots. A pair of trendy wrap-around sunglasses sat in his perfectly gelled hair. An attractive blonde man dressed in jeans and a cream fleece with two cameras slung over his broad shoulders, sat to the singer's right. Chris, Ashling presumed. The two were chatting in hushed tones like old friends and interrupted their conversation to greet Ashling.

"Hey," Paul said grinning, his even pearlies catching the light. "Ashling, isn't it? Welcome to the hot-house!"

Ashling walked over to the 'boys', avoiding a huge helium stork which was wading out of a blue box beside the bed. The blonde man stood up and offered Ashling his hand. She shook it warmly, gazing into two shockingly bright blue eyes.

"It's lovely to meet you." Ashling could feel herself blushing – they were both drop-dead gorgeous. So she got straight down to business.

"Thanks for letting me talk to you, Paul," she began in a low, quiet voice. "I know you must be tired and I can see Jackie is drained. It's not easy, is it? I'll bet those two tinies can kick up some racket when they're hungry." She gestured towards the sleeping twins.

Paul was instantly taken with her. The twins were little demons when they wanted feeding, the roars out of them would wake the dead. They had a fine pair of lungs on them!

"Hiya," Jackie's groggy voice whispered across the room.

"Oh sorry, love," the singer said with concern. "We didn't mean to wake you."

"That's OK," she replied good-naturedly, beaming at her partner. "Is this the *Courier* pair?"

Paul nodded and smiled. Ashling could see why he was the teen sensation of the moment. Paul and his band, *Lads Unlimited,* had all the trappings of real stars – looks, talent, great teeth and they were charming and easygoing to cap it all. The press loved them and the public just couldn't get enough of the four Irish homegrowns.

Paul and Jackie had been together since their early teens and made a handsome couple. The astute young woman, who owned an exclusive designer clothes shop on Grafton street, had supported the singer in his early karaoke days, before he had hit the big time. They were obviously devoted to each – the new dad was now sitting on Jackie's bed holding her hand. Ashling was envious.

Lucky things, she thought to herself. Her own lack of partner has been an overwhelming factor when Daniel was born.

* * *

"You can't register the baby now, I'm afraid," the brusque matron had informed Ashling, after the registrar had visited all the married mothers. "All unmarried babies must be registered at the office on Lombard Street. Those are the rules. Anyway, the baby's father should also sign the birth certificate. And where is the father, dear? He should be here."

Ashling, upset and mortified, had muttered something about Owen having to work abroad before the matron had strode away, tut-tutting under her breath. It was bad enough having to deal with the birth and a hungry and demanding baby, without that kind of unhelpful interference, Ashling thought to herself.

The kind mother in the bed beside her, who had given birth to her fifth child the day before, had witnessed the incident. She swung her legs over the bed and came over to Ashling.

"It's OK, love," she reassured Ashling, putting a plump arm around her heaving shoulders. "Matron didn't mean to be unkind – she just has a strange manner. Don't take it to heart."

Molly O'Reilly sighed to herself. This young scrap of a girl was going to have to get used to other people's attitudes on single mums. Things hadn't changed all that much. Ireland was still a conservative country. At least now the young ones could keep their babies these days, that was something.

Ashling smiled through her tears at the thoughtful woman, feeling alone and afraid.

One of the twins began to whimper in its sleep. Its tiny

mouth made sucking motions and its eyes started to flicker. Paul reached over, pulled back the blue cotton blanket and gently lifted the wakening baby, taking care to support the small, floppy head. He handed the baby in her soft pink babygrow to Jackie who snuggled the tiny girl under her loose pink pyjama top and began to feed her naturally.

Chris blushed. A decidedly becoming pink, Ashling mused.

"I hope you don't mind me feeding Crystal," Jackie said, smiling at Ashling and then at Chris. "The twins need to be fed a lot because of their size," she continued. "They were only five pounds each at birth."

Ashling was delighted with the self-confident new mother. If only she herself had been so laid back about feeding. "We don't mind at all, do we, Chris?"

The photographer looked sheepish. "No, not at all," he assented.

"Now can I talk to you about the birth, Jackie?" Ashling asked, her pen poised on her reporter's notebook expectantly.

"Fire ahead," she said, smiling. Jackie appreciated Ashling's genuine interest and her perceptive questions. On previous occasions before the birth of Crystal and Juniper, or Juno as he was to be known, the journalists talked to Paul and Paul only. It was as if he was giving birth and not her. It kind of pissed her off, to be honest – she was the one doing all the hard bits after all!

Paul was also impressed. This writer really knew her stuff, asking great questions about epidurals and feeding patterns. She had even given his partner some helpful hints on breast-feeding, weaning and night feeds to boot!

Chris was feeling somewhat dejected, still sitting at the window. He was fiddling with his camera and cleaning his lens with a soft cotton wipe that looked like a baby wipe. He now knew why they always said don't work with animals or children. Or breast-feeding mothers, he added wryly under his breath. The young cameraman listened to Ashling interviewing Jackie Power. The reporter was good, damn good, he realised. She really knew how to put the other woman at ease and she was asking killer questions.

"So I believe marriage may be on the cards sometime in the future, Paul?" Ashling was fluidly and effortlessly switching her questions between the partners. This, the real question on everyone's lips, she saved for Paul, asking casually, hidden in the middle of other less controversial enquiries.

Paul was taken aback. How did she know that? Jackie blushed and looked down at her baby who was now sleeping peacefully, cradled in the crook of her right arm. They had decided not to announce their engagement until Jackie was out of the hospital. But Paul liked this genuine and bright reporter and he decided to give her the scoop.

He squeezed his girlfriend's hand, looked at her and

raised his eyebrows quizzically. Jackie nodded and beamed. Paul fixed his brown eyes on Ashling's face and smiled.

"Yes," he agreed. "We've decided to get married as soon as possible. Now that the twins are here we want to be a proper family." His eyes twinkled. "I love Jackie with all my heart, and you can quote me on that!"

Yes!! thought Ashling to herself. Front page news and it's all mine.

A few minutes later, twin number two, Juniper or Juno, woke up. Chris sprang into action, posing parents and babies on the bed. His right index finger danced over the shutter. He too recognised a lead story when he saw one and he wanted to capture the best possible shots.

It was now Ashling's turn to be impressed. Chris Doyle had the gift, he was a definite natural behind the camera. He's also very cute, she caught herself thinking before brushing the idea from her mind.

A couple of hours later Chris and Ashling met in the News Room at the *Courier*. Ashling had written up the story and sent it through the computer system to the sub-editor. It was unusual to see a snapper in the newsroom, Ashling thought with interest. "How do the shots look?" she asked Chris with interest.

"Great," he replied. "One or two are excellent, and I hate to say it but the babies look angelic in the pictures. They've been blessed with their parents' photogenic faces."

"Stars of the future," Ashling laughed.

Chris nodded. "Absolutely." And after a moment's pause he smiled. "Ash, would you like to grab some lunch with me?"

It was now Ashling's turn to smile. "Yes, thanks, Chris, that would be nice."

Chapter 13

"I wouldn't have taken you for a vegetarian," Ashling said smiling. "All the photographers I know are dedicated carnivores. In fact, I think a lot of them live on greasy all-day breakfasts."

"Ah, well, I'm not your average photographer, Miss McKenna, I'll have you know. There's lots of things I'm sure you'd be surprised at."

Chris and Ashling were sitting at a wooden table in the lofty environs of the top of the Powerscourt Townhouse Centre. They were tucking into heaped plates of baked potatoes with delicious salads from the vegetarian restaurant Blazing Salads. Ashling was sipping a thick fresh strawberry and yoghurt smoothie and Chris had chosen a ginger and apple juice concoction. The photographer was excellent company and they chatted like old friends.

"How did you get into journalism, Ashling?" Chris asked, loading his fork with snap peas.

"Well I did Arts in college and like a lot of people in my class, I hadn't a clue what I wanted to do when I left. Arts courses are funny like that – you learn everything and nothing, you know?"

Chris nodded. "I have lots of friends who did Arts all right, some of them are still in college – eternal students. Sure didn't I study for a year myself – History and Philosophy. Anyway go on . . ."

Ashling continued. "When I had Dan I realised I wanted to achieve something with my life. I wanted to do something different, I suppose. It sounds silly really but I wanted my baby to be proud of me when he grew up. I guess having Dan made me more focused and a lot more ambitious." Ashling took a sip of her smoothie. "So I started writing in my final year in college, after I had Dan. Small articles, just for the college papers and some local newspapers. And I took a night course in journalism. I was knackered and a nervous wreck by the time my finals came but I got them."

"Good woman," Chris commented.

"Then I did some work experience in the *Courier*, and a few months later a staff job came up and Jim, the News Editor, encouraged me to go for it. I was offered the job and the rest as they say is history."

"Wow, a meteoric rise to stardom – you must have worked hard, Ashling. It takes some journalists years to become staffers." Chris smiled. "In fact, I think you're brilliant. You have a job you love and you're raising a cool kid too. Hey Ash, I think you're SuperMum!"

Ashling was very taken with this kind and animated

man. And he didn't seem to be fazed by Dan which was important.

"Do you think I could meet Dan one day? Hey, we could play footie together?"

"He'd like that," Ashling said, grinning. "I'm sure it could be arranged. But I warn you, he's wicked with a football, takes after his mother. Now tell me about yourself, have you always taken pictures?"

"To be honest, I don't remember a time when I didn't have my camera with me, even as a child. I was forever snapping away. Half the time the photos weren't developed – my parents were sick of shelling out money to the chemists. But I learnt to develop my own soon enough and my dad set up a little darkroom in the garden shed. It's still there, although I haven't used it for years."

"That's so sweet," Ashling said. "How come you didn't finish college?"

"Well, I really enjoyed college but I was never into the studying lark, you know? I was a bit too fond of the bar and I spent a lot of my time in the Photography Society darkroom. I took a lot of pictures for the college magazines and like you I started getting work into the local papers."

"And then . . ." Ashling encouraged.

"The summer after my first year a gang of us went to Paris for the summer. I was in my element. I spent my whole time looking at the city through a lens. God, it was a good summer – it's all a bit of a blur now. And in October I just didn't want to leave. I was making money

133

taking instant Polaroids of tourists and selling some of my prints on the street and to local galleries. I was in Paris for two years before the magic wore off. I missed my friends and my family and I decided to come home." Chris was silent for a few moments. "I still miss it though. The amazing buildings, the cafes, the whole atmosphere and the graveyards – yeah – especially the graveyards."

Ashling looked at him inquisitively. "The graveyards?"

Chris nodded, smiling. "Paris is full of these incredible old graveyards. They're not like our graveyards, they're full of art. The tombs have real stained-glass windows and most of the stones are pieces of sculpture, not just lumps of boring glassy marble. I'm sure you've heard of Père Lachaise where Jim Morrison is buried?"

Ashling nodded.

"I used to hang out there all the time and click away to my heart's content. I loved it there. When I came home all I wanted to do was to take pictures. I worked in a camera shop to get some money together and sent lots of my work to all the papers. I freelanced for a while, then the staff job in the *Courier* came up and I applied. So here I am."

They continued to talk, swapping newsroom gossip, until Ashling noticed the time. "Sorry, Chris, but I have to head. My little fellow will be wondering what has happened to me."

Chris looked disappointed. "How about a drink this evening and we can continue our conversation?"

Ashling sighed. "I'd really like to, Chris, but I'd never get a baby-sitter at this stage, sorry."

"No worries," Chris replied undeterred. 'How about I give you a few hours at home and I call in later with a bottle of wine and some food. If that's OK with you, of course?"

Ashling was delighted. Finally – a guy who was understanding and willing to compromise. "Chris, that sounds fun."

Ashling drove home, daydreaming all the way. As she reached Dalkey she stopped at Super Valu to pick up some bits – fishfingers and peas for Dan and fresh flowers for the house. Shit, the house is a state, she thought to herself as she walked briskly down the frozen food aisle. And I hope Dan behaves.

Ten minutes later she was outside her door. She lifted the shopping in, dumped it in the hall and then went out again to walk up the gravel drive to collect Dan from Tizzy's. Dalkey Manor was an imposing granite house, if you could call such a huge building a house. It had been in Tizzy's family for three generations. Mrs O'Connor, or Tizzy as she liked to be called, collected Dan from school every weekday and minded him until Ashling came home. Dan loved Tizzy and thrived in her company. As Ashling approached the house she spied the two of them in the garden, repotting Tizzy's prize geraniums.

"Hi, guys," Ashling shouted, waving.

"Mummy," Dan yelled and started running towards her. Ashling smiled, noticing his muddy bare knees. He threw himself into her arms. Ashling lifted him up, swinging him around.

"Hi pet, are you having a nice time?" Her son had smears of dried earth on his left cheek and there were strands of grass in his blonde hair. His cheeks were pink and he was the picture of health.

"Sure am, Mum," the small boy replied. "Tizzy and me, we were gardening all day long. For hours and hours. But don't worry – she made me wear my hat and I have sun cream on."

Tizzy strode towards them, her hair tied back in a Hermes scarf. She was wearing an old pair of navy canvas shorts and a light blue shirt which was knotted casually at the front. Her face was a rugged nutty brown, from days spent in her beloved garden. "How was your day, Ashling? Did you have to work?" Tizzy was well used to Ashling's erratic rota.

"How did you guess, Tizzy?" Ashling asked smiling. "It was interesting though. I interviewed Paul O'Dee from *Lads Unlimited* and his girlfriend, and they were a really nice couple."

Dan interrupted, pulling at Tizzy's shorts impatiently. "Ask Mum, Tizzy, go on."

"Dan, your mother was talking," the older woman chided.

"Oh Tizzy, I know, sorry but I'm dying to get the tent out." He looked up at her, his big blue eyes wide with excitement.

Tizzy smiled. "Ashling, Dan would like to camp out with me tonight in my late husband's army tent. It's a huge big hulking green thing but it keeps the weather out. What do you think?"

Ashling smiled. Tizzy was always coming up with mad schemes. She was worse than a child. But it sounded like fun and Dan would really enjoy it. And it would also leave the evening free for herself and the edible Chris Doyle!

"Well, I think that would be all right, Dan, but you have to wear warm pyjamas and behave for Tizzy. All right, love?"

Dan beamed from ear to ear. "Thanks, Mum, you're the best. Wait till I tell the boys in school about this. And Tizzy promised to tell me loads of ghost stories, didn't you, Tizzy?"

Tizzy laughed. "That's right, Dan. Now come and help me find this famous tent."

They spent a hour erecting the rather old and awkward canvas tent. Tizzy found an old ground-sheet, two air-beds and two sleeping bags. Dan was dizzy with excitement. Ashling fetched his brushed cotton Postman Pat pyjamas and his favourite bear. The two campers were cooking sausages and marshmallows over a camp fire, alias the brick barbecue, for their tea. Ashling left them to it. Tizzy was definitely one in a million!

It was then time to blitz the house, starting with the bathroom and moving upstairs to the open plan living-room and kitchen area. Chris was due to arrive around eight, so she didn't have much time. When she was satisfied that the place looked presentable, Ashling ran a bath, squirting in lots of her favourite fruit-smelling Body Shop Bubble Bath. She loved her baths in the generous-sized old white enamel tub. Although generally they were interrupted pretty swiftly by Dan, crashing in the bathroom door, to show his mum some newly crayoned picture or to tell her about some superhero's world-saving deeds, as seen on *Den TV*. This evening was different though – no Dan to break her peace. Ashling was blessed with Tizzy – she didn't know how she'd have coped over the last six years without her. She languidly soaped her body and then lay back to enjoy the warm, lightly scented water. A few minutes later the phone rang in her bedroom and the answering machine kicked in.

"Ash, Ash, are you there? Pick up if you are. It's me."

Ashling sighed – another shortened bath. But it was Annie, her best friend, and she wanted to talk to her. She leapt out of the bath, wrapping a large pink bath-towel around her dripping body and padded to the phone, leaving dark wet footprints on the cream carpet. She grabbed the phone.

"Annie, are you still there?"

"Sure am, Ash, I'm dying to hear all about the new snapper. Jim told me you were on a story with him today. And interviewing the delicious Paul from *Lads Unlimited* too! God, I envy you. All I get are obsessive and boring designers and most of the men are gay!"

Ashling laughed. Annie was the Fashion Editor in the *Courier* and brilliant at her job. She had a real eye for styles and trends, and was highly respected in the rag trade for being honest and incorruptible.

"Annie, it was Paul's wife who had the babies, I'll have you remember. It was a serious interview too. And

Chris Doyle is very nice thank you very much and a professional. I know your hormones are hopping these days but I don't think Harry would be impressed."

Annie's boyfriend was a dote. A wine merchant by trade, he was kind and decent and adored the quick-witted and bright Annie Brown. They had met when Annie interviewed him in her former job as the restraunt and wine critic for a women's magazine. Annie had bit the bullet and asked him out to a wine-tasting the next day and they had been inseparable ever since. A tall stocky handsome man in his late thirties with sandy blonde hair and an open, freckled face, they made a striking couple, as Annie was knee-high to a grasshopper. 'Little and Large' everyone called them.

"Go on, spill the beans. How nice is very nice? I hear he was sniffing around the news room and the two of you left together."

Ashling gave up. There was no fooling Annie – she had her finger on the pulse of every warm body in the *Courier!*

"OK, we went for lunch together and he's calling round tonight. Now are you satisfied?"

Annie whistled. "You're a fast mover, Ashling McKenna. Good on you, girl. And what have you planned for tonight, pray tell? Go on, spill!"

"Well, I'm not actually sure to be honest. He's calling over at . . ." Ashling glanced at her watch. "Shit, Annie, I have to go. I'm not dressed and he'll be here any minute!"

"That's bound to impress him, if he's a typical male,"

Annie giggled. "Go and make yourself decent and I'll talk to you in the morning. And good luck, Ash, have a ball."

Ashling flew around her room, brushing her hair with one hand and flicking through her wardrobe with the other.

Damn, she muttered to herself. Her favourite black trousers had Dan's poster paints down the front. She'd forgotten to get them cleaned. Well, it would have to be the black leather trousers. She dressed them down with a white long-sleeved T-shirt and a fleece cardigan.

Thank God for leather, she thought to herself. At least you can wipe it clean. She had just enough time to smear some lip-gloss over her lips, treat her eyelashes to a brush of mascara and spray some fresh lemony 'O' De Lancome on her pulse points before she heard a car pulling up outside.

She took a deep breath and walked to the door. Her stomach was fluttering with nerves and excitement as she watched Chris step down from a black jeep and stride towards her door. He was wearing light brown combats, a white T-shirt and a smile. Ashling's heart leapt. He really was georgous.

Chapter 14

Half an hour later, Chris and Ashling were driving down the coast road towards Wexford. When he had heard the change of plan Chris had made a snap decision to whisk Ashling away – 'into the night' as he had described it. He refused to tell her where they were headed. As Daniel was staying with Tizzy all night, Ashling felt deliciously worry-free. It was a beautiful summer's evening, warm with a light breeze. The sun still shone from the blue sky and they listened to cinema sound-tracks as they drove.

"Right, you decide," Chris had said. *"Betty Blue* or *Cinema Paradiso."*

Ashling had smiled, once again disarmed by this unusual man.

"You never cease to amaze me. First vege food, now cinema music. What's next Chris? Can you tango?"

Chris smiled. "You'll have to wait and see, my fair Ashling."

As they drove in companionable silence Ashling closed

her eyes and listened to the music. Mark loved French and Italian films, especially *Cinema Paradiso*. They had watched it together in The Lighthouse cinema on Abbey Street. Ashling had caught Mark crying at the closing sequence where the grown-up boy – Toto – looked back over his life to an accompaniment of censored film kisses. She had leant over and wiped a tear from his cheek and smiled.

"You big softie," Ashling had whispered.

"Lost opportunities and regret. They get me every time." Mark had whispered back.

She had never forgotten it – lost opportunities and regret – that about summed up their relationship or non-relationship. That and bad timing.

"Ashling, are you asleep?" Chris asked, interrupting her musings.

She opened her eyes and smiled at him."Fine thanks, just chilling out."

"We're nearly there. Have another doze if you want."

"I will so." Ashling closed her eyes. She tried not to think about Mark but ever since that invitation had arrived she just couldn't help herself. Old memories came flooding back. At least now she had Chris to take her mind off Mark.

Chris, she told herself, concentrate on Chris. But it was no use, Mark's kind, open face drifted into her mind once more. And that kiss . . . Ashling hadn't allowed herself to think about that final night for a long time. Maybe it was time she did and, as the Americans said, achieved 'closure'. But it hurt remembering it – so damn much.

* * *

"Ashling, how about Powerscourt on Saturday with Dan?" Mark had asked all those years ago. They were sitting in Ashling's flat sharing a plate of chips and watching Dan play with his toy garage in his Thomas the Tank engine pyjamas.

"But it's your last day, Mark. I'm sure you'll have a million and one things to do and people to see . . ."

"Rubbish. I'm Mr Organised and I'll have it all packed by then. And anyway I want to spend my last day with you guys."

Ashling had blushed a little. "In that case, we'd love to."

"Great. I'll borrow Susan's car and pick you both up at elevenish, OK?"

"Sounds good."

"How about dinner that evening?"

Ashling had looked at him carefully. "I though you were meeting the lads for drinks."

Mark coughed and seemed a little embarassed. "Well, um I was going to but . . . I wanted to spend the evening with you."

Ashling was taken aback. She didn't know quite what to say. "Just the two of us?"

"Yes," Mark said, fixing his eyes on Dan. "Just the two of us."

Ashling looked at Mark again and this time he returned her gaze. There were tears in his eyes. "God, Ashling, I'll miss you so much."

Ashling put her arms around Mark and pulled him towards her. They held each other for a long time until Dan leapt onto the couch and interrupted.

"Me, hug, me hug," the toddler insisted, wiggling his little body between them. The three sat on the sofa hugging each other until the light faded outside. Dan fell asleep after a while and Ashling picked him up in her arms and put him to bed.

"I'd better go," Mark had whispered on her return, noticing the young mother's stifled yawning. "I'll see you on Saturday."

Ashling saw him to the door. She watched his back as he walked down the stairs and tears welled up in her eyes again. What would she do without him?

The Powerscourt trip was a huge success. Dan loved the fountains and lake and Mark and Ashling watched with smiles on their faces as he dashed over the little wooden humpback bridges in the Japanese Garden.

"He's a credit to you," Mark said as Dan smiled and waved at them. "He's such a happy little fellow."

"Thanks," Ashling said. "I don't know what I'd do without him. He's a constant joy."

Mark squeezed her hand. "I'll miss both of you."

"Don't, Mark. Let's just enjoy the day."

"I hadn't realised how much you both mean to me and now I'm going away. Typical." Mark frowned. "You mean so much to me Ashling, I want you to know that. I think I . . ."

Just then Dan grabbed Mark from behind and held onto both his legs tightly. "Swing, swing," the little boy pleaded.

"OK, mate," Mark agreed, taking his two hands and swinging him in wide circles around and around.

Ashling smiled. Dan would miss Mark too. When the swinging finished they climbed up the grassy slopes towards Powerscourt House.

"What were you saying before Dan attacked you?" Ashling asked curiously.

"Oh nothing," Mark smiled. "I'll tell you later."

Dinner that night was in Fat Freddie's in Temple Bar. It had been one of their most popular haunts in college and reminded them both of wild nights spent laughing and boozing over a giant pizza. Annie had kindly offered to baby-sit Dan.

"I had a lovely day," Ashling smiled and munched some garlic bread. The hot herby butter covered her fingers and she wiped them on her napkin. Their table was illuminated by a large candle firmly planted in a wax-encrusted wine bottle.

"So did I," Mark agreed. "I know I've said it before but I'll miss you both so much. I didn't realise how much until the last few days. In a way I regret taking the job in Boston but . . . maybe it's for the best."

Ashling was sad. She wished Mark wasn't going but she couldn't say it to him. She wanted him to be happy and he wanted so much to succeed in Boston.

"Say something, Ashling. Will you miss me?"

Ashling looked at the pizza that the waitress had placed in front of her. The cheese was sizzling onto the wooden pizza board. It smelt delicious. She was trying not to cry but it was no use.

"Of course I'll miss you," she said as heavy drops fell onto her pizza.

"Don't cry," Mark said with concern.

Ashling raised her eyes. "What will I do without you?" she asked. "How will I cope?"

Mark was overwhelmed with feelings. Why had they left it until now to talk about their feelings? He blamed himself. He had been so concerned not to push Ashling and to give her space that he hadn't noticed how she felt.

"I'm sorry, Ashling, I had no idea . . . I thought, well you know – what with Dan and Owen and everything – that you didn't . . . Ah feck it, Ashling, I love you. I don't know why I didn't say it before. I guess I thought you knew."

Ashling stared at him in amazement. "You love me?"

"Yes!"

She took a deep breath. "Mark, you're going away tomorrow. Let's not make this any worse than it already is."

"Sorry," he mumbled, embarrassed. "You're right. I just wanted you to know."

Ashling tried to be strong. Why couldn't she tell him how she really felt? What was holding her back? "Let's eat," she stated firmly.

Later they walked back to her flat in silence. It was a beautiful evening. The stars were shining in a clear sky and the moon shone brightly over the city.

"I'm sorry," Ashling said finally as they reached Portobello bridge. "I didn't mean to be short with you at dinner."

Mark smiled gently. "I understand."

"No, I don't think you do." Ashling stopped and looked into his eyes. She leant forward and kissed him on the lips strongly yet tenderly. He pulled her towards him and kissed her back firmly. She caressed the back of his head as their mouths moved together. They had never kissed before and Ashling was blown away by his passion. They drew apart and Mark planted baby kisses on her closed eyes, her nose and her neck. He whispered her name as his lips once again moved towards her eagerly awaiting lips. She would never forget that kiss!

They stumbled towards Ashling's flat, drunk with passion, stopping at every lamppost for another kiss or caress. As they reached the door Ashling could see that the light was on in Dan's bedroom. Mark was running his hands over her shoulders from behind as she put the key in the door.

"Stop, Mark, for a second, I think Dan's still up."

Annie was waiting in the hall as they walked in. "Ashling, thank goodness. There's something wrong with Dan. He's really hot and flushed and he's got himself into a bit of a state."

Ashling followed Annie into Dan's bedroom. The small boy looked up at her from his bed with red-rimmed eyes.

"Mummy, mummy," he cried, throwing his arms around her and pulling her down onto the bed. He put his hands on his neck.

"Are you all right, Dan?" she asked with concern, sitting on his bed and holding him in her arms. "Annie says you haven't been well. Poor pet." She felt his forehead. He was burning up. "Where's sore, love?"

Dan put his two little hands on his neck. "Sore here, Mummy."

Annie was worried. "I'm sorry, Ashling, I didn't know what to do. He wouldn't tell me what was wrong. He just kept asking for you. Should I have called a doctor?"

"No, Annie, he'll be fine I'm sure. He has a bit of a throat infection, I'd say – he gets them now and again. I'll give him some Calpol and watch him all night just in case. And it's me who should be sorry. I should have rung to check he was OK. Or left you a number."

"Sure you weren't to know," Annie said kindly. "Anyway, I'm glad you're back." She noticed Mark lingering at Dan's bedroom door. "Mark, I've got the car – will I drop you home?"

Mark looked at Ashling carefully. He knew she needed to take care of Dan tonight but he wanted to stay so much. "Ashling?" he asked slowly. "What do you think?"

Ashling gazed at him with tears in her eyes. She had to think of Dan. How could she have gone out when he was obviously under the weather? He had seemed fine earlier but maybe her mind was on other things . . . "Go," she said, biting her lip and trying not to cry. "Maybe you could call in on your way to the airport and say goodbye."

Mark walked towards her and kissed her on the head. "Ashling, my flight is at five in the morning. But I'll write as soon as I can. Don't go forgetting about me now . . ."

"I won't," she promised, tears spilling onto Dan's silky head. "How could I? Now go on."

* * *

Ashling opened her eyes as Chris turned the jeep off the main road onto a small track. Her mind was brought back with a bump to the here and now. She tried to concentrate on the moment.

Soon they were driving on dirt mixed with sand. Ashling could smell the sea through the open windows. In minutes they reached a red metal gate. Chris jumped down, opened it, drove the jeep through and closed it again. In front of them was a field of tall, golden grass. As the black jeep drove to the far side of the field Ashling could see the silver and blue sea sparkling in front of them. It was a beautiful sight, the yellow grass juxtaposed against the sparkling sea.

"Here we are," Chis pronounced as they reached the sand-dunes. "Nirvana, or as close to it as you'll get in one hour."

"Where are we?" Ashling asked.

"It's my uncle's land," Chris explained. "It's quite near Brittas Bay. They have a holiday house over there." He gestured to the left, where Ashling could see a rambling bungalow, built of wood and painted light blue, with a black felt roof. "When we were kids me and my sister, Claire, came here every summer and stayed with the cousins and my aunt and uncle. We're all grown up now but we still make it down the odd time, and it's still one of my favourite places in the whole world."

Chris drove the jeep slowly towards the water's edge, stopping just before the wash met the beach. He jumped down, strode around to Ashling's door, proffered his hand and helped her down.

"It's so beautiful and so peaceful," Ashling sighed,

feeling the gentle sea breeze on her face. "Thank you for bringing me here. I love the sea."

"I thought you'd like it," Chris said, taking her hand in his. "Let's walk."

They walked to the far end of the beach, exploring the dark caves under the cliffs, where Chris swore hundreds of bats lived, and they sat quietly on the dry sand in one of the caves, until the sea began to reach the opening.

Back at the jeep, Chris lifted two plastic supermarket bags out of the back.

"I had planned a picnic in your garden, but this is even better."

He spread a black and red checkered rug on the sand and fished a bottle of red wine and two plastic cups out of the bag. He poured a glass for each of them and proceeded to unwrap cold meats, fresh white rolls, white plastic tubs of coleslaw and potato salad, paper plates and two sets of plastic knives and forks.

Now Ashling really was amazed. Chris was so organised, he had thought of everything. And to think she had only met him this morning! It seemed like a lifetime ago.

"I'm impressed," said Ashling, tucking into a filled roll. "This is just perfect."

"Wait, I nearly forgot," he sprang to his feet and pulled himself into the jeep. Seconds later the delicate strains of classical music filled the evening air.

"The City of Prague Philharmonic," he smiled.

Ashling smiled back at him. She hadn't felt quite so relaxed and content for a long time; she intended to savour every minute of this. Was this man for real? How could anyone be so perfect?

After they had eaten, he pulled her to her feet.

"Would you like to dance?"

They danced cheek to cheek, listening to the gentle sound of the waves lapping the shore, until the sun disappeared behind the sand-dunes. When Chris stopped dancing and held Ashling's face gently in his strong, cool hands, her lips were more than ready for his. They kissed, gently at first, then with a mutual intensity and passion. They then lay on the rug, hands entwined, sharing their thoughts, until all the heat had gone from the air.

On the way home, Ashling found it hard to stop smiling. It had been some evening. Wait until Annie heard the gory details!

As they drove up to Dalkey Manor Ashling began to worry slightly. She really liked Chris but she had to be careful. Sometimes guys got the wrong impression because of Dan. She didn't want things to happen too quickly.

They stopped outside the door. Chris smiled and kissed her lips tenderly.

"Bedtime for you Ashling, I think. Can I ring you tomorrow?"

Ashling felt curiously disappointed. She had been adamant that she wouldn't ask him in, but her mind was beginning to waver. And after all, she had tidied the house . . . She shook herself inwardly. Take it slowly, girl, she admonished herself.

"That would be nice, Chris," she replied. "And thank you for a wonderful evening. It really was brilliant!"

Ashling watched from the upstairs window as the black jeep drove slowly down the drive. She touched her lips with her index finger: she could still feel his mouth on hers.

He's perfect, just perfect, she thought to herself as she closed the curtains on the starry sky.

The next morning Ashling was woken unceremoniously by a heavy weight on her stomach.

"Daniel," she groaned, pushing the boy off her and sitting up. "Careful of your mother, please."

"Sorry, Mum," the small boy said. "I want to tell you all about our camping, it was so exciting!"

Groggily, she raised her head and heard a voice from outside her room.

"Daniel, did you wake your mother? You were supposed to get your Superman figures from your bedroom." Tizzy walked in.

It's just as well Chris Doyle isn't beside me, Ashling thought wryly.

"Don't worry, Tizzy, it's OK. And I'm dying to hear about the camping."

At lunchtime Chris rang. Ashling was delighted.

"How are you today?" he asked warmly.

"Fine thanks, apart from being woken at nine by my son jumping on me."

"At nine?" Chris asked slowly. "Does he always do that?"

"Ah, no. Just the odd time. He usually get up much earlier and plays in his room," Ashling replied.

"Right. Well, I was wondering if you would like to go

to the cinema this afternoon and get something to eat after. There's a new film called *Love Games* on in the multi-plex in Dun Laoghaire."

Ashling sighed inwardly. She had promised to take Dan to the Aquarium in Bray to see the sharks. Well, Dan wouldn't mind just this once – maybe Tizzy would take him. "Ashling? Ashling, did you hear me?"

"Oh, yes, sorry. Sorry, that sounds good."

"Grand, I'll collect you at two."

"Great, see you then, Chris."

Ashling walked into Tizzy's huge kitchen a few minutes later, explained about her outing with Chris and asked her to bring Dan to the Aquarium.

"Of course I will, I'd love to. Go and get Cleo some water, will you, Daniel?" Cleo was one of the many cats that inhabited Dalkey Manor.

"Is Chris the gentleman in the black jeep?" Tizzy asked when Daniel was occupied filling the cat's white metal bowl with water from the Belfast sink in the scullery beside the kitchen.

Ashling nodded.

"I don't mean to pry, Ashling, my dear, but does he know about Daniel?"

Ashling was a little irritated. She knew what Tizzy was getting at.

"I know it's none of my business, but be careful. You are your son's whole universe – you have to include him in all areas of your life. Do you understand?"

Ashling understood what Tizzy was saying but it annoyed her. Why couldn't she have something of her own? And anyway, for all Tizzy knew, Chris might be very interested in kids.

"Don't worry, Tizzy, we've only just met. Who knows what will happen?"

But Tizzy was worried. She didn't want to remind Ashling of Hugh, a crime correspondent on another paper who was crazy about her, but who happened to be 'happily' married. Or John, another photographer, who was worse than a child, wanting Ashling's attention all day and all night and who couldn't deal with her divided loyalties, even when the 'other man' in her life was her own son. Tizzy had seen Ashling through more than her fair share of man trouble. She wished someone decent and kind would come along like that Harry, Annie's beau. Tizzy liked him. But, however many doubts she had about the latest man, she couldn't live Ashling's life for her.

"OK, dear. I'm sorry for interfering, ignore me. You have a nice day and I'll have fun with Dan."

Ashling dropped Dan over to Tizzy's after lunch. Walking back to the mews she heard the phone ring. She dashed through the door and whipped up the receiver of the phone in her downstairs bedroom.

"Hi," she said breathlessly.

"What have you been up to? Running a marathon, were you?" Annie asked laughing.

"Oh hi, Annie," said Ashling, still breathing heavily. "Sorry, I was running for the phone, I'm so unfit. Hang on one second . . . right, I've got my breath back now. How are you?"

Annie blatantly ignored her question. "So spill the

beans. How was last night? And I want to know everything."

Ashling smiled. She was only too happy to tell her friend all about it. In fact she had been waiting for Annie to ring all morning.

"Annie, it was only brilliant. We went down to Wicklow in his jeep to this private beach and we ate and drank wine and danced."

She then proceeded to tell her everything, from what they had talked about on the drive down to the classical music and first kiss. Annie listened intrigued until Ashling finished.

"Right, Ash," Annie said finally. "First things first – what sort of jeep was it exactly?"

Annie was something of a car freak. Expensive cars that was, not your average Skoda or even Ford Fiesta. She loved her boyfriend Harry's top of the range Lexus and had been known to date men of questionable character on acount of their wheels.

"Well," Ashling answered slowly. "I know it was black and it was a two-seater. After that I'm not sure."

Annie sighed. Some people just didn't appreciate the important things in life, like designer suits, exclusive labels and car makes.

"Never mind." Annie resigned herself to the fact that her friend was a philistine when it came to cars. "The big question. Are you going to see him again?"

"He rang this morning," Ashling stated triumphantly. "He's picking me up at two and we're going to see a film."

Annie whistled. "Fast mover, he must be keen. Ring me later and tell me all about it, babe. Promise?"

Ashling promised and put down the receiver, grinning broadly. She glanced at her watch. It was almost two. Shit, she thought. She cast a critical eye over herself in her full-length mirror. Her dark red trousers, brown suede wedge-boots and green fitted top looked a little quirky, not something she usually worried about.

Feck it, she said to herself. This is me and if he doesn't like it then tough. She smoothed a little tinted moisturiser over her lightly tanned skin and stroked a mascara wand over her eyelashes. A little natural-coloured lip-gloss completed the effect. She was running a hairbrush hurriedly through her hair when she heard Chris's jeep pull up.

The Sorrento Lounge in Dalkey, known as Finnegan's to the locals, after the family who owned it, was buzzing. A traditionally decorated pub, with plenty of dark wood and rich upholstery, it was Ashling's favourite bar. She and Chris were sprawled comfortably, knees touching, drinking pints of cider and sharing bacon fries and peanuts, discussing *Love Games*.

"It was a complete rip-off of *When Harry Met Sally*, the long drawn-out-friendship, the whole 'men and women can't be friends' thing," Chris argued.

"I liked *When Harry Met Sally!*" Ashling exclaimed.

"So did I but that's what I'm saying," Chris continued, animatedly. "Nora Ephron was a clever scriptwriter. Her characters were real and her plot hung together. It was quite an original film, the whole split-screen thing with the late-night telephone calls and the alienation of the single person at the community rituals – weddings or New Year's Eve."

Ashling smiled. He really did take his films quite seriously.

"But the writing in this film was substandard."

"I agree," Ashling stated firmly, hoping he would now stop being Dave Fanning. She wanted to find out more about Chris the person, not Chris the film critic.

"Sorry, I'll stop now," Chris laughed. "I get the message."

Ashling smiled. He was really the most good-natured man she had met in a long time. A little later, while he was at the bar, Ashling glanced at her watch. It was nearly seven, Tizzy would be wondering where she was. Chris returned to the table with two glasses of cider.

"I'll have to head after these," Ashling said.

"No problem," Chris replied, smiling. "Do you always have to run away or is it just me?"

Ashling laughed. "It's just you, I can't stand the sight of you." Chris pretended to look hurt. "I'm sorry, it's just life with a kid is a little hectic. You can't just think about yourself. And because I'm on my own, baby-sitting is always a problem."

"Right," Chris said. He'd never really thought about it. It must be quite a responsibility.

"The thing I miss most is being able to be spontaneous. Being able to go for drinks after work or take off for the weekend. I always have to plan things."

"It must be difficult," Chris said.

"I'm sorry, I must be making it sound like a real trial. And don't get me wrong – Dan is brilliant, I wouldn't change things for the world. But . . ."

"Go on," he coaxed.

"Well, I suppose sometimes I'd like a normal life."

"Ah, sure what's normal?" Chris smiled. "Listen, I'll drop you home. I have to work tonight, a concert in the Point, but are you doing anything tomorrow? Maybe we could go out somewhere."

Ashling smiled. A small flock of butterflies tickled her stomach. She had wondered if all her serious talk about 'responsibility' had put him off? Obviously not. "That would be great." She took a deep breath. "Maybe we could bring Dan somewhere."

Chris was silent for a second before answering. "Sure, maybe. I'll ring you in afternoon."

"Perfect," Ashling said, trying not to think about his delayed reaction.

Ashling put Daniel to bed early and settled herself on the sofa with the remote control.

Typical, she thought. I have the television to myself – no *Rugrats* or *Superman* and there's nothing decent on. She decided to ring Annie at Harry's. Her friend lived in Blackrock but stayed most weekends at her boyfriend's house in Howth and it was only a matter of time before she moved in for good. But Annie refused to live 'in sin' as she called it. A thoroughly modern woman in all other ways, she was however a strong believer in 'family values' despite her own parent's messy divorce.

"Hi, Harry," Ashling said, hearing his voice. "Is Annie there?"

"Hi, Ashling, I'll just get her for you. And by the way this Chris chap sounds rather super. When will we get to meet him?"

Ashling smiled. What would Chris make of Harry? she wondered. There were at least ten years between them.

"We'll see," Ashling laughed. Annie told Harry everything – in some ways it was like having a big brother. Harry was genuinely interested in Ashling and her son and had been extremely kind to them in the three years he had known them.

Annie came on the phone. "Hi, Ash. How's the delectable Christopher?"

"Fine, thank you," Ashling replied, trying to stop the permanent grin on her lips. It was making it difficult to talk at this stage.

"How was your date?"

"Great, we went to the cinema in Dun Laoghaire and then to Finnegan's for a drink."

"And?" Annie cajoled. "What did you talk about?"

Ashling laughed. "Annie, I don't know where to begin. We talked about everything, the film, work, music, school, the works."

"Sounds promising," Annie said.

"And before you ask, yes, I'm seeing him tomorrow. We're going to take Dan out for the afternoon."

Annie caught her breath. If Ashling was allowing Chris to meet her son after only two dates she must really like this guy. Usually her friend was extremely cautious when it came to Dan, not wanting to confuse the impressionable youngster.

"Annie, Annie are you still there? You've gone very quiet."

"Oh, yes sorry, I was miles away. I'm really pleased for you, Ash, and I hope tomorrow goes well." As Annie put down the phone she had a vaguely uneasy feeling, as if something wasn't quite right. This Chris sounded a little too good to be true.

"How's Ash?" Harry asked as his girlfriend walked into the kitchen. They had been lingering over coffee, sharing a tub of Toffee Haagen Daas when Ashling had rung.

"Fine. Pretty good actually. She's seeing Chris again tomorrow."

"What's on your mind? You have that worry wrinkle on your forehead." He took Annie's hand, drew her towards him and gently smoothed out her frown with the fingers of his other hand. "Ash will be grand, don't worry about her so much. She's a big girl." Annie smiled, he knew her so well. "Come here." He placed his strong arms around her and pulled her onto his knee. He leant over and kissed her, a cold, sweet ice-cream-tasting kiss, his hands tracing patterns on her brown silk shirt. Soon his hands moved under her shirt, teasing her soft skin and moving towards her full breasts.

"Let's go upstairs," Annie suggested huskily, her brown eyes flashing with desire.

"Good idea," Harry agreed smiling. "I'll bring the ice cream."

Chapter 15

The following morning Ashling was woken as usual by Daniel, this time singing his own personal version of the theme tune to *Sesame Street* at full volume.

Ashling smiled. She was blessed – he had a bright disposition and was rarely badly behaved. And she was quite used to the early mornings.

"Morning, Daniel!" she yelled from her warm bed.

He scampered into her bedroom. He adored Sunday mornings, which he called 'pyjama mornings' because they always spent the morning slopping around the house in their night attire. They ate their breakfast snuggled together on the sofa watching Sunday morning television. Daniel could watch cartoons until *The Waltons* came on which was one of his mum's favourites. He couldn't understand what she saw in it – there were no baddies, or super-heroes. There wasn't even any singing and the children in the programme wore funny clothes and didn't seem to laugh very much. But his mummy liked it and he liked being with his mummy.

"Would you like to meet one of my friends later?" Ashling asked her son casually as Jim Bob said goodnight to Mary Ellen.

"OK," Daniel replied. "Is it Annie?"

"No, it's a new friend called Chris."

"Is Chris a boy or a girl?" he asked.

"A boy," Ashling answered, trying to sound casual.

"Sure," he said absently as an ad for a new Action Man commanded his attention.

That was easy, thought Ashling. Usually Dan was very curious, asking detailed and often scarily perceptive questions.

At noon Chris rang.

"Hi, Ash, how are you?"

"Grand, thanks."

"Listen, I was given tickets to the match this afternoon. Would you like to go?"

Ashling was taken aback. Had he forgotten about their afternoon with Dan?

"Well, I don't know if Dan would sit through a whole soccer match, he's a bit young."

The line went silent for a moment.

"I'm sorry, Ash. I'd forgotten about Dan. But listen, they're brilliant tickets – one of the *Courier* guys passed them on to me. And it's Ireland and Italy playing, you know. Why don't you ask your neighbour to baby-sit for him again?"

Ashling sighed inwardly. She was tempted but she couldn't leave Dan with Tizzy again. And she hadn't seen Dan all weekend, not really. Damn, damn, damn. Why were things so complicated sometimes?

"I'm sorry, Chris, I can't. Thanks for the offer."

"Oh right." Chris sounded disappointed. "Listen, do you mind if I go anyway? It's going to be a deadly match."

Now it was Ashling's turn to be disappointed.

"No, of course not, you go and enjoy it."

"Great. Sorry, I have to run, it starts soon. But I'll give you a ring during the week. And I thought the two of us could go to Galway together next weekend. I'll ring you, bye . . ."

Ashling was a little confused. What was he talking about? They hadn't discussed going to Galway yesterday.

"Mum, are you all right? You look sad." Dan was gazing at his mother with interest. "Is your friend sick?"

"No, love," Ashling said, attempting a smile. She was annoyed at herself for getting upset over nothing. Chris was just really into football, nothing wrong with that, she wasn't one to deprive boys of their toys and games, especially big boys! And anyway, it left her free to spend the day with her son.

"What would you like to do today, Dan?" Ashling asked.

He thought for a moment.

"I know, Mum, the zoo! Can we go to the zoo? We haven't been for ages and ages."

Ashling smiled, he adored Dublin zoo. And since its extensive renovations she quite enjoyed it herself. The animals appeared much happier and the bird and bat houses were especially impressive. The last time they had visited, they had even witnessed cows being milked in the new Pet and Farm Animals' Corner.

"Right, Dan, the zoo it is."

"Wow, thanks Mum, you're the best!" Dan flung his skinny arms around his mother.

Ashling and Dan didn't get home until after seven that evening. On the way home from the zoo they stopped in Eddie Rocket's for spicy chips, doorstopper hamburgers and deliciously thick chocolate malts. Dan had loved the zoo, especially the bats and the penguins and Ashling had enjoyed spending time with him. But at the back of her mind she wondered how Chris was and more to the point, who Chris was with.

You're just being stupid, she told herself. He's with a big bunch of lads and they're probably tucking into dirty big black pints at this stage.

It was hard not to feel very single at the zoo. Everyone else seemed to be one half of a couple or one part of a close family unit. Ashling wondered if men ever felt like that – single in a world of couples. It was even more difficult when you had a child as all the 'kiddie' sort of places – zoos, playgrounds, toy shops – attracted families in droves. Ashling had sighed to herself as they passed the elephants on the way to the hippos.

Stop it, Ashling McKenna, she said to herself. You're

bloody lucky. You have a great son, a place to live and the job you've always wanted. You can't have everything.

She was exhausted after the long day and the drive home. She was looking forward to a long soak in the bath after settling Dan in front of one of his beloved Disney videos. His favourite at present was *The Jungle Book*. He adored Mowgli and his jungle friends, and sang along to the jazzy soundtrack. As she sank into the mound of steaming bubbles, she could hear Dan laughing and she smiled, a long satisfied smile.

An hour later Daniel was miraculously in his bed. He had fallen asleep in front of the television and Ashling had lifted him downstairs and placed him as gently as she could on top of his Superman duvet. She folded the bottom of the duvet over him and planted a soft kiss on his forehead.

"Sleep well, pet," she whispered.

Ashling changed into a pair of soft light-blue cotton pyjamas and climbed under her duvet. It was only eight thirty but she needed serious rest. She read a few pages of her current 'bedtime book', a gentle, nostalgic novel about life in 1950's Ireland, before turning off her light. In minutes she was sleeping peacefully.

In the middle of the night the phone beside her bed rang, waking her up instantly.

"Hello," she answered groggily.

"Ash, it's Chris."

Ashling heard laughter and the clink of glasses in the background. She pulled back the corner of her curtains and looked at her watch in the moonlight. It was half past two.

"Ash, do you want to come to a party?" Chris slurred. "It's really good, loads of the *Courier* guys are here, well Smartie and Jacko anyway. Come on, it'll be a laugh."

Ashling was astounded. Was he completely mad? Had he forgotten about Dan or was he suggesting that she should bring him along?

"Chris, it's nearly three in the morning and Dan's asleep. Anyway, I'm working tomorrow."

Chris laughed. "Oh yeah, sorry, I forgot about Dan. Listen, how about I call in on my way home and see you? I'll leave soon, I promise."

"I don't think so, Chris, if you don't mind. I'm really tired and I need some sleep. I'll see you during the week, OK?"

"Oh yeah, right. It's just the party's in Dalkey and I thought I could stay with you. It's easier than getting a cab."

"Chris, I'll see you at work. Good-bye," Ashling replaced the phone firmly and tried to go back to sleep. What was going on in his head? They weren't students anymore and she had child to look after. She banished all thoughts of Chris and tried to keep her mind blank. Soon she was asleep.

"You'll never believe what Chris did last night."

Ashling and Annie were sitting in the *Sicily Café* on George's Street. They had just placed an order for lunch and were sipping from large bright mugs – café latte for Annie and hot chocolate for Ashling. Although it was warm outside they couldn't resist a coffee and chocolate pick-me-up.

Annie looked at her friend inquisitively.

"He rang me in the middle of the night and asked me to a party. It turned out that he wanted to stay with me. He was in Dalkey and it was less hassle than trying to get a cab."

"Ah," Annie replied.

"What do you mean, 'ah'? Do you not think it's odd?"

Annie sighed. "Ash, what age is Chris?"

Ashling paused for a moment. "He's twenty-four, nearly twenty-five."

"I hate to say it, but he sounds a little immature. Would you not go for someone older?" Annie asked.

"Annie, I like Chris, I shouldn't have told you about last night. He'd had a few drinks – you know what it's like after a game. He's a nice guy, it'll be fine. I know you'll like him. Anyway, how's Harry?" she continued, changing the subject. "Tell me about that ball you're going to next weekend, it sounds brilliant."

Annie told her friend all about the Masked Fashion Ball in Homewood Castle, in aid of a Dublin hospital, which she and Harry were attending the following weekend. She let the subject of Chris Doyle drop, but she was going to keep her beady eye on that particular photographer.

By Wednesday Ashling was starting to worry. Chris hadn't rung her so far this week, after the Sunday-night phone-call incident. She hoped she had done the right thing. Maybe she should have let him stay – it wasn't as if it would have done any harm. Damn, she thought to herself, I've blown it.

Later that afternoon Annie rang from her desk in the Features Department. Ashling had just finished researching a story about the new marina in Dun Laoghaire. She was on her way to the west pier to meet one of the marina's designers.

"Ash, I overheard Chris asking to cover the marina story this afternoon. In case you're interested." Annie knew that her friend was concerned that the photographer hadn't rung her yet this week.

"Thanks Annie, you're a star," Ashling smiled. "Maybe this afternoon won't be so bad after all."

Ashling parked her Golf beside the pier and noticed a black jeep a few yards down the road. Her stomach fluttered and she tried to stifle a broad smile. She stepped out of the car, locked it, swung her bag over her shoulder and walked over to the jeep. Chris was sitting in the driver's seat reading a music magazine.

"How's it going, Ash? Sorry for waking you up the other night. I meant to ring but it's been a busy week." Chris gave her a huge smile. He was wearing a light blue shirt and faded blue denims. Ashling's heart melted.

"It's fine, Chris, don't worry about it. If I hadn't been

so tired it would have been fun. I haven't been to a good party for ages."

Chris's eyes twinkled. "Let's go for a drink after this. I want to talk to you about the weekend."

Before Ashling had a chance to ask him what he was talking about a tall man in a dark suit walked towards them, holding out his hand, followed by a younger man in jeans and a black polo neck. It was the marina manager and the architect. Soon Chris and Ashling were hard at work, Ashling interviewing the marina designer and Chris setting up and taking the photographs. Ashling couldn't help but think what an excellent team they made. She really enjoyed working with him – he had a professional but easy manner. Tim Hawkins, the designer or marine architect as he preferred to be called, was a nice man. Young and enthusiastic, with revolutionary ideas about design. It was going to be a good, solid story and Ashling was pleased with the afternoon's work.

Chris and Ashling drove back to the *Courier* in convoy. Ashling was happy to let Chris take the lead, as it gave her a chance to gaze at him through the back window of the jeep.

I must remember to tell Annie that it's a Jeep Wrangler, she said to herself as they parked outside the newspaper's offices.

Less than a hour later they were heading out of the city towards Blackrock, where Chris lived in an apartment beside the sea with his two photographer friends, Smartie and Macker.

"What are Smartie and Macker's real names anyway?" Ashling asked as Chris returned from the Wicked Wolf's bar with two pints of cider.

"Well, Macker's name is Paul Mackey and Smartie's is Richard O'Driscoll."

"I understand Macker, but why Smartie?"

"In school, Richard was apparently a bit of a smart ass and the teacher used to call him 'Smartie' because of it and it just kind of stuck, I think."

Ashling laughed. Did boys ever grow up?

"Listen, there's this masked ball thing on next weekend, it's somewhere near Galway called Homewood Castle – I think I mentioned it to you last weekend. Jackie Power is one of the organisers and she's asked me to take the pictures. There'll be loads of celebs there and they don't want any other photographers there spoiling their fun and making them paranoid. Would you come with me? It will be a laugh. And you won't need to work. I think *VIP* magazine are the only people they want covering it."

"That sounds brilliant, Chris," Ashling said. And she stopped herself before adding anything about Dan and baby-sitting. After all it wasn't his concern, not really. And she deserved a bit of fun. Chris would warm to the idea of spending time with Dan in his own good time. She banished any niggling doubts from the back of her mind. Back home, Ashling apologised to Tizzy for being late. She had rung earlier and Tizzy wasn't too concerned.

"It's fine, Ashling, I understand about your work, you know that. It's Dan you should be worried about not me."

Ashling spoilt Dan rotten that evening, allowing him to stay up late and watch *Friends* with her on the sofa. She knew it wasn't really suitable viewing for a six-year-old, but her son loved Ross and his dinosaur obsession. And she let him sleep in her bed, after reading him some of his favourite old Dr Seuss picture books, *Green Eggs and Ham* and *The Cat in the Hat*.

"Mummy, do the boy and girl in *The Cat in the Hat* have a daddy?" he asked, after Ashling's lively rendition of the book.

"I don't know, love. What do you think?"

"Well, I think they only have a mummy like me. Mummies are cool. But Simon in school says family means mummy and daddy, not just mummy."

Ashling sighed. "Well, love, families come in all shapes and sizes. Some families have a mummy and a daddy and some don't. It depends. And you have a mummy and a Tizzy and an Annie, don't you?"

"I sure do, Mummy. I love you." Daniel yawned and closed his eyes.

Ashling lay awake for a while thinking about what her young son had said. He certainly picked his moments. He didn't ask about his father much. He seemed to accept the situation, most of the time anyway. Ashling wondered if it would get harder as he got older and started asking more detailed and direct questions.

But she had decided always to be honest and open with Dan and when the time came she would explain to him about Owen as best she could. That night she had a fitful night's shut-eye, dreaming about scheming cats and plates of green food.

"Hi, Ashling, it's Chris. It's around six on Thursday and I'm in Wicklow covering another eco-warrior story. I'll pick you up from your place at seven tomorrow. Oh, by the way you have to dress up as Juliet, from Romeo and Juliet. And we're staying in the castle. Bye . . ."

Ashling replayed the message on her answering machine. Yep, he had said Juliet. Holy Moly. How on earth was she going to put together a costume in less than a day? He was certifiable. Most definitely. She rang Annie in desperation.

"Annie, help me!"

"Hi, Ash, what's up?"

"Annie, you know the ball you and Harry are going to on Friday night?"

"Yeah . . ."

"Well, I'm going with Chris. He has to take photos at it. I intended to surprise you. You know – jump out at you with my mask on or something. But I need your help."

Ashling explained the costume or lack of costume situation. Annie had been planning her own Guinevere dress for weeks. She had had it especially made from red velvet with silver trim, and Harry had even been cajoled into hiring a Sir Lancelot outfit, real metal armour, sword and shield – the whole shebang.

"Right, it'll be too late to hire at this stage. I'm coming over with something that might just work. See you in half an hour."

Chapter 16

I still think it looks like a nightie, Ashling muttered to herself, looking at her reflection in the full-length mirror.

Annie had done a brilliant job with what was literally an old organza nightie, and yards of gold cord. She had tacked a green velvet bodice to the top of the makeshift dress and had wrapped gold cord over the sleeves in a Medieval pattern. She had also shown Ashling how to put her hair up, using the gold cord. Annie loved dressmaking and always had a store of different materials and trimmings in an old Brown Thomas hatbox under her bed.

Ashling, although she wouldn't admit it to herself, looked stunning. The gold cord brought out the golden highlights in her hair and the dress hung attractively around her hips, clinging in all the right places.

"Mummy, you're a princess. No, you're Cinderella."

Just then Tizzy knocked on the door.

"Coming," yelled Dan, running out of Ashling's

bedroom at breakneck speed. Tizzy had promised to watch *Chitty, Chitty Bang Bang* with him for the umpteenth time. It was actually the older woman's favourite film, so she didn't mind one little bit.

Ashling opened the door with an excited Dan at her side.

"Hi, Tizzy, thanks a million for letting Dan stay over, he's so excited."

"I'm dying to see that flying car again," Tizzy smiled, holding out her hand to Dan. "Let's go."

The small boy put his hand in Tizzy's and led her away.

"See you tomorrow, Ashling, enjoy yourselves."

"Thanks. Be good, Dan." Ashling closed the door behind them and walked back into her room. She threw some clothes and boots into an overnight bag, along with her make-up. She almost added pyjamas before thinking better of it. I don't think I'll be needing those, she grinned to herself.

A few minutes later Chris pulled up outside and beeped the horn. Ashling took one final look at herself in the mirror and ran out the door, slamming it behind her. Chris whistled when he saw her.

"'But, soft! what light through yonder window breaks? It is the east, and Juliet is the sun!' Wow, babe! You look amazing."

"I'm most impressed," Ashling said. "Shakespeare himself no less."

Chris shrugged his shoulders. "I did him for my Leaving. I always fancied myself in the lead role."

Ashling smiled, hitched her dress up and climbed into the jeep. She turned her head and looked straight into the eyes of her very own Romeo. Chris was dressed in a blue fitted silk jacket with a white floppy collar and matching blue pantaloons, and on his slim but well-built legs were whiter than white tights. A pair of wraparound shades completed the outfit.

"I had no idea they wore shades in old Verona," Ashling joked.

"It's my mask," Chris said. "Can't you tell?"

"Damn," Ashling said. "Hang on a sec, will you, Chris, I think it'll have to be shades for me too, I knew I'd forget something!"

The ball was a three-hours drive from Dalkey. It was a beautiful evening and Chris rolled down the jeep's top. With classical music blaring, they turned heads as they drove past. Ashling enjoyed the free sensation – she felt alive and without ties.

As they pulled up the drive to Homewood Castle Ashling gasped in amazement. The castle was stunningly beautiful. Set at the foot of a mountain, on the banks of an oval lake, it was built of granite blocks, long covered with sheets of dark green and autumnal red ivy. The castle's windows were each illuminated with a single candle and strains of a string quartet filled the air.

Ashling looked at Chris, delight on her face. He jumped down, opened the door of the jeep for 'Juliet' and offered her a hand.

"Thank you, my Romeo," she said, smiling.

"Anything for my own fair Juliet."

"Listen, Ash," said Chris, swinging his camera and camera bag over his shoulder. "I'll have to find Jackie first and take some shots for her. But it won't take long and then we can party."

A large bouncer in black tie stopped them at the door.

"Sorry, mate. No cameras allowed. Strict instructions."

Just then Jackie Power glided towards them, dressed dramatically in black, with blood-red hands.

"It's OK, Chip. Chris is with me."

Jackie led Chris and Ashling past the classical musicians playing in the hallway and up the steep stone stairway into an amazing atrium with stained-glass windows and lofty, stone rib-vaulted ceilings. A waiter handed the guests a large glass of champagne each.

"I'm delighted you could make it, Chris. And it's great to see you again, Ashling. We liked the piece in the *Courier.*"

"How are the twins?" Ashling asked.

"They're doing really well. Growing bigger by the second. We're blessed with an amazing Australian nanny. I don't know what I'd do without her."

Jackie led them into a room off the atrium which was guarded by another large tuxedoed bouncer. It was the original dining-room, complete with lofty minstrel gallery from where a five-piece Salsa band were playing. Ashling could see several A-list celebrities lingering at the bar, and a large group of B-lists dancing.

Jackie began to introduce Chris to several of the

guests, explaining that he was the 'official' photographer for the night and that the prints would be strictly vetted by the organisers before they were released to the press. Chris took it all in his stride and as he began to work, posing groups of glamorous people together and capturing them on film, Ashling wandered out of the room and down the corridor.

The castle was hopping; there were elaborately dressed guests everywhere. Ashling spotted Anthony and Cleopatra, Samson and Delilah and even Tom and Jerry. Stepping into the main ballroom she spotted Annie and Harry. They made a striking couple and were hard to miss. Harry made a dashing knight and was managing to drink through the rectangular 'hole' in his helmet's visor like an expert. Annie looked brilliant in her red velvet panelled dress.

"Hi guys," Ashling said, delighted to finally see someone she knew. "You both look great."

"If it isn't Juliet herself," Harry laughed. "And a very beautiful Juliet at that."

"Thanks, Harry," Ashling said.

"Where's Romeo?" Annie asked, looking around her.

"He's in the other room taking pictures of scantily clad women," Ashling smiled.

"Oh, the horrors of work," Harry said, grinning. "I noticed a Princess Leah in a gold bikini strutting her stuff all right."

"Not to mention a couple of Lady Godivas," Ashling added, her eyes twinkling.

"Are you serious?" Harry asked.

"No," Ashling replied. "But they may as well be – they have virtually nothing on."

"That would be Jackie Power's model friends, I presume, not mere normal mortals like ourselves," Annie decided.

"Now, now, girls," Harry chastised. "Put those claws away."

The lively band began to play an old Abba number and Annie grabbed the others and pulled them onto the dance floor.

"It's a bit early for this sort of lark," Harry complained. He wasn't what you would call a natural on the dance floor. And the armour wasn't exactly conducive to movement, let alone tripping the light fantastic.

"Come on, Harry," Annie encouraged. "Shake a leg."

Harry lasted two songs before spotting a work colleague at the bar and joining him.

"Spoilsport!" Annie yelled after him.

The two women danced on, enjoying the music. They were soon joined by three cute young men in togas.

"And who are the three of you supposed to be?" Ashling asked the fine thing dancing beside her.

"You know, I'll have to think up a smart answer to that. It was a last-minute sort of thing and sheets were the only costume to hand," he replied, smiling. "I'm Peter by the way. And that's Binner and that's Kev," he gestured towards the others.

"I'm Ashling and that's Annie." Annie smiled and waved.

Just then Harry came lumbering over, a glass of champagne in each hand.

"For you, ladies," he said. "Would you care to join us at the bar?"

Ashling and Annie looked at each other and smiled. Harry was a jealous old sod, but he was the man with the drinks.

"See you later, lads," Ashling said, following Harry and Annie towards the bar.

Several glasses of champagne later, Ashling began to wonder what Chris was up to. She excused herself from the group at the bar and made her way out the door and down the corridor to the other room. The bouncer grunted at her as she walked in. Chris was on the dance floor with Princess Leah, twisting the lithe bikini-clad girl to the music. He was still wearing his shades. Ashling had long since abandoned her own, but they suited him – he looked like a film star. Ashling watched for a few minutes. She wasn't sure whether to feel jealous or proud. After all, she had no reason to distrust Chris. Come to think of it, she had no real reason to trust him either – she really didn't know him that well, she thought to herself.

She made her way over to the duo and smiled tentatively at Chris.

"There you are, Ash, I was beginning to worry about you. This is Ronda."

Ashling smiled at the tall, leggy brunette. "Hi Ronda."

Ronda flashed a momentary toothy smile back at Ashling. "Nice to meet you. Catch you later, Romeo."

Chris and Ashling made their way to the bar, where they collected two tall glasses of champagne. "I'm missing the beer, big time," Chris complained. "Champagne is all very well, especially free champers. But they should have pints too."

Ashling laughed. "You're a philistine, Chris Doyle."

"Absolutely," he agreed. "And don't you forget it."

Jackie Power bustled over towards them.

"Sorry to drag you away, Chris, but I need you in the Smoking Room."

Chris turned towards Ashling and raised his eyebrows.

"It's grand, Chris," she said. "I'll find Annie and Harry. Come and find us when you're finished."

Chris beamed. "Right you are. See you later."

Ashling was a little miffed. She had hoped to spend more time with Chris, but she understood how demanding work could be. Especially at this type of thing. On her way back to the ballroom she was stopped in her tracks by a small blonde woman in a Native American Indian costume.

"Ashling, is that you?" The Indian lifted her mask. "It's me, Susan."

Ashling was confused. Then she recognised Mark Mulhearne's big sister, Susan. She hadn't seen her in years.

"Oh sorry, Susan! I didn't recognise you there in the Pocahontas outfit. It's been a long time. You look brilliant. How are the kids?"

Susan lived in Wicklow with her husband and young

twins – when Ashling had last met her the babies were only a few weeks old.

"Sure, they're huge now, Ashling. Big bruisers, in school and all. And how's Daniel? He must be five now at least."

"He's six now and a real little character." Ashling smiled at Susan Mulhearne. "God it's good to see you."

"I'm sorry yourself and Mark didn't keep in touch," Susan said gently.

"I did try writing," Ashling said, "but I never heard anything back. I'm sure he was really busy with work and everything. And I moved to a house in Dalkey a few weeks after he left – it was all pretty hectic."

Susan was confused. That didn't sound like Mark. He was usually good at keeping in touch – for a man, that was.

"But you know he's back in October for a St John's reunion. He's been asked to speak at it."

Ashling grinned. "I know. I got my invitation the other week in the post. I can't believe it's ten years already. It's scary."

"I'll tell him you're going, so. He'd love to see you before that, though, I'm sure. He's back a few weeks before the reunion and I think he plans to stay in Ireland for good this time."

Ashling was taken aback. She had considered the Mark episode in her life to be well and truly over. She hadn't contemplated the possibility that she might have to deal with Mark living in Ireland. Somehow it was easier when he was in Boston – it was a long way away and the possibility of bumping into him was nil. She had tried to banish the memories of Mark Mulhearne forever and she had almost succeeded. But if he was moving back to Ireland . . .

"Ashling, are you OK? You've gone very quiet."

"Sorry, Susan, I was . . ."

At that minute Chris came bounding over and put his arm around her.

"How's my favourite Juliet? Ready to party? I'm off the hook for the night now, Ash."

"This is Chris, Susan. He was taking photographs for Jackie Power."

Susan held out her hand. "Nice to meet you, Chris."

"You too," he shook it enthuastically.

Susan looked at the tipsy young man and smiled. She was glad Ashling had a boyfriend, she was a great girl and deserved someone special.

The old friends said their good-byes and Chris and Ashling found Annie and Harry on the dance floor in the ball-room.

"Jeez, it's much more crack in here," Chris exclaimed. "Posh birds don't know how to let their hair down. And the blokes are thirty or forty – they're all so old they'd have coronaries if they danced for more than ten minutes."

Harry, dancing minus his armour which lay resting against the wall like a ghostly watchman, scowled at Chris.

"Sorry, mate," Chris said. "I'm Chris by the way. Nice to meet you."

After that it took a little while for Harry to warm to Chris, but eventually he relaxed and the four danced the night away, interspersed with more than a few trips to the bar. By two o'clock Annie and Harry had had enough.

"Right, we're off to bed. Ash, I'll talk to you tomorrow," Annie said. They were staying in a B and B down the road.

Chris and Ashling lasted until four, when Chris was so drunk he could barely stand, although strangely he seemed to have no problem dancing. Ashling had gone a little easier on the champagne. She wasn't really a great drinker, since she'd had Daniel. Ashling was so used to coming home early to relieve the baby-sitter, or driving when she went out that in some way she seemed to have lost the taste for alcohol.

She managed to drag the protesting Chris up the steep winding wooden stairs to their bedroom. Their bags were still in the car and Ashling hoped that Jackie Power had stashed Chris's camera and equipment somewhere sensible. Once she had Chris in the dark room, lying on the bed, she went downstairs to fetch their bags. On returning she flicked on the light switches. What a room!

A large mahogany four-poster bed stood against one wall, with luxurious dark red tapestry drapes, and a pristine heavy cream brocade bedspread. The walls were painted a tasteful cream and adorned with original oil paintings. The curtains matched the bed's drapes and the dark brown floorboards were partly covered with exotic Far Eastern rugs. Ashling looked around in wonder. If it wasn't for a comatose and now snoring Chris sprawled on the bed, everything would be perfect. Ashling sighed. It was such a romantic room, what a shame she had no-one awake to share it with!

She removed her dress and hung it over a red velvet plushly upholstered chair. She then pulled back the bedclothes on one side, rolled Chris awkwardly onto that side and covered him.

Men are much worse than children, she thought to herself wryly. And kids don't snore, well not as loudly anyway. She climbed into bed beside Chris and switched off the light. The bed was supremely comfortable with down-filled pillows and duvet and crisp, cool linen sheets. At least I'll get a decent night's kip, Ashling thought to herself, as she drifted off to sleep.

The next morning she was woken by loud shots from outside the window.

What the hell? she muttered to herself. She looked at her watch in the gloom. It was exactly ten o'clock and she promptly closed her eyes again. Just then another shot rang out. Ashling sat up in the bed. She glanced down, Chris was sound asleep, still snoring. She prised herself slowly out of bed and made her way towards the window. Pulling back the heavy curtains she was astounded to see a gathering of people in the garden. They were all standing behind what looked like the frame of half a summer house. And in the wooden frame was a tall young man with what looked like a shotgun. Suddenly a shot rang out. Yes, it was definitely a rifle. Ashling was bewildered. The man was shooting at what appeared to be large stone frisbees. She walked back to the bed and nudged Chris in the shoulder.

"Chris, Chris, wake up." He grunted in his sleep. She nudged him again harder this time.

"Chris, Chris."

He sat up gingerly and opened his eyes. "Whaa . . . Oh mornin', Ash."

"Chris, there's someone shooting outside," she exclaimed.

"Oh yeah, forgot to tell you," Chris siad sheepishly. "There's some sort of clay pigeon shooting competition on all day. Jackie did warn me. It kind of slipped my mind, sorry."

Ashling laughed. "It's OK. I just got a bit of a fright. Anyway, how are you feeling, Mr Doyle?"

"Ah sure, I'm grand. And yourself?"

"I had a good sleep, although it ended rather abruptly. It was a great night."

Chris was gazing at her with a wicked grin on his face.

"You know, Ashling, you look a million dollars in the morning."

Ashling blushed slightly. "You don't look so bad yourself."

"Oh really?" Chris asked, leaning over towards her. Suddenly he put his arms around her and gently threw her onto the bed from her sitting position.

"Give us a kiss, Juliet," he said, beaming.

"What's wrong, Ash?" Chris asked some time later, his cheeks flushed and hair tousled.

"I'm sorry, I'm just not ready. It's a big step for me." Ashling sat up, pulling the bedclothes around her shoulders, and looked at Chris intently.

"Is it me?" he asked. "Have I done something wrong?"

"No, Chris. You haven't done anything. It's me, I need some time, that's all."

Chris stared in the direction of the window. "You know I really like you, Ashling, don't you? And we're having fun, aren't we?"

"Of course we are. But it's hard to explain . . . with Dan and everything – it kind of changes things."

"You know your having a kid doesn't bother me."

Ashling took a deep breath. She wished she had never started this conversation. She really liked Chris and she found him very attractive. So what was the problem? She knew she was feeling a little guilty about leaving Daniel with Tizzy again and not spending enough time with him. But it wasn't just that. She had this strange feeling at the back of her mind that this wasn't right – Chris wasn't right for her or for Dan. She wanted to ask Chris so many questions but it all came back to the same thing – was he prepared to spend time with her and Dan? Maybe she was just a bit hungover and tired. Maybe things would be fine tomorrow and she would wake up and feel grand. And things with Chris would be flying high again.

"Listen, Chris, don't worry about it. As I said, I just

need some more time, OK? Anyway, where were we?" Ashling pulled the bedclothes over her head and kissed her way down Chris's smooth, firm torso. She flicked her moist tongue down his chest, teasing his nipples and lapping at his belly-button.

"Would you stop that, Ashling!" Chris laughed. "It tickles."

Ashling's lips and tongue made their way slowly down towards his groin.

Chris moaned as she took him firmly in her mouth. "You're an evil woman, Ashling," he murmured.

As she moved her tongue up and down the rigid flesh he groaned in appreciation.

"Yes!" Chris cried out. "Don't stop . . . Jeez!"

On the way home, Ashling tried to shut out any negative thoughts. They chatted amicably about the past evening and Chris seemed to have forgotten the earlier awkwardness. As they drew up to Dalkey Manor Ashling spotted the small figure of her son running towards the jeep.

"Mummy," he yelled at the top of his voice. Ashling stepped down from the jeep and Dan threw his arms around her, squeezing tightly. "I missed you, Mummy."

Chris watched from a few feet away. He seemed nervous of the young boy.

"Come over and meet Dan, Chris," Ashling encouraged.

He walked over and stood stiffly beside the embracing pair with a blank expression on his face.

"Dan, this is Chris, say hello."

The boy looked at Chris with interest. "Is that your jeep?" he asked.

"It sure is," Chris replied, edging towards it. "Maybe we'll go for a drive sometime, OK? Ash, I'd better head, I'll talk to you during the week."

"Would you like to stick around for a while? We could sit and veg in the sun . . ."

Chris shook his head. "Sorry, I have a few bits to do, you know how it is."

"Oh, yeah, right. Thanks. I had fun." Ashling moved towards Chris to give him a kiss, but he drew away, looking at Dan and then back at her. He crinkled his forehead and nodded his head slowly.

"No problem," he said as he climbed into his jeep.

Ashling watched him driving away. She was quite taken aback. She had expected him to stick around for a while. And Dan would be disappointed. She wished Chris hadn't mentioned a ride in the jeep – Dan would be plaguing her about it. He wouldn't understand that Chris was just being polite, as she could tell he was. She sighed. She would have to come to terms with the fact that Chris had no real interest in Dan. But could she continue to see him when it took her away from Dan? Shit, she said to herself. Why were things so complicated? Why couldn't you have everything? It seemed to her sometimes that real happiness was dangled in front of her like a carrot, to keep her moving faster and faster forwards.

Tizzy had watched the scene with interest from the kitchen window. The blonde man, who she presumed was Chris Doyle, had seemed distant and preoccupied. He hadn't made much effort with Dan either. He's not the right man for Ashling, she thought to herself. She needs someone warm and open. Tizzy made her way downstairs, into the kitchen and out the side door. She greeted Ashling warmly.

"How was the ball? Come inside and we'll have a cup of tea and you can tell me all about it."

Ashling was supremely grateful. She needed a kind friend right at that minute. Tizzy walked inside and she followed, holding Dan's hand tightly.

A few hours later, after a pleasant afternoon spent sitting in the garden reading and watching Tizzy and Dan repotting even more geraniums, Annie rang.

"Well? Spill. What did the lovely Juliet and her Romeo get up to then?"

Ashling sighed. She had to talk to someone about Chris – it was doing her head in. She told her friend about the night, about Chris's abrupt exit and his indifference towards Dan.

"Annie, I just don't know where I am with him. We had a lovely weekend but now I'm afraid to put pressure on him in case he bolts. It's so nice to have someone around but I feel guilty about Dan."

"Would you not try talking about it with Chris?" Annie asked tentitavely.

Ashling sighed. "Annie, we've only known each other a short time and . . ."

"Ashling, you're not going to put him off by just talking to him. Not if he really cares about you."

"But that's just it I suppose," Ashling said slowly. "I don't know if he does."

"Ah pet," Annie said. "It's hard, I know. But Chris is young and maybe he wants a date, not a proper girlfriend. I didn't want to say it before, but he's not exactly the ideal boyfriend, is he?"

"Maybe it's me, Annie. Maybe I'm asking too much, being too demanding."

"Are you mad? You haven't asked him for anything. What are you talking about?"

"Well, OK, maybe not. But am I expecting too much? I just want someone to be with, you know, on Sundays and stuff. To share things with, not just to go out with on Saturday night."

It was now Annie's turn to sigh. "Ash, it's the most normal thing in the world to want someone to share things with. And one day you'll meet the right person, who wants the same things as you. But to be perfectly honest with you, I don't think Chris is that person."

Ashling was silent for a few seconds. "Maybe you're right, Annie. But sometimes the wrong person is better than no-one at all."

Dan was enjoying a large bubble bath. Ashling could still hear him talking away to himself, re-enacting a fight against evil forces involving Superman and Tommy, the baby from the *Rugrats*.

"I'd better rescue Dan from the bath, or else he'll turn into a prune. I'll see you tomorrow."

"Ash, try not to think about the whole Chris thing too much. It'll all work out, you'll see. You have to decide what you want and stick to it. If you want a proper relationship you may have to accept that Chris doesn't."

Putting down the phone Ashling made a decision. Annie was right. She should talk to Chris about how she felt, she had nothing to lose. "Except another boyfriend," she muttered to herself wryly.

Chapter 17

"We will be arriving in Dublin airport shortly, please fasten your seat-belts and ensure your seats are in an upright position."

Sally gazed out the window at the fast-approaching land. She had forgotten how green Ireland was, irregular square and rectangle shades of it, ranging from emerald green to vibrant chartreuse, like a veritable chlorophyll patchwork quilt. It was a bright and clear day in Dublin and within minutes the plane had touched down smoothly on the tarmacadam runway. The passengers clapped and cheered, delighted to be on terra firma once more.

Sally made her way with fellow passengers to collect her luggage. After a mercifully short wait she swung her two jam-packed sailing bags off the baggage carousel and slapped them onto a trolley. Then came the butterflies in her stomach. Walking through the sliding glass Arrivals doors into the main body of the airport always made her nervous. It was so intimidating being confronted with hundreds of unfamiliar faces, all waiting for someone who wasn't you.

She held her head up high and tried to appear cool and confident. Her family had arranged to meet her, but as she walked past the stainless-steel barriers in front of her Sally couldn't see them. She pushed her trolley in front of her at a slick pace, eager to avoid the re-united loving couples and the happy family scenes.

"Sally, cooee, Salleee!" a high-pitched voice made itself heard, clear as a bell above the general bustle and commotion. "Here we are dear, over here!"

Sally turned her head and looked to the right, following her mother's distinctive and easily recognisable pitch. April Hunter was waving frantically, flanked on either side by a stoic Reverend in 'civvies' and an embarrassed-looking Jamie. Her mum and dad hadn't changed a bit but Jamie, her little brother, had. He certainly wasn't little any more, for a start. He had grown even taller since the last time Sally had seen him, the day she had left, over four years ago when he was eighteen. What a transformation – if her wasn't her younger brother she would fancy him herself! Dressed in immaculate black jeans, a pressed white shirt and a loose-fitting black leather jacket, he was a head-turner. His sandy blonde hair and light smattering of freckles were offset by steely grey eyes and a lopsided, boyish smile. Jamie had certainly grown into his looks.

Sally's mum wiggled and pushed her way through the crowd in front of her, breathing exaggerated 'excuse me's' to all and sundry. She pounced exuberantly on her eldest daughter and enveloped her in an emotional bear-hug.

It's her public-display-of-affection hug, Sally thought wryly, as she patted her mother on the back and attempted to extract herself from the octopus-like grip. Sometimes April Hunter was too much. Sally was surprised that she hadn't captured the arrival of the prodigal daughter on film yet. She was a great woman for the ceremonies and family events, and each warranted a new round of photographs to record the moment. The house was full of photo albums carefully labelled with the date of each occasion.

Sally's birthdays had been faithfully chronicled on the exact day every year – August 12th – from age one, party or no party. As she grew older Sally had become more and more unco-operative, although her mother had still managed to snap birthdays number thirteen to nineteen, only missing fifteen, when her teenage angst-ridden daughter had shut herself in her bedroom for the entire day, locking the door and refusing to partake in her mother's 'pathetic, archaic ritual'.

April commandeered the trolley and briskly led Sally towards the back of the Arrivals Hall, clipping more than a few ankles on the way, to where her husband and Jamie were maintaining a low profile.

"Here she is, boys!" April announced. "James, the camera, the camera!"

Sally smiled at Jamie who raised his eyes to heaven.

"Good to see you, sis, you look great," Jamie gave her a warm hug.

"I've missed you, Sally, it's great to have you home. Emma couldn't make it but she said to say she'll see you later." James Hunter put his arms around his daughter. "And your Mum's missed you too, she's genuinely delighted to see you back," he whispered in her ear.

"Sally, James, look this way and smile, please," April's clear voice cut knife-like through the air. "James, you take the next one, Sally and Jamie together."

Sally's dad obediently took several shots of his children.

"Jamie, stop scowling please, you're not on one of your modelling photo shoots now."

Sally looked at her brother in amazement. "No one told me about you modelling, Jamie, that's gas. My brother the model – sounds impressive," she laughed.

Jamie smiled at his big sister. "Mum hasn't exactly taken to it yet, she thinks it's – how did you describe it Mum? Oh yes, a job for pretty boys and wasters, not proper men."

April spluttered, her face reddening slightly. "I just want you to have a decent job, Jamie, with prospects."

James could sense a scene brewing and interjected swiftly. "Right, I think we should make a move towards the car now. I'll take the trolley. Come on, April, we'll walk on ahead and let Jamie and Sally catch up."

Sally thanked the heavens for her peacemaking and considerate father. She linked arms with her brother and they strolled out the doors towards the carpark, letting their parents go on ahead.

"Mum hasn't changed a bit," Sally said smiling.

"How am I going to cope with living under the same roof as her, Jamie? She'll drive me demented!"

"You'll get used to it, Sal, and you can always come and stay with me in town if it gets too much. If I had a spare room, you know I'd love you to live with me, but the place is tiny."

"Ah thanks, Jamie. I might just have to borrow your sofa every now and then all right. And I want to hear all about the modelling later. It sounds brilliant."

Sitting in the Volvo on the way home, Sally was beginning to seriously worry. How could she live at home again after her years of freedom? At least Emma was still there. Emma Hunter was twenty-four, with a solid job in the bank and a solid older boyfriend called Kevin, her manager in the bank.

"I hope you haven't made plans for tonight," April said as they reached the Rectory. "I'm making your favourite dinner, peppered steak and chips."

Sally sighed to herself. She had intended to call into the yacht club and catch up on some of the old gang. Jean Kelly, her old friend from school, had promised to be there, with Peter and some of their sailing friends. Damn, she would have to ring Jean and cancel.

She missed Ginny already. They had become extremely close over the last few years, especially since the Christmas before last when Ginny's dad had been taken ill and she had been worried sick. Sally had helped her through it, encouraging her to return home and lending her the money for the plane fare. Ginny's dad had died two days after Ginny arrived in Cork, and she would have never have forgiven herself if she had not seen and spoken to him one last time. The two girls were more like sisters than friends and Sally felt the separation difficult already. It was strange, she had never had a close female friend before Ginny. At school and at college most of her friends were boys. Herself and Jean enjoyed each other's company and shared many things from sailing to boyfriends but Sally rarely talked as intimately or as honestly to her as she did to Ginny. Ginny had promised her friend she would return to Cork for Christmas and visit Sally in Dublin, but it was September and Christmas seemed an Atlantic ocean away.

As the car crunched up the driveway and pulled up outside the Rectory, Sally's heart sank. It was as grey and imposing as ever. For some bizarre reason she had thought that it might have changed, her dad might have gone wild and painted it pink or blue, or her mother might have planted tall yellow sunflowers or loopy white daisies in the flowerbeds bordering the house. No such luck. It was still dark grey, with careful, meticulously groomed flowerbeds and borders, and perfectly trimmed and cut hedges and grass.

Jamie helped his sister carry her lumpy sailing bags up the narrow stairs to the small attic room. Sally had lived under the eaves ever since she was a small child.

"Daddy, can I have this room?" she had asked when she was knee-high to a grasshopper.

James Hunter had looked doubtfully around the tiny box-

room. "It's a bit on the small side, Sally. We were going to use it as a storeroom. There's a much bigger room on the same floor as your brother if you'd like it."

She had made up her mind.

"No, Dad, I want this one, if that's all right."

The Rectory in the Dublin suburb of Blackrock was tall and narrow, four stories high, with large spacious bedrooms on the second and third floors. The family had moved from a very 'normal' semi-detached on a very 'normal' housing estate. The size of the house, Sally recognised years later, intimidated her and influenced her choice of bedroom. But although her room was small it had a killer view of Dun Laoghaire harbour and Sally grew up watching the boats in the harbour and wishing she was on the water and not in her bedroom.

The room was exactly as she had left it, except for the tall vase of lilies on the dressing-table in front of the window. Her antique dark brown mahogany wardrobe still dwarfed the room, monumental and solid like an old friend. The huge piece of furniture had been there since the family had first moved in. James Hunter had meant to remove it and replace it with a fitted wardrobe more suited to the size of the room, but he never had the energy or the inclination to haul it down the steep, narrow stairs. It was now as familiar to Sally as a childhood teddy bear or blanket. It had hidden many of her childhood and teenage secrets in its myriad interior nooks and secret drawers over the years, from diaries and love letters to cigarettes and 'Jungle Juice' – lethal cocktails of spirits stolen in minuscule liquid amounts from her parents' drinks cabinet and distilled into empty screwtop soft drink bottles.

Jamie dumped his sister's bags unceremoniously onto the white painted wooden floor and sat down on her bed, his long legs spilling untidily onto the floor.

Sally stared at him closely and grinned.

"What?" he asked self-consciously.

Sally continued to smile.

"Ah stop, what is it? Do I have spinach in my teeth or something? What is it?"

"Sorry, Jamie," Sally laughed. "I was trying to look at you in a non-sister sort of way. And you are kind of attractive, you know. Almost male model material, I would say. Or have you ever thought of joining a boy band?"

Jamie blushed and smiled, showing his even white molars. "Thanks, sis, but could you drop it please? It's just a job, you know."

"If you think for one second that I'm not going to get as much mileage as I can out of this one then you are very mistaken, young man." Sally sat down on the bed beside her brother and ruffled his hair. "I'm only slagging you, it's great to see you."

"You too, sis. And I'm not supposed to tell you this, Mum would kill me. But she's organised a surprise party for you tonight."

"Shit, not one of her 'extended family nights'?"

"Yup, complete with May and June."

Sally groaned and put her hands over her face.

"Oh come on," Jamie said. "It's not that bad. They

might have forgotten the words by now and maybe Uncle Cyril and Uncle Dick will be gardening or something. Sally, Sally, are you in there?" Jamie pulled Sally's hands away from her face, laughing.

"Anyway, she's asked some of your friends too – the sailing crowd and some guy you used to know who has some kind of cool job or something."

At this stage Sally's ears pricked up. "She's invited my friends to one of her mental granny parties? Are you serious? And what's the name of the guy?" She glared at her brother earnestly.

"Ah Jeez, Sal, I can't remember, I wasn't really listening. You know Mum – she was going on and on and . . ."

"Jamie," Sally interrupted her brother sharply, grabbing his earlobe and pinching it hard.

"Let go, you mad thing," Jamie spluttered. "I'm telling you I can't remember. She said something about school and some boy you used to like, that's all."

Sally released her killer pinch, much to Jamie's relief. "I hope to God it isn't him."

"Isn't who?" Jamie asked, rubbing his earlobe. What was his sister on about? She was obviously as nuts as ever. And she called their mother mad!

"A blast from the past," Sally said cryptically. "Right now tell me about this salubrious new career. Any babes on the scene?"

Jamie reluctantly began telling his sister about his modelling contracts, warming to the topic when he saw how genuinely interested she was.

"You're earning how much?" she asked incredulously after a few minutes. "I might try a bit of the old modelling myself."

Jamie laughed. "I've heard there's great money in lap dancing, might be more your kind of thing."

Sally landed an almighty thump on her brother's arm.

"Thanks a lot, pretty boy."

"Right, that's it, Sal – you're in trouble."

He grabbed one of Sally's pillows and started battering her over the head. A nanosecond later, she whipped up the other pillow and retaliated. They bashed each other without mercy, yelling and screaming abuse.

"Sally, Jamie, what's going on up there?" April's voice cut through the atmosphere from two floors down. Jamie and his sister fell onto the bed laughing and gasping for breath.

"Nothing, Mum, Sally's just unpacking."

Chapter 18

Two hours later, Sally was lying in the old Victorian claw-footed bath up to her neck in bubble bath foam. She was very, very apprehensive about the evening's 'surprise' party. Thank goodness Jamie had warned her. If Mark was going to turn up she certainly wanted to look her best. It was strange the way things turned out sometimes. If she could just keep him away from her mother and her two eccentric aunts, it might just be OK. Alternatively she could hide all the sweet sherry, which seemed to have a dramatic effect on her aunts and her mother. April, May and June neé Winterbottom were a force to be reckoned with at the best of times, but when they had more than two sherries in them they were lethal.

She towelled herself dry in her bedroom, put on some creased but miraculously clean underwear and dried her hair. It was still bleached blonde from the sun and salt in Antigua. Sally sighed. It wouldn't be this light for long, she thought to herself wistfully. She looked at the array of crinkly clothes draped over her chair, rescued from her stuffed travelling bag.

"Right," Sally said to herself determinedly. "Emma's wardrobe, here I come."

A few minutes later Jamie found his half-naked eldest sister staring into Emma's wardrobe, a look of astonishment on her face. He sneaked up behind her and put his cool hand on her shoulder.

Sally jumped back in shock.

"Jamie, you little shit! You nearly gave me heart failure."

"Sal, what are you up to exactly? Emma will have a fit if she finds you in here."

"She hasn't changed then," Sally grinned. "If you must know I'm trying to find something to wear this evening."

Jamie looked thoughtful. "I'm not sure Emma's clothes would be the thing, Sal. To be honest she's turned quite conservative since Kevin came on the scene."

"You're not kidding," Sally winced as she pulled out a flowery dress in shades of pink, yellow and light blue. "Hey, how about this?"

Jamie smiled as Sally held up a skimpy red silk slip dress. Suddenly he began to laugh.

"Hey, that's the nightie I gave Emma the Christmas before last. Look, it still has the Brown Thomas tag on it." A wicked glint lit up his grey eyes. "Wear it, Sal, I dare you. Emma would be mortified. It looks as if she's never worn it, it's probably too sexy for her. I'm sure

Kevin prefers flannelette nightgowns. That's if he's ever seen her less than fully clothed."

"Ah come on, Emma's not all that square, is she?" Sally asked doubtfully. "I know she's always been a little sensible but . . ."

Jamie reached into the wardrobe and pulled out a navy suit with gold buttons, a high-necked white linen shirt, stiffly starched, and a pair of light brown American style chinos.

"Right, sis, what do these clothes say to you?"

"Cooee, Sally, Jamie! Emma and Kevin are here. Come downstairs and say hello."

The partners in crime hurriedly hung Emma's clothes up and Sally ran upstairs to her bedroom. She flung on a pair of cleanish jeans and a T-shirt and bounded down the stairs. She took a deep breath and walked into the sitting-room. In front of her, sitting side by side on the sofa, smiling beatifically, was the most square-looking couple Sally had ever seen. They wore matching navy suits, his with a light blue shirt, hers with a white shirt. Their hair was shining and well-cut in classic styles, his a short back and sides, hers a shoulder-length bob. At their feet were matching black leather document carriers. And what made it really scary was the fact that this 'perfect' couple were none other than Emma and Kevin.

James and April were also in the room, along with Jamie whose shifty gaze refused to meet Sally's eyes.

Emma smiled warmly at Sally and jumped up off the sofa. "Sally," she cried throwing her arms around her sister. "It's great to have you back – I've missed you!"

Kevin was also on his feet and gave Sally a polite peck on the cheek. "Hi, Sally," he said politely. "Nice to see you again."

Sally sat down on the arm of the sofa, ignoring her mum's disapproving stare – she didn't like her prize furniture to be misused.

"I'm dying to hear all about your travels," Emma said smiling. "It all sounds so exciting. I want to hear everything."

Mrs Hunter cleared her throat theatrically. "Plenty of time for that later. Now, Sally, Emma and Kevin have something to tell you."

Sally smiled. Excellent, her perfect sister was pregnant and she wouldn't be black sheep *numero uno* anymore.

Emma blushed, gazed at her boyfriend who nodded crisply, and then turned towards Sally.

"Kevin and I are getting married. We've set the date for next May, after the end of the tax year. Kevin's very busy before then."

Sally was taken aback. She didn't really know Kevin at all, but as long as Emma was happy she supposed . . . she wasn't sure what to say, so she fell back on the old clichés.

"Congratulations, both of you. I hope you'll be very happy together. Um, it's great news." She plonked herself down on the sofa, beside Emma and gave her another hug. Kevin extended his hand towards Sally across his fiancée, and trying not to laugh she shook it firmly.

Jamie jumped up out of his chair. "Right, now that's all sorted, I'm off to have a shower." He practically ran out of the sitting-room, leaving his mother tutting and sighing in his wake.

James as usual diffused the situation. "Let's have a drink to celebrate. April, a sherry for you, dear?" He opened the drinks cabinet and took out four cut crystal glasses and a tall, elegant sherry decanter. "Your sister told us last week, Sally, but she wanted to tell you in person."

"Sherry, Kevin, Emma?"

Both nodded.

"Sally?"

Sally was confused. Since when did her sister drink sherry? Maybe the real Emma had been abducted by aliens and this strange woman with the perfect bob was from Mars.

"Um, no thanks. Could I have a vodka and tonic instead?"

April glared at her daughter.

"I don't think we have vodka," she said primly.

"How about a gin and tonic?" James Hunter asked quickly.

"Fine. Thanks," Sally answered, avoiding her mother's acid gaze. If looks could kill, she thought.

"Nice weather we're having," Kevin said inanely, considering it was a dull and showery day. "Your garden is blooming, Mrs Hunter."

"Oh, you must call me April, now that you're almost family," she twittered, blushing girlishly. "And the garden is doing rather well, thank you."

Sally watched her mother sip her Harvey's Bristol Cream at an alarming rate. She knew it was Harvey's as that was the only sherry her mother would touch. It wasn't even dinner time yet. Sally sighed. Her mother would be on her ear in no time.

When Jamie came back down a little later, the family sat down to eat in the dining-room. April had excelled herself with the table settings, using all the best plates and the heavy antique silver cutlery, polished to within one inch of its life. The Waterford crystal wine glasses and tumblers were also on the table, sparkling in the light. Even though it was bright outside Sally's mum had lit two large elaborate candelabra, whose tall red candles flickered ineffectually in the daylight. The white linen napkins were carefully ironed and starched, as Sally realised when she slid hers out of its silver-initialled napkin holder and placed it on her knee. What is it with Mum and starch? she thought to herself. Mrs Hunter was mad into the old starch – she used it on everything she could, from shirts to sheets. And now, Sally feared, her little sister had fallen into the starch trap, with her crisp white shirts. What was the world coming to? She glanced surreptitiously at Kevin's shirt – yep, starched too.

Sally tucked into a warm white roll with lashings of Kerrygold butter. She had missed Irish butter in Antigua. Her mother frowned at her and gestured with her clasped hands to the Reverend Hunter. Of course – Grace. Sally had forgotten.

James cleared his throat. "For what we are about to receive, may the Lord make us truly grateful."

"Amen," said Emma and Kevin loudly.

Sally decided to give up all hope of getting the old Emma back, the one who used to kick her under the table and try to make her laugh during Grace. That Emma had obviously been banished a long time ago. Mr Sensible Kevin McGuirk had a lot to answer for.

As the table tucked into their melon, Kevin and James discussed football, something about the Cup Winner's Cup. Sally had no interest in football, but the new Emma was hanging on Kevin's every word.

Jamie, who was sitting beside Sally, pressed her foot with his under the table. He leant over and whispered in her ear.

"Emma and Kevin are something else, aren't they? It's like they're auditioning for a bizarre soap opera about Mr and Mrs Perfect . . ."

"Well, Sally," April said loudly, interrupting Jamie's whispers – she didn't approve of whispering, especially when she couldn't hear what was being said.

"Tell us all about the exotic Caribbean. I'm sure everyone wants to hear all about it."

Sally was dumbfounded. Where should she begin?

"Come along," her mother encouraged. "It's not like you to be shy."

Sally talked for a few minutes about Ginny and her job on the boat. Jamie and her father asked sensible and interested questions about Antigua, while April, Kevin and Emma listened politely.

"It all sounds idyllic," Jamie said. "What made you come home?"

Sally was hoping no-one would ask that question until she'd had the time to concoct a feasible answer. Admitting that her main motivation had been, number one – a vague sense of unease at her carefree lifestyle and, number two – a man from her chequered past, was not something she wanted to try to explain to her parents or to the perfect couple for that matter. Jamie might understand, but he was different.

"Well, isn't it just as well I did?" Sally said, changing the subject. "Or I wouldn't have heard the exciting news first-hand. So tell me, Emma, have you made any wedding plans yet?"

This was clearly the right question to ask. The rest of the dinner, from steak to Pavlova and coffee, was spent discussing everything from the colour of the flowers to the honeymoon destination. Emma and Kevin were nothing if not organised.

"And we've asked Kevin's sister Shauna to be the bridesmaid. I hope you don't mind, Sally, but I only want one and I wasn't sure if you'd even be here in May. Anyway you'd probably feel a little awkward, me being your younger sister and all."

Sally glared at her sister. What was she implying? And Emma could always ask her now. It wasn't as if the wedding was next week or anything.

Mr Hunter stepped in as usual. "Jamie, where are you working next week? Any interesting jobs coming up?"

April snorted rudely. Jamie chose to ignore her.

"I'm in the National Gallery on Tuesday and the

Hugh Lane on Wednesday, some sort of arty sunglass promotion for *Himself* magazine."

"Kevin, have you ever thought of modelling yourself?" Sally asked mischievously. Kevin was no Brad Pitt. A small man in his early thirties, with dark receding hair and round, hornrimmed glasses, he looked at Sally carefully.

"It's never been on my career plan," he said seriously. "It's quite unstable work, you know, with no set income. Not for me, I like security. Pension plan, health insurance, company car, that sort of thing."

Sally nodded, trying to keep a straight face. "I see."

"Have I told you all that Kevin's just been given a promotion?" said Emma.

"Really, Kevin? How wonderful!" April exclaimed. "Do tell us all about it."

Kevin could bore for Ireland, Sally thought, listening to him talk about mortgage-lending. She heard a car pulling up outside and leapt up to answer the door.

"Excuse me," she whispered, careful not to interrupt Kevin's monologue.

"I'll help you," Jamie said, leaving the table and joining her in the hall.

Chapter 19

"Kevin must be one of the most tedious men in Ireland," Jamie muttered as he opened the door. "What does Emma see in him?"

May and Cyril Davis were standing on the doorstep. Sally shushed her brother.

"What was that, Jamie?" May asked smiling.

Sally popped her head around the door. "Oh, nothing, May, pay no attention to Jamie. It's all the bright lights and flashes on the photo shoots – it's getting to him I think."

Jamie elbowed his sister in the ribs.

"Don't mind Sally, May. Come on in. The others are in the dining-room." He stepped back and ushured them into the warm hall.

"Sally, how wonderful to see you! You look a million dollars – so tanned and healthy."

Sally put her arms around her godmother and held her close. She was enveloped in the familiar heady waft of Chanel Number 5. May was a confirmed Chanel addict.

Sally then hugged her uncle who was standing quietly in the background, as usual.

After the greetings, May wrinkled her heavily powered pink nose.

"You'd better give me a drink before I go in, Jamie. You're absolutely right, that man could put anyone to sleep."

Jamie smiled broadly and Sally began to giggle. She loved May, who was her godmother and more like a friend than an aunt.

"You'd better watch yourself, May – you know he's going to be part of the family soon," Sally teased.

May snorted. "Some people have no taste."

Cyril put his hand on his wife's shoulder.

"Now, May, charity, charity."

April blustered into the hall. "May, Cyril, darlings! What an unexpected pleasure," she said pointedly. She glanced at her watch and glared at her sister.

Sally smiled. There was nothing like her mum to make people feel welcome, even if May had spoilt the 'surprise'. May looked sheepish and Cyril looked embarrassed.

"It's OK, May – Jamie let it slip earlier about the party," Sally said smiling.

April Hunter sighed loudly and muttered something about Jamie under her breath. Plastering a wide smile on her face she said, "Well then, what are we still doing in the hall? Come in, come in."

She practically pushed her sister and Cyril into the dining-room.

Sally and Jamie escaped into the kitchen, ostensibly to fetch glasses for the new guests.

"It's going to be one of those nights," Sally grinned. "May and Mum rubbing each other up the wrong way and June attempting to plaster over the cracks. Excellent."

Jamie winced. "I don't know if I can cope. Still, at least we have Kevin to keep us entertained. Maybe he'll tell us about fixed-rate mortgages again."

Sally and Jamie returned to the dining-room and handed the glasses to their father.

"Where have you two been?" their mother asked frowning. "May was just telling us about her garden, weren't you, May?"

"Well, I was just saying how tedious I found gardening and how Cyril was boring me to tears this evening with his discussion on the merits of different green-fly sprays, which is why we are early. He was driving me so nuts I had to get out. Now he can bore your father instead."

April was a little flustered. Her sister had a habit of telling the truth at the most inopportune times. "No, dear. I meant what you were saying about the tea roses and Emma's wedding."

May smiled. "Oh, sorry. I was telling your mother, Sally, about the tea roses that Cyril has been growing. They'd make a beautiful bride's posy."

"I remember your roses, Cyril. And May is right, they would be beautiful." Cyril smiled appreciatively. A quiet man by nature, he let May do much of the talking

214

for him. He loved his vibrant and clever wife to distraction and he didn't mind one bit that she liked to speak her mind. It reminded him of his late mother, a strong woman if ever there was one.

April stared at her daughter. Sally grew quickly paranoid. What had she said now?

"Sally, do you intend to wear those clothes all night? We have guests coming, darling."

"You're absolutely right, Mum," Sally said, jumping out of her seat. "I'll go up and change right now."

Half an hour later Sally came down the stairs and walked into the living-room. May and Jamie were chatting on the sofa. Emma and Kevin were fingering the curtains by the window, no doubt planning soft furnishings for their future dream house. Sally could hear the sounds of washing-up from the kitchen. Her mother hated the sight of dirty crockery and pans – she always insisted on washing up as soon as a meal was over.

Jamie whistled as Sally came in the door. "Wow, sis. You look stunning. Red really suits you."

May agreed. "You'll knock 'em dead," she stated firmly.

Emma had a strange expression on her face. She stared at Jamie, who purposely ignored her gaze.

Kevin coughed and reddened slightly. "Rather risqué, don't you think, Sally?"

Sally smiled. She was delighted with the effect her appearance was having on her sister's fiancé. She was obviously making him nervous. The red 'dress' clung to

215

her body in all the right places. It stopped just on her knee, showing two tanned, well-toned legs. Sally's shoulders and chest were also lightly tanned, and her blonde sun-kissed hair swept over her shoulders attractively. She had glossed her lips and carefully applied a coral-coloured eye shadow, with a touch of mascara. Finishing the outfit were a pair of strappy silver sandals.

April poked her head around the door. "May, Cecil and James want you in the garden. Something about cats." She looked at her daughter with a fixed expression on her face. Uh, oh, Sally thought. She could hear the cogs in her mother's mind turning.

"Cover your shoulders, dear. You're not in the Caribbean now and you'll catch a chill. Emma, do you have a cardigan your sister could borrow?"

There was no way her mother was going to ruin her outfit with a naff, granny cardi of her sister's. But she didn't want to cause an argument, not on her first night back anyway.

Emma smiled. "Come upstairs with me, Sal, and I'll see if I have anything you'd like."

Doubtful, Sally muttered to herself, as she was led upstairs by her sister.

"I have a black cardigan that might do the trick," Emma said, opening the top drawer of her chest of drawers. Much to Sally's amazement she pulled out a light, see-through black top with tiny hook-and-eye fastenings down the front and fashionable three-quarter-length sleeves.

"Oh, thanks, Em," Sally said, taken aback. "That's really nice of you."

Emma smiled. "I know what you're thinking. I've never worn this, Kevin doesn't approve of see-through tops. But it's so cute I just had to buy it."

This was more like the Emma Sally knew and loved. While she had her sister on her own, she decided to ask her about the impending wedding.

"Em, well . . . um . . . I was just wondering . . ."

Emma smiled at her sister. It wasn't like Sally to be stuck for words.

"Yes?"

"I was just wondering, are you sure you want to get married? You're only twenty-four and you've got a lot of living to do. Kevin's a good bit older than you and you haven't lived together and . . . I just think . . . oh, shit I'm sorry, I'm just worried about you that's all."

Emma stared at her sister. She took a deep breath. "It's OK. You're right. Everyone else thinks it's such a great idea – Mum, my friends, Kevin. But I am a bit worried." She blushed. "We haven't even . . . you know . . ."

Sally looked at her sister in astonishment. "Are you talking about sex, Em? You haven't had sex with Kevin, is that what you're saying?"

Emma was embarrassed. "Well no, we haven't. Kevin wants to wait until we're married, he's kind of traditional that way."

Sally felt bad. She didn't want to ruin her sister's happiness. Maybe she really loved Kevin and they would be great together. But in the back of her mind she was genuinely worried. She missed the old Emma, sensible and practical but fun and willing to take risks and to break the rules if she thought it was the right thing to do. She couldn't help thinking that her sister deserved better, someone full of life who would be a challenge, a real partner. But she didn't want to upset her. After all, she hadn't even seen her for nearly four years, and she'd only met Kevin briefly before she left, when they were first going out.

"Em, as long as you love Kevin, that's all that matters."

Emma sighed. "That's just it, Sal. I do love him, but I'm not sure if I really *love* him, you know."

Sally sat down on the bed beside her sister and listened carefully.

"I mean he's really good to me, you know. He looks after me, I suppose, picks me up in the morning and brings me into work. And brings me out for dinner and buys me flowers every second Saturday. But sometimes I feel like there's something missing."

"How do you mean?" Sally asked gently.

"Well, sometimes I wish he would be a little more spontaneous – you know, buy me flowers on the wrong day, or whisk me away to Paris even instead of to *Woodie's DIY*." She paused. "And to be honest I'm a little concerned about the whole attraction thing. Kissing him does nothing for me. He's so business-like about it – one hand on my shoulder, one hand on my cheek – it's always the same. There I've said it." Emma looked at her sister. "Is that awful?"

Sally smiled. "It's hardly your fault. Us Hunters are renowned for our exceptional kissing skills – ask Jamie. And we look for high standards in our kissing partners."

Emma giggled, glad that her sister had broken the tension. "Would you stop! This is serious."

"I know, sorry. Go on."

"I'm just worried that I'll wake up one morning and my life will be over. I'll be stuck at home with kids and a mortgage and I'll be full of regrets. I'm not sure if I'm ready to settle down. What do you think I should do?"

"Honestly?"

"Yes."

Sally paused, thinking. "Kevin's a good man – a solid kind of guy. But I don't think you should marry him unless you're sure. But maybe he has a hidden passionate side. You never know. Give him a chance, he might surprise you."

Emma sighed. "I doubt it, but you're right. I should give him a chance." She grinned. "Maybe I should take my nightie back and wear it going out sometime."

"Maybe you should," Sally laughed. "But I've got a better idea . . ."

Chapter 20

Sally and Emma went downstairs again. April was standing in the hall, waiting for them.

"Well, I suppose that's a little better," she said. "Emma, Kevin is in the garden with May and Cecil. They are discussing some sort of cat repellent or something. He wants you to join him. I'm going upstairs to fix my hair."

Emma tried to look enthusiastic. "Are you coming out, Sal?" she asked hopefully.

"Sure," Sally replied. Anything to get away from her mother's disapproving glances.

The two sisters walked through the backdoor into the garden. It was a warm enough evening, if not exactly bright and sunny. At least the rain seemed to be holding off.

"Emma," Kevin called. "Come over here. Cecil is just telling us about his ingenious anti-cat devices."

Emma raised her eyebrows at Sally. The two men were standing beside an empty plastic coke bottle, which was at the edge of the flowerbed. In fact there seemed to be several empty coke bottles in the flowerbed, each partially filled with some sort of liquid.

"Tell the girls about the cats, Cecil. It's so clever."

Cecil blushed slightly. "It's simple really. You see the bottles heat up and they emit a high-pitched noise which the cats hate as the pressure increases. We can't hear it, of course, being mere humans."

May was standing beside her husband with an incredulous look on her face.

"Pay no attention to him, he's obviously lost the plot."

Kevin frowned at her. "Well, you know, May, it all sounds feasible to me. It does have some basis in scientific fact. Animals have very different hearing systems to humans, you know."

"Don't you go encouraging him, Kevin. Our garden is full enough of plastic bottles, and homeopathic slug pellets and God knows what else as it is. And, as you see, he has April convinced too. She bought bottles of coke and poured it down the sink, as she doesn't approve of fizzy drinks, as she calls them."

Sally and Emma were trying not to laugh. Cecil and Kevin were perfect together.

May took control of the situation. "Right, ladies, we are going inside to have a drink or two. Leave these boffins to talk about decomposing compost or whatever they like."

She strode into the house, whisked a bottle of gin off the kitchen counter and sat down on the sofa in the empty living-room. Sally and Emma followed closely behind.

"Thanks, May," Emma said. "I thought we'd be stuck talking about gardening for hours. Kevin does love his gardens. Not that he has one of his own yet, of course."

May poured herself a large gin. "Oops, I forgot the tonic, ladies." She jumped up and scooted into the kitchen to fetch it.

"May's still mad I see," Sally laughed. "And her hair's still lilac."

Emma smiled. May liked the colour lilac and was fond of wearing lilac from head to toe, literally. This evening she was wearing a lilac tweed suit, with an on-the-knee skirt and pink suede peep-toe shoes with kitten heels. May was Sally's hero – she had always been a true original. She came back a few minutes later brandishing a bottle of tonic and a bowl full of ice.

"Good on you, May," Sally whooped.

After three extra large G and T's had been prepared, the three partners in crime sat back into the sofa.

"Right," May began. "Tell us all about Antigua, Sally. Without censorship if you please."

Sally was more than happy to oblige. She told them about Ginny, about the wild days and the even wilder nights and the long, lazy sails around the Caribbean islands.

Emma sighed. "It sounds so beautiful, Sal, you're so lucky. I'd love to travel, I've always wanted to go to Australia. It doesn't look as if I'll get there now and Kevin says it's too far to go for a honeymoon. He wants to go to Brittany. He dosen't like cities – too noisy – and he doesn't like sitting in the sun, he comes up in bumps apparently." Emma sighed again.

"Emma, I have one thing and one thing only to say to you about Kevin, and then I'll shut my mouth," May started.

Sally was worried – what was their aunt going to say?

"Kevin is a nice man, he's solid and dependable. I can see what you like about him. In fact, he reminds me of my own Cecil at that age, although he has more hair than Cecil did, bald as a coot he was. Anyway, my parents loved Cecil, he was their golden boy, a bright young accountant with a brilliant future ahead of him. But there was this other boy, a Sligo lad who looked after the garden." May's face lit up. "Joe was his name. He had dark hair, cropped short, and a cheeky grin. And he had a small scar on his eyebrow." She touched her own eyebrow gently. "Just there. We spent many happy days in the garden, sharing our thoughts and laughing. God, he could make you laugh!"

Sally and Emma sat transfixed. May was always telling them stories about her childhood, but somehow this one seemed different.

"We were mad about each other. He taught me so much about wildlife – he loved plants and wildlife. One day my father came into the garden and found us chatting. The next day I asked my mother where Joe was, and she said that my father had let him go. I was devastated. It only struck me then how much he had grown on me and how I felt about him. I never saw him again. And I married Cecil the following summer. Years later I was in the garden with my mother and we were talking about a bush which used to be cut into the shape of a peacock, back when Joe was around. 'He came back, you know,' she said. 'Your father wouldn't let me tell you, but he came to the house three or four times. But finally your father told him you were engaged and didn't want to see him.' I asked her why he had done that and she said 'Father wanted you to marry Cecil'. As simple as that. Joe wasn't good enough for me, you see." May stopped for a second and took Emma's hands in hers. "Follow your heart, my dear. If you love Kevin, *really* love him, then I wish you all the best. I have a good marriage and Cecil is a good man. But I still wonder what life would have been like with Joe."

Jamie came bounding in the door, his arms almost pulled out of their sockets with plastic shopping bags.

"What are you three talking about?" he asked. "You all look far too serious for my liking. You could cut the atmosphere in here with a knife."

"Love," stated May firmly. "And you are welcome to join us, dear boy. Don't forget a glass."

"I'll be right with you," Jamie grinned.

Jamie dumped the heavy bags with a sharp clink on the kitchen floor.

His father followed him into the kitchen. He had decided to fetch more supplies of an alcoholic nature, prompted by his son. April's bar wouldn't keep a room full of nuns happy, let alone Sally's friends. And he wouldn't mind a dirty big vodka himself.

The doorbell rang and Jamie went out to answer it. Soon the living-room was full of their parent's friends and relations. The younger crowd were still in the pub, no doubt. Aunt June arrived with her husband Gill and the cousins, the delectable Hope and Jane, tall, willowy dark-haired girls in their late teens. Hope was a model and Jane was training to be a Primary School teacher and as the two girls wafted into the room, all heads turned.

And every time the door-bell rang, Sally grew more and more nervous. She had forgotten about Mark during the last few hours, caught up in conversations with her sister and now with May.

Jamie perched on the arm of the sofa, beside Sally.

Emma and May were in the middle of a discussion on the merits of underwired bras and push-up bras.

"Any cute men here yet?" he asked.

Sally smiled. "Not exactly, unless you count Roger, Dad's curate."

Jamie swept his eyes over the conservatively dressed young man talking to Kevin in the corner.

"Not my type, sis," he said laughing.

"I should hope not," Sally said in mock suprise. "Any cute babes for yourself, bro?"

"Well, it's a pity we're related to Hope and Jane. They are goddesses."

The doorbell rang again. Sally's heart leapt.

"Are you OK?" Jamie asked.

"Fine," Sally answered distractedly. She could hear her mother fawning over someone in the hall. She strained her ears to hear.

"She's just dying to meet you again," Sally heard her mother say. "I know you'll get along so well – you have so much in common, being in the same school and everything."

Sally caught a glimpse of a tall male figure in the hall, with his back to the doorway. He had dark blonde hair and was wearing jeans and a white shirt.

Oh my God, she thought to herself as her pulse began to race and her stomach emulated a cavern full of butterflies. It's Mark!

Chapter 21

"Are you all right, Sal?" Jamie asked again.

His sister had turned whiter than white and she was staring into the hall with a doggered concentration. But she didn't hear Jamie – her ears were tuned exclusively into her mother's high-pitched voice.

"Sally's in here, do come and say hello."

The tall man turned around. Sally nearly died. The man had nondescript pale grey eyes, thin colourless lips and a thin, sharp nose and chin. This was certainly not Mark Mulhearne, unless he had been betwitched by some sort of wicked goblin.

April strode over to her daughter, pushing the hesitant man in front of her.

"This is Cedric Hawkins – he was in your class in St John's, Sally. Isn't it nice to see him again?"

No, it bloody well is not, Sally thought to herself crossly. I was expecting my destiny in male form, not some sort of cruel joke. She forced a smile.

"Yes, nice to see you again, Cedric."

April was in her element. "Cedric was just telling me about his studies – he's training to be a clergyman. Like your father, dear," she added pointedly, just in case the obvious had suddenly escaped her daughter.

Now I remember, Sally twigged. Cedric is the geek who used to sing the hymns in perfect tenor during assembly. Everyone else made fun of the hymns, singing out of tune or belting out the wrong words. 'Praise my Goal, the King of Football' instead of 'Praise my Soul, the King of Heaven', that sort of thing. But good old Cedric had always taken the hymns very seriously. It suddenly dawned on her. Mark isn't coming, this is who Mum was talking about, the man from my past. Yeah, right! He's not bloody well coming. Sally felt relief and disappointment all mingle into one leaden lump in her throat.

"Sally, Sally! Cedric asked you a question," April interjected.

Cedric Hawkins blushed. Mrs Hunter had been insistent that he come. She had met his mother at a church fête recently and unbeknownst to him, or to Sally for that matter, the two women had practically married them off. He didn't think that Sally looked all that pleased to see him, if the truth be known. She looked rather shocked really.

"Sorry, what were you saying? I was miles away?"

"I was just wondering if you had enjoyed your time in Antigua? Your mother was telling me all about it."

Sally winced. Her mother had done this to her before, with another friend's son. She had actually gone out with Roger for a while, but he had turned out to be a lazy sod and selfish and boring to boot. Still, it wasn't poor old Cedder's fault. Many a young man had been bullied by her mother before.

Sally smiled at Cedric. "Yes, it was wonderful. I loved every minute of it."

"It must be difficult being back. It's not easy integrating into a family again, is it?"

"No, you're certainly right there," Sally replied. Maybe Cedric wasn't so bad after all.

April left them to it, delighted with her perceived 'result'.

Jamie introduced himself.

"Oh, sorry Jamie, I forgot about you," Sally apologised.

Jamie had been sitting on the sofa arm watching the awkward conversation carefully.

"Can I get you a drink, mate?" he asked in a friendly manner.

"Thank you, that would be great. A vodka and tonic if you have one."

Sally smiled again. Maybe if they all got locked it might be a bit of a laugh. That reminded her, she had business to attend to with the 'delectable' Kevin.

"I'll get it," she said. "I have to go into the kitchen anyway."

Sally sashayed over to her sister's fiancé.

"Can I get you another drink, Kevin?' she asked, flicking back her hair and beaming at him.

Kevin blushed. His glasses would steam up and steam would shoot from the top of his dinky head if this was a cartoon, Sally thought to herself.

"Oh, um, yes please Sally. Thank you," he blustered. "Fruit juice."

"Roger, how about you?"

"I'm fine thanks, Sally." Roger grinned at the bright young daughter of his 'boss'. Nice dress, he thought, before checking himself and taking his eyes off her cleavage.

"One fruit juice coming up," Sally said. With a double shot of vodka, she promised under her breath as she walked into the kitchen.

The room had started to fill up. Friends of her parents and neighbours were all chatting amicably. The sailing-club gang hadn't arrived yet. Sally fully expected them to roll in after the pubs had closed. She twisted her way though the bodies and went into the kitchen. She poured a large vodka and tonic for Cedric and sloshed some vodka in Kevin's glass, until it was almost one third full of Blue Label. She then filled the glass with orange juice, adding a wedge of lemon for good measure.

Sally gave Cedric, now in deep conversation with Jamie about music, his drink and made her way towards Kevin.

"Here you are, darling," she purred, placing her hand on his besuited arm. She was rather enjoying this.

Kevin was becoming more and more nervous and hot under the collar. He wasn't used to unwarranted female attention, and especially not from his future sister-in-law. Still, he decided, I'd better humour her. He took a deep slug of his orange juice. It had an unusually strong aftertaste but he thought he'd better drink it.

Sally watched him start into the drink. "I'll be back soon, I'm just going to circulate," she huskily told the delighted Roger and bewildered Kevin.

"What a woman," Roger muttered under his breath as she walked away.

As Sally made her way back towards her brother she spied Jean coming through the door, followed by Peter and some of the old sailing gang.

"Hi guys," she yelled over, waving excitedly.

Jean rushed over and threw her arms around her long-lost friend.

"Great to see you, Sal, you look amazing," she smiled.

"Hi, Sally," Peter said, giving her another hug. Behind him were Jimbo, Shane and a tall, slim blonde girl.

"This is Sasha," Shane introduced his glamorous companion, placing his hand on the small of her perfectly formed and evenly tanned back. The young woman was in her early twenties and was wearing a backless black dress and very high black court shoes.

"Sasha is an air hostess," he proclaimed proudly. "I met her on an Aer Lingus flight."

Sally and Jean smiled at each other. He hadn't changed one little bit. The two friends fetched drinks from the kitchen.

"God, it's so good to have you back," Jean said, pouring a triple G and T for herself. "It hasn't been the same without you, Sal."

Sally smiled at her old friend. "It's good to be back, I think," she laughed. "Mum is already driving me bonkers though. She means well but she's so overpowering. And wait till I tell you, Emma's engaged."

"What!" Jean exclaimed. "Little Emma, sure she's only young. Is it that Kevin guy?"

"Yup, the very one," Sally said, stirring her drink with her finger.

"Holy shit," Jean said. "Wait till I tell Peter, he's always had a bit of a soft spot for your sister."

"Any plans yourself on the wedding front?" Sally asked wickedly. Jean and Peter had been together for years now and were notoriously tetchy about the big M word.

"Would you stop," Jean moaned. "Mum is getting worse. She even buys me wedding magazines and drops them into the flat. Honestly, it's a nightmare. I mean if we were left alone we might consider it, I suppose, but there's no mad rush."

"You know I'm only joking, Jean," Sally smiled. "I love winding you up."

"I presume your Mum is up to her old matchmaking tricks, or did Cedders just happen to find the party as he was on his way to the church?"

Sally laughed. "You guessed it. And the worst thing is, I thought she had invited . . . someone else. I got a real fright when Cedders walked in the door. Still he's not the worst."

"Listen, I almost forgot," Jean said. "My cousin Red is staying with us at the moment. He's calling in later. I hope that's OK."

"No problem," Sally looked at her friend quizzically. "Is he cute?"

Jean grinned. "Yes, I guess he is. Glad to see you have your priorities right."

"Damn sure," Sally said firmly.

Two hours and many sherries later April, May and June had congregated at the piano in the sitting-room. April was sitting at the ivory keys, flexing her fingers in preparation to play. May and June were taking deep breaths, airing their lungs as they liked to call it. Sobering up a little, Sally thought. Jean, Peter and the others looked on with interest.

"What kind of music are they into exactly?" Shane asked nervously. He didn't want to do anything to upset his week-old 'relationship' with Sasha. She was a real babe and seemed to like him a lot, and she was a damn sight more easygoing than Breda, his last girlfriend. A strong and demanding thirty-something, with a terrifying line in put downs, he was well rid of her. No, Sasha was much more laidback, Shane thought to himself, and a stunner too.

"Well," Sally winced. It wasn't all that easy to explain. "They're all big Cliff Richard fans, the early stuff mind. 'Summer Holidays' and 'Bachelor Boy', that kind of thing."

Sasha seemed confused. "Was that before or after the Christmas song?"

Sally smiled kindly. "Before, definitely. And they're fond of old Elvis songs, with a bit of Abba and Madonna thrown in."

Shane was now more than a little apprehensive, he was downright tense.

Jean laughed. "Do you remember their version of

'Like a Prayer' New Years Eve a few years ago? It was classic. As for their 'Bohemian Rhapsody'!"

Just then Jamie wandered over with a tall blonde man. Sally automatically pulled in her stomach and lowered her chin. She had read somewhere that lowering your chin and gazing up at a man while batting your eyelashes was the ultimate flirting manoeuvre. Shit, I hope it isn't giving me a double chin, she thought.

"What are you lot talking about?" Jamie asked.

"Mum's repertoire," Sally said smiling.

"Red, this is my sister Sally, Jean and Peter, Shane and Sasha, and last but not least, Jimbo. Gang, this is Red, Jean's cousin. He's just arrived."

Everyone greeted Red warmly, and Jamie went off to fetch more bottles of wine and cans of beer from the kitchen. Sally turned to the new arrival, noticing his striking blue eyes and clear, sallow skin. He was wearing a navy short-sleeved shirt and combats – cute thought Sally, very cute.

"Where are you from, Red?" she asked with interest.

"Well, originally Galway, but my mother is Italian. I've been living in Dublin for a few years now. How about yourself?"

"I've lived in Dublin all my life, but I've been in the Caribbean for the last few years. I arrived back today in fact."

Red smiled. "You look very alive in that case. Is the jet-lag not getting to you?"

"I'm sure I'll be in bits tomorrow, but I'm running on adrenaline at the moment I guess. And the drink helps."

Red laughed. "I know what you mean." He paused briefly. "Tell me about your brother – Jean told me he's a model."

Sally was delighted. This guy must be interested if he's asking about my family, she thought to herself. They chatted amicably for a few minutes before Jamie came back with cans of Heineken hanging by their plastic out of his mouth, and several open bottles of wine grasped by the necks in either hand.

"Good man," Jimbo said appreciatively, helping him unload his wares. The gang made themselves comfortable, sitting against the wall. The room was still full, although it was heading towards one o'clock and many of the 'oldies' had retired for the evening. The heavenly trio by the piano had been singing 'Are You Lonesome Tonight?' softly, swaying along to the music. After a few similarly gentle songs April performed a loud 'riff' along the keyboards and the three broke into a lively rendition of 'Dancing Queen'.

"Hey, I like this one. Steps, isn't it?" Sasha asked. "Come on Shane, let's dance."

"Um, I don't think . . ."

"Don't be such a grampa." Sasha grabbed her boyfriend by the arm and pulled him to his feet. As she danced enthusiastically beside him, Shane loosened up and soon the pair were throwing each other around the room, in true rock-and-roll style. In minutes the rest of the gang had joined in, Sally and Jean singing along loudly into wine bottles, as Agnetha and Frieda.

"Great party," Peter enthused. "Your mum is gas."

April, May and June had decided to keep to an Abba theme and were now belting out 'Waterloo'.

Sasha led a conga out the door, through the kitchen and into the garden, Shane holding on to her for dear life. Sally and Jean watched from the kitchen window as the conga broke up and the dancing continued outside.

"Shane's got his hands full there," Jean observed. "Sasha's a real wild cat."

"About time he met his match," Sally said. "You're cousin's interesting, what does he do?"

Jean was wondering how long it would take her friend to ask about Red.

"He's a DJ on a local radio station. He seems to do everything from making the coffee and answering the phone, to hosting shows."

"Cool," Sally said, grinning. "A DJ." She began to imagine VIP seats at trendy concerts, free CDs, wild parties . . .

"He works really hard, he's rarely home."

"Where's home?" Sally asked, trying to appear nonchalant.

"He's living with me at the moment in Donnybrook. You'll have to come over tomorrow – it's the ground floor of an old house."

"Sounds great," Sally said enthusiastically. "I'm dying to see it."

"I'm sure you are," Jean laughed, digging her friend in the ribs. Sally hit her back on the arm.

"Brat," Jean said.

Suddenly they heard screams coming from the lawn.

Outside, Sasha had found the garden hose and was soaking Shane.

Sally and Jean burst out laughing – deep belly laughs. Soon they were gasping for breath and clinging to each other drunkenly.

"I like Sasha," Sally gasped. "That's the way to treat them."

Strains of Madonna's 'Like a Virgin' came wafting from the sitting-room, sung this time by a strong and tuneful tenor.

"It can't be . . ." Sally said. The two friends staggered into the room. Beside the piano stood Cedric, waving his hands in time to the music. On either side of him were May and June, gazing up at him adoringly.

"I've seen it all now," Jean said in amazement.

A couple of hours later, Jean and Sally were slumped against the wall in the sitting-room. Shane and Sasha were fast asleep on the sofa, her blonde head lying across his knee. Peter and Jimbo were discussing football in the corner, watched by a bleary-eyed Roger.

"I'm telling you, man, Roy Keane is not human. God made him, he's like, um, Jesus," Peter said, struggling to get the words out. "Sorry if that's like blast-thingy."

"Blasphemy?' Roger asked helpfully.

"Yeah, that."

Red and Jamie were upstairs, going through Jamie's vast CD collection. April, May and June had retired, dragged to bed or home by their respective husbands. Cedric now commanded the piano, singing and playing gentle Van Morrison songs.

"It's been a bloody good night," Jean slurred. "Bloody good. I'm so glad you're home, I missed you."

"Thanks. I missed you too."

"Where's Emma been all night?"

"Good question," Sally said. Where had her sister been? She had seen her leaving the room dragging Kevin by the arm, a couple of hours ago. Curiosity got the better of her.

"I'll be back in a sec. I'm just going upstairs."

Sally staggered up the stairs, helped by the sturdy wooden banisters. She crept past her parent's bedroom door, not that anything would wake her mother this evening, she thought to herself, smiling. She went up the next flight to her brother and sister's rooms. The lights were out in both. Sally pushed open her sister's door and crept inside.

Chapter 22

Emma was fast asleep on top of the covers and snoring gently. Her bare legs were dangling over one side of the bed. Her white shirt lay discarded on the floor and her long blue linen skirt was ruched up around her hips in a wrinkled clump. Sally gazed at her sister at amazement. She must have thrown back a lot of drinks to get in this state, she thought to herself. Emma always hangs her clothes up before she goes to bed.

Her sister mumbled in her sleep and rolled over violently, sending herself spinning off the bed and into a heap at Sally's feet. Sally stifled her giggles.

"What are you like?" she whispered to her now half-awake sister.

"Shit," Emma exclaimed, rubbing her head. She looked up. "Oh, hi. What time is it? I must have fallen asleep."

Sally helped her sister back onto the bed smiling.

"How many drinks did you have?" she asked.

Emma winced. "Well, I'm not sure exactly. I was trying to pluck up the courage to, well . . . you know."

Sally was intrigued. "To what?"

Emma sighed. "I decided you were right. I wanted to see if Kevin was really the right man for me. So I thought I'd . . ." She sighed. "It was stupid, I suppose."

"What did you do? Go on tell me. It's not fair to leave me in suspense like this."

"OK," Emma muttered. "But you promise you won't laugh?"

Sally nodded her head.

"You remember what we were talking about earlier? When you said you'd get him drunk and then I could hop on him." Sally nodded again. "I don't know how you did it but he was certainly the most drunk I've ever seen him. So I asked him to come upstairs to my room. I told him I wanted to show him something to do with the wedding." She paused.

Sally looked at her expectantly. "Go on."

"I can't quite remember the exact details, but once he was in here I asked him to sit on the bed and I lashed over to the door and locked it and put the key in my knickers."

Sally covered her mouth with her hand to muffle the laughs. She could just see Kevin's face. He must have been shocked!

Emma continued, her cheeks turning a delicate shade of pink.

"He was sitting on the bed with this poker face on him and glazed, drunken eyes."

Sally smiled broadly.

"He was just sitting there, staring at me with this

weird look on his face. I started to take off my shirt and his eyes were popping out of his head but he still didn't say anything. Then I stood in front of him and leant over and kissed him. But, Sally, it was awful, he wouldn't kiss me back and . . . oh shit, I'm mortified."

"And?" Sally encouraged, transfixed. *Fair City* had nothing on this.

"He just stood up suddenly and pushed me away. 'Emma,' he said in a really teachery voice. 'What has got into you? It's your sister I blame. She's the biggest flirt I've ever seen. Putting ideas in your head no doubt. I wonder if you're ready for marriage if this is how you behave.' And then he walked towards the door and tried to open it."

Sally hooted with laughter and her sister thumped her.

"Shut up, you'll wake Mum and Dad. And it's not funny."

"Was the key . . . how will I put this . . ."

"Sally," her sister frowned, trying to appear annoyed. "That's disgusting, stop it. Anyway Kevin was mortified when he got to the door and realised where the key was. And I couldn't get it out at first, so I had to try and undo my skirt to loosen it." Emma was gabbling at this stage, her face crimson. "But the hook was caught somehow and I couldn't undo it. So I had to pull my skirt up around my hips and get it that way. Kevin was just staring at me with a really smug look on his face. He said 'I hope you feel foolish now, Emma.' And he took the key. I think I called him a boring old fart and told him to feck off. Oh Sally, I could die. It's the worst thing that's ever happened to me in my whole life." Emma started crying, shoulders heaving..

"What am I going to do, Sal?" she asked. "He must think I'm a stupid floozie who can't hold her drink . . ."

Sally put her arm around her distraught sister. It was one of the funniest things she'd heard in a long time, but she recognised a soul in need of a hug when she saw one.

"Ah, pet," she crooned, "it'll be all right. Sure he might not even remember a lot of the evening with the amount of Blue Label I gave him."

Emma contiued. "I'd brought up a bottle of wine with me, so I knocked it back and I must have fallen asleep. Sally, how am I going to face him tomorrow?"

Sally sighed. Kevin had no sense of humour at all and she knew he wouldn't be in the least bit amused by any of the evening's 'entertainment'. She didn't know quite what to say.

"Emma," she began carefully. "I think you have to decide if you want to be with Kevin or not. I mean he's not going to change."

Emma looked at her sister, rubbing her eyes with her knuckles.

"I know. But it's difficult. We've been together years now and he's part of my life."

"I know it's hard. But can you honestly say you want to spend the rest of your life with him? After all, you did call him a boring old fart!"

"I don't know," Emma gulped.

"If you have any doubts at all I think you should at least postpone the wedding."

Emma's eyes opened wide. "Mum would go mad," she said.

"It's not about Mum or even Kevin for that matter." Sally began to see things clearly. The drink was wearing off with scary speed. It was amazing how quickly you could sober up when something serious happened. "It's about you and your life. You're young – you should be enjoying yourself, not worrying about weddings and bloody curtains. And old farts!"

Emma grinned and sniffed. She had stopped crying and had begun to feel better. Maybe Sally was right. She hated to admit it but all this wedding stuff was beginning to take on a life of its own. Everything was getting so complicated. The right dress, the right rings, the right church, the right food, the right . . . the list was endless. And Kevin was taking it all so seriously, and as for her mum, it was as if she was organising the Trinity Ball and the Spring Show all rolled into one the way she was going on.

Sally watched her sister with interest. She knew she was going to be blamed for this one. But it wasn't as if she was putting ideas into Emma's head. The doubts were already there. And even her mother wouldn't want Emma to marry for the wrong reasons, not to mention the wrong man. Surely she would just want her to be happy. Sally was uneasy. She knew her mother and she wasn't a woman to take major changes lightly. When she had announced her own plans to travel and sail, April had totally overreacted.

"Honestly, Em, it'll all be fine. You'll see," Sally said reassuringly.

"I hope you're right," Emma said doubtfully.

Sally opened her eyes gingerly. For a second she thought she was back in Antigua, sleeping beside the gently snoring Ginny. But within seconds she remembered, and fell back down to earth with a bump. She was on Emma's bed wrapped up in a duvet with her sister gently snoring beside her. A shaft of daylight beamed into the room as someone slowly pushed open the bedroom door. Sally looked up at the T-shirt and boxer-shorted figure before her.

"Shit, sorry," Red whispered. "I was looking for the bathroom. I didn't mean to wake you."

"Don't worry," Sally replied. "I was awake anyway."

Red glanced down sheepishly at his bare legs.

"Your brother kindly lent me his floor – I was too smashed to go home."

"I know the feeling," Sally smiled. "At least I only had to stagger up the stairs."

"Didn't make it to your room I see, or is it a Proddy thing? Sharing a bed with your siblings."

Sally giggled. "Would you stop! Listen, now that we're both awake, would you like some coffee?"

"Love some," Red smiled. "I'll just put on some clothes."

"I'll meet you in the kitchen," Sally said. "And the bathroom's the last door on the left."

Sally sat in the sunlit kitchen and gazed out the

window thoughtfully. It was strange to be home. She felt kind of out of it, as if she didn't really fit in anymore. Nothing had changed, yet in a strange way everything had changed. What was she going to do now? Sally sighed softly. She didn't think her parents would understand, especially her mother, if she said she needed some time to get her head together. She knew her mother would want her to jump straight into a job, any job.

Just then Red walked in the door.

"Penny for them," he said kindly.

"The usual hungover meaning of life stuff. You know."

"Don't I just," Red said smiling. "I'm a master of the morning-after head-wreckers. Things always seem crappy and impossible when you have a head on you."

"You're dead right," Sally grinned. This guy was really something and cute too.

Red sat down beside Sally.

"Great party," he said. "And your brother's a laugh. Tell me more about yourself and your sailing."

Sally was more than happy to oblige. They chatted for ages, sipping coffee and swopping stories. Red was utterly charming and seemed genuinely fascinated by her family.

"And your sister is engaged to that baldy guy?" he asked incredulously.

Sally filled him in on the wedding plans.

"The thing is, I may have stirred things up a bit."

"What do you mean?" Red asked.

Sally told him about the previous evening's events. Red spluttered a mouthful of coffee onto the kitchen table as she unfolded the planned seduction scene which had gone horribly wrong.

"I don't believe you! No normal red-blooded male would react like that. Your sister's a babe!"

" I know! And . . ."

Sally heard a noise outside the kitchen. Someone was coming down the stairs. She prayed it wasn't her mother, she couldn't deal with her at this hour of the morning.

Luckily it was Jamie.

"Hi folks, how are the heads?"

"Could be better," Sally grinned. "And how's the face of the new millennium this morning?"

"Make us a coffee would you, sis?"

"Only 'cause I love you," Sally said. "And it's my first morning back. God, it feels like I've been back forever."

"What were you guys laughing about? I could hear you from the top of the stairs."

"Wait till I tell you," Sally said smiling.

A short time later, Sally and Red were in Mrs Hunter's Ford Fiesta on their way to Jean's flat. They had dropped Jamie into town, where he had been summoned to a last-minute photo shoot by his agency. The sky was warm and overcast, with dark rain clouds hovering ominously over head.

"How long have you known Jean?" Red asked as they sat at the traffic-lights just past the Burlington Hotel.

"We were in school together," Sally replied. "And we were on the Irish schools sailing team together."

Red smiled. "From what Jean's told me, some of those sailing events were pretty wild."

Sally laughed. "I suppose they were. How long have you been living with Jean?"

"A few weeks. It's just until I find somewhere decent of my own. But that's not easy in Dublin."

"Where were you living before?" Sally asked.

Red sighed. "I was sharing a place on Pearse Street with a friend." He paused. "But it didn't work out."

"I see," Sally said, her curiosity aroused. "A girlfriend?" She couldn't help herself, she had to ask.

Red glanced over at Sally. Her eyes were on the road as she negotiated the Sunday lunch-time traffic. "Not exactly," he replied, leaving it at that. "Turn right here."

They drove to the end of a long leafy road and pulled in outside a large red-bricked house.

"Nice place," Sally said appreciatively.

They were greeted at the front door by Peter.

"Jean's lying on the couch, watching *Four Weddings and a Funeral*. She refuses to move, be warned. And she blames you for her hangover!"

Sally, Red and Peter walked into the sitting-room of the large ground-floor flat.

"Evil one!" Jean muttered at Sally, forming a cross with her two forefingers.

"And good morning to you too," Sally laughed. "Or should I say good afternoon?"

The gang made themselves comfortable on the

remaining armchair and the floor. Jean, true to Peter's word, refused to move from her prostrate position on the sofa.

"I love this film," Red said sighing. "It's so romantic. And when that tall Scottish guy reads that Auden poem at yer man's funeral . . . and the bit at the end when they get it together in the rain . . ."

"Red," Jean splurted. "I can't believe you've just ruined the film for me."

Red laughed. "You must have seen it before. It's been around for donkey's years."

"Well, I haven't," Jean replied irritably. "And now you've ruined it for me."

Peter cleared his throat. Jean could get very ratty when she had a hangover.

"Will I get you a cup of tea, love?" he said, attempting to dilute the situation.

Sally was having none of Jean's testiness.

"It's obvious from the start of the film that those two are going to get it together. It's only a modern-day Cinderella story." She kept her eyes from looking at Red.

"She's right, you know," Red agreed. "Sit up and I'll massage your temples, Jean. It'll make you feel much better."

What a man, Sally thought to herself. Calm, strong, gentle what more could a body ask for?

The afternoon was spent eating junk food, watching videos and drinking cups of tea, interspersed with large glasses of cold water and Lucozade. Sally enjoyed herself immensely.

"It's so nice to hang out and do nothing with you guys," she said lazily.

"And it's great to have you back," Jean said smiling. "I'm a little worried about my liver though."

Sally laughed. "You'll be grand, girl. You're out of training, that's all."

Peter held up two videos. *"Grease* or *Pulp Fiction?"*

"Are you mad?" Jean asked her boyfriend. *"Grease,* of course. That reminds me, are you going to the St John's ten-year thingy, Sal? I meant to ask you last night."

"Dead right I am," Sally replied strongly.

At least this time, she thought to herself wryly, Mark Mulhearne will definitely be there. Although I could always ask Red. She sighed inwardly. So many men, so little time.

Chapter 23

Mark Mulhearne sat at his chrome and glass desk, looking out the window of his sixteenth floor Boston office at the ant-sized traffic below. It was almost eight in the morning and already the Newton Street traffic was almost at gridlock. The sun shone down on the stationary cars in all colours of the metallic rainbow. The air-conditioned office sealed out any of the noise from the street, but Mark could hear the engines anyway and the short, sharp aggressive blasts of the horns rang in his ears.

Last night had been one of the worst nights of his life. In fact, all in all, the whole of yesterday from sunrise on had been pretty disastrous. A veritable Armageddon of a day. Mark massaged his temples gently. He had a pounding headache and his stomach was in knots. Kerry hadn't helped the situation either. What was that woman on? You thought you knew someone and bang, in seconds they threw you completely and turned your whole life upside down. Nearly four years together and now this.

"Stop thinking about it," Mark commanded himself. "It will all blow over. Things will work out."

But as much as he tried to tell himself this, yesterday's events kept running through his mind, over and over again. He had never felt so desolate or so alone.

"Mr Mulhearne, would you like some coffee?" The voice of Melody, his Texan secretary, came tinkling over the intercom just after nine.

"Please," he answered, hoping that this wouldn't turn out to be one of Melody's confessional days. She had a habit of telling him things that no self-respecting Irishman would ever want to hear. From bikini-waxes to pedicures, Melody had a bizarre need to share everything.

A few minutes later Melody arrived beside his desk with a steaming cup of coffee with cream, just the way he liked it, thick and strong. Mark knew he should go easy on the cream but his coffee didn't seem to taste the same without it.

"Here's your wake-up call," Melody said as she placed the large white cup and saucer on the desk. "Ya know it'll kill ya, cholesterol and all that," she added as if he needed to hear it. "Freeze your liver up it's so strong," she continued, on a roll. "Gotta get in control of your cravings. I heard on *Rikki Lake* last week that . . ."

"Yes, well thank you for your concern, Melody," Mark interrupted. He wasn't in the mood for her ramblings today.

She looked at him carefully from under her long and

luscious false eyelashes. Melody had a big crush on her boss but he never seemed to notice. She had tried everything from short skirts to low-cut blouses but nothing seemed to attract his attention.

"Thank you, Melody," Mark repeated firmly to her as she hovered. But she was made of sterner stuff.

"No problemo," she replied. "Hey, ya havin' sleep problems? You look kinda tired. I know this great herbal tea called 'Snooze Time'. I can go and fetch ya some if ya like."

"It's OK. Thank you for your concern, Melody," Mark said firmly. "I just . . . well, never mind. Close the door behind you, please."

Melody flounced out in a wave of musky perfume and hairspray, red kitten-heeled mules making tiny clicking noises as they hit the soles of her feet.

Mark sighed. How was he going to get through the rest of the day?

Just before lunch-time, one long client meeting later, Melody dropped the mail onto the desk in front of him. She had always been confused by the concept of In and Out trays. Mark had given up trying to teach her.

He flicked through the envelopes, mostly anonymous regular white rectangles with his name and address peeping through the clear cut-out window. One envelope caught his eye – the address was handwritten and it was from Ireland. He ran his finger over the stamp, which pictured an old-fashioned Galway hooker on a blue, blue sea. Mark hadn't received a letter from Ireland for a long time. Everyone used e-mail these days. Even his young nephews in Wicklow has learnt how to use it and they were only seven. He picked up his long silver letter-opener and slit the envelope.

Eve, he thought to himself. Eve used to write letters. She had given him the antique letter-opener for Christmas many years ago.

"Strange," he mused. " I haven't thought of Eve for a long time."

He pulled out the handwritten letter and read it. Slowly a smile came to his lips as a plan began to formulate in his mind.

"Melody," he stated firmly into his intercom. "Hold all my calls." Mark Mulhearne had a lot to think about.

"Honey, I'm home," Kerry's voice wafted in from the hall. Mark listened from the sofa as she kicked off her heels and dropped her keys into the ceramic bowl on the hall table. Familiar sounds, but this evening they seemed strangely alien and disconnected.

"How's my baby?" she purred. She padded into the living-room and he turned to look at her. "You look tense," she said, sitting down on the arm of the sofa. She began to massage his increasingly rigid shoulders. "Loosen up baby, loosen up."

Mark pulled her around to face him. "Kerry, we have to talk."

"Jeez, Mark, are you still pissed about yesterday? You know I'm sorry but there was nothing I could do. It's just business."

Mark winced. How could she say that? But he knew

he had to keep his cool. Kerry was a veritable iceberg when it came to arguments and he wouldn't gain anything by getting 'all emotional', as she liked to call it.

"How can you say it's just business, Kerry?" he began, slowly and deliberately. "You've known for months that the company you work for are not going to publish my book. You're my girlfriend, for feck's sake."

Kerry winced. She hated when Mark used bad language. What was his problem? He could write other books, it was no big deal. Anyway she couldn't have told him. It wouldn't have been professional and her neck would have been on the line.

"Kerry," he continued, breaking the icy silence, "you know how hard I worked on that book. You know how difficult I found it, the ungodly early mornings and late nights I put into finishing the damn thing on time. And Stern have decided to – how did they so delicately put it – oh yes, 'reassess their investment' in me. And to top it all I can't publish it with anyone else because it's the third book in the series. I can't believe you didn't warn me."

"You're the lawyer, Mark," Kerry stated baldly, walking into the kitchen. "You should have changed your contract if you weren't happy with it. Anyway, you got your advance and they have agreed to allow you to keep it, haven't they?"

Mark's blood began to boil. "Kerry, it's not about the money. I spent a year of my life working on that bloody book. I wrote another fucking Max Scudder because that's what Stern asked for. I've lost a whole year of my life and for what? For nothing!"

"Babe, don't be so melodramatic. You were never a real writer anyway – you have a proper job."

Mark glared at her, sparks of anger jumping in his eyes. "You just don't listen, do you? I hate my job, I don't want to be a lawyer anymore."

She sighed. Sometimes he could be such a child. "Mark, everyone gripes about work, but they don't mean it."

"Well, I mean it. And I'm leaving. I'm going back to Ireland. I've made up my mind. I've had enough."

"What are you talking about?" Kerry asked coldly.

"You heard me," Mark muttered.

"And what exactly are you going to do in Ireland?" Kerry sneered. "Write the great Irish novel. Oh please!"

Mark winced. "You have no heart, do you hear me?" He grabbed his jacket from the back of a chair and strode out of the apartment, slamming the door behind him.

Sitting in Jo's Diner beside Boston Park, Mark thought about the last two days. He had power-walked around the park after his fight with Kerry, thoughts racing through his head. Kerry's lack of sympathy and her cold, ultra-rational manner had finally worn him down. Has she always been like that? he asked himself. Well, he'd had enough. He was going back to Ireland where the women were easier to deal with. At least you knew where you were with Irish women. Maybe he should never have left. Maybe he should have waited. But the compulsion to leave Ireland and make a name for himself had been so strong. Had he been wrong to leave a girl who meant the world to him? Still, there was no point worrying about it now. What's done was done. Mark wondered if she still thought of him from time to time, the way he thought of her – with sadness and regret. He had left it too long now to contact her. And Kerry Allen – why had he chosen her? He remembered the first night they had met vividly. How could he forget?

* * *

"Mark, there's someone I'd like you to meet." Des Cotter propelled Mark by the elbow towards a tall brunette in an expensive-looking black suit at the far end of the room. Mark had been in Boston for nearly six months now and he was getting used to the regular client parties. This evening's was in honour of the renewed contract with Stern Press, a large Boston publishing house. Stern were not in his portfolio but he recognised some of the faces from the office and previous parties. But he had never seen this woman before. As they drew nearer Mark noticed her huge brown eyes, her clear, sallow skin and her chestnut-coloured hair which hung down her back like the glossy mane of a thoroughbred horse.

"Kerry, I'd like to you to meet Mark Mulhearne. He's one of the newer members of our team," Des said.

Mark held out his hand and shook Kerry's warmly. "Hi, Kerry, it's a pleasure to meet you."

"I like a man with a firm hand," the attractive woman purred. "Is that an Irish accent I hear?"

"Well spotted," Mark replied. And after a few minutes of pleasantries Des excused himself, leaving the couple alone.

"So how are you really finding Boston?" Kerry asked, her head tilted to one side flirtatiously. "Any girlfriends?"

Mark was a little taken aback. Talk about direct. "Well . . . not really. Work takes up a lot of my time and it's not all that easy to meet people in a new city."

Kerry smiled. "How about I take you out sometime?"

"I'd like that," Mark answered, flattered by this attractive woman's attention.

Their first 'date' took place the following Saturday night – dinner in an exclusive Italian restaurant overlooking the Charles river.

"So what brings you to Boston?" Kerry had asked during their prosciutto and melon starters.

"I guess I needed to get away from Dublin. I'd finished my law exams and I wanted to live a little. Dublin is small, you see. It can seem a little claustrophobic. Boston seemed a good place to kick-start my career too."

"Did you leave anyone special behind you?"

Mark paused for a while. This girl pulled no punches. It was straight to the point all the way. Different to Irish girls and refreshing in a way. "There was one girl," he began slowly. "But the timing was all wrong and she had a lot of other things on her plate. She didn't need me complicating the issue."

"Do you miss her?"

"Yes," Mark nodded. "Yes, I do." He began to feel uncomfortable. "But enough about me. Tell me about your job. It sounds fascinating."

Kerry Allen was more than willing to talk about herself – in fact talking about herself was an area she excelled in.

Later that evening Mark decided that Kerry was the ultimate saleswoman, and selling herself was no problem. She was the Marketing Director of Stern Press, one of the largest publishing houses in the States. At thirty-two she was the youngest director in the firm and one of only two females on the board. Kerry had worked her way up the ladder from lowly marketing assistant straight out of grad school to her present elevated position.

After dinner Mark and Kerry had strolled along the banks of the river. It was a cool evening and Kerry held Mark's arm firmly, pulling their bodies together.

"I've had a lovely evening, thank you," Mark said as they reached the Yellow Cab rank.

"It doesn't have to end yet, hon," Kerry flirted, looking into his eyes.

Mark had never been called 'hon' before but he thought he could get quite used to it.

Lying awake in Kerry's king-sized bed after the second highly energetic coupling, Mark watched the American woman sleep – lying on her back with one arm thrown over her head and the other holding the edge of the white cotton sheet. There was no way he was going to get any sleep – strange bed, strange woman, not to mention very strange country. Still, he thought to himself for the second time that evening, looking at Kerry beside him, I think I could very used to this.

Three months later they were living together. Mark had moved into Kerry's upmarket and very spacious apartment. He found her attitude to life refreshingly straightforward. Kerry demanded brutal honesty at all times, except when it came to things which she didn't think Mark would be interested in or need to know. It was an unusual combination, but most of the time it suited Mark very well.

Their sex life was abundant and satisfying. What Kerry lacked in tenderness she more than made up for in sheer energy, enthusiasm and skill. In fact she seemed tireless when it came to bedroom gymnastics. Although, thankfully, she tended to fall asleep after orgasm, for which Mark was grateful. It gave him time to recover in between bouts.

"We signed an Irish comic yesterday," Kerry had said one Sunday morning over breakfast. "Two-book deal. You should try it, hon, you told me you used to write in college."

"Maybe after my exams," Mark had replied. But Kerry had sown a niggling seed in the back of his mind which refused to go away. Although he was a qualified lawyer in Ireland, the American legal system was different and Mark had two years' worth of exams to get through to enable him to practise law in Boston. But often, from this time on, when he sat at his desk to study, a character began to form in his head – a man in his late forties, a football star turned private detective. And as he thought about this character a plot began to unfold before his very eyes. In no time at all the first Max Scudder book was born – *Dead Games* – a crime thriller set in the heady world of American football. Kerry had been bemused at her boyfriend's industry. She hadn't reckoned with Mark's determination and sheer bloody-mindedness. Once he started a project, by God he was going to finish it.

"Let me read it, hon," Kerry had pouted one night. "Just a few chapters. I can help you."

But Mark had been adamant. "Kerry, when it's finished you'll be my first reader, I promise. But I want to finish the first draft first. Bear with me."

Mark had finished *Deadly Games* in record time and had also managed to pass his exams comfortably. Once he had typed the last word on the black PC keyboard he saved his document and clicked the high-speed printer into action. Twenty minutes later he walked into the kitchen and placed his manuscript calmly in front of Kerry. She was sipping a tiny white cup of expresso and looked at the hefty manuscript with a smile. "The next Raymond Chandler, hey?" she said, looking up at him. "No gym for me this morning."

She gulped back the dregs of her coffee, scooped up the pages and headed off to the living-room, clutching Mark's manuscript to her chest. Now Mark was becoming nervous, too nervous to watch her read. What if she didn't like it? She would be brutally honest, and he didn't know if he could take it. Thoughts raced through his head. Shit, I shouldn't have given it to her. I should have got someone else to look at it first. Mark hovered around her like a fly, looking over her shoulder now and then to see what page she was on and pacing around the living-room restlessly.

"Mark," Kerry said eventually. "You're driving me crazy, I can't concentrate with you here. Go to the gym, babe!"

When Mark returned two hours later Kerry was still sprawled on the black leather sofa, reading. Her glasses were perched on the end of her nose and she was tapping her teeth with the nail of her index finger.

"Well, what do you think?" he asked, trying not to sound anxious.

Kerry jumped. "Jeez, Mark, you nearly gave me a heart attack." She smiled. "Oh, hon, this is really good." Her eyes sparked and she seemed animated and excited. "To be honest, I wasn't sure what to expect but you sure can write."

Mark was delighted. Kerry wasn't a woman to give praise lightly.

"Sure, it needs to be tightened up here and there but it'll sell, I know it," Kerry continued. "And I know just how to market it – modern and hip black and white jacket, heavy on the Irish author hook, especially in Boston and New York. I can see it now, 'the Irish John Grisham' . . . " She sat up and placed the page she was reading beside her. "My laptop, I need my laptop. I don't wanna lose any of these ideas."

Mark laughed. "Kerry, don't get carried away. I don't even have a publisher yet and . . ."

Kerry interrupted. "Monday morning I'll deliver *Dead Games* personally to Kate Sanders, the editor-in-chief at Stern. I just know she's gonna love it."

"Kerry," Mark said, swinging her into his arms. "You're a star."

"No, babe," Kerry replied grinning. "You're the star!"

And true to her word Kerry delivered *Dead Games* to Kate on Monday morning. And as she predicted Kate liked it and offered Mark a two-book deal with the option on another book. Kerry made sure that *Dead Games* went through editing and production at breakneck speed, taking personal control of the marketing and sales pitch. Less than a year later Mark's first book hit the bookshops and when Kerry's aggressive marketing and publicity machine went into action it soon reached *The New York Times* bestseller list.

Mark's second Max Scudder Investigation, *End Pitch*, set this time in the world of baseball, was also a success. His third book in the series had proved to be more of a problem. To be honest he had grown a little tired of his PI creation and longed to write a 'proper' novel, something more real and more personal.

Kerry was unenthusiastic about this idea. "Babe, stick to what you know. Kate wants Max Scudder, the public want Max Scudder. The market for literary fiction is difficult and anyway, I'm not sure you're ready to write the great Irish novel just yet."

Mark had thought about what Kerry was saying. Maybe she was right. Maybe he should stick to the crime genre. So he soldiered on with book number three, knowing full well that his heart just wasn't in it.

* * *

I should have followed my heart, he thought to himself as he stared out the window of the diner at a young couple who were walking hand in hand along the river bank. Mark put his hand into the inside pocket of his jacket and pulled out the letter from Ireland.

> *67 Moyville Road*
> *Donnybrook*
> *Dublin 4*
> *7 June 2000*

Dear Mark,

It gives me great pleasure on behalf of the Past Pupils Association of St John's to invite you to give the key-note speech at the class of 1990's Ten-Year Reunion Dinner Dance.

We all love your Max Scudder books and would be delighted if you could talk about your writing career at our dinner. We would, of course, cover all expenses involved . . .

Mark looked up from the handwritten letter. It was signed Vinnie Winters, who was the head boy of St John's when Mark was there and was now President of the Past Pupil's Union. His mind was made up. He'd had enough of Boston life. He was tired of waking up at ungodly hours of the morning, staggering into work and leaving after dark. He was tired of the pressure to stay fit and trim, to have perfect teeth, perfect hair, the right clothes, the right friends. Mark wanted his life back, a real life. I'm twenty-eight years old, he thought to himself, I hate my job, my girlfriend has the compassion of a barracuda and my book has just been rejected. Damn it, I want to go home.

Chapter 24

Mark handed in his notice that afternoon following lunch. His boss was less than pleased.

"I'm disappointed in you," Des said. "You're getting on well here and the clients like you. Hell, you'd have made partner in no time."

"I'm sorry, but it's something I have to do," Mark explained. "I didn't plan it, it's gut instinct I suppose."

"Hell, boy, we all have our doubts now and then. And I know you're pissed over this whole damn book thing."

Mark was confused. How did Des know about his contract?

Des sensed Mark's curiosity. "I'm sorry, maybe I shouldn't have mentioned it. Stern is one of my clients and . . ."

Mark stared at the man he considered both his colleague and his friend in amazement.

Des looked decidedly uncomfortable. "I wanted to tell you, but it wouldn't have been ethical, you know?"

Of course Des couldn't have discussed Stern's business with him directly, but he could have warned him to check his contract, or left the papers out for Mark to 'find' or . . . Well, there was no point worrying about it now. First Kerry and now Des. Both of them betraying his trust and treating him like a commodity and not a real person. His mind was now set.

"I'm sorry, I've made my decision. I'm moving back to Dublin."

"But what about Kerry?" Des asked with concern. "You've been together such a long time. Are you throwing that all away?"

Mark looked Des straight in the eye. "She's not the woman I thought she was," he replied honestly.

Mark cleared his desk after his 'chat' with Des. His boss had encouraged him to stay for a few weeks to reconsider his decision but Mark would not be swayed. When Des realised that the Irishman was not going to budge he released him immediately and arranged to attend to Mark's clients personally.

"Oh, Mark, is it true?" Melody scuttled into his office in a wave of anguish and concern, clutching the large cardboard box he had requested a few minutes previously. "Gloria, says you're leaving. Say it isn't so!"

Mark looked up from his desk and smiled. For all her annoying faults he would miss Melody. "It's true. I'm moving back to Dublin. Next week, I hope."

"So soon! Oh, Mark, I'll miss you!" Melody flung her arms around her boss, burying his face in her generous chest. Mark's nostrils were filled with heady, flowery perfume. Melody grasped the astounded man's head in her two hands.

"You were the best boss ever," she gushed. "You're just wonnerful." She gazed at his mouth and licked her cherry-red painted lips.

Mark quickly woke out of his shock and stood up, nervously. "That's very kind of you, Melody," the words rushed out of him. "I'll call you if I need you."

Melody lingered for a second before turning on her red high-heeled sandals and clipping out of the office. Mark sat back and sighed. He began to sort through his desk drawers methodically. In the end the box was only half full. He had accumulated very little in the way of personal belongings in his office: a couple of reference books, a professionally taken photograph of Kerry in an elaborate silver frame (one of last year's Christmas presents from her) and a couple of healthy pot plants which he left on his windowsill. Kerry wasn't a pot-plant kind of girl. Even spider-plants withered in her 'care'. In fact, Mark wondered if she was capable of taking care of any living thing except herself.

Mark arrived at the apartment mid-afternoon in a cab, cardboard box on his knee.

"This your place?" the cab driver asked brusquely, wondering why the tall Irishman had made no attempt to leave the hot and sticky cab.

"Oh, yes, sorry." Mark fumbled in his pocket for his wallet. He handed him a twenty-dollar bill. "Keep the change."

"Thanks," the cab driver said, smiling at the generous tip. "Wanna hand with the box?"

"It's fine, thanks," Mark replied. I'm on my own from here on in, he thought to himself.

Melody had managed to book a flight to Dublin in four days. It didn't leave much time to pack but it also didn't leave much time for him to have doubts and to change his mind. Mark had rung his sister Susan in Wicklow from his office once his flight details had been finalised. She had been shocked but delighted with the news.

"I can't believe it, Mark," she had said. "It's so sudden. I don't know what to say. I'm delighted! I can't wait to see you. Wait till I tell Pat and the boys."

Mark smiled. "I'm dying to see you all. Your sons have been telling me about their new rabbits on the e-mail – Dopey and Sugar – is that right?"

"I wouldn't like to tell you what I call them," Susan muttered cryptically. "Bloody rabbits. They've dug up the entire garden and there are horrible little rabbit droppings all over the grass. Anyway, enough about the rabbits. When are you arriving?"

Mark gave his sister the flight details and she promised to meet him at the airport.

"You'll be staying with us for a while, I hope?" she asked kindly.

"Well, if that's OK," Mark replied. "I don't want to be any trouble but I haven't had time to sort anything out . . ."

"Mark," Susan interrupted. "I'd be insulted if you

didn't. We have a lot of catching up to do, and I could do with another set of hands on the farm." Susan and her husband Pat lived on a small farm in Wicklow. Pat worked in Bray for an American computer company and Susan ran the farm which specialised in farmhouse cheeses. Pat hoped to be able to leave his job in a few years and work on the farm full-time but at the moment they needed the security of one 'proper' income.

"I can't wait to see you, Mark," Susan said excitedly. "I've so much to tell you."

Kerry walked in the door that evening, dumping her designer crocodile-skin briefcase in the hall and collapsing on the sofa. Mark had begun to sort through his belongings and there were piles of books, CDs and videotapes all over the floor.

"Spring cleaning, are we?" Kerry asked bemused.

"It's a bit late in the year for that," Mark replied darkly.

Kerry looked more closely at the debris on the living-room floor. "What are you doing exactly?" she asked, raising one perfectly plucked eyebrow. "Pretending to move out?"

"I'm not pretending. Unlike you, I don't play games. I am moving out."

"Yeah, right. There's no way you're leaving me Mark. No way," Kerry stated determinedly.

"I'm sorry to shatter your illusions. But that's exactly what I am doing. I'm flying back to Dublin on Friday morning."

"What are you talking about?" Kerry was now on her feet, fists clenched and nostrils flaring. There were sparks of fury in her brown eyes and angry red blotches were beginning to form on either cheek. "You can't leave me. No-one leaves me. I won't let you. You're the loser, Mark, not me. I should be leaving you."

Mark glared at the stranger in front of him. Kerry moved towards him and pushed him backwards forcefully, her two hands on either shoulder.

"Stop it, Kerry," he said strongly. "Calm down."

"No, I won't calm down, you bastard," Kerry screamed. She started pummelling his chest with her fists.

Mark grabbed her wrists.

"I'll be out of here tomorrow. I'm sorry it's come to this."

"Sorry!" she spat. "What do you mean sorry? You can't handle being a loser so you're running back to Ireland." A nasty sneer spread over her face. "Going home to write, are you? You've no talent. I got you that contract and I made your books sell. Me! They weren't worth the paper they were written on. It was all me."

"Stop it," Mark said again. She was destroying everything they had ever had together.

"I won't let you hurt me," Kerry shouted, storming out of the room.

Mark collapsed on the sofa and held his head in his hands.

The next few days were spent packing and avoiding Kerry. Mark slept on the sofa, making sure to come in very late after spending the evening in the local bookshop on Newton Street which stayed open until midnight. He read his way through several American short story collections, from Raymond Carver to Ernest Hemingway, unable to focus his mind on any plot more than a few pages long. He winced as he spotted copies of *Dead Games* and *End Pitch* on the shelves in the crime section.

Maybe Kerry was right, he thought to himself, maybe I can't write. He tried to block the idea from his mind.

Finally Friday come and Mark woke up feeling nervous but excited. This was it! Kerry would have been at her desk for nearly an hour by now. Perhaps he'd ring her to say good-bye. He didn't want to leave with so much bad feeling between them. Mark raised himself off the sofa, stretched his arms above his head and yawned. He padded over to the kitchen counter, lifted the phone and dialled the familiar number.

"Kerry, it's me. Mark."

Silence.

"Kerry are you there?"

"What is it? Don't tell me you've changed your mind?" she asked sarcastically.

"No, I'm just ringing to say goodbye."

"Well, goodbye."

"Kerry?"

"Yes?"

"I'll miss you."

"Piss off, Mark!" Kerry slammed down the phone.

Mark held the receiver to his ear for a few seconds. Tears came to his eyes and he stared straight ahead, trying to blink them back. Slowly, as if in slow motion, he placed the receiver back on the hook, put his arms on the counter and placed his head on the cool, marble surface. He stayed like that until his breathing became normal again. Then he stood up, walked over to the state of the art CD player and slipped in a U2 disk. Mark sat listening to 'With or Without You', trying to block Kerry's cruelty out of his mind.

A cab collected Mark and brought him to the airport. Boarding his flight after several bad coffees and one mindless hour's waiting around on a bum-numbingly uncomfortable seat he looked out at the Boston landscape one last time.

"Goodbye, Boston," he whispered under his breath.

Chapter 25

Mark walked towards the glass doors nervously. He hated the arrivals gate at Dublin Airport. It was such a short distance from the baggage reclaim and the practically non-existent customs area to the outside world. It hardly gave you time to adjust your head to being in Ireland before, bang, you were in amongst it all, crowds of over-excited relatives and agitated businesspeople collecting colleagues off the flight.

Striding through the doors, following the flow towards the exit, he was suddenly rugby-tackled around the legs and waist by two little boys. It was Shay and David, his twin seven-year-old nephews.

"Uncle Mark, Uncle Mark," they said excitedly. "Did you bring us any presents?" Shay, the darker-haired and more outgoing of the two asked.

Mark was taken aback. He wasn't used to children. He hadn't been around one for a long time, let alone two.

"Be careful, boys!" Mark's sister, Susan, appeared

beside him. "Hi love, it's so good to see you." Susan threw her arms around her brother warmly, kissing his cheek. "The boys haven't slept for days – they were so looking forward to seeing you."

Mark looked down at his nephews and smiled nervously. He wondered if life on the farm was going to be as peaceful and relaxing as he had hoped.

The drive to Susan's Wicklow farm went pleasantly. Shay talked non-stop in the car, rattling on about school, football, sharks, the weight of the human brain, the size of dust-mites and anything else he could think of.

"And how's your dinosaur collection, David?" Mark asked kindly, when Shay had paused to take a breath. "Have you got a Triceratops yet?" He knew David collected small model dinosaurs, carefully labelling each one with its name and details of its weight, what it ate and in what age they lived.

"Well," David began slowly. "Dad bought me a model in town last week. But it was a Stegosaurus."

Mark smiled to himself. He remembered being passionate about trains when he was David's age.

Shay interrupted. "Did you know that the Tyrannosaurus weighed more than a killer whale? David told me that." Shay loved his brother, and often spoke for him.

"Shay, please try not to interrupt," his mother gently chastised.

"Sorry, Mum," Shay replied smiling, quite used to this particular admonishment.

As they drove along the dual carriageway, towards

Wicklow, Mark looked out the window of the Range Rover, thinking. It was great to be back but what was he going to do now? He knew deep down that he wanted to write. But maybe Kerry was right, maybe he didn't have it in him. Her cruel and abrupt parting words still rang in his ears.

"Are you all right, Mark?" Susan asked with concern. She could see that her brother was mulling over something. It wasn't the right time to ask him about it though, what with the twins in the car. Later this evening, after dinner when the boys had gone to bed, she hoped Mark would talk to her about his unexpected homecoming.

"Sorry, I was miles away. Yes, I'm fine, thanks."

As they pulled off the main road towards the farm, the jeep was surrounded on both sides and above by a canopy of bright green branches. Sunlight glinted through the leaves, dappling the light. Mark smiled. It really was good to be back.

As they approached the farmhouse, two Labradors came bounding towards the jeep, one black and one golden.

"Hi, Honey, hi, Sam," Shay yelled out the window. As soon as the jeep stopped the two boys jumped down and started to play with the dogs. Mark and Susan lifted his bags into the cool, white hall of the old farmhouse. Built in the late nineteenth century, Crowe Farm had thick, whitewashed walls and panelled wooden doors painted dark, wine red. Susan and Pat had fallen in love with the traditional one-storey house, although it had required rather more work than they had anticipated. Mark followed his sister into the kitchen.

"Would you like some tea ?" she asked. "Sorry we don't have the iced variety here, just the normal hot stuff."

Mark smiled. "I never really took to the old iced tea in a big way. Funny acidic taste."

Susan put the kettle on and sat down at the old, pine kitchen table. She ran her finger over a fresh, deep groove in the wood. "Shay decided to cut out a dinosaur shape from card for David. He used Pat's Stanley knife, which he's not allowed to touch of course, and this was the result."

Mark smiled. "I can see you've got your hands full with him all right."

"Ah, he always means well, he's a good lad. He just doesn't think before he does things."

"He's not the only one, sis," Mark said wryly. "I'm still don't know what I'm doing here. It all happened so fast. I wonder now if I made the right choice. Maybe I should have stuck it out in Boston."

"You can fill me in on the details later, but the most important thing is that you're happy. And, to be honest, over the last few months I've felt that you weren't."

"No, you're right. But still, sometimes I wonder can we ever have it all, you know? Maybe we can only ever be 'almost' happy."

Susan looked at her brother carefully. He seemed very down, reflective and solemn, not like the usual Mark at all.

Mark attempted a smile. "Sorry, sis, I've a lot on my

mind at the moment. But it's great of you and Pat to let me stay. I really appreciate it."

"Not at all, Mark. It's a pleasure to have you, truly."

Shay and David came running in the door, each clutching a football.

"Uncle Mark, will you play football with us now?" Shay looked at Mark hopefully.

"Boys, your uncle is about to have a cup of tea, leave him alone."

"Thanks," Mark said, smiling gratefully at his sister after she had been pushed them out the backdoor. "Sorry. I'm just not in the mood."

"You don't need to apologise," Susan replied gently. "Now, can I get you more tea?"

That evening Mark joined Pat in the living-room. Susan was upstairs reading a *Thomas the Tank Engine* story to the boys. He had lingered for a little while outside their room, listening to his sister unfold the familiar and comforting story. He had given the two boys their presents from Boston – a model dinosaur for David and a baseball and mitt for Shay and both had been delighted with their gifts. Sometimes he suprised himself. The happy expressions on their faces when they'd pulled their presents out of the plastic bags had been so . . . rewarding.

"How's the writing going?" Pat said, putting down his paper. "When will we see the third one over here? I'm looking forward to it."

Mark winced. He hadn't told Susan about being dropped by his publishers yet.

"Sorry," said Pat, "have I said something . . ."

Mark took a deep breath. "No, I'm sorry. My publishers decided not to publish my third book and I'm not exactly thrilled."

"Lord. I had no idea, Susan didn't tell me."

"It's OK," Mark said. "I haven't told her yet. Everything has been a bit crazy in the last few days."

Pat looked at his brother-in-law sympathetically. He didn't know Mark all that well, but he had always liked him. "If there's anything I can do . . ."

"Thanks, Pat, I appreciate it. Just being here, with you and Susan, is enough."

Susan popped her head around the door. "What are you two talking about? You look very serious altogether. Anyway, dinner's ready."

The two men followed Susan to the kitchen, where a delicious herby smell was wafting in the air.

"Smells great, sis," Mark enthused.

"It's nothing fancy, I'm afraid. Lasagne, garlic bread and home-grown salad."

Pat grinned. "My favourite, that's my girl."

Susan swatted him on the backside with a tea-towel. "It's not all for you, you big lout. It's Mark's favourite too."

"A man after my own heart," Pat joked, opening a bottle of Chardonnay.

They sat down at the table and began to eat. Susan had done herself proud. The garlic bread was crispy and drenched with butter. The salad was dressed with a tasty mustard-seed vinaigrette and the lasagne was rich and creamy.

"This is fantastic grub, sis," Mark enthused, piling his fork with lasagne.

"Ah, she's a treasure," Pat said jokingly.

"Less of that or there'll be no Banoffi for you, Pat," Susan threatened.

"Are you trying to kill me, woman?" Pat asked. "If I eat any more I'll burst."

"I'm sure you'll find room somewhere," Susan laughed.

After dinner while Pat was brewing some fresh coffee, she turned towards Mark and took his hand.

"What's troubling you, Mark?" she asked gently. "I know there's something up, I can see it in your eyes."

He smiled. "I can never hide anything from you." He sighed. "I don't know where to start."

Susan remained silent, allowing Mark to collect his thoughts. Pat placed three small cups on the table and lingered, standing behind Susan. He felt a little uneasy, perhaps Mark wanted to talk to his wife alone.

"Will I take my coffee into the living-room?" he asked hesitantly. "I'm sure you two have a lot of catching up to do."

"Please stay, Pat," Mark said. "I'd like you to, really. I was about to tell Susan why I left Boston. I'd like to talk about it, if that's all right with both of you."

"Of course," Susan murmured and Pat nodded his assent as he took his seat at the table again.

"I suppose, to be honest, it began before any of the trouble with the book deal." Mark explained about Stern and their decision not to publish his third book. "And maybe I could have dealt with that if Kerry hadn't been so damn cold about the whole thing. It was – how did she describe it – 'just business'. The thing that killed me was she knew about the decision all along – weeks before I did. Des did too. I trusted them and they both let me down." He sighed. "After that, I guess I didn't feel at home in Boston any more. There didn't seem to be anything holding me there."

"And Kerry?" Susan asked carefully.

"It's over," Mark stated baldly. "Finished. We said some terrible things to each other, cruel, hurtful things. And she sneered at my writing . . ." He shivered just thinking about it. "Her last words to me were 'piss off!' – so I don't think we'll be keeping in touch."

"Oh, Mark," Susan leant over towards her brother and put her arms around him after he had finished talking. "That's terrible! I had no idea. I'm so sorry."

Mark could feel tears pricking his eyes and he blinked them back. He now realised with absolute certainty that Kerry was the wrong woman for him. She lacked the warmth and compassion that he recognised in his sister. Kerry had been spiky and tough, not someone to share your life with.

"Thanks. I'm sorry I didn't tell you all this before I came back, but I didn't want to talk about it on the phone. To be honest, the whole thing just came to a head and I had to get out. I realised I'd had quite enough of Boston and everything about Boston."

Pat smiled gently. "You have a bit of time and space to do some thinking now. And you know you're welcome to stay as long as you need. Are you going back to law over here?"

"I'm not sure. I'm going to try to write a different kind of book, something more personal I suppose. But if that doesn't work out, we'll see."

Susan placed her hand over her brother's. "Mark, you're a good writer, no matter what that Stern lot or Kerry think. You have to believe in yourself."

"I know, sis, but it's hard. My confidence has been shattered, you know."

"Mark, who was it said 'You have nothing to fear but fear itself'? Well, it's true. If the new book doesn't work out, so what? You've got to try though."

Mark smiled at his sister, always the practical one. "You're right, sis. I'll give it a go."

"Good on you, Mark," Pat said encouragingly. "Now where's the corkscrew? I think another bottle of wine is in order. Just as well it's Friday."

Chapter 26

The next morning Mark was woken up by shrieks coming from the bathroom.

"No, Mum! It's fine! It doesn't need a wash."

Mark listened groggily, less than delighted at being woken up.

"Shay, would you keep still for goodness sake. You are having your hair washed and that's final. "

"Ah, Mum, I have to clean out Dopey and Sugar's hutch today, and I'll get dirty again and you'll make me wash my hair again and . . ."

There was silence for a second. "Shay, you'll be the death of me, honestly. All right, we'll wash your hair tomorrow."

Mark could hear his nephew cheering loudly and splashing the bath water.

"Shay, you wet this floor and I'll change my mind."

"Sorry, Mum."

Mark got up and pulled some wrinkled jeans out of his suitcase. He'd been too tired to unpack last night so he made a start now, hanging up his shirts and suits. Mark realised that he had lots of business clothes but very few casual clothes apart from track suits and shorts for the gym. I'll have to do something about that, he thought to himself. Maybe I'll treat myself to some clothes in Dublin before the money runs out.

He showered and shaved, gingerly stepping over the puddles of bubbly water on the floor, courtesy of Shay. Putting on his jeans and an equally wrinkled T-shirt, he went into the kitchen.

"Need an iron?" his sister asked smiling, as he sat down at the kitchen table. Mark could see Pat outside, playing football with the twins.

"You know, sis, I don't think I'll bother," Mark replied smiling. "What's a few wrinkles between siblings?"

Susan laughed. He seemed in better form this morning. She had tossed and turned all night, worrying about Mark and his future. She liked things to be clear-cut – uncertainty made her nervous. She hoped with all her heart that her brother would come through this. Kerry had behaved very cruelly. Mark had talked about it more last night once he'd had a few more glasses of wine and Susan just couldn't understand the American woman's coldness. But now Mark had to put all that behind him and make a go of this new book.

"How's the head?" Susan asked. They had consumed quite a few bottles of wine last night and had stayed up talking into the small hours of the morning.

"Grand, thanks. That husband of yours is a bad influence."

Pat came in the back door. "Did I hear my name being mentioned in here?" he asked.

"Morning, Mark." He nodded at his brother-in-law. Shay and David were hot on his heels.

"Uncle Mark, Uncle Mark! Will you help us clean out Dopey and Sugar's cage?"

"Mark hasn't had his breakfast yet," Susan said. "And I'm not sure rabbits are really his thing."

Mark smiled at the two boys. "Your Mum's right – sorry boys, you're on your own."

Shay and David ran outside again and the three adults sat down at the kitchen table and began to tuck into hot buttered toast and tea.

"You'll get used to them. Wait till you have your own . . ." Susan said, the words coming out of her mouth before she could stop them. She could see Mark's face drop. "Oh, I'm sorry. That was stupid, what with Kerry and all."

"It's OK," Mark mumbled. He looked at the table thoughtfully before raising his head again. "And I would like kids some time – but I have to find the future Mrs Mulhearne first."

Susan smiled. She was relieved her brother hadn't been put off the fair sex forever.

"If you need any help looking . . ." Pat laughed.

Susan threw some toast at her husband. "Watch it you," she scolded.

Susan asked Mark to keep an eye on the twins while she and Pat went shopping in Wicklow town. The boys were standing beside the rabbits' hutch when Mark went outside. The hutch was a large wooden box raised on legs. At the front were two doors, one covered with wire mesh, the other wooden. The two rabbits were sitting happily, munching grass in a wire-covered run on the grass.

"Hi, lads," Mark said.

"Uncle Mark," said Shay, "we have to get rid of all this straw and put new straw down. But we have a problem."

Mark looked at him expectantly. "Yes?"

"Well, we're allergic to rabbit droppings. So we were wondering if you could scoop them up for us."

The two boys were something else. "Well, lads, I'd love to help you but I'm kind of allergic to rabbit droppings myself."

Shay and David looked puzzled. They had made up this particular allergy in an effort to trick their uncle into cleaning out Dopey and Sugar's cage. "Oh, I see," David smiled shyly. "I guess we'll have to do it so." He nudged his brother who nodded. "But can you show us how to play baseball after, Uncle Mark?" He looked at his uncle beseechingly.

Mark was amused. He could hardly refuse now, after getting out of helping with the rabbits. Smart kid, he thought to himself admiringly. "OK, David. You finish the hutch and I'll play baseball with the two of you."

When Pat and Susan arrived home Mark and the boys were sitting on the grass outside the house. The dogs were lying comfortably at their feet and the twins seemed uncharacteristically calm.

"What magic have you performed?" asked Susan as she lifted out the shopping. "They don't usually sit still for more than two minutes.

"We've been playing baseball, Mum," said Shay as he jumped to his feet to help his mother. "And now Mark is telling us about Boston and the Red Sox's stadium."

Susan looked at Mark and smiled.

"What?" he said. "Why are you smiling?"

"It's nothing," she replied, trying to wipe the grin off her face. "Forget it."

David and Shay staggered into the house, their little arms weighed down by the heavy plastic shopping bags.

After lunch, Mark drove the Range Rover to Glendalough and walked up the steep slopes to the top of the lake. As he looked down at the dark swirling water the image of a young man in his early twenties came into his head. The man was tall, with dark hair and dark blue eyes. Mark felt a shiver of excitement run down his spine as he realised who this character was – the hero of his new book. A young artist trying to find his way in the world – Luke, his name was Luke Ryan. Mark sat down on a clump of springy heather and began to plot the story in his head. He felt more alive than he had done in many months. Maybe things were finally starting to come together.

The weeks passed quickly on Crowe Farm. Mark was kept more than busy, helping Susan on the farm. Susan was delighted with the extra pair of hands. It made her life much easier. Mark was writing every evening, taking each day as it came. Luke Ryan's story was keeping his mind busy and he was enjoying writing more than he'd ever enjoyed it before.

"Have you heard from Kerry?" Susan asked quietly one morning, after Pat had left for work. She knew he was anxious to talk to Kerry. It upset him that they had parted on such bad terms.

"No," Mark said sadly. "I've e-mailed and rung several times but she hasn't replied."

Susan was still worried about her brother. Mark seemed to be content to help with the boys and to write – he didn't seem interested in going out. Maybe he just needed to look up some old friends.

"When's the St John's thing? That must be coming up soon."

"It's on in a few weeks. Come to think, of it I must write my speech. I explained about my third book and tried to cancel but Vinnie Winters wouldn't hear of it. 'I have no doubt that your new book will set you right back on track' he said." Mark grimaced. "I wish I shared his optimism."

"When are you sending it off to your agent?" Since the trouble with Stern, Mark had acquired an Irish agent, a decent man called Ben Woodman. There was no way Mark wanted to deal with publishers ever again. Ben was keen to send his client's new book to various publishers but Mark was reluctant. He couldn't face rejection, especially just weeks before he had to make a speech at his old school. Ben seemed to like what he had read of *Luke's Story*, the working title for the new book. He had been very complimentary about it, but Mark was still nervous.

"I'm not sure. I'm only halfway through and I don't want to tempt fate." But Mark knew that he couldn't stay with Susan and Pat for much longer. And if he wanted to live somewhere decent he'd need money. House prices and rent had spiralled in the last few years, and his savings were dwindling, slowly but surely.

"I think I'll go and see Ben next week and talk about it," Mark decided.

Susan smiled. "Good for you, Mark. Talking of St John's, that reminds me. Guess who I met on Grafton Street a few weeks ago?" Mark raised his eyebrows in interest. "Sally Hunter's Mum. Remember her?"

"Don't I just!" Mark said. "Old bag!"

"Mark! She wasn't that bad. Anyway Sally's back from Antigua this month – you should look her up."

Mark smiled. Sally Hunter, well there was a blast from the past.

"Maybe I will," he grinned.

Mark stepped off the train at Pearse Street station. He was meeting Ben in Bewley's on Westmoreland Street but he had an hour to kill before then. The Wicklow to Dublin diesel train had been quick enough and it had given Mark a chance to collect his thoughts about the new book. He was anxious about the whole contract thing, after being so badly stung by Stern. He strolled through Trinity, taking advantage of the open side gate opposite the train station. The leaves in the college grounds were falling, covering the cobbles in Front Square with a patchwork of orange and yellow. Students, who seemed to Mark to be unfeasibly young to be within the walls, sat on the steps there watching the world go by. A young girl with short dark hair walked past Mark, wrapped in a huge college scarf which threatened to engulf her.

Eve Arnold, Mark thought to himself, gazing at the girl's back. He hadn't thought about Eve for a long time – it had been a strange few days – first Sally, now Eve. Mark wondered what Eve was doing now.

Mark made his way through the Nassau Street entrance towards Grafton Street. The busy pedestrian thoroughfare had been cobbled in stylish shades of terracotta since Mark's last visit. There were still plenty of tourists milling around the Molly Malone statue, taking pictures of each other beside the bronze, amply bosomed 'lady'. As Mark strolled towards Brown Thomas he took his sunglasses out of his jacket pocket and put them on. The anonymity the dark lenses gave him was somehow reassuring. He still felt like a stranger in his own country, so much had changed since his departure. Gazing in the stylish large windows to his right he noticed the characteristic Brown Thomas logo on the glass. Confused, he looked across the street, to where his favourite shop had previously stood.

"Mark Mulhearne, is that you?" A small dark-haired woman, laden down with large black and white shopping bags stood in front of him. Mark realised with a start that it was Eve. She was wearing a perfectly cut, dark grey suit with a cerise pink silk scarf knotted carefully around her neck and high black court shoes – every inch the successful business woman, even on a Saturday. Mark removed his glasses and smiled.

"Eve, that's weird. I thought I saw you only minutes ago in Front Square. There was this young girl – she looked just like you."

Eve raised her perfectly plucked eyebrows. "Are you implying that I'm not young?"

Mark blushed. "I'm sorry. I didn't mean to imply anything of the sort . . ."

Eve laughed. "I'm only joking. Anyway it's great to see you. Have you been back long?"

"Just a few weeks. I've been staying with my sister in Wicklow."

"How is Susan?" Eve asked.

"Great, the farm is doing well."

"And what brings you back for so long?" Eve asked slowly, as if choosing her words carefully. "I know you're speaking at the St John's reunion, but are you working over here as well?"

Mark wasn't sure what to say. It wasn't exactly something he wanted to discuss in the middle of Grafton Street. He was a little nervous of Eve. They hadn't really talked properly since their break-up. Maybe it was finally time for them to clear the air. After all, they had been friends for a long time before that and besides, at this moment in time, he needed someone to talk to.

"I'm afraid I have to meet my agent in a little while,

but I'd really love to catch up," he said, stalling Eve magnificently. "How about meeting up for lunch or dinner sometime? My treat."

Eve smiled. "That would be lovely," she said. "Here's my card." She handed him a tasteful white business card. "Ring me on Wednesday or Thursday. I'll book somewhere for Friday night."

Before Mark had the chance to say anything, she leant forwards and planted a neat kiss on his cheek. She then executed a perfect turn and strode off in the direction of St Stephen's Green.

Good to see some things haven't changed, Mark thought to himself, smiling wryly as he watched Eve's grey back disappear into the Saturday shopping crowds.

Chapter 27

"Mark was thinking about me!" Eve thought to herself as she made her way back to the St Stephen's Green carpark, swinging her shopping bags jauntily as she walked along. "Things are definitely looking up. If I believed in fate, I'd call bumping into Mark fate."

Eve thought about how he had looked. Mark had always possessed boyish good looks and if anything he was now more attractive than ever. His blonde hair was now cut shorter, close to his head, and he had fine laughter lines around his blue eyes but he still had a smile to warm your heart. The scar on his lip had grown fainter with age but Eve had still wanted to reach out and run her finger tenderly over it, the way she used to when they had first got together. He filled his casual clothes beautifully, the leather jacket was perfectly cut and he looked like a movie star in the dark glasses. A warm feeling spread over Eve, and a smile rested gently on her lips. Mark Mulhearne was certainly looking good. She was looking forward to Friday night already.

Eve had bought herself a red velvet wrap and matching evening bag to finish her 'Reunion' outfit in Brown Thomas and some cream lacy underwear in a small lingerie boutique in the Westbury Mall. It was unusual for her to miss two Saturday's working in a row but the St John's event was only two weeks away now and Eve was determined to look like a million dollars. And as it turned out, it was lucky she had been in town or she wouldn't have bumped into Mark. To be honest she would have appreciated her mother's advice on the wrap – it was an uncharacteristically bright colour for Eve to wear.

"Shit," Eve thought to herself. "I must stop thinking about Mum and all that stupid Sean business. I don't need her, and as for Sean, it's disgusting . . ." Eve could feel her stomach tensing up and the skin on her forehead and around her eyes tighten. Stress was nothing new to her, but it was usually brought on by a particularly bad day at work, not by her mother. She tried to take her mind off things by concentrating on Mark, her new purchases and her new car – a gleaming red Mazda MX5.

Eve fed coins into the carpark machine, which as usual seemed to eat money, but today she didn't mind. She was floating on cloud Mark. She looked at the reflection of a smiling, happy woman in the lift and realised she was looking at herself – it had been days since she had felt anything other than wretched. She had hardly recognised her own face. Walking towards her new car she smiled again. The gleaming cherry-red

Mazda MX5 was waiting for her in all its glory. And as it was a fine and sunny autumn day, she could 'drop the top' as the young car salesman had put it.

Unbelievably Eve had made the mother of all impulse buys after one chance phone call from her desk the previous afternoon. Greg, the salesman, had been a little sceptical when Eve had arrived and bought her car in less than an hour. He had puffed out his chest and preened himself like a mating turkey in front of the other salesmen later on that morning, not realising it had little or nothing to do with his sales patter and everything to do with Eve's fragile state of mind.

"I want a sports car, what do you have? Something fast, a convertible," Eve had snapped at the young man, after what had seemed to her an excessively long wait of over three minutes listening on hold to some sort of pop drivel. It was Friday afternoon and Eve was not in the humour to be kept waiting.

"Well," Greg Delaney had stalled, looking around the desk for his calculator. "Let me see . . . are you looking for a cabriolet version of a mainstream model, a four-seater, or a two-seater ?"

Eve sighed. She hoped there weren't too many options, she didn't have the time for all this. "I want a two-seater, I have about twenty grand to spend and I don't want to wait around – I want to collect it tomorrow. Now, can you help me?"

Greg was taken aback and slightly scared by this blunt woman who meant business. He hoped it wasn't another crank call. He'd had enough of the wasters who called to talk about sports cars and demanded long test drives, only to say they'd think about it. But this lady seemed different.

"I'll come straight to the point then, shall I?" he asked. He decided to be direct and honest for once, he had nothing to lose. "The only sports cars I have at the moment that you can drive away are two Mazda MX5s – one in red and one in midnight blue. They're fast, they're smooth and sleek and with the top down they look amazing." He paused for the customer to interrupt, and was slightly unnerved to hear nothing on the end of the line. "Hello?" he asked tentatively.

"Yes, I'm still here, go on," Eve said impatiently.

Greg continued his sales pitch. "Um, well, the MX5 has a good roof system and reinforced front pillars and windscreen for driver's and passenger's protection. It's one of the most popular sports cars around, with over half a million cars out there." He couldn't think of what else to say – he usually sold cars on their looks and their performance. "Um, would you like a test drive, Miss Arnold?"

Eve thought about this for a minute. "Ms Arnold. Tomorrow morning, nine o'clock. You're on the main Blackrock road, is that correct? And fax me the details of the car – engine size, safety features, performance, fuel consumption – that sort of thing." Eve gave the startled man her fax number. He decided he'd come in an hour early, rather than attempt to change the time to ten o'clock, the garage's normal opening hour on a Saturday.

At nine on the dot the following morning, Eve was outside Global Motors. Greg Delaney drew in his breath as he looked at the attractive brunette outside the showroom's window. He opened the side door.

"Good morning, Ms Arnold, this way please." He gestured Eve towards the sparkling sports cars at the far end of the showroom. The bright red convertible immediately caught Eve's eye.

"Which car would you like to test drive, the red or the blue? The red has the stronger engine."

Eve smiled to herself. A strong engine for a strong woman. She was sold. "The red."

Half an hour later, after a nippy drive around Blackrock with the top down, Eve had her cheque book out. She had managed to haggle the price down to well under her budgeted amount. Greg, although it came directly out of his commission, was loathe to argue. A sale was a sale, and an early morning success was a coup for the new salesman. A sale before ten o'clock opening – he could deal with that!

Eve drove her new car away, towards Dublin city centre. On her instructions, Julie had spent the previous afternoon researching reputable insurance companies and had made provisional arrangements for cover with Allied Motors. Eve had simply rung the company on her mobile with the new registration number as soon as the cheque had been written.

She revelled in the appreciative looks her fellow motorists were giving her. But in the pit of her stomach she wished she had someone to share her exciting new purchase with. She pushed the thought to the back of her mind and thought about what new CDs to buy to play in her car – Van Morrison definitely, some jazz and some classical music, perhaps some opera . . .

Later that afternoon, Eve pulled up outside her house. For the first time since she had lived there she opened the double gates to the left of the path. The bolt was stiff at first, but with a few firm wiggles it opened. She then drove the red convertible into the drive, put the black roof up with the flick of a switch and activated the alarm. Eve stood at her front door and gazed at her new car lovingly. Pushing open her front door she swaggered in, dropping her shopping bags at the foot of the stairs. The red light on the answering machine flickered at her accusingly. Eve pressed play and waited.

"Hi, love, it's me. I know you're probably still angry with me and I'm sorry. I was wondering are you coming over tonight? I was going to cook something nice, or maybe you'd like to out for dinner? Anyway, give me a ring."

God she has a nerve, Eve thought to herself, fuming. Is she mad? There's no way I'm going over there after what she's done.

She stomped around the house for an hour, putting away her new purchases, listening to her new CDs, skipping from song to song erratically. At around seven she ate some pre-packed salad with walnut bread and lashings of butter and treated herself to a glass of chilled Australian white wine from the fridge. She then walked to the local video shop and chose two suitably romantic films, and picked up a tub of extremely fattening chocolate-chip ice cream from the local Spar.

Halfway through *When Harry Met Sally* Eve began to cry. Meg Ryan, in her autumnal brown hat, always reminded her of her mother who had a similar hat.

"Shit," Eve muttered to herself through her tears. "I can't get away from her." She paused the video, walked into the kitchen and poured herself another glass of wine. This time, she brought the bottle into the living-room with her. Towards the end of *Jerry Maguire* Eve started crying again. In front of her on the coffee table were an empty bottle of wine and an empty carton of ice cream. "You had me at hello," Tom Cruise's 'wife' was saying, before launching herself into Mr Perfect's arms. Eve wiped her tears away and sighed. She imagined herself falling into Mark's strong, protective arms. Eve practised saying 'You complete me' and 'You had me at hello' in a soft, sexy American accent. By the time the credits were rolling she was fast asleep on the sofa in a mist of chocolate and alcohol.

The next morning when Eve woke up her neck was throbbing from sleeping at an awkward angle and her head was muzzy from the wine. She felt terrible. Dragging herself to a seated position she scrunched up her eyes for a second before rubbing them vigorously. She crept slowly over towards the window and looked out. There in front of her, shining in the gentle morning sun, was her new baby. Eve smiled and decided at that moment to take a long, long drive somewhere, it didn't really matter where. She was doing fine on her own without her mother and from now on Sundays were car days.

Driving past Sandymount a little later, she couldn't help but notice that her mother's blinds were down. Eve slowed down as she passed the house. She was sorely tempted to forget everything and call in, but she just couldn't.

"It's her loss," she muttered to herself grimly as she pressed on the accelerator and shot past the house. She had a shiny new sports car and she was going out for dinner with Mark Mulhearne next weekend, what more could she want?

The week crawled by for Eve and by Wednesday late afternoon she was all raw nerve-endings. She had snapped at Julie all day.

"Have there been any calls for me?" she had demanded at regular intervals.

"No, Ms Arnold," Julie had replied each time. By the end of the day she was getting a little tired of her boss's abrupt and accusing tone. Finally Julie had bravely asked, "Ms Arnold, are you expecting a particular call?"

"No," Eve had snapped back. "Certainly not." She had paused for a second before attempting to vindicate her behaviour. "I mean yes. An Italian bank, I'm expecting them to ring."

"Ms Arnold," Julie replied smoothly. "If you receive any calls from an Italian or any other man I'll be sure to put them through immediately."

"Make sure you do," Eve replied curtly, slamming down her phone.

The experienced secretary had a feeling that Eve Arnold wasn't waiting for any business call. First the silver dress, now this, there was definitely someone on the cards. Julie smiled deliciously to herself. If she could just find out some of the juicy details, the girls would be all ears. Especially that Catriona Miller, Mr Duke's PA. Her boss was having an affair with his children's nanny – now that was real gossip. Julie was desperate for some juice to give the others at lunch-time. Maybe old chilly knickers Arnold would surprise them all.

Relax, Eve said to herself. He'll ring, it's only Wednesday. She chastised herself for not assuming control as she usually would by asking for his number. But she was not taking any chances this time. According to the 'rules' of dating you had to let the man ring first, it was a power thing, a men-are-from-Mars thing. She wanted things to work more than anything this time.

Eve sat at her desk, unable to concentrate. She began to mull over her recent love life – if you could call it that, she thought wryly. Recently the dates had begun to drop off. There had been a few dinners with work colleagues from other banks, many only here for weeks or months which at first suited Eve. Her job meant everything to her and she was damned if she was going to let a mere relationship stand in the way of her success. However, although Eve was loathe to admit it, she was an old-fashioned girl at heart and as time went on she hoped for a decent, strong man who she could respect and who loved her.

Many of the men she dated seemed to expect sex on

the first date and were quite put out if they weren't invited in for 'coffee' after an expensive dinner. Eve enjoyed matching her wits against a fellow banker, discussing politics, the financial markets and the housing shortage. But when it came to the end of the evening things tended to become more difficult. Intelligent conversation went out the window and all the respectable suited men wanted was a quick grope on the sofa before some 'bedroom gymnastics' as one of the more recent lawyers was apt to call it. Once Eve relented and was treated to ten minutes of rough thrusting and an evening of snoring for her trouble. Of course he hadn't been able to kiss – he was a specimen of the saliva, flabby lips and washing-machine-tongue variety – not a pleasant combination.

In Eve's opinion, if a man couldn't kiss he was unlikely to be able to do anything else. Bad kissing equalled bad sex in her book. And she'd dated quite a few bad kissers in her time. From Alex the barrister with his short, stubby tongue and fat lips, to Stephano the Italian banker with his permanent 'manly' stubble and measly thin, tight lips, and Diarmuid the accountant with his false teeth and rough moustache.

Most of the time Eve had had quite enough after one date. George had been particularly persistent, sending flowers by the basketful. He had proposed after three dates – two dinners and a drive in the country to see the ancestral home. Eve had refused him kindly yet firmly. She couldn't imagine a lifetime of bad kissing and worse.

In fact, since Mark she had enjoyed kissing only once – with a Corkman called Robin who turned out to be married. Robin had been very charming, lavishing her with expensive dinners and thoughtful presents from all the best stores. He had even taken her to Paris for one whirlwind weekend last spring. Eve had adored the city with its spectacular architecture, inspirational galleries and glorious food. The two had spent their time wandering through the streets of the city, when they weren't in bed of course. Robin kissed with his heart and his soul – long lingering, playful kisses, exploring Eve's mouth with his strong, firm tongue. The sex was equally mind-blowing – Robin was a generous lover, exciting and in control. He paid attention to Eve's body and respected her shyness, putting her at ease. His large warm hands knew exactly where to touch and stroke his lover's body, sending shivers of pleasure running up and down her spine.

Unfortunately Robin was 'happily married with two young children and another one on the way', as he had admitted to Eve one evening a few weeks later.

Eve had looked at him in disbelief. They were sitting in an Italian restaurant, surrounded by full tables. "What?" Eve had spluttered, swallowing her wine the wrong way. "Why are you telling me this now?"

"Well, the new baby is on the way and I won't be able to see you as much. I didn't want you to think I was going off you. I'm not, not at all." He smiled widely, a wolf in sheep's clothing. "We don't sleep together any more – well, not very often."

Eve had carefully stood up, picked up the plate of pasta in front of her and tipped it neatly on his lap. *"Fuck. Off,"* she had said loudly and succinctly before walking slowly out of the restaurant, all eyes on her.

That evening she had cried herself to sleep. She had never heard from Robin again. She read in *The Irish Times* that the sick bastard had called his new baby daughter Eve.

"Ms Arnold, phone call for you," Julie's voice broke into her thoughts. Eve picked up the phone immediately.

"Hello?" she heard a male voice ask uncertainly. " Is that Miss, I mean Ms Arnold?"

"Yes," Eve answered impatiently, instantly aware that it wasn't Mark Mulhearne on the other end.

A few minutes later she rang her secretary in a fury. "Julie, what in hell's name were you thinking of putting that life insurance salesman through to me? Are you mad? I'm a busy woman."

"Sorry, Ms Arnold," Julie mumbled to herself. How was she supposed to know he was a salesman, for all she knew the man could have been Eve's new beau. He did know her name after all. Although come to think of it a man with a similar voice had rung half an hour earlier asking for her boss's name. Narky old cow, it wasn't her fault the boyfriend hadn't rung.

"Thick girl," Eve muttered, slamming down the phone again. She threw herself into a particularly nasty market analysis and within an hour was caught up in a world of options and bonds.

Eve enjoyed her work and was bloody good at it, one

of the best in the business. She had pinpointed many problems for Viva Notre bank over the years saving them a small fortune, and she had an uncanny knack of finding loop-holes in the Irish tax system. A lot of her success was down to the long tedious hours she put into studying the figures, but she also had a distinctive flair for the job. Eve Arnold was highly respected in the company and had been steadily promoted since starting with the bank straight after college. She had obtained first place in her accountancy exams – the highest marks ever recorded.

But as the years went by, she began to get less and less satisfaction from her gruelling work. She wondered if she should change to a different department or move to the head office in Paris? But in her heart of hearts she knew it wasn't the job that was the problem, it was her life.

On Thursday afternoon Julie finally put Mark through. "Call for you on line one, Ms Arnold. It's a Mr Mulhearne, he says it's *personal*." Julie took great delight in emphasising the 'personal'.

"Hi, Eve, how's work?" Mark asked.

Eve melted as she heard Mark's mellow tones over the phoneline.

"Hi, Mark, it's fine thanks. Busy but under control. And how's the writing?"

"It's going OK so far, touch wood," Mark replied. "I'm almost finished and my agent has a deal waiting for me in London. I just have to sign on the dotted line."

"That's wonderful news. You can tell me all about it on Friday. Julie, my secretary booked La Stampa for eight, I hope that suits."

Mark smiled. Eve was nothing if not organised. "That sounds great. Is it all right to meet you there? I have an appointment in town in the afternoon."

"Of course," Eve replied. "I'll see you in the restaurant."

"I'm looking forward to it," Mark said before hanging up.

Eve held the receiver to her ear for several seconds after the phone went dead, as if to prolong the conversation. "So am I," she whispered into the phone. "So am I."

Eve was staring at her bed in disgust. It was Friday evening, she had to be in town in less than an hour and she hadn't a stitch to wear. Well, that wasn't strictly true. She had an extensive wardrobe, full of designer labels, many carefully chosen for her by professional shoppers in some of the best stores in Ireland. However, nothing seemed exactly right this evening. On her bed were two dresses – one long and black with spaghetti straps, one short and red, a black trouser suit, two black skirts and a gold sequinned elasticated top or 'boob tube' as her mother would have called it. Eve put on the gold top and looked at herself critically in the full-length mirror. OK, this looks good, she thought to herself, turning around and studying her back. A little dusting of gold powder on the cleavage I think. But hell, which skirt?

Eventually she decided on the fitted black trousers from the trouser suit – the short black skirt looked tarty and the long looked too 'Black Tie-ish'. Eve finished off the outfit with a pair of black strappy Nine West sandals and a black velvet wrap.

She kept her make-up minimal, with the barest dusting of powder, some gold eye-shadow and a smattering of gold cream highlighter on her cheekbones and on her lips. A gentle wanding of black mascara completed the look. Eve gazed at herself in the mirror and she liked what she saw. She sprayed herself with a liberal dose of Chanel Number 5, grabbed her black evening bag and skipped jauntily down the stairs. As she closed the door behind her she took a deep breath and pouted, "You had me at hello".

Chapter 28

Eve walked up the steps of La Stampa just after eight. The restaurant was buzzing – even the waiting area was packed. Eve was greeted warmly by the blonde hostess, Jo, as she entered.

"Ms Arnold. A pleasure to see you again. Table for two, is that correct?"

Eve nodded. "Thank you."

"Your friend is already at the table." Jo brought Eve to the table after taking her wrap and hanging it up carefully. "Enjoy your meal."

"Thank you, Jo," Eve said smiling. Viva Notre used La Stampa to entertain their clients and Eve was a familiar face to all the staff.

Eve looked at Mark. His eyes were twinkling in the gentle candlelight. He was wearing a dark blue shirt which complimented his colouring. He beamed at Eve and stood up while she was seated by a tall Italian-looking waiter.

"Hi, Eve, you look beautiful." Mark leaned over and

kissed her cheek. Eve felt his familiar firm, cool lips on her skin and a shiver ran down her spine.

"Thank you, you don't look too bad yourself," she replied grinning.

"Nice place," Mark said looking around him. "Do you come here often?"

Eve laughed. "Do you always use that line?"

"I didn't mean it that way." Mark smiled. "Ah, Irish wit, I've missed it. God, it's great to see you, who would have thought? After all these years we can still be friends. Isn't it great?" Mark reached over and took Eve's hand in his.

"Friends, yes. Isn't it great," Eve replied carefully. She hoped that after this evening that they would be a lot more than 'friends'.

They ordered and then Eve said, "So tell me all about Boston, I want to know everything."

Mark talked about his life in the States, about his job, his writing and about Kerry and her betrayal and ultimate rejection of him, interrupted only by the waiter bringing their starters – deep-fried goat's cheese for him and chilled chicken-liver pate with raspberry coulis for Eve.

Eve listened with interest.

"All along I thought she was the one." Mark sighed.

"And?" Eve encouraged.

"She wasn't. Not even close."

"Does that mean you're looking?" Eve asked, running her finger around the top of her wine glass.

"I guess I am." Mark agreed. "The future Mrs Mulhearne is out there, I hope. I just have to find her."

"That's very honest of you," Eve smiled. "I like a man who knows what he wants. And Kerry sounds unreal. Was she out of her mind, letting a wonderful man like you go?"

"She must have been," Mark replied wryly. "There aren't too many Mark Mulhearnes out there. And what about yourself?" he asked gently. "No wedding ring, I see."

Eve smiled. "I've been waiting for the right man," she replied. "Some day my prince will come and all that."

"I hope you don't have to wait too long," Mark said kindly.

"So do I," Eve replied, gazing into his eyes.

Mark lowered his eyes and concentrated on his food. The conversation was getting a little . . . intense. He decided to change the subject. "And work. How's work?"

Eve filled him in on Viva Notre. "I love work, Mark. It's exciting, stimulating and it suits me. It's everything I've ever wanted it to be, I suppose."

"But . . ." Mark coaxed gently.

"I guess I'm looking for something more at the moment."

Mark was beginning to feel uneasy. Eve was letting her guard down more and more every time she spoke. He wasn't quite sure what she'd say next. Luckily their main courses arrived and they began to tuck in, both savouring the rich and aromatic tastes and smells of their baked salmon in lemon butter sauce.

"I've really missed Irish butter," Mark said, trying to steer the conversation onto safer ground.

"What else have you missed?" Eve asked, looking at Mark from under her eyelashes.

Mark took a deep breath. He decided to ignore Eve's obvious flirtation.

"Susan and the kids. And Pat. I've really enjoyed staying with them. And friends, I suppose. Real friends."

"Special friends?" Eve asked.

Eve just wasn't going to let go. Mark decided he'd better clear the air before things got out of hand. Anyway, there was something he wanted to know.

"Eve, it's lovely being here with you. But if we're going to be friends I think there's a few things that need to be said. For a start there's something I'd like to ask you."

"Yes?" Eve leaned towards Mark eagerly.

"In college, you really hurt me you know. I just wondered was there someone else? It was just all so sudden. One minute we were fine and the next minute . . ."

Eve sighed, "Oh, Mark, I'm so sorry. No, there was no-one else. I was just young and stupid. I thought that my career was more important than a college boyfriend. I wish it hadn't happened. I shouldn't have put exams and work first like that. What can I say?"

Mark winced, he was opening a whole can of worms but he didn't seem to be able to stop. It seemed false to him, sitting here all pally with the girl who once broke his heart. "Did I really mean that little to you? Just a college boyfriend?"

"I don't know quite what to say. You meant a lot to me of course, but I had my whole future to think about and I now know I made a mistake. I hope you can . . . forgive me and maybe we can . . . I guess what I'm saying is that I regret what happened but I'm a different person now and maybe this time things could be different." Eve paused and stared at him intently. "I still find you very attractive and at this point of my life I'm ready for a relationship. There, I've said it." She studied Mark's face carefully. His eyes were fixed on hers, with a slightly bemused look. "What?" she asked irritably. "Why are you staring at me like that?"

Mark smiled. "You haven't changed one bit."

"What do you mean?"

"Well," Mark continued, taking a gulp of his wine, "you still don't stop to think of other people. You still think that what's good for Eve is good for everyone."

"Are you saying I'm selfish?"

"Not selfish exactly. You just don't consider other people's point of view."

"So you *are* saying I'm selfish." Eve was getting angry at this stage.

"OK – if you have to put a label on it, yes, call it selfish. And another thing, this is the first time we've seen each other for years and you seem to have forgotten the past like it didn't exist. Our 'college fling', as you seem to have written it off as, affected me badly. In fact, I might not have gone to America if it hadn't been for you and maybe things would have been different."

"What things?" Eve's voice had begun to take on a diamond-hard edge. "You can't blame me for your life going wrong in the States. Any choices you made were your own choices."

Mark sighed. "Let's not argue. I'm not here to rake over the past."

Eve was livid. "And why are you here exactly? To humiliate me? To get your own back for some old hurt?"

Now Mark was beginning to lose his temper. "Eve," he said strongly. "I thought we could have a nice dinner, two old friends getting together. I didn't realise you had read a little more into it and I'm sorry if I've wounded your pride. But I seem to remember you have a fairly thick skin, so deal with it!"

"How dare you!" Eve spluttered, trying not to raise her voice as she noticed the couple at the next table were looking on with interest. "Don't come on the innocent with me. You asked me out to dinner and you've been more than attentive all evening. Telling me your Kerry sob story and how you're looking for Mrs Mulhearne."

"OK, I'm sorry," Mark said in a kinder tone. "I didn't realise that you still have feelings for me and I should have . . ." Mark was interrupted by the waiter.

"Is everything all right, sir?"

"Yes, thank you."

Eve stared at her dinner. She hadn't eaten much of her salmon. She pushed the food around the plate, attempted a few mouthfuls and then gave up. She really didn't feel much like eating right now. Mark was trying to catch her attention but she ignored him.

Mark watched her in silence. She was refusing to meet his gaze and was absorbing herself in her food. He finished his salmon and looked around him. Happy couples and groups of friends were enjoying their meals.

"Would you like to see the dessert menu?" The waiter asked.

"No, thank you," Eve stated firmly. "Just coffee. One black and one with cream."

Mark tried to stifle a smile.

"What?" Eve asked finally. "You're doing it again."

"Eve, let's stop this bickering. It's stupid and it's not achieving anything. I think we should both accept that we're different people now and move on." He took a deep breath. "Perhaps we can finally be friends."

Eve stared at him as the waiter placed a cup of steaming black coffee in front of her. If she wasn't so annoyed, she'd be mortified at this stage. Friends, yeah right.

They sipped their coffee, trying not to look at each other.

Eve finally broke the silence. "Mark, I'm tired, I've had a long week. I'd like to go now."

Mark was relieved. He didn't know quite how long he would be able to sit feeling so awkward. He felt as if he'd done something wrong, as if all this unpleasantness was his fault. He hadn't done anything wrong and he was damned if he was going to let Eve make him feel bad – again.

"Let me walk you to your car."

"No, it's fine, it's only down the road."

Mark insisted on paying the bill and followed Eve into the lobby where she was wrapping her velvet throw around her shoulders, like a safety blanket. They walked out together, both aware of an icy chill surrounding them, threatening their fingers and toes with frostbite.

As they reached the bottom of the La Stampa steps Mark turned towards Eve.

"I know I've said it before but I really do hope we can still be friends . . . it would mean a lot to me. . . . Things change, Eve. I'm not the same person as I was in college. You deserve someone special, but it's not me."

She could hear his voice ringing in her ears.

Oh, just shut up, Mark she thought to herself. I just want to get out of here.

She shivered as a dart of wind whipped under her wrap. As she pulled the luxurious textured material closer to her body she allowed her mind wander, a defense mechanism to cover the hurt inside. I wonder will there be a Louise Kennedy sale soon? I'd love a new linen suit, they had beautiful light blue ones in recently. Eggshell blue really, with those nice long-line jackets and little silver buttons with the blue insets. I wonder how they make those buttons . . .

"Eve . . . Eve, do you understand, are you listening?"

She tuned back into what Mark was saying. Now more than irritated, she took a deep breath and forced a smile to her face. She had been faced with worse disasters than this. For heaven's sake, she had survived some serious currency crises. There was no way she was going to lose face over this minor skirmish.

"Mark, Mark," she crooned, changing tack. "Don't worry yourself on my account. Just a little misunderstanding, that's all."

She reached out a hand and touched him on the arm. Her chunky silver bangle glistened.

"Please go home, it will be fine. And of course we can be friends, I'd like that. I must dash, I've a busy weekend ahead. *Ciao*, darling."

She leant over and kissed the bewildered man on the cheek, turned on her heels and walked briskly down Dawson Street towards the carpark under the Kilkenny Design Centre.

Mark gazed after her in astonishment. Women, he thought to himself. Mad, the lot of them.

As his eyes followed Eve's slim back they misted over ever so slightly. He gave himself a quick shake and started walking towards St Stephen's Green to find an elusive taxi.

Strange how thing work out, he muttered to himself.

Eve lowered herself into her new red MX5 and threw her wrap and black-beaded evening bag on the seat beside her. She clutched the wheel with both hands and stared fixedly in front of her. The carpark was deathly silent, enveloping her in a dark cocoon. Her whole body was as tense as a tightly wound spring. Her head throbbed and she could feel tears pricking at the back of her eyes. She screwed up her eyes, held them like that for a few seconds and opened them.

She pulled her car out of the parking space, flicked on the headlights and drove up the ramp and out into the real world.

As she drove the short distance home her mind was spinning.

How could I have been so stupid? she said to herself. Damn, I'm so embarrassed he must think I'm just a pathetic female . . .

Also running through Eve's mind was the feud with her mother. Now she had no-one to talk to about the evening and Mark's behaviour. At this moment she missed her mother more than anything. It was as if a huge hole had been left in her heart with nothing to fill it.

"Well, I'm damned if I'm going to let any of them get to me," she muttered to herself, severely.

She approached the traffic-lights at Lincoln's Gate. As she continued through the green lights she noticed headlights coming towards her.

That's strange, she thought to herself.

A moment later she realised that the car was heading straight towards her at speed and it wasn't stopping.

Chapter 29

Eve's heart thudded in her chest. Her first reaction was to brake, hard, but it was too late. She heard the sickening crunch of metal and shattering of glass as her car was hit. The impact to the passenger side sent her car spinning a full 360 degrees. Eve's body was lurched brutally forward.

Her life flashed before her eyes. It was as if the split seconds had been set in slow motion. The next thing she knew the MX5 shuddered to a halt and she was thrown back against the contoured seat and headrest.

Then everything was suddenly silent and still. Eve raised her head and looked out her windscreen. There in front of her was a blue car, with a badly damaged front. The headlights were smashed, the bonnet was crumpled back and the car's windscreen was shattered.

Before Eve could collect her senses properly, the other car started to move. To Eve's amazement it picked up speed and drove past her to the right, scattering glass and plastic from the windscreen and broken lights everywhere. As the car passed she noticed several passengers packed into the back seats and a young boy, no more than twelve or thirteen, at the wheel.

Eve removed her hands from the steering wheel which she had been gripping as if it were a lifebuoy. Her whole body started shaking, from the tips of her fingers, up her arms, through her shoulders and neck and right down to her toes.

A hot, salty tear ran down her numb cheek. Followed by another tear and another, until in a matter of seconds her whole face was wet with them. She began to sob uncontrollably and was having difficulty breathing, she was crying with such intensity.

She became aware of outside noise and a cold breeze as her car door was opened.

"Are you all right, love?" asked the disembodied voice.

Eve nodded, holding her head in her hands.

"Now, it'll be fine," the kind voice continued. "I've rung the Guards and they'll be here in no time. Out you get, and come and sit in my car. It's warm and I have a nice rug to throw over you. Full of dog-hairs, mind, but we won't worry about that, dear, will we?"

Eve rubbed her swimming eyes with the back of her hands and looked up. A large lady with a round, pink face, wearing a green Barbour jacket, smiled down at her. Beside her was a tall, thin man in a matching jacket. She allowed herself be eased from her driving seat and helped into a Range Rover Jeep which was parked to the right of her car. The man supported her gently and carefully. Glass crunched under his feet and Eve winced at the sound.

The faint sound of a police siren wailed in the distance.

"That'll be the guards, love," said the lady softly.

Eve was placed gingerly in the back of the jeep and covered with a large, brown fluffy rug. It smelt of dogs and was indeed covered with wiry white hairs.

"What happened?" she whispered. "I was going quite slowly, I didn't see them until it was too late and I . . . I . . ." she began to cry again.

"Hush now, dear," the lady said. "It wasn't your fault. Giles and I saw the whole thing. This is Giles by the way." She lady gestured at the man who was now sitting in the front of the jeep and watching Eve's face with concern. "And I'm Rose. You have nothing to worry about, there was nothing you could have done. Young hooligans, should be locked up. About six or seven of them in the car. But hush now, here's the guards."

Eve turned her head towards the window. Two marked squad cars, blue lights flashing, pulled up beside her car.

Several uniformed guards stepped out of the cars. They surrounded her MX5, talking into radios. Noticing Rose gesticulating wildly, two young guards strode over to the jeep.

"Officer, you'll want to talk to this lady. She was in that car." Rose pointed to the MX5. "Some young boys went through the red lights and straight into her, joy-riders, I've no doubt. She's all right, but rather shaken."

One of the guards stared in at Eve. He smiled. "Are you all right, miss?"

Eve was touched with the guard's concern. His eyes looked completely sincere and genuine.

"Are you OK? Are you hurt in any way?" he repeated. Eve shook her head. She noticed a soft accent, Kerry perhaps or Cork. Why was she thinking about a guard's accent? She was confused. What was happening to her? Eve felt out of control, emotional. She started crying again. She had been through so much in the space of a few hours, she couldn't help herself. She cried for Mark, for her car, for the ruined night, for her lack of control, for everything.

The guard climbed into the jeep and put his strong arms around her.

It was strange – John Redmond had been a guard for many years now but he couldn't remember ever reacting in this way to anyone. But this young woman seemed different. She really needed him. And it felt right. He held her firmly in his strong arms. John felt her heart beating fast and erratically, her breath jagged and irregular.

He held tight, soothing her with whispered reassuring words and phrases until her crying had slackened off and her breathing had become more regular.

It was only then that he looked into Eve's blurred red and blotchy eyes and noticed how beautiful she was, blotches and all.

John Redmond shook himself inwardly and removed his arms. He was now embarrassed.

"Thank you," Eve whispered. She was amazed that a man she had never met before could be so thoughtful and tender.

He sidled out of the jeep and jumped to the ground.

"I'll have a look at your car," he muttered.

Eve felt strangely disappointed. Another guard with red hair and a perky smile then took her details, Rose and Giles filling in many of the blanks.

"They were joy-riders I'm afraid, Mrs Arnold," the second guard said. "Young local kids messing. The car was reported stolen earlier from along the quays."

Eve nodded. She was too exhausted to explain that she was Ms not Mrs.

"I don't think you are in a fit state to drive your car. I'll have one of the other guards drive it to the station and a garage can pick it up from there in the morning. How's that?"

Eve murmured assent.

"I'll take her home officer, if you like," Rose offered.

Eve heard a voice call over from beside her car.

"Dave," came the clear, deep tone. The young guard looked over. John Redmond walked towards the group. "I'll take Mrs Arnold home."

Eve stared at the guard's back. "John Redmond," she said to herself.

The guard had gruffly introduced himself while opening the back passenger door of the squad car for her. He was tall, with dark brown hair cut closely to his head. His ears stuck out a little. Eve smiled to herself as she noticed this. What was she thinking, sizing up a guard like this?

Guard Redmond made some perfunctory remarks during the drive. Eve found herself wondering about the real John, the man behind the uniform.

They reached her town-house quickly.

"I'll see you in, Mrs Arnold," John said formally.

Eve smiled. "It's Eve, please call me Eve. And I'm not married."

John took her hand as she stepped out of the car. "Eve," he repeated, "That's a lovely name."

Their eyes met and they both held the gaze for a long, lingering moment. He blushed, a delicate shade of pink spreading across his cheeks.

"Thank you for being so nice," Eve said, blushing herself and eyes glistening in remembrance of his strong embrace. She couldn't believe she was being so . . . so female. Where was her toughness, her hard shell, her invincible nature? Surely she wasn't rattled by a stupid car crash and teenage tearaways. Why was she almost in tears again? What was happening to her? Thoughts raced through her mind. All she knew was that at this precise moment she wanted someone to look after her, to care for her and help her. Was that so awful?

John noticed Eve's eyes flickering. What is she thinking about? he wondered.

Eve reached into her black evening bag, searching for her keys.

"Here." The guard handed her the keys.

At that moment Eve knew. She was tired of being the

tough, strong woman. She wanted to change her life. As she turned the key and opened her yellow door she heard John's voice behind her.

"Is there someone at home to keep an eye on you? You're still in shock."

"Well, no. But I'll be fine. Thank you."

John looked dubious. "I'll call in to you tomorrow to check you are OK and to sort out the car and that. Take a few days off, won't you? You'll need to rest."

Eve looked into his warm brown eyes and nodded. "Yes, you're right. I will."

"And you should get your neck and back checked at the doctor's first thing in the morning. Promise me you will."

Eve smiled. "I promise. And thank you. For everything, I'll see you tomorrow." She closed the door behind her and listened to the patrol car driving away. Her house was deathly silent. The light on her answering machine was steady, showing no new messages. Eve felt very, very alone. She fetched a glass of water from the kitchen and made her weary way up the stairs to her bedroom. Her eyes hurt from crying, and looking in her dressing-table mirror, she winced as a red and blotchy face with panda mascara eyes stared back at her. She looked a state. What must that guard have thought of her? She sat at the mirror for several minutes. Her mind felt numb, while her whole body was beginning to ache.

She pulled off her clothes, kicking them into a ragged pile at the foot of her bed, roughly rubbed off her make-up with cotton wool and splashed palmful after palmful of cold, fresh water over her face, trying to relieve her puffy eyes and skin. She felt more weary than she had ever felt before. She climbed into bed in her underwear and fell into a deep sleep within minutes.

Her night's sleep was riddled with nightmares – Mark laughing at her, her mother laughing at her, her car crashing over and over and over again, glass and plastic flying above her head and into the sky. She woke up at six in the morning in a hot sweat. Unable to get back to sleep but not wanting to take a sleeping tablet at this late stage, her mind began to work overtime.

I'm so stupid, stupid. Why did I make a fool of myself with Mark like that? What was I thinking of? I should have read the signals. Tears began to prick at her eyes once again and eventually she gave in to them. She lay in bed for hours holding herself and sobbing so hard she thought her heart would break.

Chapter 30

Ashling was sitting at her desk in the newsroom on Monday afternoon when Annie rang. It had been an eventful morning. She had covered the opening of a new travel shop on Henry Street, Wilde Holidays, who were offering a free American 'Dude Ranch' holiday to the person dressed in the best cowboy costume. It was won by an American who looked like he had just stepped out of the original Marlboro ads, tall and lean, with leathery tanned skin, wearing a gleaming white Stetson, leather-tasselled chaps, denim shirt and leather holster complete with two shining silver guns. Ashling asked him if they were real.

"Yes, ma'am, here you have Betty and Marge, my trusty sure-shooters. On hand to stop any cattle ranchers or poachers on my land, you know how it is."

Ashling had smiled. He was certainly in character. "And you're from where, Mr Yorke?"

"Call me Dwight, Little Missy. To answer your question I'm originally from Texas, but I've set up ranch

325

in Kildare now. Me and the lady – she's from Naas."

Ashling was intrigued. "And where did you meet?"

"I came over to work as her stable manager – got the job over the Internet. And it was love at first sight."

Ashling was delighted. This would make a great story. She instructed the *Courier's* photographer, Jack O'Dowd, to take some shots of Dwight. "Is your lady here by any chance?" Ashling asked.

"No, ma'am, she's at home running the ranch and running after the little 'uns."

Just then, the manager of Wilde Holidays stepped up to the microphone. "Ahem, I'd like to announce the results of our competition. The choice was unanimous. The winner is Mr Dwight Yorke. And now I'd like to present the prize of two week's holiday for two on a 'Dude Ranch' in Texas to Mr Yorke. Can you come up to the microphone, Mr Yorke?"

Dwight had swaggered up to the microphone, to much cheering and clapping and was handed the tickets. "Thank y'all. Myself and the little lady will be visiting the folks back home now!"

Ashling smiled as she sat at her desk that afternoon writing up the story – *Cowboy Wins Reunion Trip*.

"Hey, what are you up to this afternoon?" Annie asked.

"Well, I've just finished my cowboy story and I have a few garda reports to follow up, but apart from that it's pretty quiet. Why do you ask?"

"I'm covering a book launch in Fred Hanna's Bookshop. Jo is off on holidays and they need a colour piece for tomorrow. Want to come?"

"Can you give me half an hour?" Ashling asked.

"No problem. It doesn't start for an hour or so. And you know these book things, they never start on time. I'll come down and get you at three. And Ash?"

"Yes?"

"You can fill me in on the cowboy thing. It might give me a few ideas for a fashion page!"

Ashling laughed. "Will do, see you at three."

Walking down Nassau Street, on their way to Fred Hanna's, Ashling filled her friend in on Dwight Yorke.

"Hey," Annie said enthusiastically. "We could do a photoshoot on his farm. Get him to wear his cowboy gear – and we could use some natural-looking models and dress them in Western gear. I'll call it *Cowboy Chic.*"

"Sounds good to me," Ashling replied, smiling. Annie could make anything look fashionable, and she had a real talent for picking trends before they hit the streets. Hell, she made trends.

"Heard from Chris today?" Annie asked casually as they approached the door of Fred Hanna's Bookshop.

Ashling sighed. "No, but it's only Monday. If he hasn't rung by Wednesday I'll ring him myself."

"That's my girl," Annie said strongly. "Don't take any shit."

"Dead right," Ashling replied, sounding much more assertive than she felt.

There were crowds of people streeling into the bookshop, the young and trendy set. Ashling spotted a couple of young stage actors smoking on the steps into the shop.

"Annie, I forgot to ask you. What's the book being launched?"

She grimaced. "Good question, Ash. I'm not used to doing these things and I've forgotten to bring the Press Release. It's some sort of fiction by a young Galway author."

They squeezed themselves into the crowded bookshop and made their way to the desk where some black-suited women were congregated.

"One of these women will know," Annie stated authoritatively. "One of them is bound to be the PR woman."

"Hi, I'm Annie Brown from the *Courier*." She held out her hand to one of the women in black.

"Annabella Pollox from Picador House. Delighted you could make it. Can I introduce you to Hailey Bagshaw and Floss Jones from the Marketing Department and Owen's editor Max Rider-Smith?"

Ashling stifled a giggle. Marketing and PR people always had such marbles-in-the-mouth names. She wondered if it was a prerequisite for the job.

"And this is Ashling McKenna, also from the *Courier*," Annie said, pushing her into the fray.

"And here comes the man himself, Owen O'Sullivan," Annabella said, a beaming smile plastered on her immaculately made-up face. "Oh, he's been stopped by a fan." She giggled. "Well, he'll be here in a second."

Ashling felt faint, a sudden rush of adrenaline hit her, sending her heart racing. Surely it couldn't be the same Owen O'Sullivan, Dan's dad? From where she was she couldn't see. She looked over at Annie. There was a look of total shock on Annie's face as she stared into the crowd. Ashling followed her gaze. And there, moving towards her through the throngs, was her Owen.

"Jesus, I'm sorry, Ashling," Annie hissed, holding her friend's arm firmly. "I had no idea it was him. Little bastard. Are you OK?"

"I . . . I don't know," Ashling whispered.

She could hear Annabella's voice clearly over the hum of noise. "And Owen, can I introduce Annie Brown and Ashling McKenna from the *Courier*?"

Owen was now standing just in front of Ashling. She looked up at his familiar face and attempted a smile. Owen seemed as shocked as she was. His face had turned pale under the tan, making his freckles stand out like tiny brown and golden flecks. His brown hair was cut tight to his head and he was wearing an expensive-looking black leather jacket, black shirt and indigo blue denims.

"Damn, he looks so well," Ashling thought to herself. "He must be boiling in that jacket. Dan looks just like him – it's uncanny."

"Ashling, Ashling, are you OK?" Owen asked gently.

Ashling tuned back into earth. "Sorry, I was miles away. What did you say?"

"I asked how you were," Owen repeated, looking at her carefully.

Annabella interrupted. "How wonderful, and how

Irish! You all know each other! You must come to dinner tonight. We're taking Owen out and it would be wonderful to have some of his friends join us. Say you'll come."

Annie looked at Ashling. She looked flushed now. Her cheeks were glowing and Annie could see tiny flecks of anger beginning to form in her eyes. "Thank you for the offer, but I don't think . . ." Annie began.

Ashling interrupted. "Annabella, we'd love to join you this evening, it sounds like fun." She glared at Owen. "And Owen and I have lots to talk about, don't we, Owen?"

Owen had the grace to look sheepish. In fact he was starting to feel more than a little anxious. He hoped Ashling would keep her cool in front of his publishers. He'd be mortified if she caused a scene. Shit, he thought to himself. Why is Dublin so bloody small?

Annie was eager to get Ashling away from Owen. She spotted the *Courier* photographer coming through the door of Hanna's and breathed a sigh of relief. "Sorry, folks, we have work to do." She took Ashling firmly by the arm. "Come on, our snapper's over there."

"We'll see you tonight then, eight o'clock at *La Dolce Vita. Ciao!*" Annabella said, smiling. "Don't forget your Press Pack." She handed Annie a bright orange folder with Owen's face grinning on the front.

"We wouldn't miss it," Ashling said sardonically, smiling at Owen as best she could. "I'll see you later, Owen. It's such a nice surprise to see you back in Dublin. "

Annie dragged her away, worried what she would say next. Holding onto Ashling's arm for dear life, she pulled her towards Jack O'Dowd.

"Hi, Jack, listen, Ashling's not feeling too well. I'm going to see her home. Can you get me some shots of the author and of any of the usual. There's a gang of baby actors outside and one of the RTE weather girls is knocking around somewhere."

"No problem, Annie." Jack looked at Ashling with concern. It wasn't like Ashling to be sick – she did look rather flushed and agitated. "Go home and get some rest, love," he said kindly. "It looks like you may be coming down with something."

"Thanks, Jack," Ashling replied. "I think you're right, there's a couple of nasty bugs around. There's one in this room, in fact."

"Right," Annie said quickly. "See you, Jack." She pushed Ashling towards the door, across the road to Trinity College and didn't stop until she had reached a wooden seat in Fellow's Square. She put her arms around Ashling and held her tight.

"I'm so sorry, Ashling," she whispered.

Ashling began to cry and soon her body was heaving and shuddering, and huge tears were dropping from her eyes.

"Bastard!" she hiccuped through the tears. "Fucking bastard! I hate him!"

"It's OK, Ash," Annie crooned. She didn't know what to say. It was such a shock to see Owen. What must Ashling be feeling?

"And the worst thing is," Ashling cried, "Dan's the spit of him. It's so unfair. And how can he be in Dublin, knowing he has a son here? He didn't even ask about him. Bastard."

"Ashling, it wasn't a good place to talk. His publishers were all around him . . ."

"Why are you sticking up for him?" Ashling asked, her tears subsiding.

"I'm sorry," Annie replied. "You're right. He's a prick. He should have stayed away and not come back to haunt you. Ashling, what can I say? I wish I could make it all better for you, but I can't."

"Thanks," Ashling smiled through her tears. "You're a good friend. And Annie?"

"Yes?"

"Will you come to the dinner with me this evening?"

"Ashling, I don't think . . ."

"Please, Annie? It's something I want to do. Please just say yes."

Annie sighed. She knew Ashling wasn't up to it. And she was damned if she was going to let her get hurt.

"I'm sorry, Ashling, but neither of us is going. I'm bringing you home to Dan and I'm going to stay the night. And that's final!"

"Annie," Ashling began to cry again. "But what if I never see him again? And what do I tell Dan when he gets older – your dad lives in Dublin but he doesn't want anything to do with us?"

A huge wave of sadness swept over Annie. She'd kill Owen O'Sullivan for putting her friend through this again. Abandoning her once, leaving her alone and pregnant was one thing. At least he'd had the common decency to stay away. But how he had the audacity to return to Dublin, knowing he had left Ashling and their child behind – he had a bloody nerve. Well, Annie was damned if she would let him away with it, not if she had anything to do with it!

"You'll see him again, love," Annie said. "I'm sure of it."

"Annabella, this is Annie Brown, we met earlier at the launch."

"Darling, how are you? We're looking forward to seeing you tonight," Annabella gushed.

"Listen, I'm really sorry but we can't make it tonight, something's come up. But I wondering if you could give me Owen O'Sullivan's number. I'd like to interview him."

"Of course, I'm sure he'll be delighted to talk to you." The woman gave Annie his home and mobile numbers.

As Annie put down the phone she whispered, "I'm sure he will be delighted. Just delighted!"

"So, Dan, would you like to go out for dinner tonight? My treat."

"Yippee, Burger King please!" Dan replied.

Annie was playing *Rugrats* with Dan while Ashling was having a bath. Annie was worried about her friend. She had been very quiet in the car on the way home. Annie had insisted on driving Ashling's Golf. Her friend was in no fit state to take the wheel. Harry had kindly offered to collect Annie's own car later.

"Is she all right?" Harry had asked with concern when Annie had rung him from Ashling's.

"No, not really." Annie had replied. "I think she's still in shock. She got a terrible fright."

"No wonder," Harry had said. "Is there anything I can do?"

"No thanks, love. I'll talk to you tomorrow." Annie had smiled, putting down the phone. She was very lucky to have Harry around – he was such a decent guy.

Dan was pretending to change the nappy of Tommy from the *Rugrats*. Annie watched him carefully and gently wrapping the white toilet roll around his toy. Dan's blonde hair was its usual untidy thatch and he had mud on his left cheek and on his jeans. How could anyone abandon Dan? she asked herself.

Ashling padded into the room, wrapped in a soft white towelling bathrobe and wearing huge grey furry elephant slippers. "How's my favourite boy? Have you been good for Annie?"

"Mummy," Dan yelled, bounding over to Ashling and giving her a huge hug. "Annie is taking us to Burger King."

Annie smiled. "Sorry, Ashling, but it was his first choice."

"That's fine," Ashling said. "I could do with a serious injection of junk food right now."

An hour later they were all tucking into burgers and chips. Ashling was trying to get her mouth around a

Whopper, creamy mayonnaise sauce squirting out and shredded lettuce falling everywhere.

"Mummy, you've got sauce on your cheek. Here, have a napkin." Dan, who had ketchup all over his T-shirt and in his hair, handed his mother a wad of paper.

Ashling laughed. What was the expression? Oh yes, the pot calling the kettle black.

"Ah, junk food," Annie sighed, licking salt off her fingers. "You can't beat it."

Ashling looked at her friend. "Thanks, Annie."

"For what?"

"For the food, for everything."

Annie smiled. "Anytime, you know I'm always here for you."

Tears pricked Ashling's eyes.

"Mummy, did you burn your tongue?" Dan asked. "I cry when I burn my tongue."

"Something like that, love," Ashling replied. "Give your mummy a hug."

Chapter 31

"Hi, is Ashling there, please?"

Ashling had been sitting at her desk on Tuesday afternoon when the ringing of the phone cut through her muddled thoughts. She had considered taking the day off, but Annie had convinced her that she was better off at work. She'd been right as usual. At least her mind had been taken off Owen this morning as it was so busy.

"This is Ashling."

There was silence on the line for a second. "Ashling, it's Owen."

Ashling was stunned. What did he want?

"Ashling, are you still there?"

"Yes," she whispered.

"I was wondering if you'd meet me – we have a lot to talk about," Owen began nervously. "It was a bit of a shock seeing you at the launch. I'm sorry I didn't get to talk to you properly."

"I'm sorry too," Ashling said.

"You're very quiet, Ash, are you all right?"

"I'm fine," she replied, trying not to snap at him. "I've just got a lot on my mind."

"Yes, of course. I'm sorry."

Ashling took a deep breath. "You haven't asked about your son."

It was Owen's turn to be quiet now. At last he said, "I was waiting for you to bring it up. Of course I want to know all about him. Everything. And I'd like to meet him if you'll let me, as soon as possible. I've never stopped thinking about him."

Ashling sighed. She didn't know how to deal with all this. Should she let Owen see Dan? Should she tell Dan who Owen was? She knew he had a right to know who his father was, but he was so young. Would he understand?

"I'm not sure how I feel about all this. Can you give me a few days to think about it?"

"Of course, but can we meet up? Just you and me. We need to talk."

Ashling gritted her teeth. How dare he come swanning back into her life like this? Of course they needed to talk. They had needed to talk all those years ago when she was pregnant, when Dan was born, when Dan broke his leg and was in plaster for six weeks. Not bloody now! She was bringing up Dan the best she could and she didn't need Owen interfering at this stage.

"Ashling, I know you're angry with me and you have every right to be. I acted immaturely and I ran away. I know that now. But I've changed – things are different now. Please, I'd really like to see you."

"All right," Ashling muttered. "Friday afternoon in The Club in Dalkey – four o'clock."

"Fine, I'll see you then. And Ash?"

"Yes?"

"I really am sorry."

As soon as she put down the phone to Owen, Ashling rang Annie. "Are you busy?"

"Nothing that can't wait." Annie heard the distress in her friend's voice. "I'll be right down."

As she walked towards Ashling's desk she cursed herself. Maybe she shouldn't have talked to Owen. She had given him a right earful earlier and he had promised to ring Ashling. But maybe it had been the wrong thing to do.

"Ash, are you OK?"

Ashling looked up at Annie. Her eyes were filling up with tears again. She didn't seem to be able to help it. "Oh, Annie. Owen rang and I'm so confused. He wants to see Dan. And he wants to meet me on Saturday but I don't know if I want to talk to him. I don't know if I'd cope."

Annie took a deep breath. "Listen, I think you two will have to talk. You never really got Owen out of your system."

"But . . ." Ashling began.

"I know he ran away on you and everything. But you've never really talked about the whole situation, what he said to you, how he reacted. You need to let it

338

all out. Scream at Owen if you have to. Or scream at me, I don't mind. But you have to let it all out and deal with it." Annie was in her swing now. "Take charge of your emotions, let him know how he's hurt you. Closure, that's what you need, closure on the whole situation." She stopped triumphantly.

"Jesus," Ashling said, a smile forming on her lips, "have you ever thought of becoming a chat-show host. Rikki Lake has nothing on you."

Annie smiled. "Would you stop! I'm only trying to help."

"I know," Ashling laughed. "You just sounded so serious."

"Anything to make you smile, my dear. So you're going to talk to Owen?"

"Yes."

"Do you want me to come with you?"

"No. You're right, this is something I need to do on my own."

The week crawled by for Ashling. On Wednesday she covered a long and tedious Dublin County Council meeting on the future of planning in the city. Thursday was taken up with a dog show and an interview with the new Miss Ireland. Ashling was disappointed when Chris hadn't rung by the end of the week but in a way she was relieved. She knew she'd told Annie that she'd ring him but she had enough on her plate with Owen returning.

Walking down to The Club, Ashling's mind raced. She had no idea what she was going to say to Owen. She decided she'd let him do most of the talking. After all, he had a lot of explaining to do. Pushing open the heavy wooden door just after four, Ashling made her way to the bar.

"A pint of Bulmers, please," she said to the young barman.

"Make that two." Owen was sitting at the bar, reading *The Irish Times*. "Hi, Ash," he smiled nervously. "It's good to see you." He leant towards her and planted a soft kiss on her cheek.

Ashling blushed. She hadn't expected a kiss. "Hi," she said sitting down beside him on a bar stool. "You look well." He was wearing a tight dark blue T-shirt and combats.

"Thanks. You don't look so bad yourself."

Ashling smiled. If only he knew. She'd spent hours trying on different outfits, trying to capture the right look. Casual and together. A girl in charge of her life yet not afraid of having fun. As if it mattered what she wore. But as Annie was fond of saying – 'look right and you'll feel right'. Ashling had settled on her black leather trousers, a cerise 'skinny fit' T-shirt and a snow-white fleece.

There was silence for a few long minutes. The barman slid the pints towards them over the dark wood bar. Ashling took a long gulp of her pint and looked at Owen. He was watching her carefully.

"I suppose you're wondering what I'm doing back?" he asked tentatively.

Ashling nodded. "And where you were in the first place," she said calmly.

Owen reddened. "You know I was in Australia. Everyone knew."

"Owen, your friends told me. You never told me yourself."

"I'm sorry, that was wrong of me. But I was scared, you know, of the whole thing."

"What 'thing'?" Ashling asked quietly.

"Jesus. The whole thing, the baby, our relationship, the future, everything. I just wasn't ready for all of that, I wanted to be free."

"I know all that. You made it quite clear to me and I haven't forgotten it." She looked at Owen with a stony expression on her face. "Dan means the world to me and I love him more than anything. You hurt me more than you'll ever know, but I've got over it. But if you hurt my son I'll kill you."

Owen was taken aback. He knew Ashling had had a boy but knowing his name made it all so real. "Dan? My son's name is Dan?"

"*My* son," Ashling said quickly. "Don't think you can waltz back into our lives just like that. He has no idea who you are, you're nothing to him. You hear me, nothing!"

Owen sighed. "I'm sorry, this is all pretty intense. I didn't mean to upset you. I was going to settle in and get things sorted before I contacted you. But meeting you and Annie at the launch – well, everything's happening a little too quickly."

"So you intend to stay in Dublin? And how long have you been back anyway?"

"Only a few weeks, and I'm not sure if we're staying. I don't know how to say this, Ash, but it's not really just up to me anymore." He paused.

She stared at him. "What do you mean?"

"Do you want another drink? Another pint?"

"Don't change the subject. Do you have a girlfriend?"

He frowned. "Not exactly."

"Jesus. You haven't changed. Getting information out of you is like getting blood out of a stone."

"I'm sorry. I'm just not sure how you're going to take this . . . I'm married."

"You're what?" Ashling asked in shock.

"She's called Fiona and she's from Perth. I met her when I was over there."

"Fiona?"

"Yes. And there's something else." Owen wasn't looking forward to this part. He took a photograph from his pocket and handed it to Ashling. She stared at the photograph of a tiny baby with long fingers gripped around a large hand. The baby looked just like Dan! How did Owen get a picture of Dan?

Ashling's eyes filled with tears. "You carry a picture of Dan?"

"No," Owen replied slowly. "That's Josh. He's six months old now. He's my other son."

"I . . . I have to go now." Tears were streaming down Ashling's face. She jumped down from the bar stool and ran out the door. She didn't stop until she'd reached Dalkey Park. She sat down on wooden bench and looked out towards Dalkey Island. She pulled her knees towards her chest and rocked backwards and forwards. She felt wretched. She pulled her mobile phone out of her fleece and pressed in the familiar name.

"Annie, I need you. Can you come and get me?"

"Where are you, love?"

"In Dalkey Park, the one down by the sea."

"OK, stay put. I'm in Blackrock and I'll be with you in fifteen minutes."

The next thing Ashling knew, Annie's strong, warm arms were around her.

"Annie, he's married and he has a baby."

Annie cursed Owen O'Sullivan under her breath. "I'm taking you back to my place. I'll ring Tizzy and ask her to keep Dan for the night."

Annie put Ashling into her car and rang Tizzy.

"Is Ashling all right?" Tizzy asked in concern.

"Well, she's just met Owen and well, she's had some unexpected news."

"Owen O'Sullivan, Dan's father?" Tizzy asked, confused.

"Had she not told you? I'm sorry, Tizzy. Owen's back in Dublin with a wife and baby in tow."

Tizzy was bewildered. It wasn't like Ashling to keep things from her. "I had no idea. Owen being back is a big shock in itself. But married and with a baby, poor Ash!"

"I know, it's too much to take in really. But I'll take her home with me. But Ash is a toughie, she'll be fine."

Tizzy sighed. "You're right, I suppose. But she doesn't deserve all this. Life is so unfair sometimes."

"You've said it, Tizzy."

Annie drove to her apartment in Blackrock, stopping at SuperValu in Dalkey on the way to collect some provisions.

"Ashling, you're very quiet," Annie said when they were stopped at traffic-lights in Sandycove.

"He married her but he wouldn't marry me," Ashling said in a whisper. "He didn't love me enough."

"You were both very young," Annie said. "Do you really think marrying Owen would have been the right thing to do?"

Ashling hiccuped. She had stopped crying now but her eyes were still throbbing and her breathing was still erratic. She hadn't cried so much since she had found out she was pregnant. "I don't know. I suppose not." Her mobile phone rang in her pocket.

"Hello, Ashling McKenna."

"Hi, Ash, it's Chris."

"Hi," Ashling said. He was the last person she wanted to talk to at this precise moment.

"Are you all right? You sound like you have a cold."

"I'm fine."

"Right. Do you want to come out tonight? There's a party on in town in Merrion Square. I thought we could mosey on in, have a few pints in The Duke first or something."

"I don't really feel like it, Chris," Ashling said. "Another time."

"Right, right," Chris replied. "Are you sure you're OK? You sound funny."

"Do I?" Ashling asked sardonically. "Really? And what do you care?"

Chris was uneasy. This wasn't the carefree and fun Ashling he was used to. He was fucked if he wanted a heavy scene on a Friday evening. He had partying to do! "Well, I have to run. Smartie's waiting. See ya."

Ashling looked at the phone in disgust. "Annie, I'm sick of men! They're all fucked in the head."

Annie sighed. It was going to be a long night.

Later that evening the two friends were curled up on Annie's sofa, watching *Good Will Hunting*. An empty pizza box lay at their feet, together with two empty cartons of Ben and Jerry's icecream and an empty bottle of wine. Ashling felt much better. She wondered if she had been in extended shock since Monday? And now the 'married with a baby bombshell'. But maybe Annie was right, maybe she needed to 'close' the whole Owen thing. He was married now and he had his own family to think about and maybe he'd finally grown up. God, things were complicated.

"Thanks for having me here," Ashling said, as Matt Damon licked Minnie Driver's stomach.

"Shush," Annie replied. "It's just getting to the good part."

Ashling laughed. "You have a one-track mind."

"Don't I know it? Anyway, are you feeling better?" Annie asked, dragging her eyes off the screen and Matt's muscular chest.

"Yes, I really am. It's just been one hell of a week. But I've made a decision. I'm going to let Owen see Dan."

"Are you sure? You don't have to, you know."

"I know. But it's not about me or even Owen, Annie. It's about Dan. The more people he has around him that love him the better."

Annie smiled hugged her friend. "Jesus, Ashling, you have the biggest heart of anyone I know."

"And another thing," Ashling said. "Tomorrow I'm going to tell Chris what I want. And if he doesn't like it, then tough!"

"Good on you," Annie smiled. This was the Ashling McKenna she knew and loved.

Chapter 32

Ashling woke up on Sunday morning with a knot in her stomach. Had she really said all that last night to Chris? Bloody hell. It had all started innocuously enough. She had rung him on Saturday afternoon and suggested drinks that evening.

"Hi, Chris. Listen, sorry I wasn't up to much last night, I was tired. But what are you up to tonight?"

Chris was relieved. Things seemed to be back to normal, the way he liked them, easy and hassle-free. "I've nothing planned. I'll give you a ring later and we'll get together."

"I'd like that," Ashling said. "And Chris?"

"Yes?"

"Just you and me, OK?"

Chris was silent for a second. "Oh, yeah. Fine. But we might hook up with the gang after, yeah?"

Ashling sighed. "Whatever. Talk to you later."

Chris rang back from the pub. Ashling had almost given up on him but she was damned if she was going to ring him. In fact in another half an hour she would have been resplendent in pyjamas and fluffy slippers, make-up removed and in full slob-out mode. Dan had already been deposited at Tizzy's and Ashling had just decided between watching a previously videotaped episode of *Dawson's Creek*, or *Breakfast at Tiffany's* for the umpteenth time (*Dawson's Creek* had won). Instead she checked her face and hair in the bathroom mirror and pulled a white fleece over her black vest top. It was spitting rain outside so she grabbed a red corduroy *Gap* hat from the hall table and pulled it on as she walked out the door.

They had arranged to meet in The Club in Dalkey, where Chris was already ensconced. Ashling was uneasy when he'd suggested the venue. After all it was only yesterday that Owen had dropped the bombshell in the very same place. Still, she thought to herself, after she'd put the phone down, it's only a pub and I have to bury the ghosts sometime. No time like the present. She grimaced. And I suppose Chris is already there after all. She wondered what sort of state he'd be in when she arrived.

It was a ten minute walk, but tonight Ashling managed it in five, eager to avoid the drizzle. The Club was packed. Throngs of bodies lined the bar three or four deep. Every available seat was taken. Ashling looked around. She couldn't see Chris anywhere, maybe he was upstairs. She made her way up the solid dark wooden staircase, after pushing her way through a gaggle of short-skirted girls who were drinking bottles of Ritz and giggling. As she reached the top she heard a familiar voice.

"Ash!"

It was Owen, sitting alone at a small table with two pints of Guinness in front of him.

Ashling felt a shiver down her spine. She took a deep breath before bravely making her way towards him. He looked at her kindly and gestured towards the second stool. "Sit down. Can I get you a drink?"

"No, no, I'm grand, thanks. I'm meeting someone but I'll stay for a second." Ashling sat down. "What are you doing here anyway?"

Owen looked a little embarrassed. "Well, I kind of liked it yesterday, despite the circumstances and we're living quite near, in Shankhill."

"And where's the lovely Fiona?" Ashling asked. Owen raised his eyebrows. "Oh, I'm sorry Owen, that come out wrong. I didn't mean to sound sarcastic."

"That's OK. Fiona's gone to look for a phone. She wants to check up on Josh. He's with the next-door neighbour, who's had masses of her own – seven, I think, but she worries. You know how it is."

"Yes, I do," Ashling replied slowly. "I think I'd like to meet her – Fiona I mean."

Owen smiled. "You'll like her."

Ashling looked around her. She felt uneasy and wanted to leave. She wondered where Chris had got to. Damn him.

"Are you all right?" Owen asked.

"What? Oh, yes." Ashling concentrated on talking to Owen. "Listen. I'm sorry about running out on you yesterday. I just felt . . . well, it was a bit of a shock."

Owen was silent, allowing her to speak.

"It was all too much for me," she continued. "Seeing you at the launch like that and you being married and Josh and everything . . ."

"You don't have to explain. I understand. At least I think I do. And you don't have to apologise. Jesus, if anyone is apologising it should be me." He ran his hands through his hair. "I behaved really badly and believe me if I could change things I would. I abandoned you when you needed me because I was scared. It was all just too much for me. There's no excuse. I don't know what to say."

Ashling knew that Owen wasn't finding this easy. He had never been much of a communicator at the best of times. Maybe he had changed.

Owen continued. "But I really am a different person now and I'd like you to give me another chance. With Fiona and Josh and all, I think now that I'm ready to be a good dad to Dan if you'll let me."

"I think I'd like Dan to get to know you, but only if you're going to stick around. He needs some stability in his life, not someone who will flit in and out of his life when it pleases them. Are you planing to stay in Dublin?"

"I am now," he said strongly. "I really want to be

involved in Dan's life. I know I've left it late but he'll be one of my top priorities from now on, I promise. We're looking for somewhere to rent in the Sandycove or Dun Laoghaire area, a house with a garden for the kids hopefully. And I'm around a good bit during the day, what with the writing and all, so maybe I could help with baby-sitting and stuff."

"I don't think it's called baby-sitting when it's your own son," Ashling laughed, beginning to feel a little less awkward. "But that sounds good. I'm sorry I forgot to say it to you before, but congratulations on the book. I look forward to reading it."

"Thanks," Owen grinned. "It was an idea I was kicking around for years in the back of my mind. And I suppose it was Fiona really who lit a fire under my ass. She sent the first few chapters to Picador and they liked it and offered me a deal. Then I had to sit down and finish the thing."

"Good woman," Ashling said genuinely. She of all people knew how difficult it could be to motivate Owen at times. "And are you working as well or just writing?"

"I'll be working part-time next month. I was teaching in Australia and I'm starting in a school in Blackrock in two weeks."

"Teaching?" Ashling asked amazed. "Children?"

"Don't be so shocked, Ash." Owen blushed a little. "I'll be teaching fifth class. It's funny, if you told me a few years ago that I'd end up teaching ten-year-olds I'd have laughed. But I love it. They are so interesting at that age and I feel I'm doing something valuable. It sounds like a cliché, but I'm building the future in my classroom."

"You always were a great one for the lectures all right," Ashling joked. "Although in those days they tended to be on Socialist Workers Party stuff and free college fees for all."

"And wasn't I right?" Owen asked smiling. "Even the government agreed on the old fees thing. But I've mellowed out a bit in my old age. I've decided the way to change the world is to get them young. And anyway the hours suit me. I'll be working mornings only which gives me loads of time to play with Josh and Dan. Then I can write in the evenings."

"If you have any energy left," Ashling laughed. "And are you sure the school knows that you intend to indoctrinate little Socialist Workers?"

Owen laughed. "I'll teach them to make up their own minds about the world, including politics. So don't you worry."

"I'm glad to hear it," Ashling said. "And what about Fiona? Is she working?"

"Not at the moment. But when we're a little more settled she's hoping to set up her own catering company. Dinner parties and that sort of thing."

"Did I hear you talking about me?" A tall brunette approached the table and put her hand on Owen's shoulder. Owen held her tanned hand and turned towards Ashling.

"Ash, this is Fiona. Fiona, Ashling McKenna."

A sharp irrational dagger of jealousy pierced Ashling's heart but she smiled through it.

Fiona gave a wide smile and held out her hand. "It's good to meet you. You're Dan's Mum." She shook Ashling's hand warmly.

"I've seen a picture of Josh and he's only beautiful," Ashling said.

Fiona continued. "I hope they can meet each other one day. Family is important. It would mean a lot to us both." She looked at Ashling, her dark brown eyes honest and sincere.

Ashling admired her open and direct manner. It's funny, she thought to herself. By rights I should hate her, but I don't. She seems . . . nice.

Fiona sat down at the table.

Owen smiled. "I've told Ash that we plan to stay in Dublin for good so that I can be close to Dan. It looks like we'll be spending some time together."

Fiona looked at Ashling and back at Owen and beamed. "That's brilliant. Thank you, Ashling. I hope we can all be friends. And maybe Dan and Josh can play together when they're older."

"Definitely," Ashling replied. "They are half-brothers after all."

"Yes, they are," Owen nodded. "Thanks, Ash." A lump was forming in his throat, it had been quite an evening.

"I want to thank you too," Fiona added. "None of this can be easy for you but you're dealing with it so well."

Ashling smiled to herself. If only they knew. It was killing her to see them together. Owen, if she was honest with herself, had always been in her heart and in her mind. Every time she looked at Dan it reminded her of Owen. Sometimes it hurt and sometimes it didn't. But, she mused, time was a good healer.

"The more people Dan has around him who care about him the better," she said. "I just want to do what's best for him."

Just then Ashling's mobile rang. "Excuse me," she murmured, moving towards the stairs so that she could hear. "Hello?" she answered.

"Ash, it's me, Chris. Can you hear me? I'm in The Queen's."

Ashling sighed. Chris was really getting under her skin this week. "Chris, I thought we said The Club."

"Yeah, well, I met a mate and we came here instead. Are you coming over?"

Ashling gritted her teeth. "I'll be there in five minutes," she muttered and clicked off her phone. Chris really was impossible.

Ashling made her way back towards the table where Owen and Fiona were now holding hands and talking earnestly. They looked up as she approached the table.

"I have to leave now," Ashling said. "Duty calls."

Owen smiled. "Me and Fiona are really grateful, Ash. You're being really cool about the whole thing."

"Dan's a lucky boy," Fiona added.

"I was wondering, could I give you a ring

tomorrow?" Owen said. "We still have a lot to talk about."

"Sure, I'd like that." Ashling scribbled her home number onto an old receipt from her wallet and handed it to him.

"It was really good to meet you," Fiona said, standing up.

"You too," Ashling said. And maybe one day I'll mean it, she said to herself.

Chris was holding up the bar in The Queen's with a young dark-haired man who Ashling recognised as Damien from the sports department in the *Courier*. They had obviously been at the pints for several hours.

"Howaya, Ash," Chris bellowed when he spotted her. "Pull up a pew."

As there were no bar stools free, Ashling went to the far side of the bar and carried one over. Although Chris's eyes had a rather hazy appearance, he still managed to look well. His blue eyes twinkled at Ashling and he gave her a lopsided grin. "What are you having?" He ordered her a pint of cider and went back to talking to Damien about Man United's chances in next year's Premiership.

Ashling sat listening for a while but it was hard to concentrate on their inane drivel. She began to get annoyed. After all, she had arranged to meet Chris. And on his own at that. Now she was being made to feel like a spare part – an unwanted girlie on male territory. What was Chris's problem?

"Chris," Ashling interrupted. "There are seats over there. Are you coming?" A couple had just vacated a corner table opposite them. Ashling knew Chris preferred to sit at the bar, directly in front of the Guinness tap if at all possible. "Shortest possible route to the black stuff," he liked to say.

Ashling jumped down from the bar stool and stood behind Chris.

"My cue to leave I think, mate," Damien said. "The girlfriend will be wondering where I am."

"Don't leave, Damien. Have another drink," Chris cajoled and looked at Ashling for her approbation. Ashling said nothing. "Right so," Chris muttered moodily. "See you Monday."

Chris sat down at the table beside Ashling. "You should have encouraged him to stay," he said, grumpily. "He would have if you'd asked him."

"I didn't want him to stay," Ashling stated firmly.

Chris looked at her suspiciously. "Oh." He decided not to ask her why. It would only cause grief. Staying quiet was the easy way out. "D'ya want another pint, Ash?" he asked.

"No thanks." Ashling's pint of cider was sitting in front of her almost full. She wasn't in the mood for drinking, not tonight. She took a deep breath. "Chris, we have to talk." The words came out of her mouth before she could stop herself. It was such a cliché – we need to talk.

Chris now looked nervous. He wasn't into 'talking' –

not now, not ever. It was all right when you first met a girl. You had to ask all the relevant questions – life story, favourite music, favourite colour – it was kind of expected. But when you'd been out a couple of times it was unnecessary, wasn't it? He was only twenty-four after all. There was plenty of time for 'talking' when he was in his thirties or forties even, no rush.

"Um," Chris replied. Maybe it was better to let her have her say. It was probably her time of the month or something. Girls went a bit weird then, didn't they? Anyway, hopefully, she'd get whatever it was off her chest and they could get on with the serious matter of the evening – drinking. "Go on," he said tentatively.

"What do you want from me?" Ashling asked, looking at him carefully.

Chris was confused. He wasn't quite sure what she was getting at.

Ashling noticed the blank expression on his face and started again. "Let me rephrase that. Do you want a proper relationship?"

Chris thought about this for a second. If by 'proper' she meant sexual the answer was yes. But maybe she meant something else. He decided to hedge his bets. "Ash, you know I like you and you're very attractive. And you're great *craic*." Usually, he thought to himself wryly.

"I know all that, Chris." Ashling was now losing patience. "OK, I'll tell you what I want. I want someone to stay in and watch videos with, to go out for dinner with, to take long walks with. And someone who likes spending time with me and Dan, not just me."

Chris looked at her silently. Ashling continued. She had nothing to lose now and Chris Doyle was losing his appeal rapidly.

"Ah, um . . ." he began awkwardly. "I'm sorry, Ash, but walks and playing with kids aren't really my scene."

Ashling smiled with her lips but not with her eyes. "So you want someone to go drinking with, to have a laugh with at the weekends and to have great sex with?"

"Yes!" Chris said emphatically. Maybe this wasn't going to be so bad after all.

Ashling had thought as much. "Well, I'm sorry but I don't think this is going to work out. We're too different."

Chris had the good grace to look sad. His mouth turned down at the sides and he began to pout. "But we can still see each other the odd time, right?" he asked hopefully, raising his eyebrows.

Damn, he was cute, Ashling thought to herself. But I have to be strong. "No," she said firmly. "We'll see each other in work, that's all."

"Oh." Chris was disappointed. He genuinely liked Ashling but he wasn't ready to slow down his life yet. "Right, I understand."

"Chris, it's just timing. We're at different stages of life. Having Dan made me grow up a lot quicker, that's all."

They were silent for a while, Ashling finishing her

pint and Chris not knowing what to say. Finally he broke the ice. "Would you like another drink?"

Ashling smiled at him. "No thanks, I'm going to head now." She got up and gave him a kiss on the cheek.

Chris watched her walk out of the pub before pulling out his mobile. "Smartie, where are you?" Smartie was in another pub in Dun Laoghaire. "Yeah grand, I'll see you there in half an hour." Life had to go on after all.

Ashling walked home from The Queen's by the coast road. She felt sad, yet relieved. In her heart of hearts she had known that Chris wasn't right for her, but it had been fun while it lasted. It's all for the best, she thought to herself. Passing Dalkey Island she remembered Annie's kindness only two days previously. If I'm on my own it's no big tragedy. I don't need a man in my life to complicate matters, she told herself firmly, wishing she truly believed it.

Chapter 33

"I did it," Ashling told Annie the following morning.

"What time is it?" Annie mumbled, reaching for her alarm clock. "Ash, it's not even ten yet."

"I'm sorry," Ashling replied, contrite. "I'll ring back later."

Annie sat up in her bed and rubbed her eyes. "Don't worry. I'm awake now. We just had a bit of a late night."

"Annie, can I call over later? I've loads to tell you."

Annie looked at Harry's sleeping body, comatose beside her. He was playing golf later with some old college friends so her afternoon was free. "Sure. Why don't you and Dan call over for late lunch at around two. Harry will be on the golf course by then and we can have a good gossip."

"Great," Ashling said. "I'll see you then. Would you like me to pick anything up on the way?"

"No, don't worry. I have to do a shop anyway. See you at two."

Ashling put down the phone. "Right, young Daniel McKenna," she said, chasing her son around the living-room. "Bath and hair-wash for you."

"Tomorrow, Mum," Daniel shrieked. "I promise I'll have a bath tomorrow."

"No way, young man. You've got Coco Pops in your hair and chocolate all over your face. Bath, now!" She marched him down the stairs into the warm bath which was waiting for him, filled to the brim with his favourite strawberry-scented bubbles. Back in the living-room, she sat down on the sofa, fished the latest Tina Reilly from under the cushion behind her and began to read.

The phone rang. Ashling put down her book and padded over to the phone.

"Ash, it's Owen."

"Hi, how are you?"

"I hope it's not too early to ring, but with Dan I presumed you'd be up already."

"We've been up for hours," Ashling said smiling. "How are Fiona and Josh?"

"Great," Owen replied. "She's feeding him now. I was wondering could I call over one evening this week?"

Ashling took a deep breath. "Sure," she said. "How about Wednesday evening at about six? I'll ask Tizzy to give him his tea early."

"That sounds great. I'm really nervous about meeting him. Do you think he'll like me?"

Ashling wondered but thought it best not to make

Owen too nervous. "Of course he will. It'll take him a little while to get used to you, that's all."

"Thanks, Ash," Owen said, relieved. "I'll see you on Wednesday."

Ashling gave Owen directions to the house and put down the reciever just as Dan came up the stairs wrapped in a large pink bath towel.

"Dan, you're dripping all over the floor," she said. "Come here to me and I'll dry you."

"Who was that on the phone, mummy?" Dan asked as Ashling rubbed his hair dry. "Was it Annie?"

"Did you use shampoo on your hair, Dan?" Ashling asked, changing the subject and looking at his hair which didn't seem that clean.

"No," Dan replied smiling. "I used bubbles."

"Back to the bathroom with you," she laughed, "and we'll use shampoo this time."

Dan smiled. He didn't mind, not really. He liked when his mum washed his hair. She was always gentle and he liked it when she rubbed the shampoo all over his head. It was much more fun than doing it by yourself

Two hours later Ashling and Annie were sitting at the kitchen table in Annie's apartment. Dan was playing with Lego in the adjoining sunroom, pieces of multi-coloured plastic all over the terracotta-tiled floor. The two women were tucking into warm chicken salad with crusty French bread.

"So what happened with Chris?" Annie asked. "Tell me everything."

Annie poured herself some Aqua Libra and sat back

to listen. Ashling filled her friend in on the previous evening's events, from meeting Owen and Fiona to breaking up with Chris.

When she had finished Annie whistled. "That was some evening, Ashling. Talk about eventful. It must have been hard seeing Owen with someone. You never really had a chance to get over him."

"No, you're right, I guess," Ashling sighed. "And it was hard seeing them together . . . holding hands and being so damn happy. But it'll get easier, I hope."

"And how do you feel now about the whole Chris thing?"

"Relieved mainly. I should have listened to you. He wasn't right for me, our lives were too different."

Annie topped up their glasses. "I know it's not easy for you, what with work and Dan and all. But the right man will come along, you'll see."

"I'm not holding my breath," Ashling said smiling. "And in the meantime I'm going to enjoy spending time with Dan. I feel kind of guilty that I haven't been giving him all my attention recently."

"When are you going to tell him about Owen?" Annie asked gently.

"Good question," Ashling sighed. "He's calling over on Wednesday so it'll have to be soon. I just don't know what to say."

"Children are very adaptable," Annie reassured. "Dan may suprise you. My guess is that it won't be as difficult as you think. What have you told him so far?"

"That his father lives in Australia. We don't talk

about it much, to be honest. It tends to crop up when something about families is on the television or in a book. Then he asks about his dad the odd time."

"Suppose you tell Dan the truth?" Annie said. "That Owen has decided to live here now so that he can be close to him. I'm not sure that time means the same to children as it does to adults. I'm no expert but I think Dan may just accept that Owen is around now and soon he won't even remember the last six years without him."

Ashling looked at her friend thoughtfully. "I hope you're right Annie. But Dan's so used to things the way they are. And I'm worried that it may affect the relationship we have together. What if he likes Owen more than he likes me?"

"That's just silly. You will always be the most important person in Dan's life. That's not going to change."

"I know," Ashling said. "You're right. There's just so much to think about."

"Dan will take his lead from you. So you have to be strong and decide how you are going to deal with it all. If you take everything in your stride so will he. How are you going to explain Fiona and Josh for example?"

"I guess I'll have to be as honest as I can with Dan. He deserves to know the truth and it will be better for all concerned in the long run."

Dan came running into the kitchen and Annie and Ashling quickly changed the subject. "How's the spaceship coming along, Dan?" Ashling asked, ruffling his hair.

"Great, but it's thirsty work. I need a drink," Dan replied.

Ashling glared at him. "I need a drink, what?"

"Orange juice or apple juice," Dan said innocently.

"I think your mum was talking about the magic word, Dan," Annie said smiling.

"And I don't mean *Abracadabra* either," Ashling added.

"Please," Dan said beseechingly, his blue eyes wide. Annie poured some orange juice into his Winnie the Pooh glass, kept in the cupboard especially for his visits.

"Thanks," he said, turning towards the sunroom.

"Walk, Dan, don't run. You'll spill your juice otherwise," Ashling admonished. Soon he was caught up in a galaxy far, far away, creating the ultimate space ship.

"He's in flying form," Annie said, putting the juice carton back in the fridge. "Would you like some ice cream? I've got Strawberry or Caramel Surprise."

"Have you ever known me to say no?" Ashling replied, smiling.

"Lots of both so."

"Cream on mine if you have it."

"You're an awful woman."

"Don't I know it," Ashling laughed.

On Monday evening Ashling and Daniel were curled up on the sofa reading *Charlie and the Chocolate Factory*. Dan loved the book and the especially the strange Oompa-Loompa characters. He loved singing the Oompa-Loompa song with his mum every time they came into the story. As Ashling finished the chapter she was reading, she closed the book and turned towards her son.

"Dan, I have something to tell you."

"Can we have another chapter?" Dan asked.

"In a minute, love. But I want to talk to you first."

Dan wondered had he done something wrong. The last time his mum had talked to him like this was after he'd stuck a pencil in Davey O'Brien's head. He hadn't meant to, they were playing sword fights with their pencils and he had missed. His teacher, Miss Sweeney, hadn't been amused. Davey hadn't minded too much. It had made him a bit of a hero in class and he liked that.

"It's about your dad," his mother said.

Dan was relieved and pleased he wasn't in trouble. He paused, thought for a second and then asked, "My dad?"

"Yes, love," Ashling said gently. "Your dad has come back to Ireland and he's going to live here now."

Dan didn't seem all that interested. "Can I have the next chapter now?" he asked, unfazed by the news.

Ashling tried again. "Owen – your dad – has come back to be near you, Dan, and he'd love to see you. He had a Australian lady with him – her name is Fiona – and a little boy called Josh who's six months old."

"A baby?" Dan asked, suddenly paying attention. "Younger than me? Can I play with him?"

Ashling smiled. "Of course you can. He's your half-brother. He's small now so you'll have to be careful with him though."

"Cool," Dan stated. "Thanks, Mum, that's brilliant. When can I see the baby?"

"And your dad," Ashling pointed out.

"Him too. When can I see them?"

"Your dad is calling in on Wednesday – that's the day after tomorrow. So you can see him then. And maybe you can meet Josh on Saturday."

"Do you think he'll bring a present? My dad, I mean," Dan asked smiling.

"Daniel McKenna, what kind of child are you?" Ashling asked laughing. She squeezed him, her two arms wrapping snugly around his small body.

"Mum, stop, stop," he squealed, giggling maniacally. He loved being squeezed really.

Ashling read Dan the next chapter of his book before putting him to bed. She could see he was tired. Three new relations in one day were quite enough for any six-year-old!

As Ashling tucked his Superman duvet around his body he looked up at her. "Mum, will they be living with us – my dad and the baby?"

"No, love," Ashling said thoughtfully. "Your dad and Fiona and Josh will be living together. And you and I will be living here together."

Dan beamed. "That's OK. I was worried it might be a bit crowded. And you know something, Mum?"

"What, love?"

"The baby might swallow my Lego and it might get stuck in his tummy. Isn't that right?"

"Yes, absolutely right." Ashling leant over and kissed him on the forehead. "Sleep well, my love."

"I love you, Mum."

"I love you too, pet." Ashling walked out of her son's bedroom with tears in her eyes. I'm so lucky to have such great kid, she told herself. And Annie was right about him accepting things.

Lying in bed that evening Ashling thought about the previous few days. So much had happened, it was hard to get a handle on it all. She hoped she had made the right decision about Owen and Dan. Only time would tell.

Chapter 34

Ashling collected Dan from Tizzy's on Wednesday at six on the button. She had gladly excused herself from a tedious bank shareholder's meeting which she was covering for the business pages of the *Courier*. She had rushed home to tidy the house, not to mention Dan, for his father's imminent visit. Owen had rung earlier. Fiona was exhausted. Josh had been up all night teething, so he was bringing the baby with him to give her some time out.

"Dan's so excited," Tizzy said smiling, handing Ashling a cup of tea in her kitchen. They were sitting at the large antique pine table watching Dan play with Cleo, his favourite of Tizzy's cats, outside the window. Ashling took some time to fill her in on the weekend's events. Tizzy was concerned for both Ashling and Dan. But she trusted the young mother's judgement. She knew that Ashling always tried to put her son's best interests before everything and she agreed that the more people that loved and cared about Dan the better in the long run. So, like Annie, Tizzy decided to be both positive and supportive about Owen and the whole situation.

"He can't wait to meet his 'baby Josh'," Tizzy said. "He hasn't stopped talking about him all day."

Ashling grimaced. "He's more excited about Josh than he is about Owen."

Tizzy put her hand on Ashling's and smiled. "It will all work out fine. Don't be nervous."

A blue car pulled up outside the house, tyres crunching on the gravel. The two women looked out.

"It's Owen – he's early," Ashling said, standing up. "And Dan's a state and the house is a mess." Ashling hadn't quite got around to cleaning either yet.

"Owen won't mind," Tizzy laughed. "He's a man, he won't even notice!"

They watched out the window as Dan ran over to the car. Owen stepped out and walked towards him. Dan looked up at him and smiled.

"Hiya, are you my dad?"

"I am," Owen said firmly. "And are you Dan?"

"Yes," Dan replied.

Owen smiled broadly. "It's good to meet you, Dan."

"Can I play with Josh?" Dan stared into the car with interest.

"Well, he's asleep at the moment. But you can later when he wakes up."

"Can I play with you then?" Dan asked.

"I'd like that."

"I'll just get my football so. You make goals and I'll be back in a minute." Dan pointed to the grass to the side of the house as he ran in the opposite direction. "Over there," he yelled.

"Right," Owen replied smiling. He walked over to the grass, took off his jumper and made one goal post. He lifted an empty terracotta flower pot from the side of the grass and made another.

Inside, Tizzy looked at Ashling. There were tears in the young woman's eyes. Tizzy smiled and gave her a hug. There was no need to say anything, the astute older woman understood.

"Mum, I got forty-four goals and Dad only got thirty-seven," Dan gabbled as Ashling pulled his mud and grass-stained white T-shirt over his head. "And he said that I could join the football club in Dalkey and that he'd take me to matches and . . ."

"Slow down, love," Ashling said smiling. "Hop into the bath like a good lad, you're covered in mud." Her son had been talking non-stop since Owen's departure a couple of hours earlier. She watched as her son stepped into the bath and lowered himself into the clear, warm water. It immediately turned pale brown.

"No bubbles, Mum?" he asked disappointed.

"No, sorry, love, we've run out. I didn't get to the shops last weekend. But I'll buy you more this week, I promise." Ashling sat down on the lowered toilet seat and scrubbed her son with his Body Shop pink elephant sponge. He really was filthy. He was covered in mud from top to toe. Once she had given him a good scrub, she retreated into her bedroom to ring Annie.

"Well, how was the visit?" Annie asked immediately as soon as she recognised the voice.

"Fine," Ashling said. "Actually it was more than fine. It was great. Josh was asleep for most of the time and it gave a chance for Owen and Dan to get to know each other. They played football in the garden for ages and then the three of us played *Operation*. Owen was really good with Dan, and they seemed to get on really well."

"And how did you feel about the whole thing?" Annie asked carefully. "Seeing Owen and Dan playing together must have been weird."

"It was a bit strange all right," Ashling agreed. "At first I was kind of sad. I suppose it made me think about how it would be if Dan had a proper family, and a dad who was around all the time. He's never had someone to play football with. I mean I've tried all right, but I've no real interest in it and Dan knows that."

"Ashling," Annie said gently. "You're doing a brilliant job with Dan. He has everything he needs. Don't go beating yourself up about the lack of a male around the house. Sure don't you have a fine big wheelie bin and doesn't Tizzy cut the grass? What else would you need a man around the house for? They only get in the way!"

Ashling laughed. "Would you stop, Annie! I'm trying to be serious."

"I know," Annie replied contritely. "I'm sorry. But I mean it. Dan has everything he needs in you. You're a brilliant mum."

"Thanks," Ashling said, smiling.

They chatted for a while about their days. Annie had had an unusual day, with a photo shoot for autumn knits. The three male models had been double-booked by their agency and Annie had pulled three young men off the street to stand in.

"You know the funniest thing," Annie said. "It was a lot easier to deal with them than the real models. They were really enthusiastic and co-operative. And they looked great too. I'm thinking of using a lot more real people as models in the future. And the shots are suberb. Really gritty and natural." Annie was on a roll – she loved her work and it showed. "I could use you and Chris . . ." Annie stopped mid-sentence. "Sorry, I forgot. Don't mind me, it was stupid. Mouth before mind."

"It's fine. I haven't thought about Chris all week. There've been so many other things going on. Dan is dying to see Owen and Josh again so we've arranged a trip to Burger King and the park next weekend."

"Sounds like fun. I'm so glad things are working out for you. You really deserve it, and I hope Owen appreciates it."

"I hope he does too," Ashling said.

On Saturday Owen collected Ashling and Dan at twelve. Dan had been sitting at the window for over an hour waiting for Owen's car to pull up the drive.

"Do you think he'll bring Josh, Mum?" he kept asking. Or "Can we go to the toyshop in the shopping centre, Mum?" Dan had his eye on a new Action Man figure who swam underwater.

As soon as he spotted the blue car he ran downstairs and pulled the front door open.

"Daddy!" he yelled, looking into the car.

Ashling followed him out. She had mixed feelings about Dan's enthuaism. On the one hand she wanted him to know his father, to love and respect him. But on the other hand she felt a little jealous. She knew this was silly. Her son was just excited at the newness of everything. After all, it wasn't every week that you met your dad for the first time. She tried to surpress her feelings and accept that Dan would bond with Owen and that she wouldn't be the only parent in his life anymore. Damn, it was hard to let go.

Ashling had had similar feelings on his first day at school. Dressing him in his blue school uniform and putting his little red rucksack on his back, she had shed more than a few tears. He wasn't her baby any more, he was now a boy. He would learn things that he could chose to tell her or not to tell her. He would have his own life outside their home, his own friends and his own activities. Ashling smiled as Owen stepped out of the car and gave Dan a warm hug.

"Hi, Owen," she said. "Where's Josh today?"

"He's with Fiona," Owen replied. Dan frowned. "It means we can do lots of things for big boys," Owen added quickly. "And I thought I might buy you a present, if that's all right with your mum." He looked at Ashling who nodded. "After all, I have a lot of birthdays to catch up on."

"And I know exactly what I'd like," Dan said with delight.

"I've no doubt you do," Owen laughed. "Now everyone into the car, the burgers and chips are waiting."

It felt strange sitting in the front of Owen's car, Ashling thought. Dan was in the back, seatbelt on and playing with an action figure. Happy families, she thought wryly. If only! She'd tried not to think about the past, about how Owen had hurt her, but it was difficult. He was Dan's father and like it or not she still had feelings for him. But she had to learn to deal with them. But it wasn't in her nature to bury her emotions, she preferred to bring them to the surface, confront them and move on. So now sitting in the car, she allowed herself to mull over the past one more time.

"Ashling . . . are you all right?" Owen's voice broke through her thoughts.

"Sorry, I was miles away."

"I was just asking you where in the shopping centre the toy shop is."

"It's on the top floor, beside the bookshop."

"That's what I said, Mummy," Dan interrupted. "He doesn't believe me."

Ashling frowned. "Don't be rude, Dan," she snapped.

"Of course I believe you," Owen said, keeping the peace. "I was double-checking, so I'd know where to park."

Dan was satisfied with this and went back to his imaginary game.

"Are you sure you're OK?" Owen whispered. "Have I done something wrong? You seem very quiet."

"Honestly, it's nothing. I'm fine."

As they stopped at the traffic-lights at the edge of Dun Laoghaire, Owen turned towards her. She was gazing out the window with tears in her eyes. It was all catching up on her, Chris and Owen and the whole thing.

"Ash, I don't know what to say. But if you want to talk about it I'm here."

"Thanks," Ashling said. "It's just been one hell of a week and I'm tired. There's nothing to worry about, I promise. Forget it."

Owen parked the car on the top of the shopping centre and they made their way down the stairs to the shops on Level three, where the toy shop was located. Dan found the coveted Action Man toy within minutes and Owen bought it for him, plus a range of Action Man accessories – clothes, hang-glider and hovercraft. Ashling was quite aware that Dan didn't need any more spoiling – she was quite good enough at that herself. But she hadn't the heart to disappoint her son. And it seemed to make Owen happy too. But what was that old expression? You can't buy love. Owen had to earn Dan's love. And in time she hoped he would.

They stuffed themselves full of junk food at Burger King before walking to Dun Laoghaire park. The playground was alive with the noise and action of hoards of children. Dan immediately made friends with a boy a little smaller than him, and they started happily playing commandos together on the wooden climbing frame.

"Kids are brilliant the way they can make friends just like that," Owen observed from the wooden bench where himself and Ashling were watching.

"They don't have the same inhibitions that adults do, I suppose," Ashling agreed.

Owen wasn't sure whether to bring it up, but he was concerned that he had made Ashling unhappy and it had upset him to see her crying earlier. "Ash," he began. "Is everything OK? I know you don't want to talk about it, but if it's something I've done I want to know. I wouldn't hurt you again for the world."

"How do I know that?" Ashling asked, her eyes flashing. She felt suddenly angry. How dare he say something like that to her after all he had done, or not done. "I'm trying really hard to trust you, but how can I? You say you've changed, that you're a different person now, and I'm trying to believe you. But it's hard."

"You're right. I'm sorry, I know this is all very hard for you. And, as I've said before, you've been brilliant. But you have to trust me this once. Please. I only have Dan's best interests at heart. I admit it, I was an immature little shit and my behaviour was beyond reprehensible. Tell me how I can make it all up to you."

Ashling began to cry silently, the tears spilling down her flushed cheeks. "No, I'm sorry. I broke up with my boyfriend last weekend and I suppose I'm feeling sorry for myself. And I do trust you. I'm just a bit tender today."

"Everyone has bad days, and you're right to get angry with me. I deserve it. I can be really selfish sometimes. And I'm sorry about the boyfriend. Come here." Owen put his arms around Ashling and held her tight. Ashling allowed herself to be hugged. It was comforting, having a man's arms around her like that, even if it was only for a brief minute. She longed for someone special to be there for her, to hold her close and to comfort her when she needed it.

"You'll find the right guy soon, Ash. You're a rock star and if things had been different . . . anyway, you deserve the best. It'll all work out, you'll see.

"Thanks." Ashling wiped the tears from her eyes with the sleeve of her fleece. They sat in silence, watching their son hanging upside-down from the monkey bars and hurling himself down the slide. It was a crisp autumn day and the sky was clear. Ashling began to feel better. Dan came running towards them, a clump of fallen leaves in his hands.

"It's raining leaves," he shouted as he threw them at Owen's head.

Owen jumped up and chased Dan. "Come here, you little messer!" Within seconds they had started an intense leaf fight. Ashling laughed as Dan stuffed leaves down the back of his dad's jeans. They ended up rolling on the grass, Dan giggling manically.

From the coffee shop overlooking the playground Mark Mulhearne intently watched the scene below him. He was waiting for his agent who lived nearby. He had noticed a couple sitting on a bench below him earlier and the thought had flashed through his mind that everyone in the park seemed to be part of a couple except him. Now he realised with a start that the woman was Ashling McKenna. The boy playing in the leaves must be Dan. And the man – it appeared to be Owen O'Sullivan, Dan's errant father, but it couldn't be, could it? Mark looked harder. It was Owen! That was a turn-up for the books.

Happy families, Mark thought to himself. Ashling looked really well, she hadn't changed a bit. It suddenly seemed like days not years that they had been apart. He suddenly missed her so much, it was like a slither of ice piercing his heart. Mark considered going over and saying hi but he couldn't bring himself to do it. Waves of regret flooded his mind suddenly. Ashling McKenna . . . he pulled his eyes away from the happy scene, put his sunglasses on and began reading *The Irish Times* lying in front of him. But he couldn't concentrate. He wanted to talk to Ashling badly but he stopped himself from raising his head again. When he finally couldn't help himself, they had gone.

"Thanks, Dad. I had a brilliant time," Dan said, jumping out of the car. "Can I show Tizzy my new toys, Mum?" He ran towards the back door of Dalkey Manor before Ashling had a chance to say no.

"He's a real bundle of energy. I don't know how you do it," Owen laughed. "No wonder you look so fit."

"You're telling me. Who needs the gym when you've got kids?" Ashling agreed.

"I had a great time. Thanks for coming with us."

"My pleasure. And thanks for being so nice, you know, in the park. I appreciate it."

Owen smiled. "That's what friends are for. That is, I hope we can be friends."

"Of course. And it'll be nice to have someone around to take away some of Dan's energy. Wait till Josh is a toddler, then you'll be in trouble. Keys down the loo and yogurt and crayon all over the walls."

"I look forward to it, sounds lovely," Owen laughed. "And it'll be great for Fiona to have someone around with some experience. Listen, I'll have to head home now, Fiona will be waiting. But I'd like to see Dan again next week if that's all right with you."

"You know it is, but thanks for asking. Maybe we could set up regular days, it would be easier for Dan, and for me too."

"Good idea. I'll ring early next week and we'll talk about it," Owen said. "And Ash?"

"Yes?"

Owen took Ashling's hand in his and held it firmly. "You're one of the strongest and most together people I've ever met. If you need help you just have to ask."

"Thanks," Ashling said, looking up at him. This time she believed him.

Chapter 35

"I saw Ashling McKenna today in the park," Mark told his sister, trying to keep his voice level and calm. They were sitting at the kitchen table, steaming mugs of coffee in front of them.

"That reminds me," Susan said. "I bumped into her at a ball recently in Homewood Castle. She was asking for you."

"Was there anyone with her?" Mark asked, unable to contain his interest.

"Yes, there was. A tall young man, he looked a little younger than her. It was a fancy dress ball so I didn't get a good look at him, mind you."

"Oh," Mark replied, disappointed. Thinking about it on the way back to Wicklow, he had almost convinced himself that Ashling and Owen were just bringing Dan out for the day. But if Susan had seen them together at a ball they were obviously sharing more than an interest in Dan.

"Why?" Susan asked. Mark and Ashling had been

very close at one stage, before he had left for Boston. She had always liked Ashling and had hoped that some day the couple might become more than friends. But things never worked out the way you planned.

"I was just wondering. Anyway she looked well."

"How is her job going? Is she still in the *Courier*?"

"I don't know. I didn't talk to her."

Susan was confused. "How do you mean?"

Mark was silent for a few minutes. But it made no difference now. He couldn't turn back the clock. She was with Owen now and that was all that mattered.

"Mark . . . Mark! Earth calling Mark, come in, Mark."

"Sorry, I was miles away. Ashling was with Owen and Dan and I didn't like to intrude."

"I don't think the man at the ball was called Owen, but I could be wrong," Susan said. Susan could sense that her brother was troubled but she didn't want to pry. If he wanted to talk about it he would. She sipped her coffee and waited, giving him time.

"I suppose I've never really got Ashling out of my system. We were so close and I could never understand why . . . anyway, I suppose seeing her today just brought it all back." Mark stood up abruptly. "I'm going for a walk. I'll help with dinner when I get back."

Susan watched the solitary figure of her brother stomp down the lane. He definitely had a load on his mind – his shoulders were hunched over and his hands were thrust deep into his pockets. Susan was worried about him. Seeing Ashling seemed to have brought back a lot of memories. After all, he had been through a lot in

Boston what with the book and Kerry and all. Maybe it was natural for him to be a bit out of sorts. But she worried that he had too much time on his hands to think. Being a writer was certainly not a job she would choose. All that sitting on your own, trying to motivate yourself. Give me farming any day, Susan thought to herself, as she poured Mark's untouched coffee down the sink.

Thoughts went racing through Mark's head as he marched down the lane, thoughts that had lain dormant for many years. Life wasn't exactly going to plan at the moment. What if he and Ashling had managed to keep in touch? Would things be different now? Should he talk to her? Perhaps it wasn't too late. But she had her own life now. He hadn't been a part of it for many years. Maybe he would bump into her at the St John's reunion.

Sally Hunter would be at the reunion too – she was always good for a laugh. Mark smiled, remembering some of the mad times they'd had together. And no-one kissed quite like Sally!

Shit, the reunion, Mark was suddenly jolted back to earth. It's only two weeks away, he thought, and I haven't written the speech.

And to top it all he was sure that Eve would be there. Another confrontation with her was more than he could take at this stage. But she had looked well. And he wondered in time he could warm to her again? After all – they had been very much in love . . .

* * *

"What do you think, Susan? Does it sound a bit 'new age-y'?"

"Read me the Emerson quote again," Susan said. "I liked that."

"Only if you give me your honest opinion on the rest."

"Agreed." Susan had always loved being read to. As a child she had often made Mark read her chunks of her favourite poems or books.

Mark cleared his throat and began to read his speech.

"Well?" he asked when he'd finished. He was getting anxious about the reunion. Since Saturday he had thrown himself into writing his speech, reading countless books of quotations and books on public speaking. To be honest it was good to have something to keep his mind off Ashling.

"Some of it is excellent but . . ."

"Not the dreaded but!" Mark exclaimed.

"I think it could be a little more personal, that's all. You've used a lot of 'the writer' in the third person the whole way through and very few 'I's. I think people would like to hear more about how it feels to be a writer, where your ideas come from, that sort of thing. And don't forget to say how excited you are to be back in Ireland again. Irish people love to be reminded how wonderful living in Ireland is!"

Mark smiled. "You're very cynical, Susan. But I think you may be right on the personal thing. I'm still playing around with ideas at the moment. Next thing is hiring a suit."

"Is it black tie?" Susan asked.

"Yes, why?"

"Pat has a tux and I'm sure it would fit you fine. It's a nice one too and it only sees the light of day for weddings so he hasn't worn it much."

"That sounds perfect."

"Why don't you try it on now? That way if it needs to be altered at all there is plenty of time."

Upstairs she unzipped the tuxedo from its suit bag and found a dress shirt, cufflinks and a black bow tie and handed them to Mark who was watching her with interest.

"Are you sure Pat won't mind?"

"Of course not."

Mark put on the shirt and suit and looked at himself in the mirror in his bedroom. He looked reasonable, he thought, a little pale perhaps, but he'd have to get used to being paler now he was living in Ireland again. He definitely needed a haircut though. The back of his hair was creeping over the collar of the shirt. He wanted to look his best. What was it about school reunions, he wondered? He was unnaturally nervous about what people would think of him. He wanted to appear the picture of success and happiness to his classmates. But did it really matter? He hadn't really kept in touch with anyone from school, so what did he care what they thought. But he knew that, as a speaker, all eyes would be on him. Shit, he thought to himself, I should have turned it down. Who am I to stand up in front of the class of 1990 and talk about my success?

"How does it look?" Susan walked into his room and gave a wolf whistle. "You scrub up well. It fits perfectly. Turn around to me for a second while I do up the bow tie."

Mark could never get his fingers around do-it-yourself bow ties. At the debs Sally had completed it for him.

"Remember the night of my debs, sis?"

"You brought Sally Hunter, didn't you?"

"That's right."

"A bit of a dancing-on-the-tables kind of girl, wasn't she?"

Mark grinned. "That's right. I hope she's at the reunion. Liven the place up a bit."

"Mummy, we're back," Shay yelled up the stairs. Seconds later two familiar heads popped around Mark's door. The boys had been walking the dogs with their dad.

"Uncle Mark, you look like James Bond," Shay said admiringly. "Can you come and play spying with us outside?"

"Not in my suit, he won't," Pat laughed, ruffling Shay's hair affectionately. "It looks good on you, Mark."

"Thanks, I hope you don't mind me borrowing it for the reunion."

"Not at all, I'm glad to see it's coming to some use. And I'm bloody glad it's not me who has to wear it. I hate monkey suits."

"Why is it a monkey suit, Dad? Do you turn into a monkey when you wear it?"

"I hope not, Shay," Mark laughed. "Although it would be a good excuse not to turn up – sorry, I've turned into a monkey."

"Sure don't we have our very own monkeys in this very house," Susan smiled, looking at her sons. "Come on, you two, you can help me set the table for dinner."

"Are you nervous about your speech?" Pat asked when Susan and the boys had left the room.

"Yes, I guess I am," Mark agreed.

"Sure you'll be grand," Pat encouraged. "Won't you know them all?"

"That's what I'm worried about," Mark said ominously.

Chapter 36

"Sally Hunter, what have you done? Poor Kevin has just broken the news to us. Come home immediately, young lady!" April bellowed down Jean's phone.

"Mum, what are you talking about? What news?"

"Don't act the innocent with me! You know jolly well what I'm talking about."

Sally sighed. "Mum, I really don't. Tell me what's happened."

"Kevin's just gone and broken it off with Emma, that's all," April said angrily. "He says she's not the girl he thought she was and he's worried about marrying into a family with – how did he put it – 'loose moral fibre and lack of common decorum'. He thinks that you're a bad influence on Emma and he's concerned that she'll turn out like you!"

"He said what?" Sally spluttered. "The little fecker."

"Sally," her mother scolded. "Less of that gutter-talk.

388

Did you or did you not tell her that she should having fun and enjoying herself while she's young?"

"Yes, but . . ."

"And Kevin tells me you spiked his fruit juice."

"Well, I guess so but . . ."

"And you encouraged her to lure him into her room."

Sally couldn't believe that Kevin had told her mother all the gory details. "Now come on, that was nothing to do with me. That's unfair, Emma did that by herself."

"Um," April muttered doubtfully. "Anyway, the damage is done now."

Sally was beginning to lose her cool. "How dare he? He should get down off his high horse. Sanctimonious baldy! He should be thanking his lucky stars for such a babe of a girlfriend. He's an idiot. Emma's well rid of him."

"There's no need for that now. And besides, I think if Emma apologises Kevin might forgive her."

"What do you mean – if she apologises? It's him that should be apologising. To Emma and to me," Sally said loudly, trying to keep her cool. "And why should she marry him now? He's just proved what a boring old fart he is! She's better off on her own."

"Sally, I won't tell you again. Language, please."

"Sorry, Mum. But I can't believe you still want Emma to marry him. Can't you see she's not happy? Isn't it obvious to you?"

The line went deadly silent for a long second.

"Sally," April began in a steely tone, "the only thing that is obvious to me is that everything between them was fine until you came home. Now explain that."

Sally sighed again. There was no way she was going to win this one. Her mother was set on making her a scapegoat.

April continued. "I want you to come home and talk to Emma. Make her see sense."

"I don't know if I can do that," Sally said honestly. "I don't think Kevin's the right man for her and I won't lie."

"You'll come home right now, young lady, and you'll do exactly what I tell you to!"

Sally took a deep breath. "I'm sorry, Mum, but you can't talk to me like that. I'm not a child anymore and I think what you're doing is wrong. Emma's not happy with Kevin and if you talked to her properly you'd know that. She's scared of you but I'm not. I'm staying right here."

April slammed down the phone. How dare she! Sally had always been trouble but this was the limit. If she couldn't make her see sense then James would. She made a quick call to Jean's mother, for the second time that morning, and then called her husband in from the garden.

"James, James, you have to go and collect Sally! She's at Jean's flat in Donnybrook. I got the address from her mum."

"Is there any hurry, dear? I'm in the middle of deadheading the roses."

April Hunter focused her eyes on his. They were sparking with anger and two patches of deep red inflamed her cheeks. He paled. He hadn't seen her this physically angry for a long time. Not since Sally had dropped the bombshell about dropping out of college, in fact. James was relieved that Emma and Kevin had broken up. He'd never really warmed to the chap. Something too serious about him, bossy too. Reminded him of someone . . .

"James, hurry up, please. It's important." He picked up his car keys from the hall table and grabbed his green Barbour jacket. Twenty minutes later he was in Donnybrook, outside Jean's flat. He turned off the engine and sat in the Volvo for several minutes, mulling over what he was going to say to his daughter. Finally he made a decision. He started up the car again and drove back to The Rectory. It's about time that things changed around here, he thought to himself.

"He what?" Sally asked incredulously.

"OK, I'll start at the beginning," Emma said excitedly. "Dad walked in the door and Mum was waiting in the hall. She asked him where you were and he said – get this – 'April, into the kitchen please, we to have talk', in a very un-Dad-like voice."

"And . . . go on," Sally encouraged. She was still at Jean's flat and was listening intently to her sister on the other end of the telephone.

"Well, I listened at the door of course. It was about

me after all. Dad was telling Mum how he'd been thinking on the way over to Jean's to collect you and he thought you were right. Kevin wasn't the right guy for me and she was wrong to interfere."

"Wow," Sally drew her breath in. "Did Mum have a fit with him?"

"He didn't stop there, Sally. He went on to say that Mum only wanted the wedding for herself, to impress the neighbours, that she wasn't thinking about my long-term happiness at all and that she was being overbearing and selfish."

"No!" Sally exclaimed. Her dad had never stood up to his wife in this way before. What a turn-up for the books! "And did Mum not eat him alive?"

"That's the funny thing," Emma continued. "She stayed quiet the whole way through, letting Dad speak."

"She was probably too shocked to say anything," Sally smiled.

"And then he said that Mum had to apologise to you, because it wasn't your fault at all and that you'd only had my best interests at heart."

"And what did she say?" Sally asked. Her mum had never apologised to her for anything, especially when she was in the wrong.

"I'm not sure. I think she may have been crying. She was very quiet."

Sally sighed. "I'd better come home. But if Mum's waiting for me at the front door with a wooden stake I wouldn't be too surprised."

Emma laughed. "April the Vampire Slayer – it has a certain ring to it!"

Sally stood at the front door of The Rectory. Damn, she thought to herself, I don't have a key. She rang the doorbell. A contrite-looking April opened the door.

Her eyes were red and her cheeks were flushed pink.

Sally was taken aback. "Mum, " she said gently and before she could stop herself she started apologising. "I'm sorry, I didn't mean to be rude. I just . . ."

"No," her mother interrupted. "It's me who should be sorry. I had no right to speak to you like that. You were quite right. Emma should be on her own at the moment. I see that now. You were only trying to help her."

"It's OK, Mum. Let's forget about it. As long as Emma's all right about the whole business, then it's grand."

Emma had been listening at the top of the stairs. She made her way down the stairs into the hall, her hair loosely piled on top of her head, wearing a tight pink top and black Capri pants. "I'm bloody relieved, to be honest. What was I thinking of? I'm only twenty-four after all. Years of partying in me yet!"

April looked at her younger daughter. She was wearing make-up and some sort of glittery 'disco' type stuff on her cheeks. April bit her lip. Now wasn't the time to criticise Emma's appearance. After all, her daughter was also wearing a broad smile and looked carefree and happy for the first time in ages.

James came into the hall from the garden, where he'd been cutting the grass. "How are my favourite girls?" he asked, looking at his wife.

"I think we're going to be fine, Dad," Sally replied.

"Where are we going tonight?" Emma asked that evening. "I'm gagging to go clubbing, I haven't been out in an age."

Sally was nervous. It was nice having the old Emma back, but she could smell trouble.

Kevin had called in earlier, asking for his ring back. "Scabby bastard," Sally had muttered, as Emma had handed back the 'tastefully' tiny diamond engagement ring. He had also asked for all the CDs he had given, or 'lent' her, as he had delightfully put it. Emma had put all the Elton John, Neil Diamond and Queen CDs in a plastic shopping bag and handed them to Kevin.

"To be honest, Kevin," Emma had told him, smiling, "they're not really my thing. I'm not mad on ageing rockers. I like dance music, something with a bit of bite. And while you're at it, you can have this back." She thrust the leather document case he had bought her in his face. "Where I'm going I won't need a briefcase."

"And where are you going?" he had spluttered.

Emma was enjoying herself now. "I haven't quite decided yet. Maybe Sydney or Perth. Or New York or Paris. Somewhere exciting and fun and a million miles away from you!"

Kevin had looked at her in astonishment. "I'm glad I've found out what you are really like before I married you."

"And I'm glad I've come to my senses!" Emma retorted. "Goodbye, Kevin, close the door behind you!"

Sally smiled thoughtfully."There's a party on in Mount Merrion, one of the guys from the sailing club. How about that?"

"Will there be lots of men there?" Emma asked, grinning wickedly.

Sally laughed. "Yes, but I can't vouch for their morals."

"Excellent!" Emma exclaimed. "Lead on, McDuff!"

Chapter 37

"And who's this lovely young lady?" Shane's brother asked. Alex was just nineteen and as cute as a button, with a shock of white-blonde hair, piercing blue eyes and perfect sallow skin.

"This is my sister Emma, Alex," Sally said.

"Come and dance, Emma." Alex whisked her into his arms and spun her around the dance floor. Sally smiled. She loved seeing Emma enjoying herself.

"Hey, Sal!" Jean called from the far side of the room. Sally made her way towards Jean and Peter who had taken up residence beside the drinks table.

"Red or white, darling?" Peter asked in his poshest voice. "Or a little spot of Red Bull and vodka perhaps?"

"That'll hit the spot," Sally replied. "Make it a double."

Peter splashed a large swig of vodka into a glass and filled it with the potent 'red lemonade'. "Here you go, get it down you."

"I see Emma and Alex have hit it off. Does she know what age he is? And what about Kevin?" Jean asked, a little confused.

Sally laughed and watched her sister, who now had her hands on Alex's tight boyish buttocks. "I don't think that would bother Emma at the moment." She filled Jean and Peter in on the day's events.

"So Emma's young, free and single again?" Peter asked, grinning.

Jean dug him with her elbow. "Don't get any ideas, Peter," she laughed.

He leant over and kissed her on the cheek. "As if I would, darling. I know you'd kill me."

"Dead right," Jean replied smiling.

"Want to dance?"

Sally turned to look at the tall man standing beside her. He didn't look a day over twenty, shaggy brown hair framing his strong-jawed face. He was wearing a dark blue cord shirt, and striking square-rimmed glasses framed his eyes.

"Sure," Sally replied, taking his hand. "I'm Sally."

"George," he said, pulling her towards him. "I hope you like Salsa."

The heady strains of The Buena Vista Social Club filled the room. Sally loved Salsa and had become quite an accomplished Salsa dancer in Antigua. Herself and Ginny had often danced on table tops in the local bar. In fact the music was making her feel quite nostalgic. George was an excellent dancer. What he lacked in technique he made up for in enthusiasm, throwing himself into the music, waving his long arms and expressive hands in the air and moving his supple body against hers. Sally was really enjoying herself. She noticed that Emma and Alex were now wrapped around each other on the couch, holding hands and gazing into each other's eyes.

"Hey, babe," George whispered into her ear. "You dance like an angel. Have I seen you dancing in my dreams?"

Sally smiled. Boys, you had to love them. George, it turned out, was a twenty-five-year-old teacher. Young but legal, Sally thought to herself.

"So, what do you do when you're not dancing?" George asked. They were taking a break from their energetic dancing. The garden was illuminated by tall candles and lanterns on bamboo sticks. Strings of white fairy-lights twinkled on the wooden garden shed in which they were sitting on deck-chairs, surveying the grass and flower beds through the two fly-splattered windows. It was a magically clear evening. They had brought a bottle of vodka with them and a few cans of Red Bull and were filling their glasses at increasingly frequent intervals.

"Nothing, at the moment," Sally answered honestly. "I've just come back from the Caribbean. I'm going to take some time out to think about what I want to do."

George nodded sagely. "You're dead right. No point

in rushing into work for the sake of it. Life's too short to waste time doing something you don't like."

Sally smiled. This guy was uncomplicated, nice and cute too. He took her hand and ran his fingers up and down the inside of her palm, sending shivers up her spine. She jumped as he put one of her fingers in his mouth and began to caress it with his tongue. She turned her head towards his and kissed him firmly on the mouth. His lips and mouth tasted deliciously of Red Bull. She moved her tongue over his teeth, taking his upper lip between hers and sucking gently. George moaned. He kissed her back urgently, holding her head in his hands. Sally pushed herself off her deckchair and lay her body on top of his. But the combined weights were too much for the striped canvas chair, which gave way, depositing them on the wooden floor of the garden shed with a bump.

"Shit," Sally exclaimed, laughing. "Are you all right?"

George grinned beneath her. "Apart from a bruised arse, I think so. Come here, you vixen." He pulled Sally towards him, his hand climbing under her black top and purple cardigan and cupping her breast. He began to caress her gently, moving his fingers over her firm flesh. Sally moved her body over his, feeling him responding and hardening underneath her. George's hands turned their attention to her skirt, and soon the purple velvet was ruched up around her waist, like a thick belt. Sally moaned as George crept his warm fingers inside her lace G-string and began to explore. Shit, he's good, Sally thought to herself, her mind turning to jelly. He stopped for a second and pulled out his wallet.

"Will I get a condom?" he whispered, smiling at Sally.

"Good idea," she said, unbuttoning his jeans. She pushed up his shirt, revealing a slim, toned chest and ran her hands over his skin, stopping just millimetres above his hard-on. He had a great torso, firm and smooth. Sally hated great big hairy brutes.

She tried not to giggle as she watched him rolling the condom over the taut skin. Condoms were so damn ungainly – it all seemed so inelegant, the whole rubber thing. George had chosen a particularly nice yellow one, banana-flavoured and scented. Sally could smell the sickly sweet aroma. She had had a run-in with a luminous willy in the Caribbean, quite an experience.

"What are you smiling at?" George asked when he had the condom in place.

"You," Sally smiled. "Come here." She pulled him towards her, taking a firm hold of his banana hardness and guiding it into her waiting body. She gasped as he entered her. He moved slowly and smoothly, building up speed and pressure and Sally cried out as she came, waves of pleasure sweeping over her. Afterwards, she fell contentedly asleep on the wooden floor, her arms wrapped around a gently snoring George.

"Sally, Sally, are you out here?"

Sally sat up. It was getting light outside and George

was still snoring beneath her, trousers still undone. She climbed off him, careful not to wake him and stepped outside, pulling her skirt down and running her hands through her hair.

Emma was outside, looking at her in amazement.

"What were you doing in there?" she asked, smiling.

Sally stood back as her sister peered into the half-light of the shed. "Cute," Emma proclaimed. "Not as cute as Alex of course."

Sally smiled. "And where is the delectable teenager?"

Emma blushed. "He's asleep on the sofa. I came out to see if you were OK. I saw you go out here earlier."

"I'm grand," Sally said.

"I can see that," Emma replied. "You look like the cat that got the cream. Lucky bitch."

"Are we heading?" Sally asked.

"You can't leave your man in the shed."

"Why not?"

"Well, he'll wonder where you are."

Sally smiled. Like hell she couldn't. "Let's walk, it's a beautiful morning and it might help clear my head."

"You're awful. Has anyone ever told you that?"

"Yep."

They started walking towards Blackrock, stopping in a garage to buy icecream and water, Sally's hangover cure.

"Alex works in the Irish Sailing School in Dun Laoghaire. He was saying that one of their instructors was leaving and they need someone."

"At this time of the year?" Sally asked.

"Apparently they teach a lot of secondary school classes, Transition Year mainly. Would you be interested Sal? You have your instructor's cert."

Sally thought for a minute. "Maybe. It sounds interesting."

"I have Alex's number – you can give him a ring about it."

"Oh, you have his number, do you?" Sally asked her sister. "Are you going to see him again?"

Emma blushed. "I think so."

Sally put her arm around her sister. "You don't waste any time. We're a terrible pair."

Emma smiled. "It's good to have you home."

"Hi, Alex, this is Sally, Emma's sister."

"Hi, Sally, she said you might be ringing. You have your instructor's cert, I hear, and to be honest we're a bit desperate. Any chance you could start tomorrow? One of our girls left on Friday unexpectedly and we're really stuck."

Sally smiled. Why not? It wasn't as if she had anything else to do and she might even enjoy it.

"Sure, what time do you want me down?"

"Thanks, Sally. You're a lifesaver. Come down at around half eight and I'll fill you in on the kids and the boats."

"Fine, I'll see you then."

"And Sally?"

402

"Yes?"

"Tell Emma I'll ring her tonight."

"Who was that on the phone?" Jamie asked from the kitchen. Sally joined him at the table and poured herself a glass of orange juice.

"Alex, Emma's latest."

Jamie whistled. "She doesn't waste any time does she? Bloody hell. Why were you talking to him?"

"Don't be so nosy," Sally scolded. "If you must know he asked me to teach sailing in the sailing school he works in."

"And are you going to do it?" Jamie asked.

"Yes, for a while anyway. Then we'll see. How are you this fine day? Were you out last night?"

Jamie looked at Sally carefully. "Yes, myself and Red were in The George."

"What were you doing there?" she asked.

Jamie stared at his glass. "Hanging out."

Sally thought for a second. The only time she'd been in The George was with a gay friend from college who had dragged her along to the Gay Bingo night. Suddenly she had a thought. No way. They couldn't be!

"What are you telling me?" she asked.

Jamie raised his head. He was more than a little embarrassed. He presumed his sister knew. Or guessed, at least. "Do I have to spell it out?"

Sally started laughing. She couldn't help herself. She'd thought that Red had been interested in her! No wonder he'd asked so many questions about her brother! Of course, it all made sense now. God, she was thick sometimes. And delusional.

"Why are you laughing?" Jamie asked. "It's not funny."

"Sorry Jamie, it's just I thought Red was into me not you. He kept asking all about the family the other night."

Jamie brightened. "So it's OK?"

"What are you talking about? It's a big loss for the female race, of course, and it'll take some getting used to. But you've got good taste at least. Red's very cute!"

Jamie grinned delightedly. "Thanks, Sal."

"Does Emma know?"

"I don't think so."

"She won't have a problem with it," Sally assured him. "Tell her. But just one thing, Jamie."

"Yes?"

"I wouldn't tell Mum at the moment. She's got enough on her plate what with Emma and Kevin and all."

"Sally, I don't know if I'll ever be able to tell Mum," Jamie sighed. "It's not exactly the kind of thing she'd be able to boast about to the Mother's Union."

Sally grimaced. "I suppose not. How long have you been . . ."

"Gay?" Jamie added. Sally nodded. "Always, I guess. I've never really felt at ease with girls at all."

"What about Rona Gallagher?" Sally asked. Rona and Jamie had been together for nearly a year.

"We were more like best friends than anything else," Jamie said. "Nice girl, but she did nothing for me."

"And have you had boyfriends?" Sally asked. Had she ever imagined herself asking such a question!

Jamie smiled. Typical Sally. This was proving to be less difficult than he thought it would be. "A few, but no-one serious. It's not that easy to meet the right type of guy."

"Tell me about it," Sally said wryly.

Chapter 38

"Hey, Miss, you're better looking than our last teacher, Lisa. She was a dog."

"Thanks, Marcus," Sally said uncertainly. It was her first day of work in the sailing school and she'd been given a group of four teenage boys from a local school to teach the rudiments of boat handling to. No mean feat. This particular group, Alex had warned her earlier, had forced their last teacher's resignation. Lisa Godkin had been well out of her depth. A serious, quiet young woman, the boys had shocked her with their fruity language and stories of joy-riding and shop-lifting.

Sally had been very apprehensive when she met the boys. They had looked her up and down, some of their eyes lingering on her chest a little too long for comfort, in her opinion.

"They're a difficult bunch, I won't lie to you," Alex had said earlier. "But one of them in particular, Tommo, is really keen to learn. The key is to earn their respect and not be frightened of them. Poor Lisa didn't know how to deal with them at all."

Sally had coughed nervously. "Alex, they're not, um . . . dangerous, are they? I'm not going to get stabbed or anything?"

Alex had paused for a second. "It's only happened once and that was a male teacher." He had smiled on seeing Sally's shocked expression. "Jeez, Sally I'm only joking. No-one's been stabbed, ever. The worst thing they've ever done is pushed Lisa in and sailed off without her."

Sally looked doubtful. "I guess that's OK then."

She had led them down to their boat which was moored in the Coal Harbour in Dun Laoghaire. She climbed down the wall into the boat, ignoring the boys who were pretending to push each other into the water and shouting.

"Get off, ya fecker!" Niall, a short lump of a boy with ginger hair and freckles, yelled at Tommo, who was flicking the main sheet at him.

"Right, you lot, into the boat now please," Sally commanded, sounding a lot more self-confident than she felt. "You're not scared of a bit of wind, are you?" It was blowing a good force four and the wind was beginning to whistle in the halyards. "Ever capsized?" The boat they were going out in had a keel and wasn't going to turn over in any circumstances but the boys didn't know that.

"Lisa said these boats couldn't capsize, Miss," Tommo said looking at her suspiciously.

"Let's go out and see, will we?" Sally said. "Last one in the boat's a chicken!"

The boys scrambled into the boat, Tommo eagerly sitting beside Sally. She showed them how to hoist the sails and allowed Tommo to sail the boat out the difficult Hell's Gates, as the mouth of the Coal Harbour was known. Two of the lads, Anto and Deco, both small and wiry with scowling faces, sat at the front of the boat, smoking insolently. Sally chose to ignore them. They were quiet enough and as long as they kept the cigarettes away from the sails they could blacken their lungs all they liked.

"Lisa never let me do this, Miss," Tommo stated, delighted with himself. "She said it was too dangerous."

"You're doing well," Sally said, praying that he wouldn't hit one of the expensive cruisers in the harbour. They sailed out into the harbour. "Right gybe now, Tommo."

"Are you sure, Miss?" Tommo replied anxiously. "Annie never gybed on windy days."

Sally smiled. "Tommo, Lisa's not here now, is she?"

Tommo grinned. "I like you, Miss."

Sally felt warm inside. It was stupid being pleased by a spotty teenager liking her, but it felt good. She felt she was doing something useful for once in her life. Sally explained to the boys about tell-tales and how to spot wind shifts. She also told them all about Antigua and Tommo was well impressed.

"Jeez, Miss, that sounds cool. Do'ya think I could do that one day?"

"Tommo, you learn all you can about boats and sailing and I don't see why not."

"They wouldn't want someone like me, Miss," he had continued. "They'd want some posh kid."

"Tommo, they wouldn't care who you were in the Caribbean as long as you worked hard."

"Is that right, Miss?" Niall asked, listening in to the conversation.

"Yes," Sally had said firmly. "And please call me Sally, you're making me feel old."

"Sure you're ancient," Tommo said smiling. "At least twenty-five."

Sally filled a bailer full of cold seawater and dumped it unceremoniously over his head.

"You shouldn't have done that, Miss," he said, handing the helm to Niall. Sally shrieked as he put his arm in the water and flicked water all over her. Soon the two of them were splashing each other and shrieking wildly.

"Watch me smoke!" Anto yelled. "You'll put it out."

But they ignored him.

After another hour's sailing they walked back up to the sailing school, soaked and shivering, but laughing. Alex met them at the door.

"Are you all right, Sally?" he asked nervously, noticing her wet hair and damp oil-skins.

"Grand," Sally smiled.

"Can we have Sally tomorrow, mister?" Tommo asked Alex. "She's fuckin' cool."

A familiar figure walked into the staff room of the sailing school at lunch-time. Sally buried her head in the latest copy of *Afloat* magazine and prayed she was seeing things.

"Sally, this is George, one of the teacher's in St Ronan's. You had some of his boys out this morning," Alex said.

Sally raised her head. It was him! She hoped she didn't have coleslaw on the edges of her mouth. She'd just finished tucking into a large cheese and salad roll.

George smiled and put out his hand. "Nice to meet you," he said, grinning at her knowingly.

Sally blushed. Saturday evening came back to her in all its colourful detail, banana aromas and all. "Hi, George," she managed.

"The boys really liked you. I'm impressed. Usually they moan about getting wet and cold. But they had a blast this morning, thanks," he said.

"No problem," she said, smiling. "They're good kids. I look forward to having them out next week."

"Will you be working here long?" he asked, with interest. He had been disappointed on waking up on Sunday morning. He had really taken to Sally – she was a true original and sexy as shit. He'd been a little miffed that she'd done a legger, to be honest.

Sally looked at Alex. "It depends."

Alex smiled. "Sally, if you've kept the St Ronan's lads from killing each other you can cope with anything. I'd say you'll be running this place in no time at all."

"Maybe we can go for lunch next week, if you're free?" George asked her, his brown eyes lingering on her tanned, salt-encrusted face.

"Maybe," Sally replied, eyes twinkling. "We'll see."

Sally staggered in the door of The Rectory, her stripey McWilliam bag weighed down with wet oilys and sailing boots. Emma came out of the kitchen to greet her.

"How was your first day?" she asked. "Would you like some coffee?"

"Love some," Sally said, dumping her bag at the back door. She'd hang out her dripping gear later. "I'm knackered."

"Well?" Emma asked again. "How was it?"

Sally grinned. Emma was always so impatient. "Good. I liked it. The kids were a bit of a handful at first but grand once you got to know them. And you'll never guess who I met."

"Who?" Emma asked.

"The guy from the party – George. He was the one of the group's teachers."

Emma smiled. "Alex did say something about that all right."

"I'll kill you. I can't believe you didn't say anything to me, you bitch," Sally scolded good-humouredly. "Anyway, we might be going for lunch next week."

"Sounds good," Emma said. "And how is Alex?"

"Besotted," Sally admitted. "I hate to say it, Emma, but he's mad about you. Didn't stop asking about you all day. In fact I think he only gave me the job because of you."

Emma grinned broadly. "So now we both have toy boys."

Sally raised her coffee cup. "To toy boys!" she said.

"To toy boys," Emma agreed, clinking her mug against her sister's. "Long may they last! In every way!"

"Hey, you can bring George to your school thingy," Emma said. "The reunion yoke."

"The guy's a teacher," Sally reminded her sister. "He's hardly going to want to go to a school function. And anyway I'm quite looking forward to meeting some old friends," she added cryptically.

"Sounds interesting," Emma said, her curiosity aroused. "Anyone in particular?"

"That would be telling," Sally said. "But come to think of it, it's less than two weeks away. What the hell am I going to wear?"

"You could wear my nightie again," Emma laughed. "But it's a great excuse to go shopping. How about Thursday night?"

"You're on," Sally said. They hadn't been shopping together for years. It would be fun.

Emma collected her sister from the sailing school on Thursday. Alex had been delighted to see her, thinking Emma was paying a surprise visit. He had been disappointed to learn that the girls had planned a shopping trip without him.

"I'll carry the bags, I'll be very useful," he had cajoled. Emma had been playing it very cool with him, keeping their phone calls short and sweet and refusing to see him before the weekend. He was gagging for her attention at this stage.

"Lover boy has it bad," Sally commented, shutting the door of Emma's Peugeot 206.

Emma smiled. "Great, isn't it?"

They drove into Dublin, chatting about work and men. Sally was looking forward to seeing George next week, although she was loathe to admit it.

"Right," Emma said after they had parked the car in the Dawson Street carpark. "What type of dress are you looking for?"

Sally thought for a moment. "Something dramatic and different but classy. Not black."

"A little pink dress?" Emma asked. "Or red perhaps. Something strappy?"

Sally nodded.

"I know just the place." Emma frogmarched her sister into several different shops before they finally found the perfect dress in Brown Thomas. It was a pink satin dress by Miu Miu, tight and fitted on top, with tiny pink ribbon straps and a dramatic, floaty purple and dark pink chiffon skirt. It clung to Sally in all the right places and suited her tanned skin to a T.

"It's a bit expensive," Sally grumbled, looking at the price tag.

"But it looks like a dream," Emma said. "You have to buy it. It's an investment. And I guarantee there'll be no-one there in a dress to touch it."

Sally sighed. "I bet they'll all be wearing really exclusive Chanel or Dior dresses. The women are probably all married to fabulously rich husbands and do nothing all day but paint their nails and do lunch.

413

And I'll have absolutely nothing to say to any of them."

"Jean will be there, won't she?" Emma asked. "And Peter and Shane and the guys you used to sail with. And isn't Mark Mulhearne speaking or something?"

Sally smiled. "He is."

Emma studied her sister's face carefully. "You used to go out with him, didn't you? And then you went out with his friend in UCD – what was his name?"

Sally winced. Emma made her relationship with Mark sound so inconsequential. As if he was only one in a long line of boyfriends. "I brought Mark to my Debs."

"Did you?" Emma asked. "There were so many boys and so many Debs, I find it hard to remember."

Sally punched her sister in the arm and laughed. "Listen, Miss Vestal Virgin, less of that, thank you. I'm a changed woman now."

Emma smiled. "I must ask George what sort of woman you are."

Chapter 39

On the way home in Emma's car, shopping bag at her feet, Sally thought about her Debs.

"Sally, Mark is here," April Hunter had called up the stairs that October evening, ten years ago. "Don't keep him waiting. Your Dad has the camera ready."

Sally pulled the black velvet bodice of her dress up again and looked in the mirror. Her hair was backcombed to within one inch of its life and held in place by a large black velvet bow. Long, droopy diamante earrings sparkled in her ears, pierced three times in each lobe. Her mother never allowed her to wear more than one earring in each ear, so she had two more pairs of little plastic button earrings, black and red, in her bag ready to insert into her ears when she was out of her mother's sight. Sally didn't see what the problem was – they were her ears after all – but her mother said it looked 'common'. The skirt of her dress was red taffeta, held stiff by layers of net underneath. On her feet were black suede stilettos and she had black tights on, covered with a pattern of little bows and with tiny diamante bows at the back of each ankle.

Emma had done her make-up. Her lips glistened with pearly pink lipstick. Emma had carefully applied bright blue eyeliner inside her eyelids and the same bright blue mascara on her eyelashes. Two diagonal streaks of carefully chiselled blusher completed the look. Sally pulled on her black elbow-length nylon lace gloves and looked at herself in the mirror. A mixture of Madonna and Kate Bush – excellent. Pretty but provocative. She grabbed her black velvet bag and her herringbone three-quarter-length coat and made her way down the stairs.

Mark whistled as her saw her. "You look great, Sally," he said admiringly. He handed her a white rose corsage and a box of Milk Tray chocolates. Sally thanked him and pinned the flower onto her dress.

"You look great too," Sally replied. Mark's tuxedo fitted him perfectly, figure-huggingly tight around thighs and backside, and the red satin cummerbund, with matching bow tie and handkerchief were very flash.

April clicked her tongue. "I presume you're going to brush your hair, young lady?" she asked.

James stepped in. "Mark, Sally, can you go into the sitting-room for a photo, please?" He took two quick photographs in front of the good curtains, sensing the couple's impatience. "I'm sure you two youngsters will want to get on now. Have a good night."

A taxi was waiting outside to take Sally and Mark to

Blackrock Castle Hotel where the Debs was being held. As soon as they sat in and began to move away Sally whipped her extra earrings out of her bag and pushed and twisted them into her ear-lobes.

"For fuck's sake, my mother would drive you mad. Do you want some vodka? I have some in here." Sally pulled out a small naggin of Smirnoff and unscrewed the top. She took a hefty swig and handed the bottle to Mark.

"I'm OK thanks, Sal," he said, handing it back to her. "I'll wait for the pints."

They drove to Jean's house to pick her and Peter up. Jean was almost in tears getting into the car. "I told you to get me a white flower, Peter. Red clashes with my dress." Jean was wearing a salmon-coloured taffeta dress with a puff-ball skirt. Her hair was swept up on top of her head. Peter's cummerbund and bow tie were made of the same material, courtesy of Jean's mother. He found the whole thing a little embarrassing – after all it was a Debs, not a wedding, but he decided he'd better go along with it. Jean was weepy enough this evening without adding to it.

"Jean, why don't we swap?" Sally asked kindly. "You have my corsage and I'll have yours. Red would suit my dress."

Jean smiled. "Are you sure you don't mind?" She wanted the evening to be perfect right down to the last detail.

"Not at all."

The two girls swapped flowers. Mark squeezed

Sally's hand and smiled at her. It was a kind thing to do. Sally surprised him at times.

The drive to the Blackrock Castle went quickly.

"Do you think Shane will get it together with any of the teachers?" Sally asked wickedly.

Jean choked on a mouthful of Sally's vodka. "Sally!" she exclaimed. "Don't be stupid. There's no way any of the teachers would go near him."

"I don't know, Jean," Peter mused. "I think you underestimate him. Remember all that business with the student teacher, what was her name?"

"Lucy," Sally said firmly. "I'm telling you, Jean, he's Tom Jones and Casanova all rolled into one. We don't take him seriously because he's our mate. And we know exactly what he's like."

Mark laughed. "I'd go with Sally on this one. Who's on for a little flutter? Ten quid says Sally's right."

Jean looked at Mark carefully, her eyes narrowing. "You're on. But I still think you're all mad!"

"We'll see," Sally said. "Hey, here's the castle." A large hotel with 'turrets' came into view in front of them. They pulled up outside and the taxi driver held the door open for them.

"Have a crackin' night," he said. "And tell yer man good luck with the teachers!"

The gang made their way into the hotel laughing. Sally and Jean already felt a little drunk – the vodka had gone straight to their heads.

"We're just going to the Ladies'," Sally called to Mark and Peter.

"See you in the bar," Mark replied. "What are you both drinking?"

"Vokda and orange for me," Sally replied. "A double, please."

"I'll have the same," Jean said.

The Ladies' was packed with St John's girls. Most of their year had brought someone from the school to the Debs, but there were a few new faces.

Georgina Higgins pulled Sally and Jean aside as soon as she spotted them coming in the toilet door. Georgina had an unhealthy interest in other people's business. "You'll never guess who's coming with Shane McCarthy?"

Sally and Jean looked at each other. They knew who Shane had asked: Nicola Andrews, the best-looking girl in the school, a tall, leggy blonde who had an annoying habit of flicking her mane away from her face and back again and giggling. But she was a stunner. She'd already modelled in some fashion shows and featured in soap ads which were currently showing on RTE.

Sally sighed. "Nicola Andrews, yes, we know."

Georgina looked triumphantly at Sally. "It's not Nicola Andrews," she gloated.

"Well, go on, tell us. Who is it then?" Jean asked impatiently.

"Fifi Andrews!"

"What?" Jean and Sally said in amazement. "Are you serious?"

Georgina was delighted. She loved being the bearer of interesting news. She nodded. But Sally and Jean had already lashed out the door, heels clicking. They found Peter and Mark in the bar.

"Where's Shane?" Sally asked breathlessly.

"Haven't seen him yet," Mark said suspiciously. "Why?"

At that moment the hotel bar began to buzz with excited chatter and all eyes had turned towards the door.

"Holy shit!" Mark exclaimed.

"No way!" Peter gasped.

Jean and Sally looked at each other and smiled. "Good on you, Shane," Sally said.

Shane McCarthy had just walked in the door with the current Miss Ireland, Fifi Andrews, Nicola Andrew's sister. A six-foot beauty, with striking green eyes, strawberry blonde hair to her waist and legs that went all the way to her armpits, Fifi was a cool twenty-one and one of the highest paid models in the country. She was wearing a long, white sheath dress which clung to her hips and breasts like a second skin. Shane was wearing a white tuxedo jacket and also looked amazing. Shane saw the gang at the bar and made his way over, hand placed protectively on the small of Fifi's back.

"Hi, guys," he beamed at the shocked group.

"Hi, Shane," Sally said, looking at him expectantly.

"Oh, yeah, this is Fifi, Nicola's sister," Shane said smiling at his date. "Nicola has the flu and Fifi kindly stepped in at the last minute."

"That was lucky," Mark said, trying not to sound envious. "And how's your sister?" he asked Fifi.

"She's getting better thanks," Fifi said. "She's really annoyed at missing the Debs though. She was really looking forward to it. But I've promised to behave myself with Shane."

Shane laughed. "Fifi, that's unfair. You have to score at your Debs. You don't want to ruin my reputation, do you? Nicola won't mind."

Fifi fixed her green eyes on his and smiled. "Good try, Shane, but you're not my type." She patted his cheek affectionately. "But I'll pretend to be mad into you when everyone's looking, OK?"

Shane was disappointed. He'd thought he was well in there. But still, there was always the lovely   Miss Ryan, his history teacher. Now there was a woman . . .

The bar was filling up quickly with ex St John's students. Sally and Jean checked out the girls' dresses and dates.

"Would you look at Alicia McDevitt?" Sally exclaimed. "Talk about low-cut! Poor old Jimbo, or maybe I should say lucky old Jimbo!"

"We should go over and rescue him," Jean said. "Look at the way she's holding onto his arm. There's no way he'll be able to make an escape on his own."

"Good idea," Sally replied, following Jean towards the group of giggling girls in the corner.

" Hi, Jimbo," Jean greeted her friend. "Hi, Alicia. Listen, the others are over by the bar. Would you both like to join us?"

Alicia stared at Jean. Alicia's tight black dress left nothing to the imagination and her dark blonde hair had been dyed an unnatural shade of orange with the help of a rather large dose of Sun-In. Her make-up matched her hair – orange, with pink eye-shadow and lipstick. Jimbo had kindly agreed to accompany her as a favour to his mother, who was Alicia's mother's best friend. He was regretting it now however. She wouldn't stop talking and her friends were just as bad. He couldn't stand that Georgina Higgins, she had such a chip on her shoulder.

"I'm sure Jimbo's just fine where he is, thank you," Alicia stated firmly, tightening her grip on his arm. "And anyway I can't leave my friends, it would be rude."

Jimbo coughed. Damn, he wanted to join his friends, but he was too polite to say it.

Sally recognised a man in trouble when she saw one. "Fifi Andrews would love to meet Jimbo, Alicia."

Alicia hesitated. Meeting Miss Ireland would be something to boast about for years. Seeing Georgina's face, jealousy etched all over it, she changed her mind. "Well, I suppose we can join you for a little while," she simpered.

"Grand. I'll bring Jimbo back over in a while," Sally linked her arm through Jimbo's and looked pointedly at Alicia. "I'm sure Fifi will understand that you can't leave your friends, Alicia."

Alicia was fuming. "But, I . . ."

Georgina cut in. "It's a shame you won't meet her, isn't it? But Sally is right – you did say you couldn't leave your friends, Alicia."

Alicia was caught. She couldn't leave now. She unlinked her arm from Jimbo's and watched Sally, Jean and her date join Miss Ireland at the bar. And Shane McCarthy was with them too. Damn! Alicia had a big *grá* for Shane.

"Thanks, Sal," Jimbo whispered as they walked away from 'the coven' as Alicia's gang were known. "Alicia is so painful. I hadn't realised how annoying she was. And she keeps planting kisses on me in front of all her witchy friends. It's scary."

Sally laughed. "Don't worry, she'll get the message soon enough and turn her attention to someone's boyfriend like she usually does."

"Hey, Jimbo," Shane gave his friend a manly hug. "This is Fifi, Nicola's sister." Jimbo blushed. He'd seen Fifi on the television and in photographs but she was even more stunning in real life.

"Hi, Jimbo," Fifi smiled. "It's lovely to meet you."

The hotel staff began to usher the guests into the dining-room.

"Where's our table, Jean?" Peter asked. Jean had been on the organising committee and had arranged the seating plan.

"Down the back, beside the bar. The rugby club gang are on one side and the teachers on the other."

"The teachers?" Sally asked in horror.

"Don't worry, Sal. There's method in my madness. Jill, one of the organisers last year, told me that the teachers were worse than any of the students last year. It's the younger gang like Murphs and Tonka and Miss

Ryan. Apparently they buy loads of drinks for everyone and are brilliant *craic* once Mr Greene leaves at midnight." Mr Greene was headmaster at St John's.

"Midnight," Shane groaned. "You mean we have to wait till then to misbehave?"

"Not exactly," Jean beamed. "You see, I put Mr Greene at Alicia's table."

"What?" Jimbo asked. "Thanks a lot!."

Jean smiled. "But the tables only seat eight so I put you at our table, Jimbo, with Murphs. Alicia will have to entertain old Greeney all by her lonesome."

"You're not serious?" Sally asked, laughing.

"That's my girl," Peter smiled at Jean. "Not just a pretty face."

Soon all the guests were seated at their tables. Alicia had nearly had a coronary when when she realised who was sitting beside her, but she couldn't make a fuss in front of Mr Greene. Damn that Jean, she thought to herself. Stupid cow! Still, Jimbo was hardly love's young dream. And Georgina's date Daragh was quite cute. She smiled over at him, much to Georgina's annoyance. Maybe she'd play footsie with him later. He was conveniently sitting opposite her at the table. It must be fate, she thought to herself, smiling. As she tucked into her melon starter, Jimbo was almost forgotten.

Chapter 40

"How are my favourite sailors?" Sheila Murphy asked. "Any news? How's college going for you all?"

"Great thanks, Miss Murphy," Sally smiled.

"Please, call me Sheila. I'm not your teacher anymore."

"OK," Sally agreed. "UCD is great. So many men, so little time, you know how it is."

Mark frowned. He was having problems keeping up with Sally at the moment. She was always out at some ball or rugby club or boat-club thing. He was in Trinity and tended to hang out in the Pav, the sports bar on the grounds. Sally didn't really like the Pav – she said it was boring. He wasn't sure how long their relationship would last at this stage. He got the feeling that she didn't want to be tied down.

"And what are you up to, Shane?" Sheila asked.

"I've set up a computer company with my brother. We bring in American computers and sell them over here."

"Sounds interesting," Sheila said. "Good for you."

They all tucked into the beef that was put in front of them.

Sally giggled to Jean. "I can't taste, my tongue is numb from the drink."

"I know the feeling," Jean said. "I don't know how we'll last the night."

"Keep an eye on Tonka," Jean said quietly. "I'm sure he's flirting with Fifi." Tonka was the St John's rugby coach, a thirty-something ex-Irish rugby international.

"I think you're right," Sally agreed. "And have you seen Miss Ryan staring at Shane? It's unreal. I think you've lost your bet."

"It's going to be one hell of a night," Jean laughed.

After the dinner Mr Greene gave a short speech and left. As soon as he exited a loud cheer went up from the teachers' table.

Miss Ryan stood up. "It's tequila time!" she cried and came back from the bar wielding a large tray on which sixteen small glasses, salt in a silver shaker and a plate of lemon slices were precariously balanced.

"Let's join the tables up with these degenerates beside us," she suggested. "If that's OK with you lot."

Shane and Fifi were the first to say "Yes" and Tonka wasn't far behind.

"Right, down in one," Sheila commanded. "And don't forget the salt and lemon." She showed the gang how to take the lemon slice between the fingers and place the salt on the licked fold of flesh beside the thumb. "Go."

Sally and Jean spluttered as the potent spirit hit the

back of their throats. Mark grinned at them. "Good women."

Tonka came back from the bar with a whole bottle of tequila and sat down beside Fifi. Soon they were chatting away.

"Hey, Tonka," Louise, as Miss Ryan had told everyone to call her, yelled at him from the other table. "Get on with pouring the drink and stop chatting up that poor young one."

"I'm coming, don't be so impatient," Tonka said, smiling. He was delighted with himself. Fifi Andrews was a babe and really sound too. He poured another round of drinks into the small glasses and sat back down beside Fifi.

Shane had given up on his Miss Ireland now and decided to turn his attention to Louise. He turned on his brightest smile and walked towards her. "Hey, Louise, would you like to dance?" The DJ was playing 'Wherever I Lay My Hat That's My Home' and Shane held Louise closely to him as they began to sway to the music.

Jean and Peter were also dancing. Sally and Mark watched the couples on the floor.

"Who's that with Headboy Vinnie?" Sally asked with interest. They always called Vinnie Winters by his full 'title'. Captain of the rugby team, he was known as a bit of a womaniser.

Mark stared at the small dark-haired girl. "It's Eve Arnold," he said in amazement.

"I didn't recognise her without the glasses," Sally said. "She looks great."

"She sure does," Mark replied thoughtfully. "Will we dance?"

At five in the morning Sally, Mark, Jean and Peter were lying on a large velvet sofa at the back of the room. Jimbo had fallen asleep slumped across their table soon after the end of dinner, and Shane was nowhere to be seen. The music was still playing and they sang along to 'Wake Me Up Before You Go Go'.

"Sally?"

"*Don't leave me hanging on like a yo yo . . .*" Jean interrupted Sally's singing.

"Yes?"

"There's something moving under the table over there."

"Don't be silly," Sally slurred. "'Sonly a dog or shomethink."

"You've lost it, Sal," Jean laughed. "No, I'm serious, look over."

Sally looked over at the table where they'd been sitting earlier and sure enough there was something or someone under it.

"We'd better investigate," Jean decided giggling. She held her hand out to Sally. "Come on, they won't even notice we've gone."

The boys continued to sing. "*You spin me right round baby, right round. Like a record baby, right round . . .*"

Jean and Sally crawled along the floor towards the table. "Don't want them to see we're coming," Jean had decided. "Have you got the camera?"

"Yep, loaded and ready."

As they neared the table they could hear muted giggles. Jean lifted the long tablecloth and Sally got the camera ready. They could make out a naked male back in the gloom. The bright flash startled the couple whose lips parted. It was Shane and Louise.

"How's it going, girls?" Shane beamed. Louise was still lying under Shane on the floor, grinning. "Louise is a bit tired. It's been a long night, you know." Louise raised her hand and waved it drunkenly at the girls.

Sally and Jean laughed. "We'll leave you to it." They crawled out from under the table and collapsed on the floor, laughing. Jean rested her head on Sally's shoulder.

"D'ya think Shane'll ever change?" Sally asked, hiccuping.

"I hope not," Jean replied. "I hope none of us do."

"Let's be friends for ever and ever," Sally said. Jean's eyes were closed. She was fast asleep.

Eve looked at her two classmates, Sally and Jean, asleep on top of each other at the back of the room. Although they looked a state, dresses crumpled, tights laddered and shoes discarded, Eve felt envious. She would like a friend she could fall asleep on. She looked around her. Everyone seemed to be with someone. Her own date, Vinnie, had disappeared with Georgina Higgins over an hour ago. Alicia had 'stolen' Daragh from right under her nose and Georgina was damned if she was going to worry about Eve Arnold.

Eve sighed. She was chillingly sober now and not enjoying herself at all. Maybe she should just go home.

She stood up, pulling her green silk dress back into place. These off-the-shoulder dresses are more trouble than they're worth, she thought to herself. She walked towards the door to order a taxi.

"Hey, Eve," Mark said loudly as she passed himself and Peter, "is everything all right?" He'd never really talked to Eve. She had tended to keep herself aloof at school.

She stopped and looked at him carefully. "Fine, thanks. I'm just on my way home."

"Where's Vinnie?" Peter asked.

Eve pointed towards the dancefloor.

"Over there." Vinnie and Georgina were slowly moving to the music, their mouths firmly locked together.

"Oh," Peter muttered, embarassed. "Sorry."

Eve smiled. "Don't worry. I don't mind, not really."

"We're going in to breakfast soon, will you join us?" Mark asked kindly. He didn't like to see her on her own.

Eve paused for a second. "Thanks, I'd love some food, I'm starving. If you don't mind . . ."

"Of course not," Mark said. "We could do with a hand waking up the girls. And we seem to have lost Shane."

A little while later Mark, Sally, Jean, Peter, Shane and Eve were sitting in the dining-room. There was no waking either Jimbo or Louise, and Fifi hadn't been seen for hours.

Plates of sausages, eggs and bacon sat in front of them. Peter, Mark and Eve were tucking in. Sally and Jean looked on dubiously.

"Are you sure our stomachs can take this, lads?" Sally asked.

"It'll make you feel much better," Mark stated. "Food is a great hangover cure." He lifted up his egg and sausage-laden fork and dipped it into a pool of waiting tomato ketchup. He placed it in his mouth and licked his lips dramatically. "Delicious."

Jean's face was beginning to turn a delicate shade of green. She stood up and rushed out the door. Sally followed her.

"Was it something I said?" Mark laughed.

Eve smiled at him and he smiled back. He's lovely, she thought to herself.

"What are you doing with yourself now?" Peter asked her, interrupting her thoughts.

"I'm in Trinity," Eve said. "Doing ESS."

"That's strange," Mark mused. "I haven't seen you. I'm in Trinity too. We should meet for coffee some day."

"I'd like that," Eve said earnestly. I'd like that a lot, she thought to herself . . .

Chapter 41

The day following the accident Eve took a taxi to her GP, Dr Ryan. Her head still throbbed and her neck was stiff and tender.

"If you weren't in such good shape, Eve, your poor old body would be in trouble. As it is there is some soft tissue damage and the muscles and tendons at the base of your neck are a little strained. But overall you were very lucky. A touch of whiplash, but it could have been a whole lot worse." The doctor smiled. "I'll give you a prescription for some muscle relaxants and some painkillers. Take a few days off to rest and come back to me if anything hurts. Some physiotherapy or massage would be a good idea to get that neck back to normal."

"Thanks, Dr Ryan."

He looked at Eve carefully. "Is everything else all right, Eve? You look exhasted. Is there anything you'd like to talk about?"

Shit, Eve thought, I'm going to bloody cry again. She gulped back the tears. "The crash just gave me a bit of a fright, that's all. I'll be fine. I guess I'm still in shock."

Dr Ryan smiled. "Well, take it easy. Oh, by the way, my wife met your mother in the supermarket last week. I believe congratulations are in order. Tell her I sent my very best wishes. When's the big day going to be?"

Eve was taken aback for a minute before she remembered what she'd been trying to block out of her mind – her mother's engagement. "I don't think they've set a date yet," Eve said, trying to sound enthusiastic. "I'll pass on your good wishes to Mum."

As she sat in the waiting-room, watching out the bow windows for a taxi, Eve missed her mother more than ever. Most of the anger she felt towards her had now subsided but she was still full of hurt pride. I can't ring her, she thought to herself miserably. It's up to her to apologise, not me. I'm damned if I'm going to make the first move now. It's not as if I've done anything wrong. She had conveniently forgotten that her mother had called in and rung her on several occasions.

At midday Eve heard a knock at the door. As she walked into the hall she saw the shadow of a tall male figure through the frosted glass to the right side of the door. For a split second she thought it was Mark, coming to apologise, before she realised that Mark wasn't that tall.

She opened the door and was surprised to see John Redmond. And even more surprised to find herself blushing on seeing him on her doorstep. "Garda Redmond," she said, uncertainly, not knowing quite what to call him.

He smiled. "Please, John is fine. Can I come in?"

Eve stood back from the door. "Oh, yes, sorry. I'm still not myself. Of course, please come in. Would you like some coffee?"

"I'm on duty so I shouldn't really." He paused. "But, I suppose if I'm quick . . . that would be nice, thanks." John followed her into the kitchen. "Great place you have here. Did you decorate it yourself?"

Eve smiled. "Yes, I did."

"You have a good eye."

"Thanks."

Eve was pleased. For some strange reason she wanted this man's approval more than anything right at this minute. He sat down at the kitchen table while Eve brewed some fresh coffee.

"You should see our place in Dun Laoghaire," John continued. "Three country lads in one small house, you can imagine!"

Eve laughed. "Sounds chaotic all right." She paused, wondering whether it was 'allowed' to ask a guard personal questions. "Um, where are you from?"

"West Cork originally, a tiny place called Castletownsend. But I've been in Dublin for over ten years now." Eve placed a mug of steaming coffee in front of him. "Thanks, this smells great. We tend to have lots of plastic cups of coffee at the station and it's great to have the real stuff. How's your neck? Did you go to the doctor's?"

Eve smiled. He sounded genuinely concerned. It was nice to have someone to talk to and she felt comfortable with this man, even though they had just met, and he was on 'official' business.

"I was lucky, just a touch of whiplash. He said it could have been a lot worse."

"The doctor was right. I've seen some fairly nasty cases in my time, believe me. By the way, I've arranged for a local garage to have a look at your car if that's all right. The owner, Joe, is a friend of mine and he'll do a good job. As the other car was stolen it's probably best to claim through your own insurance for the moment until the whole mess is cleared up."

"That sounds fine to me," Eve said, relieved not to have to deal with it herself. "Where's my car now?"

"It's at the station in Ringsend. It'll have to stay there for a few days until we get an assessor to look at the damage. That's the procedure I'm afraid. Then Joe will tow it to his garage and repair it for you. I'd say it will take about ten days in total."

"Thanks for your help," Eve said. "I really appreciate it."

"It's a pleasure," John replied, looking at his half-finished coffee with regret. "I'd better be off now." He stood up and Eve showed him to the door. "I'll give you a ring if we have any news about the other car or anything. Bye now."

Eve watched from the door as he drove away. "Bye, John," she whispered, closing the door.

Shee went for a short walk to the shops after lunch. On her return she saw the little red light flashing on her answering machine. She hoped it was her mother. Eve was ready to forgive her now. Her heart gave a jump when she recognised John Redmond's voice.

"Hello, Eve. This is John Redmond. Just rang to say we caught three of the boys who were involved in the crash last night. The driver and two others. They were arrested in another stolen car in the small hours of the morning. Thought you'd like to know. If I have more details I'll ring."

Eve spent the rest of the day with a smile on her face. She replayed the answering machine tape several times, listening to John's voice. "God, I'm being so stupid, but I can't help it," she thought to herself. "He's just doing his job. And he's a guard, for heaven's sake!" But there was something in his manner that made her wonder. Surely guards didn't blush all the time or smile so much? Maybe it was a new garda directive.

Even dealing with the insurance company went swimmingly. Luckily the car was comprehensively insured, but as Eve listened to the young man from Allied Motor Insurance her thoughts were elsewhere.

"Sorry, what was that? Oh yes, a quote from the garage. John Redmond is dealing with that. I'll see they are sent on to you." She couldn't help adding, "He's a guard, you know. He's been great, really helpful."

Eve was shocked with herself. What was she saying? The insurance guy must think I'm nuts, she thought. But I don't care!

The following day Eve was sitting at her kitchen table, drinking a cup of tea and staring into space when John Redmond called.

It was almost one o'clock. As she walked towards the door she recognised the familiar tall, figure and a smile played over her lips.

"Hello, John, I wasn't expecting you." He was wearing a blue shirt and dark denims and he looked even better out of uniform.

"I'm off duty and I was just passing and I've got some news about the joy-riders. I thought you might be interested."

"That's very nice of you," Eve said, a little uneasily. "Won't you come in?"

"Am I interrupting your lunch?" John asked, frowning. He seemed nervous.

"Not at all. I hadn't started making it yet." Eve paused. What was the protocol involved in inviting a garda for a bite to eat even if he was off duty? He had been very kind to her and she would like to repay him in some way. She decided to bite the bullet and ask anyway.

"Would you like something to eat? It won't be anything too exciting, just an omlette and some salad."

John took a deep breath. There was something about this woman that he liked. It was completely against the rules to visit people on garda business when off duty.

But he had felt compelled to see Eve again and it was worth the risk.

"That would be lovely, Eve, if it's not too much trouble."

John filled her in on the joy-riders while she cooked a large Spanish omlette. It felt oddly 'normal' and relaxed, seeing as she didn't know this man from Adam.

"They found the rest of the boys involved in the incident. The driver will be charged with reckless driving, leaving the scene of the crime and theft. He's looking at some pretty serious charges."

Eve looked at him with a worried expression on her face. "Will he go to prison, do you think?"

"He's not old enough. But he'll be put in State care of some sort." John paused, watching Eve's face carefully. "I'm sorry, you probably don't need to know all the details, I just thought . . ."

"No, I want to know." Eve said firmly. "The whole thing has shaken me, that's all. I didn't sleep at all last night, I had nightmares about the crash. And I keep going over and over the whole thing in my head. I keep thinking if I hadn't been there, if I hadn't gone out . . ."

"It's quite normal to feel like that. You're still in shock. It'll be fine. I promise." He smiled up at her and she felt better.

She tossed some honey and mustard-seed dressing on the green salad and served it with the omlette. She poured two large glasses of apple juice.

Other conversation was a little stilted at first but in a

while they were talking openly. Eve listened to John talk about growing up in a small village, fascinated with his gentle ease and confident good humour. They discussed a recent government scandal and the political implications and other current hot topics. She had never talked to a guard before, except on 'official business' and she was surprised by his intelligence and wit.

"And why did a country boy like yourself decide to join the guards?" she asked.

"It's always been at the back of my mind I suppose, ever since I was a child," John replied. "I loved all the old police shows – *Starsky and Hutch, Dad's Army* . . ."

"*Dad's Army!*" Eve laughed.

"They weren't police exactly, I guess. But they had uniforms of sorts. Oh yeah, I loved *Charlie's Angels* too."

"John Redmond, Charlie's Angels had nothing to do with the police force and you know it. Next you'll be telling me that *Wonder Woman* was another major influence on your chosen career."

"Well, she was! And the *Bionic Woman!*"

She laughed and without thinking leant over and punched him playfully on the shoulder. He grabbed her hand and held it tightly.

"Now, now. No violence please or I'll have to arrest you. I have handcuffs in the car, I'll have you know."

"Promises, promises," Eve teased before she could stop herself, pulling her hand out of his grip and offering her two hands outstretched in front of her for him to handcuff.

"You're an awful woman," John laughed. "But stay there and I'll nip out to the car. I'll be back in two secs."

Eve joined in the laughter, unable to stop herself and soon tears were running down her face. "Stop," she pleaded. "My sides hurt from laughing." She hadn't had so much fun for ages. In fact, she couldn't remember when she'd felt so happy and at ease with a man. Pity he wasn't her type.

"So, tell me about yourself, Eve," he said when they'd stopped laughing. "I know about your hot-shit job but tell me about your family. Where did you grow up?"

Eve told him about her mum, about her father's death and about Betty's recent engagement. She hadn't talked about it with anyone before and it seemed strange opening up to someone she hardly knew.

"Your mum sounds great," he said, after listening carefully.

"Yes," Eve replied, trying not to sound wistful. "She is great. We're very close, more like best friends than anything else."

"And she's getting married again you say? Isn't that great now! You must be delighted for her." John trod carefully. He could sense that Eve was uneasy about her mother's recent engagement.

" I'm thrilled of course, it's just . . ."

"Yes?" John coaxed.

"Well, he's a lot younger than her and it's all a little awkward. I suppose I feel that they're both doing something wrong, that Sean's trying to muscle in on my father's place in the family, that I should be getting married not her . . ." Eve was shocked that she'd said aloud what she had been trying not to admit to herself – that she was, at the end of the day, jealous of her mother. What would John think of her?

He was silent for a moment. "It's perfectly natural to feel hurt when you and your mum have been so close. In a way I'm sure you feel that Sean's taking your place, and you feel out in the cold. Give yourself a little time. It'll all work out and I'm sure you and your mum will be as close as ever soon. And Eve, your day will come."

Eve smiled. She could see now that her mother's happiness was the most important thing. She'd been childish and selfish and she resolved to ring her mum that evening. "You're right, thanks. I suppose I had blown the whole thing a little out of proportion."

There was a long silence.

"You're very easy to talk to John," she said at last. "I hope I haven't kept you from anything . . ."

John coughed nervously and smiled. "Not at all, it's been a pleasure. I've enjoyed lunch very much." He stood up.

"I'll see you out," she said.

As they approached the door Eve was disappointed. She wouldn't have minded if he had stayed for a little longer. But he probably had a nice Cork girlfriend hidden away somewhere, a teacher or nurse or something. He paused at the door.

"I was wondering . . ." John began, a boyish blush beginning to creep up his neck and onto his cheeks.

"Yes?" Eve smiled.

"Can I ring you?"

"About the crash?"

"Yes . . . no. Not about the crash."

"Oh." Now Eve was blushing.

"I thought we could go out sometime."

Eve was taken aback. A guard had just asked her out. She didn't know what to say. He was very nice, of course, but . . . she couldn't go out with him – it wouldn't be right.

"I don't think so, sorry."

"Right." He seemed mortified. "Better be going," he muttered and went out quickly.

"Bye," Eve said, closing the door behind him.

"Hello, Mum?" Eve asked uncertainly. "It's Eve."

Betty was silent for a second. She hadn't expected to hear from Eve for a while. She knew exactly how stubborn her daughter could be when she wanted to.

"Eve! It's so good to hear your voice. I've missed you so much."

Eve felt terrible. "Mum, I'm sorry, I shouldn't have reacted in the way I did. What can I say?"

"Eve, it's all right. I understand. It was a shock to your system. I should have told you earlier. I'm sorry too. Can you forgive me?"

"There's nothing to forgive. And I've missed you too. I've so much to tell you."

"Why don't you call over? I'd love to see you."

"I'd like that. Will Sean be there?"

"I'll send him out, love, don't worry."

"No, Mum, I want to congratulate him. Please ask him to stay."

There was a long pause.

"Eve, are you still there?"

Eve mumbled through her tears. "Yes. Can I come over now?"

Betty started to cry. "Of course you can, love!"

Chapter 42

Eve sat at her desk staring out the window. She was thinking about John Redmond. She'd told her mother about the kind garda and had been surprised at her response.

"Eve! He sounds lovely. Why won't you go out with him? It must have taken a lot of guts for him to ask you."

"Mum," Eve began, "he's a guard. I can't go out with a guard . . ."

"Why not?" Betty interrupted.

Eve thought for a moment. "I'm not sure, I just can't."

"Don't be so ridiculous!" Betty exclaimed. "I'm going out with a builder. It's the person that counts."

"We'd have nothing in common . . ." Eve protested.

"I thought you said you chatted for ages over lunch."

"Yes, but . . ."

"It's worth a chance," Betty smiled. "Do you believe in fate?"

"Not really," Eve replied.

"Well, maybe you should!"

As she gazed out the window a garda van drove past, sirens blaring. "Mum would say that's fate!" Eve whispered. "Feck it!" She had nothing to lose. She picked up the phone.

"Julie, can you get me the number of Ringsend Garda Station, please?"

During dinner with John on Saturday evening Eve realised that she hadn't been so calm and relaxed for a long time. At work on Thursday and on Friday she had left at six on the button, much to the astonishment of Julie.

"Are you feeling all right, Ms Arnold?" her secretary had asked on Friday as Eve had walked out of her office into the reception area.

"Yes, Julie, I'm feeling very well thanks," Eve had replied smiling.

"It's just that the weekly accounts haven't gone through yet. I thought you'd want to check the details."

"It can wait till Monday morning I think, but thank you anyway, Julie."

Julie gasped audibly. She looked up at her boss through her shaggy 'Rachel' fringe. Ice Eve, another of Julie's pet names for her, had never left the accounts until the morning, let alone Monday – a whole three days away. Wait till she told the girls.

"And Julie," Eve added as she strode towards the entrance. "Forget about working tomorrow morning, I won't be in."

This time Julie gasped even more loudly. Eve was missing the second Saturday in a row. She was genuinely astonished. "Something must be up, and I'm going to find out what," Julie said to herself, packing away her emery board and nail-buffer in her bright pink handbag.

Eve waltzed through the door, down the marble-floored hallway and out into the fresh air. She felt good. No, she felt great.

Saturday morning was spent in the beauty salon, where Eve treated herself to a facial, eyebrow-plucking and full manicure with hand massage and French polish. On leaving the beauticians' she felt wonderful. There were tiny butterflies fluttering in her stomach all afternoon and she spend an unprecedented two hours in the supermarket and shops in the Merrion Centre, happily dithering over body lotions and bubble baths, and filling her trolly with gloriously coloured fresh fruit. Saturdays were usually spent in the office or catching up with paperwork at home. This was a brand new experience for Eve and she was stangely taken with it.

Late that afternoon, she had delicious soak in her new calming aromatherapy bubbles, which wafted lavender scent around the bathroom. She chose a pair of black trousers, with a gold knitted cardigan and sprayed herself liberally with Chanel No 5.

When Eve had rung John's station he had been out on a call. But he had rung back that evening and they had talked for over an hour about everything from their collective days' work to music. John liked some pretty dodgy tunes, as he admitted himself, and had insisted on singing a few choice morsels to Eve, who retaliated with her own favourites.

"Seriously, Eve, this one's called 'Drop Kick Me, Jesus, Through the Goal Posts of Life'." He sang a few bars. "Have you ever heard it? It's great."

"OK, how about 'I Don't Care if it Freezes as Long as I've Got My Plastic Jesus Sitting on the Dashboard of my Car'," Eve asked. "Do you know that one?"

"You made that up!"

"I did not. It's a real song. Are you calling me a liar?"

"Would I?"

"Yes!"

"Eve, can I take you out this weekend. Please?"

"Yes," Eve said, "I'd like that."

"You're sure?"

"Yes!"

"You're not going to change your mind on me?"

"No!"

"I'll ring you tomorrow, just to make sure," John laughed.

Eve put down the phone with a wide grin on her face. So what if he was a guard? He was the first man in a long time to make her smile. Anyway, it was only a date. There was no way she could get serious about him, it wouldn't be right.

He also rang on Thursday and on Friday, ostensibly to make final arrangements but really just to say hello.

As Eve sat and waited for him to collect her on Saturday evening she began to get more and more nervous. She hadn't felt this way about anyone for a long, long time. "Now if only he can kiss . . ." she thought to herself smiling.

"I was half-expecting the squad car," Eve said smiling, stepping into John's Honda Prelude.

"I'll save that for a special occasion," John promised.

As they drove along Sandymount Strand Eve pointed out her mother's house. "Herself and Sean are thinking about buying a bigger place. Mum would love to live out of the city, Wicklow or somewhere."

"How would you feel about that?" John asked.

"I haven't really given it much thought. It's not that far, I suppose," Eve replied. "And I could still visit at the weekends."

"Did you make up with your mum, then?"

Eve looked at John's face which was fixed on the road. "How did you know we were fighting?"

"It was in your eyes," he mused. "Anyway, I'm glad everything's fine now."

"So am I," Eve agreed.

John had refused to tell Eve where they were going, so she was mystified when he pulled into the carpark at Dalkey train station.

"I didn't know CIE were known for their *haute cuisine*," Eve joked.

"Don't be so smart," John said, locking the car and putting his arm out for Eve to hold.

"This way, Madam."

They walked through Dalkey village, past the pet

shop where budgies and love-birds were chattering and cooing in the window and towards PD'S Woodhouse.

"Have you been here before?" John asked as he pushed open the door.

"No," Eve replied. "But it looks lovely."

They were greeted warmly at the door and shown to their table. The restaurant was dark and cosy, subtly lit and simply decorated.

They tucked into the tasty dips on their table while they waited for their food – oak-grilled chicken for Eve and steak for John. Soon they were chatting like old friends.

"Eve, there's something I have to tell you," John said eventually, playing with the skin of his now demolished baked potato.

Eve looked at him expectantly. Thoughts of Robin came flooding back. She hoped to God that John wasn't married. "Yes?"

"I shouldn't have called in to you last weekend."

"What do you mean?"

John looked sheepish. "It's against the rules to – how will I put it – mix business and pleasure. It's actually a sackable offence. But I just had to see you again. There's something about you . . ."

Eve smiled. "I'm glad you called in and I won't tell anyone. And I know this sounds strange but in a way I'm glad I had the car crash. It's helped me put a lot of things into perspective."

John took Eve's hand and kissed it gently. "It was worth the risk then."

"Yes," Eve said, embarrassed now. She looked at her plate.

"I hope I can see you again after tonight," John said, sounding suddenly anxious. "I really like you."

"I like you too," Eve replied lightly, trying to ignore his serious tone. "Now, let's order dessert. The brown bread ice cream sounds delicious."

Eve rang her mother as soon as she got up the following morning. Although she'd had several large glasses of wine the night before, she felt wonderful. John had dropped her home straight after dinner. In the end they'd chatted for nearly an hour in the car, loathe to leave each other's company.

"Can I take you out next weekend?" John asked.

"Well, I have to ... but maybe ..." began Eve tentatively.

"Yes?"

"I know it's short notice, but my school reunion is coming up next weekend. Would you like to come with me?"

John smiled. "Eve, I'd be honoured." He touched her cheek tenderly. "Now, I'm sorry but I really, really have to go. I'm on a long shift tomorrow, but can I call in after work on Monday evening?"

Eve smiled. He was keen. "I don't think so. I'll have to work late and play catch-up, you know how it is. But give me a ring."

"I'll do that," he said, a little disappointed.

He kissed her forehead. She looked into his deep blue eyes. He really was a most attractive man. He leaned towards her, cupping her chin in his hand. He kissed her gently on the lips. "I've had a wonderful evening, thank you."

"So have I," she replied.

He walked her to the door. They paused on the doorstep and he put his arms around her and held her closely against his chest.

"Oh, Eve," he murmured into her hair, his lips brushing her neck. "You're so lovely."

"I'll talk to you during the week," she smiled, pulling back.

"I'll ring you tomorrow from work," he promised, dragging himself away from her. "'Bye." She stepped into her house and watched as he walked towards his car. He waved before driving away. She pushed the door closed with her back and leant against it, grinning widely. That night Eve slept better than she had for years.

"Hi, Eve, it's John. It's Sunday afternoon. I was just ringing to see how you were." There was an embarrassed cough. "I'll talk to you tomorrow, I guess." The answering phone clicked off.

Eve stood staring at the flashing red light. She should have talked to him, it wouldn't have hurt. But something was holding her back.

She heard her mother's car pull up outside. She grabbed her jacket and keys and opened the door.

"Eve," Betty yelled from the car. "Are you ready?"

"Just coming," Eve shouted, slamming the door

behind her. She climbed into Betty's shiny new metallic blue Volkswagen Beetle.

"Good to see you," Eve said, leaning over and planting a kiss on her mum's cheek. "Love the wheels."

Betty smiled gratefully. "You don't think it's a little much?"

"Not at all," Eve smiled. "It's cool! And I love the flower." Betty's tiny dashboard 'vase' held a large fake sunflower.

"It's got a 2 litre engine, so hold onto your hat!" Betty laughed as they turned onto the Stillorgan dual carriageway.

They drove towards Wicklow, lapping up all the attention from the other Sunday drivers. The small car was still a novelty on the Dublin roads.

"Mum, it drives like a dream, I'm so jealous!"

"You could always trade in your Mazda," Betty stated. "I think a Beetle would suit you."

Eve beamed. "Maybe you're right."

"You're in good mood today. Tell me all about your date. I want to know everything."

Eve smiled. She'd wondered how long it would take her mum to ask about John.

"It was great, Mum. He's a real gentleman. We went to PD's Woodhouse in Dalkey."

Eve told her mum about the food, about their conversation and about John's 'keen-ness'.

Betty was silent for a few seconds after Eve had finished.

"What?" Eve asked.

"Don't shut John out," Betty began carefully. "He sounds like a good man."

"He is," Eve sighed. "I'm just not sure if he's for me."

"Why not?"

"Lots of reasons."

"Give it a chance, love," Betty said gently.

"You're right, Mum," Eve said, looking out the window.

That evening Eve rang John at the station.

"Hi, Eve. How was your day?"

"Great. I went driving with Mum in her new Beetle."

"Lucky thing, they're great cars. Good engine on them. Cute too! Listen, I've almost finished my shift. Can I call in on my way home?"

Eve hesitated for a second. "Yes," she said finally. "Can I make you some dinner?"

"Eve," John said, "that would be lovely!"

The week passed quickly and Eve couldn't remember when she had last felt so happy. But at the back of her mind she was worried about letting John get too close. Maybe there was someone out there who would be more 'suitable' for her. After all, as she kept telling herself, John really wasn't her 'type'.

Chapter 43

"Did you go to your Debs, Eve?" John Redmond asked. It was Saturday afternoon and they were sprawled on the sofa in Eve's house. It was blowing a gale outside and harsh rain was whipping at the bedroom window. They had been talking about the reunion that following night and about Eve's schooldays.

"I did," Eve said thoughtfully. "It was a strange night."

"Why?" John asked.

"Well, Georgina Higgins went off with my partner for a start . . ."

John laughed. "There was a lot of that going on at my Debs too."

"I wonder how many of my year will be at the reunion." Eve mused. "It will be really interesting to see what everyone's doing."

"A lot of the time it's only the people who've made something of their lives who go to their school reunion," John said wisely.

"Really?" Eve asked.

"Think about it," John continued. "The whole night people will be asking you what you're doing, are you married, have you got children . . . that kind of thing. If you'd spent the last few years doing nothing it would be difficult. No-one wants to feel a failure."

Eve thought about this for a minute. "I suppose you're right. Now you're making me feel nervous."

"Why?" John asked gently. "You've got a great job, a house, a boyfriend who loves you. People will think you're the luckiest girl in the world." Eve went quiet. "Eve, are you all right? Was it something I said?"

Eve smiled and turned towards him. "Yes, you said you loved me."

"Well, I do," John stated firmly. "Very much."

"But we haven't known each other that long," Eve began nervously. She knew she liked John but love . . .

She snuggled up to him and kissed him firmly on the lips. She hoped he hadn't notice her lack of response.

"Are you looking forward to tonight?" Betty asked her daughter on the telephone that afternoon. John had gone to play indoor soccer with some of his friends and Eve was slouched on the sofa watching *Little House on the Prairie*.

"Yes and no," Eve replied hesitantly. "I'm a little nervous to tell the truth. It will be strange meeting everyone again after all these years."

"Eve," Betty started, she wasn't sure how to bring up the subject of Mark Mulhearne. Eve had told her everything about their dinner together and she knew her daughter was still embarassed about the whole thing. "Will Mark be there?"

"You know he will, Mum. He's one of the speakers." Eve sighed. "I'm going to apologise to him for . . . well, for everything. I behaved stupidly, I see that now."

Betty was taken aback, Eve had really changed in the last few weeks. "If you think that's the right thing to do, love. Would you like a hand getting dressed? I could blow-dry your hair."

Eve smiled. "That would be great. John's collecting me just before eight, so how about six?"

"Done," Betty said. "See you later. And Eve?"

"Yes, Mum."

"Don't think I've forgotten about your mystery date last night. I'll expect to hear all about it!"

"I'm off to Eve's now," Betty told Sean, who was flicking through the newspaper in the kitchen.

"Fine, love, what time would you like dinner?"

"About eight if that suits. What are we having?"

Sean smiled at Betty. "Now that would be telling."

Driving towards Eve's house, Betty thought about Sean and their forthcoming wedding. She was blessed. Sean was the kindest man she had ever met. She wouldn't have got over the trouble with Eve if he hadn't been around. Now that things with Eve were better than ever, Betty felt on top of the world. She stopped at the local florists and bought a huge armful of lilies. She knew it was extravagant but they were Eve's favourite flowers. If you couldn't spoil your only daughter, then who could you spoil?

"Mum," Eve shrieked as she opened the door. "You're mad! You must have wiped the florists out. I'll never have enough vases. Thanks." She smiled warmly at her mother.

"I thought you'd like them, love. I'll put them in the sink for the moment," Betty said.

"Let's have a cup of coffee before I do your hair." They sat down at Eve's kitchen table. The heady scent of the lilies began to fill the air.

"How was last night? Tell me everything," Betty said. She knew that John had planned a surprise for Eve last night. Eve had called over to borrow a fleece jacket and hiking boots in honour of their evening out. John had told her to wear warm clothes and comfortable shoes.

Eve laughed. "We went on a picnic up the mountains. John's completely crazy – you'd make a good pair. He collected me and we drove to Enniskerry. Of course the whole way he wouldn't tell me where we were going." She took a sip of her coffee.

"Go on," Betty urged.

"We drove to Glencree and we walked to beside a bog lake. He carried the picnic basket and rugs. And he went swimming in the lake – honestly, Mum, he's psycho! It was freezing!"

Betty laughed. "Sounds like fun."

"We had some salmon and brown bread and wine. And then we lay on the rug and looked at the stars."

"Sounds romantic," Betty said.

Eve blushed. "It was lovely. If a little cold. And then he drove me back."

"And?" Betty asked.

"You're so nosy." Eve scolded. A smile lingered on Betty's lips. "What?" Eve asked irritably.

"Did he, you know . . . stay the night?"

"Mum!" Eve exclaimed. "Of course not. I'm not ready for that kind of relationship. We hardly know each other."

"I'm sorry," Betty said contritely. "You're right. Anyway, I'm pleased for you – he seems a nice man."

"He is, Mum." She looked at her watch. "He's a nice man who's collecting me very soon. My hairdryer awaits."

* * *

"I'm really sorry, Sal, but I told George about your reunion tonight," Emma said contritely. "I didn't mean to. We were talking about school and it just kind of slipped out. He was upset that you hadn't asked him. He didn't really understand why you hadn't mentioned it." Emma, George and Alex had been hanging out together for the last few weeks. George was good fun and after the initial lunch they had seen each other on a regular basis. Sally was amazed at how attentive he was being and she wasn't sure if she was ready for it. She liked him a lot but she didn't want to get serious about anyone for a long time to come. And after the reunion who knows how she'd feel about him.

Sally sighed. "I'm not really into bringing him, to be honest, Emma. He's a nice guy but it would be a pain in the ass. I'd have to sit with him and talk to him all night and I want to have a bit of a laugh with Jean and the gang, you know?"

Emma didn't know, not really. She and Alex had become very close and if it was her reunion she'd definitely want him there. But Sally had always been different. Sometimes Emma wondered if her sister had more male hormones than normal – she acted like such a boy at times. "He really likes you. If you don't feel the same way you should tell him."

"I suppose I'd better talk to him," Sally muttered. Life was complicated sometimes.

* * *

"Are you nervous, Mark?" Susan asked gently. His St John's reunion was tonight and he had been a little withdrawn in the last few days. They were sitting at the kitchen table reading *The Irish Times*.

"I'm OK, thanks," Mark replied. "The sooner it's over, the better. I'll start looking for a flat next week. You and Pat have been amazing but now that I've got some money it's time for me to move."

"You know you're welcome to stay as long as you want," Susan said.

"I know, but it's time I got on with my life. Living here is too easy in a way. You gang have become my family. But looking at you I suppose I see how much I want my own family," Mark said truthfully.

Susan put her arms around him. "I know. It's hard being on your own. But you'll find someone soon, I just know it."

Mark lowered his eyes and went back to flicking through the *Weekender* supplement. His eye came to rest on a familiar face, the author of a new book. It was Owen O'Sullivan. "Look who's in the paper," he said slowly.

Susan stared at the photograph. "I don't recognise him," she said. "Who is he?"

"That's Ashling's boyfriend, Owen," Mark said slowly. "Didn't you meet him at a ball?"

"That's not the guy from the ball," Susan said. "He was much younger, with a slimmer face."

"Oh," said Mark thoughtfully. So Ashling and Owen weren't together after all.

Susan took a deep breath. "Mark, I know you don't like talking about it and I promise I won't mention it again but would you not tell Ashling how you feel?"

Mark looked at his sister carefully. "I don't feel anything for her," he said sharply. "It's ancient history."

"I'm sorry," Susan whispered. "I didn't mean to upset you."

Mark sighed and reached out to hold his sister's hand. "No, I'm sorry. I shouldn't have snapped at you. I just have a lot on my mind at the moment, that's all." He just wanted this damn reunion to be over with so he could put her out of his head once and for all.

Susan looked at her brother's tense face. If she could live his life for him she would. But this was something that Mark had to go through himself.

Chapter 44

"Annie, it's Ashling, if you're there pick up! Please, it's an emergency." Ashling was at the end of her tether. Everything seemed to be conspiring against her in the last few days. Yesterday morning her car wouldn't start and she had to get the postman to help her push it down the hill to jump-start it. He'd been very nice about it luckily. She'd also been very late for work because she'd had to drop Dan to school herself as Tizzy was visiting one of her sons in America. Connor and his wife Janet had just announced 'their' pregnancy and Tizzy was thrilled. Although she loved Dan with all her heart, a grandchild of her own was something she had longed and hoped for. Connor had been talking about coming home to Ireland to raise his family and Tizzy was determined not to leave New York without a definite promise that he would return home within the year. She planned to give them the house and build a smaller house for herself on the grounds so that she could help with the baby. Ashling was delighted for her but a little apprehensive about how it would impact on her own life. Maybe Connor wouldn't be as keen as his mother was to have herself and Dan around. Why was life so complicated?

"Hi, this is Annie, I'm not in right now, please leave a message."

Damn, damn, damn, Ashling muttered to herself. This morning the local girl who Ashling had booked to baby-sit for Dan had rung.

"I'm really sorry to do this to you, Ashling," Milly had rasped. "I seem to have come down with some sort of chest and throat infection. I've been in bed the last few days. I though I'd be better by today but . . ." She broke off to cough violently. "I'm really sorry."

Ashling could hear that Milly was in a bad state. "It's OK, Milly, I understand. It's not your fault you're sick. I hope you feel better soon." Putting down the phone Ashling was filled with a mixture of disappointment and self-pity. Things had been getting on top of her in the last few days. She hadn't realised how much herself and Dan had come to rely on Tizzy's help on a daily basis.

"Are you sick, Mum?" Dan asked, walking into her room. "You look funny." Ashling was trying not to cry. She rarely let everything get to her like this but Milly had to be sick today of all days! Although she'd been trying not to think about it too much, if she was being honest with herself she'd have to admit that the school reunion had been constantly on her mind. The thought of seeing Mark again was both exciting and depressing at the same time. He'd disappeared out of her life at a time when they'd started to become very close. Ashling wanted to exorcise his lingering ghost once and for all.

"I'm fine, love, it's Milly who's sick. She won't be baby-sitting tonight."

Dan stared at her anxiously. "Who'll be looking after me then, Mum?"

"Don't wory, Dan. I may just have to stay in, that's all."

"But you bought that pretty dress for the ball, Mum. You have to go."

Ashling smiled. Dan was convinced that the St John's reunion dance was like the ball from his Cinderella story. "It's not a big deal, Dan," she lied. "Now, are you going to finish tidying your room, young man?" She patted him playfully on the bottom. "I found a half-eaten chocolate-spread sandwich under your bed the other day. I hope I don't find any more surprises today!"

A couple of hours later and Annie hadn't returned her call. Ashling had tried her friend's mobile but it was switched off. She had rung two other girls, schoolfriends of Milly's but Saturday-night baby-sitters were like golddust. Dan was 'helping' her clear away leaves from outside the house when the phone rang. Ashling prayed that it was Annie.

"Hi, Ash, it's Owen."

"Oh, hi, Owen."

"Don't sound so disappointed."

"Sorry," Ashling apologised. "I thought it was Annie, that's all."

"Is anything wrong?"

She sighed. "My school reunion is on this evening and my baby-sitting plans have fallen through. I was very shy in school, and well, this probably seems stupid, but I wanted to . . ." Ashling went silent.

"Go on," Owen encouraged.

"It's hard to explain really. I suppose I just want to tell people about Dan myself, not be the subject of some after-dinner gossip. And I want to show everyone that I've done all right – you know, with work and all."

"Ashling, you don't need the approval of strangers," Owen said gently. "You are amazing. Dan is a real credit to you. I don't know how you've managed in the last few years but you have."

"I know, and I suppose you're right," Ashling said thoughtfully. "But there's someone I have to see, just once."

Owen sensed that the evening was very important to Ashling. He wasn't sure who the mystery person was and he didn't like to pry. Maybe he could help. After all it was the least he could do. "Ashling, why don't I take Dan for the evening? He could stay overnight. I'm sure Fiona wouldn't mind."

"I couldn't ask you to do that. Josh is so tiny – you guys have enough on your hands without Dan too."

"I insist," Owen said. "Anyway, it will be fun. And you deserve a good night out, Ash. And from now on I'm here to help you in any way I can."

"If you're sure," Ashling replied smiling, with tears in her eyes. Maybe her luck had changed.

"And Ash?"

"Yes?"

"Good luck."

"You look lovely, Mum. Like a princess."

Ashling smiled. She gazed at herself in the full-length mirror again. She had twisted her hair in sections and piled it on top of her head, held in place by a mountain of hair clips and practically a whole can of hair-spray. Tiny silver butterfly hair-clips twinkled, highlighting the effect. The white *Ghost* dress swirled sensuously around her body and the dark pink pashmina draped over her upper arms looked sensational.

Not bad, she said to herself.

"Right, Dan, do you have your bag ready?"

"Yes, Mum."

"Did you pack your slippers and your toothbrush?"

"Mum, I've got everything," Dan replied. Sometimes his mum could be a real fusspot. "Let's go." He was excited about staying over at his dad's house. Maybe they'd let him stay up late and eat breakfast cereal without any milk. He loved that!

Ashling bundled him into the car, holding her dress around her hips with one hand and her dark pink evening shoes with the other. She was wearing her boots as she couldn't drive in her high heels. As Ashling parked the car Owen was waiting at the window with Josh.

Dan ran up the path to meet his dad who was now standing at the front door.

"Hi, " Owen smiled as he gestured her inside. "You look great, I like the hair. Very Zoe Ball."

"Thanks, I think," Ashling laughed. "Now are you sure this is all right?"

"Of course," Owen said. "It'll be fun. Won't it, Dan?"

"Sure will!"

"Why don't you go and find Fiona in the kitchen. She's feeding Josh."

Dan ran into the kitchen to find Fiona, in the hope of getting something nice to eat.

"Walk, Dan," Ashling shouted after him. "These are his things. He usually goes to bed around nine. I really appreciate this." She handed Owen Dan's overnight bag.

"Can I get you anything, a cup of tea or something?"

"Thanks, but I'd better get going. There's a drinks reception before the dinner."

Fiona came out of the kitchen with Josh on her hip, followed by Dan who was munching on a biscuit. "Sorry, Ashling, I gave Dan a custard cream. I hope you don't mind?"

Ashling smiled. "Not at all. He's a divil for the biscuits." She planted a kiss on Dan's cheek, trying to aviod his now crumby and sticky mouth. "Be good, love. I'll see you tomorrow."

"Have a good time," Owen called from the door as she stepped into her car.

"Thanks, I hope I will."

Chapter 45

"Who's that?" Shane asked Sally, gazing at the small blonde who had just walked in. "I don't remember her from school."

They had taken up residence in the corner of the St John's entrance hall, beside the door where the wine was being poured out and served. Easier to get a drink quickly if you were beside the source, they had all decided. Jean and Peter were discussing the price of houses in Dublin with their old Economics teacher, Mr Brady. Sasha had wisely chosen not to accompany Shane. He wasn't sure how he felt about this – he was curiously torn between relief and disappointment.

Sally had come on her own after having 'a talk' with George earlier that evening – "I'm sorry, it's not you, it's me . . . I'm just not ready for a commitment at the moment . . . I really like you but it's unfair to make you wait around . . . you're wonderful and if the timing had been right . . ." She couldn't seem to prevent the old clichés from pouring out. George had been upset but

467

had brightened considerably when she had added, "But we can still sleep together."

She had felt curiously hollow afterwards. Still, George was only her 'transitional man' as Meg Ryan would have put it and not the 'real thing'.

Sally looked at the woman who was holding Shane's attention. She looked familiar but she couldn't quite place her. Then it came to her. "I think that's Ashling McKenna, you know, the one who had the baby."

"No way," Shane said in amazement. "She didn't look like that in school. I would have noticed."

Sally laughed. "I'm sure you would."

Jean and Peter walked back over. "God, that man could still bore for Ireland," Jean moaned, slugging back the dregs of her white wine.

"He's not that bad," Peter said. "At least it wasn't Ratty."

"Don't speak too soon," Jean warned. "I think he's over there, talking to Georgina and Vinnie Winters."

"They're married?" Sally asked incredulously. "Someone married her?"

Jean laughed, "Don't say that so loudly, Sal, she'll hear."

"I don't care." Sally smiled. "The night is young, Jean. And I intend to enjoy myself. And there's Alicia McDevitt, what is she wearing? And what is that thing on her arm?"

Shane miaowed and rasped his fingers in the air, like claws.

"It's her husband," Jean giggled. "Would you stop, Sal."

"No way," Sally stated. "I intend to get my money's worth tonight. And if Alicia comes out wearing a 'Dolly Parton meets the Adams Family' dress, it's her own fault."

Jean looked Alicia up and down. She was squeezed into a black leather dress, fringed with silver and black tassels. Her calves were contained by high-heeled black leather boots. "I see she hasn't thrown away the Sun-In," Jean commented.

"Or the orange foundation," Sally added.

Shane and Jimbo decided they might as well join in.

"Her husband looks like a real computer geek," Jimbo said.

"Hey, watch who you're calling a computer geek," Shane complained.

"You're not a real computer geek," Jimbo explained. "You're a computer mogol."

"Right, thanks," Shane replied, not quite sure what his friend meant.

"We should really mingle," Jean said. "Catch up on all the news and stuff. If we stay here much longer we'll all be totally smashed in a little while."

"I'm already a bit drunk," Sally warned the gang. "Maybe you should be my chaperones," she continued pointing to Shane and Jimbo. "Otherwise I might get myself in trouble.

"No problem," Shane agreed. "I think we should find Ashling McKenna, I'd like to talk to her."

Sally looked at Shane darkly. "You have a girlfriend, Shane McCarthy. Or have you conveniently forgotten that?"

"I just said I'd like to talk to the girl. Where's the harm in that?"

Jean and Sally laughed.

"What?" Shane demanded. "Why are you laughing?"

"Talk," Jean giggled. "When was the last time you just 'talked' to a girl?"

"I'm hurt," Shane said, trying not to smile.

Sally linked his and Jimbo's arms and pulled him away. "See you later, guys," she said to Jean and Peter. "We're off to 'talk' to people."

"Will we be joining the others for drinks?" Mark asked his ex-headmaster.

"No," Mr Greene answered. "We don't really have time, I'm afraid." The grey-haired man winked at Mark and continued. "How's young Sally Hunter these days? You pair were doing a line, weren't you?"

Mark was amused. That was a long time ago. Mr Greene had a memory like an elephant's. "I don't know, to be honest. We lost touch in college. But I hope to meet her again later."

Mr Greene dug Mark in the ribs with his elbow. "I'm sure you do."

Shit, Mark thought to himself. Get me out of here. He spotted a tall, elegant woman standing alone in the corner. "Excuse me," he said to Mr Greene, and walked towards her.

"Hi," Mark smiled, holding out his hand. "I'm Mark Mulhearne."

The dark-haired woman smiled back at Mark. "I'm

Alison O'Reilly, nice to meet you. You're one of the speakers tonight, along with my husband."

"That's right," Mark said. "I'm a little nervous."

"So's Gerry," Alison replied kindly. "Our two boys are in St John's junior school and he wants to make a good impression on their future headmaster and teachers."

"What age are they?" Mark asked.

"Seven and eleven," Alison replied. "Do you have children yourself?"

"No," Mark replied. "But I've got two nephews."

Gerry O'Reilly appeared beside his wife and grinned at Mark. A tall thin man with a shock of dark hair, a lopsided mouth and a deep, chocolately voice, he was 2FM's unlikely heart-throb. "You're a great writer, man. I love Matt Scudder, he's cool. When's your next book out?"

"Well," Mark began. "I'm working on something different at the moment. Something a little more personal, I suppose you could say."

"Sounds interesting, man," Gerry said. "Tell me about it. I could put you in touch with Pat Kenny. He loves writers on his *Late Late* gig."

Mark smiled. Gerry and his wife were really nice. Maybe this evening wasn't going to be so difficult after all.

Eve felt strange walking up the St John's drive with John on her arm. The school brought back such vivid memories.

"Are you OK?" John asked gently as they approached the entrance.

She squeezed his arm and smiled at him. "Just a little nervous, I guess."

"Eve, you look stunning," he said. "You'll blow them away."

"Thanks," Eve smiled.

As they walked into the school Eve spotted faces she recognised. It was strange, everyone looked different, the men especially. She spotted 'Headboy Vinnie' and Georgina talking to Alicia and a wiry man with glasses. Vinnie had put on a huge amount of weight and his hair was receding fast. He was wearing a white tuxedo jacket which really didn't suit him. Georgina's red dress was far too tight – it clung to her spare tyres without mercy.

"Eve, how are you?"

Eve turned towards the voice. Jean and Peter were standing beside her. They hadn't changed a bit.

"Hi," Eve said smiling. She'd always liked Jean. "It's nice to see you. This is my boyfriend John." John shook their hands warmly. "And this is Jean and Peter."

"How are you?" Jean asked. "You look amazing, I love the dress."

"Thanks," Eve said. "I'm very well. And you?"

"Grand," Jean replied. "I saw your name in the paper recently, something about banking I think."

Eve smiled. "I write for the papers now and again on investments. Nothing very exciting."

"Nonsense! It sounds really interesting," Jean said. "Tell me about your job."

The two women talked about work for a while and

the men swapped Manchester United stories. Jean was amazed at the change in Eve. She used to be very serious and intense. She seemed less scary now, more approachable.

"Will you sit with us at dinner?" Jean asked as they heard one of waiters summoning them in to dinner.

"That would be nice, thanks," Eve replied smiling.

"I'll just warn you," Peter said. "Sally will be sitting with us. And Shane and Jimbo. And knowing that lot I think it may be quite a noisy table."

John grinned. "Sounds good to me! And I thought this was going to be a boring evening."

Eve looked at him and saw the twinkle in his eye.

"I'm just kidding, love," he said, putting his arm around her shoulders.

Ashling had been cornered by Georgina and Vinnie. She had been having an interesting conversation with Sheila Murphy and Jules who were telling her about their baby son, Pierre. Jules had moved over to Ireland a year after he had met Sheila in La Rochelle and he was now teaching sports in a school in Blackrock.

"Ashling McKenna, I do declare," Georgina bustled into the group. "Haven't you changed!"

Sheila and Jules excused themselves rapidly.

"Hello, Georgina, Vinnie," Ashling said, plastering on a fake smile. "How are you both?"

Vinnie looked at Ashling and was tempted to tell the truth. She looked stunning. He had definitely married the wrong woman. Georgina never stopped moaning and spent his money like water. And she was useless with the children, Spencer and Amelia, spoiling them rotten. He couldn't understand why they needed a nanny. After all, it wasn't as if Georgina worked or anything. She seemed to spend her time lunching with 'the girls' and shopping.

"Oh, we're great, aren't we, Vinnie?" Georgina replied. "Vinnie has just been promoted in the bank and we've just come back from a luxury holiday in Bali."

"How long have you been married now?" Ashling asked.

Too long, Vinnie thought to himself.

"Seven blissful years now," Georgina replied. "And where's your husband this evening?"

Ashling was confused. "I'm sorry?" she asked.

"Oh, silly me," Georgina continued. "I forgot. It's a baby you have, not a husband."

Vinnie winced. His wife could be such a bitch when she wanted to be.

Just then Sally, Shane and Jimbo joined them. "Hi, guys," Sally smiled. "And how are the happily married couple? Enjoying life? Keeping Georgina out of trouble, are you, Headboy Vinnie?"

"We're very well, thank you," Georgina purred. "And Shane, how are you? How nice to see you."

"Fine, thanks," Shane muttered before turning his attention to Ashling. "You look incredible. You were always attractive, even in school, Ashling. But now . . . words escape me."

Ashling smiled. She had no interest in Shane McCarthy, but she was flattered by the attention. She also knew that Georgina had always held a torch for him. "Flattery will get you everywhere," she laughed.

"I've read lots of your work in the *Courier*," Vinnie said. "You write very well."

"Thank you," Ashling said.

"But you don't get the *Courier*, darling," Georgina admonished. "You get *The Times*."

"I get the *Courier* in work, dear," he said.

"Do you write features, Ashling, or little stories?" Georgina asked condescendingly.

Sally glared at Georgina. She hadn't changed one little bit. "Where have you been, girl? Ashling is one of the top new reporters in the country. She's one of St John's success stories. I've been out of the country for years and even I knew that." Sally wasn't sure if Ashling was good, but she knew she'd got the news bit right.

"Sally's right, dear," Vinnie agreed. "Ashling is a very highly respected journalist. And she manages to look after her son too. Quite a wonder-woman."

Georgina was mortified. Her attempt at belittling Ashling had gone badly wrong. "Can't be easy on your own, Ashling," Georgina continued. "I have two so I should know. Even with the nanny it's difficult."

"Where do you work, Georgina?" Sally asked.

"Work? Oh no, I don't need to work," Georgina replied smiling smugly. "Vinnie makes more than enough for both of us."

"Better make sure he doesn't leave you then," Sally said ominously. "You'd be in trouble then."

Georgina giggled nervously, hoping that Sally was

joking. "It's just as well that Vinnie is devoted to me then, isn't it?"

Vinnie grunted.

"Well, we must say hello to darling Alicia and Tony. He owns Vitol Computers, he's very rich," Georgina smiled and pulled Vinnie away from the group. "So nice to talk to you all."

"Yeah, right," Jimbo muttered after they had left. "That woman would give anyone ulcers. I pity poor Vinnie."

Ashling smiled at Sally, Shane and Jimbo. "Thanks for coming over. Georgina has always made me feel so small. She's as bad as ever."

"I feel sorry for her, really," Sally said thoughtfully. "She has such a huge inferiority complex, always had. She was always such a green-eyed bitch. Anyway, I'm glad she's gone. Vinnie seemed very taken with you, Ashling."

Ashling blushed.

"And he's not the only one, Ashling," Shane said smiling. "I hope you'll dance with me later."

"I see you haven't changed either, Shane," Ashling laughed. "I'd be happy to, but only if we can dance right beside Georgina's table."

"Good girl yourself!" Sally encouraged. "A woman after my own heart."

"Will you sit with us at dinner?" Jimbo asked. "I'll warn you it might get a little rowdy though."

"That sounds like fun," Ashling laughed. "I'd love to. Thanks for asking."

Chapter 46

"Right," Jimbo stated as they had all taken their seats at tables in the St John's sports hall, which had been decked out in streamers and balloons for the occasion. "What's on the menu?" Sally passed him the white menu card, embossed with the school's eagle emblem. "Very posh," Jimbo commented, running his finger over the eagle. "Let me see. Mediterranean salad with goat's cheese, breast of chicken stuffed with herbs and served on a bed of balsamic rice. What's that when it's at home? And Banoffi. Sounds all right."

"What's the meat?" Shane asked.

"It's chicken," Sally said.

"That's not meat," Shane said, putting on his best 'cave-man' voice. "Us men need meat."

"I'd have to agree with Shane," John added. "Chicken isn't meat. We're growing lads."

Sally laughed. "Would you keep your man under control, Eve? He's not allowed to encourage Shane and Jimbo. They're bad enough as it is."

"I'll try," Eve said, smiling at John. She was really enjoying herself. Sally's personality had been a bit too wild for her liking in school, but now she found it refreshing and deliciously dangerous.

"Red or white?" the waitress asked Jimbo.

"One of each," he replied. "In fact you can leave the bottles."

"I'm not sure if . . ." the young waitress stuttered.

Shane gave her one of his special smiles. "I'm sure it will be OK. If there's any hassle I'll take responsibility." The waitress placed the bottles on the table.

"I suppose it's all right," she smiled at Shane. He reminded her of Ronan Keating.

"And maybe you could bring us a few more bottles?" Shane cajoled.

"I'll see," she said, cautiously.

"More glue, vicar," Sally said, laughing.

"I warned you it might get a little messy," Jean whispered to Eve who was sitting beside her.

"It's fine," Eve replied. "I haven't had so much fun in ages."

"Why is the table over there empty?" Peter asked, pointing at the centre of the room.

"Must be where the speakers and the Board are sitting," Eve replied.

"Mark Mulhearne's speaking, isn't he? Have you seen him recently?" Jimbo asked Sally innocently. Both Eve and Ashling pricked up their ears at the mention of his name.

"Na," Sally said, trying to think coherently. She'd

have to take it easy on the wine, it always went straight to her head. "I haven't spoken to him for years. We lost contact during college, I suppose. I'm looking forward to seeing him tonight though. I wonder is he still cute? I'm sure he's with someone though – he was always a bit of a serial monogamist."

"Sally!" Jean warned, glaring at her friend. Sally knew all about Eve and Mark's former relationship – she'd told her herself. She couldn't have forgotten already.

"What?" Sally asked.

Jean looked at Eve who seemed totally composed. The penny dropped for Sally.

"Oh, sorry, Eve, I didn't mean anything by that . . ."

Eve smiled. "It's fine, Sally, no offence taken."

Sally was relieved. She had a habit of putting her foot in it. Her friends were used to it but she didn't know Eve at all.

"That's all right so," Sally said. "He was a great snog though, wasn't he?"

"Sally!" Jean reprimanded. Everyone laughed.

Eve's eyes sparkled. She decided she might as well enter into the spirit of things. "Sally's right, he was. But he's got nothing on John."

"Can I try John later, so?" Sally asked grinning.

"Certainly not!" Eve countered. "He's all mine."

John laughed. "I'll see you at the bike sheds after dinner, Sally," he joked, winking at her.

Eve thumped him on the shoulder as the waitress came towards the table with four bottles of wine.

"A girl after my own heart," Shane said, wondering what age she was. "Thanks."

"Dangerous," Ashling said, smiling, as Shane poured her a large glass of white wine. She was thinking about Mark. It was like that bit in *Four Weddings and a Funeral* where Hugh Grant's character has to sit at a table with three ex-girlfriends. At least Mark would be saved that embarrassment.

"Did you ever kiss Mark?" Sally's voice rang out across the table. Ashling looked at her nervously. Luckily she was asking Jean and not herself.

"Don't be stupid," Jean giggled. "Sure haven't I been with Peter practically my whole life. When would I have got the chance?"

"Charming," Peter said, pretending to be hurt.

"You know I'm joking, chicken." Jean kissed Peter on the cheek.

The room went gradually quiet as Mr Green appeared, followed by Gerry O'Reilly. Other men and women trailed behind them.

Ashling's heart jumped as she spotted Mark. His hair was peppered with a few grey hairs and his face looked a little more lived-in but overall he looked great. On his arm was a tall woman, elegantly dressed and smiling felicitously at him. Well, what was I expecting? Ashling asked herself, feeling disappointed.

"Ashling?" Jimbo asked. "Are you feeling all right? You've gone a bit pale."

"I'm fine thanks," Ashling replied.

Eve studied Mark's face carefully. He really was most

attractive. Did she still have feeling for him, after everything that had happened? And what about John?

John watched Eve's face. Her eyes were fixed on one of the men who was sitting down at the speaker's table. She looked anxious, as if something serious was on her mind. John was worried. That afternoon he had opened his heart to her and told her how he felt about her. But she hadn't reciprocated.

Sally stared at Mark. Fuck, he still looked good! She took a large gulp of her wine. It was going to be an interesting evening.

Mark looked around the room as he walked into the hall. So many familiar faces – it was very unnerving. How was he going to get through the evening? Before he sat down he noticed Sally and Eve at a table behind him, with some of the gang from the sailing club. He caught Sally's eye and smiled broadly. She waved and smiled back. He must talk to her later. To both of them, in fact.

He hoped Eve wouldn't go all funny on him again though – he didn't know if he could take it tonight.

"You're on after Gerry," Alison said kindly, noticing his agitation and mistaking it for nerves. "He'll only talk for a few minutes, he's under strict orders from me."

Mark smiled at her. "I'm dreading it, but the sooner it's over with the better."

They tucked into their food, chatting amicably, interrupted now and again by loud laughter from Sally and Eve's table. At least they were enjoying themselves, he thought wryly.

As the coffee was served Mr Greene stood up and cleared his throat into the microphone.

"Ladies and gentlemen, or should I say boys and girls? It seems like only yesterday that you were all running around, playing kiss-chase in the playground." The crowd laughed.

"That was you, Shane," Sally said. "In sixth year."

Shane smiled. "Actually, I think he's talking about you, Sal."

"Who would have guessed that you would all have turned into such delightful adults," Mr Greene continued. "And not a criminal among you." He cleared his throat again, remembering suddenly that Richie Malone had been charged with tax evasion and was now living on the Isle of Man. "And now I'd like to introduce you to a man who needs no introduction – Mr Gerry O'Reilly." Everyone clapped loudly as the popular DJ strode up to the microphone.

"Um, hiya," Gerry began. "I'd like to thank Mr Greene for inviting me here tonight. To be honest the only reason I'm here is so he'll be nice to me nippers when they're in senior school. I thought, you know, if he was going to suspend them or something I could remind him of tonight." Everyone laughed and clapped enthusiastically. Mr Greene wasn't quite sure how to react so he decided he'd better join in. "Seriously though, I think St John's, as schools go, isn't bad. The teachers are cool enough and the whole school embraces kids who are a little different. The kids come out knowing that they don't have to be a rocket scientist or an all-Ireland rugby player. As long as they do their best and are happy, that's all that matters. I have two kids and neither of them are brainy. In fact one of them had really bad trouble with the old reading until recently. But they were looked after and the teachers let them both progress in their own good time. That was how Miss Lynch, that's the youngest lad's teacher, put it. She said 'Gerry, he'll progress in his own good time. When he's gained the confidence in his reading he'll fly along.' I liked that. She's a nice lady." Gerry paused and took a sip of water. "I wasn't much of a school head myself. I left at sixteen and stuff. But I know I want me kids to have the education I didn't have and I think St John's is the best I can give them. So thanks, Mr Greene, you have a good school here. Now enjoy!"

"Thank you for your heartfelt sentiments," Mr Greene said. He was impressed with Gerry O'Reilly's honesty and he liked his straightforward delivery. "And now I'd like to introduce one of St John's success stories, the lawyer and bestselling author – Mark Mulhearne!"

Mark stepped up to the microphone, holding his speech nervously. He looked around the room. All eyes were on him. He recognised most of the faces – the boffins from the computer and chess clubs, the rugby and hockey players, his fellow debating-team members, and Sally and the gang from the sailing. As his ex-classmates clapped, he stared at Sally's table more closely. He thought he saw Ashling sitting beside Shane. But the clapping had subsided and everyone was waiting eagerly for his speech. He couldn't take another look.

Mark stood up pokerstraight and began. "Like Gerry, I'd like to thank Mr Greene for inviting me here tonight. Firstly, it meant I didn't have to pay." The crowd laughed warmly. "And it also meant I got the chance to meet Gerry and his lovely wife Alison." He gestured at the couple who smiled up at him. Ashling sat up sharply. The woman who walked in on Mark's arm was Alison O'Reilly! "I'd like to thank Gerry for his speech. He's right about St John's – it's a school that really cares. And in this day and age I think that that's something to cherish." The crowd clapped again. "I was lucky enough to be a pupil here for six very happy years. And I owe my interest in English and in writing in part to Mr Cahill who, although my mother cursed him at the time for taking up so much of her time hearing my poetry and Shakespeare speeches, fostered the love of English literature in me. I can still remember poems I learnt at that time and I re-read many of the novels he introduced me to such as *The Great Gatsby* with wonder and awe." Mark paused. "I write because I have to write. And I write because I love to write. It's not an easy job. The hours can be long and lonely. Sometimes when things are going badly it can seem like a chapter or even a sentence will never be finished. But above all it's a privilege. To call myself a writer and to have my books published is a blessing that I never take for granted. I'd like to read to you from my new book. As most of you will know my previous books have been crime novels, based around a character called Max Scudder. This book is a little different. It's called *Luke's Story.*" Mark paused for a second to collect his thoughts and began reading. *"Luke Ryan pulled his long, heavy wool coat around his body and lowered his head into the wind. It was a bleak day, the wind whipped around him, like whip-cracks, chilling him to the marrow. The night street was deserted. As he drew nearer Alice's house he became more and more anxious. He had been away for so long but she had never left his mind, not once in almost six years. Luke could still picture every intricate detail, her honey-blonde hair, her gentle smile and her laugh that wrapped itself around your heart and never let go . . ."*

There was deathly silence as Mark read. Even Sally was humbled into silence. Ashling closed her eyes and listened to Mark's familiar voice telling the heart-breaking and romantic story. Ashling thought about the past, their late-night talks, discussing the troubles of the world, their shared meals and shared days out. It hurt her just to think about it.

Mark finished his reading and there was a moment's silence before the genuine, booming applause.

"Good one, mate," Gerry smiled as Mark sat down. "Can't wait to read it."

"I'd like to thank Mark for that wonderful reading. *Luke's Story* will be out in the spring. And now I'd ask you to bear with us as we move the tables for the dancing."

Mark looked over at Sally's table again. The group were on their feet, hovering as their table was shoved against the wall by a young waitress, helped enthuastically by Shane and Jimbo. Watching the proceedings from the sidelines and chatting to Jean and Peter was Ashling. So he hadn't been seeing things earlier! She looked beautiful. He couldn't take his eyes off her.

"Mark?" His thoughts were interrupted by Eve who slipped into Gerry's seat beside him. Gerry was talking to one of the waiters about getting into radio.

"Hi, Eve," Mark said nervously.

"I just wanted to say sorry," Eve said sincerely. "I know I gave you a hard time, but anyway . . . things are different now."

"That's all right," Mark said. "Maybe we can really talk sometime."

Eve looked at his face carefully. She felt . . . nothing. Before the last time they had met in La Stampa she had convinced herself that Mark was the man for her – no questions asked. But that was before John. She had created an image of Mark in her head that had nothing to do with the real Mark. And now it was time to finally let go of that ideal man and get on with her life.

"I'd like us to be friends, real friends," Eve said genuinely. "And I'd like you to meet my boyfriend, John, later," she continued, smiling. "You'll like him."

"I'm sure I will," Mark replied.

"I'll see you later," Eve stood up. "I'd better get back to John."

As he watched her walk back towards her table his eyes met Ashling's. He was transfixed. He smiled at her and she looked away. He wasn't sure what to do. Right at this moment he wanted to talk to her more than anything in the world. He stood up and excused himself from the table. Slowly and purposefully he made his way towards her, never once letting her out of his sight. Just before he reached her Sally stepped in front of him.

"Hi, Mark." Sally looked at him closely, his expressive, kind eyes and his highly kissable mouth. With George there were butterflies in her stomach, rushes of adrenaline, heightened sensations. Sally dismissed it as 'hormones' but perhaps a good dose of 'hormones' was important in a relationship. Maybe Mark wasn't the man for her after all. Anyway, no harm in giving it a try, Sally thought to herself.

"Sally, nice to see you. How have you been?" He tried not to seem as distracted as he felt. He examined her face and tried to concentrate. She still had a movie-star figure, and tonight it was poured into a tight red dress which left nothing to the imagination.

"Great, thanks. I hear you're back from Boston for good now."

Mark nodded. "That's right. I'm staying with my sister and her family at the moment – you remember Susan?"

"Yes, she was a couple of years ahead of us, wasn't she?"

"Three. I'm looking for a flat though. Somewhere on the southside, near the sea," Mark went on.

"I'm looking for a place myself at the moment," Sally laughed. "Myself and Emma are going to share a place. Mum is driving us both mad."

Mark smiled. He wasn't surprised. He remembered Mrs Hunter only too well. "Well, I hope it all works out for you. Where are you working?"

"I was in the Caribbean the last few years," Sally explained. "Working on boats. And I'm teaching in the sailing-school in Dun Laoghaire at the moment. I like it there so we'll see what happens."

"You're making me jealous," Mark said wistfully. "I haven't sailed for years. I really miss it."

"If you like I'll take you out sometime. We could have a trip to Dalkey Island or Howth on one of the sailing school boats and catch up on old times."

"Sally," Mark grinned. "There's nothing I'd like better. I'll hold you to that."

"On one condition," Sally added.

"Yes?"

"You let me call the shots."

Mark laughed. "Absolutely! Now, how about a dance?

Sally grabbed his hand and led him onto the dance-floor. "I thought you'd never ask!"

She tried not to compare his moves with George's but it was hard. She tried to push George from her mind, determined to enjoy herself with Mark. After a few dances Sally decided it was no use, Mark was a lovely guy but . . . she wanted George. Right now!

"Excuse me," she shouted to Mark over the music. "There's something I have to do, I'll see you later."

Mark watched Sally's back as she walked over to Eve and left the hall clutching the other woman's silver mobile phone. Women were all mad! He'd enjoyed dancing with Sally, but he'd forgotten how exhausting she was.

Feeling alone, he finally made his way towards Ashling who was at the table with the now seated Eve. Ashling's head was down, almost touching her knees.

"Hello, Ashling," Mark said, trying to sound more confident than he felt. "Are you all right?"

"Mark," Ashling raised her head suddenly. She could feel a shock of adrenaline racing through her veins. She tried to keep her breathing normal and even. "I was just checking my phone for messages – Dan's staying with Owen tonight for the first time. I'm sure he's fine but I worry about him . . . sorry, you don't want to hear all this."

"Yes, I do," Mark stated firmly before he could stop himself.

Ashling blushed. She wished he would just go away and leave her alone. She couldn't cope with this. Seeing him again after all this time was hard. It brought back feelings that she had spent years dealing with and trying to forget.

"How is Dan?" Mark asked, after an awkward pause.

"Do you really care?" Ashling snapped, lashing out before she could stop herself.

"Ashling!" Mark was shocked. This wasn't like the Ashling he used to know.

"I'm sorry," she whispered. "I don't know why I said that. It just came out."

"My question was genuine."

Ashling was embarrassed. She barely trusted herself to speak. "He's fine, thanks."

"Right," Mark persevered nervously. "And where are you working now?"

"The *Courier.*" Shit, she thought to herself. Why am I being like this? Snap out of it, Ashling.

"In what department?" Mark continued, growing more and more uneasy. This was like getting blood from a stone. It wasn't meant to be this hard.

"News."

"Do you want me to go?" Mark asked, looking at her carefully. Her lips were pressed together, forming a thin line and there were lightly furrowed lines on her brow.

"Yes."

"Have I done something wrong?"

"I . . ." Ashling didn't know what to say. Emotions crashed over her like waves over jagged rocks. They threatened to engulf her and drag her down into their cold, stormy depths. Tears welled up in her eyes. "I can't talk to you right now." She was mortified. Mark must think I'm seriously unhinged, she thought to herself.

"I . . . I'd really like to talk to you, Ashling," Mark stumbled over his words. "Could we take a walk outside?"

"What, now?" Ashling asked in confusion.

"I guess," Mark said uncertainly. He wanted to talk to her alone so badly that it hurt.

"No," Ashling whispered. "I'm sorry." She stared down at her hands which were clasped around her mobile. Her knuckles were white.

Mark stood up in a daze. He felt physically sick. He walked slowly away, oblivious to everyone around him. Music and laughter assaulted his ears but the loudest noise in the room was the sound of his own heart thumping in his chest.

"Mark," Gerry O'Reilly shouted over from the side of the hall. "Come and join us."

He gritted his teeth and made his way across the crowds.

Ashling watched, her eyes blurred from hot, stinging tears as Mark left her without saying a word, finally sitting down at a table at the far end of the hall.

She pulled herself quickly to her feet and made her way as fast as the crowds would allow to the girl's toilet in the corridor outside. She dabbed the corner of her eyes with the edge of the cotton handtowel which hung from the wall. Sitting down on one of the closed toilet seats, she placed her hands on the white wooden door in front of her. It felt cool to the touch. She took several deep breaths, willing herself not to cry

Why didn't I go outside with Mark? It wouldn't have killed me, she thought to herself. After all, he is the reason I'm here. I have to talk to him one last time.

Ashling stared at the graffiti on the walls. *Kitty loves Rollo*, it read. *Boys are all mad*, said another. *Andrew Blake is a ride*, read a third. She tried to smile. She wished she had a pen now. She'd never have dared to write on the walls in school, but things were different now. *You have nothing to fear*, she'd write, *but fear itself . . .*

Ashling sat bolt upright and stared straight ahead of her. She now knew what she had to do, but would she have the courage to go through with it?

Chapter 47

"George, lower your voice. Someone will hear us," Sally whispered. "These are the teachers' toilets. We shouldn't be in here."

"I can't help it. You're so fucking sexy," George wrestled with Sally's dress, pulling it up over her hips. The cubicle was tiny so he was having a few problems.

Sally kissed him forcefully. "God, I want you," she moaned. She reached down and unbuttoned his black Levis.

George groaned with pleasure as she firmly gripped his hardness.

"This might be easier," Sally whispered, as she twisted around, her back facing George. She placed her hands in the toilet cistern and turned to look at him, grinning wickedly.

"Oh, baby!" George exclaimed.

"I can't believe you're going out with a guard!" Jean squealed.

Eve laughed. "I know, I know."

The two women were sharing a bottle of wine. Peter and John were discussing cars at the far side of the table. They were interrupted by a flushed-looking Sally, who was staggering towards them, a tall dark-haired man in tow.

"Hi, guys," Sally beamed. "This is George. He's . . ." She smiled at George and pulled him towards her, throwing both her arms around his neck. "He's my lucky boyfriend."

George was delighted. He didn't know why Sally had had such a change of heart – after all she'd said. But he was seriously in lust with her. Hell, it might even be love! He kissed her on the cheek and waved happily at her friends.

"Hi," he beamed. "Nice to meet you all."

"This is Jean, my best friend," Sally nodded at Jean. "And her fiancé, Peter." Jean and Peter both protested loudly.

"Sally!"

"Well, you've both admitted to wanting to marry each other sometime."

"That's true, I suppose," Jean began doubtfully. "But we're not engaged."

"A mere technicality," Sally stated firmly. "Anyway, moving swiftly on – beside Peter is John . . ."

"Or, Garda Redmond, as you may have to call him sometime soon, Sally," Jean added threateningly. "Unless you decide to behave!"

"Doubtful," George laughed.

"You're not a guard!" Sally exclaimed. "You're too good-looking. And you don't have that strange midlands accent."

"There are lots of things about me that would surprise you, Sally," John said cryptically, winking at Eve.

"And finally, John's girlfriend, and my new friend, Eve." Sally sighed. "Now, after all that taxing brain-work, I need a large drink."

A little later, Sally touched Eve on the arm.

"I nearly forgot, here's your phone. Thanks a million."

"No problem," Eve replied. "Hey, I like George, he's great fun." George was 'dancing' with John, Jean, Jimbo and Shane, leading a long, snake-like Conga around the hall, weaving in and out of the tables.

"John seems nice too."

Eve smiled gratefully. "Yes, he is. It took me a little while to overcome the whole guard thing, to be honest. But he's a good man and I . . . I love him very much."

"I can tell he adores you," Sally said gently. "I hope it all works out for you."

"So do I."

"Did you ever think ten years ago that we'd be sitting here like this – chatting like old friends?" Sally asked thoughtfully.

"Never!" Eve laughed.

"You've changed a lot since school," Sally said, slowly. "You know what we all used to call you?"

"Ice Eve," Eve smiled. "I hated it then, but it doesn't bother me now. I'm not surprised, really. I was very stand-offish in school. But you're right, I have changed. And you have too – you're much more approachable now. Still mad though, I'm glad to see!"

"Thanks, I think," Sally laughed. "Listen, how about a boozy lunch next week? And you can tell me all about Garda Redmond – the whole, uncut story."

"You're on," Eve beamed. "But only if you reveal all the details of your own Prince Charming."

"I'd be delighted," Sally giggled. "It may be a little X-rated though, I warn you."

Eve raised her eyebrows in mock horror. "Sounds intriguing, I can't wait."

"Let's have another glass of wine," Sally said, a dangerous glint in her eyes. "After all, we both have lots to celebrate." She filled Eve's glass to the brim before topping up her own.

"To friends, old and new," Eve declared, raising her glass in the air.

Sally clinked her glass to Eve's. "To friends!"

In dismay, Ashling stared at the table where Mark had been sitting. He had gone! A wave of disappointment washed over her, disappointment and regret. She pulled herself together and slowly criss-crossed her way through the crowded hall, back to her table where she would make polite goodbyes, order a taxi and go home. She hoped no-one would ask any awkward questions about her early departure, but she had Dan as an excuse.

She smiled half-heartedly at classmates she recognised as she passed them, sitting at their tables, laughing and enjoying themselves. She tried not to think about Mark but it was impossible. *Damn, damn, damn,* she thought to herself. Why didn't I talk to him? At least it would have put my mind at rest.

As she approached her table she eyes focused on a lone seated figure who was running his hands over her pink pashmina, which stood out starkly against his dark dress-suit. Her heart leapt and pounded in her chest as she recognised him – it was Mark! She reached out and touched him gently on the shoulder.

"Jeeze!" He jumped as her hand grazed his shoulder. "Ashling, you startled me. I was waiting to talk to you." He looked at her carefully. Did her eyes have a red tinge? It was hard to see in the dimmed lights.

"Yes?" Ashling whispered.

He looked at her beseechingly. "Please come outside."

She nodded. Mark stood up and draped the pashmina over her shoulders. Ashling shivered as his hands brushed her bare upper arms. It felt deliciously intimate.

"I'll follow you out," she said nervously. She was oblivious to the noise around them. All she could think about was her own thumping heart. She knew he couldn't have any feelings for her after all this time, but she couldn't stop herself.

They made their way around the edge of the dancefloor and out the main doorway. Several people stopped to congratulate Mark on his reading, so it was several minutes before they were outside.

As soon as they stepped outside the door Mark linked Ashling's arm in his. She almost shrugged his arm away but thought better of it. The sky was clear, stars twinkling and an almost-full moon shining, throwing muted yellow light onto the school and playing fields. They walked down the drive in silence until they reached one of the benches overlooking the hockey pitch.

"Will we sit?" Mark asked. "Hang on – I don't want you to get your dress dirty." He took off his jacket and placed it on the wooden bench.

"Thanks," Ashling murmured, sitting down. She had no idea what Mark wanted to say to her and she didn't trust herself to speak.

"This is kind of hard for me," Mark began. "So I'll say what's on my mind quickly and get it over with."

"Sounds painful," Ashling attempted a smile.

Mark began. "Susan told me about meeting you at Homewood Ball and that you wrote to me in Boston." He sighed. "This sounds terrible but I never got your letters. I moved soon after I arrived and I didn't leave a forwarding address in the old apartment. Stupid really."

Ashling was taken aback. It was so long ago. She'd tried to forget about it and get on with things. She'd presumed that he'd lost interest or had been too busy to reply. "I see. You don't have to explain. It's not a big deal," she said slowly.

"But it is," Mark continued. "I thought you'd forgotten about me and found someone else. I didn't want to push it and after a while I tried to put you to the back of my mind. And it worked for a long time."

Ashling stared at her hands. She allowed him to continue uninterrupted.

"But as soon as I got back to Ireland everything began to remind me of you. And I just wanted to tell you that . . ." Mark's voice dropped to a whisper. "That . . ."

"What?" Ashling asked gently. That he'd managed to forget her finally? That he was over her? That he regretted kissing her all those years ago?

Mark tumbled the words out. "That I've never stopped loving you."

Ashling raised her head. There were tears in her eyes. "You can't do this, Mark," she said. "You can't come back and say things like that. It's not fair."

"Why not?" Mark asked.

"You left me. I really needed you and you left me. You can't come back now and expect me to be waiting for you."

Mark sighed. She was right. He shouldn't have left her – but he was young and it was something that he'd had to do. He took Ashling's hands in his and held them tightly. "Ash, if I could change things I would, believe me. But life doesn't always work out the way you want it to. I don't know what to say. I think we're supposed to be together. I've never met anyone who I can talk to the way I can talk to you. I love being with you. I love everything about you. I see that now."

Ashling's head was racing. She wanted Mark back in her life more than anything but it still hurt to think that he hadn't been there for her over the last few years. Could she ever trust him again?

"Mark," she said slowly. "That was a long time ago, things change – I've changed and I'm sure you have too. This is all too much. There is too much – history . . ."

There was deafening silence for a few minutes. "I understand," Mark said, finally. "I'm sorry, but I just had to tell you how I felt. I've been thinking of nothing else since I saw you in the park with Owen and it's doing my head in."

"In the park?" Ashling asked, confused. "Dun Laoghaire park?" Mark nodded. "Why didn't you say hello?"

"You were with Owen and Dan, and I thought . . . well, I didn't want to intrude."

"We're not together," Ashling said quickly, surprising herself. "He was there for Dan, not for me."

"I'm glad," Mark began. "For Dan, I mean." He added. "Shit, Ash, this is so difficult. Can't you just think about it?"

"There's not just me to consider, there's Dan too. It's not the right time . . ."

"Dan isn't a problem for me. He never has been – you know that. And what if it's never the right time? Are you prepared to risk that?" Mark demanded. "Ashling, there's no-one else for me. There never has been. I need you in my life. Please . . ."

"Let's go back inside," Ashling said quietly. "Mr Greene will be wondering where his star turn is."

"Only if you promise me one thing." Mark said earnestly.

"Yes?"

"The first dance."

Ashling smiled. "You never give up, do you?"

"I'll never give up on you, Ashling, no matter how long it takes. I promise you that."

Mark put his arm around her shoulders and this time she didn't consider shrugging it off.

"Who's that on the table?" Ashling asked Mark as they walked in the door of the sports hall and fixed their eyes on the two animated figures.

"I think it's Sally and Eve!" Mark laughed as they made their way towards the girls who were dancing to 'Tainted Love', waving their arms and singing loudly. He'd seen everything now!

Peter was throwing Jean around the dance floor and John, Shane and Jimbo were sitting at the table the girls were dancing on, huge smoke-billowing cigars in their mouths, leaning on the wooden surface to prevent it from up-turning.

"What a motley crew," Mark smiled. "Will you dance?" He pulled her gently by the hand to the edge of the dance-floor.

"Yes," Ashling whispered, wrapping her arms around him and drawing him closely towards her. He rested his cheek on hers. She smiled behind his back.

"Now I know I've come home," he murmured into her ear.

"Me too," Ashling said, before she could stop herself. "Me too!"

THE END

It Had To Be You

This one's for my sisters, Kate and Emma.

Thanks

To all my family and friends, especially Mum and Dad, Kate and Richard; Emma, Peter, Luan and Charlie; Ben, Sam and Amy-Rose; Nicky, Andrew and Tanya.

To my agent Ali Gunne, for her advice and enthusiasm. And to Milly Gosworth for all her help.

To all in Macmillan – especially my editor, Imogen Taylor, David North, Emma Bravo, David Adamson and Trisha Jackson. And to Cormac Kinsella in Repforce.

To Councillor Mary Elliott and Deputy Fiona O'Malley for the invaluable insights into the world of local councillors and Irish politics.

To the staff at Dalkey library, especially Trish Byrne and Niall Brewster for all the help in finding just the books I needed for my research, and for never asking why I desperately needed information on dating, shoes and pregnancy all on the same day!

To all my writing friends – especially Martina Devlin, Martina Murphy, Clare Dowling and all the Irish Girls. It's a pleasure knowing you and thanks for all the fun lunches, dinners, e-mails and phone calls.

To all those in the Irish book trade who have always been so encouraging – especially Tom Owens, Eoin McHugh, David O'Callaghan, Alan Johnson, Maria Dickenson, Cathal Elliot, Bert Wright and all the Eason gang.

And to all the booksellers I met on my last book tour – especially Seamus Duffy in Westport – thanks for all the support and kindness.

And finally to you, the reader. I hope you enjoy reading *It Had To Be You* as much as I enjoyed writing it. I love hearing from my readers so do drop me an e-mail. You can contact me through my website – www.sarahwebb.info.

After writing *It Had To Be You*, my sister, Emma, told me about an area near Greystones, Co. Wicklow called 'The Burnaby'. I've become so attached to my own fictional village, Burnaby Village, that it would break my heart to change it – so Burnaby Village it stays. But, for the record, there's no Happily Ever After in 'The Burnaby', or anywhere else in Ireland for that matter – and more's the pity!

'Make good use of bad rubbish'
Elizabeth Beresford

Chapter 1

Molly

The minute Anita walked through the door of Happily Ever After bookshop that fateful Monday morning, Molly knew that something was up. Although Anita looked perfectly normal – her long red hair tied back in its customary loose chignon, her floor-sweeping black jersey dress clinging in all the wrong, bumpy places – there was a strange expression on her face. Her usual Monday wrinkled brow looked a little less furrowed and her gait was loose and almost girlish, unlike her more normal heavy-footed loaf. She smiled at Molly as soon as she swung open the door, sending the small bell into wild reverberations.

'Hi Molly, how are you this fine morning?'

Molly studied her boss carefully. Was Anita *really* smiling? It suited her: more's the pity that she didn't do it more often.

'Anita. You're early. I wasn't expecting you until lunchtime.'

Although Anita lived in an apartment directly above the bookshop, she wasn't know to be an early riser. She rarely lifted her head from her anti-allergy pillow until after ten, and without exception never made it down the stairs and through the shop door before noon, though she was usually just in time to be taken out to lunch by whichever publisher's rep was currently courting her. Anita was crotchety and ill-tempered at the best of times but she also had an unerring talent for spotting bestsellers. Every day she received at least ten couriered packages or jiffy bags containing manuscripts and proofs from various publishers – some from as far away as America and Canada. She was the best-kept secret in Irish bookselling and, as publishers had been telling her for years, she'd missed her calling as an editor. What they didn't know and what she'd never divulged was that she *had* worked as an editor for a large British publisher many moons ago and the experience had been enough to put her off the publishing business for life.

Anita sniffed. 'Yes, well, I have some news. Where's the other poor unfortunate?'

'In the back going through the Eason's order.'

'I see,' Anita said dreamily.

Molly looked at her carefully – Anita was behaving most strangely this morning.

The bell on the door finally stopped ringing and Molly breathed a sigh of relief, grateful for the peace once again. As if to compensate, Anita picked up a stapler off the counter and began to play with it – pressing it together and watching as closed staples fell uselessly onto the fake pine with whispery rattles.

Molly coughed. Anita looked at her. She knew how much Molly hated her fidgeting. They'd had many minor arguments about it over the past few years. Molly had been working in Anita's bookshop for nearly six years now – ever since she'd left college – progressing from lowly part-time assistant to the lofty heights of shop manager. She and Anita were like chalk and cheese and it was amazing that they hadn't killed each other yet.

Molly brushed the wasted staples onto her right hand and dropped them purposefully into the bin under the counter. She resisted the temptation to pull out the duster to polish the fake pine. It was only ten o'clock after all and they'd only just opened. Not even one greasy customer fingerprint to warrant such action yet.

'Felix came in especially early this morning to get the new orders processed,' Molly said. Felix was the other full-time staff member. 'It's really busy at the moment what with the Rosemary Hamilton reading and the Book Club meeting, both on the same day.' She looked at Anita pointedly.

Anita ignored her and instead picked up yesterday's copy of the *Sunday Ireland* newspaper and began to flick through it. Molly sighed and went back to cutting up *The Times* book pages, continuing her usual Monday morning review selection for the bookshop's large notice board. Anita had booked Rosemary to read and sign, forgetting that it would clash with the Book Club, which met religiously on the first Saturday morning of every month. And by the time Molly had realized the mistake, it had been too late to cancel Rosemary's event. Meaning yet more work for Molly. Still, she was looking forward to meeting the popular American writer.

Rosemary Hamilton was starting to break through in Ireland and the UK. She wrote big, generous, kind-hearted romantic sagas, exactly the kind of books that both Anita and Molly liked to read. It was one of the few things that they actually had in common. Rosemary had been described as an 'American Maeve Binchy' and there had been terrific response to the event which they'd advertised in the local press and which had been picked up by some of the nationals, even the *Irish Daily* who weren't exactly renowned for their love of romantic fiction.

Anita Vickers had opened Happily Ever After to cater for readers like herself – voracious readers of popular fiction, especially romantic fiction, thrillers and crime novels. And although the shop had a decidedly female slant, including its very own pink-couched 'Romance Room' packed full of all kinds of women's fiction from Mills and Boon to Jane Austen, they also had many loyal male customers who travelled to Burnaby

Village, to find books by their favourite American crime writers which were difficult to come by in mainstream bookshops.

Happily Ever After was just off Burnaby's main street, tucked between Coffee Heaven, and Slick Harry's – Irish floral-design legend Harry Masterson's shop which specialized in unusual plants and shrubs and catered to the well-heeled market. Burnaby Village, nestled on the south Dublin coast, was a Mecca for shoppers with a taste for the unusual. Hidden within its windy, cobbled laneways was the tiny yet perfectly formed print and art gallery, Halo; Presents of Mind, a gift shop crammed full of all kinds of delights including a miniature stone Buddha carved from pink, black and white marble; funky American cloth bags decorated with Andy Warholesque prints for the discerning grocery shopper; not to mention Baroque, the uber-trendy shoe emporium stocking everything from Converse and Camper, to Gina and Jimmy Choo.

The bell rang and Molly looked up. Their first customer of the day.

'Morning.' She smiled at the tall, white-haired woman.

'Hello. Have you got the new Ivy White book? I believe it came out today.'

'You might be in luck. We've just received an order of new titles and it should be in one of the boxes. Let me check for you.'

'Thanks,' the woman said gratefully. 'I'm going on my holidays today and I was hoping to take it with me.' Molly went into the back room to find it for her.

'It's good,' said Anita thoughtfully while the customer waited. 'She writes wonderfully about affairs of the heart, don't you think?'

'Yes.' The woman nodded. 'Quite.'

Molly came out smiling, holding the spanking-new book out in front of her. 'Here we are. The very first copy. We haven't even priced it yet.'

After the woman left, happily swinging her dark pink

Happily Ever After bag by her side, Molly looked at Anita. 'What were you saying about having news? I got distracted by a scathing review of Paddy O'Hara's new thriller.'

'I'm not surprised, it was very harsh indeed,' said Anita. 'And completely undeserved, poor man.'

'Your news?' Molly pressed.

'Ah, yes. I was just coming to that. Can you get Felix?'

'Can't you tell me first? Please.'

'Of course.' Anita smiled easily, unnerving Molly yet again. 'I've just sold the shop.'

'You've what?' Molly stared at her incredulously.

'Sold the shop.'

'You can't have.'

'Ah, but I did.'

'To who?'

'To whom, you mean?'

'Anita!' Molly was reeling with shock and didn't need a lesson in grammar right now.

The bell on the door rang again and Molly cursed inwardly. This was unbelievable. Anita *was* Happily Ever After, the bookshop wouldn't exist without her. And Anita almost wouldn't exist without the shop – the shop was her whole life.

Molly heard a discreet cough. Anita was staring at her. Patricia Simons, the Trinity publisher's sales rep was standing in front of them, glammed up to the teeth as usual in a perfectly-pressed navy suit with cream and red pipe-edging, a dazzling sheen on her immaculately bobbed blonde hair and her lips painted a perfect rosebud pink. 'Penny for them,' Patricia smiled.

Molly looked at Anita's face which somewhat unnervingly wasn't betraying any emotion at all, and back at Patricia. 'Sorry, I was miles away,' she said. 'Anita just told me some rather surprising news.'

'Oh, really?' Patricia's eyes lit up. She loved news, and she loved being the purveyor of it to all her customers. Nothing like a juicy bit of gossip, ahem, news to make the day go a little faster.

Anita glared at Molly. Had Molly taken leave of her senses? Telling Patricia anything guaranteed that it would be all over town in the blink of an eye. Bush fires had nothing on this publisher's rep.

'Well?' Patricia tapped her red nails on the counter-top impatiently.

Molly could feel the heat of Anita's stare and chose to ignore it. She wasn't stupid – she knew exactly how big Patricia's mouth was and she had no intention of telling the woman anything. She just wanted to make Anita sweat. 'Harry Masterson is thinking of opening a lap dancing club in the basement of Slick Harry's. What do you think of that?'

'Really?' Patricia asked with unabashed interest. 'But that's just beside you. It could bring in some interesting new business, I suppose.'

Molly laughed. 'Could do. But I'm only joking! Harry isn't exactly the lap dancing type.'

Patricia frowned. Molly often poked fun at her expense and she didn't like it one little bit. She sniffed. 'He's a business man though. It wouldn't be the worst idea in the world.'

'Would you like some coffee?' Anita interrupted. She knew there was no love lost between the two women.

'Love some,' Patricia smiled gratefully. 'But why don't we pop next door? My treat. I have a manuscript that I'd love you to read. A young Irish author straight out of college that Trinity's looking at acquiring.'

Anita looked at Molly who shrugged her shoulders. 'We'll have that meeting as soon as I get back,' promised Anita. 'I won't be long.'

'Fine. I have plenty to be getting on with.' Molly turned

towards Patricia. 'Are we doing the order for the December new titles today?'

'I'll do the order with Anita if that's all right. There's nothing of much importance, to tell the truth. December is a pretty dead month for us.'

'Fine,' Molly said curtly. It was her job to order the new titles for the shop from the sales reps and Patricia knew this. Patricia was no fool. The experienced rep knew she'd get a far larger order than was strictly necessary from Anita – who always got carried away in the face of glossy new fiction titles and blew their budget for the month with one single publisher. Which was precisely why Anita and Molly had agreed years ago that Molly would do all the 'front list' or new title ordering.

As soon as Anita and Patricia had left the shop Molly picked up the phone and dialled nine for an outside line.

'Paige? Pick up if you're there. It's Molly.'

Paige, a Burnaby County Councillor and Molly's best friend, was notorious for screening her calls. She said it was a necessity in her business when all the local nutters had both her work and home numbers and were likely to call at all hours of the day to complain about anything that took their fancy – from blocked drains and leaking pipes, to noisy neighbours and dog poo on the streets.

'Hi, Molly. How are you this fine morning?'

'Do you have me on speaker phone again?'

'No.'

'You do, don't you?'

'Well yes, but I'm in the middle of typing a document and . . .'

'No buts. I demand your 100 per cent concentration. It's important.'

Paige picked up the receiver. 'OK, you have it. Now what's up?'

'I can't believe you never told me about Anita selling the shop.'

7

'Happily Ever After?'

'Yes! What other shop would I be talking about?' snapped Molly.

'Keep your shirt on. I didn't know. I would have told you if I'd heard anything.'

'But you know everything about Burnaby!' Molly protested. 'That's your job.'

'And you're sure she's sold it?'

'Yes! She told me herself only a few minutes ago.'

'Why didn't you ask her who she sold it to then?' Paige said trying not to sound condescending. She regretted the question as soon as she'd asked it.

'I would have if she hadn't left the building. She's gone out for coffee with Patricia Simons who walked in as soon as Anita had broken the news to me, bloody nuisance of a woman. And she'll be gone for a while I imagine. I'm dying of curiosity here. I thought you might be able to put me out of my misery.'

Paige sighed. 'I'm sorry I can't be more help. It must have been a private sale. But it seems a bit out of the blue. Two weeks ago she was telling me about her plans for the October events. Is she selling it as a going concern?'

'A what?' Molly was confused.

'You know – will it still be trading as a bookshop?'

'Goodness, I hadn't even thought of that.' Molly sat down on the stool behind the counter and began to run her left fingers up and down the coiled flex nervously. 'You mean the new owners might close the shop? And I might lose my job? I'm hardly qualified to do anything else. That would be terrible. What would I do?'

'Stop right there,' commanded Paige. 'There's no point worrying about things that may never happen. Anita's no fool. There's no way she'll see you out in the street – or Felix for that matter. Talk to her as soon as she comes back. I'm sure she'll put your mind at rest.'

'You're probably right. But what if . . .'

'Molly!'

'Sorry. Listen, I'd better go. I can see a customer approaching out the window.'

'Ring me when you've talked to Anita.'

'OK.'

'Promise?'

'Promise.'

'And Molly?'

'Yes.'

'Stop worrying. I'm sure your job is safe.'

The bell on the shop door rang, interrupting their conversation.

'I'll try. I have to go.' Molly put down the phone and smiled at the man in front of her. 'Hello, how can I help you?'

'Are you Molly?'

She studied the short, shiny-headed man in front of her. He was wearing an expensive-looking black wool polo neck and dark brown cords and as he held out his hand, a heavy gold bracelet slid down his wrist towards his hairy hand. She nodded. How on earth did this stranger know her name?

'Yes, how can I help you?'

'I'm Milo Devine, the new owner of this shop, since you ask. And the question is – how can I help *you*?'

Molly stared at him without saying a word. She could feel the blood drain from her face and her palms began to feel cold and clammy.

'Are you all right?' Milo asked with concern. 'You seem a little pale.'

'Um, yes, fine,' she mumbled.

'I'm sorry, my dear, has Anita not told you about me?'

Molly shook her head. 'No. Not a word.'

'Ah, I see.' He looked a little embarrassed. 'Maybe I should have waited . . . but still, now that I'm here, why don't you show me around? Tell me about the kind of books you stock. I'm not much of an expert on romance I must admit, but I have seen *Gone With the Wind*.'

Molly had been decidedly unsettled by Milo's unannounced visit and, in Anita's continued absence, had rung her friend Paige again to discuss it. Paige had sighed, saved her half-written document on the computer and picked up the receiver. Molly gave her a description of the man – gold chains, wide Hollywood smiles and all – and told her what he'd said in one breathless gasp.

'Milo Devine, first of all, what kind of name is that?' Paige scoffed when she'd heard the details. 'Sounds like a dodgy American detective.'

Molly laughed. 'It does rather, I suppose, but he's actually Irish. He gives me the creeps to be honest. He reminds me of a wide-boy car salesman – all smiles and platitudes but always on the make. I have a bad feeling about him, Paige, I really do. He mentioned a few of his plans for the shop, but it's what he didn't say that I'm worried about.'

'When's Anita back?' asked Paige looking at her watch and biting her lip. Much as she loved talking to Molly she really did have rather a lot of work to do today.

'Soon, I hope. I have a lot of questions to ask her.' The bell rang again. 'Damn, I have to go.'

'Ring me later,' Paige insisted. 'But not for about an hour if you don't mind, I have to get this bloody document finished before lunchtime. This is better than *EastEnders*. I'm dying to hear more.'

'Excuse me. Have you seen my dad?' a deep, treacle-rich voice asked Molly as soon as she'd put the receiver down.

Molly looked up. This day was getting stranger and stranger. There in front of her was the face of an angel – a rugged, no-shoes and dirty-faced kind of angel, but an angel nonetheless.

His dark blonde hair hung in messy curls around his strong square face. Molly had read about 'chiseled cheekbones' in many of her romantic novels but she'd never come face to face with them in real life. His must have been carved by Michelangelo – they were that sharp and that perfect. One of his front teeth was slightly chipped and his full dark-pink lips were lopsided – all adding to his attraction in Molly's eyes.

Stop staring and say something, she told herself.

'Um, your dad?' Brilliant, Molly, just brilliant. Inspired.

'Milo Devine?' The man smiled. 'I was supposed to meet him in here but I'm running a bit late.' He coughed nervously and glanced at his watch. 'Well, very late actually.'

The new owner's son. This was all she needed. 'He was here but he left a while ago,' Molly said. 'Sorry.'

'I see. I'm Sam. And you are . . . ?'

'Oh, sorry.' She could feel hot prickles running up the back of her neck and spreading towards her cheeks. 'I'm Molly,' she managed eventually. 'Molly Harper. I'm the manager.'

'Ah, yes, of course. I've heard all about you from Anita.' He smiled again.

Molly noticed that the pocket on his dark blue shirt was torn and had an irrational urge to touch it, and an even more irrational urge to offer to take it home and mend it. What was happening to her?

'This must all have come as a bit of a surprise to you – the shop being sold and everything,' he said kindly.

She nodded. 'Yes.'

'But Dad's only going to make one or two minor changes. And I'll just slot in – you'll see. You won't even notice me. Of course I'll need your help at first – I've never run a bookshop before. But I'm sure I'll get the hang of it quickly enough.'

Molly felt decidedly faint. What did he mean – run a bookshop? She was the manager here. Did he not know that? She'd had enough. Was no one going to tell her anything? Wait until

11

she got her hands on Anita, she'd had an emotional roller coaster of a morning thanks to her.

'Have I said something wrong?' He looked at Molly carefully. She was staring at him and her large blue eyes seemed to be swimming with moisture.

A large tear dropped from her right eye and twinkled down her cheek. She wiped it off swiftly with the back of her hand, mortified. 'Sorry,' she murmured. 'Something in my eye. Excuse me.' She brushed past him, pushed open the door at the back of the shop and stepped through it.

Felix looked over. He was sitting outside the back door catching a few surreptitious rays of morning sun.

He stood up quickly. 'Are you all right, Molly? I'm just waiting for the Macmillan delivery. The driver rang to say he was on his way.'

'I'm fine, thanks. I don't want to disturbed.' Molly walked past him and into the office, closing the door behind her.

Felix shrugged his shoulders and sat back down. He'd been working in the bookshop for almost five years now, so was well used to Molly and knew to keep out of her way when she was angry or upset. After a moment, he heard a knock on the door which led on to the shop floor. 'Hello, is anyone there? Molly?' A tall figure walked through the doorway and blinked in the brightness. Felix stood up again. 'Can I help you?'

'Do you know where Molly went?' the man asked.

Felix gestured towards the wide open back door. 'She went out, mate,' he lied smoothly. 'Gone to get a coffee, I'd say. I'm just on my way in to look after the shop. Can I help you?'

'No, never mind,' he said. 'Tell her Sam said goodbye.'

'Sam. Sure thing.'

Sam turned swiftly on his heels, took one last lingering look at the dark pink bookshelves and left the shop, the bell ringing loudly behind him.

As soon as Molly heard the bell she gingerly opened the office door a slit. 'Is he gone?' she asked Felix in a low voice.

'Sam?'

'Yes.'

Felix nodded. 'He said to say goodbye.'

'Thanks,' she said. What a relief. The tears had stopped just as soon as they'd started and she felt stupid. It was just a reaction to the sudden news, she told herself, nothing to worry about, just shock. She still felt a little funny though.

'I'll look after the shop for a while,' Felix said, noticing the slightly manic look in her red-rimmed eyes. 'You stay in the office. I'm sure you have work to do.'

'Thanks.' She smiled gratefully. Felix never asked questions, that was one of the reasons she liked him so much. A silver-haired early retiree from the civil service who had got bored at home, he'd been working in Happily Ever After for almost as long as she had, pottering along at his slow yet solid pace, getting everything done and rarely making a mistake.

Half an hour later Anita opened the door of the office and found Molly rifling through one of the drawers of the tall grey filing cabinet – the top drawer where Anita kept all her private papers.

Anita coughed quietly. Molly jumped.

'I was just looking for . . .' Molly began and then stopped.

'For what?' prompted Anita.

Think of something, Molly willed herself. Anything. She couldn't – her mind had gone completely blank. 'I was looking for information about the sale,' she said truthfully. 'About Milo and his son. About my job.' She stared at the dark blue carpet tiles, bit her lip and willed the tears away. Could this day get any worse?

Anita put her hand on Molly's shoulder. 'I'm so sorry,' she said. 'Sam rang my mobile and left a message. He was worried that he might have upset you.'

Molly pushed her back against the drawer, sending it clattering home. 'When were you going to tell me about the new owner?'

'This morning,' Anita said gently. 'You know that. Milo just pre-empted me, that's all. He's quite . . . um, how will I put this?'

'Pushy?' Molly suggested.

'Not exactly the word I was going to use. Forthright I suppose.'

'Pushy,' Molly said again.

Anita ignored her. 'His son seems nice though – Sam. Did you like him?'

'Sam, the new manager, you mean?' Molly glared at her.

'Is that what he told you?'

Molly nodded silently.

'I see. You'd better sit down.' Anita waved at the sofa opposite the desk.

Molly did as requested.

'Sam will be working here with you. You will be the Book Manager – in charge of everything to do with the books and the events – just as you are now. Sam will do what I've been doing – staff rotas, holidays, the accounts, tax returns, that kind of thing. His official title will be Shop Manager, but it doesn't mean he's over you. Not at all. Milo promised me that we'd all keep our jobs and that the shop would stay as it always has been with one or two minor changes, nothing drastic, he promised.'

'We?' asked Molly. 'Are you staying?'

'Yes, I'll be working at the weekends and on Thursday evenings. Just to keep my hand in. And I'll still be living upstairs so you'll see me all the time. Now do you feel any better? I'm so sorry you've had such a stressful morning, my dear. I didn't mean for it all to come out this way.'

'I understand. But you should have told me earlier.'

'I know.'

Molly cocked her head to one side. 'One more question. Why did you sell to him?'

'He offered me a good price,' said Anita honestly. 'He's taken early retirement and has always wanted to own a bookshop in the area.'

'And?'

'And what?'

'Don't give me that, Anita. There must be another reason. You love this place.'

'No other reason, honestly.'

'There is, and I know it. And if you won't tell me I'll find out anyway.'

Anita smiled. 'You'll be disappointed.'

'We'll see.'

'Feeling better now?' Anita asked. She put her hand on Molly's shoulder and gave it an affectionate squeeze.

'Yes,' Molly said. 'Much better. But please tell Felix before Milo or Sam get to him, OK?'

'I'll tell him right now.' Anita smiled. 'I promise.'

Chapter 2

Kate

Kate looked up, sipping her lukewarm coffee and saw the man she assumed to be her new client, Angus Cawley. He'd described himself on paper as 'tall and dapper, with an eclectic dress sense'. Eclectic, she thought, looking him up and down, more like downright bad. He was wearing what she presumed were once black jeans but which had now turned an unsavoury shade of greeny-grey, a grey cotton polo neck and the pièce de résistance – a black silk waistcoat decorated with what looked like bright red cherries. To top it all he was also wearing red suede brothel creepers on his large feet and some of his hair was greased back in a type of poor man's duck's-ass, the rest falling lankly around his face. Kate sighed. She had her work cut out for her with this one.

Kate had been running 'Dublin Dummy Dates' ('Dummy Dates' for short) for over six months now and it hadn't been quite the 'nice little earner' she'd imagined when she'd set it up. In fact, most days it was downright disheartening – there were a lot of sad lost male souls out there all too in need of her services. After an initial consultation, like this morning's meeting, she took men out on dummy dates and put them through their paces – from grooming and clothes, to conversational openers (otherwise known as 'chat-up lines') and learning to listen without interrupting – building their confidence and preparing them for future 'real' dates. Many of the men on her books had gone on to have successful 'real' dates and one, Ken, had even announced an engagement a month after meeting his 'ideal woman', a dog groomer from Rialto, which, although it had been cancelled after three weeks, still counted as an engagement (on Kate's promotional blurb anyway).

Her plan had been to start the company, get it running smoothly and then fade back into a purely administrative role, allowing her hand-picked employees to deal with the actual dates. But herein lay the problem. The company hadn't actually made enough money for Kate to employ anyone, so she'd ended up taking out all the clients herself, which wasn't exactly ideal. Alex and Matty O'Connor, the sibling owners of Coffee Heaven where she held most of the initial meetings with the prospective dates, thought she was some sort of compulsive man-eater until Kate had explained what her work entailed.

In the afternoons and on Saturdays, too, Kate worked in Baroque, the local designer shoe shop, but mornings and evenings she turned into Ms Dummy Date. She advertised her services in the local newspaper, *Burnaby People*, and in several Dublin magazines. The phone hadn't stopped hopping from the second week on after she'd appeared on the Brenda Jackson morning radio show talking about her services. Brenda had been intrigued and had sent her intrepid reporter Missie O'Donaghue along on a dummy date with Kate and one of her clients – a rather showy man from Howth called Bryan – 'Bryan with a y, mind, not an i, mind'. Bryan had turned out to be a compulsive liar, the most sexist man either woman had ever encountered and was basically a lost cause. Awful as he was, he had made compulsive radio listening and the company had gained the best free nationwide advertising ever. After the show, Kate had been interviewed by *Sunday Ireland*, the *Irish News* and the *Dublin People*.

She raised her hand and waved at her new client who was looking around the coffee shop anxiously. He caught her eye and smiled. Kate smiled back. He made his way towards her, tripping over a buggy and slopping a mug of coffee all over a table. 'Sorry,' he murmured to the owner of the coffee who was glaring at him.

Kate tried not to sigh. An awkward, socially inept specimen – she'd seen it all before. He probably had a stutter or a stammer and voted Green Party to boot. Stop it! She chastised herself. That's not nice. You are here to help this man, not to make fun of him. Just because you had a disagreement with Trina already this morning doesn't mean you can take it out on this poor individual, even if he is pathetic.

Trina was the rich and rather batty owner of Baroque whose taste in shoes was, as Kate liked to say rather crudely, 'up her ass', and who couldn't tell a Manolo Blahnik from a Gina Couture – quite a failing in a designer shoe buyer. She had far more money than sense and Kate was convinced that Trina's husband, Dublin and London property magnate Farrell de Barra, only bankrolled the shop to keep his darling wife out of his hair and away from his office. Trina ran the shop with the help of her 'VBF', Cathy Philips, another trophy wife, married to snooker hall and leisure plex owner 'Flames' Philips. Unlike Trina, who was Burnaby old-money born and bred, Cathy was from Limerick and had worked as an Aer Lingus air hostess for three years before serving 'Flames' champagne on a memorable trans-Atlantic trip. He'd whisked her away from her life in green, but after two children ('Axel', boy and 'Lolita', girl) she'd decided she needed to get out of the house more and going into cahoots, otherwise known as 'business' with Trina seemed like a good idea at the time.

Shoes, after 'Flames', were Cathy's great passion – and the

more expensive the better. Kate had no complaints about Cathy's taste, it was Trina who had chosen the bright orange '70s inspired wedge sandals and the chunky 'Bjork' inspired white tap dancers with the thick dark brown heels and soles for this season, when all their customers were clamouring for was sexy dark pink stiletto sandals and neat '50s peep-toes with kitten heels.

Angus stuck out his hand in front of her face. 'Kate, I presume? Sorry I'm late.'

'Not to worry. Please sit down. I've ordered you a coffee.'

He pulled the chair back from the table, catching the back legs on the wooden floor with a loud dragging noise. 'Sorry. I'm a bit nervous.'

'No need to be.' Kate said kindly. 'I'm here to help you. Think of me as your sister.'

'I haven't got a sister,' he admitted as he sat down.

'Your aunt then.'

He shook his head again.

This man was beginning to annoy her and he'd only just arrived. 'Your mother then.' She fixed a smile on her face. 'You have one of them, don't you?'

Angus looked down at the table. 'I did. She died last year.'

Kate's heart sank. Please let him not be a crier, she pleaded. I couldn't deal with that today.

'But she was a great woman,' he continued looking up and smiling back.

'You have nice eyes,' she said, studying him properly for the first time. His quiff had collapsed, dark brown hair tumbled shapelessly around his face. His steel-rimmed Germanic glasses did nothing for him, but his dark brown eyes shone brightly and intelligently from his slightly sallow skin. Maybe Angus wasn't going to be such a difficult nut to crack after all. She glanced at her watch and jotted down the time at the top of her foolscap sheet. 'Bang on quarter past ten – let's get started shall we?'

'Fine.'

Alex arrived at the table with a large mug of coffee and placed it on the table in front of Angus. Terminally nosy, she always enjoyed having a look at Kate's latest client. 'Enjoy,' said Alex looking him up and down. She wasn't impressed. Too skinny and what was with that hair?

'Thanks,' he said, oblivious to Alex's critical gaze.

'Thanks, Alex,' added Kate.

Alex lingered within hearing distance, flicking a cloth ineffectually at the table beside them and rearranging the milk jug and sugar bowl several times. But Kate was having none of it. She waited patiently until Alex had sniffed audibly and retreated into the kitchen, allowing Angus to take a few calming sips of his coffee before continuing. She promised her clients absolute confidentiality and that was what she gave them.

'I just need to get one or two details from you before we begin our session,' she said poising her pen at the top of the page. 'How old are you, Angus, if you don't mind me asking?'

'Not at all,' he said. 'I'm twenty-nine.'

'Really?' she raised her eyebrows. Her clients had a habit of stretching the truth a little and he looked a lot younger than that.

'OK,' he admitted, 'I'm twenty-six. But I much prefer women who are a few years older than me, so I usually say twenty-nine just to be on the safe side.'

Kate looked him in the eye. 'Let's get this straight from the very start. I'm here to help you. You're paying me to be honest with you. The process won't work unless you tell me the truth – do you understand?'

He nodded. 'Yes, I'm sorry, I understand, really. Please continue.'

She tried not to laugh. He really did look rather contrite; his head hung low, almost disappearing into his shoulders and his hands were clasped on the table in front of him.

'Do you work?' she continued.

'Yes, um, well no.'

'Which is it – yes or no?'

'I'm not sure. I went back to college to take my teaching diploma which I've nearly finished. I'm working part-time in a primary school at the moment as work experience – does that count as work or not?'

'Yes, I guess so. Are you training to be a primary school teacher?'

He nodded sheepishly.

'You're embarrassed by this?' she asked.

'A little.'

'Why?'

He shrugged his shoulders. 'Not very manly is it – teaching four- and five-year-olds?'

'I don't know,' Kate said thoughtfully, 'some women like men with a sensitive side. It's a very useful job and you're obviously not in it for the money.' She looked him in the eye. 'Why are you in it exactly?'

He held her gaze for a few minutes and then looked away. 'My mother was a primary school teacher. I like children and I think I'll be a good teacher. I know it's not very fashionable and to be honest, I get more than my fair share of snide comments from people who don't know me, which frankly I find a little upsetting. Implying . . . well, things.'

'I can imagine,' Kate said. She was ashamed that she'd been thinking along the same lines herself. 'I'm sorry, but I need to get to know you a little so that I can help you.'

'I understand. But honestly, I want to be a teacher for all the right reasons. Trust me.'

Something in those eyes made her believe him without

question. She scribbled some preliminary notes on the foolscap pad. In this job, her two years studying psychology in UCD came in extremely useful – not that she could remember many of the technical terms. *Training to be primary school teacher*, she jotted down. *Wears heart on sleeve. Over sincere? Could be a problem. Too intense? Scaring women away? Mother complex? Oedipus thingy?*

'What are you writing?' asked Angus.

'Just notes, nothing for you to worry about.'

'I'll stop trying to read upside down, then.'

She smiled. 'Yes. Better not to. Where are you studying?'

'Trinity College.'

'And your last date was?'

'Excuse me?'

'Your last date – when was it exactly?'

'That's a bit personal isn't it?'

'Angus, it's only me you're talking to.' She lowered her voice. 'Kate from 'Dummy Dates', remember? I'm not here to judge you. I'm just trying to help, honestly.'

'Sorry,' he murmured. 'I know. OK, it was last year.'

'Can you give me some of the details? How do you feel it went?'

'Terribly. We had nothing to talk about and halfway through the meal she excused herself to go to the Ladies.' He stared at his hands.

'And?' Kate asked gently.

'She never came back. I waited for half an hour and then left. I never saw her again.'

'Right,' Kate said a little more brightly than she'd intended. 'That does happen. Two of my other clients have had exactly the same experience. One in a cinema and one in Wales.'

'In Wales?'

'Yep. They went over to Wales on the ferry to spend a romantic weekend in a hotel. My client's date excused herself while they were having a drink in the hotel bar and Bob's your uncle.'

'What happened?' he asked with interest.

'She'd gone upstairs, packed her bag and got the last ferry back to Dublin.'

'No!'

'Honestly. He was devastated. Poor man.'

'I can imagine.'

'But he got over it. In fact he got engaged to a lovely girl only two months later.'

'Really?'

'Yes, really. So, you see, there's hope for you all.' She thought it prudent not to mention that the engagement had been broken after only a few weeks.

Angus considered this for a brief moment. 'For us all, you mean?'

'No, for you all. All my clients.'

'Have you already found your own true love then?' he asked.

'My own true love?' she repeated slowly. She had a right one on her hands here.

'Yes, you know, your soulmate.'

Kate smiled indulgently. 'Let's crack on, shall we?'

'Maybe you'll tell me later?'

She raised her eyebrows and ignored him. 'Can you tell me a little about your previous dating history? Before the one who did the legger.'

'OK, point taken. We're here to talk about me not you, right?'

She nodded curtly. 'Dating history?'

'Right, well, there hasn't been a huge amount of it to tell the truth. I find it very difficult to talk to women. I tend to get nervous and clam up.'

'You're talking to me,' she pointed out.

'But that's different. You told me to pretend I was talking to my mother.'

'True. Sorry, continue.'

'There was Sandy in school, we went out for two weeks just before the debs. She was in the Computer Club with me.'

'And what happened?'

'She dumped me at the debs for a guy from the debating team. Then there was Dina.'

'Dina? Tell me about her?'

'She was from Bangor. I studied Computer Science in college and I met her there. We were together for two years. Dina was special.'

His voice became wistful and Kate allowed him time to collect his thoughts.

'She married my best friend last summer. I'd asked him to keep an eye on her while I was in Germany for two months working on my Master's. I never believed he'd betray me like that. Anyway he did and after that, there was the legger woman as you called her and that's about it.'

Let down and hurt badly by friend and ex-girlfriend ('Dina'), Kate jotted down, *self-esteem problems?, honest, seems sincere.*

'Thank you for sharing that with me,' she said, putting down her foolscap pad. 'And now can I ask you – what are you looking for in a woman? What qualities do you find important?'

Angus considered for a moment. 'Honesty,' he began hesitantly. 'I'd like someone I can trust, and someone kind. She'd have to like children, I guess, and have a big heart. Someone a bit pretty maybe, but I'm not too bothered.'

'You said you liked older women?'

Angus shrugged his shoulders. 'I don't know why I said that to tell the truth. I just thought someone a little older might be less inclined to judge me and might accept me for who I am.'

'And is that important to you – acceptance?'

'Of course, isn't that what everyone wants – to be accepted and loved for who they are?'

'I suppose so.'

He stared at the table and then looked up again. 'This isn't how I thought it would be, you know.'

'What?' she asked.

'You, I suppose. All this. I thought you'd just give me some hints on how to dress and some killer chat-up lines.'

'But you could get that from a book or a magazine. I try to get a little deeper, get down to the root of the problem.'

'And what's my problem, Doctor?'

'I'm not sure yet,' she said honestly. 'You seem a very decent young man and . . .'

'Why did you call me that?'

'What?'

'Young man? You can't be much older than me.'

'I don't know why,' she replied. 'I don't suppose I am.'

'To establish professional distance?' he suggested.

'Maybe.'

'What age are you anyway?' he said. 'If you don't mind me asking.'

'Actually I do. And as I keep reminding you, I'm not the one we're here to talk about, am I?'

'Sorry, I just find other people far more interesting than myself, I guess.'

'So do I. But I get paid for finding out about other people and you don't. So let's move on.' She glanced at her watch. 'We only have another ten minutes before this session is over.'

'What's next?'

'I'm going to advise you on your appearance and then we're going to set up a dummy date so that I can get a feel for how you behave on a first date. Then I'll give you a full report with some recommendations.'

'And then?'

'It's up to you to use the information I've supplied.'

'And will the dummy date be with you?'

'I'll have to check my diary. I think all my employees are pretty much booked up for the next few weeks. I presume you'd like the date as soon as possible?'

'Yes.'

'Well then it will be me all right.'

'Good.' He smiled.

'So, appearance,' she said trying to veer the conversation back onto safer ground. 'What do you think women like men to wear?'

'I'd say they like them to look smart and coordinated. And clean,' he added as an afterthought.

'Good. And what type of clothes do you wear generally?'

'This kind of thing,' he said gesturing to his chest. 'Although I keep this waistcoat for special occasions. Normally it's just the polo neck or maybe a checked shirt.'

'I see.' Kate bit the top of her pen.

'You don't approve of the waistcoat, do you?'

'No.'

'Why not?'

'Honestly?'

He nodded.

'It's too loud. And not very fashionable.'

'Oh. Mum made it for me. It's my lucky waistcoat.'

'Right.' She could hardly tell him how awful it was now.

'If I said it was a post-modernist joke would I get away with it?' He tilted his head to the side.

'Not really.'

'I see. I won't wear it again then.'

'I didn't say that. Just don't wear it on the first date, OK?'

'Understood. And how about the shoes? You don't like them either, do you?'

'Truthfully?'

He nodded again.

'No, I think they're terrible,' she said.

'They're going in the bin then. I've no major attachment to them and besides they're not all that comfortable. What about the jeans?' He looked at her face. She was wrinkling her nose slightly. 'Another no-no. So give it to me straight – what should I be wearing?'

'On a first date you want to look smart yet not too formal. Clean, classic, ironed clothes always impress. As you're twenty-six I'd suggest something fashionable but not too over the top. Think Next or TopMan rather than cutting edge. A nice white shirt, a pair of jeans that fit properly – Levis, or something like that, not cheap chain store jeans, girls hate them; brown or black boots, and, if the budget will stretch to it, a nice simple well-made leather or suede jacket. And you'll need to get a haircut and maybe think of changing the frames of your glasses for something less severe.'

Angus whistled. 'Serious make-over stuff. I'm way off the mark, aren't I, Kate?'

'Just a little,' she admitted.

'And does all that really make a difference – the haircut and the clothes?'

'Yes, it really does. Most people judge on first appearances whether they admit to it or not. It can make or break a first date.'

'Well, I'll have a go. I have jeans that might be OK and runners, are runners acceptable?'

'Not really. They can be a bit scruffy.'

'I think the budget might just about stretch to a pair of boots and a haircut. I have a white shirt – I'll get it pressed in the dry cleaners. And I have contacts instead of the glasses, should I wear those?'

'Definitely.'

'Then I'm pretty much set.' He smiled widely. 'This is going to change my life, Kate, I can feel it in my bones.'

'Great. Your time's up, I'm afraid. When would you like your dummy date?'

'How about next Wednesday night?'

'Fine.'

'Where would you suggest?'

'It's usually best to go somewhere casual on the first date. I wouldn't always suggest dinner, unless you're confident that you can eat and talk without getting too nervous. Women do like to be taken out to dinner but sometimes a drink can be a little less intimidating for you both. Arrange it for the early evening – say sevenish – and if you're getting on well with your date you can always suggest dinner after the drink. Or maybe she'll even suggest it – if she's interested.'

'And how will I know that?'

'I'll explain how to read the signs on the dummy date.'

'Great. So how about seven in O'Connor's pub on Wednesday?'

'Perfect. I look forward to it.'

'Really?'

She smiled at him. 'Sure. Now I'm afraid I have a lunch appointment so you'll have to excuse me.'

'A date?'

'Angus!' She laughed. Maybe she should try setting him up with Alex – they were as bad as each other.

'Sorry.' He stood up and held out his hand.

She took it in hers and shook it. His grip was surprisingly firm. 'Bye, Kate. See you on Wednesday.'

'See you.' She watched as he walked towards the door, managing to reach it safely and without incident this time.

Alex buzzed over to Kate's table as soon as he'd left. 'Well, what's he like?'

'As always, Alex, I'm afraid I can't tell you. Client

confidentiality and all that. But I would like a Chicken Caesar Salad and a fresh cup of coffee, thanks.'

Alex sniffed. 'Fine,' she said and flounced away.

Kate reached into her bag and fished out her *Irish Times*. She loved Thursday's edition – the property pages and the new film reviews – lots to interest her. She began to read about a bijoux cottage in Burnaby, which sounded about as big as a shoebox, which was selling for over three hundred thousand euro. She'd never be able to afford to buy in Burnaby at this rate. The townhouse she shared with Molly was tiny and they spent the whole time trying not to get under each other's feet – which was difficult as there wasn't even enough room to pass comfortably in the hall and they shared a tiny shower-room. Damn, she remembered, I promised Molly I'd get a new bulb. The bathroom had no window and they'd been having showers by candle light for the last two days – romantic but not very practical. She got on well with her housemate but sometimes Molly could be a little anal about cleanliness and tidiness. It was best just to keep out of her way when she was on one of her regular 'spring, summer, autumn or winter' cleaning sprees.

Kate had arrived back in Dublin nearly a year ago, after ten years living and working in Boston. But that was all in the past. Her new life lay in Burnaby – making enough money to buy a house in the area that felt like home, near her beloved Granny Lily. She got on fine with her mum and dad who had moved to Connemara after her dad had retired, but it was Lily who she'd always felt closest to. Her parents had had a rather tempestuous marriage when Kate was growing up, and she had loved staying in her granny's peaceful and cosy Burnaby house, away from her parents' continuous arguments and shouting matches. Her father, Billy, had always been a bit of a bully, with a furious temper, which had mellowed with age, thank goodness, and Cleo, his wife and Kate's mum, had walked out on him several times over the years. But she always came back and they'd stayed together, mainly for their daughter's sake. Now, in their early sixties, they seemed to have come to some sort of strained truce.

Kate had written to Lily every week when she was in the States, and once her granny had learnt how to use the Internet at evening classes there was no stopping her. They conversed every day on-line, sometimes several times a day. In fact, it was Lily who had advised her to come home to Ireland before 'all the good men are snapped up', as she'd put it. If only Lily knew the whole story. Kate had no intention of letting a man get close to her ever again – American, Irish or any other nationality for that matter. But she was enjoying being home and knew she'd made the right decision. Besides, Lily hadn't been all that well recently and Kate wanted to be there for her – especially as she was her only grandchild.

'Here you are,' said Alex.

Kate moved the newspaper to allow Alex to place the steaming mug of coffee and large white plate in front of her. The plate was heaped full with light green lettuce, croutons and strips of juicy looking chicken. The dish was topped with a generous amount of Parmesan shavings and dusted with freshly ground black pepper – just the way Kate liked it.

'Thanks, Alex,' she said. 'That looks great.'

'Have you any more clients coming in today?' asked Alex hopefully.

'No.' Kate smiled.

'Pity,' Alex said, walking away.

Kate tucked into her salad with relish and thought about Angus. He was an interesting one all right. She really was quite looking forward to Wednesday to tell the truth – in her professional capacity of course. She wondered what he'd look like with a haircut and contacts. As she speared a piece of chicken with her fork she remembered that she'd have to talk to Trina again today about the shoe lines that weren't selling. She'd tried talking sense into the woman earlier this morning, but they'd ended up arguing. Kate had pointed out that it made no sense waiting until the end of the summer season to sell skimpy sandals and white shoes – they might as well cut their losses early. Maybe that way they'd shift them all before July was out but Trina was having none of it, control freak that she was.

Sometimes Kate wished she had Molly's job – books could be returned to their publisher with no questions asked. Light bulb! she thought suddenly. She'll kill me if I forget again. She pulled a blue ballpoint out of her bag and wrote the word in capital letters on the back of her left hand. *LIGHTBULB!!*

Chapter 3

Paige

'What do you mean you're closing "Little Orchard" for August?'
Paige demanded. 'You can't close for a whole month – what will
I do?'

Clodagh sighed. 'I'm sorry, Paige, but we can't get staff to
cover us in August, and me and Ethel badly need a holiday.'

'What about Connie? Will she not be around? You must be
able to do something!'

'Connie's going back to Sydney for the month. And before
you ask, Marta's English isn't good enough yet to run the place.
Even if it was, she's only been here three months and she'd need
at least six staff to keep the place open. We just can't do it – I'm
sorry – we have tried, believe me.'

Paige felt bad – it was hardly Clodagh's fault she had to close.
'No, I'm sorry. I didn't mean to jump down your throat. It's just
I rely on you to be able to work, that's all.'

'I understand, honestly. But there's nothing we can do.'
Clodagh, who ran the crèche and after-school club had had this
exact conversation with many of the parents. But her hands were
tied – she had to give her staff holidays. She couldn't afford to

pay them as well as she would like to, so a month's holidays in the summer was the least she could do.

'Do you have any suggestions?' Paige asked. 'Is there somewhere else open that you can recommend?'

'Not really,' said Clodagh. 'You could try Nora Hilton's place in Sandybay but I think it's full to tell the truth.'

'Do you have the number? I'll give it a try.'

Clodagh flicked through the large desk diary, wrote down Nora's number on a yellow sticky note and handed it to Paige.

'Thanks, I appreciate it,' said Paige. 'And you're open again . . .?'

'Monday the third of September. The first day of school for most of the older children. I've booked Alfie and Callum in already – Alfie into the baby room and Callum into Montessori and afternoon care – is that right?'

'Yes.' Paige nodded. 'We'll see you on Monday. And sorry for being short with you.'

Clodagh smiled. 'Not to worry. I know how busy you are, Paige. I read all about the proposed refugee centre on Burnaby Crescent. Good luck with it anyway.'

'Thanks. I hope it gets resolved soon. Everyone's getting a little heated about the whole thing.'

'But the Crescent would be ideal for the families wouldn't it? I know a lot of them have young children and it's just beside the park. I can't really see what the problem is.'

'Not everyone sees it like that,' Paige said evenly. 'I have to represent all my constituents and they have all kinds of views. Especially the Crescent residents.'

'I can imagine. Mrs Calloway from the gallery lives there, doesn't she?'

Paige nodded but said nothing. Connie Calloway was the current thorn in her side and the over-opinionated woman was calling into Paige that very evening – a prospect that didn't exactly fill her with joy. 'Anyway, I'd better collect my little monsters before they think I've abandoned them.'

Clodagh led her towards the baby room at the back of the building. Paige looked through the glass at the top of the door and studied the row of baby seats, looking for Alfie. She spotted him almost immediately. He was crying and Marta was crouching beside him, offering him a bottle. He hit her hand away, sending the bottle flying across the room.

'He's been a bit cranky today,' said Clodagh leading her in. 'Teeth coming through I expect.'

Paige sighed. 'Tell me about it. He was like a demon last night – wouldn't settle at all. His poor little gums were sore and he was dribbling like a dog. We didn't get a wink of sleep. I was hoping he'd be better today.'

'You never know,' Clodagh said kindly as they walked towards him. 'He might be all right by this evening. Fingers crossed.'

Paige bent down, unclipped Alfie from his chair and lifted him up. 'There, there, little man. What's bothering you?' He'd obviously been crying for a while – his face was red and blotchy and his breath was uneven. Paige felt a stab of guilt pierce her heart. She shouldn't have left him here all day. He hadn't been happy this morning when she'd got him ready and he'd cried all the way to 'Little Orchard'. She was a terrible mother. She held him close to her.

Marta handed her another bottle. 'Try this one,' she said gently in her accented English, 'it's nice and warm.'

'Thanks, Marta.' Paige swung Alfie around so that he was nestled in the crook of her left arm and put the teat in his mouth. He sucked immediately, his crying forgotten.

'He would have been the same at home,' said Clodagh, as if reading Paige's mind. 'He's just having a bad day. Marta's been great with him – rocking him in his seat and walking him around the room in the buggy. He was in good hands.'

Paige could feel tears prick the back of her eyes. Clodagh really was a find – she knew exactly the right thing to say at exactly the right moment. 'Thanks,' she murmured gratefully.

Clodagh smiled. She knew how difficult it was for working mums. 'That's what I'm here for. Now, let's find Callum, shall we?'

Clodagh helped Paige gather together all Alfie's bits – baby bag, bottles, food containers, buggy and baby seat. She clicked the seat into the buggy expertly and pushed it in front of Paige who was still holding Alfie.

As they entered the other, larger room Callum came crashing towards them and hurled himself at his mother's legs.

'Callum!' she scolded. 'You nearly knocked me over and I'm holding Alfie.'

'Sorry, Mum.' He looked up at her, beaming. 'Can I see Alfie?'

'Sure.' She bent down and showed Callum his brother's face. 'Now don't poke him or anything, he's not a very happy camper today.'

'Why not?' asked Callum. 'Does he have a poo in his nappy?'

'No, he doesn't!' Paige tried not to laugh. 'His little teeth are coming through his gums, that's all. But if he did have a smelly nappy I'd make you change it.'

Callum wrinkled his nose. 'Yucky!'

'Let's get you both to the car,' said Paige. 'Say goodbye to Clodagh now and go and put your coat on, there's a good fellow.'

'Bye, Clodagh Woda,' he shouted as he ran towards the coat pegs. 'See you later, alligator. Not too soon, you big baboon.'

'Hey, that's my line.' Clodagh laughed.

'Sorry,' Paige said. 'His manners are getting really bad.'

'I'm quite used to it. He's by no means the worst. He's just lively.'

Paige smiled. 'I'd love to ask you who was but I'm sure you wouldn't tell me.'

'Try guessing,' Clodagh suggested with an evil glint in her eyes.

Paige lowered her voice. 'I'd say Axel and Lolita Philips, am I right?' naming the ultra-spoilt children of one of Burnaby's best know socialites, Cathy Philips, co-owner of Baroque shoe shop.

'I couldn't possibly say.' Clodagh gave a tiny nod and grinned widely.

'You've made my day.' Paige laughed. 'I'll see you on Monday morning.'

'Bright and early.' Clodagh opened the main door for Paige and helped her down the three steps with Alfie's buggy.

'Bye poo-face,' Callum said loudly as soon as she closed the door behind them.

Paige glared at him. 'I hope she didn't hear that. You are a very rude little boy and there'll be no telly for you this evening. Do you hear me? Tea, bath and straight to bed.'

'Muuumm!' he moaned. 'That's not fair.'

'Quiet!' she snapped. 'Mummy's tired and she won't take any more nonsense from you, young man, do you hear me?'

He nodded.

Alfie began to cry again.

'Now look what you've done.' Paige pushed the buggy down the gravel drive towards the car. Callum trailed behind her. 'Sorry, Mummy. Can I have a treat on the way home?'

'What do you think, Callum?'

'Yes?' he asked, his little face upturned hopefully.

She ignored him, unlocked the car, unclicked Alfie's seat from the buggy and lifted it onto the back seat, all the while listening to his ever-increasing roars. 'Please, let me just get home sane,' she murmured. 'You're OK, Alfie,' she soothed, lodging his bottle into his mouth and cupping his plump pink hands around it. 'Here's your bottle. There's a good boy.' He looked at her for a moment, contemplating whether to continue crying or not, then decided he was actually quite hungry and began to suck. 'Thank you, baby.' Paige let out a sigh of relief. She turned around to tell Callum to get in beside his brother but he'd disappeared. She put her hand to her head. Not again. Callum had a habit of playing hide-and-seek at the most inopportune moments. Her nerves were frayed enough as it was today, she didn't know if she could take any more.

'Callum!' she shouted. 'Come here right now or there'll be trouble. Do you hear me?'

She leant her back against the car. It was just as well that she wasn't premenstrual or she'd have started crying right about now. In fact, she thought suddenly, have I had my period this month? I must have had, but I don't remember it. She heard gravel crunching on the far side of the car.

'Come on, Callum. Get into the car, please.'

'Boo!' He jumped in front of her and waved his hands above his head.

'Very funny, now what have I told you about wandering off?'

'But I was beside the car, you just couldn't see me. I was doing good hiding.'

Paige held him by the arm to stop him running off again.

'That hurts, Mummy!' he protested. 'Leave me alone.'

'I'll give you hurt if you don't get into the car this instant, young man, do you hear me?'

He climbed in and sat on the booster seat.

'Keep still, I'm trying to fasten your seat belt.'

'I hate seatbelts!' He wriggled again.

'The guards will arrest you if you don't wear your seatbelt,' she threatened.

'They never wear theirs,' he retorted. 'I've seen them.'

'Yes, they do,' Paige lied, thinking that her son had a point. 'Most of the time anyway. But sometimes they need to be able to jump out of cars quickly to catch robbers and things, that's all.'

'I need to catch robbers,' he said, wriggling again.

'No you don't,' she said firmly. 'And for the last time, stay still.' She finally managed to click him in, tucking the seatbelt clasp under the upholstery of the back seat just as her husband Tom had shown her. It was the only way to stop Callum unclicking himself as soon as she started driving. They'd had to use duct tape over the clasp up until last weekend when Tom had made the loose upholstery discovery while cleaning her car for her.

As Paige sat behind the steering wheel and turned the key in the ignition she could feel pressure building behind her temples. Great, she thought, a tension headache. Just what I need before a meeting with Madame Calloway.

'Tom, are you in?' Paige shouted as she walked into the hall. 'Tom?'

'In here.'

She walked into the kitchen. 'Be an angel and give me a hand with the kids, will you? They're still in the car and Connie Calloway will be here any minute.'

He groaned. 'Could she not have met you earlier or this evening? Dinner time is not exactly convenient, is it?'

'I know, and I'm sorry. But she insisted on meeting me today and she has some kind of gala charity do later this evening.'

'So as usual you're expected to bend over backwards to suit her, is that it?'

'Something like that.' Paige smiled wryly. 'I'm sorry. But with the elections coming up soon . . .'

'I know, she's a well respected member of the community with a lot of contacts, I understand. But the sooner the bloody elections are over the better.'

'Not long now,' Paige promised. 'The polling date is due to be announced any day, it's only a matter of time.'

'Good! I've saved up all my holidays to help you, but at this stage I'm getting itchy feet.'

'I know and I really appreciate it, my love. You'll make a great campaign manager.'

'I don't know about . . . is that Alfie screaming?'

They ran outside the house.

'Callum, what are you doing?' asked Tom.

Callum quickly took Alfie's bottle out of his mouth and hid it behind his back. He smiled sheepishly. 'I was having a drink, I was thirsty. Mummy wouldn't get me a treat in the shops.'

'Give your brother back his bottle this instant,' said Paige testily. 'Will you take Callum inside, Tom? I'll deal with Alfie.'

'Sure.' Tom unbuckled the seatbelt and let Callum free. Callum jumped up, sprung out of the car and ran into the house. Tom immediately followed him. Callum on the loose in this kind of humour was no joke.

'He's not allowed any telly,' Paige shouted to their disappearing backs.

'Come on, little man,' she said to Alfie, 'let's get you out.'

'Connie, how nice to see you, won't you come in?'

Connie Calloway stepped over the bulging baby bag which had been unceremoniously dumped in the hall, past the litter of outdoor shoes and overcoats heaped to one side and noted the broken radiator cover that was hanging from the wall by a single hinge.

Paige led her into the sitting room to the right. Connie studied the seat of the leather sofa carefully before she sat down. She took in the small painting beside the window – a reasonable attempt at a still life, practically worthless, of course, but pleasant enough, and the random pieces of rather fine antique furniture – gifts from relatives no doubt. She wouldn't have thought of Paige as a collector.

'Would you like some coffee?' asked Paige politely.

'Please, black, no sugar.'

As Paige walked into the kitchen she frowned. Callum was

sitting at the kitchen table, eating some toast and watching television.

'Sorry,' Tom said sheepishly. 'I said he could watch one episode of *Rugrats*. I need to get Alfie ready for bed.' Alfie was sitting in his little chair with a fresh white Babygro and vest by his feet.

'Don't worry about it,' Paige said mildly. 'I probably would have done the same myself.' She flicked on the kettle, luckily still warm from Tom's cup of tea and put some biscuits on a plate. 'I was talking to Clodagh today. They're closing "Little Orchard" for August. She can't get extra staff to cover the holidays.'

Tom whistled. 'Not good news for us. Any ideas?'

'She gave me the number of a place in Sandybay, I'll try that tomorrow.'

'Otherwise?'

Paige shrugged her shoulders.

'My mum might help if we asked her,' Tom suggested. 'She'd take Alfie anyway.'

'That would be great but Callum's the problem,' said Paige.

'I'm not a problem,' Callum insisted.

'Little pitchers and all that.' Tom smiled. He turned towards Callum. 'No love, we were talking about another Callum.'

'Oh.' Callum accepted this immediately and went back to watching *Rugrats*.

'Would there be any students around for the month do you think?' asked Tom. 'We could pay them well.'

'I'm not sure,' Paige said doubtfully. 'Do you think they'd be able to cope?'

'You never know. If we found the right person.'

'It's a possibility. I'll put an ad up in the supermarket tomorrow. Can you type something up for me later?'

'No problem. I have a bit of work to do anyway after dinner.'

'Not again,' Paige sighed. The kettle boiled, she poured the steaming water into the cafetière, lowered the plunger, pulled out a tray and put the coffee, two mugs and the biscuit plate on it.

'Sorry, love. August will be quieter, I promise.' Tom was a manager in the Castle Building Society in Dun Laoghaire, in charge of the mortgage department. It was a highly responsible and very busy job, and one he was becoming less and less enamoured of as time went on. He'd love to spend more time with the children but it just wasn't possible these days. He had to cover their own mortgage after all. Not to mention the bills. As a local councillor, Paige was only paid a nominal salary. She got reasonably generous expenses on top of this but, in total, it didn't even cover the crèche fees. It was Tom's salary that supported the household, a fact he never alluded to, being the kind and decent man that he was.

'Into the fire.' She kissed him on the cheek before picking up the tray.

'Here you go, Connie,' Paige said, walking through the door.

'Thank you. I thought you'd forgotten all about me.'

'Sorry, had to wait for the kettle to boil.' Paige placed the tray on the coffee table, sat down in front of it and began to pour.

Connie said nothing.

'So,' Paige opened, 'you wanted to see me.'

'Yes. And I'm sure you know exactly what it's about.'

'The refugee centre?'

'Precisely. We just can't allow it to happen in the Crescent. You understand that, don't you, my dear?'

Paige refused to be drawn. 'Why don't you explain your objections and I'll just jot them down.' She took a notebook and pen from the desk by the window.

'Right, first of all, they're all foreigners, aren't they? We don't know what kind of diseases they may have brought with them, do we?' Connie sniffed.

'Objection number one: foreign diseases. Any foreign diseases in particular, Connie, or just diseases in general.'

Connie looked at her. Was Paige trying to be funny? She wasn't smiling but Connie got the distinct impression that she wasn't exactly taking this matter as seriously as she should. 'Aids, my dear girl, for one. And malaria and typhoid, things like that. And smallpox.'

Paige wrote everything down.

Connie continued, 'And the Crescent doesn't have the car parking spaces for lots of extra cars. It's already a big problem.'

'I don't think the refugees will own many cars, to tell the truth,' Paige said evenly. 'Most of them won't have been in the country very long.'

'Well then,' said Connie, 'they won't even have any English, will they?'

'Probably not. The centre would offer English lessons to all age groups, including children.'

'Another problem. Children. It's a busy road and there's no pedestrian crossing to the park.'

'And will I put down house prices?' Paige suggested.

Connie stared at her. 'That isn't one of our main reasons, but it is a factor, yes. The residents are worried that it would affect the value of their properties.'

'Especially you, I would imagine, as you're right next door to the proposed centre.'

'*All* the residents,' Connie stressed.

'And is everyone in agreement on this?' Paige asked. 'The objections, I mean.'

'Everyone except one or two,' Connie admitted. 'But they're new to the area, they don't really count.'

'Who are new?'

'Harry Masterson and Darcy Wallis.'

'Darcy has lived in Burnaby for years,' said Paige. 'She's hardly a newcomer.'

'But she's only been on the Crescent for three,' Connie pointed out. 'Making her a newcomer.'

'Right, I see.' Paige glanced at her watch. She was starving. 'Any more objections, Connie? I know you have a dinner to go to later.'

'My dear, I've only just started. The dinner can wait. This is far more important.'

Paige sighed inwardly. It was going to be a long evening.

Chapter 4

Molly

Molly slipped the key into the lock of Happily Ever After and turned it. She stepped inside, closed the door behind her and quickly made her way to the office where she disabled the alarm. It wasn't even eight yet and the rest of the staff wouldn't be in for at least another hour but she'd slept really badly – tossing and turning all night and finally waking up for good at six a.m. She'd lain in bed for a while but had only got to worrying about the future of the bookshop and about last night's rather unnerving phone call from her ex-boyfriend, Denis – both good reasons for her fretful slumber.

Molly sat down at the desk she shared with Anita. She'd come in early to try to get some writing done. For several years now she'd been cutting her teeth on a succession of short stories – building up her confidence and learning how to make her characters and stories come to life. What she really wanted to write was a big, romantic saga, like *Gone With the Wind*, only set in nineteenth-century Ireland, encompassing all the sweeping political and social changes that had taken place at that time. She had a main character in mind – a feisty heroine who would start off as a kitchen maid and go on to become actively involved in the 1916 Easter rising, finally meeting and marrying a fictional tragi-hero, not unlike Michael Collins. She even had a title – 'The Price of Gold'.

Molly had only told two people in the whole world about her writing – Anita, who had been hugely supportive and had offered to read her work at any time, and Denis, who had laughed, patted her on the head and said 'Stick to the bookselling, Molly, you're not a writer. You don't have it in you'.

After fifteen long minutes staring at a blank computer screen, Molly gave up and pulled a blank yellow-sheeted foolscap pad towards her. If she couldn't write, she may as well do some work instead. She found a pen in the top drawer and wrote 'Saturday 12th July – Book Club Meeting and Rosemary Hamilton Event' on the top of the first sheet in large capitals, intending to make a list of all the things she needed each member of staff to do as soon as they all came in. She then put the pen down, sat back and sighed. Her brain just wouldn't click in this morning. Coffee, she thought, that's what I need, strong, black coffee. Matty would definitely be in Coffee Heaven baking or making soup or something, even if they didn't open till nine. He always was. You could set your watch by him. She stood up, took her wallet out of her bag and walked out of the office. She decided against setting the alarm – she'd only be a few minutes after all.

'Morning, Molly, I was wondering who was banging so insistently on my door,' Matty smiled. He brushed his sandy-blonde hair out of his eyes, sprinkling flour onto his freckled temples in the process.

'Sorry, Matty,' said Molly. 'Hope I wasn't interrupting anything.'

'Just the usual early-morning scone-making, nothing important. Coffee is it?'

She nodded and smiled. 'How did you guess?'

'Come on in. I've just put on the first brew of the day – Columbian all right?'

'Perfect.'

He poured the rich steaming-hot liquid into a large paper cup, popped on a plastic lid and handed it to her.

'Thanks, how much do I owe you?'

He waved his hand at her. 'Nothing. On the house.'

'Are you sure?'

'Yes. Sorry I can't stop and chat but I have soup to prepare.'

'That's OK. Thanks again.'

As she unlocked the bookshop for the second time she got the distinct feeling that someone was watching her. She turned around and looked up and down Burnaby's main street. It was completely empty. She must have been imagining it. Although Denis had been known to follow her. In fact that was how they'd first met.

The Molly and Denis saga had begun almost twelve years ago. When Molly and Paige reached the ripe old age of sixteen they were finally allowed to take the train home from school – Loreto Convent in Killiney – on their own. There were one or two rules, of course. They weren't allowed to talk to strangers, including the boys from the neighbouring Christian Brothers' College, Killiney (CBC) and had to come straight home after their after-school activities. What their collective parents didn't know was that neither of the girls were actually members of the debating club, the school magazine, or the choir. They both played hockey all right for the Senior Thirds, and now and again Molly wrote articles for 'The Loreto Killiney News', usually detailed and somewhat hyperbolic accounts of hockey matches – *The crowd went wild as Paige Brady flicked the ball into the back of the opponent's net with all the grace and fury of an African gazelle . . .* – mainly to throw the parentals off the scent. Because after school all the Loreto girls congregated under the green bridge in the train station, on the southbound platform, shielded from nosy neighbourhood eyes, and smoked until they were green in the face, matching their putrid-coloured green uniforms perfectly. The station platform was also where they met the CBC boys – small in height compared to themselves, kitted out in purple and grey, and far more nervous of the girls than the convent girls were of them, however cool and together they seemed.

Molly always felt a bit of an outsider with the station gang. She didn't smoke for one thing – she didn't see the point really. It tasted nasty and made you feel ill – what was to like? Paige made it look cool of course. She could even French inhale, inhaling the smoke through her nose. The CBC boys were very impressed. When Paige learnt how to blow large smoke rings, she was considered the bee's knees.

Paige had lots of boyfriends – she changed regularly and was currently working her way through fifth year CBC after cutting her teeth on the boys her own age. Molly had never had one, apart from Garvan Evans, if you could count him. He'd only gone out with her for two hours in order to talk to Paige. But Paige had been so unimpressed with his treatment of her best friend that she'd completely ignored him when he'd introduced himself. But Denis was different.

Paige had noticed him first, not in the way she usually noticed boys though. Denis wasn't exactly what you'd call good-looking. Smallish and thin, with wispy dark brown hair that always looked as if it could do with a good wash, and eyes that were almost permanently fixed on the ground in front of him. The other boys pretty much ignored him at the train station but he always insisted on standing only a few feet away from them, as if some of their social skills with the convent girls might be transferred to him by osmosis if he stood close enough. Paige had also noticed him because, according to her, he was always staring at Molly. Molly refused to believe this of course. Why would he be staring at her for goodness sake? She was plain and didn't wear any make-up unlike the other girls. Her skirt was the regulation length, instead of hiked up towards her armpits, and even her shoes were boring – sensible brown lace-ups instead of the kitten-heeled black suede stilettos of her peers. Or, if you were very cool like Paige, flat black impossibly pointy winkle pickers with dinky fake silver zips adorning the toes.

One day when Paige was at the dentists getting fitted for a brace (which, to Molly's knowledge, she wore once then hid at the bottom of the kitchen rubbish bin, under some carrot and potato peelings and claimed she'd lost it) Molly was left to make the journey home alone. It was a nice enough day and she didn't mind too much to tell the truth. It meant she could go straight home instead of pretending to have debating. She'd just started a new Virginia Andrews novel and was dying to get stuck into the strange and warped world, which she found totally addictive. Her head was stuck in her book at the station and on the train. Two stops later she'd arrived in Burnaby, crossed the railway bridge and had started to make her way home, her nose still stuck in her book. She'd discovered many years ago that if she progressed slowly, she could read whilst walking. Once she'd walked into a concrete bollard and grazed her knees and she'd often narrowly missed being mowed down by a fast-travelling baby buggy, but generally she got home in one piece after managing to read a chapter or two of the current favourite.

Today, as she read, she could hear footsteps behind her. She waited for the person to catch up with her and overtake her plodding pace but it didn't happen. They stayed behind her. This began to unnerve her and she began to walk even more slowly, tucking herself into the side of the pavement, willing them to pass. But they didn't. Finally she'd had enough. She was nervous, scared and more than a little cross. Who was trying to keep her from her book? She took a deep breath and turned around.

'Oh,' she squeaked in surprise.

'Hello,' said Denis, blushing furiously.

'Are you following me?'

He coughed nervously. 'Um, no.'

'What are you doing then?'

'Um, I don't really know.'

She put her finger in her book to keep her place and stood up straight. 'Are you a stalker?'

'A what?'

'You know – do you follow people all the time? A stalker. Famous people have them.'

He still looked confused.

'Never mind,' she sighed. 'Do you live in Burnaby?'

'No, Bray.'

'So you are following me!'

'Maybe.' He shrugged his shoulders and stared at the pavement in front of him.

'Why?' she asked in amazement. She'd never been followed home before, except by a lost dog, but that didn't count. In fact, even Paige hadn't been followed home.

'Because I wanted to meet you,' he said still staring down. 'You look nice. Not like the other girls.'

'Oh!' Molly was completely taken aback. She hadn't expected that at all.

From that moment on they were inseparable – almost thirteen years in total.

Until April this year that was, when Molly had had a change of heart and Denis, in turn had his heart broken. She'd made the decision that there must be more to life than having a safe, comfortable relationship and a safe, comfortable job. She wasn't even sure she still loved Denis, and she'd stopped fancying him ages ago, so being with him had just become a habit. And encouraged by Paige, after several long, agonizing days she'd finally managed to convince Denis that she really meant it when she said she didn't want to be with him any more. When he'd called into her house and proposed in May after a month apart and daily phone calls, her heart had sunk to the pit of her stomach, leaving her even more convinced that she'd made the right decision. It was only then that he'd left her alone.

But last night he'd rung her mobile, knowing that it was rarely on in the evenings and had left an extraordinary message. 'Hi, Molly. Just to say, you don't have to worry any more, I'm completely over you. I've met a lovely girl called Carrie and things are going great. We're getting quite serious. I just thought I should tell you. Bye . . .' Bastard! He knew Molly had a jealous streak as green as the Incredible Hulk. But this wasn't going to make any difference this time, her mind was set. She was very happy that he'd met someone else and she wanted the best for him. And she was going to ring him later and tell him so.

'Molly, Molly.' Anita's voice rang out loud and clear as a bell from the shop floor.

She raised her head from the computer where she'd been reordering books for the crime department and looked at her watch. Ten to nine, almost time to open. Seconds later the office door swung open. She'd taken to rising earlier now that she was no longer in charge of the shop.

'There you are,' said Anita. 'Did you not hear me?'

'I did, I was finishing an order.'

'Already? How long have you been in?'

'A little while,' Molly admitted. 'We have a busy day ahead and I wanted to be prepared.'

'Milo and Sam are coming in this afternoon for the event. Just to warn you.'

'Checking up on us?' Molly saved her work, sent the order down the line and stood up.

Anita ignored her. 'They won't be here for the Book Club but said they'd both try to make the next one.'

She stared at Anita. 'Why would they do that?'

'I don't know, out of interest I suppose. What's wrong?'

'Reading is not a spectator sport. If they want to attend a meeting they'll have to read the book, same as everyone else.'

'Fine, I'll tell them. I won't ask what's wrong with you this fine morning as you'll only bite my head off.'

'Sorry. I didn't sleep very well, that's all. I'll be fine in a while, honestly.'

'You'd better be. I think I hear Felix at the door, I'll just let him in.' She turned on her heels leaving Molly in the office.

Molly leant against the desk. She thought of ringing Paige but didn't want to wake her up. Tom usually took the two boys for a walk to the shops on Saturday morning, leaving Paige to have a lie-in before the Book Club meeting. Still, she'd see her later and maybe they could have coffee together before the Rosemary Hamilton event kicked off at three. The phone rang, interrupting her thoughts.

'Hello, I wanted to find out about the event this afternoon. Is it booked out?'

'No, not quite,' Molly replied. 'Will I take your name and reserve you a seat? It starts at three.'

'Please.'

Molly scribbled down the woman's details. 'Thanks for ringing. See you later.'

The phone rang again almost instantly. She sighed. At least it would keep her mind off Denis, she thought.

'Is everyone here?' Paige asked the rest of the Book Club members, looking around the room.

'Harry's not coming, he sent his regrets,' said Anita. 'He has a wedding today and they want seven extra cactus arrangements for the tables apparently. He's doing his nut.'

'Cactus arrangements at a wedding?' sniffed Trina. 'Surely not? Whose wedding exactly?'

'No idea,' Anita replied.

Kate came flying into the side room where the Book Club meetings were held. 'Sorry I'm late, guys, have you started?'

'No,' Paige said. 'Out late were you? Another dummy date or a real one?'

'Dummy,' Kate said.

'She doesn't do the normal kind, remember?' added Trina who thought that Kate's other job was very peculiar indeed. She'd much prefer if the girl would commit to Baroque on a full-time basis but there was no talking to her on the subject. She'd threatened to leave completely if Trina didn't stop going on at her. And that was the last thing Trina wanted. Kate might be odd but she was a damned fine salesperson whatever way you looked at it, and she sure as hell knew her shoes.

Kate ignored her. 'I've only got halfway through the book, I'm sorry,' she admitted as she squeezed in between Molly and Anita.

'That's OK,' Paige said quickly before Trina had a chance to butt in. 'Let's get going, shall we? Who'd like to start?' She looked around the table. This month's choice had been a sweeping literary saga by Booker award nominee, Francesca Scata.

'I will,' said Cathy, 'as I chose it. I was a bit disappointed to tell the truth. I loved her other books, which is why I suggested this one. But it's not as strong. I found the main character Elena a little unbelievable. I mean, if she was as stunningly beautiful as the author portrayed her, why didn't anyone realize that she was a woman masquerading as a man? It didn't make sense.'

'You're right.' Anita nodded. 'It was a little unbelievable.'

'But in those times wouldn't it have been so unbelievable

that she would have got away with it?' Molly suggested. 'It would have been such an outrageous thing to do in the nineteenth century, especially in England, to pose as a man and work in a newspaper, maybe it just wouldn't have crossed anyone's mind to question it. Nowadays, yes, she would have been questioned, but perhaps not then.'

'But what about Oliver, her eventual husband?' Cathy demanded. 'Surely he would have copped? He said he was attracted to her from the moment he realized she was a woman – that's rubbish! How can he suddenly have feelings like that? It doesn't make sense.'

'Again, maybe not now, but this was set almost two hundred years ago,' said Molly. 'Things have changed. It wouldn't have been acceptable then to admit that you found a person who you thought was the same sex as you attractive.'

'Maybe,' Cathy allowed. 'But the way their relationship was described and the sex scenes . . . I mean really, what baloney.'

'I liked those,' Anita said. 'They were gentle and tender. We're just used to stronger stuff in modern books. But I thought the sex scenes were very much in keeping with the period. And I love her writing, it's so descriptive.'

'She has a way with words all right,' Paige said. 'Remember that scene set in the corn field – that was stunning.'

An hour and a half later they'd finished dissecting the book and were trying to decide on a text for the following meeting, which always provoked much discussion.

'Not Anita Shreve again, please,' Trina moaned. 'I know you like her, Cathy, but we've read her to death.'

'Trina has a point,' said Kate. 'How about Anne Tyler? She has a new one out.'

'Harry's not that keen on her, remember?' Molly said.

'But he's not here, is he?' Paige smiled. 'How about something different? Alan Frost has a new book out – *Stradbrook* – we could try it. It would be more literary than some of the books we read.'

'Wouldn't mind giving it a go,' Cathy said. 'He's a Booker winner, isn't he?'

'That's right – for one of his earlier books. *Stradbrook* sounds interesting, have you heard much about it, Anita?' asked Molly

Anita nodded. 'The book's been getting some rave reviews in the press all right, but that doesn't always mean much. The book's out in paperback next month but I might be able to get early copies off the rep if I ask nicely.'

'Excellent!' Paige looked around the table. 'Now are we all agreed?'

Everyone nodded.

'I'll order it and ring you all when it comes in,' Anita promised.

'How much will it be?' Trina asked.

'About ten euro, I think.'

'Fine.'

'You'll treat us all then, Trina, I presume?' Cathy said smiling. Rich as she was, Trina was known for her Scrooge-like tendencies.

Trina kept quiet. She knew Cathy was only teasing her.

'Who's coming for coffee?' asked Paige. 'It's on me.'

'We have to get back to the shop,' Cathy said, looking at Trina pointedly. 'We're supposed to open at twelve.'

'Only on Book Club days.' Trina sniffed. 'Otherwise it's strictly ten o'clock, that's what we agreed.' Although if she'd had her way she would have made Kate miss Book Club and open up on Saturdays without them. Kate had Cathy wrapped around her little finger.

Molly turned to Anita. 'Is it OK if I pop out for a few minutes?'

'Of course,' Anita said. 'But don't be too long. Milo and Sam will be here soon.'

'Don't remind me,' Molly groaned. 'I'll be back before one, I promise.'

'So, how are things at home?' Molly asked Paige as they walked into Coffee Heaven. 'Tom has the kids, I presume.'

'Yes, poor man. Callum's being rather difficult these days. He was like a devil this morning. He took a swipe at me with his shoe earlier and really hurt me.'

Molly's eyes widened.

'Don't look at me like that,' said Paige. 'He's five. Five-year-olds do that sort of thing, it's quite normal.'

'But maybe you should . . .'

'Drop it,' said Paige. 'I'm not bringing him to see anyone, especially to some child psychologist who will make him even worse. He'll grow out of it.'

Molly wasn't so sure. He was due to start school this September and she pitied his poor teacher.

'How are my favourite Saturday customers?' Alex smiled at the small group. 'I've booked a table for you in the back.'

'Thanks, Alex,' said Molly.

'No Harry today?' Alex asked.

'Busy with a wedding,' Molly explained.

'I see. And what can I get you all?' Alex pulled out her small notepad and pencil.

'The usual, I'd say,' Kate said, 'two cappuccinos and a latte, is that right, ladies?'

They all nodded in the affirmative.

As soon as they'd settled into their coffees, Paige heard a familiar shrill voice behind her.

'I need to talk to you urgently, Paige,' Connie Calloway mock whispered. 'It's about . . . well, you know.'

'The refugee centre,' Paige said, trying not to sigh.

'The *proposed* centre,' Connie corrected her.

'Would you mind terribly if I finished my coffee? I'm with my Book Club friends you see.'

'Not at all,' Connie replied. 'I'll just sit behind you here and wait.' She pulled a chair over and did exactly that – sat directly behind Paige, Kate and Molly, tapping her fingers together impatiently. After a few minutes Paige admitted defeat and moved to a table at the far side of the shop to talk to her in private.

'Poor Paige,' Kate said to Molly after she'd gone. 'Does that happen a lot?'

'Unfortunately yes.' Molly drained her coffee cup and placed it back down on the table. 'She's far too nice to people like that if you ask me. I'd tell them where to go.'

Kate laughed. 'You wouldn't go very far in politics then, my girl. Paige is contesting the next election, isn't she?'

'How do you know that? It's supposed to be a secret.'

'Cathy told me. Her husband is backing Annette thingy apparently and Annette thinks Paige will be her main opposition.'

'Annette Higgins? Wasn't her dad done for tax evasion a few years ago?'

'I believe he paid it all back, according to Cathy anyway.'

'Let off by his political cronies more like.'

'Shush, someone will hear you.'

'Don't care if they do. Paige is so decent and hard working. It makes my blood boil that someone like Madame Higgins can swan in and win elections on her father's rather dodgy name.'

'She was a councillor for a while, like Paige,' Kate pointed out.

'Yes and a pretty terrible one from all accounts,' Molly snapped.

'I didn't realize you felt so strongly about politics,' Kate said. 'It's a whole new side of you.'

'I don't really, except when it comes to Paige.'

'Fair enough. Listen I'd better get going or Trina will have my guts for garters. Will I see you this evening?'

'I'm having dinner at Paige's but I won't be too late. Have you anything planned?'

'If you're going to be out I'll probably call into Granny Lily and make her dinner.'

Molly smiled to herself. Kate was so good to her gran, it was quite something. 'Why don't I get a video and we can watch it when I get back. Something lame and girly.'

'You're on. But to be honest I'd prefer a thriller if you don't mind.'

'Not at all. I can pick something up from the video shop later. See you around tennish, OK?'

'Perfect, see you later. Tell Paige I said goodbye.'

'Will do.' Molly watched her housemate leave. She'd known Kate vaguely when they were both teenagers as they'd played hockey against each other, and Kate and Paige had liked the same boy at one stage. Luckily there had been no hard feelings when Paige had won the particular boy's heart, as usual. Molly had been pleasantly surprised when Kate had arrived at her doorstep one evening after answering an ad for a housemate – Molly thought she'd recognized the voice on the phone but hadn't been sure at the time as she hadn't asked for her surname.

They'd hit it off from the very beginning – it was nice to have someone to do things with, especially after breaking up with Denis. But Molly always felt there was something that Kate wasn't telling her – there was something about her return from Boston that didn't quite fit. Molly wasn't one to meddle and so she'd let it lie and Kate was very private and rarely volunteered any personal information about her past, or her present for that matter – especially when it came to men. And as time went on she'd almost forgotten about it. Until now. Because Molly had had a rather strange phone call from someone with a decidedly American accent. Someone looking for a 'Cat'. It was only afterwards that she'd realized that maybe the

'Cat' he'd been looking for was actually Kate. But as she hadn't even got a name from him it would be foolish to even mention it to Kate – wouldn't it?

As Molly walked back into the bookshop she was surprised to find Sam and Anita behind the front desk.

'I'm just showing Sam how to work the till,' said Anita. 'Then maybe you could show him how to take a special order.'

'Um,' Molly murmured noncommittally. He still looked stunning. His hair was falling foppishly over his face and he was biting his lip in concentration. She walked past them towards the side room where Felix was unstacking the folding chairs.

'Hi, Molly.' Felix looked up. 'How do you want the room set up? How many are you expecting?'

'About sixty, I think, but there could be a few extra late-comers who haven't booked. If you put the lectern at the far end of the room and curve the chairs around it in a semi-circle. It will look less formal that way. Rosemary said she'd like a comfortable chair for signing afterwards, one with arms.'

'I'll get one of the chairs from the office for the signing, will I?' asked Felix. 'No need to take it out yet.'

'Perfect.' Molly surveyed the room. Felix had adorned the room with pink and purple balloons and large banner-style posters advertising Rosemary's new book, and he had also placed a large glass vase of white lilies on the table beside the lectern.

'Is it OK?' Felix asked. 'Anita said just to fire ahead with the posters and balloons.'

'It looks great,' Molly replied. 'Couldn't have done better myself. I'll do a display of her books on the front table as you come in the door and then we should be pretty much set.'

'Is she a Ripley Barker do you think?' he asked nervously. 'Or is she normal?'

Molly smiled. Ripley Barker was an American crime writer, one of three writers who had taken part in last year's 'Murder on Burnaby Street' crime event. The other two authors had been charming but Ripley had been an eye-opener. Arriving in a black stretch limousine, wearing an Armani three-piece suit and a black Stetson, he looked like a Hollywood film star. He'd had three minders with him – two from the publishers and one from the film company who had optioned his latest book – and had demanded ultra-special treatment from the minute his silver-tipped cowboy boot had stepped in the door of the bookshop. Felt tip pens in dark blue only, no biros – he couldn't write with them; no flowers – he was allergic to them; French mineral water, not Irish, and only in blue bottles, not green – he hated the colour green; and vegetarian food with no mushrooms or peppers.

'And M&M's with all the brown ones taken out, I suppose,' Anita had quipped to his American publicist, who had not been amused.

'No,' Molly smiled at Felix. 'Not another Ripley. Rosemary's lovely apparently.'

'Good.' He breathed a sigh of relief. It had been his job to source the vegetarian food and the French mineral water in a blue bottle and he'd never forgotten it. Ripley hadn't even said thank you and had asked Felix not to look at him while he was eating as it interfered with his digestive system.

Molly felt a tap on her shoulder and jumped.

'Sorry,' Milo beamed. 'Didn't mean to startle you.' His eyes lingered on the balloons and the posters. 'Very pink, isn't it?'

'The cover of Rosemary's new book is pink,' Molly explained. 'They tend to use the same image and colour scheme on the posters and display material.'

'I was talking about the shelves. Have they always been pink?'

'Not always. They were natural brown to start with but

Anita updated them several years ago when the shop started specializing in romantic fiction.'

Milo nodded slowly, a thoughtful expression on his face. 'I see. What type of bookshop was it previously?'

'A general one really. It stocked a bit of everything. But we decided it was a good idea to specialize, as most of our customer base was female. It made sense really. So we have a large range of fiction mainly aimed at the female market plus most things you'd expect in your average bookshop as well – books on gardening, health, reference books, children's books and a very strong crime section of course.'

'But the figures have been slipping slightly in recent months, do you think it's time for another change?' he asked. His thick black eyebrows rose. 'Say a crime bookshop for example, or a literary bookshop?'

She hesitated for a moment. Was he fishing for a reaction or was he serious? 'There's already a crime bookshop in Dublin – "Murder Books" on Callow Street.'

'Is there a literary bookshop?' he asked.

'No, for very good reason. It's not . . .'

'Molly, are you ready to show Sam how to take a special order?' Anita interrupted. 'I have to help a customer with children's books.' She looked from Molly to Milo and back again. 'Sorry, were you in the middle of something?'

'Milo was just asking me what I thought of changing the shop into a literary bookshop. You know, Anita, lots of serious hardbacks, Booker novels, IMPAC nominees, black shelves, jazz music, that sort of thing. What do you think?'

Milo put his hand on Molly's shoulder before Anita had a chance to reply. 'Now, Molly, it was only a thought. No need to get hot under the collar, my dear.'

She shrugged off his hand. 'I'm glad to hear it.'

'As long as the figures start improving you have no need to worry,' Milo continued.

'And if they don't?' Anita demanded. He hadn't said anything about drastically changing the shop when he'd made his offer.

'We'll have to see, won't we?'

'I think we need to talk, Milo,' Anita said gravely. 'There are one or two things about Happily Ever After that you don't seem to understand.'

'Ah, yes,' Milo smiled a little too widely, showing two large gold-capped wisdom teeth, "Happily Ever After", now as names go . . .'

'We'll talk later, Milo,' Anita snapped, interrupting him mid-flow. 'Right now we have a shop to run. Why don't you help Felix and Declan with the chairs?'

'As long as I don't get dirty, I'd be happy to.' Milo brushed his hand over the front of his black polo neck. 'Cashmere does have a habit of picking up dust.'

'There are several publisher's T-shirts in the back,' Anita said. 'I can get you one if you like. Save your good clothes.' She emphasized the word good, trying not to wrinkle her nose in the process. Milo might be an attractive man for his age and most charming when he wanted to be but today he was seriously starting to annoy her.

He held up his hands. 'That won't be necessary.'

'Then let's get back to work, shall we?'

Molly led Sam towards the back desk where the second computer lay waiting.

'Customer orders are an important part of our business,' she began. 'We can order books from America or the UK in a matter of days but you have to be careful not to promise too much.'

'I'm sorry about Dad,' Sam said, not really listening to her spiel on special orders. 'When he gets an idea into his head he can be quite bullish.'

'I just hope he doesn't change the bookshop for the sake of

it,' she said. 'We've spent the last few years building the business up and tweaking things to get it just right.'

'I understand, really I do,' Sam said. 'But he's got it into his head that the figures should be better.'

'What line of business was he in before he retired?' Molly asked.

'Property. Money isn't a problem. He's just a stubborn old businessman who wants the shop to be as profitable as it can be.'

'I see. He's the owner. And you're his son. And to be honest, I don't feel all that comfortable talking about this with you. Can we just drop it?'

'Of course. But one last thing.'

She looked at him with interest. Damn, he had the loveliest eyes. But maybe in time she'd become immune to his physical charms. 'Yes?'

'Stand up to him. He likes a challenge.'

'OK.' And his son? Does he like a challenge? Please tell me I didn't say that out loud, Molly begged. Please, please. 'OK,' she said again, realizing that blessedly she hadn't. 'I'll stand up to him.'

'Good. Now what were you saying about special orders?'

'Do you really want to know?'

'Honestly?' he asked.

She nodded.

He smiled broadly, his eyes wrinkling most attractively around the edges. 'Not today, if you don't mind. I'm sure it's all very interesting and everything . . .'

'It's not,' Molly laughed. 'Why don't I show you around the different sections instead and how to tell if a book's in stock or not. You'll need to be able to find the books if you're going to be working here, won't you?'

'Absolutely! And you can tell me all about yourself in the process.'

'Another day,' she said. 'First, the crime shelves.'

He felt deflated but he tried not to show it. He was only trying to be friendly. Molly Harper was proving to be the Brazil nut of all nuts to crack.

'How did your event go?' Paige asked Molly that evening while standing over the sink. 'Sorry I couldn't make it, I had council business.'

'Not to worry, it was packed,' said Molly. 'Just over eighty people in total. And Rosemary was a pet. She stayed around for ages after the talk – signing people's books and chatting to them.' She picked a black olive from the bowl on the table and popped it in her mouth.

'Good. And how's Anita? It must be strange for her working in the shop when she's no longer the owner.'

'Especially when the new owner's the spawn of the devil.' Molly licked her fingers.

'Molly! You don't mean that.'

'Yes, I do,' she said. 'He's terrible. A big greasy lump of a man, in his cashmere polo necks and his bloody literary book-shop.'

'Hold it right there, what are you talking about?' Paige stopped washing the cherry tomatoes and turned around.

'He wants to change Happily Ever After into a literary book-shop.'

'You can't be serious?'

'He said unless the figures improved he was going to make changes. I'm telling you. Ask Anita.'

'Unless the figures improve?'

Molly nodded.

'Are they bad?'

'Not especially. The whole book trade is in a bit of a slump at the moment – it happens sometimes. There haven't been as many big titles as there usually are in the first half of the year and people are spending their money on other things, that's all.'

'No new Harry Potter or footballer spilling his guts you mean?' Paige asked.

'Exactly!'

Paige for silent for a few minutes.

'Paige?' Molly asked eventually. 'What are you cooking up in that brain of yours? I know you.'

'Nothing.' Paige smiled broadly. 'Absolutely nothing. Now let's eat. Tom!' she shouted out the door. 'Dinner's ready!'

'Coming!' he shouted back. A minute later he joined them in the kitchen. 'Callum's locked himself in the bathroom and I can hear all the taps running. Can you talk to him? I've tried till I'm blue in the face but he won't listen to me.'

'I'll give it a go,' Paige sighed. 'What's wrong with him?'

Tom shrugged his shoulders. 'I have no idea. And I'll kill him if he wakes up Alfie, I've just got him to sleep again.'

Paige kissed him on the cheek. 'You're an angel and I don't deserve you, do you know that?'

'I do.' He flopped down on the kitchen bench beside Molly.

'Keep an eye on the lasagne,' Paige said. 'I'll be as quick as I can.'

As soon as she'd left the room Molly turned towards Tom. He was slumped over the table, his head in his hands.

'You have to talk to her about Callum,' Molly began. 'He's getting worse and it's draining you both.'

Tom sat up and rubbed his eyes with his knuckles. 'I know, but she won't listen to me. Why don't you try again?'

'It won't do any good. What about her mum?'

'She said she doesn't want to get involved. And mine's as bad. Sometimes I think Paige is right – maybe he will grow out of it – but he may send one of us to an early grave in the process.'

'Tom! Don't say that.'

'You haven't had the day I've had. First he punched Alfie in the stomach on the way to the shops, then he had a tantrum in the supermarket, and then he ran across the road without looking and nearly got himself killed. It's no joke looking after him, Molly, believe me.'

· She put her hand on his. 'I know, I understand, honestly. But unless Paige is prepared to do something about it nothing will change, you know that.'

'I know.'

'And I don't really want to be having this conversation with you for the rest of his childhood.'

'I'll talk to her again.'

'Promise?'

'Yes.'

'Good. Now you'd better check the lasagne. I'm the guest, I'm not allowed to move. I have to sit here and eat all these delicious olives.'

'Do you now?'

'Yes. And I'd love another glass of wine while you're up.'

'You're early. How was dinner?' Kate asked as Molly walked into their small sitting room.

'Great. Except for Callum.' She sat down in the armchair, flicked off her runners and curled her feet under her body.

'What did he do this time?'

'Flooded the bathroom. Paige had to break the lock to get in.'

'Poor Paige.'

'No kidding.'

'I hope you don't mind but I mentioned Callum to Granny the other day. I thought she might know someone who could help.' Granny Lily knew everyone in Burnaby and the surrounding area, and was a fountain of knowledge when it came to almost every subject from gardening to psychology.

'I don't mind at all. But don't tell Paige for heaven's sake. You know how touchy she is about Callum.'

'I know. But Lily would never say anything to anyone, you know that. She's the soul of discretion.'

'Did she have any ideas?' Molly asked hopefully.

'Not really, but she said she'd have a think about it.'

'Tell her thanks.'

'I will,' Kate replied. 'Now are you ready to watch Ben Syles?' Ben was the latest Hollywood hunk.

'Always. Bring on the eye candy.'

Chapter 5

Kate

On Wednesday evening, Kate checked her profile in her full-length mirror, and was satisfied that she looked presentable. Her Dummy Date clients always made a huge effort to spruce up and she saw no reason to let them down. This evening she was wearing a plain white cotton wrap-around shirt, neatly ironed and starched, and a dark pink silk skirt, which clung to her slender frame in all the right places. She was also wearing her favourite pink shoes – delicious leather and canvas sandals with sky-scraper heels that had cost her two week's wages even with her generous discount. But they were worth it – she always felt like a million dollars when she wore them and they were exceptionally comfortable for such a high shoe. She was a little over-dressed for the local but to hell with it, she thought as she looked in the mirror again, who cares?

It was only ten minutes on foot to Burnaby and, as it was a dry and reasonably warm evening she decided to walk, heels or no heels. She clicked her way towards the village, past her Granny's ambling Georgian cottage with its slightly haphazard-looking front garden. Her Granny did have an on-off gardener who was almost the same age she was, but he was decidedly more off than on these days because of a clicky hip. She'd have to find someone else or the garden would go to pot, Kate thought. Maybe Harry would have some local contacts.

As she walked into O'Connor's pub she looked around. There were several couples sharing drinks, a group of men and women in suits – an office crowd no doubt – but no men on their own, apart from one with very short hair and his head buried in a newspaper. She sat down at one of the tables overlooking the street and ordered an orange juice from one of the lounge girls. From experience, she needed all her wits about her this evening if she was to be of use to her client and even one glass of wine had a bad effect on her as she had no tolerance for alcohol. To tell the truth she was a little tired – Trina had been her usual obstreperous self this afternoon and they'd had several disagreements about the winter stock.

Trina wanted to stock leather boots in all colours of the rainbow for the winter season. Kate was trying to reason with her – all women really wanted was the perfect black or dark brown boot. They didn't want purple, cream, pink or green. It would be a waste of time stocking the whole colour spectrum. Trina wouldn't see reason. Eventually she'd said 'we'll see what Cathy has to say' and Kate had dropped it. She happened to know that Cathy had already bought most of the entire winter collection – including lots of different styles of brown and black boot as suggested by Kate – while Trina was on holiday in South Africa for three weeks in the spring, and she couldn't wait to see the sparks flying when Trina found out.

Kate pulled out her Filofax and checked her appointments for the following week. She had a Monday morning meeting with Ralph, a new client who worked with animals and sounded all right; and two evening dummy dates, one on Wednesday and one on Thursday. She was going to be busy. She looked at her watch. Angus was now officially late. She looked around the room again, her gaze settling on the man reading. As if sensing her, he raised his head. She recognized the eyes, even if they weren't hidden this time behind Germanic frames. It was Angus. He smiled over at her and waved.

'Stay there,' she said loudly. 'I'll come over.'

He nodded and folded up his newspaper.

She put her Filofax back in her bag, picked up her drink and made her way towards him.

'I didn't recognize you,' she said, standing in front of him. 'You look very . . . um . . . different.'

'Different good or different bad?' he asked, an anxious edge creeping into his voice.

'Good,' she said decidedly. 'Nice haircut.'

He ran his hand self-consciously over his head. 'I asked the hairdresser what she'd recommend and she scalped me. I'm not sure about it at all. I look like I'm in the army.'

'You're lucky, you have an evenly shaped head. Some men have lumpy heads and they can't carry it off. But you're head isn't bumpy at all.'

'Thanks, I think,' he said smiling.

'Now, aren't you forgetting something?' she asked.

He thought for a second. 'My glasses?'

'No, not your glasses, although now that you mention it, you look much better without them. You have nice eyes, there's no point in hiding them.'

He thought again. 'A drink, I haven't offered you a drink.'

'No you haven't. But that would come next. You need to greet me first. Pretend this is a proper date, remember?'

'I'm so sorry, how rude of me.' He stood up suddenly. 'Lovely to see you Kate, won't you sit down?'

'That's better. Standing up was a nice touch.'

'Now would you like a drink?' he said, relieved that he'd got over the first hurdle, albeit retrospectively.

'I already have one, thanks, but you can get the next one.'

'Do I have to pretend you're my date right now or can you just be Kate for a while?'

'I'm your date from the very beginning,' she said firmly. 'You can call me Betty if you like, would that make it easier?'

'Not really. I'd prefer Kate if you don't mind. Can I start again then? You've caught me a little off guard.'

'OK, if you think it would help. Pretend you've just greeted me and I've just sat down. Start from there.'

'Have I offered you a drink yet?'

'Yes.'

'So we're actually at exactly the same place as we were before I asked could you be Kate for a while?'

She looked at him intently. It was going to be a long evening if he insisted on analysing every little detail as they went along. 'OK, how about this? I'll be Kate for a few minutes, you can get any pressing questions out of the way and then I'll be your date again.'

'Great!' He beamed. 'First of all, what do you think of the clothes? I took your advice.'

She looked him up and down. White shirt tucked loosely into faded Levis, dark-brown lace up boots, dark brown leather belt. He was slim and toned, she noticed, with a real waist. She wondered did he work out? Most men of his age were starting to lose their waists unless they were actively fighting against it. 'So I see,' she said finally. 'The belt is a nice touch. It matches your boots perfectly.'

'So the lady in the shop said. It cost me an arm and a leg but she said it was a good investment.'

'She was right.'

'So you approve?'

'Yes, quite a transformation. As I said, I didn't recognize you.'

'And you look lovely too. I like the sandals.'

She smiled. She loved it when people noticed her shoes and it didn't happen that often, especially not with men. 'Thank you. Now do you have any other questions or will we press on?'

'If I think of more can I ask them as we go along?'

'Not really, it would interrupt the flow of the date.'

He seemed disappointed. 'Oh, I see.'

'But you can save them up and ask me at the end.'

'I might not remember them all.'

'Well, they can't be important if you can't remember them.'

'I don't know, I haven't thought of them yet.'

Kate said nothing. She couldn't win.

'You're annoyed with me, aren't you?' he asked. 'I'm doing everything wrong.'

'No, you're not,' she said kindly. She hadn't meant to make him feel ill at ease. 'Let's just have a conversation. And if you have questions ask away as they come to you. How's that? I don't normally allow it but I'll make an exception for you.'

'Thanks, Kate,' he said. 'I appreciate it. So how will I start?'

'Ask me something about my day. About work, or if I don't work how I've spent the day.'

'That's a good one. Will I tell you what I did first?'

'No, Angus, ask *me* first. It's much more polite.'

'Oh, right. How was your day, Kate?'

'It was fine thank you, Angus.'

He looked at her intently. 'That's not a great answer. What am I supposed to ask now? I expected you to go on for at least a few minutes. I haven't even thought of my next question yet.'

'No, you're right, it wasn't a great answer. But I'm testing you. Try saying – tell me a little about your work, Kate.'

'OK.'

'Well.'

'Well, what?'

She sighed. 'Say it.'

'Again?'

'Yes, again.'

'The thing you've just said about telling me about your work?'

'Yes, Angus!' She was trying not to get exasperated but he was starting to wear her down.

'OK, tell me about your work, Kate. Do you meet many interesting people during the day or is it boring?'

'It's boring.'

'But there must be something interesting about it. Sure, aren't you working there? There must be some redeeming factors. Sorry to interrupt the flow, Kate but do I know where you work or not?'

'Yes, I work in a shoe shop and you met me at a party and we talked briefly. Does that make it easier?'

'Yes, thanks. Will I continue?'

She nodded.

'What are your favourite shoe designers?' he asked. 'I've heard of Manolo Blahnik all right, do you sell his shoes?'

'Good,' Kate said. 'I love Manolo, these are actually his.' She couldn't help raising her foot and pulling up her skirt slightly.

'You have lovely feet,' he said admiringly. 'Very dainty. And I like the pink nail polish.'

'Thank you. Do you like shoes yourself?'

'Um, not particularly.'

'What do you like?'

'Books, films.'

'Anything else?'

'I thought I was supposed to be asking the questions.'

'At first, to get things going. After the first few minutes conversation will hopefully just come naturally. But don't worry if it doesn't. Just keep talking and letting her talk.'

'OK. What do I say next?'

Kate looked at the table for inspiration. This was one of the hardest dummy dates she'd ever had. Usually her clients got the swing of it much more quickly and treated her as a real date.

Angus seemed to be having problems getting his head around the whole concept. Her eyes fell on his newspaper. 'Tell her about something you read in the newspaper.'

'Her?'

'Me! Tell me! Your date!'

'Sorry. Are you annoyed with me again?'

'No,' she lied. 'So was there any interesting news today?'

'A man in his eighties swam the English Channel for charity. Is that interesting?'

'Yes, very,' she said. 'Go on.'

'Um, I only read the headline, I'm afraid. But he's someone famous's grandfather, I remember that much. Um, do you have any grandparents?' he asked, floundering for something to say.

'Yes, actually I do. One granny – she's nearly eighty. And she swims in the sea every day. She's never swum the Channel though.'

He whistled. 'Impressive. I don't have any unfortunately – more's the pity. They all died quite a few years ago. I always felt closer to them in a way than to my own parents. I could really talk to them, you know, without being judged.'

'I know exactly what you mean. It's an easier kind of relationship, isn't it?'

'Yes. Do you get on with your own parents?'

Kate drained the last of her drink and put it back down on the table before answering. 'Sort of. I don't see them that much to tell the truth. Dad took early retirement and they moved down to Connemara.'

Angus leant forward, his head on his hands. 'This is going well, isn't it?' he said in a low voice. 'Do I ask you for dinner now or later?'

Kate laughed. 'Angus!'

'Sorry, have I annoyed you again?'

'Stop asking me that! Please!'

'OK. But what about dinner?'

'Honestly?'

'Yes.'

'If I was your date, yes, this is a good time to ask. We are getting on well. But as for me, I'd have to say I'm not so sure.'

'Why?'

'I don't know if I have the energy to continue counselling you all night.'

'Are you suggesting I need counselling? Am I that bad?' He seemed a little upset by her comment.

'No, of course not. It was the wrong word to use. I should have said helping, advising.'

'I'm tiring you out.'

'Yes. I'm afraid you are.'

'Oh.' He stared at the table, his hands clasped together in prayer position, the tops of his fingers touching lightly.

'Angus, I'm sorry. I didn't mean to upset you. I shouldn't have been quite so direct.'

'You didn't upset me, not really. I was coming on too strong, wasn't I? You don't like me, do you?'

'That's not it at all. You were doing great. I do like you – as a client. And as I said, if I was your date I'd definitely go for dinner with you.'

'Really?' He looked up, his brown eyes catching hers and reminding her of something. 'How about we just go to dinner as friends?' he suggested eagerly. 'We could drop all the dummy date thing and . . .'

'I don't think so, but thanks for the offer.' She was often asked out by her clients and she made it a policy not to meet them outside 'office hours'.

'Have I overstepped the line again?' he asked.

'A little.'

'I didn't mean a date. Just dinner.'

'Stop right there,' she said. 'Please. I can't have dinner with you, OK? I have other plans.'

'That's OK. I'm a complete loser, I know. Why would you want to have dinner with me?' He stared at the table.

'Ah, Angus, you're not a loser. You're just a little different. Tell you what – let's meet again next week and talk – for coffee this time. What do you think? I'll give you your report and we can talk it through. Usually I send the report out in the post but I'd be happy to meet you if you think it would help.'

'Thanks,' he said. 'That would be great. I do appreciate your help, really I do. I'm finding this a bit difficult, that's all. Maybe dummy dating isn't for me. Please be nice about me in your report.'

'I'll be honest,' she said evenly. 'That's all I can promise.'

'Can I ring you to set up a time? I don't have my diary on me.'

'Of course.' She stood up. 'It was nice to see you again, Angus. And you did well.'

'Thanks. I'll see you next week.'

'Yes. Ring me.'

A bushbaby, Kate thought as she walked home. That's what his eyes remind me of, an African bushbaby – dark, chocolatey brown. All wide-eyed and innocent.

The following night Kate had an even stranger dummy date experience. She was sitting in O'Connor's pub again, this time with another client, Clive, chatting about cars and four-wheel drives (he was a car salesman who was trying to get his dating confidence back after coming out of a long relationship) when, out of the blue, a red haired woman poured a pint of cider over her head.

'What the hell!' Kate exclaimed standing up and leaning forward, her head dripping onto the carpet.

'Bitch!' the woman screamed. 'I should have known there was some reason Clive was going off me.'

'Going off you?' Clive demanded, standing up. 'I loved you.

You broke up with me, remember? Eight years and then wham, you said it was over.'

'Only because I thought you didn't love me any more. You never told me, how was I to know?'

'Excuse me,' Kate interrupted. 'I'm going to the bathroom to dry off. Clive talk to . . . sorry what's your name. Tell her how you feel.'

'Linda,' Clive said.

'What are you talking about?' the woman demanded. 'How do you know how he feels?'

'I'm his counsellor,' Kate lied smoothly. 'The electricity is off in my office so we had to meet here instead. He was just telling me how much he missed you at our session, weren't you Clive?' She stared at him, willing him to agree.

'Yes,' he said, rather convincingly. 'Kate has been great. A real professional.'

'Shit, I'm so sorry,' the woman said looking genuinely shocked. 'I saw you both over here together and I realized how much I missed Clive. I thought . . .'

'Never mind,' Kate said quickly. 'No harm done. Now I'll leave you both to it, shall I?'

'Thanks, Kate,' Clive said sincerely. 'Thanks for everything.'

'My pleasure. It's all part of the service.'

The following morning there was a knock on the door and as Kate answered it she was almost knocked out by the heady smell of lilies.

'Kate Bowan?' the man holding the huge bouquet asked.

'Yes?'

He thrust the flowers towards her. 'For you.'

'Thanks.' She stepped inside and managed to wrestle the tiny card out of its envelope.

'To Kate,' she read. 'Who's no dummy. Getting married to Linda in the spring. Thanks for everything, Clive.'

She smiled to herself. Another happy customer. The same

morning she got another surprise delivery – this time from the postman. She started as she recognized the familiar sharp, angular writing on the envelope and the American stamp. Her immediate reaction was to tear it up, but curiosity got the better of her. She walked into the kitchen, sat down at the table and stared at the envelope in her shaking hands. Just then the phone rang. She let the answering machine take it.

'Hi, Kate, hoping we could meet up on Tuesday at lunchtime. Say half twelve in Coffee Heaven? Give me a ring if it doesn't suit. Oh, this is Angus by the way. Your mad but keen client. Remember to say nice things about me in your report. Bye.'

She put her head on the table and let the solid wood cool her brow. Angus and a letter from America. She didn't know which was worse.

'What's wrong with you?' Trina asked as soon as Kate had stepped in the door of Baroque that afternoon. 'You have a real sourpuss face on you.'

'Thank you very much, Trina,' she said evenly. 'Nice to see you too.'

'Out late last night, were you? Had a few tequilas too many?'

'No, I just have a lot on my mind. Where's Cathy?'

'She'll be back in a minute. She's gone out with Flames for coffee and then I'm off. There's this charity lunch in aid of some local arts thingy that Connie's running. I promised I'd go for a while.'

'You can go now if you like, I'll hold the fort. But don't forget we all have to finish talking about the summer sale and the winter collection later.' Kate would be glad to see the back of her for a while – sarky cow.

'I won't forget.' Trina grabbed her black leather coat and Gucci bag. She kissed her hand and blew it at Kate. '*Ciao!*'

'Bloody *Ciao* to you too,' Kate said as soon as Trina had breezed out the door in her wafts of Gucci perfume. She looked at the desk and on the floor. As usual there were at least twenty assorted shoeboxes to be put away. Trina never cleared away after herself, leaving Kate and Cathy to do all the real work. She got stuck in, replacing the toe-stiffeners and foam in all the shoes and wrapping them back into their tissue cocoons before closing them into their boxes. At least it would keep her occupied. The letter this morning had really unnerved her.

At half past four Trina flung open the door and staggered in. Her eyes looked wild – her pupils dilated and the whites blood-shot. She was a terrible drinker – she couldn't take a glass of wine without looking like the mad Lady Macbeth.

'Uh-oh,' Cathy whispered. 'I'll run out and get some black coffee. Want anything?'

'No, thanks. But don't leave me with her in that state,' Kate said. 'I'll go.'

Cathy patted her arm. 'She'll be fine. She's a pussy cat really.' She turned towards Trina who was tottering towards them. 'Sit down, darling. I'm going on a coffee run. Back in a tick.'

Trina plonked herself down on one of the two large red-velvet covered sofas which ran down the centre of the shop, back to back.

'That's better,' she said, kicking off her impossibly high gold sandals. 'My feet are killing me.'

'Don't say that if any customers walk in,' said Kate. 'Those sandals are one of our best sellers.'

'Crappy things.' Trina ignored her. She began to massage the ball of her right foot. 'What have you been doing all afternoon anyway? Talking on your phone as usual, I suppose. Anyone would think you had a boyfriend the way you carry on.'

Kate stared at her but said nothing.

'Oh, no, too high and mighty for that sort of thing, aren't you? Think you're so superior with your vamps and your uppers and moulded soles – who gives a damn how shoes are made as long as they fit? I certainly don't.'

Kate ignored her again. She'd seen Trina drunk before, but she'd never been this bad.

'Answer me, girl!'

Kate had had enough. 'Don't speak to me like that, Trina, I have no intention of answering you, you stupid woman. Look at the state of you, it's embarrassing. You should go home.'

'No, I won't go home. And don't *you* speak to *me* like that. I'm your boss, remember? Now get me some water, I want some water.'

'Get it yourself, you know where the cooler is.'

'How dare you! Get me some water.'

Kate turned away and began to price some sale stock.

'Damn you!' Trina shouted.

Kate felt something hit the back of her head and then her shoulder. 'Ow!' she looked down. Trina's shoes were lying on the floor beside her. She turned around and glared at the woman angrily.

Trina had a nasty smile on her lips.

'Did you just throw your shoes at me?' asked Kate angrily.

Trina threw her head back and laughed manically.

'What's going on here?' Cathy asked walking in the door with two large cups of coffee in her hands.

'She threw her shoes at me and hit me on the head,' Kate explained.

'What?' Cathy stared at Kate in amazement. She looked down at Trina. 'Did you?' she asked crossly.

Trina nodded, still smiling.

'What's got into you? I'm ringing Farrell.'

'Don't do that. He'll be cross. I'm not supposed to be drinking – the injections . . .' She tailed off sheepishly.

Cathy stared at her again. 'Are you having fertility treatment again?' Silence. 'Answer me!'

Trina looked down at the floor.

'You stupid thing, you know you can't drink when you're having treatment, you know that. I'm ringing Farrell.' She put the coffee down on the counter, pulled out her mobile and had a quick conversation with Trina's husband. 'He's coming straight over. Could you get her some water, Kate? I'll lock the door and put the blinds down. I don't want anyone to see her like this. I'm sorry I left you, I hadn't realized how bad she was.'

'Yes, get me some water,' Trina cackled.

'Trina!' Cathy scolded. 'Not one more word out of you, do you hear?'

'OK.'

Kate felt like refusing but she knew none of this was Cathy's fault. She went into the office and came back a minute later with the water.

'Thanks, I appreciate it. Would you like to go home now? You look a little shell-shocked if you don't mind me saying. And take tomorrow and Saturday off.'

'Are you sure?'

'Yes. I'll be fine on my own in the morning and Trina will be in in the afternoon whether she likes it or not. And all day Saturday.'

Trina groaned beside her. 'Don't feel too well,' she said.

'I'm not surprised,' Cathy handed her the water. 'Drink this.'

''S'not alcohol is it?'

'No, most certainly not.'

Trina drained the cup. 'Didn't know you designed shoes, Kate,' she slurred. 'Lady at the lunch told me you used to work for Sin in Boston. You were one of their top designers.' She hiccupped loudly. 'And then you left suddenly to come back to Ireland.'

'She must have me confused with someone else,' Kate said calmly. She walked into the back room and collected her jacket and bag.

'Ring me if you need me tomorrow, Cathy,' she said before she left. 'Otherwise I'll see you on Monday.'

'See you then,' Cathy said to Kate's back. A shoe designer at Sin, the most cutting-edge of the American shoe design houses, now that was interesting, Cathy thought. And it made sense.

'So, Angus, how are you?' Kate asked after they'd sat down in Coffee Heaven.

'Good thanks. And what did you get up to over the weekend?'

'This and that.'

He cocked his head to one side. 'Why don't you answer the question? It wouldn't kill you.'

She shrugged her shoulders. 'Would you like some coffee?'

He nodded.

She caught Alex's eye. 'Two coffees,' she said loudly. 'Thanks, Alex.'

Alex smiled. 'Coming up.'

'You're very evasive,' said Angus, picking up a sugar packet from the table and playing with it, rolling it backwards and forwards in his fingers. 'What are you hiding?'

'Angus! I'm not hiding anything. We're here to talk about you, not me, OK?'

'Fine. I was just trying to be friendly. That's all.'

'Sorry . . .'

'Sorry what?' he asked.

'Angus!'

'I thought you were going to say something else there,' he explained. 'You know, like sorry but I don't find it easy to open up to people. Or sorry, but I prefer to keep my private life to myself, or sorry . . .'

'I get the picture. And if you must know I was going to say – sorry, I'm not in great form today.'

'Why?' he asked gently. 'If you don't mind me asking.

Although I know you probably do. But I'm asking anyway because I like you, Kate and I'm genuinely . . .'

'Stop! OK, I'll tell you if you're really interested.' Anything to shut him up, she thought. 'There was a bit of an incident with my boss on Friday – I work in a shoe shop some days, did I tell you that?'

'Yes, on our date.'

'Dummy date.'

'Sorry, of course, dummy date. Although I wasn't sure if it was you who worked in the shop or Betty.'

'Betty?' What is he talking about, Kate wondered.

'You know, you asked me did I want to call you Betty.'

'Right.' Kate was losing patience. 'Do you want me to tell you or not?'

'Yes, sorry. Go on.'

'Well, she's been trying to contact me all weekend. It's been driving me nuts. She sat in her jeep outside my house for ages on Sunday waiting for me. I had to get my housemate to go outside and tell her I was away for the whole day.'

'What did she do on Friday?' Angus asked, intrigued.

Kate sighed. 'I shouldn't really tell you.'

'I'm not likely to know her,' he pointed out. 'And I'm very discreet, honestly.'

She studied his face. For some reason she trusted him – he was kooky, said all the wrong things and was most inappropriate with his questions – but she had a gut feeling that he wouldn't betray a confidence.

'OK then. She threw a pair of shoes at me and hit me on the back of the head. Oh, and she verbally abused me.'

'Wow! Supermodels eat your heart out. Welcome to the spicy and vindictive world of Kate's shoe shop. Why did she do that?'

'A heady cocktail of alcohol and fertility drugs apparently. Gets them every time.'

'Are you serious?' he asked.

She nodded. 'The lives of Burnaby's rich and famous – who needs Hollywood?'

'No kidding. And are you all right? It must have really shaken you up.'

'It did,' she admitted. 'But I'm OK now.'

'And you haven't talked to her since – allowed her to apologize?'

'No, I'll see her later though. Unfortunately.'

'I presume you're not going to sue her. You don't seem the type.'

'No, I'm not. Life's too short.'

Alex put two large mugs of coffee on their table.

'Sorry about the delay,' she said. 'We're pretty short staffed at the moment. Rona's just gone on holiday for the whole month and Peter's out sick.'

'Not to worry.' Kate smiled up at her.

Alex leaned towards her. 'Heard about the shoe incident. Cathy told me. Are you all right?'

'Fine,' she said shortly. She hoped Trina didn't think it was *her* spreading the gossip. She would have to have words with Cathy. 'I think it would be best if you kept it to yourself, Alex, if you don't mind. For Trina's sake.'

Alex looked at her for a second. 'You're a good person, Kate. I won't say a word.'

'Thanks.' As Alex walked away Kate focused her eyes on her coffee cup – adding milk and sugar and stirring furiously.

'You should talk to Trina,' Angus said, breaking the silence. 'Clear the air.'

She raised her eyes. He was smiling gently at her. 'It would make work easier. You need to allow her to atone and to make amends.'

'You're probably right. I don't know why I'm worrying about it, it's her who should be embarrassed, not me.'

'I'm sure she is.' Angus picked up the small ceramic jug on

83

the table and poured more milk into his already very white coffee.

Just then, Molly came in the door and bustled over towards their table.

'Thank goodness,' she said breathlessly. 'I thought you might be here. I couldn't get through on your mobile and I've been home already in case you weren't answering the phone.'

Kate gestured towards Angus. 'I'm having coffee with Angus. Angus, this is my friend, Molly.'

He smiled up at her. 'Hi, Molly.'

'Hi, Angus. Nice to meet you. Sorry to interrupt, Kate, but you need to get to St John's Hospital as soon as you can. It's Lily.'

'Granny?' Kate asked faintly.

Molly nodded. 'Yes. She fell over this morning after swimming and she broke her ankle. But I think she also bumped her head.'

'Is she all right?'

'I'm not sure. They seemed a little concerned about concussion and wanted you to get there as soon as possible.'

'Why did the hospital ring you?' Kate asked in confusion.

'Lily suggested it when they couldn't get through to you. Your mobile was off apparently.'

Kate pulled her phone out of her bag and was greeted by a blank screen. 'No wonder, stupid thing is out of juice again.' She banged the phone ineffectually on the top of the table.

'I can get an hour off if you need a lift over,' Molly said, aware that her friend was in a bit of a state. 'I'll call into Anita – I'm sure she'll cover for me.'

Kate stood up and picked up her bag. 'OK. Thanks.'

'Listen, I'll take her,' Angus offered. 'I'm not working at the moment and I wouldn't mind, honestly.'

Molly looked at Kate. She was pale and seemed very shaken, but she didn't protest at the man's offer. Molly didn't recognize him but she presumed he was a good friend of Kate's to offer his services like that. Maybe even a new boyfriend. As Kate never shared her private life with Molly she had no idea if Kate had met someone recently. 'Is that all right with you, Kate? I'll call over to the hospital straight after work. Would you like me to call into Cathy for you and tell her what's happened?'

'Yes, if you wouldn't mind.'

'Not at all. And, Kate, ring me if you need anything later, understand,' said Molly. 'Anything.'

'Thanks.'

Molly looked at Angus. 'And you're sure this is all right?'

'Honestly, it's fine. I'll drive her over and stay with her for a little while to check she's OK.'

'Great, I appreciate that. Kate, I'll see you later.'

After Kate and Angus had left Molly ordered three coffees from Alex.

'He seems nice,' Molly said as she watched Alex pour. She was fishing for information and felt sure that Alex would know something. 'Kate's friend. Haven't met him before.'

'He's actually one of her clients,' Alex said. 'They left very suddenly. Everything all right?'

'Kate's granny's been taken into hospital with a broken ankle. She might have concussion too.'

'Granny Lily? I hope she's OK. Lovely woman. Mum knows her from the church flowers.'

'I should have driven Kate to St John's myself,' Molly said a little anxiously. 'I hadn't realized he was a client. But she seemed happy enough to let him drive.'

'Then don't worry. He seems sweet. He's been in here a lot over the last two weeks. Must have moved into the area.'

'You're right. I'll stop fretting and get back to work.' She paid and picked up the tray of paper cups. 'Thanks for the coffee.'

'Any time.' Alex smiled. 'Give my best wishes to Lily when you see her.'

'Will do.'

It was only a twenty-minute drive to St John's Hospital in Sandybay but Kate worried the entire journey. Angus tried to talk to her and keep her mind off her granny's fall but she was so preoccupied that he gave up after a few minutes and flicked on the radio instead. The presenter was discussing people who had strange collections – the lady he was talking to collected ceramic toads.

'Do you collect anything, Kate?' Angus asked as he negotiated a large pothole on Burnaby Hill Road. The hill between Burnaby and Sandybay, nicknamed 'Swiss Cheese' by the locals, was notorious for its lumps and bumps. He may as well give conversation one more go – he had nothing to lose.

'Sorry?' she murmured.

'Do you collect anything?' he repeated. 'You know – like model cars or cacti?'

'Shoes,' she said absent-mindedly.

'What kind of shoes?'

'All kinds,' she replied, still staring out the passenger window.

'Like what? New shoes, old shoes. Borrowed shoes, blue shoes? Blue suede shoes, dancing shoes?' he was trying to lighten the mood but it didn't seem to be working.

'Old ones,' she said after a long pause. 'Foreign ones. I pick them up on the internet and at car boot sales and sales of work.'

'What's your favourite pair?'

'I have some nineteenth-century Lotus shoes my granny gave me for my birthday a few years ago.'

'Lotus shoes?'

She sighed. 'Do you really want to know or are you just making conversation? Because if you're not really interested I'd prefer not to talk if you don't mind.'

'I was just making conversation to begin with,' Angus said,

ignoring her short tone. 'But now I'm interested. Very interested. Please go on.'

'Fine. Lotus shoes were worn by Chinese women. You've heard of foot binding?'

'Yes,' said Angus. 'Mao banned it in 1949.'

'Did he? How do you know that?'

'Read it somewhere. I'm a mine of useless information. Go on anyway.'

'A "Golden Lotus" was a foot measuring three inches or less. That's where the name of the shoe came from.'

'So they're basically tiny shoes.'

'Mine are tiny black shoes covered in pink and white embroidery to be exact.'

'Where did your granny find them?'

'In an antique shop in town. It was pure luck.'

'How long have you collected shoes for?'

'Years.'

'How many pairs do you have?'

'I'm not sure really. Lots.'

'What is your second favourite pair?'

'Angus! Enough! Stop the questions, please. I'm not in the mood for talking this morning, I'm sorry.'

'Worried about your granny?'

Kate said nothing.

'Sorry, stupid question.' He kept quiet until they drove into Sandybay.

'You can drop me outside St John's,' said Kate evenly. 'I'm fine from there.'

'I'll bring you in, it's no trouble.'

'But . . .'

'Kate, you might need me to go and get something for your granny. You probably won't want to leave her.'

'Like what?'

'Coffee or a newspaper.'

'Angus, she might have concussion, and if she has, she'd hardly be able to read a paper, would she?'

'Sorry, I wasn't thinking.' He sounded subdued.

'That's all right. I shouldn't have snapped at you. You're only trying to help.'

'I'm coming in with you whether you like it or not. You're in shock. I insist.'

'Fine.' She didn't have the energy to argue.

As they walked into Lily's ward Kate thought she could hear her granny's laughter from behind some drawn flowery curtains which encircled one of the hospital cubicles.

'Excuse me, I'm looking for Lily Bowan,' she said to a nurse.

The nurse pointed to the curtains. 'In there, love, talking to Dr Martin.'

'Thanks.' Kate pulled back the curtains and looked in. A white haired doctor was sitting on a stiff-backed hospital chair. Her granny was sitting upright in the bed, a blue cotton hospital gown covering her tanned chest.

'Hello, love.' Lily beamed. 'Coming to join the party? This is nice Dr Miles Martin. He'll be operating on my ankle in a few days. Isn't that right, Miles?'

'You must be Kate,' Miles said. 'Lily was telling me all about you.'

'That's right,' Kate faltered. 'And is Granny all right? I was told she might have concussion.'

'Not me.' Lily knocked her knuckles against the side of her head. 'Tough old nut, I have.'

'We think your granny passed out from the pain of breaking her ankle. We can't find any evidence of concussion but we're keeping an eye on her just in case.'

'That's a relief,' said Kate. 'And her ankle?'

'Cooee, I'm still here,' Lily reminded them, 'you can ask me, you know.'

Miles stood up. 'I'll let Lily fill you in on all the details. She knows almost as much about the procedure as I do from all accounts. Who was it had the same operation, Lily?'

'Old Mr Carmody from swimming,' Lily replied. 'Old fool slipped on seaweed a couple of years ago. Went into all the details at the time, let me tell you.'

'Thanks, Doctor,' Kate said.

'No problem. I'll be back to check on her later. Your granny is a great friend of my mother's, you know.'

'From the chess club,' Lily explained. 'See you later, Miles.' She waved at him.

'Granny, were you flirting with that poor doctor?' Kate smiled as she sat down on the bed.

'Ow,' Lily squealed sharply.

Kate jumped up immediately. 'Oh, my God! Did I sit on your bad ankle?'

Lily winked at her. 'Only joking,' she said, her eyes twinkling mischievously.

Kate frowned. 'I'll sit on the chair just in case.'

'What's ailing you, love?' asked Lily. 'You seem a little out of sorts.'

'I was worried about you. I thought you were concussed. I wasn't sure what to expect.'

Lily patted her hand. 'Sorry to disappoint you, chicken, but apart from my ankle I'm as fit as a fiddle.'

'And what will they have to do with it exactly – your ankle I mean?'

'Put pins in it,' Lily said. 'I'll be like the bionic woman. When you cremate me you'll have to take out the pins before you sprinkle my ashes on the sea.'

'Granny, don't talk like that!'

'Why not? Everyone dies in the end. Not much we can do about it. Might as well just enjoy ourselves while we're here. Kate, is there someone outside the curtains? I can feel something. Can you have a look?'

Kate got up and pulled the yellow and pink curtain open. Angus was standing patiently against the wall at the far end of the ward. She'd forgotten that he'd followed her up.

'One second, Granny.' She walked towards him. 'What are you doing?' she asked a little crossly. 'I'm here now and everything's fine. There's no need for you to wait for me.'

'I'll go then,' he said. 'I just wanted to make sure . . .'

'Bring the lad over,' Lily said in a loud voice. 'I'd like to meet him.' Kate hadn't closed the curtain behind her and she and Angus were in full view of Lily's hospital bed.

Angus immediately made his way towards Lily.

'You can't stay,' Kate hissed following closely behind him. 'She's very weak.'

'She looks it,' Angus said just before he reached the curtain. 'Hello, you must be Lily.' he smiled. 'I'm Angus. I'm . . .'

'Angus is a friend of mine,' interrupted Kate. 'Before you ask, he's a primary school teacher and he's on his summer break. He very kindly drove me over and he's just about to leave, aren't you, Angus?'

'No, I can stay for a little while.' Angus beamed angelically at Kate.

Kate felt like hitting him. Why was he being so obstinate? This was her granny, her hospital visit, her life for goodness sake. What the hell was he doing interfering?

'That's nice,' Lily said. 'I'm a bit bored to tell the truth. The nurses are pets but they're much too busy to chat. And all the other old dears in the ward are a bit doddery if you know what I mean.'

Angus stayed standing. 'Sit down, Kate. I'll go downstairs and fetch us all some tea, will I? Make myself useful. I'm sure you'd like to talk to your granny on your own.'

'I've tea coming out my ears. Do you know what I'd love, young man?' asked Lily.

'A nice big gin and tonic?'

Lily laughed delightedly. 'Apart from that. Some nice cold bottled water. The water they give you in here is lukewarm and tastes mouldy.' She pointed at the plastic water jug by her bed. 'And I'd love some sweets, toffees if you can find them.'

'Your wish is my command.' He bowed. 'And for you, mademoiselle?' he looked at Kate.

Really he was too much. 'I'd like a bottle of water too. Still please. And Granny likes sparkling.'

'Matches my personality,' Lily winked at him.

'I think you're right.' He laughed.

As soon as he'd left the ward, Kate sensed that the second interrogation of the day was about to begin.

'He's adorable!' Lily enthused. 'Such a thoughtful lad. Very endearing and such good manners. Where did you meet him?'

Kate thought quickly. 'Tell me about the operation, Granny. All the gory details.'

Lily was torn – she wanted to find out all about Angus but she knew she wouldn't get another chance to tell her usually hyper-squeamish granddaughter about her operation. She opted for the blood and guts.

'I won't bore you with too many details – but first of all they give you some sleeping pills, then the anaesthetist puts you to sleep,' Lily began. 'An injection. Hate them. They can never find my veins. I'm too slim you see, my toned figure is a curse.' She snorted and Kate smiled. 'They'll be paranoid putting me under, of course – convinced I won't wake up again on account of my age, you see.'

'Granny!'

'Then they'll cut through the skin and the . . .'

Kate tried to block out the procedure her gran was describing while still appearing interested. Maybe she should have told her about Angus after all and got it over with. But what was there to say – he's a lost cause, Granny, and I'm trying to help him get a girlfriend. Still, he had brought her to the hospital and he was doing an errand for them. But it didn't redeem his peculiar behaviour. And it wasn't lovable or endearing, not one little bit.

'Are you listening, Kate?' Lily asked. 'You seem a bit away with the fairies.'

'I'm fine, just a bit preoccupied with things at work, that's all. Please, continue. We got to the bit where the doctor was fitting the pins.'

Chapter 6

Paige

'Hi, Molly, you'll never believe what happened at the council meeting this evening,' Paige began. She was picking up Callum's clothes from the kitchen floor, the portable phone jammed between her shoulder and her ear. He'd insisted on warming his naked body in front of the aga before putting on his pyjamas and had dumped his clothes unceremoniously on the tiles. 'Davorka Ferata arrived.'

'The Bosnian opera singer?' Molly asked intrigued.

'The very same. Apparently she's also an award-winning photographer. She's in Ireland for the Wexford Opera Festival and one of her old friends, Besnik something or other is living in a B&B just outside Burnaby. He's a famous tenor in his own country.'

'What's he doing here?'

'He's an asylum seeker. He and his family were forced out of their home by the Serbian army.'

'Was Connie Calloway at the meeting?'

'She was.'

'You are infuriating sometimes. Where is all of this leading?'

'It was amazing. Davorka stood up and . . . Shit! What's that

Sarah Webb

smell? Hang on a second, Molly.' Paige ran up the stairs and sniffed the air in the upstairs landing. The strong, heady odour was coming from Callum's room. She put her hand over the receiver. 'Callum, what are you doing in there?' There was no answer.

'Paige!' Molly protested.

'I have to go,' said Paige. 'There's a really strong smell coming from Callum's bedroom, suspiciously like Chanel No 5. I'll kill him if it is. He's supposed to be asleep.'

'Paige, you can't leave me hanging like this. Tell me what Davorka said. Please.'

'I'll ring you back in a few minutes,' she promised. 'I really have to go.' She put down the receiver, took a deep breath and walked into Callum's room.

He was nowhere to be seen. There was a telltale puddle of dark yellow liquid on the floorboards and as she bent down to investigate she was nearly knocked out by the fumes. It was her Chanel all right, but where was the bottle?

'Callum? I know you're in here. Are you under the bed?' She pulled up his duvet which was hanging over the side of his lower bunk bed and looked underneath. He wasn't there. However she did spy the pieces of broken glass and the plastic spray insert and metal top amongst the dust balls, once her perfume bottle. He'd obviously kicked them under there to hide the evidence. She stood up and pulled open his closet, another of his favourite hiding places. He smiled up at her nervously, knowing he'd done something very bad this time, but at the same time shocked at his own audacity and bravery.

'Get out,' she said in a dangerously low voice. She pointed at the pool of perfume on the floor. 'What happened?'

'I was on the top bunk and the bottle kind of slipped out of my hand,' he explained. 'It wasn't my fault.'

'And whose fault was it then exactly?'

'Um, Alfie's.'

94

'Why was it Alfie's fault?'

'He was annoying me.'

'But he's in his room asleep, Callum.'

'He was still annoying me. He's a shit.'

'Callum! Don't use that language in this house.'

'You do. I just heard you on the phone.'

'That's different.'

'Why?'

'It just is.' She sighed deeply. 'And what were you doing with my perfume anyway? You know you're not allowed to take things from Mummy and Daddy's bedroom, don't you? And why does the hall smell of perfume too? Tell me the truth. It'll be a lot better for you if you do. I know when you're lying to me, young man.'

He had the good grace to look a little contrite. 'I was using it as a magic potion. You know, like Harry Potter. I was making myself grow bigger. I put some on my head. It didn't work. I was standing on the stairs so I could listen to you on the phone, then I came up to my room. I dropped the bottle when I was climbing onto the top bunk.'

She leant down and smelt his hair. It reeked of perfume. 'Oh, Callum, what am I going to do with you?'

'Smack me?' he said nervously.

'No, I'm not going to smack you. We don't smack in this house, you know that. But you have to understand that you can't take things without asking and then break them. Or listen in to my phone calls.' She sat down on the side of the bed. 'I'm tired of all this, love. Can't you just be good for a change?'

'I'll try, Mummy.'

'You need a bath and a hair wash. Your hair stinks.'

'Can we use Fruit Alive Shampoo for Kids – "Makes hair washing fun for all the family"?' He sang the shampoo's distinctive jingle loudly.

'No, we'll use the normal shampoo. You watch too much telly, Callum.'

'No, I don't!' he shouted.

'Why did you just shout at me?' she asked in exasperation. 'You said you were going to be good.'

'Sorry, Mummy.'

'Now, I'm going downstairs to get some kitchen roll and a plastic bag to put the glass into. And then you can help me mop up the perfume, OK? Now sit on your bed and wait for me like a good boy.'

He nodded eagerly.

When she walked back into Callum's room three minutes later she found him crouched over the perfume puddle.

'What are you doing?' she asked.

'Helping.' He smiled up at her.

She looked down at the floor and to her horror saw that he'd been mopping up the perfume with his new white towelling dressing gown.

'Callum! What the hell are you doing? You'll ruin your dressing gown, you idiot.' She knelt down on her hunkers and put her head in her hands.

'Are you crying, Mummy?' he asked with interest.

'No! But I will be in a minute. You're driving me mad! Get out of here.'

'Where will I go?'

'I don't care. Out!'

'I'll go and watch telly, will I?'

'Yes, whatever. Just get out!'

'You shouldn't really shout at me, Mummy. Daddy doesn't like it.'

'Daddy isn't here. He's at the gym. And if you know what's good for you, you'll get out right now, Callum and stop annoying me. And stop answering me back, do you hear? Go!'

Callum skipped down the stairs to the television room. His

mummy got a bit tired sometimes, she didn't mean to shout, that's what Daddy said.

Paige sat on her son's floor, moving her legs from beneath her as they started to get pins and needles. She heard a faint cry coming from Alfie's room, then a stronger one. I know exactly how you feel, Alfie, she thought. She pulled some kitchen paper off the roll and began to mop up the perfume. She'd become immune to the strong smell by this stage. But as for Callum, she was far from immune to his fatal charms at the moment. As soon as Tom got home their son would get a strong talking to, she'd see to that. She didn't have the energy to do it herself. Besides, after cleaning the mess up and soothing Alfie back to sleep she'd be fit for nothing except her bed.

Paige rang Molly back an hour later.

'Is Callum OK?' Molly asked gently.

'No comment,' said Paige. She explained what had happened to her favourite bottle of perfume.

'Is he asleep now?'

'Yes, Tom gave him a bath and settled him down.'

Molly took a deep breath. 'It might be time for you talk to someone about Callum. For your own sake if not for his. He's wearing you down and it's not right.'

Paige didn't reply.

Molly broke the silence. 'I'm sorry, I shouldn't have said anything, you're probably exhausted. Bad timing.'

'No, you're right,' Paige said finally. 'It's getting beyond a joke and he doesn't seem to be growing out of it, in fact he's getting worse.'

'I hope you don't think I'm interfering because I'm not. I just care . . .'

'Stop! Honestly, it's all right.'

'Good. And you never finished the story about Davorka,' Molly reminded her.

'OK. To cut a long story short, she's going to hold a fund-raising concert in St John's Church next month to raise funds for the refugee centre.'

'I bet Connie is only too thrilled.' Molly snorted.

'No kidding. But she seems to have had a bit of a change of heart.'

'Oh?'

'Davorka's no fool. Apparently her friend Besnik filled her in on the details. Davorka called into Connie's gallery and offered her the very first showing of her photographs in Ireland. Connie was delighted and accepted immediately. But Davorka had one condition.'

'Let me guess. That Connie drops her objections to the refugee centre.'

'Darling,' Paige drawled in her best 'posh' Connie voice, 'now that a famous tenor is involved in the arts centre how could I refuse?'

'Arts centre?'

'Gas, isn't it? Connie agreed on the condition that the refugee centre be called the Burnaby Arts Centre and that Davorka be its patron.'

'Brilliant! But they'll still be teaching English and helping the refugees find jobs, like you wanted.'

'Yes. As well as holding multicultural music and drama evenings, exhibitions, festivals and events for children. So everyone wins.'

'Including you.'

'Exactly!'

'Another triumph for Councillor Brady.'

'Why, thank you, Molly.'

The following day Paige visited Lily in hospital.

'Hi, Lily, I hear this place is driving you bonkers.' She

smiled, leant down and kissed Lily's cheek. 'I thought I'd come in and say hi.'

'How lovely to see you, Paige. And how is your mum? Still teaching the flower arranging? I haven't seen her for a while.'

'She's great, thanks. And yes, still teaching, mainly evening classes these days. It keeps her out of trouble.'

'I took one of her classes last year, it was a one-off thing in the church hall for the Flower Festival. She was very good. Very organized. Perfectly symmetrical arrangements – amazing. I was useless of course, mine kept drooping to one side.'

Paige sat down on the chair beside Lily's bed. 'So how are they treating you in here?'

'Very well. My doctor is a dear – Miles Martin – do you know him?'

Paige shook her head.

'Lovely man. His mother is an old friend of mine.'

Paige smiled to herself. Lily knew everyone in Burnaby and had more friends than anyone she knew.

'And how are you, Paige? You look a little tired.'

'Things are busy enough, Lily. Alfie was teething last night so I didn't get much sleep to tell the truth.'

'And how's Callum?'

'Fine. Still a handful.'

Lily looked at Paige carefully, tapped the tips of her fingers together and then smiled knowingly. 'And when's the next one due? Kate didn't say anything to me so it must be early days yet. No wonder you're tired.'

Paige could feel the blood drain from her face and she became suddenly lightheaded. She swayed dangerously in her chair.

'Put your head between your knees and take deep breaths,' Lily commanded. 'That's it, good girl, take it easy.'

Paige sat back up after a few minutes and Lily handed her a

glass of water. 'I'm sorry, I shouldn't have said anything,' Lily said. 'Forgive me.'

'No, it's not your fault, really. I just . . . I hadn't realized to tell the truth. But I think you're right. No, I know you're right. It all makes sense. I've been really tired in the last few weeks and I've had to eat all the time or I've felt faint and sick. How could I have been so stupid? What lousy timing!' Fat tears began to roll down Paige's cheeks.

Lily pulled some tissues out of a box on the cluttered bedside table and handed them to her. 'It will all work out, you'll see.'

'But the elections are coming up soon and I've no one to mind the children in August and . . .' She began to cry, her sobs catching in her throat and making it hard to breathe.

Lily patted her on the shoulder. 'There, there, love. Things are never as bad as they seem. Stop crying now and we'll see if Lily can help, will we? I know a lovely primary school teacher who might be available. A young man called Angus who would be wonderful with Callum I think, from all appearances a kind and gentle soul. Don't cry, Paige, we'll sort it all out, you'll see.'

Paige looked at Lily, her eyes still full of tears. 'A primary school teacher. Do you think he'd be interested? It would be a godsend, really it would. I've interviewed all kinds of people, mostly college students, and older women, but none of them were quite right. Some had no experience of children at all, and there's no way they'd be able to cope with Callum. Mum has offered to take Alfie, but . . .'

'Let's just see, will we?' Lily smiled. 'God moves in mysterious ways. Leave it with me.' She patted Paige's hand. 'Now you go home and have a little lie down. You've had a bit of a shock. Ring that nice husband of yours.'

A couple of hours later Kate rang Paige on her mobile.

'Granny says you're looking for Angus's number,' she said, a slight edge to her voice.

'Are you OK, Kate? You sound a little strange,' Paige asked.

'It's nothing.' Kate had had a flaming arguement with Lily less than an hour ago and it was still affecting her. She couldn't believe that her granny wanted to ring Angus. She knew it was in a good, no an excellent cause, and she knew in her heart that her granny was right – Angus could be just what the doctor ordered for Callum – but Lily had no right to involve Angus in their lives. He'd actually had the nerve to visit Lily off his own bat the previous day – bringing her grapes and two bottles of sparkling water. It wasn't on. He was a paying client – nothing more and nothing less and she was damned if she was going to start treating him as a real person. 'Here's the number. Granny's already had a chat with him and apparently he is available in theory. But he said to give him a ring.'

'Brilliant! Kate, Lily is an amazing woman. If you see her this evening tell her how much I appreciate this.'

'I will.' Kate put down the phone, her blood boiling. Yes, Granny was amazing – amazingly interfering. And she'd had almost enough. She had a good mind not to visit her this evening out of spite. Her mobile phone beeped. It was a text message from her. She should never have bought Lily a phone in the first place – it was a bad idea. But after her fall, she'd been worried, and had presented her with a brand new mobile the day after her ankle operation and making her promise faithfully that she'd carry it whenever she left the house. Now she was using it to harass her – typical.

Can u bring in your posh moisturizer this eve? Skin drying out – bloody hospital. Granny.

That evening while lying in bed, Paige filled Tom in on all the events of the day. Callum and Alfie were both asleep, much to their parents' relief. She had tried to ring Tom earlier but he'd been in meetings all afternoon and evening. She'd decided to save the momentous news – the news about the baby – till last. She had no idea how he was going to take it and she was afraid that he'd be annoyed and upset. After all, it did have huge consequences for both of them, and the way things were at the moment, they were just about hanging on to their sanity by the thinnest of threads.

'So you talked to this Angus guy and he's agreed to come and meet Callum?' Tom asked with interest.

'Yes. He said it was up to Callum. They would spend some time together and if Callum liked him he'd do it.'

Tom smiled and shook his head. 'The man has no idea what he's letting himself in for, does he?'

Paige glared at him. She didn't appreciate Tom's flippancy. 'Callum's not that bad. I'm sure he'll be on his best behaviour when Angus meets him.'

Tom said nothing. In his opinion, Callum was likely to play up when confronted with Angus – he'd be Denis the Menace and Just William all rolled into one just out of mischief.

'And he'll bring over his references. He was working in the local national school in Killiney last term and has several character references – including one from the priest in Sandybay.'

'Sounds good,' said Tom. 'You'll check them all out, of course.'

'We'll check them all out, you mean,' Paige said, her voice dangerously low. Tom had a habit of leaving things for her to do and she wasn't in the mood for his passing the buck, not today. 'You can't be too careful. And he is a man after all.'

'If I'd said that you would have accused me of being sexist,' Tom pointed out.

'You're right, I probably would.'

'Did he sound nice on the phone?'

'Very.'

'Well, I'm happy if you're happy. And it certainly solves the babysitting problem for August. Mum's already agreed to take Alfie, bless her. And Paige, I heard on the news on the way home that they announced the date for the general elections. I would have rung you but . . .'

'I know, I know. You don't like using the phone in the car. As I keep telling you, you have a handset, Tom, it's legal you know. Anyway I heard about the elections earlier.'

'And as I keep telling *you*, I still prefer to concentrate 100 per cent on my driving. There are an awful lot of nutters on the roads these days and talking on the phone while driving is a distraction no matter how legal it is.'

Paige sighed. When Tom got an idea into his head there was no budging him on it. Besides, he was probably right. 'We'll have to start getting organized,' she said. 'I've already ordered the printing of the posters and flyers. And I'll have to start the doorstepping next week if I want to get around the whole neighbourhood by early September.'

Tom nodded. 'You're probably right. At least we've drawn up the provisional plan of action so we're fairly on top of things. And the Arts Centre issue has been a bonus. You managed to keep everyone happy and come out of it smelling of roses in the process, clever woman.'

'And I have a few more tricks up my sleeve which should keep the media interested,' she added.

'Really, and they would be?' Tom asked. This was news to him.

'I'll tell you tomorrow. I don't have any energy left right now.'

'No energy at all?' He smiled wickedly at her, his blue eyes flashing.

'Well, maybe a little,' she admitted. She flicked off the reading light on her bedside table and turned towards him. She had hoped to tell him about the baby but that could wait until tomorrow.

He kissed her firmly on the mouth and she responded instantly. No matter how often she kissed Tom she never tired of it. She was lucky she'd found him – a best friend and a lover all rolled into one. And what a lover. He was kind and considerate, yet powerful and strong when she wanted him to be. This evening she wanted to feel loved and cherished and he sensed this – taking things slowly and languorously, his hands moving expertly over her smooth skin with lingering, caressing touches.

Suddenly they heard something.

'What was that?' Tom asked.

'I don't know, it sounded like a thump.'

Tom sighed. 'I'd better go and see.' He pulled on a pair of boxer shorts and went into the hall.

'It was only Callum,' he told Paige as he got back into bed a few minutes later.

'Did he fall out of bed?'

'No, he'd pulled his mattress onto the floor so that he could play magic carpets.'

'What?'

'Don't ask. I remade his bed on the floor and told him he could stay there as long as he went straight to sleep.'

Paige smiled despite herself. 'Let's hope he stays there. Now where were we?'

'Right about here, Councillor,' Tom said, kissing her again.

The following day Molly rang Paige just before nine. 'Have you seen the local newspaper yet?' she asked.

'No, why?'

'I think you'd better take a look. Ring me back as soon as you've bought a copy. And try not to worry, it's only a newspaper. I have to run, the shop's about to open. Bye.'

'Molly, what are you talking about?' But her friend had cut her off.

Paige was intrigued. She made two pressing phone calls – one about rubbish collection or lack of it on one of Burnaby's cobbled pedestrian side streets, and the second about a gas leak on Collins Avenue – and then she walked down to the newsagents to buy a copy of the *Burnaby News*. She could have sworn that the young girl behind the till smirked at her as she bought her copy but Paige decided she was just being paranoid. She flicked through the pages as she walked home. The banner headline read 'Proposed Burnaby Rubbish Dump – Local Councillor Says No'. Was this what Molly was talking about? She stopped on the path and read on. No, this article was all about Paddy Burns, the local People's Party councillor and election candidate. Paddy was a decent man and Paige had a lot of time for him. He was a little 'old school' for her taste but he wasn't easily swayed and was a good ally to have. She was standing as an independent candidate and as soon as Paddy had heard the news he had rung to wish her good luck. 'We could do with some fresh blood in the constituency,' he'd said. 'But is there any chance you might stand for the People's Party, Paige, do you think? Any chance at all? A woman like you would live long and prosper in the party, mark my words.' She'd been flattered but unmoved.

Paige turned the page. Immediately the offending photograph struck her straight between the eyes. She felt like she'd been slapped in the face – her cheeks began to burn and she turned around her to see if anyone was staring at her, feeling distinctly paranoid. This was what Molly had been talking about. She closed the newspaper quickly and had to stop herself from running home. Once back in the house, she closed the hall door behind her, hurried into the kitchen, opened the newspaper on the table and stared at page three. How could this have happened and where on earth did they get that photograph? She felt sick to the stomach. She sat down and forced herself to read the tabloid-like headline. *Councillor and Election Candidate in Flashing Shocker.*

Local County Councillor and independent election candidate, Paige Brady, has quite a checkered past as this recent photograph clearly shows. Is this the type of person we want representing Burnaby at national level? Councillor Brady was unavailable for comment when we contacted her last night, but Councillor Annette Higgins, another independent election candidate, had this to say – 'I think it's a disgrace, Ms Brady exposing herself like that. I have no idea where the picture was taken but I just pray there were no children present.' Ms Brady who lives in Burnaby has two young children and Ms Higgins feels that she should not be putting herself forward as a candidate in the September election in light of this exposé.

Paige stared at the photograph. It was her all right. Football shirt pulled up, showing a rather nice lacy white bra. She remembered the occasion only too well – the UCD team, under her captaincy had just won the all-Ireland university title and had been chosen to represent their country in France the following month. The whole team was over the moon and had pulled their shirts over their heads in true football fashion to celebrate. Unfortunately the shot had been taken as her shirt was on its way to her head and not covering her face. But why had they printed only her mug shot – where was the rest of the team? And why had they given so much space to Annette Higgins' rants? And most importantly – where had they got the photograph?

Paige sat down at the table and took a deep breath. This is only the beginning, she thought. I've put myself on the line by becoming an election candidate. I have two choices – I can fall at the first hurdle or I can fight back. Her mobile phone rang and she pulled it out of her pocket. It was Tom.

'Oh, Paige. It's all my fault, they rang last night. You were working on the computer and I never gave you the message, I'm so sorry,' he said all in one rush.

'The newspaper you mean?'

'Yes, they rang and I forgot to give you the message.'

'It's most certainly not your fault, Tom,' she said firmly. 'Who rang exactly?'

'The editor – Millie thingy.'

'Millie O'Shea?'

'Yes.'

Paige knew Millie from way back. She was a decent enough sort but very ambitious. Paige knew she'd do anything to sell papers but she hadn't expected this. She made a quick decision. 'I'm going to ring her. Tell her the real story behind the photograph. Insist that she print the whole photograph and not just the cropped version. That will put everything in context. I have a strong feeling that Annette is behind this whole thing, Tom, mark my words.'

'You're an amazing woman,' Tom said in admiration. 'And if Annette is behind this she'd better watch her back. No one messes with my wife and gets away with it.'

'Thanks, Tom. Now I'd better get moving 'cause I want them to run a front page retraction tomorrow.'

'Are you sure you're all right, Paige? Is there anything I can do?'

'No. I'm fine, honestly. For a brief moment there I was a bit upset to tell the truth, but I've decided not to let this get to me. I'm stronger than that. And this is only the start of it, Tom. I intend to win a place in the elections – I deserve it – I've worked bloody hard for this constituency and no one is going to deny me the chance.'

'Good woman, I'm proud of you. And Paige?'

'Yes?'

'I love you.'

'Love you too.' She clicked the phone off with a smile on her lips, walked into the sitting room which she also used as a study, bringing the copy of the *Burnaby News* with her. She dialled calmly.

'Hello, is that the *Burnaby News*? I'd like to speak to Millie O'Shea please. Tell her it's Councillor Brady and that it's urgent. She's in a meeting? Well you can tell Ms O'Shea that it's in her best interest to talk to me right now, or she can deal with my lawyers instead. Because I'm sure she doesn't want a libel case on her hands now, does she?'

Chapter 7

Molly

Molly smiled widely as she read the lead story in the following day's *Burnaby News* – 'Councillor Brady All-Ireland Soccer Hero', which was accompanied by the large and extremely striking photograph of the UCD Ladies' Soccer team, each team member with her shirt lifted over her face in celebration of their all-Ireland victory. She read on:

Councillor Brady is proud of her impressive sporting achievements, including three all-Ireland medals and one European silver medal. At only twenty-two she was awarded the most prestigious college sporting award in existence – the Golden Griffin – for her dedication and tireless promotion of the sport. Councillor Brady, an independent candidate in the forthcoming election, says she will wholeheartedly support all the local GAA and soccer clubs if elected, and might even be cajoled into coaching the ladies' youth team. We think that Councillor Brady is just the sort of politician needed to represent Burnaby on a national level, and we apologize unreservedly for any embarrassment caused by yesterday's unfortunate photograph, which had been cropped in error, and the corresponding article. Ms Brady has graciously accepted our apology.

Molly immediately rang Paige. 'Paige, that's a brilliant article –

how on earth did you get them to print it? You're a miracle worker.'

'I threatened them with a libel suit, no more and no less. Millie O'Shea is no fool – the paper isn't exactly rolling in it and a libel suit is the last thing she needs on her CV.'

'You'll make some politician,' Molly said with respect. 'There'll be no messing with you.'

Paige laughed. 'That's what Tom said. Let's hope I get in. So, are you free for lunch? I feel like celebrating.'

'I surely am. Coffee Heaven at one, or would you like to go somewhere more swanky, you sports hero, you?'

'Coffee Heaven is perfect. See you later.'

As Molly put down the phone and folded up the paper which was lying on her desk, she murmured jauntily 'Hi ho, hi ho, it's back to work we go'. As she walked out of the office and onto the shop floor she found Sam on his hands and knees in the small children's section at the back of the shop, sorting through picture books. He looked up at her.

'What are you smiling about?' he asked. 'Must have been a good joke.'

She told him all about Paige's article.

'Phew.' He whistled. 'She sounds like a tough cookie, your friend. But she's dead right – the press shouldn't get away with printing things like that. Good on her.'

'And what are you up to?' Molly asked. 'Are they not a bit young for you?' She nodded at the picture books fanned out on the floor.

'I'm alphabetizing them,' he explained. 'I wouldn't have started if I'd realized what a big job it was.'

'No kidding. Now you see why it doesn't get done as often as it should.'

He smiled. 'At least I now know what we have in stock. So it hasn't been a complete waste of time.'

'I wouldn't tidy them too well or you'll be stuck doing it till kingdom come. Unless you like children's books, of course.'

'I like all books. To paraphrase the late, great Dr Seuss – "a book's a book, no matter how small."'

Molly laughed. 'Not bad, Mr Devine, not bad. And how are you settling in? I'm sorry I didn't have much time to spend with you over the weekend, but it was pretty hectic.'

'Hectic but fun,' Sam said. 'And I liked Rosemary, she was a real lady. Are there any more events lined up?'

'Loads,' Molly said. 'So keep your diary free.'

'Are they always at weekends?'

'Not always, why?'

'Weekends can be difficult for me, that's all.'

Molly looked at him. Was he being funny? Weekends didn't exactly suit *her* either but she just got on with it, along with the rest of the staff. She hoped he didn't expect special treatment just because he was the owner's son. Just when she'd started to like him too – typical.

'Sorry,' he said after a moment. 'That came out wrong. I know working weekends is part of the job. It's just . . .' The bell rang on the front door.

'Excuse me,' Molly said to Sam as she broke away and strode towards the front of the shop.

'There you are!' It was Anita – looking in buoyant form – a huge grin plastered on her face. 'How's my favourite bookseller?'

'Not too bad. And to what do I owe this honour? It's not often I see you so early on a Monday morning. Especially as Monday is now officially one of your many days off, you lady of leisure, you.'

'I have news, my dear, good news. Paige tells me you're meeting her for lunch. I'll be joining you and we're going to talk about . . .' she leant towards Molly and whispered conspiratorially in her ear 'our plan.'

'What plan?' Molly asked in her normal voice. She refused to whisper. Anita was being very Nancy Drew-ish and she wasn't having it.

'Shush!' Anita hissed.

'Anita, what are you talking about? There's not a soul in the shop.'

'What about Sam?' Anita whispered.

Molly stared at her. This time she did lower her voice. '*What* about Sam? What are you talking about?'

Anita put her finger to her lips. 'Don't tell him a word.'

'I can hardly tell him anything as you haven't exactly told *me* anything now, have you?'

Anita winked at her. 'See you at one in Coffee Heaven.' She walked towards the door.

'Oh, no, you're not leaving,' Molly protested. 'That's so unfair. Tell me what's going on. I want to know.'

'See you later,' Anita said breezily, completely ignoring her.

'Anita!' It was no use, Anita was strolling down the road, swinging her shopping basket at her side.

'Who was that?' Sam asked.

'Anita. She just called in to say hi.'

'Nice woman.' Sam smiled broadly but said nothing else.

'What?' Molly asked.

'Nothing.'

'Why are you smirking?'

'Am I smirking? I don't mean to. Ignore me, it's nothing.'

'Sam! Go on. It's something about Anita, isn't it? You'd better tell me or I'll jump to all sorts of conclusions.' She studied his face carefully. He looked a little flushed. 'You don't . . . no!'

'What?' he asked. 'I don't what?'

'You know – like her.'

'Me!' he spluttered. 'Of course not. Not me. No offence, but she's at least twenty years older than me.'

'So? Some men like older women. She's very attractive.'

112

'I agree – she's just not my type.'

'Really? And what is your type exactly?'

'How did I get myself into this?' He laughed. 'You're a pretty straight shooter, aren't you, Molly?'

'Straight shooter?'

'You ask very direct questions.'

'Does it bother you?'

'No, not really.'

'So are you going to answer my question?'

'No, not today. Maybe some other time.'

'Fair enough. But at least tell me about your father's crush on Anita.'

'Molly! I never said that.'

'Do you deny it? It's true, isn't it? If it's not you, it must be him. It's hardly Felix, he's very happily married.'

He smiled. 'I'm saying nothing. My lips are sealed.'

'I'm going to be keeping a good eye on your dad, just in case,' she said. 'Smooth operator that he is.'

'Promise you won't say a thing to Anita,' he pleaded. 'Dad would kill me.'

'I promise. But you owe me one.'

'I do not.'

'You so do.'

'OK, I'm not going to argue about this. Now shouldn't we do some work?'

'*You* should,' she said. 'The Panda rep is due in at any minute and we'll be in the office for about an hour ordering the new titles.'

'Can I sit in?'

She shook her head. 'Sorry, someone has to keep an eye on the shop and Felix won't be in until twelve.'

'Fine.' He seemed a little put out.

'Tell you what,' Molly said. 'You can sit in on the session with Dunwoody Press this afternoon? How about that?'

'Thanks. Is there anything you'd like me to do in the mean-time?'

'Tidy the tables and put out the stock titles. They're on the trolley in the Romance room.'

'Will do.'

'I have a few things to do in the office, so can you send the Panda rep in when she arrives?'

'Sure. How will I know her?'

'She's tall with blonde hair. She's called Mona.'

Molly sat down at her desk and stared straight ahead of her. Sam was definitely growing on her. Now if he hadn't been late this morning and given such a feeble excuse she might even . . . no, that was stupid. He was Milo's son for goodness sake. Just because Sam didn't wear cashmere polo necks it didn't mean that he wasn't another charmer. Like father like son. Still, he was nice and she missed having a man around. She liked her independence and enjoyed her evenings in with Kate or Paige, but it wasn't quite the same. She missed having someone to snuggle up to on the sofa, someone to bring her chips and bottles of wine, someone to watch videos with, someone . . . Stop it! She told herself. You're a disgrace to modern women. You are perfectly fine on your own and much better off without a man to complicate things. She turned her attention to the computer screen and checked her e-mails. One new message in her in-box jumped straight out at her. It was from Denis and the subject was 'Missing You'. She knew she should delete it immediately without reading it but curiosity got the better of her. As she opened the message she heard a gentle knock on the door.

'Come on in, Mona.' She smiled up at the rep as she entered. 'You're bang on time as usual.'

'Creature of habit,' Mona replied.

'Sit down,' Molly said. 'Make yourself comfortable.'

'In this place?' Mona laughed. 'Never!'

Molly liked Mona very much. She was a no-nonsense kind of

woman with a razor-sharp mind and she was damn good at her job. Meetings with her were always a pleasure. Molly dragged her attention away from her e-mail and concentrated on the job at hand.

'Who's the new assistant?' Mona asked with interest. 'Not bad.'

'That's Sam Devine. The new owner's son no less. You've heard the news I presume?'

Mona nodded. 'Patricia told me. I hope they don't change the shop – it's perfect as it is.'

'Thanks.' Molly smiled gratefully. 'You say all the right things.'

'That's my job, honey buns. What's he like – the new guy?'

'Sam? I haven't quite decided yet. I'll tell you when I have.'

'He's a good-looking man. I wouldn't mind working with him myself, let me tell you.'

'You're welcome to visit any time.'

'Better get back to business,' Mona sighed. 'I have some crackers for Christmas too. Wait till you see.'

'That's terrible!' Molly groaned.

'What?'

'Crackers for Christmas, Mona, I expect more from you.'

'I'll try harder next time,' Mona grinned. 'Now, let's talk food – de-da!' She pulled a large hardback out of her large black-leather rep's bag. 'The new, all singing, all dancing *Panda Sinful Chocolate Cook Book*.'

As Molly walked towards the till a little later, passing several customers who were happily browsing, Sam was standing beside one of the front tables. 'What do you think?' he asked as she approached.

She looked at the table. He'd changed the books around so that they faced the front of the shop, not all four sides as they usually did. He'd created a raised area in the center of the table with one of the most popular hardbacks of the week. 'It look great. Thank you.'

'I quite enjoyed it. It's a bit like building, isn't it?'

'I suppose it is.'

'Mona seemed nice. She introduced herself.'

'Oh, really?' Molly said. 'Your sort of woman, is she?'

He sighed deeply. 'Molly! Stop. I was just saying she was nice that's all. I'm not in the market for a girlfriend at the moment thank you very much. And I'll keep my observations to myself in future.' He looked at her with a serious expression on his face

Molly felt that she'd overstepped the line and was mortified She hadn't meant to embarrass him. 'Look, I'm sorry, I promise I won't ask you any more personal questions, all right?'

'No, I'm sorry, I didn't mean that to come out the way it did. He stopped for a second as if deciding what to say next. 'I had a bad experience with someone last year to tell the truth and haven't quite got over it. That's all. So, go easy on me.'

'I'm sorry,' she said, contrite. 'I really am. I don't know wha to say.'

'It's no big deal. Let's talk about something else. Where do you live, Molly? Is it near here?'

She smiled at him gratefully. She told him about the town house she rented in Burnaby Grove and about Kate, making sure she kept the whole conversation on level ground. They were interrupted once or twice by customers asking questions or paying for books but it didn't seem to interrupt the flow.

'And where do you live?' she asked him after she'd wrapped a book in gift paper for a customer.

'In Sandybay, near the beach. I own a little cottage – it used to be a railway worker's cottage – it's small but fine for one. I've spent the last few years doing it up, it was in a complete state when I bought it. It's handy for Burnaby too – I can walk or get the train if I'm feeling lazy.'

'You're so lucky,' Molly said enviously. 'I love Sandybay beach. I often walk along it in the evenings.'

'So do I. Maybe we'll bump into each other one of these days.'

'Maybe.' Another customer walked in. Molly smiled at them and then looked at her watch. 'Listen, I have to fly. Felix said he'll come out onto the floor to give you a hand. I'm off for lunch with Anita and my friend, Paige. I'll be back in an hour.'

'See you later.'

Molly stopped outside Coffee Heaven for a moment. She turned around quickly. She could have sworn someone was staring at her, she could feel it, but that was stupid – there was no one there. She looked across the road. There were a few people on the far pavement – a young woman pushing a buggy and a well-dressed older man talking to Connie from Halo – none of whom were paying her the least bit of attention. She pushed open the door to the coffee shop, breathed in the familiar warm, coffee smell and felt better instantly. Paige and Anita waved at her from their favourite table at the back of the shop. She smiled and made her way over. I was just being stupid, she told herself. But the sensation of being watched had unnerved her and it took a few minutes to shake it off. But as she listened to the two women's plan unfold she forgot all about it. Their startling idea for the bookshop was quite something – but could they pull it off?

After their heady and productive lunch Paige walked Molly back to the bookshop.

'Come in and meet Sam,' Molly insisted.

'Can't – I have to run. I've a meeting with . . . hang on, this is Sam Devine, the owner's son? Anita says he's very attractive. Maybe I'll just stick my head in for a minute. Just to be polite. Why didn't you tell me he was good looking?'

'It wasn't relevant,' Molly sniffed.

'Since when are good-looking men in Burnaby not relevant?'

Paige laughed. 'Get a grip. It's not as if the place is exactly crawl
ing with them.'

'You're a married woman,' Molly reminded her.

'Doesn't mean I can't admire a nice bod when I see it.'

'Paige!'

Paige ignored her and waltzed in the door. She went straigh
to the front desk. 'You must be Sam.' She smiled warmly and
held out her hand. 'I'm Paige, a good friend of Molly's. Nice to
meet you.'

'Hi, Paige.' Sam smiled back. 'You're the "Sport Billy". Molly
was telling me about the article this morning. Good on you –
like your style. Newspapers get away with too much these days
It's good to see someone fighting back.'

'Thanks. Listen, I have to run. But welcome to Burnaby. Are
you a local?'

'If you mean can I vote, then the answer is yes. And you have
my vote, Councillor Brady.'

'Fell straight into that one, didn't I?' Paige grinned. 'You'll
have to excuse me, it's election time after all.'

'Best of luck with it. Hope you get elected.'

'Thanks.'

Molly had been listening to the whole exchange with interest.
She walked Paige out. 'You're shameless,' she hissed at her outside the door.

'And he's lovely,' Paige whispered back. 'If I were you . . .'

'I don't want to hear it.' Molly glared at her. 'Talk to you later,
Councillor.'

'Later, lover.' Paige winked at her.

'I wouldn't be winking at me like that. Annette Higgins might
have you outed as a lesbian.'

'Wouldn't put it past her. I wonder what she'll come up with
next.'

'Next?'

'Who do you think sent the *News* the photo?'

'No!' Molly exclaimed. 'Really? How did you find out?'

Paige tapped her nose. 'I have my sources.' She glanced at her watch. 'Now I really do have to go. Later, Babe.'

As Molly turned towards the door she felt a hand on her shoulder and jumped.

'Sorry,' a familiar voice said, 'I didn't mean to frighten you.'

'Denis,' she said, staring at him in astonishment. 'I thought we'd agreed . . .'

'I had to see you, Molly. It was a matter of life and death.'

'Hardly. And I'm working, Denis. This is not a good time.'

He looked at her carefully. 'Tonight then. It's important, please.'

'No, Denis. Not tonight and not any night, understand? We have to get on with our lives. We can't go backwards.' She sighed. 'We've been through all this. And anyway, I thought you'd met someone.'

He looked sheepish. 'Yes, well that's over now.'

Molly stared at him in amazement. 'That was quick.' She narrowed her eyes. 'Hang on, Denis, there never was anyone, was there? You were just trying to make me jealous.'

'There was!' he protested. 'It just didn't work out.'

Molly knew better than to argue with him. 'I have to go,' she said firmly, walking away as she spoke.

'I'll drop in tomorrow.' He turned on his heels and scooted away quickly before she had a chance to say anything.

'Denis,' she called after him. 'Don't come into my work again, please.'

But to no avail. He'd rounded the corner and was now out of sight.

'Shit!' she muttered. Her hands were shaking. She leant against the shop front and took a deep breath. A few minutes later, when her heart had stopped thumping quite so hard in her chest, she went inside.

'Everything all right?' Sam asked. He'd seen her talking to a man outside and the exchange didn't seem too friendly. He didn't like to mention it, as he shouldn't have been spying on her.

'Fine,' she lied. 'Just fine and dandy.'

Later Molly opened yet another e-mail from Denis. *Darling Molly, why don't you stop this madness? You know we belong together. Don't fight it. I won't give you up. I love you with all my being. Denis.* She shivered. It was all going to start again, she could feel it. But this time would be different – this time she'd have the strength to say no. She'd made a promise to herself, not to mention to Paige. There was no way in high heaven she was going to get back with him. No way! It was time for her to move on – finally.

'Callum, please stop kicking my seat,' Molly said crossly. She glanced at Paige. 'Sorry,' she mouthed at her. She didn't want to get him in trouble but it was getting annoying and she had asked him several times.

Paige swiftly pulled into a parking spot. 'Callum, you'd better behave in the puppet show, I'm warning you,' Paige turned around and told him. 'Do you understand?'

'Yes, Mummy,' he said with an angelic smile and nodded his head vigorously.

'I'll get you a treat afterwards if you're good,' Molly said. Paige had been through a busy time in the last week, what with the unsavoury exposé in the *Burnaby News* and the corresponding aftermath and Molly was determined to make this afternoon as easy for her as she could. Paige had had to be convinced to come out in the first place – she was exhausted but felt guilty that she hadn't spent any time with Callum this week.

'Can I have Skittles?' he asked hopefully. His mummy never let him have Skittles and they were his favourite sweets.

'No,' Paige said firmly. 'They're full of E numbers, they

always send you up the walls. You can have some popcorn or crisps.'

'Pringles are crisps,' he said firmly. 'Aren't they, Molly?'

Molly said nothing. Most of the time it was best not to interfere when it came to Paige and Callum.

'We'll see how good you are,' said Paige.

A few minutes later they were entering the large red wooden gate of the Hayward Puppet Theatre in Blackrock.

'I haven't been here since I was a child,' Molly reminisced. 'It's changed quite a bit but I remember it clearly. Dad used to take me every Christmas until I was seven. Then he said I was too old for puppets and he stopped. I remember being really upset and Mum having to comfort me. He didn't replace the trip with anything, you see, and I didn't understand. I thought I'd done something wrong and that he was punishing me.'

'That's a shame,' Paige said. 'He can be quite . . . how will I put this – black and white, your dad.'

'Tell me about it.' Molly frowned. She didn't much like talking about her dad. Fergal Harper was a strong, overpowering man who had been deeply disappointed that his only daughter hadn't followed him into the family printing business. Even though she was twenty-eight, he still made Molly feel like a child when he talked at her. She got on well with her mother, Laura, but had never really forgiven her for not standing up to him more and for never taking her side when she was growing up. Molly, rightly or wrongly, blamed her lack of self-confidence and her feeling of inadequacy on her childhood.

'Have you seen your folks recently?' Paige asked as she paid for three tickets.

'Not really. I spoke to Mum last week, she seems fine. I sent her out the list of books we've read in the Book Club. She's just started one up with some of her Mothers' Union friends.'

'I didn't think she was a great reader,' Paige said, watching

Callum, who was walking in front of them, like a hawk as they made their way towards the puppet theatre.

'She used to read a lot apparently, before she had me. Then she kind of got out of the habit.'

'Callum!' Paige said loudly. 'Sorry, Molly. I'll be back in one second.' Callum had run on ahead, bumping into a tall man and his son and sending the young boy flying sideways. He came to a halt at the theatre door and leant against the wall to wait for his mother, oblivious to the trouble he'd caused.

'I'm so sorry about my son,' Paige said to the man. He turned towards her. 'Oh, it's you,' she said in surprise.

'Sorry?' he asked.

'We met briefly last week in the bookshop. I'm Paige, Molly's friend. Molly's just . . .'

'Here,' Molly finished for her.

'Of course. Paige. I didn't recognize you out of your suit. So this is what you do on your days off, Councillor.' Sam smiled at Molly. 'And Molly, not what I would have expected from you at all – going to puppet shows.'

'I'm here with Paige and her son, Callum,' Molly explained. 'He's the one who knocked . . . um . . .'

The boy had been watching and listening to the adults with interest. He was small, with white-blonde hair and steel-rimmed round glasses, but from his face Paige reckoned he might be five or six.

'This is Hugh,' Sam said. 'My son. Say hello Hugh.'

Hugh said nothing, clutched his dad's hand and hid behind his legs.

'He's a little shy.'

'You didn't tell me you had a son,' said Molly. She was more than a little taken aback to tell the truth. She'd presumed from what Sam had been saying over the last week that he was single. She was confused. Hadn't he said he lived on his own? She'd obviously got the wrong end of the stick. Still, it did explain some of his late mornings she figured – he was probably dropping his son to school. It also explained why working weekends might be difficult for him.

'You didn't ask,' he said evenly in answer to her question.

Paige snuck a look at Molly. Molly seemed a little flushed and flustered.

'What age are you, Hugh?' Paige bent down and asked the boy.

Still no reply.

'He's nearly six,' Sam answered for him.

'Mum!' Callum shouted from the doorway. 'Hurry up.'

'Sorry, I'd better go and get him,' Paige said. 'But we might see you both afterwards.'

She and Molly walked towards Callum, excusing themselves to the people queuing in front of them.

'Mum!' Callum beamed as she reached him. 'Who's the little boy you were talking to? I've been waiting ages.'

'That's the little boy you knocked down when you dashed over here,' she said sternly. 'He's called Hugh.'

'Sorry,' he murmured, knowing from her tone of voice that he was in trouble again.

The woman taking the tickets smiled at Paige. 'Go on in,' she said. 'The lad's dying for the show to begin. Can't wait, he told me, didn't you, pet? He's been as good as gold waiting for you.'

Callum smiled up at his new friend.

'Thanks,' Paige said gratefully, handing the woman the tickets.

'Enjoy the show, young man,' the woman said to Callum.

As they sat down on the small wooden seats in the dim auditorium Paige leant over to Molly.

'You never told me he was married,' she whispered.

'I didn't know he was. He's not wearing a ring and I could have sworn he told me he lived alone. Still, it makes no odds to me.'

'Really?'

'Yes, really. And stop looking around. He'll think we're talking about him.'

'We are.'

Molly sniffed. 'Not any more we aren't.'

'Message received and understood.' Paige smiled at her knowingly.

'My Action Man says that when you pull the string in his back,' Callum said.

Paige grinned at Molly. 'Little pitchers,' she said.

'Have big ears,' Callum finished for her.

'Yes, thank you Callum,' said Paige. 'That's what your daddy always says too. Now you tell me when the curtain opens, will you?'

'Do you not have eyes, Mum?'

'Just watch the curtain, Callum, OK?' Paige said curtly, ignoring his rudeness.

'OK, Mum. But can I go . . .'

'No!'

'OK, OK.' He sat slumped with his arms folded in front of him and pulled his face into a huge scrunched-up frown. He started jiggling his feet up and down on the floor.

'What's wrong, Callum?' Paige asked with a sigh.

'I only wanted to ask could I go to the loo. I really need to pee. It's an emergency. If I don't go I'll wet —'

'Yes, thank you, Callum,' Paige interrupted. 'We get the picture.'

'I'll take him,' Molly offered quickly.

'Are you sure?' Paige asked. She could do with a few minutes' peace.

'Not at all. Come along, Callum.'

'Tell her I'm allowed in the boys' loo, will you, Mum?'

'Is he?' asked Molly.

Paige shook her head. 'Bring him into the Ladies with you, if you don't mind. He has a habit of talking to strangers and you wouldn't know . . .'

'I understand,' said Molly. 'You can't be too careful. Now, hurry up Callum or we'll be late for the show.'

On the way back, Molly saw Sam and Hugh sitting on the right-hand side of the auditorium. Hugh had his head on his dad's knee and Sam was talking to him or telling him a story, she couldn't make out which. He noticed her and waved over. She waved back and took her seat again.

'Was Callum OK?' Paige asked.

'Fine,' Molly replied biting her lip. He'd actually tried to soak her with water from the tap but her friend didn't need to know that.

After the show, they met Sam and Hugh again in the foyer.

'Did you all enjoy that?' Sam enquired.

'It was great,' Callum answered. 'I want to be the prince.' He stood with his two hands together in front of him. 'Look, I can cut down that forest for the princess lady, no trouble.'

'Sleeping Beauty,' Hugh said quietly. 'She was called Sleeping Beauty.'

'That's right,' said Paige. 'Did you like the show, Hugh?'

He nodded eagerly. 'I have a puppet theatre at home. Daddy made it for me. It's wood.'

Paige and Molly looked at Sam with interest.

'You made a puppet theatre?' asked Molly.

Sam shrugged his shoulders. 'I like woodwork. I'm good with my hands.'

'He made my bed too,' Hugh added proudly. 'And my desk and my shelves.'

'Yes, well, we'd better be going.' Sam put his arm around Hugh. 'Have to get you home, young man.'

'Do you need a lift?' Paige asked kindly.

'No, it's only around the corner, we'll walk. But thanks for the offer.'

'Not at all. See you around.'

'Yes, and see you tomorrow, Molly.'

'Yes,' she replied distractedly. 'Tomorrow.' She could have sworn he said he lived in Sandybay. How could they walk that far? It would take hours. It was all very strange.

'What's up?' Paige asked as they got onto the car. 'You seem a little out of it.'

'Nothing,' Molly said. She had no intention of telling Paige that she'd been thinking about Sam. 'Just work stuff, you know.'

'Don't let it get you down. As I told you, once our plan is in action there'll be absolutely nothing to worry about. Honestly.'

'Thanks,' Molly said gratefully. 'I'll stop worrying, I promise.' Easier said than done, she thought. 'And how are you?'

'Fine, well almost fine. We're a right pair, aren't we?'

Molly laughed. 'That we are.'

'At least I don't have to worry about Callum this month. Angus starts tomorrow.'

'Kate told me. I don't think she's too thrilled to tell the truth. She doesn't like to mix business with pleasure.'

'Is there something going on between them?' Paige asked. 'Is that what you mean?'

'No! Sorry, pleasure was probably the wrong word to use. Angus is one of her dummy dating clients and ... oops, you knew that, didn't you?'

'Not exactly. Lily said they were friends. She didn't say how they knew each other.'

'Trust me to put my foot in it. I'm sorry, I should have kept my mouth shut. Kate is very particular about client confidentiality. Don't say anything to Angus, please?'

'I won't,' Paige said. 'And if Kate and Lily like him that's all that matters to me. The fact that he can't get a date and resorted to using Kate's help has no bearing on my views of him. No, none at all.'

'Paige! Promise me you won't say anything.'

'I already have. It just seems kind of sad though. Sad and funny at the same time.'

'I guess it does,' Molly said thoughtfully. Although the way her own arid love life was looking, she could probably do with a helping hand herself.

Chapter 8

Kate

Kate stood on the doorstep and put the key in the lock. She heard a noise behind her – a slight rustle in the bushes and she swung around to have a look. Nothing. Must have been a cat or something, she reasoned. Then she heard it again. It sounded bigger than a cat, more like a person moving through the leaves.

'Hello?' she said nervously. 'Is anyone there?'

There was no reply. She turned the key quickly, let herself in and closed the door firmly behind her. Safely in the hall, she leant her back against the door, her breath catching in her throat and her heart thumping. Was there someone out there? She left the living-room light off, tiptoed towards the window and looked out. She gasped as she saw a shadowy figure crawl from under the rather scraggly hedge and walk towards the gate. Who the hell was that and what were they doing? The figure paused for a moment before walking out the gate and down the road. Kate watched him in astonishment. Because it certainly was a him and not a her. She noticed the lenses of his glasses flash under the street lamp as he sloped away.

'Molly?' she shouted upstairs. 'Molly, are you in? Quick!'

She heard a muffled noise from upstairs. 'Coming!' Molly

yelled. She appeared at the top of the stairs, resplendent in her dark pink towelling dressing gown, her hair caught up in a clashing light pink towel. 'I was washing my hair. Is everything OK?'

'Not really. There was a man hiding in the front garden. I opened the door and he went away. I saw him from the living-room window.'

'A man?' Molly asked with concern. 'Where exactly in the garden?'

'Behind the big straggly bush.'

Molly looked at her blankly.

'The one beside the gate.'

'Oh, that one.' She walked down the stairs and looked carefully at Kate. 'Nothing happened did it? He wasn't a flasher or anything?'

'No, I don't know what he was doing. Just watching the house, I think. He just gave me a fright, that's all.'

'And you're all right?'

'Fine. I think I should ring the guards though. He might be dangerous. He could be a burglar or something.'

'Maybe,' Molly said, a thought coming into her mind. 'What did he look like? Did you recognize him?'

Kate shook her head. 'No. He was quite tall and thin and wearing glasses, that's all I know.'

'I see,' Molly said slowly.

'What?' Kate demanded. 'Do you know who it was?'

'I might,' she replied slowly. 'I'll find out. Give me one second.' She walked quickly back up the stairs.

'Molly . . .' Kate shouted after her but it fell on deaf ears.

'I'll kill him,' Molly muttered as she picked up her mobile from her dressing table and punched in the familiar number. 'Denis, is that you? Where are you?'

'Um, nowhere,' he said a little nervously. 'Where are you?'

'You know damn well where I am. Just answer me this one

question – are you spying on me? Were you outside the house a few minutes ago?'

'Um, no.'

'What do you mean, no?' she asked, her voice rising to a dangerous level. 'I know you're lying. And before you say anything you may like to know that my housemate saw you and is able to identify you.'

'But I've never met her,' he protested. 'How could she . . .'

'Got you,' Molly screamed. 'Don't you ever, ever scare her like that again, do you hear me?'

'But I was just dropping in a letter,' he said meekly. 'Then I just thought I'd wait for a little while to see if you came out. I wanted to talk to you. You haven't been answering my phone calls and . . .'

'Too right I haven't, you nutcase. And if I ever catch you stalking me again I'll report you to the guards, do you understand?' She didn't wait for his answer.

She sat down on the bed and took a deep breath. Men! There was a knock on the door.

'Molly? Are you all right?' It was Kate.

'Come on in.'

'I heard the shouting and I was worried.'

Molly looked up at Kate. 'I should explain – that guy in the bushes earlier was my ex – Denis. I'm so sorry he frightened you. I wouldn't say he'll do it again in a hurry. I gave him a right earful.'

'At least it wasn't a burglar, I suppose. But he gave me a real fright. My heart is still thumping.'

'I'm so sorry.'

'It's OK, it's not your fault. And this was on the hall floor. It's addressed to you.' Kate handed her a red envelope.

Molly handed it straight back. 'It's from him. Bin it for me.'

'Are you sure?'

'Positive.'

It Had To Be You

Kate took it back, sat down on the bed beside her friend and cleared her throat. 'Is Denis, how will I put this, a little highly strung?'

'As in totally crazy?'

Kate nodded. 'Does he often do this kind of thing?'

'I'd have to say yes. But hopefully it's all over now.'

'Hopefully,' Kate murmured. She didn't want any more unnerving experiences – she got quite enough of those at work, thank you very much.

'I'm sorry about all this,' Molly said. 'I don't know what to say. He's a strange one.'

'And I never even had the pleasure of meeting him,' Kate said. 'Listen, don't worry about it. I'm going to bed now. I'm tired to the bone.'

'How was your date?'

'Brutal. He was a total male chauvinist and kept calling me babe.'

'That good?'

'Sad thing is he'll probably have no problem finding a date – some women love that kind of thing. Plus from all accounts he's rolling in it.'

'Always helps.' Molly smiled.

'No kidding. The more I learn about men the less I like them.'

'You don't mean that,' Molly said. 'You must have met some decent ones along the way. What about that Angus – Callum's nanny? Paige has been singing his praises.'

'I'm sure he'd be delighted to be referred to as a nanny,' Kate said. 'I must tell him that. He's OK, I suppose.'

'Only OK?' Molly looked at Kate, a smile lingering on her lips.

'What are you implying? Stop looking at me like that.'

'Like what?'

'You know.' Kate stood up abruptly. 'I'm going to bed.'

'Sweet dreams,' Molly said, still smiling.

'Yeah, Yeah,' Kate muttered. She walked into her room, th
red envelope still in her hand. She threw it into her waste pap
bin and stared at it. Men! What a waste of time and energy. Sh
walked over to the window and stared out. No one lurkin
under the street lamp or in their garden as far as she could tel
She closed the curtains and sat down on the bed. Angus! As
she'd be interested in someone like Angus – what a joke!

The following lunchtime Kate called into Coffee Heaven befor
work. She'd had a blissfully free morning with no client mee
ings and was making the most of it. She'd gone for a long wal
this morning up Killiney Hill, followed by a shower and som
yoga and she hadn't felt this good in a long time. Last night
date was long forgotten and she even had a whole evening t
herself – one of her clients had cancelled his date and she'd trie
not to sound too delighted when he'd rung with his apologies.

'You look happy,' Alex said as she placed a steaming bowl
carrot soup in front of her. She raised her eyebrows. 'Anyon
new on the scene?'

'Alex!' Kate scolded. 'I don't need a man to be in a goo
mood.'

'Sorry.'

'Don't worry about it. So how are things? Any news?'

'Well actually,' Alex leant down and lowered her voice, 'I di
want to talk to you about something, are you free in a few min
utes? I won't keep you long.'

'Sure.' Kate was a little taken aback. She didn't know Alex al
that well and wondered what on earth she wanted to ask he
about.

'I'll be back in a minute. I'll just get Matty out of the kitche
to cover for me.'

A few minutes later Alex sat down at Kate's table and smiled
nervously at her. 'How's the soup?' she asked.

'Good.' Kate smiled back. 'Is that what you wanted to ask me?'

'Um, no, not exactly.' Alex blushed and leant forward. 'I wanted to ask your advice on, um, dating, I suppose. There's this guy I like and I don't know what to do about it.'

Kate put down her soup spoon and looked at Alex carefully. 'I don't know if I'm the right person to ask. I normally help men, you see. I've never helped a woman before.'

'I'd pay you,' Alex said quickly. 'What's the going rate?'

'Don't be silly.'

'But you're a professional, Kate,' Alex said firmly. 'I insist.'

'How about a month's supply of free coffee? And the odd bowl of soup?'

'Done!' Alex grinned. 'So, will you help me?'

'I'll try. Tell me about this man. What's happened so far?'

'Well nothing's happened really. Nothing at all. In fact he never seems to notice me at all. He's very busy and . . . um, I'm sure I don't make much of an impression on him. He's only ever seen me in my apron.'

'He's a customer?'

Alex nodded. 'If I tell you will you promise to keep it a secret?'

'Of course, everything you say is completely confidential, you have my word.'

'Thanks.' Alex looked around to check there was no one listening and then whispered, 'It's Harry from the plant shop.'

'Harry Masterson?' Kate asked in amazement.

'Shush, lower your voice. Yes, that Harry. He's amazing and I'm totally mad about him. And Kate, he doesn't even know I exist.'

'But he will,' Kate said and patted her hand. 'He most certainly will.'

Ten minutes later, after arranging another meeting with Alex, Kate put the first germ of her plan into action. This was going to

be an interesting one. Because just the previous day she'd take
on a new client – none other than Harry himself. Alex and Harr
would be a rather unlikely couple – he lived his life at brea
neck pace and personally Kate found him rather spiky. Alex wa
far more laid back, a nice girl with a good heart, if a little nosy
but stranger things had happened.

Swinging open the door of Slick Harry's after lunch she wa
greeted by a shout.

'Watch the bloody cactus!' Harry came running over. 'Sorr
Kate. But I need it for the *Des and Shelly Show*. They are holdin
some sort of Western Special and I have to talk about cacti. Tha
cactus is the centrepiece. So what can I do for you?'

'Two things,' Kate said coming straight to the point, knowin
how busy Harry always was. 'Firstly, I'm looking for a new ga
dener for my gran, she's coming home from hospital next wee
but she has to rest her ankle for six weeks. I wanted someon
to look after the garden for her. Someone who wouldn't min
being watched and advised.'

'Might know the very woman,' Harry said. 'Cecily Ham
mond. She's from Bray – nice woman and very sensible.'

'A woman? That would be great. Do you have a number fo
her?'

'Certainly.' He strode towards the large stainless steel desk
flicked through his large Filofax and scribbled a mobile numbe
on the back of one of his cards.

'Thanks,' said Kate, pocketing it. 'I appreciate it. And th
other thing was that Alex in Coffee Heaven was looking fo
some new plants for the shop. I suggested she called in o
Thursday morning to have a look. Will you be here?'

He flicked through his Filofax again. 'Should be, yes, I thin
so. Is Alex the blonde girl?'

'Yes,' Kate said, hoping she didn't sound a little too eage
'Lovely girl, great cook too.'

'Thought it was her brother who did all the cooking?' asked Harry.

'In the shop, yes. But she trained at Dunmore House, with Rena Travis.' Rena was a well-known Irish celebrity chef who ran her own cookery school.

'Really?' he seemed to be losing interest so she didn't push it.

'And I'll see you on Thursday evening for our, um, meeting,' she said moving towards the door.

'Yes, indeed,' he said a little nervously. 'See you then.'

As soon as she'd left he stared after her. To tell the truth he was a little embarrassed about using Kate's services, but as he'd had nothing but disasters on the dating front recently he'd decided that it was time to take matters into his own hands and do something positive about it. All he seemed to meet were models, television presenters and would-be actresses. And what he was really looking for was someone like his mother – a kind, decent girl who could take care of him and slow his life down. It had got far too fast for his liking and at times he longed to retire to the country with a Range Rover and a couple of dogs. And a nice, pretty wife and two adorable children – a boy and a girl. Not that he'd ever admit this to anyone of course. In everyone's eyes he was Harry Masterson, plant genius, daytime-television darling, and man about town.

'Hello, Kate,' Cathy said looking up from the desk in Baroque. 'Mind if I go on my lunch straight away? Trina's at the doctor's and I'm starving.'

'No problem. Just give me a second to dump my bag in the back.'

'You look well today,' Cathy said to Kate she returned onto the floor. 'I like the suede skirt.'

'Thanks, it's Molly's. She claims it's too tight on her so she gave it to me.'

'Listen Kate, Trina is a little, um, upset. She says she keeps trying to apologize to you but that you won't . . .'

'I don't really want to talk about it,' Kate said firmly.

'I understand, but Trina is my friend. She may be an old boot some of the time but she's not that bad really underneath it all. She's been very good to me over the years.'

'But she hasn't been good to me, has she Cathy? In all honesty?'

Cathy looked at the ground. 'No, I suppose not,' she admitted. 'But people change. Give her a chance.'

'That's just it, I don't believe they do. Not really.'

'Just let her apologize properly, please? It would mean a lot to her. And it would make working here with the two of you a damn sight more bearable.'

'Has it been awful?' Kate asked, suddenly realizing that it had probably been no picnic for Cathy over the while with the two of then sniping at each other.

'Yes, to tell the truth, it has.'

Kate sighed. 'I'll see what I can do. I'm not promising anything, mind.'

Cathy smiled. 'Thanks, Kate.'

As soon as Trina opened the door of Baroque that afternoon Kate made a decision. What both Cathy and Angus had said had made her think. She stood just inside the door waiting in case she changed her mind. Trina looked pale and slightly frazzled. She looked at Kate expectantly.

'Yes?' Trina demanded. 'Are you going to have a go at me already? Can you not wait till I'm in the door?'

'I want to talk to you,' Kate said mildly, ignoring the barbed questions. She flicked the sign on the door from 'open' to 'closed' and pulled down the blinds.

'Oh? What about?' Trina asked, her interest piqued.

'Sit down,' Kate replied firmly.

Trina did as she was told for once, without comment.

'I accept your apology,' Kate began. 'I know all about the fertility treatment – Cathy told me. The injections sound horrible and I'm sorry you have to go through all that.'

Trina nodded, too stunned to say anything.

'I want to declare a truce,' Kate continued. 'I've had enough of the bickering, it's tiring and neither of us needs it right now. So can we agree to be civil to each other?'

Trina nodded. 'Yes, absolutely.'

'And no smart comments from either side?'

'Agreed. On one condition.'

'What's that?' Kate asked.

'That you think about designing a shoe collection for Baroque.'

Kate began to protest. 'But . . .'

Trina put her hands up. 'I just said think about it, OK? I have a contact in Italy who runs a shoe factory. They specialize in soft leathers. I know you were good, Kate, one of the best. I talked to my contacts in Boston and they remember you well. Let me know when you're interested.'

'Don't hold your breath.'

'And last thing,' Trina added.

'Yes?'

'I think there's definitely a market out there for Irish designer baby shoes – soft leather ones. "Baroque for Babies", what do you think?'

'I don't think it would work,' Kate said calmly. She opened the blinds and let the sun back into the shop. Designer shoes for babies, now that would be a fun project – if she were interested, of course, which she was most certainly not. She hadn't designed a shoe for a very long time. Not since Boston. Not since . . . she blocked it out of her mind. No point thinking about the past, she had to move on.

Later that afternoon Cathy was delighted to find the two

women working together at the desk at the back of the shop – putting the final touches to the sale banners and showcards.

'Looking good, ladies,' Cathy said surveying the assorted dark pink signs. They'd had them printed in the local printers – dark purple lettering on a rich pink background, all in 'Baroque'-style lettering of course – to which Kate and Trina were adding pink feathers and assorted sequins and plastic jewels. 'How many more are you going to do?'

'We're almost finished,' Kate said with a smile. 'Thank goodness. I've glue all over my fingers.'

A customer walked in the door. 'I'll get it,' Cathy said. 'Councillor Higgins, how are you? How can I help?' Cathy knew that Annette Higgins liked to be referred to by her proper title and she tried not to smirk as she said it. It had been plain old Annette up until a year ago, before she'd gone all high flying. And now that she was on the verge of being elected to the Dail, the Irish government (in her own mind at least), Annette was becoming unbearably pompous.

'I'm looking for something comfortable but smart for canvassing,' said Annette. 'With a low heel, I think.'

'I have just the shoe,' Cathy said. 'What colour – black, dark brown . . . ?'

'Navy,' Annette said firmly. 'All my suits are navy.'

'Fine,' Cathy said. 'And you're a size . . . ?'

'Six.'

'Right then. Give me a moment and I'll pull out the shoe I'm thinking of.'

'Rather her than me,' Trina murmured to Kate as Cathy walked past them into the small storeroom. 'I bet her feet smell.'

'Trina!' Kate giggled. 'I'm sure they don't.' She smiled to herself – maybe being nice to Trina wasn't going to be as difficult as she'd thought.

*

'Hi, Angus, thanks for coming.' Kate gestured at him to sit down.

'Two coffees please, Alex,' she shouted over.

'Coming right up,' Alex shouted straight back.

'My pleasure.' Angus sat down, nudging the table a little and spilling some milk from the small white jug. 'Oops, sorry. So, am I in trouble? What does my report say – "will never amount to much", "if Angus spent as much time at his work as he did clown-acting he might do better in class"?'

'Report?' Kate murmured in confusion. Then she remembered. Of course – that was why they'd arranged to meet for coffee last week – before Molly had found them and they'd rushed off to hospital. She'd forgotten all about it. 'Sorry, I left it at home. I'll send it to you in the post. Is that all right?'

'Fine,' he said. 'So, you decided you couldn't live without me, it that it?'

'Not exactly.' Kate stifled a laugh. 'I wanted to talk to you about Paige. I understand she's asked you to mind Callum.'

'Yes, I'm going over to meet him tomorrow. I hope he likes me.'

Kate smiled. 'I'm sure he will. But do you think it's such a good idea? I don't feel all that comfortable with it to tell the truth.'

'What do you mean? Thanks,' he mouthed to Alex as she put down their coffee. He added milk and four spoons of sugar to his cup.

Kate wrinkled her nose. 'How can you drink it so sweet?'

He took a slurp and smiled. 'Easy. But stop trying to change the subject. Why does it bother you? Because Paige is your friend? Because in some strange convoluted way you've got it into your head that it compromises your position? Because you're scared that if you see too much of me you actually might start liking me?'

'No!' she protested. 'Nothing like that. I'm just thinking of *you*.'

'Oh really?' He raised his eyebrows. 'How's that?'

'As I'm sure Paige has pointed out, Callum is a bit of a handful. I just think you should know what you're letting yourself in for, that's all.'

'That's not it, is it, Kate?' he said gently. 'I know you better than that, even though you won't believe me. I know you care about Paige and Callum, too. And from what Lily told me the little lad could do with some attention right at the moment. And maybe I can help. Would you begrudge him that just because you feel uneasy about having me around?'

'I don't feel uneasy . . .' she began.

'Face it, Kate, you're beginning to like me and it scares you.'

'Angus! That's not it at all. You're being ridiculous.'

'Am I? Think about it, Kate. I'll see you around.' He stood up, pushed the chair towards the table, spilling both cups of coffee in the process and strode away.

Kate watched him leave, dumbfounded.

'Is he coming back?' Alex asked a few minutes later as she wiped the table down.

'Um, no,' Kate said. 'I don't think so.'

'Right, I'll take away his coffee so. Anything wrong, Kate? You look a little perturbed.'

'Just thinking.'

'Any news on Harry?' Alex asked in a low voice.

'Yes, actually. I forgot to tell you. He's expecting you to call in on Thursday morning about some plants for Coffee Heaven. So be sure to slap on some lip-gloss. Maybe put your hair up. You could bring him some muffins or biscuits or something. And make sure to tell him you made them yourself.'

'That's a little extreme isn't it?' Alex said. 'Bringing him food. He doesn't even know me.'

'Ah, but he does,' Kate corrected her. 'He said some very

complimentary things about you and he was most impressed when I told him about your Dunmore House training.'

'Really?'

Kate could see this gave Alex confidence and made her more sure of herself. She nodded firmly. 'Play it cool. Ask his advice on new plants for the shop, but don't decide on anything. That way you can call back another day.'

'Great, thanks. I hope I don't go all red and get tongue-tied.'

'If you do, just take a deep breath and smile at him. You have a lovely smile. No man minds a little blushing. In fact, they think it's quite sweet.'

'Really?'

'Really. And it would do no harm to drop into the library and take out a few books on plants. Drop in a few Latin names to impress him. Show him you have a shared interest.'

'I quite like gardening to tell the truth, and that's a great idea.' She leant forward and kissed her on the cheek. 'Thanks, Kate. I appreciate it.'

On Thursday Kate had two unexpected visitors to Baroque.

'Harry,' she said, surprised to see him as he walked in the door. 'You know we only do ladies' shoes. Unless you're looking for something in a larger size.' She winked at him.

'No, I'm not here for shoes. Although I'd love to try some on for the giggle. But someone might see me. You know how small Burnaby is.'

'Don't I just.'

'Are Trina or Cathy here?'

'No, I'm on my own this afternoon.'

'Good.' He sat down on the red sofa. 'I think I'll cancel our meeting this evening, if that's OK with you.'

'Fine,' she said. 'I'll refund the money.'

'Why don't you just hang on to it, I might need you at a later date.'

'And, if you don't mind me asking, what has changed your mind?'

'Um, I kind of met someone.'

'Really?'

'The girl from the coffee shop, you know, Alex. She called in this morning and I haven't been able to get her out of my head.'

Kate beamed. Yes! she thought. Instant success. You're good, Kate Bowan, damn good.

'She called into the shop and she looked so different. Her hair was pinned up with curly bits hanging around her face and she has the loveliest smile, Kate. I was trying to rush her through choosing some plants but she offered me one of these amazing chocolate bun things that she'd cooked – they'd just come out of the oven and they were still warm. I started to eat it on my feet and she said it wasn't good for my digestion to eat that way and that I should sit down.'

Kate stifled a grin. Alex telling Harry what to do – now there was a first.

'She waited until I'd finished eating and then we talked about plants,' he continued. 'She's quite into gardening, you know. She's just signed up for an evening course in Sandybay Community College on indoor plants.'

'Really?' Kate asked, most impressed. Alex had done her homework impeccably.

'And she even knew the Latin name of one of my favourites – the *Citrus mituis*.'

'Sorry?' asked Kate.

'It's a small tree that grows baby oranges. I suggested it for the coffee shop. She was a real breath of fresh air to tell the truth. I wanted to ask your advice. Do you think she might like to go to the Burnaby Flower Festival with me? It's on over the next weekend. Do you think I should ask her?'

'Yes, I definitely think you should.' Kate put her hand on his. 'If she's interested in plants she'd really enjoy it and it would give you both a chance to get to know each other better. The Flower Festival sounds lovely.'

'Thanks, Kate. I'll ask her tomorrow.' He jumped up. 'Must dash. Radio tomorrow morning and I haven't got anything prepared. I'm supposed to be talking about bushy succulents and their medicinal properties. Don't ask. See you.'

'See you.' Kate smiled to herself. Her plan had worked like a treat. Maybe she should take on more female clients. Pity she couldn't fix her own love life while she was at it. She popped herself onto the stool behind the desk to lodge the last two sales in the stock book – one pair of pink strappy sandals and a pair of red size three boots left over from last spring that they thought they'd never get rid of. Cathy and Trina would be delighted. Another customer came in the door. Before she had a chance to raise her head she heard a familiar voice. 'Cat? Cat?' She recognized the soft American accent instantly and her heart began to pound in her chest. She leant towards the desk, her eyes fixed on the stock book. The numbers and letters swam before her eyes. Was this some sort of elaborate nightmare? Would she wake up any second now sweating and head thumping.

'Cat?' The voice drew nearer.

She forced herself to look up. There he was, standing in front of her, smiling – the man who had almost ruined her life. Still as damn attractive as ever.

'Jay?' she whispered. 'What the hell are you doing here?'

Chapter 9

Paige

Paige lay in bed wide awake. It was only six o'clock in the morning but she couldn't get back to sleep.

'Tom?' she whispered. 'Are you awake?'

No answer. She nudged him in the side. 'Tom. I need to talk to you.'

He grunted.

'Tom!' she said again, a little louder this time.

'What's wrong?' he asked groggily. 'Have we slept through the alarm?'

'No, it's still early. But I have to talk to you.'

'Can't it wait?'

'No.'

He sighed and rolled over to face her. 'What is it then?'

She looked at him in the half light and wondered how he was going to react to the news about the baby. It was nearly a week since she'd visited the doctor and had had her home test confirmed and she'd been putting it off ever since. But she couldn't keep it to herself any longer.

'I'm pregnant,' she blurted out.

'What?'

'Pregnant. We're having another baby.'

Silence again.

'Tom? Say something.'

'I can't. I'm in shock.'

She started to cry. Getting the news off her chest was a relief but she'd hoped he'd be pleased.

'What's wrong, love?' he asked putting his arms around her. 'Are you not pleased? It's great news. I know it's a bit quick after Alfie, but it'll be fine.'

'Do you really mean that?' she asked. 'You're not annoyed?'

'Annoyed? Why would I be annoyed? Of course not. I'm delighted. You know I want a big family. It's a bit of a surprise, that's all.'

'No kidding.' She sniffed. 'Think of how I feel. What with the elections and everything.'

'It doesn't change a thing,' Tom said evenly. 'How many months gone are you?'

'Three, I think. I'm not sure of the dates.'

'So you're over the worst of the tiredness and the sickness, aren't you?'

'Yes, Dr Spock. Since when are you the great expert?'

'I've been through it twice before, remember? You won't be all that big for a while yet. And there's no reason to mention it to anyone until after the elections.'

'Is that not lying by omission?'

'Not at all. Your health is your own business. If anyone asks you directly you can answer them honestly. If they don't ask don't proffer the information. It's as simple as that.'

'Spoken like a true campaign manager.'

'Absolutely. Speaking of which, in the circumstances, are you really up to doorstepping this week, love?'

'Yes,' she said firmly. 'I'm going to do everything I can to win this election, Tom. Everything. Including drawing the raffle at the Burnaby Flower Festival, opening the new library in

Sandybay National School, and holding an open questions and answers session on my policies in the new Burnaby Arts Centre in the spirit of openness and transparency, as suggested by my campaign manager.'

'Are you really sure?' Tom asked again.

'Yes, positive.'

'Then I'm behind you all the way.'

'Thanks,' she said gratefully. 'I love you, Tom. You're so good to me.'

Tom held her hand to his lips and kissed it. 'Anything for the mother of my soon to be three children. Now seeing as we're up so early, Councillor.' He moved his hands over her arms and she could hear the smile in his voice. 'And we don't have to worry about time, let's make the most of it.' He nipped her ear playfully with his teeth.

'How about a big cuddle?' Paige asked. 'I'm not really up to anything else this morning, to be honest.'

'A cuddle it is.' He smiled warmly. 'Come here you.' He put his arms around Paige and hugged her tightly.

She hugged him back and smiled to herself. Maybe Tom was right. If she could just get through the next few tense and super-humanly busy pre-election weeks, then everything would be fine.

Paige and Tom started their first day of doorstepping at nine o'clock that very morning. 'Come in, young lady, come in. I've just put the kettle on,' said Mrs O'Brien, an elderly Burnaby Grove resident as they stood in her hall at ten o'clock. They'd already covered the High Burnaby estate and were now moving down Burnaby Avenue towards the village. 'Would you like a cuppa?'

Paige looked at Tom who shrugged then nodded.

'That would be lovely, Mrs O'Brien,' he said. 'But we don't want to put you to any trouble.'

'Not at all. I insist.' She showed them into the sitting room, then toddled slowly out the door.

Tom smiled at Paige when Mrs O'Brien had left the room. 'This doorstepping is taking longer than I'd planned. I hadn't realized how much people like to talk.'

'I know. But it means a lot to some of them, especially the older ones.'

'Next week Molly and Kate have promised to help. And I've roped in your mum too. And Lily's going to ring as many of her friends as she can. She said if she wasn't incapacitated at the moment she'd be burning shoe leather with us.'

'Lily's such a sweetie. I must give her a ring.'

After a few minutes, Mrs O'Brien returned carrying a tray. 'Here we go,' she said.

Tom jumped up. 'Let me help you.'

'It's fine, young man. But thank you anyway.' She placed the tray carefully on a small coffee table in front of them and began to pour tea from the elegant light blue china pot with matching tea cups, sugar bowl and milk jug.

'What lovely china.' Paige smiled. 'Where did you get it?'

Mrs O'Brien beamed. 'How kind of you to ask. My late husband gave it to me for our fiftieth wedding anniversary. I use it whenever I have special guests over. He was a wonderful man you know, such a gentleman. Let me tell you about our wedding day. When I saw him standing at the altar waiting for me I thought I'd pass out. He looked so handsome . . .'

As they left the house forty minutes later Tom smiled at Paige. 'You only managed to tell her about one of your policies but she adored you. You've definitely got her vote.'

'Wasn't she sweet? Imagine, they were married fifty-seven years, isn't that just something?'

'It is, quite something.' Tom looked at the list on the wooden clipboard in his hands. 'Burnaby Manor next. Should be interesting.'

As soon as they walked in the door of the old people's hom‹ they heard loud piano music which sounded suspiciously li‹ 'Knees Up Mother Brown'.

'That's Lily Bowan playing.' The matron smiled warm‹ 'She's here every Monday morning running the weekly sin‹ song. The residents love it.'

'Isn't she supposed to be resting?' asked Paige. 'She's just o‹ of hospital.'

'You try telling Lily to rest,' the matron snorted.

Paige laughed. 'I know what you mean.'

'Paige!' Lily cried as she and Tom entered the large fro‹ room. 'How nice to see you. I hope you're all voting for Paig‹ ladies and Mr Fowler. She's an old friend of mine.'

'Give us a song and we'll vote for you,' a woman with pir‹ hair quipped.

'Yes, go on, give us a song,' another added. 'That Annette o‹ refused. Said she didn't know any. But you do, don't yo‹ Paige?'

Tom pushed her firmly towards the piano. 'She's a wonderf‹ singer,' he assured them.

'Tom!' Paige hissed.

'Do the one you do for the kids. The one about the moon.'

'"Moon River"?' she asked.

'That's the one.'

'I don't think . . .'

'I know that,' Lily surprised her. 'Audrey Hepburn i‹ *Breakfast at Tiffany's*, wasn't it? Let me see.' She played a fe‹ notes on the keys. 'Got it. On you go, girl.'

Paige began to sing the opening bars, wobbling a little at firs‹ She had a clear, low-pitched voice which suited the song pe‹ fectly. As she sang the residents began to sing along, some mor‹ than a little out of time but it didn't matter, they were obviousl‹ enjoying themselves. As she finished everyone gave her a rou‹ ing round of applause.

'Well done, Paige.' Lily smiled widely. 'That was great. And
now Tom.'

'Oh, no!' Tom protested.

'Go on,' Paige said. 'Do "Summertime".'

'I know that one too.' Lily started to play.

'Go on,' Paige cajoled. 'Do it for the votes, please,' she
whispered.

He smiled. 'Just for you.' He sang in his lazy, easy manner
and many of the residents joined in.

'He's great,' the matron whispered to Paige as he began the
second verse. 'Thanks for being such good sports, you've made
their day. I think they found Annette a little dry. She kept dron-
ing on about her policies and bored them all stupid.'

'I'll have to remember not to do that.'

'I don't think you could bore people if you tried. You have a
nice easy way with people. And Lily is always singing your
praises.'

Paige smiled. 'That's lovely to hear.'

'I hope you get in. Burnaby could do with someone like you.
Best of luck.'

'Thanks.'

Leaving the home an hour later after more tea and more
singing Paige felt like she was walking on air.

'That went really well, Paige,' Tom said. 'If you keep that up
you'll have the whole of Burnaby voting for you in no time.'

'Here's hoping,' she replied. 'Fingers crossed.'

The following morning Paige was one of the guests on Chat
FM's political and local news programme, *What's Going On*. The
presenter, Wella Davis was a tall, attractive blonde in her late
twenties, who was known and loved by the listeners for her
sharp tongue and her 'take no prisoners' approach to interviewing. She was also known in the radio world for being brutally
ambitious – many young producers and researchers had been

cut to the quick by her bruising criticism and downright ru
manner. Her current researcher, Rita Farrell, rumoured also to
Wella's girlfriend, had rung Paige the previous evening to a
her to appear on Wella's radio show.

'Late notice isn't it?' Paige had asked.

'Wella likes to spring things on people – it's part of her styl
Rita explained.

'Who else will be in the studio?'

'Annette Higgins, Paddy Burns, Miles McGreinna, Mark Ti
and Jackie Pile.'

Paige whistled. 'Bring on the heavy hitters. And you want n
as well?'

'Wella likes some of your policies. She thinks you have a go
chance of winning a seat if the liberal vote comes through f
you.'

'Really?' Paige was flattered.

'So we'll see you tomorrow at quarter to ten in the studio? [
you have the address?'

'Yes, I've been in a few times before. See you then. An
thanks, Rita.'

'No problem. See you tomorrow.'

As Paige drove towards Dublin city on the way to the studi
she listened to Wella laying into a representative from a
Internet company who had been less than scrupulous with the
on-line competitions. The show started at nine, and Paige an
her fellow politicians were on at ten. Apparently, the Intern
company had been making quite a habit of giving their to
prizes to friends and family, angering many of their on-line cus
tomers who, by all accounts, had really won the competitio
and had documentary on-line proof of the same. Paige wa
impressed by Wella's technique. Her legal training obviousl
served her well – she cleverly extracted enough damning info
mation from the interviewee to sink them and then stuck th
knife in – making them admit to their wrongdoings. By the en

of the piece the company had promised to recompense all the aggrieved parties and had given an unconditional apology to all their clients into the bargain.

Paige gripped the steering wheel tightly. Wella was not to be trifled with. She decided there and then that the only way to deal with Wella was to be open and honest – completely transparent – and to hope to goodness that Rita was right and that Wella really did like some of her policies. She wasn't going to get into any slanging matches no matter how tasty the bait.

Paige parked the car on Merrion Square, luckily finding a spot almost straightaway. She fed coins into the parking meter and stuck the ticket onto the inside of her driver's window. Bending down, she contorted her upper body to check her lipstick in the wing mirror. As she suspected – telltale dark cherry red stains on her teeth. She rubbed them with her finger, then popped a finger in her mouth, pursed her lips around it and drew it back out. That should deal with the rogue lipstick, she thought, shouldn't have put it on so hastily. She brushed down the front of her slightly wrinkled black pencil skirt and began to walk towards the radio station's building.

'Hello,' she said a little nervously into the intercom.

'Chat FM. How can I help you?' A disembodied female voice asked.

'Paige Brady. I'm on Wella's show at . . .'

The intercom gave an almighty screech and Paige heard the door lock click open.

'Push the door. We're on the third floor,' the voice said crisply.

Standing in the dimly lit lift Paige stared at her reflection in the grimy mirror. She looked pale. She ran her hands over her stomach. It was starting to take on a gently rounded shape. Soon she'd be in maternity clothes but hopefully not too soon. Luckily it was looking hopeful – with both Callum and Alfie she'd never got huge. She always felt sorry for the women who looked like baby elephants – their swollen bellies causing them to waddle in a most ungainly fashion, their breath short and laboured.

As the lift door opened she walked into the hall and looked around. There was no obvious indication of where she should go. Wooden swing doors led in three different directions. Then she spotted a small Chat FM sticker on one of the doors. She took a deep breath and pushed it open. Sitting on the lurid green sofas in front of her were Annette, Paddy, Mark and Miles.

'Hi, Paige.' A young woman with short dark hair came rushing towards her, her hand outstretched. 'It's lovely to meet you. I'm Rita. I spoke to you on the phone.' She turned towards the other guests. 'And you know everyone, I presume?'

Paige nodded. 'Yes, thank you.'

'Would you like a cup of coffee before we start? We're just waiting for Jackie and then we'll move into the studio during the news.'

'I'd love one,' Paige said gratefully. She could feel her hands begin to shake.

'Come and sit down, Paige.' Paddy smiled up at her. 'Take the weight off your feet. Not that you have any weight of course. Young slip of a thing like you.' He looked around the room. 'Or am I allowed to say things like that in this day and age? Annette will probably accuse me of being sexist.'

Annette scowled at him. 'And are we allowed to make comments about your weight, Paddy?' she asked.

'You can if you like,' he said mildly, holding his stomach in. He was fond of the good life and this had taken its toll on his girth and his jowls over the years.

'How's the anti-dump campaign coming on?' Mark Tine asked, aware that Paddy and Annette didn't exactly see eye to eye at the best of times. Mark was the local Green Party representative, an idealistic young man in his late twenties. This was his first time to contest an election.

'Good, Mark, good. And thanks for all your support, and

yours, Paige.' Paddy nodded at her and ignored Annette and Miles who had both deemed local environmental issues beneath them.

'I saw an interesting photograph of you in the paper last week, Paige,' Miles said, his sharp nasal voice cutting through the air. Miles McGreinna was the local Irish Party representative and Paige didn't like him one little bit. He was fixated by 'family values' and the destruction of morality by the liberal agenda. He'd spoken out vehemently against both divorce and abortion when the relevant referenda had come into play and he was firmly right of centre, a die-hard conservative and vocal Roman Catholic. His policies were positively prehistoric and Paige hated his creeping anti-working woman stance. Annette also took this stance. Which was unsettling since she was one in theory, although her children were grown up.

'Would that have been the one of my team winning the all-Ireland?' Paige said feigning innocence. She knew damn well which one he was referring to.

Before he had a chance to answer, Rita came flurrying back. 'Everyone ready? Let's get you all into studio. Jackie rang to say she was stuck in traffic. We'll have to go ahead without her.'

Miles led the way, followed by Annette and Paddy. Mark and Paige brought up the rear. The studio was small and they all had to clamber over wires, old jugs of water and discarded ring folders to get to their places around the large table. Rita handed each guest headphones.

'I hate these things,' Paddy complained. 'They always pinch my ears.'

'Me too,' Mark agreed.

Wella smiled at them. 'Welcome. They're playing the ten o'clock news at the moment and we'll go into our slot straight afterwards. I'm going to ask each candidate a question on their policies and there will be a little time for open discussion at the end. Please try not to hog the air space and give everyone a chance to speak.'

They all nodded.

'Here we go,' Wella said. She leant in towards the large furry grey microphone in front of her. 'Welcome back to *What's Going On*, the topical news programme on Chat FM, with myself, Wella Davis. This morning in the studio we are privileged to have the leading Dun Laoghaire Rathdown candidates in the forthcoming September election – Deputy Paddy Burns from the People's Party; Councillor Annette Higgins, Independent; Mr Miles McGreinna, from the Irish Party . . .'

Miles interrupted her. 'Doctor Miles McGreinna,' he said pompously.

'Ah, yes, I'd forgotten about your Open University doctorate in ancient history,' she said cuttingly. 'Sorry *Doctor* McGreinna.'

'London School of Arts,' he corrected her. 'And it was in philosophy not ancient history.'

Paige caught Mark's eye. He winked at her. She looked down at the table and tried not to laugh. Miles was so annoying.

'To continue,' Wella said, 'Mr Mark Tine from the Green Party and last but not least, Councillor Paige Brady, also Independent. I'd like to start with Deputy Burns. Deputy, there has been a lot in the papers recently about the proposed Burnaby dump, can you fill the listeners in on some of the issues please?'

'Certainly, Wella,' Paddy said warmly. 'Be glad to.'

As Paddy explained the risks involved in locating a dump near a residential area, Paige's mind began to drift. She was dog-tired today and she could have done without the mad dash into town to tell the truth. She was due back in Burnaby in two hours to talk at a Lady's Lunch in the Burnaby Golf Club and then Angus was calling in that afternoon to meet Callum and she was a little worried about it. She so wanted them to get on and . . . She was brought back to earth with a bump when Wella asked her a question.

'What do you think, Paige?'

Damn, she thought, what were they talking about – the dump? Or had they moved on from that? Openness and honestly, she reminded herself.

'Can you repeat the question, Wella?' she asked with a smile.

Wella looked at her for a second, and noticing Paige's drawn, pale face and dark shadows around the eyes decided to cut her some slack. 'Of course. Do you think you are a good role model for young people? I was thinking specifically about the recent photograph in the *Burnaby News*.'

Paige had been dreading this question, but figured if Wella hadn't asked it, Miles would have weaseled it in somewhere anyway.

Paige took a deep breath. 'Interesting photo, wasn't it?' She smiled at Wella.

Wella laughed. 'Yes, it was.'

'To answer your question in one word – yes. I am an excellent role model for young people. I was introduced to sport from an early age, thanks largely to my father, Lorcan Brady, who also played soccer for his country, and who set up the local Burnaby Soccer Club in his time. I've played soccer at the highest level and have also been involved in both college and school coaching. I am very involved in the community and was instrumental in setting up the new Burnaby Arts Centre.'

'And you have two young children I believe, Councilor Brady, is that right?' Wella asked.

'Yes. And one of my key policies is to lobby the government to provide affordable childcare for all working women in the country. At present Irish parents pay out over twenty per cent of their wages on childcare, way above the European average of eight per cent.'

Miles snorted at this.

'Do you have a problem with women working, Dr McGreinna?' Wella asked, knowing full well that he did.

'I have no problem with women working *per se*,' he said smoothly. 'It's women with young children who work I object to. Children shouldn't be abandoned to strangers for large portions of the day. It's causing huge problems in our society – teenage drinking, delinquency, rise in crime rates . . .'

'I agree,' Annette interjected. 'Women should take full responsibility for their offspring.'

'What about men?' Mark asked. 'Surely they should take equal responsibility.'

'Quite,' Miles said with a sneer on his face. 'But you wouldn't know anything about taking responsibility, Mr Tine, would you?'

'Sorry?' Mark asked. 'Would you care to explain that last comment?'

'Yes, Dr McGreinna,' Wella said, delighted with the way things were heading. Nothing like a whiff of scandal to boost the ratings. 'Please explain what you're trying to say. I for one would like to hear it.'

'Mark Tine is having a baby out of wedlock with a married woman.' Miles stared at Mark with an evil glint in his eye. 'Deny it if you can.'

Mark was silent for a moment. His eyes were flashing and there were two angry red spots on his cheeks. 'Of course I don't deny it. I *am* having a child with my partner of four years, it's true. And for your information, Miles, she's divorced . . .'

'An English divorce,' Miles said snidely. 'Not recognized by the church in this state.'

Mark stared at him. 'She's Protestant, so her divorce is recognized by her own church. But of course you don't believe there is any other church in this country except for the Roman Catholic one, do you Miles?'

'The Roman Catholic church has a very important role to play in —' Miles began.

Wella held her right hand up. 'We're not really interested in the church's role this morning, thank you. Now let's get back to Mr Tine. Is there anything else you'd like to say on this matter, Mr Tine?'

'Yes, Wella, there is. I'd like to say that I am overjoyed at the prospect of being a parent. My partner suffers from polycystic ovaries and she didn't think she'd ever have children, so it was a delightful surprise for both of us. And we hope to get married next year when we've found a new house.'

'Thank you for being so honest, Mr Tine.' Wella smiled at him.

'If I were you, Mr Tine . . .' Miles began.

'And do you have children yourself, Dr McGreinna?' Wella asked quickly.

'Um, no.'

'Or a wife?'

'No.'

'Then you're not really in a position to give advice are you, Doctor?'

'But . . .' Miles was livid. How dare that young pup speak to him like that?

'Can I cut in here?' Paddy Burns said.

'I haven't finished . . .' Miles blustered.

'Yes, you have,' Wella said, glaring at him. 'Please allow Deputy Burns to speak.'

'I'd like to congratulate Mr Tine on the news and wish him and his family all the best in the future.'

'Thank you,' Mark said gratefully.

After the slot had finished, they all walked through into Chat FM's hall together.

'Outrageous,' Annette said. 'Call that a radio show? I only got to talk about my garden winning a prize in the Tidy Towns competition for a brief moment and didn't get to mention the new computer call centre I have planned for Dun Laoghaire borough at all.'

'Terrible woman, that Wella,' Miles grumbled. 'Most unprofessional.'

Paige put her hand on Mark's arm. 'Well done,' she said in a low voice. 'You handled that very well.'

'So did you,' he said. 'Exhausting, wasn't it?'

She nodded.

There was an awkward silence as they all waited for the lift in the small hallway.

'So, who's for the Burnaby Flower Show on Saturday?' Paddy asked in a jovial voice, breaking the atmosphere. 'You're doing the draw, aren't you, Paige?'

'That's right.'

'Hardly fair,' Annette muttered.

'Sorry, what was that, Annette?' asked Paddy.

'They should really have asked me you know. After all, my garden did win a prize . . .'

'At the Tidy Towns, yes, I think we all know that by now, Annette. But I'm sure you're going to go along anyway, aren't you? Shame to miss an opportunity to meet the punters.'

'I might,' Annette admitted sniffily.

'And I'm running the bottle stall for my sins,' Mark said.

'Well, I'll definitely see you then, Mark.' Paddy laughed and rubbed his hands together. 'Hope you have some nice Irish whiskey. I feel a lucky streak coming on.'

Paige opened the front door and smiled at Angus. She felt decidedly nervous. Callum was in high spirits and was currently dashing around upstairs with no clothes on, nothing new. 'Come in.' She led Angus into the kitchen. Bright sunlight was flooding in the windows and she gestured towards the small flowery sofa. 'Please, sit down. Would you like tea or coffee? Or a soft drink?'

He smiled. 'Nothing for me, thanks. I'm fine. This is a lovely house, is it Georgian?'

'Yes. It was in rag order when we bought it but Tom's a bit of a DIY nut – he did a lot of it himself. And luckily he works in a mortgage company or we never would have been able to afford it. This part's an extension. They weren't mad into big kitchens in those days. The one we replaced was small and didn't get much light.'

'Liked keeping the servants in the dark, did they?' He grinned. 'I'm sure they would have had servants in a house this size.'

'You're probably right.' She was beginning to feel more at ease. Angus had a nice calm manner and a wonderfully warm smile. It was impossible not to smile back. 'I'll just go upstairs and get Callum.'

After she'd left the room Angus looked around. The kitchen was country-style wood complete with dark blue Aga and had a warm and homely feel. In front of the sofa where he was sitting was a large Victorian dresser crammed full with books of all shapes and sizes, framed photographs, a jar full of coins, plastic toys in various states of distress and candles in wooden and wrought iron holders. There were larger framed photographs on the walls, along with an attractive oil painting of Burnaby's coastal Martello tower, the sea stretching out shimmering blue in the background. The most striking photograph on the wall was of two laughing teenage girls in scary eighties outfits – one in a pink and blue ra-ra skirt, with legwarmers, lace-up boots, and a string vest over a yellow T-shirt; and the second fashion victim in a tiny stonewash denim miniskirt, her slim legs in fishnet tights and her hair piled up on top of her head and fastened with some sort of bright blue netting. Hang on a second. He got to his feet and walked towards the photograph. Leaning forward and looking even closer, he snorted. It was Paige and the girl from the bookshop, Molly.

Just then he heard a noise behind him and swung around. 'Great, isn't it?' Paige asked.

'Sorry, I didn't mean to . . .' Angus stammered.

'Don't worry, it catches everyone's attention. Molly gave it to me for my birthday last year. It was taken when we were thirteen. We thought we were the bee's knees.'

'Mummy looks silly, doesn't she?' a little voice piped up.

Angus smiled at the little boy who was holding his mother's hand tightly. He looked angelic with his white blonde hair and open, round face. 'You must be Callum. I'm Angus.'

'Mummy told me there'd be no telly if I was bold so I have to be nice to you,' Callum said. He then gave an almighty sniff and wiped his nose on the sleeve of his red sweatshirt.

'Callum!' Paige glared at him. 'That's nasty. If you need to wipe your nose go and get a tissue.'

Callum let go of her hand and toddled off into the hall.

'Sorry about that . . .' Paige began.

'Paige, I'm here to help. I'm well used to it, remember? I usually have twenty five or so of the little darlings at the one time.'

'Thanks,' she said gratefully. Callum came back into the room pulling a long tail of toilet paper behind him. 'Callum, what are you doing?' she asked in exasperation. 'I told you to get a tissue.'

'Couldn't find one. And the loo paper wouldn't break off.'

'That's just not true, is it young man?' she asked.

'It is, honestly, Mummy.'

She said nothing. What must Angus think? She tore off a piece of the white tissue paper, handed it to Callum with a stern look on her face and began to pick up the remainder of the roll off the floor. 'I'll be back in a second,' she said to Angus as she followed the paper out of the room.

As soon as she'd gone Angus looked at Callum. 'Do you like the Andrex ad where the boy gets the toilet paper stuck in his jeans and runs it all around the house?' he asked calmly.

Callum smiled knowingly and nodded. 'Are you going to give out to me?' he asked after a few seconds.

'Not at all,' Angus said. 'Sure, why would I? I'm only here to play with you, not to give out to you.'

Callum's eyes widened. 'Is that right?' he asked. 'That's not what Mummy said. She said you were here to mind me and that I was to be good.'

'You don't have to be good,' Angus said. 'Except at our games. You have to be good at them.'

'What sort of games?' Callum asked with interest, cocking his head to one side.

'All sorts – hide and seek, mountain climbing, making a tree house, making a camp fire, bungee jumping . . .'

'Bungee jumping!' Callum was amazed. 'I've seen that on telly. They jump off bridges and stuff. Mum would never let me do that.'

Paige, who was standing in the hall listening to the conversation with interest, stiffened. Bungee jumping? Callum was quite right. What was Angus thinking of?

'It's not real bungee jumping,' Angus explained. 'It's a bungee trampoline. You're attached to these rubber pulleys and you can jump up and down and go amazingly high. They have one on Sandybay seafront.'

Paige who suddenly realized that she'd been holding her breath, felt a huge wave of relief flood her body. For a second there she'd begun to wonder about Angus's suitability.

'Cool!' Callum grinned. 'Can we go now?'

'So you want me to play with you when your mum and dad are at work?' Angus asked.

Callum nodded firmly. 'Yes.'

'There's just one thing, Callum. Every morning you'll have to tidy up your room before we play and do one nice thing for your mum and dad.'

'Like what?' Callum asked suspiciously.

'Nothing major. Give your mum a kiss, pick up Alfie's toys

for him, blow your own nose, get up and dressed yourself like a big fellow, that kind of thing.'

Callum thought about it for a minute – it didn't sound too bad really. 'And then you'll take me bungee jumping and all the other cool things?'

'Yes, I promise. Bungee jumping or one cool thing every day. I'll make up a star chart and every morning I'll ask your mum and dad to put a star up if you've been helpful and nice. And then we play for the whole day. Is it a deal?'

'Sure,' Callum said. 'As long as Mum doesn't mind.'

Mind? Paige smiled to herself as she rested her forehead against the wall, the plaster deliciously cool against her skin. She felt weak with relief – had they finally found someone who understood how to deal with Callum?

Angus started on Monday and sure enough, encouraged by the idea of bungee jumping and other 'cool' activities, Callum behaved himself on Monday morning. After staring intently at the new star chart for several minutes, which Angus had dropped in over the weekend, he ran over and kissed Paige on the bottom.

'Callum!' Paige squealed and whipped around. She was rinsing the cereal bowls in the sink at the time and was taken quite unawares.

Callum smiled up at her. 'I kissed you, Mummy. Angus said that was being nice. Can I have my star now?'

Paige laughed. 'Yes, I suppose so, but next time try kissing me on the cheek. OK?'

'OK, Mummy.'

'He just got the wrong kind of cheek, love,' Tom grinned.

'Talking of cheek,' Paige said to Tom. 'Less of that, you. You're supposed to be showing your son a good example. How's Alfie getting on with his breakfast?'

'He's nearly finished. I'll drop him off to Mum's this morning if that would help.'

'That would be great, thanks. And you're all right for campaigning at the train station at five?'

'Grand, I'll meet you there. Looking forward to it.'

'Being belted by commuters' brollies, I'd say you are.'

'Surely it doesn't get violent.'

'Not usually, no.'

Tom looked at her and she broke into a smile. She walked over and kissed him on the cheek. She was feeling decidedly chipper this morning, all things considered. 'I'm going into the office to make some phone calls. See you later, alligator.'

'In a while, crocodile,' said Tom.

'Not too soon, you big fat baboon,' Callum joined in.

'Callum!' they both chorused.

'Have I lost my star?' he asked anxiously.

'No, but I'd watch it young man,' Paige said ominously.

'I'll go and tidy my room.' Callum ran out the door and thundered up the stairs.

'Whatever that Angus has done, God bless him,' Tom said.

'No kidding,' Paige agreed.

Chapter 10

Molly

'Who are we waiting for?' Paige asked the rest of the Book Club at the August meeting.

'Just Harry, I think. Trisha can't make it,' Cathy said. 'I'm no sure about Kate.'

'No, Kate's not coming. She sent her apologies, she's watching Lily swim,' Molly explained. 'She doesn't trust her on he own.'

'Is Lily's ankle better then?' Paige asked.

'Not quite. But there's no stopping her. She says she's having withdrawal symptoms from the lack of her daily swim.'

'Hello, everyone. This is the Book Club I presume?' Milo asked.

Everyone looked up.

'This is Milo Devine, the new owner of the shop,' Anita explained. 'He's going to be joining us today.'

'Have you read the book?' Molly asked a little too sharply.

'Yes,' he said. 'And I thought it was most . . .'

Paige put up her hands. 'Stop! We haven't started yet.'

'Sorry,' Milo said. Duly chastised, he sat down beside Anita.

Molly nudged Paige in the side. She'd already told her about Milo's crush. Paige smiled back at her and nodded discreetly.

Harry came blustering in. 'Sorry, sorry, last minute order came in. Sent the wrong bloody pots of course, idiots. Still, I'm here now.' He sat down beside Molly. 'And how are we all this fine day?' He looked around the table, his eyes stopping when they came to Milo. There hadn't been a new member of the Club for quite some time.

Paige noticed Harry's interested gaze. 'This is Milo, Harry. He's the new owner.'

Harry raised his hand and waved casually at Milo. 'Hi, welcome. Nice to have another man on board.'

'Will we get started then?' Paige asked. 'Who'd like to begin? Anita?'

Anita grimaced. 'I was hoping you wouldn't ask me first.' She sighed theatrically. 'I have to say I hated it. Absolutely hated it.'

'Thank goodness,' Cathy joined in. 'I thought it was just me. I couldn't make head or tail of it at all. What nonsense.'

'Pretentious rubbish,' Molly agreed. 'Practically unreadable in parts.'

'What I can't understand,' Harry added, 'is how the man won the Booker a few years ago. Had the judges gone mad?'

'The one that won the Booker – *Regret* – wasn't so turgid,' Anita said. 'In fact it was excellent in parts. But this one . . . *Mamma Mia*!'

'Tell us why you didn't like it, Anita,' Paige encouraged.

'Where to start? First of all – the plot was very weak. Nothing really happened the whole way through the book. It was supposed to be about the narrator revisiting the village he grew up in – a presumably fictional place called 'Stradbrook' which sounded like a small town in the north of Ireland. But it was so bloody boring. I couldn't stand the narrator – he never stopped moaning about how his life had stagnated in the place and how he'd never been able to make anything of himself because of his

upbringing. And the other characters were completely wooder
I couldn't empathize with any of them, let alone understan
them.'

'Old Mrs White was particularly unbelievable, wasn't she?
Cathy asked. 'She was like something out of *Ryan's Daughte*
with the white lace shawl and the thatched cottage. I mear
please.'

'She was supposed to be the narrator's sort of surrogat
mother, wasn't she?' Molly asked. 'But she wasn't a very pleas
ant character.'

'That's right,' Harry said. 'She had no time for her own chil
dren and when her youngest son died – what was his name?'

'Johnny,' Anita said.

'That's right, Johnny,' Harry continued. 'She didn't seem too
bothered.'

'Another thing I can't understand is how the book got so
many good reviews. It's complete hogwash,' Anita said. 'I
would make you wonder what the reviewers were thinking
about.'

'May I say something?' Milo asked Paige.

'Of course,' Paige said. 'Sorry, it is hard to get a word in edge
ways at times. Fire away.'

'I thought the book was wonderfully written,' Milo began. 'So
atmospheric. You could almost touch the mist on the bogs and
smell the turf burning in the old hearths. I think Frost has a
touch of genius when it comes to describing the way life was in
Ireland in the last century.'

'Really?' Anita asked a little scornfully. 'Did you not think his
descriptive passages went on a bit?'

'No, I enjoyed them. Some of the sentences were exquisitely
crafted. You could almost smell the sweat that went into writing
some of them.'

'But surely writing shouldn't be like that!' Anita cried. 'Over
crafted and arty. Surely it should flow and be artless. I think the

best writers are the ones who make writing look easy. Frost spends far too much time crafting perfect sentences and not enough time creating a strong plot and real, believable characters.'

'I agree with Anita,' Harry said. 'I found his writing most frustrating. I just wanted him to get on with the story, not waffle on about dew catching the light on spider's webs.'

'But this is literary fiction we're talking about here, not story-telling,' Milo insisted. 'Surely you see the difference. Maybe you're more used to reading popular fiction, that's all. Maybe your reading tastes are a little unformed, a little unrefined.'

'Rubbish!' Paige said a little more vehemently than she'd intended. 'We read all kinds of things in this Book Club, including some damn fine literary fiction.'

'Indeed,' Anita said angrily. 'All kinds of things. But we also read good popular fiction, we're not snobbish. A good book is a good book no matter what genre – crime, sci fi, historical saga, fantasy, whatever. Maybe you just haven't read enough good books to recognize *Stradbrook* for what it is, pretentious rubbish.'

'Well really!' Milo said looking a little red in the face. 'I'm not here to be insulted about my reading tastes. Maybe I should leave.'

'Please don't,' Paige said. 'And don't take anything personally. We often have quite heated arguments about books, it's quite normal. Stay. We'd all like you to. Please.'

Milo looked around the table. Everyone nodded. Even Anita.

'Sorry,' Anita mumbled. 'I got a little carried away there.'

'Yes, well . . .'

'Have I missed anything?' Sam asked, walking towards the table. Everyone stared up at him. 'Sorry I'm so late.'

Paige laughed. 'Not much, Sam. Please do sit down. Welcome. Did you get a chance to read the book?'

He nodded. 'Yes, but I only got about halfway through. There's not much of a story to it, is there? I got bored of it to tell the truth. Picked up *Lucinda's Tale* instead. Anita had recommended it to me when I started in the shop. Now, there's a book.'

Within minutes, the group was eagerly and noisily discussing *Lucinda's Tale*, which had been an earlier Book Club choice. Paige breathed a sigh of relief. She had enough squabbling children to deal with at home.

'So, what did you think of your first meeting?' Paige asked Milo after the meeting had finished.

'Interesting,' he said. 'Very interesting. I learnt a lot.'

'About books?' Paige asked.

'Among other things,' he said quietly. He looked over towards Anita who was deep in conversation with Cathy about next week's book. 'I don't think she likes me,' he said, gesturing towards the two women.

'Anita?'

He nodded.

'You'd be surprised,' Paige said. 'She just gets very passionate about books, that's all. I honestly don't think it was anything personal.'

He said nothing.

After lunch, Anita and Molly met in Coffee Heaven to discuss their plan for the bookshop. Paige had excused herself – she had an interview with one of the radio stations and a photo call for the Flower Festival.

'I'm worried about pulling off a Book Festival of this size,' Molly began. 'I know you and Paige are confident but there are so many things that could . . .'

'Molly, have some faith.' Anita smiled at her. 'It's going to be a lot of work but it'll all come together, you'll see. Especially now that we've found such a great second venue. Paige has arranged everything with Tara, the new arts administrator in the Burnaby Arts Centre and she's mad keen to get involved. She wants to run a special Love Bean event for the children with African storytelling and dancing. And best of all, she'll organize the whole thing herself.'

'What's a Love Bean when it's at home?'

'It's an African friendship token. It's literally a large, brown bean. You give it to someone you like.'

Molly sighed: 'I just don't . . .'

'Molly! What's wrong with you?'

She sighed again. 'I don't know. Sorry, I'm all over the place today.'

'Is that ex-boyfriend of yours pestering you again?'

'Not really. He's been fairly subdued this week to tell the truth.'

'Good. Don't let him get to you. Be strong.'

'I'll try.'

'And how's the writing coming along?'

'Not great,' Molly admitted. 'I haven't been able to concentrate for a few weeks now. Maybe I'm not cut out to be a writer.'

'Maybe not. But you should at least give it a go. You'll regret it if you don't.'

'I suppose.'

Anita put her hand on Molly's. 'Have some courage, Molly. Be brave for once in your life. You have it in you, I know you do. Reach inside yourself and find your inner strength. I really do think that there's a writer in there.'

Molly felt like crying. She had no idea why Anita believed in her but it was comforting to know that she did.

'Now, let's go over our list,' Anita said gently, sensing Molly's emotionally fragile state of mind. 'Who do we have for Saturday morning?'

Molly studied the sheet in front of her. 'We blast off with two of the biggies – Rose Lovett and Jennie Tracker.' Rose and Jennie were the American and British Queens of romantic fiction.

Anita whistled. 'That should draw the crowds. Followed by . . .?'

'The Literary Lunch.'

'Of course, that should be fun. And Matty and Alex have agreed to do the catering?'

Molly nodded. 'And Harry has offered to decorate the tables for free.'

'How sweet of him.'

'It is decent of him, isn't it? After lunch we have the panel discussion on "Getting Published – Tips from the Top".'

'Has Bonnie Evans agreed to sit on the panel?' Anita asked.

'She has.' Molly smiled. 'Should be interesting.' Bonnie was one of Burnaby's most famous locals – a flamboyant romantic saga novelist who spent most of her time in the South of France. She was well known for her strong opinions on everything from writing to poker and horse racing and always had something outrageous to say. The media loved her – a glamorous woman in her early fifties, she ate interviewers for breakfast and had rendered even Terry Wogan and Gay Byrne speechless in her day.

'Should be,' Anita agreed. 'It's going to be wonderful, really Molly. You and Paige have done Trojan work putting it all together.'

'Thanks, I hope it will work.'

'It will. No doubt about it. Especially now that Brenda Jackson's researcher has confirmed Rose and Jennie for the radio show the week before the Festival to talk about their work.'

'That's great news.'

'Isn't it?' Anita said. 'And talking about the media, did Millie from the *Burnaby News* get back to you?'

'She did,' Molly said. 'She agreed to run a short story competition to tie in with the festival. And she'd like you to be one of the judges, along with Bonnie.'

'No problem, could be a bit of fun. I hope you're going to enter, Molly.'

Molly wrinkled her nose. 'I couldn't. It might be a conflict of interests.'

'Perhaps. But think about it. Is there anything in the rules to say you can't?'

'Don't know,' Molly said thoughtfully. 'You haven't written them yet.'

Anita laughed. 'Then we'll have to see what we can do.'

'There's no need, I'm not going to enter.'

'OK.' Anita knew better than to push her. She looked at her watch and sighed. 'I suppose we'd better get back to the shop.'

'One last thing. Cathy and Trina have offered to sponsor Jennie's flights. And they said they'll do a window advertising the event in their shop. And Harry and Alex offered to put up posters in their shops too.'

'Excellent!' Anita beamed and put her hand on Molly's. 'It's all coming together. I knew we could do it Molly. Now let's see if the press will sit up and take notice, shall we?'

'And Milo,' Molly added.

'And Milo.' Anita nodded solemnly.

That evening Molly decided that some fresh air would do her good. She grabbed a fleece and headed out the door straight after her dinner. Kate was out on yet another dummy date and as it was a sunny, warm evening there was nothing to keep Molly in the house. As she walked down Burnaby Lane towards Sandybay beach she thought about a short story she'd been working on. It was set on a beach in West Cork and involved a chance encounter between a lobster fisherman and an American tourist. Molly wanted to use the Selkie story as a basis for her tale – the legend of how seals came out of the sea and became women on land. But she was having difficulties sewing the traditional strands into her own short story without it being too 'clunky' and obvious.

Crossing over the railway bridge, she stood for a moment

gazing at the sea stretched out in front of her. It glistened in the evening sun – the light dancing merrily on the tips of the waves. There was a good breeze which whipped at her hair, threatening to pull it out of its loose ponytail. She walked down the steps and her feet crunched onto the stony beach. She strolled down the beach at a brisk pace in the direction of Wicklow, swinging her arms by her sides and taking in deep breaths of the tangy, salty air.

After a while, she heard a familiar voice behind her.

'Hey! Molly! Wait up!'

She turned around and shielded her eyes from the sun. She smiled as she saw Sam being pulled along by a large black Labrador.

'Are you walking him or is he walking you?' She laughed.

'I'm not altogether sure.' The dog stopped at Molly's feet and began to jump up, putting it's wet paws on her thighs.

'Sorry,' Sam said. 'This is Tara, she belongs to my neighbour. She's just been playing in the waves, she's a bit wet.'

'So I can see.' Molly bent over and patted her head. 'Hello, Tara. Are you enjoying your walk?'

Tara wagged her tail eagerly and began to bark.

'I think she likes you,' Sam said. 'Sorry, are we interrupting your walk?'

'Not at all, it's nice to have the company.'

'In that case, mind if we join you?'

'Not at all.'

Molly began to walk and Sam fell into step beside her.

'You like going at a fair lick, don't you?' he asked after a moment.

'I know. Paige is always complaining. Sorry, I'll slow down.'

'Don't on my account. Tara likes it and I'll get used to it. I've been looking out for you when I'm walking but this is the first time I've seen you.'

'I've haven't been walking in ages,' Molly explained. 'Too busy. You know how it is.'

'Don't I just? But Hugh loves the beach. So we're usually here every weekend whether I like it or not.'

Molly said nothing. She hadn't asked any questions about Sam's private life since she'd touched one of his raw nerves in the shop – she'd been too nervous of annoying him again.

'You can ask me if you like,' Sam said, sensing her unease. 'I won't bite your head off this time, I promise.'

'About what?'

'About Hugh.'

'I'm sorry – you must think I'm awfully nosy.'

Sam laughed. 'You're not the worst. Must be the writer in you. I hear you're all a very curious bunch.'

'How do you know I write?' she asked quickly.

'Anita told me.'

'Anita?'

'Sorry, I didn't realize it was a secret. I'd love to read some of your work if you'd let me.'

Molly stared at the sea.

'Molly? Sorry, have I said something wrong?'

She shook her head. 'I just don't like anyone knowing about my writing, that's all. Anita shouldn't have said anything to you. Not that's there's much to know to tell the truth. I haven't written a word for weeks.'

'Why not?' he asked gently.

She shrugged her shoulders. 'Haven't felt in the right frame of mind I suppose.'

'Not centred enough? I have the same problem myself sometimes.'

She looked at him in surprise. 'You write too?'

He laughed. 'Me? Heavens, no. I make furniture, that's all. But I can only do it if I'm in a good mood.' He picked up a stone and kicked it into the sea.

'I remember now, Hugh said you made him a puppet theatre.'

'That's right. I make other things too. It's my hobby I suppose – I dabble in it. Not like your writing.'

'What do you mean?'

'Well, Anita told me you're quite serious about your writing. How many short stories have you finished?'

'Twenty-seven,' she mumbled. 'And half a novella.'

He whistled. 'That's really something. Twenty-seven. I'm impressed.'

'Don't be. It's won't come to anything.'

'Why do you say that?'

'I just know.'

'You should have some confidence in yourself. Maybe some of them are good.'

She frowned. 'I doubt it.'

'Let Anita read one or two. At least you'd know then.'

'Maybe I'm happier not knowing. Have you thought of that?'

Sam stopped walking and looked at her. She continued on without him, realized that he wasn't beside her, and stopped. 'What?' she asked sharply. 'What are you smiling at? Tell me.'

'You,' he said finally. 'You're one big mass of contradictions, Molly. Do you know that?'

'I have no idea what you're talking about.' Molly was getting more than a little uncomfortable at the direction this conversation was heading. She decided to change the subject. 'Tell me about Hugh.'

'What do you want to know?' Sam let Tara off the lead to play in the surf again, put the lead in his pocket and caught up with Molly.

'Are you married?' she asked before she could stop herself.

'Married!' He laughed. 'I suppose it's a fair enough question. No, I'm not married. I thought about it at one stage – to Hugh's mum in fact, but it wouldn't have worked out. What about yourself?'

'I was asked once,' Molly admitted. 'But like you, it wouldn't have worked out.'

'The guy outside the bookshop?' Sam asked astutely.

'You saw us?' she asked, embarrassed.

Sam nodded. 'He seemed a little upset.'

'That was my ex, Denis. He's all right really. Just gets a bit over-emotional at times.'

'I know the feeling, Brona is a bit like that.'

'Brona?'

'My ex, Hugh's mum.'

'What happened? If you don't mind me asking?'

'No, it's fine. We were in college together – Arts in UCD. She was in my philosophy class and we met on the very first day of term. She was wearing the most amazing yellow coat with a huge furry yellow collar – you could hardly miss her.'

'Love at first sight then?'

'You could say that. She sat down in the row in front of me during the very first lecture and I couldn't take my eyes off her. Afterwards I asked her for coffee and one thing led to another.'

'And Hugh?'

Sam was quiet for a moment. 'He wasn't exactly planned. Brona was in bits when she found out. Her family are quite strict Catholics and she was dreading telling them. At one stage she considered not having it but neither of us felt it was the right thing to do.'

'What age were you?' asked Molly.

'I was twenty-two and Brona was twenty-one.'

'It must have been hard.'

'It was I suppose, but we managed. We lived together for a while but things didn't work out. She moved back in with her parents nearly two years ago. She and Hugh live in a self-contained apartment in their basement now – so it's all worked out for the best really. He gets to see his grandparents every day while Brona's working and I get to see him every weekend.'

'What does she do?'

'She's an actress. She does voice-over work, radio ads mostly and she has a small part on *City Lights* as Jude's on-off girlfriend. You know, the soap opera.'

'Don't watch it I'm afraid.'

'Neither do I.' He took Tara's lead out of his pocket and walked towards the edge of the water. 'Here, girl!' he shouted. 'You've had enough now.' Tara barked and stayed in the water.

Molly laughed. 'You have great control over her.'

'I know. Still, she probably has the right idea.' He sat down on the stones and began to untie his boots.

'What are you doing?' Molly asked.

'Going paddling. Come on!'

'No way. It'll be freezing.'

'No it won't.' He pulled off his boots and socks and rolled up the bottom of his jeans. He walked boldly into the water, trying not to wince as the icy water lapped his ankles.

'Told you,' Molly said.

'It's not that bad,' he insisted. 'Come on. I dare you.'

Molly looked at the water which was rippling and bubbling over the shingle. It did look rather inviting. 'OK.' She joined him, dipping in one foot gingerly, followed by the other.

'You liar, it is freezing.' She grinned.

'Freezing but fun.'

After two minutes Molly's toes had had enough. She stepped out of the water and walked slowly towards her shoes and socks. 'My feet are practically numb,' she said. 'I blame you.'

'It's good for you,' he said. 'Toughen you up.'

She sat down on the shingle, waved her feet in the air to get rid of the drips and pulled her socks over her damp feet. As she tied the laces of her runners, Sam sat down beside her.

'When was the last time you paddled?' he asked.

She shrugged her shoulders. 'No idea. Ages ago.'

'You should do it more often, keeps you young.'

'Is that right? What happened to you then?'

'Very funny,' he grinned back. 'Um, what are you up to this evening?'

'Do you know, I think I might attempt to do some writing.'

'Good idea.' He jumped up and walked towards the sea. 'Here, Tara,' he shouted at the dog who was still enjoying the waves. 'Come on, girl. You'll freeze if you don't get out now.'

Molly watched him from her seated position as Tara ran towards Sam, her tongue lolling out of her mouth. He wrestled with her good-naturedly on the stones, Tara yelping enthusiastically as he held her down and rubbed her tummy. He looked over at Molly and smiled, his eyes crinkling attractively at the corners.

Damn, Molly thought. I do believe Sam was going to ask me out. And I blew it. She looked at Tara and back at Sam. Oh, to be a dog, she thought. Life would be so much simpler.

Chapter 11

Kate

'Hello. There are no free tables anywhere, mind sharing?'

Angus looked up in surprise at the attractive blonde woman in front of him. 'Um, no, not at all. Please sit down.'

'Thanks.' She said, placing her coffee mug on the table and sat down. 'It's busy in here today, isn't it?'

'Um, yes, very. Saturday shoppers, I suppose.'

'Yes, of course.' She looked at him and smiled. 'I've seen you in here a few times.' She held out her hand. 'I'm Patricia. Patricia Simons. And you are . . . ?'

Angus took a deep breath. Stay calm, he told himself. 'Angus Cawley.' He shook her hand firmly. 'Nice to meet you.'

'And you.' Patricia smiled again.

Angus smiled at her shyly and was about to go back to reading his newspaper when she asked him another question.

'Are you working today?'

'Sorry?'

'Working?' Patricia asked again.

'Oh, no. Just having lunch.'

'I see. I'm working.'

'Oh.'

'I'm a publisher's rep. Do you like reading yourself?'

'Yes, I suppose so. I don't get much time to read books though. Not whole ones anyway.'

'You are a scream.' She patted his arm playfully.

Angus wasn't sure why what he'd said was funny, but he played along with it anyway. He thought Patricia was a little pushy and there was something slightly off-putting about her perfectly set hair and immaculately made-up face but talking to her would be good practice. He was sure that Kate would approve.

'Your job sounds interesting,' he said, remembering Kate's advice on talking to women. 'Tell me about it.'

Patricia was only too pleased to oblige. She loved talking about herself. And Angus was really rather good-looking, with those lovely chocolate brown eyes. There was a Booksellers' Ball being held the following weekend and she just might ask him to escort her.

'What?' Kate asked incredulously. 'Angus is going out with who?'

'Patricia,' Molly said evenly. 'Patricia Simons. I'm sure I've told you about her before – she's one of my least favourite publisher's sales reps – she has a mouth the size of a car boot. She called into the shop this afternoon to drop in some catalogues and some car stock. Apparently she met Angus in the coffee shop, they got talking and she asked him to the Booksellers' Ball next weekend.'

'Are *you* going?' Kate asked.

'I wasn't planning to. Why?'

'No reason.' Kate was silent for a few moments. She tapped her teaspoon against the side of her mug. They were sitting at the kitchen table, having just finished sharing a Chinese takeaway.

'You're not jealous, are you?' Molly asked, trying not to smile.

'No!' Kate insisted. 'Of course not. What's she like anyway? This Patricia woman.'

Molly described the elegant, blonde sales rep.

Kate listened in stony silence. 'Good for him,' she said curtly before standing up. 'I'm glad he's met someone.'

'Where are you going?' Molly asked. 'I thought you were staying in this evening.'

'I've changed my mind. There's something I have to do.'

'But I rented a video.'

'Sorry. We can watch it tomorrow evening. How about that?'

'Fine.' Molly folded her arms across her chest. Kate had been in a funny mood all week. Molly had blown out dinner at Paige's to stay in with her this evening in the mistaken belief that Kate might like the company. Kate was a strange one sometimes. There was obviously something bothering Kate but she didn't seem to want to talk about it. 'Whatever,' Molly sighed to herself.

Kate strode into the lobby of the Killiney Arms appearing a lot more confident than she felt. She'd made a special effort to look nice – light brown on-the-knee suede skirt, brown leather high-heeled boots, fitted black shirt. Her hair was freshly blow-dried and she'd carefully applied a layer of foundation, glittery gold eye shadow and strong, red lipstick – her 'war paint'. Because this evening, above all other evenings she was certainly going to war.

She sat down in an armchair where she had a good vantage point of the whole lobby and glanced at her watch. Good, she was five minutes early, enough time to collect her thoughts. Because she knew exactly what she was going to say – she'd been rehearsing it over and over for the past week. But as a familiar dark suited figure walked down the stairs, caught her eye, smiled and walked towards her, she was rendered speechless. Damn, she thought, he always does this to me.

'Cat.' He grinned at her, his impossibly white teeth gleaming. 'You look a million dollars. Let me look at you.' He held both her hands firmly and looked her up and down. He whistled softly. 'Still a beauty.'

'Um, thanks,' she managed to say.

'Would you like a drink? A glass of white wine?'

She nodded wordlessly.

'Wait there,' he commanded her.

Kate watched as he walked towards the bar to the right of the lobby. His suit was immaculately cut, his smart black leather boots shone as if they'd just been polished, and his dark-brown hair was freshly shorn. As always, Jay Sweetman looked good, too damn good.

One of the top American fashion promoters, Jay's job took him all over Europe and he always dressed to impress. In fact, he was so stylish if you didn't know him you'd think he was Italian or Spanish, not Boston-Irish. Kate had first met him two years ago in the Diva, a glitzy hotel in Boston, at the launch party of a new range of Sin 'streetwear for feet', which included several of her designs for funky pink, light blue and moss green sneakers. She'd caught his eye across a crowded room and had blushed as Jay had smiled and winked blatantly at her.

Later that evening, to her delight and after several hours of heavily loaded exchanged looks, he'd asked her to dance. They hit it off immediately. He was her ideal man – charming and polite, strong-willed and intelligent. They had talked all night and once he'd kissed her in their shared taxi home, her fate was sealed. He kissed like an angel. Or should that be a devil? Either way, he kissed too well to be strictly human.

'Here you are.' Jay put a full glass of wine down in front of her. He sat down beside her, put the bottle in its silver cooler and his own glass on the table and put his hand on hers. She pulled it away quickly.

'Don't be like that,' he said. 'It's good to see you again. I've missed you, Cat.'

As soon as he uttered his pet name for her again, the way he always said it, lingering over the 'C' and caressing it with his tongue, Kate knew she shouldn't have come here this evening. Her stomach was already full of butterflies. She tried to keep calm and looked at him squarely in the eye.

'What are you doing here, Jay?'

'I came to see you.' He lifted his glass and took a long sip of wine.

'And?'

'And I have a couple of business meetings in Dublin.'

'Why did you want to see me?'

He raised his eyebrows, his normally baby-smooth forehead wrinkling slightly. 'Why do you think, Cat?' His eyes bored into hers, dark pools of intensity, burning straight into her soul. She looked away quickly and stared at the table.

'I'll cut the bullshit and get straight to the point. I still love you, Cat. Surely you know that. We had something, something real, something . . .'

'Stop!' Kate insisted. He'd always had the gift of being able to throw himself full force into every conversation and completely catching her off guard. 'We can't go back, Jay. You know that.'

He was silent for a moment. 'But things have changed. I've changed.'

'No you haven't.'

'How would you know? You vanished off the face of the earth. Never even said goodbye. I was distraught.' He ran his finger up the stem of his glass. 'I had a terrible time trying to find you. But I'm here now and . . .'

'How did you find me exactly?' she asked.

'Reena at Sin. You asked her to forward on your last pay cheque. It took me months to get your new address out of her.'

Kate winced. She thought she could trust Reena but obviously she'd been wrong. Although knowing Jay, he'd woven Reena some elaborate tale to cajole the address out of her. He had a way of doing that as Kate knew only too well.

'You shouldn't have bothered.' She gulped back the last of her drink.

Jay poured her another glass of wine. She didn't protest – she sure as hell needed some Dutch courage right now.

'I haven't been in Ireland for nearly two years,' Jay said ignoring her last comment. 'I've missed it.'

She said nothing.

'Would you like to go for a walk?' he asked. 'It's a beautiful evening. We could climb Killiney Hill.'

'I'm not really dressed for it.' She nodded at the heels on her boots.

'Why don't we go somewhere a little more private then? I have a hot tub on my balcony – and it has fantastic views.'

Kate stared at him. Had he been listening to a word she was saying? She wanted nothing more to do with him – couldn't he get that into his thick skull. 'I don't think so,' she muttered. 'I'm going.' She stood up abruptly.

'Leaving without saying goodbye, Cat?' he asked smoothly. 'Again? Your manners are appalling.'

'Don't talk about my manners.' She'd had quite enough of his arrogant behaviour. 'Manners! I'll give you manners.' She picked up her glass and poured the contents over his head.

'Cat! What the hell!' He grabbed her wrist, his hair and jacket soaked. 'What's all that about? You left me, remember? Or have you conveniently forgotten?'

'Yes, I did. And you remember why of course?' her voice was raised to a dangerous level.

'Let's take this upstairs,' he said calmly. 'People are beginning to stare.' He brushed his wet hair back with his hand, tendrils beginning to cling around his flushed face. Even soaked in wine he still looked good and remained poised and composed. Typical, Kate thought.

'Let them.' She looked around. He was right, the two women at the table beside them were staring wide-eyed and the reception staff had also noticed the commotion. It would be just her luck if someone she knew was listening. She suddenly remembered that Trina's husband owned half the hotel and she was reluctant to have her personal life gossiped about all over Burnaby Village but she hadn't finished with Jay quite yet. 'OK then,' she decided quickly. 'Let's go. Your room, now! I have one or two things I want to say to you, Jay Sweetman, in private.'

He strode ahead of her towards the stairs, drips of wine still falling from his head, and powered up them at break-neck speed. Kate found it difficult to keep up in her heels and tight skirt but she was determined not to let him get the better of her. That was Jay, always too impatient to wait for the lift. On the third floor, he stopped outside a door and opened it with a card swipe. Kate was relieved; her heart was pounding in her chest both from the exertion and from the bubbling anger she felt.

Jay held the door for her. She walked in and looked around. It was a stunning room, dominated by a huge bed dressed in sparkling white linen, with a mountain of different sized velvet and satin cushions in shades of gold and beige, and a luxurious fur throw draped over the foot. The dusky evening light bounced off the white walls and Kate could see the large sunken hot tub on the balcony, steam rising in swirling snakes from the top of the water.

'Great view, isn't it?' Jay asked calmly. He gestured towards the balcony. 'I'm going outside for a smoke. Care to join me? Then you can lay into me.'

Kate looked at him incredulously. Was he serious? She followed him out wordlessly.

'You're some piece of work, Jay, you know that?'

He nodded but said nothing. He took a rolled cigarette out of his inside jacket pocket, lit it and inhaled deeply.

'What's that?' Kate asked, smelling the air suspiciously.

'Don't act the innocent.' He smiled at her. 'Would you like some?'

'No! You know I don't smoke.'

'Sometimes you do. At least the old Cat used to. Or have you become a cheerleader, *Kate*?'

She ignored him, folded her arms in front of her chest and stared out at Killiney Bay, stretching out in front of them as far as the eye could see. The hotel was practically on the beach and Kate could smell the tang of salt in the air. Jay handed her the joint. She looked at it for a few seconds before deciding what the hell? She took it from him without looking at him, and took an almighty drag, the thick smoke hitting the back of her throat, making her cough.

Jay patted her on the back. She felt the smoke fill her lungs and she immediately began to feel a little lightheaded.

'So what did you want to say to me?' Jay asked mildly.

She shook her head, took another calming drag, then began. 'I hate you. You fed me a long line of bullshit and like a fool I believed you. I left Boston because I had to. I wanted to have people I could trust around me, decent people. Honest people.'

'I never treated you badly, Cat, it's just . . .'

'It's just what?' she asked. 'You were married, Jay. Married! And you never told me. I had to find out the hard way.'

'I never meant to hurt you, Cat. My marriage was over, *is* over. Cindy and I were never meant to be but I couldn't leave her. Not just then. You never let me explain.'

'Explain what?' Kate demanded.

'Cindy was pregnant. She broke the news to me soon after I'd met you and I didn't know what to do. We'd been trying for kids for a few years but it looked as if it was never going to happen. I knew even before I met you that I didn't love her any more. I was on the verge of telling her about you and me, but after she broke the news about the baby – what could I do, Cat? It's what she'd been dreaming of all that time – a baby of her own. I couldn't leave her, not then. I'm not that big a bastard. But I loved you so much, not seeing you would have broken me. I had no choice, I had to keep Cindy and the baby a secret. Don't you see?'

Kate listened to him, staring at the sea and not knowing what to think. All kinds of things were racing through her mind.

She looked him in the eye. 'So, as I keep asking, what are you doing here, Jay? What about Cindy? What about your child?'

Jay stared at his hands. 'She lost the baby,' he whispered. 'Just after you left Boston. Things were difficult after that. Cindy was distraught. I couldn't help her get through it, although I did try. She moved back to Maine to be with her family and met up with her childhood sweetheart, a dentist. They fell in love and the rest is history. I lost my baby and I lost you, all in one fell swoop. I was completely alone.' He paused for a moment to compose himself and swallowed. 'As you can imagine I was devastated.'

Kate didn't know what to say. Whatever explanation she'd expected, it hadn't been this. She was bowled over by anger and something else, something bordering on sympathy. He'd made her feel sorry for him and she hated him for it. How dare he?

'Why are you telling me all this?' she demanded. 'Are you

under the impression that I still care about you, Jay? Because as you've probably realized by now, I don't.'

Jay looked at her. 'You've asked me what I'm doing here. Well, I could ask you the same question, Cat. If that's true, what are *you* doing here? Why did you come here?'

'That's easy, Jay!' Kate said, her voice raised to a dangerous level. 'I loved you, really loved you. When you asked me to marry you I was so happy. And then that Christmas Eve . . .' She took a deep breath. Tears threatened and she was damned if she was going to let him see her cry. Not like this. 'I came here this evening to tell you to keep away from me. Pure and simple. I never want to see you again, do you understand? I didn't think I could do it on the phone. Not properly.'

She looked at Jay and was shocked to see that he was crying. Unashamedly. Tears were pouring down his face and he wasn't even bothering to brush them away. 'I'm sorry.' He shook his head. 'I'm so sorry you had to find out the way you did, it was unforgivable. But Cat, don't give up on us, please. I beg you. I love you. I've missed you so much.'

'How can you say that?' She stubbed out the joint in a plant pot and sat on the edge of the hot tub as she was feeling decidedly strange – hot and light-headed. 'You asked me to marry you when you had a wife already! That's bigamy, Jay. What were you thinking? You don't love me. You don't know the meaning of the word. And you certainly never respected me, or your wife for that matter.'

'Yes, I do,' he whispered. 'I love you, honestly.' He put his head in his hands. 'But I've lost you, haven't I?'

'Yes. I'm afraid you have.'

'The one person in the whole world who means the most to me. How could I have been so stupid? If only I'd met you earlier, before, things would have been different.'

'But you didn't,' Kate pointed out. 'Did you? And then you lied to me.'

He shook his head. 'And now that I've given up everything to be with you, you don't want me. How ironic is that?'

'What did you just say?' Kate asked.

He looked her straight in the eye. 'I'm in the middle of a divorce settlement and I'm selling the apartment. I came over here to tell you. In a few weeks, I'll be a free man. My meetings in Dublin are about moving over to Ireland. I thought that we could buy a house, be together, get married as we'd planned. Maybe have a family. Start again. I know how much you want to be near your granny and I respect that, Cat. Family means everything and I thought we could start our own family here in Dublin.'

Kate felt as if she'd been hit by a train. How dare he bring Lily into this? And what the hell was he talking about? She hadn't contacted him since coming home and now this. Was he mad? 'What?' she cried. 'I don't understand. Is this some sort of sick joke?'

'It's not a joke. You heard me. I'm free to marry you now. And I'll move to Ireland to be with you.' There was a strange intensity in his eyes. 'So I'm asking you again, Cat – will you marry me?'

'Are you serious?' she asked furiously. 'After everything you've done, you still think I'll come running? Are you crazy? We haven't spoken for almost a year, did it not occur to you that I want nothing more to do with you? Well, Jay?'

'Don't be like that, Cat.'

'Like what? You're some piece of work.'

'Cat, I know you're scared and you have every right to be angry with me. But this time it's different, trust me. I'm a free man. No more deceit, I promise. Just you and me, we were made for each other, you know that. I love you.'

Kate stared at him. 'Don't,' she whispered. She put her hand into the hot tub and moved her fingers through the clear warm water. She should never have come here this evening, it was a mistake.

He walked over and sat down beside her. 'I know you still love me, Cat. I can see it in your eyes. And I love you so much. Why can't you trust me?'

Kate sighed deeply. She felt suddenly exhausted. 'Jay, stop! I can't do this again. It nearly broke me the last time, but I'm OK now. Please, just let it go.' She could feel her defences weaken. He always had this effect on her, Jay was her one big weakness. But she wasn't going to give in, not this time.

He put his arm around her shoulders but she immediately shrugged it off.

'Cat,' he said softly, brushing her hair back with his hand.

'Don't touch me!' she insisted tetchily.

He ignored her and continued stroking her hair. 'Let me take care of you. It could be like it was in Boston, the way it was before. We belong together. Do you remember what you used to call us, "soulmates"?'

'I remember,' she murmured, feeling her resistance starting to fade even more. The joint and the wine weren't helping. Why didn't I refuse it and stay clear-headed? she chastised herself. Stupid, stupid, Kate. Always so stupid. Her mind raced. Wouldn't it be easier just to give in to him? I think about him all the time, from the moment I wake up, to last thing at night. I thought I was over him, prayed I was over him, but who am I kidding? And what does it matter anyway? He's going to win in the end, she thought woozily, he always does. Or why not have one last night with him, get him out of my system? She laughed out loud.

'Why are you laughing, Cat?' he asked.

'I'm laughing at you,' Kate replied woozily. 'At us.'

He ran his hand along the side of her face. 'My beautiful Cat.' He kissed her on the cheek.

She felt her heart somersault. 'Don't,' she said softly.

He silenced her with a firm kiss on the lips.

'Jay!' she protested and pushed him away. But he wasn't giving up that easily.

'Let me love you, Cat,' he said. He cupped her head in his hand, and smiled at her. 'Don't fight it.'

The next time he leant forward to kiss her, Kate couldn't help herself. She could feel her lips respond to his kisses, and a delicious warmness spreading from her lips, down her neck and suffusing through her body.

He put both arms around her and held her tightly. 'Cat,' he whispered in between kisses, 'my lovely Cat.' She felt powerless to resist, overcome by her own pent-up emotions. At that precise moment she didn't care about anything other than Jay's hands and lips, both sending her whole being into divine ecstasy and leaving her wanting more. God, how she'd missed him. He was right – she'd never stopped loving him – no matter what he'd done, the lies he'd told, the fool he'd made of her. And she still wanted him – more than anything. But she certainly didn't trust him.

While still kissing her, he gently and expertly pulled her top over her shoulders and undid her bra.

'Jay,' she said nervously, crossing her arms over her full, naked breasts. 'We can't do this. Please . . .'

'Just getting into the hot tub, my sweet, that's all,' he promised her. 'It will relax you, then we can talk some more.' He slipped off his own jacket and shirt, took off his boots and socks, leant over and kissed her bare shoulder. She felt a delicious shiver down her spine. As if in a trance, she pulled off her boots, socks and skirt, feeling exposed in just her black lacy G-string. Although it was a warm evening, she still shivered.

'Everything off.' Jay grinned at her. 'That's cheating.'

'What about you?' she asked.

He shrugged his shoulders, dropped his trousers, stepped

out of them and whisked off his pristine white boxers. 'As naked as a jay-bird.' He laughed.

He moved towards her, lifted her up in his strong arms and dumped her unceremoniously into the tub.

'Jay!' she spluttered.

He laughed again and stepped in. 'Come here.'

She stayed where she was, the water suddenly sobering her up. 'Jay, this isn't right. I can't . . .'

He moved towards her and kneeled in front of her. Cupping her face in his hand once more he kissed her on the forehead, on both cheeks and then ever so gently on her lips. She could feel them tingle beneath his.

'You know you want me, Cat. Let yourself go. Just concentrate on how you feel right now. Let go of everything else. Just let go.' He put his hands on her shoulders and pressed her against the back of the hot tub. 'Lie very still,' he whispered. He pressed a button behind her and jets of warm water began to fill the tub, snaking upwards and hitting her back, her buttocks and the tops of her thighs. 'Now open your legs.'

'Jay!' she cried.

'Just humour me, it'll be worth it. Please?' He kissed her again, this time his tongue caressing and teasing her lips and tongue and making her gasp. Her heart was racing and her whole body felt warm and on tenterhooks. As he nuzzled her neck, he moved his hands down her body, removed her G string and spread her legs. Then he lifted her up slightly in the water and repositioned her over a firm, strong jet of water. Kate could feel the warm, forceful jets against her most sensitive area. She closed her eyes and gave in to the delicious sensations. Jay held both her hands in his and kissed her all over her face and neck, whispering into her ears.

'That's it, Cat,' he crooned. 'I knew you wanted me. Just like I want you.'

After a little while the jets began to feel stronger and

stronger, warmer and warmer, until Kate's body had taken its fill. Her back arched and then she flopped forwards as limp as a rag doll, completely sated.

She opened her eyes and Jay smiled at her. Without saying a word he turned to sit, lifted her body onto his knee, light in the warm water. She wrapped her legs around his torso, pulled him close and began to kiss him ravenously, clutching and massaging his muscular shoulders and back in her hands.

'Cat!' he said. 'You're back.' She'd always been the most passionate and exciting woman he'd ever been with.

'Yes, I am,' she murmured. 'Now, shut up and kiss me.' For old times sake, she thought as she kissed him passionately, there's no way I'm letting Jay back into my life, no way in high heaven.

'Cat, I have to go now, I have a meeting in town.'

Kate opened her eyes and rolled over. Jay was standing in front of her, fully dressed in his signature dark suit. He looked fantastic as usual.

She looked up at him, rubbing her eyes. They hadn't had much sleep the previous evening and she felt a wave of regret that she had let things escalate to such an extent. She should have left straight after the hot tub. In fact she should never have been in the hot tub in the first place. Or in the hotel for that matter. What was she doing? She should have been stronger – the joint and the fact that she hadn't had sex since the last time she'd been with him in Boston were some excuse, but Kate was ashamed of herself. 'What time is it?' she asked.

'Eight,' he said. 'Don't get up. I'm sorry I can't stay but you know how it is. I have a breakfast meeting in The Morrison Hotel at nine.'

'On a Sunday?' she asked.

'I know, tell me about it,' he said, ignoring her suspicious tone. 'But I'm only over for the next three days and you know what us Americans are like about breakfast meetings.'

'It's fine, I understand.'

'I'll see you this evening. Dinner here at eight? I'll book the restaurant.'

'I don't think so, Jay.'

'Please, Kate, it would mean a lot to me. I know what happened last night wasn't . . .'

'I don't really want to talk about it, Jay, OK? Just leave it.'

'Can I at least ring you later?'

She sighed. 'I suppose so.'

He pulled out his mobile and stood waiting, his fingers hovering over the keys.

She dictated her mobile number.

He smiled at her. 'I'll see you later.'

'Jay . . .'

He kissed his fingers and lay them gently on her lips. 'Just humour me,' he said with a grin.

Soon after he'd left, Kate fell into a deep dreamless sleep. When she woke she felt deliciously refreshed. Standing in the shower, powerful jets of hot water spiking her body, she thought about Jay and about the previous night. And much to her disgust she felt happy. Happy that he still loved her, happy that he still wanted her. Because she knew deep down that she'd never stopped loving him. Lies or no lies. What was she going to do?

'You're in good form,' Lily said as she and Kate walked down the steps towards Forty Foot bathing place in Sandycove that afternoon. 'You haven't stopped smiling all day. What's up?'

Kate shrugged her shoulders. 'Nothing in particular.' She looked at the greyish-blue water stretched out in front of them. 'I can't believe you've talked me into this.' She laughed. 'I must be mad.' There were several people of all ages in the water – from young children with their parents to groups of teenagers and older swimmers. Some were jumping and diving in and others were sitting on the edge of the steps, chatting amicably in bathing suits with towels draped around their shoulders. The sun was hiding behind thick cloud cover but the air was warm.

'You'll enjoy it once you're in,' Lily said. She led them towards the right where there were concrete seats. Several people nodded or said hello to Lily as she walked past. She sat down.

'How's the ankle today?' Kate asked, sitting down beside her.

'Not too bad. Healing nicely. I should be able to go naked in the next week or so.'

'Naked?' Kate asked with interest.

Lily smiled. 'Without a bandage.' She opened her bag and pulled out her togs and towel. 'Come along,' she said to Kate. 'Don't just sit there. Unless you intend to swim in your clothes.'

'Maybe I'll just watch,' Kate said uncertainly. 'It looks a bit cold and . . .'

'A bit of cold never hurt anyone,' Lily said dismissively. 'Now that you're here you may as well try it.'

'I suppose so.' Kate was still very reluctant. To tell the truth her legs were still a little shaky after last night. She tried not to smile as she thought of Jay but it was proving difficult. Jay had held her in his arms and promised her that everything would be all right. Last night Kate had blocked out the voices in her head telling her that she was mad to get involved with Jay again. That he was a liar and a cheat, and a danger to her mental health. That he'd hurt her again, just like he did the last time. Today, as the afternoon had progressed the voices were becoming dimmer and dimmer. In fact she almost couldn't hear them any more. And one more evening with him couldn't hurt, could it? He was hardly serious about moving to Dublin and, after all, he was single this time – if he was telling the truth about his ex-wife and the loss of his baby. But Kate was sure that even Jay wouldn't lie about something like that.

'Kate? What do you think?' Lily asked again.

'Sorry, I was miles away. What did you say?'

'Would you like to go out for dinner this evening? To Bistro Nova?'

'I have to meet an old friend, Gran. Maybe next weekend.'

'Who?' Lily cocked her head. 'Anyone I know.'

Kate shook her head. 'No.'

'It's not that nice Angus is it?' Lily persisted.

'No!' Kate laughed. 'What made you think that?'

'He's a decent young man. And he seems very keen on you. Whenever he calls he always asks all about you.'

'He still calls in?'

'Yes. This week Callum was with him. Lovely child – he's really growing into himself. Angus is working wonders with him.'

'Well, I'm certainly not dining with Angus.'

Lily smiled gently. 'You could do worse. He's a good lad. You could trust him, Kate. He wouldn't break your heart like that American. What was his name again?'

'Gran!' Kate wanted to change the subject right now. She didn't feel at all comfortable with the direction this conversation was heading. 'You know I don't like talking about him. Just drop it, OK? It's all in the past.'

Lily looked at Kate carefully. 'Is it?'

'Gran! Are we going swimming or not?' Kate pulled her togs and towel out of her bag and began to get undressed, using her towel to protect her modesty. She winced as her bare feet hit the concrete but decided it was her penance for last night's excesses. They'd polished off three bottles of champagne between them, although a large part of the third bottle hadn't been drunk – it had been liberally sprayed over each other and over the sheets.

'We most certainly are,' Lily said. As she changed, Lily thought about Kate. She had a strong feeling that the American was back in town. She noticed a couple of fresh scratches and bruises on her granddaughter's arms, back and inner thighs. She wasn't born yesterday. And if it was the American and she was under his spell again – it spelt trouble for Kate. Trouble with a capital 'T'.

Chapter 12

Paige

Paige lowered herself onto the sofa. The house was blissfully quiet and, if she was lucky, she could catch a few minutes shut-eye before Callum and Angus arrived home. She rested her head against the side cushions and let her weary eyelids droop closed. A little while later she was wakened by a loud bang in the hall. It was the front door being slammed shut.

'Callum!' she heard Angus scold. 'What did I say?'

'Close the door gently,' Callum replied.

'And was that gently?'

'No,' Callum admitted. 'Please don't tell Mum and Dad. I've been really good today, haven't I?'

'Yes. And I'll let you off this time. But run upstairs and hang your coat on the back of the door, there's a good lad. And change your trousers, those ones are filthy.'

Paige heard Callum scamper up the stairs. Angus walked into the living room.

'Sorry,' he said, noticing her stretched out on the sofa. 'Did we wake you?'

'That's OK.' She yawned. 'I have to get up anyway. More

doorstepping this evening, I'm afraid. Are you still all right for babysitting?'

Angus nodded. 'Fine.'

Paige sat up slowly, rubbing her eyes. 'Thanks. You've saved my life. Mum was supposed to do it but . . .'

'It's no trouble, honestly. I could do with the money to tell the truth.'

'So what did you both get up to today?' asked Paige.

'We went to Bray on the train. Walked along Bray head and then had a few dodgem rides at the amusement park. Callum got a bit muddy rock climbing so I sent him upstairs to change.'

'Callum was rock climbing?'

'Sure. Rock scrambling more like. He's pretty talented – he has great balance and he's very agile.'

Angus looked at Paige's face. She looked a little anxious.

'It's good to stretch him, Paige. Don't look so worried, I'd never take him anywhere that wasn't safe, honestly.'

'Sorry, I know you wouldn't. So what's the plan for tomorrow?'

'The waterfall at Powerscourt. Thought we could do some dam building in the stream. There's a great playground there too – should run off some of Callum's steam.'

Paige smiled. 'You're full of great ideas, Angus. We were lucky to find you. Callum hasn't been so easy to deal with for I don't know how long. We really appreciate it, you know that.'

'I know. And he's a good kid – lively but bright. Just needs some one on one attention.'

Paige sighed. 'I wish me and Tom had more time to spend with him, but with the election coming up, and Tom's work . . .'

'It's difficult to juggle everything but . . .' Angus began.

'But what?' asked Paige.

He shook his head. 'Nothing. Forget it.'

'Please. Tell me what you were going to say.'

Their conversation was interrupted by Tom. 'Hello, everyone. How's my favourite councillor? Ready to visit some mad constituents?' He strode into the room and kissed Paige on the top of her head.

'Are you all right, love?'

'Fine. Just resting.'

Callum came bounding down the stairs and threw his arms around his dad's waist. 'Hi, Dad!'

'Hi, Callum. Have you been good today?'

'Very. Angus promised to show me how to use the washing machine this evening. How to put in the cleaning stuff and everything. All by myself. So I can help Mummy with the washing.'

Tom looked at Angus. 'Is Callum serious?'

Angus nodded. 'He's really interested in machines. I'd be surprised if you didn't have a little engineer on your hands, mate.'

'Sounds good to me,' Paige said. 'They're never too young to learn. I'll show you how to put on the dishwasher next young man, if you're good.'

'Thanks, Mum!'

Tom glanced at his watch and sighed. 'We'd better get something to eat, Paige. We need to leave in twenty minutes or so. The Killen Estate is huge – it will take us all evening to cover it.'

'Molly and Kate offered to cover some of it with us. And Molly said that Alex and Harry have also offered to help.'

'Harry from the plant shop? The guy from your book club?'

Paige smiled. 'Gas, isn't it? We should send him round the houses with the big gardens. Maybe he'd hand out some free gardening tips – that might win us some brownie points.'

Tom smiled back. 'No kidding, he's really popular on the

radio. I wouldn't have thought he was the political type though.'

'Molly was saying it has more to do with Alex's influence than anything else. Kate worked some sort of magic there apparently. I'll tell you all about it when we're walking.'

'Sounds interesting.' He turned towards Angus. 'You know Kate, don't you?'

'Yes.' Angus blushed slightly. 'Yes, I do. Lovely girl. I haven't seen her for a while but I called into her granny's a few days ago with Callum. I hope that was all right.'

'Of course,' Paige said. 'Lily's a pet, isn't she? And Callum adores her.'

'I'm hungry,' Callum interrupted. 'What's for tea?'

'Callum!' Angus, Paige and Tom said in unison.

'Sorry,' Callum replied meekly.

'How about we make some toasted sandwiches for everyone?' Angus suggested kindly. 'And then your mum and dad can have a sit down for a few minutes.'

'OK,' Callum said. 'Can we use the whirr thing to grate the cheese?'

'The food processor?'

'Yes!' Callum said eagerly.

Angus looked at Paige, who nodded assent. 'I suppose so. But you'll have to help me wash all the bits afterwards, deal?'

'Deal.'

The doorbell rang shrilly.

'That must be Mum with Alfie,' Paige groaned. 'No rest for the wicked.'

'I'll get it!' Callum ran out of the kitchen, past his parents and towards the door.

Tom patted Paige's hand and smiled at her. 'And we're having another? Are we quite mad?'

She laughed. 'I think we just might be.'

*

'You take this side of the road and I'll take the far one,' said Tom. 'Try not to spend too much time with each person. We have a hell of a lot of houses to call on this evening.'

'Right,' Paige replied. 'I'll try to keep focused and not get sidetracked.' She looked at the number of the house in front of her and checked her clipboard. 'I'll start with the Kavanagh household.'

'Good luck. I'll wave at you from across the street.'

Paige walked up to the door and rang the bell. A thin, dark-haired girl of about nine answered the door.

'Yes?' She stared at Paige suspiciously. 'What are you selling?'

'Um, nothing. I'm Paige Brady, one of your local councillors. I'm looking for your support in the forthcoming general election.'

'I'll get Mam. Mam!' she shouted into the house.

'Coming.' A dark-haired woman appeared at the door from a doorway at the back of the hall. She looked at Paige. 'You're the one who's campaigning for childcare, aren't you?'

Paige nodded. 'That's right. Among other things.'

The woman said nothing.

'Do you have any questions for me?' Paige asked evenly.

Again nothing. The woman was completely tongue-tied.

'Anything at all?'

Her daughter nudged her mother. 'Ask her about a playground,' she hissed. 'Go on.'

'Oh, yeah. We need a playground in the estate. The kids have nowhere to play since the green was taken over by the council for new housing. I have five kids and the garden is tiny.'

Paige jotted down a note in her diary. 'I'll certainly check it out for you, Mrs Kavanagh. As they haven't started building yet, maybe some sort of arrangement can be made with the builders. Insurance is usually the big problem with play-grounds, but I'll do my best. I promise.'

'Fair enough.' The woman was about to close the door when Paige stopped her.

'I'll make some enquiries and I'll ring you back within the next two weeks about it. Maybe in the meantime you could talk to some of the other parents, and if they feel the same way you could start a petition.'

'Good idea.' The woman looked a little taken aback. 'You're really going to ring me?'

'Yes,' Paige promised. 'I really am.'

'I'll vote for you if you do.'

'Thank you,' Paige said. 'But you don't have to.'

'No, you're grand, I will. And I'll make sure my husband does too. He works nights but he votes before he comes home.'

'Thank you, Mrs Kavanagh.'

As Paige walked away from the house she put two discreet ticks beside 'Kavanagh' on the list. She knocked on the door of the next house as the bell seemed to be broken.

'Jeeze, would you give me a chance,' she heard a voice mutter in the hall. Through the safety glass she could see a tall shadowy figure. 'Who is it?' a male voice asked.

'Paige Brady, one of your local councillors.'

'What do you want?'

'Would you mind opening the door, Mr Cole? I could explain then.'

'How do you know my name?'

'I have a list of all the registered voters in the estate. Your name is on my list.'

'It's like fecking *Big Brother*,' he shouted at her. 'Go away.'

'If I could just . . .'

He opened the door and glared out at her. 'Did you not hear me? I said go away. I have nothing to say to the likes of you.'

'What do you mean – the likes of me?' Paige asked in

astonishment. 'I'm an Independent candidate, Mr Cole. I don't belong to any political party.'

'I'm not talking about politics. I'm talking about women!' he practically spat at her. 'No bloody good – the whole lot of you. Spawn of the devil. Go to hell!' he slammed the door in her face.

Paige stood on the doorstep for a moment in complete shock. He was obviously quite barmy. She shook herself, took a deep breath and crossed a heavy line with her pen through his name. 'Mad!' she wrote to the far right of the line.

The next few houses had more normal occupants thankfully – even if two of them were staunch People's Party supporters and had already promised their votes to Paddy Burns.

'How's it going, Paige?' Tom crossed the road to talk to her.

'Not too bad.' She looked down at her clipboard. 'Five definite yesses, two for Paddy, seven undecided and one mad man.' She told Tom about her experience with Mr Cole.

'Take care of yourself, Paige,' Tom said with concern when she'd finished. 'There are a lot of nutters out there. Maybe we should do the next set of houses together.'

'It would take twice as long that way,' Paige pointed out. 'I'll be fine, honestly.'

'If you're sure.'

She nodded. 'And how are the others getting on? Have you heard from them?'

'Harry rang to find out about your policy on the proposed "Educate Together" school for Burnaby. Oh, and Molly got several requests for a playground for the estate. Apparently they're building on the green where the kids used to play.'

'Interesting,' Paige said. 'I got the same request. There might be something I can do about that.'

He linked her arm. 'You're going to make a great Deputy, Paige. Do you know that? You really care, don't you?'

'Of course.' She widened her eyes. 'What are you suggesting, Tom? That not all politicians care?'

'Not at all.' he winked at her. 'Would I?'

'No comment,' she smiled. 'Now let's get back to work. We have a long evening ahead of us.'

Paige sat down at the kitchen table the following morning. Tom had already got Alfie and Callum up and was feeding Alfie in his highchair.

'Morning, Sleepyhead.' Tom smiled at her as she poured herself a bowl of cereal.

'Thanks for letting me sleep on,' she said. 'I just couldn't get out of bed this morning.'

'How are the feet?'

'Not the best,' she admitted. 'I could do with a foot rub. Any offers?'

'I'll do it,' said Callum, immediately jumping under the table and crawling to his mother's feet.

He took her left foot out of its slipper and held it in his small hand.

She winced. 'Callum, your hands are freezing. Warm them up, please.'

'How will I do that?' he asked from under the table.

'Blow on them and rub them together,' Tom suggested.

'OK.'

Tom looked over at Paige and smiled. She smiled back, put her chin in her hands and waited. A few minutes later she felt a slightly warmer hand on her foot.

'Is that better, Mummy?'

'Yes, thanks, Callum.'

'Now what do I do?'

'Rub your mum's foot gently but firmly from the heel to the toes,' said Tom. 'Don't tickle her, OK?'

'OK.'

Callum stroked his mother's foot as directed. Paige was surprised, he was actually quite good.

'How is it?' Tom whispered.

'Not bad,' she whispered back.

'Will I pull your toes a little, Mummy?' Callum popped his head up from under the table. 'Kind of stretch them. I saw a lady on *Richard and Judy* doing that to someone's toes.'

'*Richard and Judy*?' Paige asked. 'When were you watching that?'

'When Angus and me were making toasties last night. They were talking about modern art and Angus told me to watch and tell him what I thought of the pictures.'

'Really?' Tom asked. 'Did you like them?'

'I liked the one of the snail by the French guy. The one made from all the bits of paper. Angus said the man did it like that because he was sick and his fingers couldn't hold a paintbrush properly. I think his name was Massey something or other.'

'Matisse?' Paige asked.

'That's it,' Callum said. 'Matisse.'

Tom shook his head. 'Amazing,' he murmured. 'Our son the art critic.'

'We're going to go to the gallery next week,' Callum continued. 'Angus said there's lots of pictures of animals and a cool computer thing that explains the paintings. Have I been to the gallery before, Mum?'

'No, I don't think so. But you've been to the stuffed animal museum and it's right beside it.'

'Maybe Angus will bring me there too. How's your foot, Mummy?'

'Better,' Paige said truthfully, wiggling her toes. 'You're doing a great job.'

'I'll do your toes.' He popped back under and after pulling Paige's toes gently for a moment asked 'Will I do the other foot now?'

'Please.'

'And will this get me an extra star, do you think?'

'It just might.' Paige laughed.

While Tom dropped Alfie over to his mother's, Callum sat on the end of the double bed watching his mother dress. She was currently standing in her bra, pants and tights, trying to decide what to wear.

'When will Angus be here?' he asked impatiently.

'Soon,' Paige promised. She looked at her watch. 'Very soon, hopefully.' She was due in the *Now TV* studios at half past nine and it was now five past. With Dublin traffic the way it was, she'd be lucky to get there on time. She breathed a sigh of relief as the doorbell rang.

'I'll get it!' Callum ran out the door and thundered down the stairs.

'It's a man,' he shouted up to Paige. 'He says he's your taxi driver. What will I do?'

'Nothing!' Paige shouted back. 'I'll be down in a second.'

'I'm here too, Paige,' Angus shouted up. 'Sorry I'm late. I asked the driver to wait in the cab for two minutes. Is there anything I can do to help?'

'No, thanks. I'm almost ready.' She looked in the mirror again. 'Thank goodness Angus is here,' she murmured. She quickly pulled a black top out of her wardrobe, held it up against her body, decided it would be too much with her black suit and threw it down on the bed with the other tops. 'Why didn't I choose my outfit last night?' she asked herself as she rummaged through the tops hanging on the rail. 'Damn, damn, damn!'

She picked up her mobile and keyed in Molly's number.

'Hello, Paige?'

'Molly. You've got to help me. I'm on *Now AM* this morning and I'm running late. What the hell will I wear?'

Molly thought for a second. 'Is your dark pink trouser suit clean?'

'Yes, but is it not a bit . . .'

'Wear it with a plain white top and some heels. You don't want to wear black on the television – everyone does and it's instantly forgettable. You want people to sit up and remember you.'

'I suppose.'

'What time are you on at?'

'Ten.'

'I won't keep you, so. Are you taping it?'

'Yes.'

'Cool, I'll be over later to watch it this evening. Good luck.'

'Thanks.'

Paige pulled a plain white top over her head, and stepped into the dark pink trousers. She hoped Molly was right. Paige usually wore this suit at parties, not for work. Still, she didn't really have time to think about it. She threw on the pink jacket, wiggled her feet into her matching dark pink court shoes, grabbed her large brown leather bag, ran into the bathroom and swept her make up and hair brush into it.

'Mobile, wallet, keys,' she muttered as she collected them all together and threw them into the bag. She looked at herself in the mirror. Her cheeks were flushed from all the rushing around, matching her suit. But she had to admit she looked pretty good. Luckily her stomach was still reasonably trim, otherwise she'd never have been able to wear the closely fitting trousers.

She walked quickly down the stairs into the kitchen, her heels clicking noisily on the tiled floor.

'You look nice, Mummy,' Callum said, looking up from the table-top.

'Thanks.' She smiled at him and ruffled his hair. He was

playing a game of Junior Scrabble with Angus. 'Be good now. I'll see you later.'

'*Now TV* this morning, right?' Angus asked.

Paige nodded. 'Ten o'clock.'

'We'll be glued. Hope it goes well.'

'Thanks. I have to run. See you later.'

'We'll be watching you, Mummy!' Callum shouted as she closed the hall door behind her.

She opened the door of the taxi. 'Sorry to keep you.'

'Not at all, love,' he said, folding away his paper. 'We'd better get going though. We have to pick up Ms Higgins on the way.'

Paige's heart sank. That was all she needed. She pulled her bag onto her knee and rummaged through it to find her foundation and her powder compact. She didn't want Annette to see her looking like a dog's dinner. She carefully poured some creamy base onto her fingers and holding the small compact mirror in front of her face, she began to smooth it onto her skin, taking care to cover the pasty, greyish skin around her eyes. Heavens she looked tired. She pulled out her tube of liquid concealer, dotted it on the dark circles and patted it in gently. Then she finished with some powder, mascara and lip-gloss. She looked at herself critically. She'd do – thank goodness for make-up. She knew she'd be given the full treatment in the make-up room of the studio, but she didn't want to go in there looking like death warmed up. Now at least she looked slightly presentable.

'Feel better now?' the taxi man asked.

'Sorry?'

She caught the taxi man's eye in the rear-view mirror.

'A lot of my fares do their make-up in my cab.' He smiled kindly. 'I think it helps them to wake up. Must be important in your line of work too. First appearances and all that. You're standing in the next election, aren't you?'

'That's right.'

'My wife says she's voting for you. She likes your policies on childcare.'

'And what about you?' Paige asked. 'Who will you be voting for?'

'Haven't really decided yet. Paddy Burns has always been a decent sort. Says what he means. I like him.'

'Would you think about giving me your second preference?' Paige asked directly.

'Sorry?'

'Putting me in as number two.'

'Ah, I might. I'll certainly consider it.'

'Thanks.'

'But what would you be doing for the average working man like myself?'

'That's a good question,' Paige said, wishing she'd never started this conversation. 'A lot of my policies relate to childcare, funding for schools, improved services – water supply, upgrading roads . . .'

'Upgrading roads?' he asked. 'Like making the roads better to drive on?'

'Exactly. Some of them are in a right state and I think it's unacceptable. And something positive has to be done about traffic congestion.'

'I think you're dead right. Let me tell you a story about traffic congestion . . .' he began. Paige sat back against the seat to listen. She'd obviously hit the right note. After a ten minute monologue, he pulled up outside a red brick townhouse and beeped the horn.

'The wife's not that keen on your one Higgins,' he admitted. 'She thinks she's stuck in the Dark Ages. And she wouldn't be my choice either.'

Paige smiled to herself.

Annette opened the door and walked towards the taxi. She

was immaculately turned out in a sombre navy suit with a frilly white blouse underneath. Her hair was perfectly set in a static halo around her head.

She climbed into the front seat of the car. The taxi man said nothing. He knew this one all right – she was the old boot who had called taxi drivers 'lazy' last year. How could he forget? He pulled swiftly out into the Dublin traffic.

'How are you this morning, Paige?' Annette asked crisply, turning around to face her.

'Very good, thanks.'

'You look a little tired. Not sick are you?'

Paige could have hit her. 'No, I'm fine. Just canvassing until late last night, you know how it is.'

'Oh, I leave a lot of that door-to-door stuff to my supporters,' Annette said breezily. 'Too busy myself. Far more important things to be doing.'

The taxi man grunted.

'Sorry?' Annette asked him icily. 'Did you want to say something?'

'No,' he muttered. He didn't like this one's attitude at all. Snooty cow. Too busy to meet the common people – like himself.

'Who else is in the studio, do you know?' Paige asked Annette.

'Jackie and Hilda.' Hilda Murphy was another Independent. She wasn't expected to win a seat, but had appeared on many radio chat shows expounding her rather extreme right wing views. She could always be relied upon to get under the listeners' skin.

'Just the women?' Paige asked.

'Just the women.'

'Should be interesting.'

'Quite.'

Paige looked out the window as they approached Dundrum,

where the studio was based. As they pulled up outside the buildings, she rubbed her finger over her teeth to check for any stray lip-gloss and pulled the hairbrush through her hair.

Stepping out of the taxi, she thanked the driver.

'Not at all,' he said. 'And I'll give you my number two,' he promised her.

'Thanks,' she smiled.

'And I'll get your number one, I presume?' Annette asked arrogantly, listening in to their exchange.

'Are you joking?' he snorted. 'You're the one who was giving out about taxi drivers, last Christmas in the *Southside Sentinel*, remember?'

Annette's face reddened. 'That was a long time ago. Besides, you can't believe everything you read in the papers,' she said sniffily.

As they walked into the lobby, Paige could feel butterflies in her stomach.

'Those taxi drivers,' Annette muttered as they approached the large curved desk. 'Not to be trusted.'

Paige ignored her and smiled at the receptionist. 'Paige Brady and Annette Higgins. We're here for *Now AM*.'

'Please, take a seat. A researcher will be out to you in a moment.'

'Thanks.'

Fifteen minutes later, Paige was sitting in the brightly lit *Now AM* studio, her lips sticky with freshly applied gloss and her short dark hair neatly stuck down by a generous soaking of hairspray, which had nearly asphyxiated her in the small make-up room. Her eyelashes felt heavy with mascara and her hands were hot and clammy with nerves. This was the very first time she'd appeared on national television. Jackie leant over and squeezed her clasped hands.

'Don't worry,' she said kindly. 'Once we're on air you'll forget your stage fright. Anyway, a bit of adrenaline never hurt anyone. Better than being as cool as a cucumber and dead on the screen.' She gestured towards Annette pointedly who was sitting calmly on the sofa opposite them.

'Thanks,' Paige said gratefully.

A moment later the presenters – Frank Ryan and Dee Kelly arrived and sat down.

'How are you all this morning?' Frank asked, smiling at the four would-be politicians.

'Fine, thank you,' Hilda replied for them all. 'And I hope this is going to be a fair and equal debate. I know this station is very left-wing and I want to —'

'This station isn't left wing, Hilda,' Dee cut in. 'Or right wing for that matter. It has no political allegiances whatsoever.'

'And we're not really having a debate, Hilda,' Frank explained. 'This is breakfast television after all. We'll be keeping it light.'

Annette muttered something under her breath.

'Sorry, Annette?' Dee asked. 'I didn't quite catch that.'

Just then the female floor manager strode over. 'We'll be on air in two minutes, after the news headlines. Is everyone set?'

They all nodded.

'And everyone's been wired for sound?'

More nods.

'Good.'

'They're all very young in here,' Jackie whispered to Paige.

'And mostly women,' Paige replied. 'Great isn't it?'

'Absolutely!' Jackie said. 'Wish more companies were like that.'

Dee looked at Jackie and put her finger to her lips.

'Oops, better be quiet,' Jackie said to Paige.

Paige stared at the coffee table in front of her which held two bright yellow *Now AM* coffee cups. The weather had just come on and she knew their slot was next. She raised her head and tried to stay calm. Her stomach was doing somersaults and she could feel a dull flush spreading down her neck and face. Hopefully the heavy television make-up would stop it being too noticeable. Damn, her cheeks would clash with her suit. She should have worn black – it would have been safer. What was she thinking of?

'And welcome back.' Dee smiled at the camera. 'We are very privileged to have the four women who are standing for election in the Dun Laoghaire Rathdown constituency in the forthcoming general elections – Deputy Jackie Pile of the New Alliance, Councillor Annette Higgins of the Democrats, Ms Hilda Murphy, an Independent, and Councillor Paige Brady who's also an Independent. Welcome to you all.'

'Thank you.' They all smiled and nodded.

'Let's start with Deputy Pile,' Frank said. 'Deputy, you've held a seat in the government for the past ten years, is that correct?'

'Eleven years,' she corrected him.

'Eleven years,' he continued. 'And in that time you've seen a lot of changes, especially for women. Could you tell us a little about your work on the Women's Health Bill and what that will mean for the women of Ireland?'

'Certainly, Frank,' Jackie said.

As Jackie explained the proposed bill, Paige's mind drifted. She watched Jackie as she talked and wondered if she'd ever be so poised and so confident in front of the cameras.

'And Councillor Brady, many of your policies involve women's issues of various sorts. Am I correct?'

Paige took a deep breath and looked at Frank. 'That's right, Frank. Ireland is way behind most other European countries when it comes to the provision of childcare facilities. If I win a seat, I intend to lobby the government to provide affordable childcare for all those women who wish to work. I also intend to lobby for funding of the "Educate Together" schools. I think it is important, especially in this day and age, that our children are educated with other children of different religions and different cultural backgrounds.'

'That would be a complete waste of money!' Hilda Murphy interrupted. 'We already have a fine network of primary schools in this country who all could do with extra funding. It would be foolish to start funding new schools.'

'But most of the traditional schools are run by the churches,' Paige pointed out calmly. 'Both Catholic and Protestant. I'm talking about a different sort of education – where all children can be taught together, no matter what religion they are.'

'What's wrong with religion?' Hilda spluttered. 'Do you have something against it, Councillor Brady?'

'Of course not,' Paige said, sounding calmer than she felt. 'But just because something has always been done in a certain way, it doesn't mean it's right.'

'Quite.' Jackie nodded. 'I think Councillor Brady has a good point. There is certainly a place for "Educate Together" schools in Ireland and her ideas on childcare are spot on.'

'Two opposing candidates agreeing,' Dee said. 'How unusual.'

'Well I don't agree at all,' Annette said firmly. 'I think Councillor Brady should stop trying to encourage mothers back into the workforce. A lot of Ireland's current social problems stem from mothers going out to work.'

'That's ridiculous!' Paige said. 'There are no approved statistics to back that up. How can you say that?'

'Look at your own son, Callum,' Annette looked Paige straight in the eye. 'I hear he has a lot of behavioural problems. Am I right?'

'That's unfair!' Paige raised her voice. 'There's nothing wrong with my son, how dare you?'

'Ladies,' Frank interrupted. 'I think this is all getting a little personal. Let's concentrate on your polices, not on your private lives. Oops, it's time for a break. We'll be back in a few minutes with more of this election special on *Now AM*. Don't go away now.'

As soon as Paige heard the ads come on she glared at Annette.

'How could you, Annette?' she asked. 'How could you drag my son into this? There's nothing wrong with him.'

'That's not what my contact at his crèche said. She told me all about his terrible record at Little Orchard. Calling the teachers names and running riot. Oh, I know all about Callum's behaviour, Paige, believe me.'

Paige was dumbstruck.

'That's all a bit below the belt,' Jackie said. 'Let's keep this clean. I have no time for dirty politics and I don't wish to be associated with them.'

'I'd have to agree.' Hilda nodded.

Annette pulled herself up bolt upright on the sofa. 'All's fair in politics, ladies.'

'If you don't mind me saying, I don't think it shows you in very good light, Annette.' Dee joined in.

'Really?' Annette raised her eyebrows and said nothing further.

As soon as they were back on air, Paige's heart sank.

'Now we have a viewer on the line who'd like to ask Councillor Brady a question.' Frank looked at Paige. 'Will you take the question, Councillor?'

'Um, I suppose so,' said Paige nervously.

'Hello, my name is Peggy and I wanted to ask the Councillor if she's having a baby. I saw her in Holles Street last week and I was just wondering.'

'Um, well . . .' Paige took a deep breath. Tom has told her to be honest and open if this ever came up, so that was how she was going to play it. 'Yes, yes I am. I haven't made the news public yet because . . .'

'I think it's a disgrace,' Annette piped up. 'Mothers should be at home with their children, not gadding about the place looking for votes. She's putting the baby's life in danger.'

'Yes, yes,' Hilda agreed. 'Women of Ireland, listen to me. I'd like to talk about the rights of the unborn child. In my day . . .'

Paige felt like crying. First the comments about Callum, now this. It was most unfair.

'I'd like to say something.' Jackie leant forward, interrupting Hilda's rant. 'We are not here to discuss Councillor Brady's personal life. What's Irish politics coming to if that's all we think the voters are interested in? Let's not insult their intelligence. Let's talk about what really matters – how we can get this country back on its feet. How we can improve the standard of life for the large percentage of the country who are living below the poverty line. How we can educate our children better. These are the things that matter, not the Councillor's personal life.'

'Well said, Deputy,' Frank said. 'And now we have another call. This time for Councillor Higgins. And I believe it's someone you know, Councillor.'

'Hello, Mum,' came a voice down the line. 'It's Chantal, your daughter. Remember me?'

'Um, yes, hello Chantal. And what are you doing, dear? Why are you ringing?' Annette's face began to pale and her eyes flicked around the studio nervously, before settling on her knees.

'I've been watching the programme and I'm ashamed of you, Mum.'

'Chantal!' Annette said. 'What are you saying?' She looked at Frank. 'I think you should cut her off. This is not my daughter. This is an impostor.'

'Mum, it is me. You know it is. And how can you be such a hypocrite? You worked the whole way through both your pregnancies and we never saw you when we were small because you were always at some meeting or other. Dad brought us up. And how could you say that about that woman's little boy? What kind of person have you become? We don't even talk, Mum. You haven't said one word to me in over two years, maybe you'd like to tell everyone why.'

'Um, yes, well, I've learnt from my mistakes, haven't I? And I don't think they'd be interested at all in our little stand-off. Goodbye, Chantal.' Annette looked visibly shaken.

'But —' Chantal said.

Frank stepped in, worried about the legal implications of what she might say. 'I'm afraid we'll have to leave it there as it's time for a commercial break. Thank you, ladies, for coming into the studio this morning. It's been most, um, interesting.'

'Join us after the break for the amazing story of Gina, the surrogate chimp mother.' Dee smiled broadly at the camera.

'Talk about getting personal,' Jackie whispered to Paige as soon as the ads had come on. 'I've never known an election like it. Remember Miles laying into Mark on the radio the other week?'

Paige nodded. 'How could I forget?'

Frank looked at all the candidates. 'That was quite something. I don't know what to say really.'

Annette stood up. 'You should never have accepted my daughter's call. It was most unprofessional of you. I'm, I'm . . .' With that she stormed out of the studio.

Hilda, looking almost as pale as Annette for some reason, followed her out.

'Phew!' Dee said. 'I wouldn't be surprised if some of that ends up on this evening's news. Explosive stuff. What do you think her daughter was going to say?'

'Who knows?' Frank shrugged his shoulders.

'Thank you for having us on,' Jackie said. 'Sorry it all got a little heated.'

'Not to worry, it's good for the ratings,' Frank said.

I'm sure it is, Paige thought to herself. But it's not good for my nerves.

Chapter 13

Molly

'Are you expecting someone?' Paige asked Molly who's eyes kept flitting towards the door of Coffee Heaven.

Molly looked at her. 'No, why?'

'You keep staring at the door, that's all.'

'Oh, do I?' Molly drained the last of her coffee. 'Would you like another cup? I'm getting one.'

'Please. And a chocolate muffin if there are any left.'

Molly pushed her chair out and made her way to the counter. Alex flew past her with two heaped plates of salad and a steaming bowl of soup.

'Back in a second,' she told Molly. Alex placed the food in front of its owners and bustled back to Molly. She blew a stray piece of hair out of her flushed face.

'Busy?' Molly smiled.

'No kidding. I hate lunchtime. Especially when it's raining and everyone wants to eat in. What can I do for you?'

'Two coffees and a chocolate muffin.'

'No problem.' Alex glanced over at the door, looked back at Molly and grinned.

'What?' Molly asked.

'Nothing. I'll bring your coffees over in a few minutes.'

'Thanks.' When Molly turned around, she understood why Alex had been smiling. Sam was now sitting at the table with Paige. Alex had it in her head that there was something going on between herself and Sam. Try as she may, Alex just wouldn't believe Molly when she explained that they just enjoyed having lunch together, that was all, nothing more.

'Oh, yeah?' Alex had asked. 'Every day? And coffee too?'

'We just get on well as friends, that's all!' Molly had protested. But it hadn't done any good. Alex still had the two of them pegged as the next Rhett and Scarlet. She just wouldn't listen.

'Hi, Sam,' Molly said as she sat down beside him. 'I thought you were on a day off today.'

'I am, but I got these this morning and I knew you'd want to see them straight away. But I don't have long I'm afraid, I have to collect Hugh soon.' He patted the large brown envelope which was resting on the table.

'What's that?' Molly asked.

'The designs for the Book Festival,' Paige said excitedly.

'Have you already seen them?' Molly asked a little miffed.

'No, we were waiting for you, of course,' Paige said. 'Will you show us now, Sam?'

'Certainly.' He opened the envelope and pulled out three sheets of A4 paper. 'My friend, Dora did three different designs. She said there's no problem changing anything you're not happy with – the colour, lettering, lay-out, that kind of thing.' He spread the three sheets on the table. 'What do you think?'

Paige looked at Molly. Molly was smiling broadly.

'They're great!' Paige said. 'Just what we wanted. Bright and fun, with a romance theme. Which one do you like best, Molly?'

Molly studied the three designs carefully. They were all very different. One was an old fashioned design in the shape of a heart with a lacy border and filled with what looked liked pink and red pick and mix sweets. The next was more modern –

another heart, this time filled with tiny books, all spilling over each other. The third was very striking – little pink cherubs flying up and down the page, their hair highlighted in gold, each holding a book.

She pointed at the cherubs. 'That one.'

'My choice too.' Paige nodded.

'What do you think, Sam?'

'I'm not really your target market, am I?' he said. 'But I'd have to agree with you. The cherubs are really eye catching. And the lettering and the slogan in the cloud is a great idea.'

Paige read it aloud. 'The Burnaby Book Festival in association with Happily Ever After Bookshop. Bringing Books Alive.'

'And best of all,' Sam said, 'Dora showed the designs to her boss in the design house who turned out to be a dedicated reader. Her boss offered to sponsor the printing of the posters and flyers for the event if we bung some free tickets her way and put their company's name on all our promotional material. And Ink Press offered to print the programmes for free as part-sponsorship.'

'Really?' Molly asked. 'That's excellent news. Thanks, Sam.' She felt like kissing him but thought against it.

'How can we thank you?' Paige said. 'That's the best news I've had all day. No, all week. You're an angel.'

'A cherub?' Molly laughed.

'Exactly.' Paige smiled. 'A cherub.'

After Sam had left, Molly and Paige finished up their coffee.

'He's so nice,' Paige commented.

'Sam?'

'Yes, Sam.'

Molly looked at her and smiled. 'I know. He's lovely, isn't he?'

Paige leaned closer towards her. 'Has anything happened that you haven't told me about?'

Molly shrugged her shoulders. 'Unfortunately not. But we're

going out to the cinema on Saturday, so you never know. Fingers crossed.'

'How did that happen? Did he ask you out again?'

'Not exactly. He mentioned there was a film that he'd like to see and I said I'd love to see it too but that no one would ever go to subtitled films with me. Not even you.'

'Liar!' Paige snorted.

Molly laughed. 'I had to think of something.'

'What are you going to see?'

'A new French film. It's supposed to be really romantic.'

Paige raised her eyebrows. 'Did he choose it?'

Molly nodded.

'Sure, you're away on a hack, girl, in that case. I look forward to hearing all about it.'

On Saturday night, Molly started getting ready early. She wanted to look her best but she didn't want to look like she'd put too much effort into it. If only men knew how long it took to apply 'natural looking' make-up, they'd be shocked. She'd fake tanned her body earlier and had spent most of the last hour walking around the house half-naked, worried that it would streak if she got dressed. Luckily, Kate was out for the night, though she'd been very coy about where she was going. All that she'd divulge was that she was meeting an old friend and wouldn't be back until the following afternoon. Molly was intrigued but try as she might, she couldn't get any more information out of Kate.

'I'll tell you when I can.' Kate had kissed her on the cheek, her eyes dancing with happiness.

'It's good to see you in such flying form,' Molly had conceded. 'But could you not just tell me his name, please?'

Kate had smiled and shaken her head. 'You'll be the first to know, I promise. OK?'

Molly smelt her arms. They still reeked – the sweet acidic

smell of flesh turning golden brown she hoped. She'd wait for a little while longer, then have a shower. She studied her legs carefully, turning them this way and that. They seemed a little browner all right, but it was hard to tell really.

Striding down the stairs two hours later in a flowery summer skirt, dainty slip-on sandals which flattered her feet, a white vest top and her fitted denim jacket she felt great. She'd piled her hair on top of her head, allowing a few tendrils to falls down on either side of her face to soften the effect, and her make-up was deceptively natural.

She waited for Sam in the living room. He'd kindly offered to collect her at home. Molly was delighted with this – it made it seem like a real date, not just two friends going to the cinema together. After spending a few minutes watching television, the doorbell rang.

Molly jumped up and went into the hall to answer it. As soon as she opened the front door she instantly regretted not checking through the tiny security peep-hole first.

'Hello, Molly,' said Denis. 'Can I come in?'

'What are you doing here?' she demanded, still holding the door half open.

'That's no way to greet an old friend.'

'Denis, I'm sorry but I'm on my way out. I'll ring you tomorrow, how about that? We can talk.'

'Why not now?' he asked persistently. 'I miss you, Molly. I can't get you out of my head. I'm so sorry things turned out the way they did. But if you'll only . . .'

'Denis, please stop.' Just then a car pulled up outside the gate. 'I think this may be my lift. It's better if you . . .'

Sam walked in the gate. Molly waved at him. 'I'll be with you in a second,' she said loudly. 'Denis,' she said, turning her attention back to him, 'you have to go now.'

'I see,' he stared at her, and she felt as if his cool, blue eyes could cut her in half, they were that sharp. 'Am I that easily replaced?'

'It's not like that,' Molly said. 'Sam is a friend from work. We're going to the cinema together, that's all.'

'Why are you so dressed up then? You never wore skirts when we were together.'

'Yes I did, you're being ridiculous,' Molly said. 'Now I have to go, I'm sorry.' She closed the door in his face, not knowing what else to do, grabbed her bag and waited a few seconds. Denis was still there when she opened the door again. 'I'll walk you to the car,' he offered.

She said nothing. There was no point in arguing with him, it would only make things worse. As they approached the car, Sam stepped out and held the passenger door open for Molly.

'Quite the gentleman,' Denis observed. He held out his hand formally. 'I'm Denis, I don't think we've been introduced.'

'Sam,' Sam said without betraying any emotion at all. 'Nice to meet you. And that's my son, Hugh, in the back of the car.'

Molly looked into the car in surprise. 'Oh,' she said waving at Hugh who waved back in reply. 'I didn't realize he was coming with us.'

'A family outing,' Denis said, an unpleasant look on his face. 'How sweet.'

'We'd better get going, Molly,' Sam said glancing at his watch. 'Nice to have met you, Denis.'

'And you.'

As the car drove away, Molly breathed a sigh of relief.

'Sorry about all that,' she said.

'Not to worry.' He lowered his voice. 'And I'm sorry I had to bring Hugh. His mum was called away on a voice-over job unexpectedly. Some ad she'd recorded got accidentally wiped by the studio and they have to re-record the whole thing. And his grandparents are away. I did try Dad but he's busy.'

'It's OK. But he won't be able for the subtitles, will he? And the film's not really suitable anyway.'

'Um, no. I was hoping we could go to the new Harrison Ford action film instead. Would that be OK? I know I should have rung you first but we were in such a rush and . . .'

'Sam, that's all right, honestly. We can go to the French film next week or something. I'm quite partial to Harrison Ford to tell the truth.' She turned around. 'Do you like Harrison Ford, Hugh?'

'Is he the old guy who plays Indiana Jones and who was in *Star Wars*?'

'Yes, that's right. I wouldn't have thought of him as old though.'

'He's got white hair, like Grampa.'

'But with a much younger girlfriend,' Sam added.

'Grampa has a girlfriend?' Hugh asked with interest.

'No! Harrison Ford.' Sam laughed. 'You have to watch what you say with Hugh,' he whispered to Molly.

'So I see,' she whispered back.

'What are you saying?' Hugh asked.

'Just talking about the film.'

After dropping Hugh back to his mum's, Sam drove back to Burnaby along the coast road.

'How's the writing going?' Sam said. 'Or am I allowed to ask?'

'You are this week.' She smiled. 'Because it's actually going all right, fingers crossed. I've almost finished the story I've been working on. I just have to get the ending right. I always find endings so difficult.'

'They are kind of important, aren't they?' He smiled back. 'But I'm glad it's going well.'

'Thanks.' Molly looked out of the window. Sam was very easy company. She never felt she had to fill the silences with him.

If they didn't feel like talking they didn't seem to need to. 'Look at that moon,' she said staring up. 'Isn't it amazing? So bright.'

'We should take a walk along the beach,' Sam suggested. 'It's such a beautiful evening.'

Molly's heart leapt. 'Yes, why don't we?'

Sam drove down the slip road to the beach and parked the car. 'You won't be too cold, will you?' he asked as they stepped out of the car. 'I have a jacket in the back if you like.'

'That would be great. Thanks.' He handed her a dark blue fleece and she put it on. The sleeves were much too long for her so she rolled them back. 'I look huge in this,' she laughed.

'No you don't, it suits you.' He locked the car and took her hand. The steady heat of his skin against hers made her feel safe and warm.

They crunched down the shingle towards the edge of the sea and walked along the firmer, damp sand. The waves were lapping at the shore, with gentle wet swishes, and the moon illuminated the water, giving it an otherworldly, unearthly glow.

'About Denis,' Sam began nervously. 'I'm not causing any problems there am I?'

'Not at all. He's having problems accepting that it's over between us, that's all. We were together for ten years on and off and I guess he figured we'd end up together eventually. But it's definitely over.'

'If there's anything I can do – talk to him for you, keep out of the way . . .'

'There isn't, but thanks for offering. He's harmless, just annoying. Anyway, let's not talk about him this evening. Did Hugh enjoy the film do you think?'

'Yes. He was a bit freaked out by the giant spiders, I think. He was gripping my hand so hard I thought he'd break my fingers at one stage, but he seemed to like the rest of it. Thank you for being so nice to him.'

'He's easy to be nice to,' Molly replied. 'He's a good kid.'

'He really took to you. He's not always that chatty with people. Actually he's usually quite shy.'

'We were talking about books mainly. He's quite the little reader, isn't he?'

Sam nodded. 'He started reading at four and he's been flying through them ever since. He's reading *The Hobbit* at the moment.'

'So he told me. That's quite some child you have, Sam.'

'I know, I'm very lucky.' He lifted her hand towards his face and kissed it softly. 'But thank you. And you're quite something too, you know.'

Molly didn't know what to say. She could feel her face redden but hoped Sam wouldn't notice in the half-light. 'Um, thanks.'

'You're not used to compliments, are you?' he asked.

'I suppose not.'

He stopped walking. 'Come here,' he said quietly.

Molly's heart leapt. His eyes were warm and kind and they drew her in, encouraging her to move towards him. He put his arms around her, touched her cheek tenderly, then ran his arms up and down hers, warming her through the fleece. 'You're cold,' he said. 'We should go back to the car.'

'I'm OK,' she protested, not wanting him to stop. 'Really.'

He smiled at her. 'Really?' he cocked an eyebrow.

I could drown in those eyes, she thought, staring into them. His blonde curls were falling over his face and he looked edible. Kiss me, she urged. Go on, kiss me.

He stroked her face again and ran his fingers over her lips. Molly thought her legs would melt from under her. She couldn't take much more of this. She could feel her breath becoming faster, and her heart skipped a beat as he planted a tiny kiss on the edge of her mouth. That was it – she'd had enough. She put one hand behind his head and pulled his lips towards hers. They kissed gently at first, exploring each other's mouths, growing more passionate with each lingering lip caress. Molly pressed her body against Sam's and felt him respond instantly, tighten ing his grip on her. They kissed for what seemed like hours before drawing away and holding each other, Sam's firm hand cupping the hollow in Molly's lower back.

'You really are something,' he whispered into her ear.

'You're not so bad yourself,' she whispered back.

They walked back towards the car, lingering to have one final look at the beach before driving away.

'My house is just up the road,' Sam said as they pulled out o the side road. 'Would you like some coffee or something?'

Or something, Molly felt like saying but she refrained herself 'Sure,' she said instead. 'That would be nice.'

As soon as they stepped into his house she knew he wasn' like other men. For one thing, from what she'd seen of the house so far it was incredibly tidy, except for an area of toys to one side of the living room, and shelves and shelves of slightly disorgan ized-looking books of all shapes and sizes. Children's books, Molly decided on closer inspection.

'Sorry, that's Hugh's play area,' Sam explained. 'It's always a bit of a mess.'

'It's a lovely room,' Molly said. She unzipped the fleece, pulled it off and handed it to him. He hung it on the back of the sofa. 'Sit down,' he said. 'I'll put the kettle on. Or would you like a glass of wine? I've a bottle of white open in the fridge.'

'I'd love a glass of wine.' She smiled up at him. 'Thanks.'

After he'd left the room, Molly had a good look around. The black fireplace had an intricate boarder of patterned tiles to either side of it and above the mantelpiece was a most unusual mirror, framed in what looked like driftwood. On either side of the fireplace were white wooden built-in shelving units, filled with all manner of objects – small wooden sculptures, a silver tankard, silver candlesticks, framed photographs of Sam and Hugh, some ornamental glass paperweights and a small block of wood decorated with painted-on primroses and forget-me-nots.

Sam came back in holding two generous glasses of wine. He handed one to her, put his own down on the wooden coffee table between the two cream sofas and sat down on his hunkers in front of the fireplace. He began to build a fire, placing firelighters on the grate and putting pieces of wood and small logs around them.

'I love real fires,' he said as he worked. 'They're a bit of a pain, but worth it.'

'We don't have one in our house, and I do miss it,' Molly said. 'We have a gas one in the living room but it's not really the same, is it?'

'It's a good substitute.' Sam stood up, brushed his hands on his jeans and picked up his wine.

'I love your mirror,' Molly said as he sat down beside her. 'Where did you get it?'

'I made it,' he admitted. 'I made most of the furniture in the house.'

'Really?' Molly said in surprise. 'Even the coffee table and the shelves?'

'Sure.' He nodded. 'They were quite easy. Hugh's bed was the hardest. He had a very fixed idea of what he wanted.'

'What did he want?'

'Harry Potter's castle.' Sam grinned. 'Complete with spiral staircase and turrets.'

'No! And you made it? Hogwarts isn't it?'

'That's right. I did, my impression of it anyway.'

'Can I see?'

'OK.' Sam stood up and held out his hand for her. He led her down the narrow hallway, opened a door and flicked on the light.

'Sorry it's such a mess.'

Molly stepped over the Lego pieces and walked towards

Hugh's bed. It was one of the most incredible things she'd eve
seen. It reached from the floor right up to the ceiling, two dar
green towers with purple turrets and a bed perched in betweer
Below the bed was a desk and a wardrobe, and against the fa
wall was a wooden puppet theatre, the puppets in an adjacen
open wooden box.

'It's amazing!' Molly said. 'I've never seen anything like it
Are the towers hollow?'

Sam nodded. 'One has steps and the other has a spiral slide
Hugh loves sliding down it in his pyjamas when he's supposec
to be in bed.'

'I'm not surprised, what fun. And you made all this?'

Sam nodded and shrugged his shoulders modestly. 'It took
me a while, but yes, yes I did. I'm quite good with my hands.'

'I'm impressed.'

'Thanks. Now let's go back into the sitting room. Knowing
my luck, the fire will have gone out.'

They sat back down on the sofa and Sam put his arm arounc
Molly's shoulders. The fire hadn't gone out, as Sam had fearec
and they sat in companionable silence gazing into it and sipping
their wine.

'Thank you for a lovely evening,' Sam said after a while.

'My pleasure.'

He leaned over and kissed her again, trailing his hand dowr
her cheek and caressing her neck and shoulder.

Sam's right, he really is good with his hands, Molly though
as they kissed. *Damn good.*

The following afternoon, Kate still hadn't arrived home. Molly
tried her mobile but she wasn't answering. Molly had also rung
Paige this morning, bursting to tell someone all about her
evening with Sam, but Tom had answered the phone and said
Paige was writing up some report for the County Council meeting on Monday evening and had asked not to be disturbed.

Molly toyed with the idea of visiting her parents – but why spoil a great weekend she decided. She would have loved to have spent the day with Sam but he was working in the book-shop. They'd have to start getting their rotas in synch, she thought. Thinking about Sam she smiled. She could still feel his lips against hers. He had dropped her home at four in the morn-ing, after waking her up. She'd fallen asleep on the sofa, head resting on his shoulder, lulled to sleep by the warmth of the fire, the wine and the heady passion of the evening. He'd offered her a bed, but she wasn't quite sure what he'd meant by this and had opted to go home instead. She hated waking up in someone else's bed after spending the night unexpectedly, last night's make-up sunk into her pores, yesterday's stale clothes, no clean underwear. She never felt at ease in someone else's shower either – if it worked that was – she liked things to be clean and had had horrible experiences of standing on the slimy, hair rid-den shower tray in Denis's house. She always ended up cleaning out that particular shower before daring to step into it. Yes, boys' bathrooms could be a downright health hazard, although Sam's, from what she'd seen of it, was remarkably clean, except for some toothpaste residue on the sink and the mirror which were only minor hygiene crimes in her book.

After having a shower in her own, ultra-clean bathroom and getting dressed in her most comfortable grey tracksuit bottoms and an off-white fleece, she walked to Burnaby Village to pick up a bagel and the papers.

Sitting down at the kitchen table half an hour later, she started flicking through the *Sunday Times* supplements while munching on her cream cheese and salmon filled bagel, washed down with some freshly squeezed orange juice. After she'd finished eating she looked at her watch – three o'clock. Still a large part of the day to fill. She thought about catching the afternoon showing of the French film at the Cineplex in Dun Laoghaire, but she had promised to go with Sam. She could always see it twice she supposed – no, that would be stupid. She knew damn well what she really should be doing and going to the cinema would just be a delaying tactic. She stood up, cleared away her plate and stacked the papers neatly on the table. She poured herself a glass of water, and made her way out of the kitchen, up the stairs and into her bedroom. She stared at her desk for a few seconds before sitting down.

As she turned on her computer and waited for it to boot up, she thought of Sam again. Sam walking on the beach, the wind in his curly hair, Sam paddling in the sea, Sam on his hunkers, building a fire, Sam's lips on hers ... If she wanted to get any work done, she'd really have to stop. Think of your story, she admonished herself, not Sam.

She clicked on Microsoft Word for Windows and opened the short story she was working on – 'The Fisherman'. She read over what she'd written, changing words or sentences here or there and trying to get into the story. It was almost finished but she was having problems with the ending. For almost an hour she tried to think of some sort of logical and fitting conclusion, but ultimately failed once again.

She sighed deeply, began to bite at the skin around her thumb before picking up a pen and fiddling with that instead. 'Come on,' she told herself. 'Think of something.' She was about to turn off the computer in disgust when an image came into her mind, an image of a laughing, smiling man. Who is he? She asked herself. What does he look like? He's called Arthur, she decided. Arthur, um, Arthur, what? She tapped her teeth with a pen. Arthur Logan, Art for short. And he's tall, with messy black hair and dark blue eyes. Well built. She began to form his character in her mind. He works in the local library but he's also a painter, no a sculptor. A girl joins the library staff, Lisa. She's extremely quiet and no one can get much out of her, except for Art. They become friends and gradually he finds out why she's so quiet – her daughter died over a year ago and she hasn't even started to deal with it. Art helps her to come to terms with her loss and they fall in love.

Molly smiled to herself as she typed her notes frantically onto the keyboard. The story seemed to flow out of her from nowhere. The story of a woman and her road to recovery through the love of a good man. Sure, it was sentimental and maybe a little over optimistic, but hell, why not? People needed a bit of light relief and a little hope. Life was hard enough without having to read depressing stories all the time. There was definitely a place for some optimism in the world. Not to mention love.

She jotted down some more notes on her characters and her plot and then began to launch into the opening paragraph.

Molly read over what she'd written and smiled. Not a bad opening if I say so myself, she thought. She continued typing, drawing out Lisa and Art's story. By the time she looked up again, she was astonished to find it was almost seven o'clock in the evening. Over the last while she'd found writing a bit of a chore to tell the truth, but today the story had just told itself. Once she'd started, the characters had simply taken over, telling their own tale. Something that hadn't happened to Molly for a long, long time. She stretched her arms over her head and yawned. She saved her work and shut down the computer, happy and content. As she collected up her laundry – one of her usual Sunday chores – her mobile rang. She checked the screen – it was the shop. Sam was closing up today – she hoped there wasn't any problem.

'Hello?' she answered tentatively.

'Molly,' Sam said warmly. 'It's me, Sam.'

Her heart leapt. 'Hi, Sam.' She sat down on the bed, all thoughts of laundry forgotten.

'Sorry I didn't ring earlier,' he said, 'but it was really busy in here. You know how it gets on a Sunday.'

'Don't I just. Are you only closing up now?'

'Yes, unfortunately. Listen, what are you up to? Can I call over?'

'Sure, that would be nice. Would you like something to eat? I was just about to start making something.'

'If it's not too much trouble.'

'No trouble at all.'

'I've been thinking about you all day,' Sam said.

'I've been thinking about you too,' Molly admitted, surprising herself. 'See you in a while.'

'Would you like me to bring anything?' he asked.

'Just yourself.' She smiled as she put down the phone. Sam was delightfully straightforward and didn't seem to believe in playing games which was refreshing after Denis, who seemed to think that their relationship was a protracted game of Snakes and Ladders with a little Poker and Cluedo thrown in for good measure.

Chapter 14

Kate

On Sunday morning Kate woke up and opened her eyes. Feeling the unusually firm mattress beneath she remembered where she was – in the Presidential Suite of the Killiney Arms with Jay. Jay was lying beside her, on his back fast asleep and snoring gently. The previous week had gone by in a blur and she couldn't think when she'd last felt so happy. After a remarkably civilized dinner the evening after the hot tub incident – where she and Jay had talked and talked all night, ending up in bed together again – Kate had decided to take each day as it came and, after some initial reservations, concluded that maybe Jay had changed. She'd decided to give him the benefit of the doubt and to enjoy the short time they had together. Because once he left, it was over for good. They would just have this one last week, that was all she promised herself. Just one last, very final fling. To get him out of her system.

Jay had stayed in Dublin for four extra days just to be with her, and he'd already asked her to spend Christmas with him in Boston, which she had no intention of doing, of course. Christmas. As Kate lay in bed, thinking about Jay her mind drifted back to last Christmas Eve, a day she'd tried to block from her memory and had almost succeeded.

They'd intended to spend last Christmas together but on Christmas Eve things had taken an unexpected turn. On that fateful day, Kate had finished up work early and joined her colleagues for drinks in the local watering hole. She'd tried ringing Jay several times as they were due to meet that evening, but his mobile had been turned off. Up until then they'd always met at her house, and looking back on it of course it seemed strange to Kate, but caught up in the romance of their relationship, it was one of many signs she hadn't spotted until it was too late. Her place was nearer where they both worked and it suited Kate well – it meant she didn't have to remember to bring fresh underwear and toiletries in her bag every time they met. But that particular evening, tired of waiting for him and sensing that something was up, after some dithering she made up her mind to call into Jay's apartment. It was a good half an hour's walk away from the bar but it was a fresh, crisp night and she decided she could do with the fresh air after the hectic day she'd had and the smoky atmosphere of the bar. She said goodbye to her colleagues and left, looking forward to seeing Jay.

Kate approached his apartment, her cheeks tingling from the cold and pressed his bell. No answer. She tried his mobile again – it was still off. Where the hell was he? A tall dark-haired woman approached the communal door and opened it with a key. She looked at Kate for a moment as if deciding whether she was dangerous or not.

'Are you all right?' the woman asked Kate.

Kate nodded. 'Visiting a friend. He's late.'

'Wait inside, it's a chilly night.' The woman held the door open for Kate.

'Thanks,' Kate said gratefully. She was beginning to get cold.

Kate walked inside, took a seat on the red couch in the lobby and watched as the woman's back disappeared into the lift. All around her was deathly quiet. She pulled out her mobile and tried Jay's number again. Nothing. She sat there for a few minutes turning over the mobile in her hands, hoping it would ring at any moment, not knowing quite what to do if it didn't. Since meeting Jay she hadn't seen much of her other American friends and now she was beginning to regret it. She could always go back to the bar, she supposed, but she knew she wouldn't.

Just then, she heard a car pull up and voices outside the door. She looked out. A dark-coated man was stepping out of a yellow cab. It was Jay! Kate jumped to her feet to get the door for him as his arms were laden down with multi-coloured shopping bags. So that's where he was – shopping – of course! She was relieved and delighted to see him. As he approached the door he saw her and his face froze. He stared at her and then looked behind him at the elegant blonde woman, also holding several shopping bags, who was leaning over, paying the cab driver. Kate's heart sank. Who was the woman and why was Jay frowning like that?

Kate opened the door and held it for him as he walked through into the lobby.

'Jay?' she said quietly. 'Are you all right?'

'No.' He looked at her intensely. 'I'll explain everything later, I promise. Right now please don't say anything to . . . um . . .' He gestured towards the woman. 'Stay right here and I'll be down in a moment, OK?'

Kate was too shocked to answer.

'Sit down,' he commanded. 'I'll only be a moment.'

Kate was so dumbfounded and so confused, she did as he requested. Surely there was some rational explanation for all this – an out of town college friend back for the day, a long lost sister . . . but why hadn't he introduced them? Kate feared the worst. Still, she just sat there, silent as stone.

As Jay and the woman walked past her, Kate watched them like a hawk.

'I'm exhausted,' the woman said in a strong Boston accent. 'I could fall asleep on my feet, honey. No more shopping, ever, OK?' She put her head on his shoulder as they stood and waited for the lift.

'Sure,' Jay replied. They both stood with their backs to Kate and it suddenly all fell into place. He had another girlfriend. He'd replaced his little 'Cat' with a more glamorous model. How could she have been so stupid? Jay was much too good for her, she'd known that all along.

She strained her ears, trying to hear what Jay and the woman were saying, but to no avail. She watched them both step into the lift and as they turned towards her, Kate looked at Jay's face. It was betraying no emotion whatsoever. Kate felt a sharp stabbing in her chest. How could he ignore her like that? What was she doing sitting there, watching him when he had another woman by her side? She stood up abruptly, determined to say something. But it was too late, the lift doors closed just as she was galvanized into action. She waited for the lift to come back down, determined to follow him up to his apartment. But as soon as the doors opened again she realized to her surprise that Jay was still in the lift.

As he stepped out she began to flood him with questions.

'Where were you, Jay? I've been trying to ring you all afternoon. Who was that woman? Why is she in your apartment? What's happening? You were supposed to —'

'Cat,' he interrupted. 'There's a perfectly good explanation for all of this. Let's take a walk.' He put his arm around her but she shrugged it off.

'No! I want to see your apartment. Do you realize in all this time that I've never been inside it? You've always had some excuse or other for me not to see it.'

'You're being silly,' he said smoothly. 'Let's go outside and get some air. Have you been drinking?'

'No, not really. Stop trying to twist things. Jay!' He was walking towards the door.

He turned around and smiled at her. 'Come on,' he said. 'Join me.'

She followed him, not knowing what else to do.

'Who's the woman?' she asked again as soon as they were outside. 'Tell me now, Jay, I need to know.'

Jay said nothing for a few minutes, just kept walking towards the end of the block. Kate walked beside him.

'Jay?'

He stopped and looked at her, his eyes dark and restless, unable to focus on hers for more that a brief moment. Kate knew immediately that it was over. He was smiling but his eyes were cold. 'I don't know how to tell you this . . .' he began. He put his hands on her shoulders and rested them there. Kate could feel them pressing down on her, like a dead weight. 'She's my wife.'

'What?' Kate could feel the blood draining from her face and she began to feel quite faint. She shrugged off his hands and took a step back from him. 'I don't understand. You never told me you were married.'

'It never really came up.'

'What do you mean?' she said again. 'Never came up. You're joking, right?'

Jay shook his head. 'I never meant to fall in love with you, Cat. But I did. And it's changed everything. My marriage was rocky before I met you but now it's practically over. But I can't leave yet, Cindy's . . .'

'Cindy?' Kate demanded sharply. 'Is that her name? Cindy?' She snorted. 'As in Sindy doll?'

'You're overreacting, Kate. As I told you, my marriage is over, we haven't been close for a long time. But this week she . . .'

'I don't want to hear it,' Kate said icily. 'You're married and your wife is waiting for you. It's Christmas Eve, why wouldn't she be waiting for you? God knows where you've told her you've gone, you lying bastard. So go on, go back to her.' Kate turned to walk away from him but he held on to her upper arm tightly.

'Cat, please let me explain.'

'No! Get your hands off me!'

'There's no need to be like that. If you'll just listen . . .'

'I've been listening to your lies for quite long enough. I don't want to hear another thing from you.'

'I understand that you're annoyed with me but . . .'

'Annoyed? Annoyed doesn't even begin to explain how I feel. I'm so angry, Jay I could hit you.'

He looked at her in alarm.

'Don't worry, it's not really my style. I just want you to leave me alone.' She turned away from him again and began to walk quickly down the street, not looking back.

'Cat! I can explain,' he shouted after her. 'Cat! Don't leave like this.'

But she ignored him. As soon as she'd turned the corner of the block she stopped and put her back against the cold grey concrete wall of an anonymous apartment block. Only then did she allow herself to cry in huge, heaving sobs, engulfing her whole body.

Kate sat alone in her Boston apartment that evening, staring at the large package wrapped in jaunty Christmas paper still sitting under the small artificial tree. It was Jay's carefully chosen present – a simple but hideously expensive black cashmere scarf. Jay had rung both her mobile and her apartment several times but she'd eventually turned the mobile off and taken the other phone off the hook. Her eyes were red and swollen from crying and her heart felt torn to shreds, so torn that it would never heal. She wanted to go home. Back to Dublin, back to people she could trust.

'Cat?' Jay murmured and her thoughts were dragged back to the present.

'Hi, Sleepyhead,' she said, trying to forget what she'd been thinking about. 'I was just about to have a shower.'

'I'll order breakfast and then I might join you.' He grinned. 'What would you like?'

'I'm pretty hungry,' she admitted. 'I fancy some scrambled eggs with salmon and some toast. And coffee, lots of it.'

'Your wish is my command.'

As she stood under the shower she heard Jay talking on the phone but she couldn't quite make out what he was saying. Must be ordering breakfast she mused, putting her head under the hot jets of water and letting it stream down her face and hair. God, she loved hotel power showers. Moments later Jay joined her, his tanned naked skin a sharp contrast to her paler body.

'Hello, stranger.' She smiled through the steam.

He moved towards her, a bar of soap in his hands. 'You look a little dirty,' he smiled back. 'Let me fix that.' He lathered up the soap and began to smooth it all over her shoulders and her upper arms, moving slowly downwards towards her chest and stomach.

'Turn around,' he said, 'I want to do your back.'

She did as requested and gasped as he ran his soapy hands up and down her legs, lingering deliciously on the tops of her thighs. He stood closely behind her, so close that she could feel his breath on the back of her wet neck.

'You're amazing,' he whispered. 'Do you know that?' He began to caress her stomach, moving his hands in tantalisingly slow circles on her skin. She began to turn around but he stopped her with his strong arms and pressed her gently against the white tiled wall in front of them. She put her hands against the tiles, feeling the damp coolness on her palms. He held her firmly, one hand circling her waist and resting on her stomach, the other free to caress her most intimate area. She surrendered to the sensation, her heart beating faster and faster and her legs almost buckling weakly beneath her.

He took his hands away, turned her around smoothly and entered her, making her gasp in surprise.

'Did I hurt you?' he asked tenderly, wiping water away from her face.

'No, don't stop,' she whispered back.

'I won't,' he promised. He was as good as his word.

'That was amazing,' Jay said as they tucked into breakfast, wrapped in the hotel's fluffy towelling bathrobes. 'I can't believe I have to go this evening.'

'Then don't,' Kate suggested. 'Stay another night.'

'You know I can't.' He took her hand and stroked it gently. 'I have to get back to Boston – I have a big meeting with one of the sports wear companies tomorrow. I'm sorry. But I'll be over as soon as I can.'

'Jay!'

'I'm coming back to see you, you know I am. I keep telling you . . .'

Kate groaned. 'And I keep telling *you*, this has to stop. I want to get on with my life and you're just confusing things.'

'Really?' he asked with a smile. 'You didn't seem too confused in the shower, Cat.'

Kate blushed and ignored him. 'I'm serious, Jay, OK. I don't want to see you again after this week. We've both had our fun and now it's back to real life.'

'Is that really what you want, Cat?'

'Yes,' she said definitely. More definitely than she felt. 'It is.'

'I'm going to ring you every day,' he said. 'You'll change your mind, I know you will. I know you.'

'No, you know the old Kate, not the new one.'

'Kate?' He laughed. 'I guess my little kitty Cat has all grown up then?'

'Don't make fun of me!'

'I'm not. You're just being so serious.'

'Life is serious, Jay, for some of us at least.'

'It doesn't have to be.' He leant over and kissed her on the cheek. 'Life with me would be a whole lot of fun, Cat, sorry, Kate. You'll miss out.'

'I'm willing to take that risk. I don't just want fun, Jay, I want something more.'

'Like what?'

Kate looked at him and then looked away. She wasn't quite sure. But being with Jay didn't feel safe, she could never really relax around him. 'I can't explain,' she said finally. 'Just something.'

'OK, I'm not going to push you. Let's just enjoy the remainder of the time we have together.' He kissed her hand. 'What will we do this afternoon? I have a few presents to buy, but apart from that, I'm all yours.'

'Presents? For who?'

'My secretary, she's expecting another baby in a few weeks. And I might even get you one if you're good.'

'Oh, I'll be good,' Kate said seductively, glad that he'd stopped grilling her about the future.

'Really?'

Kate nodded. 'Oh, yes.'

The following day, Kate was lying in her own bed again, in the doldrums. Jay was gone, her whole life had been turned upside down and being on her own again was a huge anticlimax. The previous week seemed like a distant dream. Had she done the right thing by letting him go? Her head said yes, but her heart . . . she was trying not to think about it.

Molly had been sweet to her this morning, bringing her a cup of tea and toast in bed. Kate still hadn't told Molly about Jay and she was sorely tempted to, but she didn't want to talk about it in her current fragile state. She missed him so much and they'd only been apart for mere hours. How was she going to cope? She began to think. What if she'd made a huge mistake? What if he had changed? He wouldn't be single for long, not a man like Jay. In a few months' time he'd probably be married again, or engaged at the very least. She had to know for sure. Maybe seeing him on his home territory in Boston would help her decide. She'd never met his family for goodness sake, or his friends for that matter. If he really was serious about loving her, surely he'd introduce her to them all – it stood to reason. Then she'd know for sure. Kate sat up. That was it. That was how she'd know if Jay really had changed. He'd bring her to visit his family. Ha! She'd book a flight for the very next weekend and surprise him. She began to feel instantly better.

'I saw you yesterday,' Lily said, looking at Kate carefully.

'Oh, really? Where?'

'On the main street, you were coming out of Presents of Mind.'

'Oh.' Kate knew that if Lily had seen her she'd also seen Jay, as they were holding hands at the time. He'd just bought a gorgeous silver picture frame for his secretary and a wooden toy for her little son. They should have been more careful – shopped in Dun Laoghaire or Bray – she should have known someone would spot them in Burnaby.

'The man with you – was that Jay?' Lily asked calmly.

Kate sighed. There was no point lying to her granny and besides, she was dying to tell someone. 'Yes.'

'You looked very happy,' Lily observed. 'Is he still here?'

Kate shook her head. 'No, he left yesterday.'

'Missing him?'

'Yes.' Kate stared out of the window. It was the early evening and they were sitting in her granny's kitchen, drinking tea.

Lily said nothing.

'Before you say anything, he's changed, Gran, he's not the man he used to be. He's so much more caring, more considerate . . .'

Lily snorted. She couldn't help herself. 'Is he still married?'

'Don't be like that, Gran, please.'

'Well, is he?'

'He's almost divorced. His wife moved back to Maine, she's with someone else, a dentist actually. Does that satisfy you?'

Lily again said nothing. She wondered why her perfectly reasonable granddaughter was so blinded by love.

'Gran! Don't look at me like that.'

Lily sighed. 'Be careful, Kate. I don't want to see you hurt again, that's all.'

Kate smiled. 'I won't be, Gran. I'll make sure he's serious this time, before I get involved.'

Lily felt uneasy. Why would a man who had just come out of a bad marriage want to get involved again so quickly? It didn't make sense. Lily had a bad feeling about all this, a very bad feeling. But she held her tongue. Kate had to find her own way in the world. She wasn't a little girl any more and Lily couldn't protect her.

'Say something, Gran, please.'

Lily reached out her hand and placed it on Kate's. 'I just want you to be happy.'

'I am, very happy.'

'Good.'

'In fact, I'm going over to Boston next weekend to see him. It's pretty quiet in the shop and I'm going to ask Trina and Cathy for a few days off and cancel my dummy dates.' Kate seemed so elated that Lily didn't have the heart to caution her.

'I hope you have a lovely time, dear,' she said instead. 'Take care of yourself. Boston's a big place.'

'Gran,' Kate smiled, 'I lived there, remember? Don't worry, I'll be fine.'

I hope so, Lily thought. God I hope so.

*

'I'm worried about Kate,' Lily said to Angus the following morning, handing him a mug of tea. They'd become firm friends in the last few weeks, and this week Angus had taken it upon himself, with Callum's 'help', to repaint her hall in a glowing yellow, replacing the rather drab white which had become decidedly off-white over time. He'd decided this was a good project for his young ward to undertake and a nice thing to do for Lily, who he'd become terribly fond of.

Callum was delighted with this of course, he'd never been allowed near the walls when his own house was being painted, in fact he'd been banned from the house outright when he'd trod in the paint tray and walked red footprints all over the beige carpet on the stairs. But today he had his own small paintbrush and mini-roller and he was dressed in an old dress shirt of his dad's, an old pair of ripped-at-the-knee jeans and a baseball cap, turned backwards to protect his hair. He was merrily and carefully applying the primrose yellow paint to the edges of the walls and the corners, taking extreme pains to 'stay within the lines' as Angus called it – on the walls and not on the skirting boards.

Angus sat down on the stairs and gingerly took a sip of the steaming hot tea. 'Why?' he asked. He glanced over at Callum to check he wasn't listening.

Lily sat down beside him.

'It's a long story,' she said. 'But I think she's involved with a less than honest man.'

Angus raised his eyebrows. 'I didn't know Kate was seeing anyone.'

'She wasn't until the last week or so, from what I can make out. Then this man reappeared, a man from her past. But I'm afraid his intentions are not honourable.'

Angus tried not to smile at her old-fashioned phraseology. 'Is there anything you can do about it?' he asked kindly.

'I don't think so. Just be there to pick up the pieces I suppose.'

She told a little about Jay and what had happened on the previous Christmas Eve in Boston.

'Poor Kate,' Angus said when she'd finished. 'Maybe it will all work out this time, you never know. Maybe he has left his wife.'

'Maybe,' Lily agreed. She didn't believe it for one second. 'Oh, I'm sorry, I shouldn't have burdened you with all this. And I know you like Kate, I can see it in your eyes. What was I thinking of?'

Angus shrugged his shoulders. 'That's all right. Anyway, I don't think she's ready for someone like me,' he said evenly.

'Someone decent you mean?' Lily said astutely.

Angus shrugged his shoulders.

'Maybe not quite yet,' she agreed. She looked over at Callum who was still stuck into his painting. 'So, have you any spare rollers? I thought I might give you a hand.'

'Lily, you're supposed to be resting.' Angus smiled.

'Resting, pah!' Lily swatted the air. 'You're only young once. Besides, I've my old worn-out tracksuit on, you don't think I'm dressed like this for nothing, do you?'

He laughed and handed her a fresh roller. 'OK, but take it easy. You'll have to share a paint tray with Callum though.'

'That's just fine. And how was your date last weekend? The ball?'

'How did you know . . .?'

She tapped the side of her nose. 'I know everything that happens in Burnaby.'

'It was terrible to tell the truth. Patricia is stunning looking but she's . . . how will I put this? Difficult.'

'Selfish and demanding?' Lily asked. 'I remember her as a small child – always terribly spoilt. I'm afraid she hasn't really changed.'

'It was an experience anyway,' Angus said. 'The meal was

nice and I had fun dancing with some of the other book trade people. They're a nice gang.'

'Were Molly or Anita there?'

'No, but the guy who owns Happily Ever After was – Milo. He was sitting at our table. Interesting man.'

'Yes, so I hear.' She rolled her brush in Callum's paint tray. 'That's great, Callum,' she said, studying the work he'd already done.

'I'm being real careful, like Angus said,' Callum said.

'Yes you are, poppet,' she ruffled his hair affectionately. 'You're doing great. I'll tell your mum and dad what a good little painter you are the next time I see them.'

After painting a large section of one side of the hall, Lily took a break and made more tea for her and Angus. He followed her into the kitchen to collect it, glad of the break. His shoulders had started to ache from lifting his arms over his head to reach the high spots.

'Would you like me to talk to Kate?' he asked as Lily put fresh tea bags in their mugs.

She looked over. 'About Jay?' she asked.

'Yes.'

Lily thought for a second. Her first reaction was to say no, but something made her change her mind. Maybe this gentle man would be able to get through to Kate. It couldn't do any harm – could it?

'You could try,' she said finally. 'I'm not sure if she'd listen to you though.'

'You never know.'

Kate opened the door early that evening and was surprised to find Angus standing there smiling at her.

'Hi, Kate, have you got a second?'

'Um, yes, sure. Come in.' She stepped back from the door, let him in and closed it behind them. 'Would you like some coffee?'

'Thanks.' He followed her into the kitchen and sat down at the table.

She flicked on the kettle and stood leaning against the counter. 'So, what can I do for you? More dating advice? I hear you've been seeing Patricia. How's it going?'

'I went to a work do with her,' he said evenly. 'That's all. We didn't really click to be honest.'

Kate felt strangely relieved. 'Oh, I see.'

'I'll get straight to the point, will I?'

She nodded, her curiosity piqued.

'Your granny is worried about you and the American guy. She told me a little about last Christmas. She doesn't want to see you get hurt again you see and —'

'The American guy, as you so delightfully call him, is called Jay,' Kate interrupted. 'And what right do you have to come here and lecture me about my choice in men? So Gran put you up to this. I can't believe she told you about me and Jay.'

'No. It was my idea. I just thought you might want to talk about it, that's all. Sometimes it's easier to talk to someone on the outside . . .'

Kate looked at him incredulously. 'I know damn well what you're doing here and it won't work. Coming over here all kind and caring. Trying to muscle in on another man's territory. You're just as bad as the rest of them. And I thought you were different.'

Angus was taken aback. That thought hadn't even entered his mind. He really did just want to help. 'No, Kate, you've got this all wrong. Lily was worried about you, that's all. I thought I could help. I'm sorry if . . . maybe I should leave. But I'm always there if you need to talk, remember that. I'm there for you no matter what.'

'Isn't that a boy-band song?' she asked disparagingly. 'I can look after myself thank you very much. I'm going over to see Jay this weekend and . . .'

Angus raised his eyebrows.

'Don't look at me like that,' she continued. 'You'll see, you'll both see. Now I think it's best if you do leave.'

Angus stood up. 'I'm sorry if I upset you. I didn't mean to question your judgement.'

'Yes, well, that's not what it sounded like to me. And you can tell Gran to keep my private life just that in future – private.'

After she showed Angus out, Kate leant her back against the door. She was furious with both Angus and Lily. She grabbed the phone from the hall-stand and dialled Jay's mobile number. His mobile was turned off. Typical! She dialled her gran's number instead but cut it off after two rings. She was too annoyed to speak to her. Still, at least she only had three more days until she saw Jay again. Three long, lonely days.

Chapter 15

Paige

'And this morning I'd like to welcome Finbar White, Chief Political Correspondent of the *Irish News* for our election special,' Wella announced on Chat FM.

'Shush, Callum!' Paige hissed. He was singing 'Twinkle, Twinkle Star' to Alfie at full volume.

'Sorry, Mummy. I'll go up and get dressed, will I?'

'Yes, good lad,' she said distractedly, trying to listen to the radio.

Tom turned the volume up, sat back down beside Alfie and began to spoon mashed apple and banana into his eagerly waiting mouth. Finbar White was the single most important and most highly respected political commentator in Ireland and his opinion counted. With only one week to go until the election, what he said this morning could sway the public's vote. Paige hadn't been able to sleep last night and was on tenterhooks this morning, waiting for his verdict on her possible election result.

'We'll start with the North Dublin constituency. Finbar, who's in the running there?'

Paige turned towards Tom. 'This is agony,' she said.

'Don't take what he says as gospel,' Tom advised. 'He's only one person. You have thousands of supporters out there, you know that, Paige.'

'I know, but so many people listen to him.'

Tom nodded. 'But at least he tends to be fair. And he has no bias towards the male candidates like some of the commentators. Or towards the People's Party.'

'I suppose so.' Paige chewed the skin around her thumb and listened again.

'And Dublin West, Finbar?' Wella asked.

The doorbell rang. Paige stood up quickly. 'I'll get it.'

Angus was on the doorstep.

'Hi, Angus,' she said.

'Are you all right, Paige? You look a little anxious.'

'I'm listening to Finbar White on the radio. He's predicting the outcome of the elections.'

'Phew!' Angus said. 'Are you sure you should be listening?'

'I don't know. At least this way I'll hear it from the horse's mouth. It'll be all over the evening papers later and I'd prefer to know the worst before that.'

'Or the best,' Angus pointed out. 'He might say that you're bound to get a seat.'

'He might,' Paige said doubtfully.

'I'll help with doorstepping this week,' he offered. 'And I could galvanize a few others too.'

'That would be great,' Paige said. 'Thanks. It all helps.'

'Paige!' Tom shouted from the kitchen. 'Dublin South after the ads.'

'Coming!'

'Welcome back,' Wella said. 'And this morning I have Finbar White from the *Irish News* with me, making his election predictions.'

'Get on with it,' Paige muttered under her breath.

'Dublin South next,' Wella said. 'Now that's an interesting one, isn't it Finbar?'

'Yes, certainly, Wella. Some changes could well be seen there.'

Tom looked over at Paige. 'Breathe,' he told her.

She smiled at him.

'There are four seats to be filled there and the first two, in my opinion, will certainly go to Deputy Paddy Burns, the People's Party stalwart and a very popular man. And Deputy Jackie Pile, another popular name with the punters. They have both been good, solid representatives and I can't see them losing their seats.'

'And Miles McGreinna?'

'I think Deputy McGreinna has had his day to be frank. From what I've observed over the last year, he's lost a lot of his support. I can't see him being re-elected.'

'And of course, Deputy Ryan, of the Green Party is retiring so he's not standing this time around,' Wella observed.

'Quite. I'd be surprised if Mark Tine didn't win the Green seat back. A bright young man, and a popular politician. The Green Party could do very well in this election if they play their cards right.'

'So that leaves McGreinna's seat,' Wella pointed out. 'Who's in the running?'

'Well there's Annette Higgins of the New Democrats, already a well-known Councillor in Burnaby. She is, of course, Ray Higgins' daughter. She has a good chance on the back of that alone.'

'Even after her father's tax scandal?'

'Yes, he's still fondly regarded by most, even after the revelations in the last tribunal.'

'And Rex Reximus?'

'Ah, good old Rex is back again, on his usual "Legalize Cannabis" ticket,' Finbar said. 'I don't think so, Wella. Do you?'

'I'm sure you're right,' she laughed warmly. 'And Hilda Murphy?'

'Again, she's not a runner. Too right wing for most people's taste.'

Paige looked at Tom. 'They've forgotten me.'

'No, they haven't,' he said reassuringly. 'Keep listening.'

'And finally, Paige Brady,' said Wella. 'Another Burnaby Councillor, running as an Independent. What do you make of her chances?'

'Reasonably good,' Finbar replied. 'She's very popular on the ground, she's not afraid to voice her opinion and she will certainly be in line for a good chunk of the liberal vote. I'd say she has a good chance of taking the fourth seat. It's between her and Annette Higgins.'

'Interesting. Now let's move out of Dublin and on to Tipperary South. Feelings on that, Finbar?'

Paige unclenched her hands and sat up.

'That was great!' Angus said. 'Your man said you have a good chance of getting elected. You must be pleased with that, Paige.'

'I suppose,' Paige said thoughtfully.

'What is it?' Tom asked. 'There's something on your mind.'

'If Finbar's calling it correctly and it is between me and Annette, I just wonder . . .'

'Yes?' Tom said impatiently.

'Whether she had anything else up her sleeve,' Paige sighed. 'I'm not sure if I can cope with any more surprises.'

Tom noticed that Paige's face looked pale and drawn and she had dark circles etched under her eyes. He put down the small plastic spoon he'd been feeding Alfie with and put his arm around her. 'Don't worry,' he said. 'It'll all be over soon. Just one more week to go – hang in there.'

Paige gently shrugged off his arm. 'I'd better go upstairs and get ready. I'm presenting the prizes for the Ladies' Cup at the Burnaby Sailing Club today. And I have a meeting with Connie before that.'

'She's not still on about the Art's Centre is she?' asked Tom.

'No, she wants a word about environmental waste charges apparently.'

'Exciting stuff.' Tom grinned. Just then, Alfie started to grizzle.

'Will I have a go at feeding him?' Angus offered.

'That would be a help, if you don't mind,' Tom said gratefully. 'I have a few things to go over for Paige in the office.'

'Not at all. Where's Callum? Is he still in bed?'

Paige smiled. 'He's upstairs getting dressed. He's been rather a long time though. Heaven knows what he's getting up to.' She walked towards the kitchen door and shouted up the stairs. 'Callum! Callum! Angus is here. Come down, please.'

A moment later she heard him dash across the landing. 'Slowly, please,' she said firmly.

As he appeared at the top of the stairs Paige had to hold back her giggles. He was wearing the most mismatched outfit she'd seen for a long time. Stripy blue and white trousers, with a red and white short-sleeved gingham summer shirt over a long sleeved black T-shirt.

'Angus is waiting for you in the kitchen,' she said and followed him in.

'Hi, Angus,' Callum ran over. 'Can I help you feed Alfie?'

Angus nodded. 'If you're careful.'

'I got dressed all by myself this morning,' Callum said proudly. 'Mum hadn't left any clothes out like she normally does so I got them out of the wardrobe all by myself too.'

'Well done,' Angus beamed. 'And you didn't pull everything else out too, did you?'

Callum looked a little worried. 'Um, not really. Some shirts fell down but that's all.'

Angus said nothing and continued to feed Alfie.

'Do you think I should put them back in the wardrobe?' Callum asked after a moment.

'Are they still on the floor?' asked Angus.

'Yes,' Callum admitted sheepishly.

'I think you should,' Angus said gently. 'That would be very helpful.'

'I'll give you a hand, love,' Paige said, smiling gratefully at Angus. 'I have to go up and get changed anyway. I can hardly go out in my pyjamas now, can I?'

'You could, Mummy.' Callum laughed. 'Sometimes I leave my pyjama bottoms on under my tracksuit bottoms if it's very cold.'

'Do you now?' Paige smiled grimly. 'I didn't need to know that. Come along, young man. Let's go upstairs and sort out these shirts, will we?'

Callum nodded solemnly.

After a brief tidy-up in Callum's room and another type of wardrobe crisis in her own room, Paige was finally ready to leave. She'd decided to play it safe and wear a plain black suit today – she didn't want to upstage any of the lady sailors after all. Unbeknown to Tom, she was actually squeezing in a trip to her GP, Dr Adams, this morning before meeting with Connie. She didn't want to worry Tom, but she'd been having sharp pains in both her sides and she wanted to get it checked out.

Dr Adams, or 'Jilly' as Paige called her, having been in school with her, gave Paige a thorough examination – blood pressure, weight, glands, stomach – before sitting her down in the old-fashioned dark red leather chair.

'Now, Paige, I don't think there's anything to concern yourself with. As there don't seem to be any other symptoms like bleeding or nausea, the pains sound to me like your pelvic muscles moving and stretching. It's perfectly natural during pregnancy. It's caused by the pregnancy hormones surging around your body at the moment, and it can cause some discomfort. But as long as you take it easy and don't go overdoing things, you'll be fine. Are you taking your iron tablets?'

'When I remember.'

'Well, remember,' Jilly said firmly. 'It's important or you'll become anaemic. Your iron count is quite low as it is. And have you been getting enough rest? Or should I ask?'

'Probably not,' Paige admitted.

Jilly looked her in the eye. 'I know it must be hard, what with elections coming up and everything, not to mention Callum and Alfie, but you must take it easy. Promise me you will? You'll put the baby's health in danger otherwise, not to mention your own health.'

'I promise.' Paige smiled.

'Good. And if the pain moves or gets worse, or you have any other worries ring me immediately.'

'Thanks, Jilly.'

As Paige walked out of the surgery and unlocked the door of her car she sighed. Take it easy, Jilly had said. How on earth was she going to take it easy over the next week? Let alone after that. Maybe Annette was right, maybe she was wrong to be contesting the election when she was pregnant. She tried to block the thought out of her mind as she stepped into the car. As she drove towards Burnaby Crescent to meet Connie, she listened to Wella's morning show.

'And after the news we'll have more details of the shock exposure which will appear in this evening's papers. Orla Murphy, daughter of the election candidate Hilda Murphy has given an exclusive interview to the *Evening Tatler* on her relationship with the daughter of another candidate, Councillor Annette Higgins and their foreign adoption hopes. This is not good news for either of the candidates.'

Paige couldn't believe her ears. If it was true, no wonder Annette and her daughter didn't get on. She pulled the car over and dialled Tom's mobile number.

'Did you hear the news?' she asked.

'I'm just listening to it on the radio. It's unbelievable, isn't it?

This country gets stranger and stranger every day. What possessed the girl to talk to the papers?'

'Who knows?' Paige asked. 'Sick to the teeth of her mother's piety probably. But it might mean Annette will stop digging up my past. From all accounts she has plenty of her own skeletons to contend with.'

'No kidding. How was the meeting with Connie?'

'I'm just on my way. I got talking to an old school friend in the street. You know what Burnaby's like.'

'Don't I just. I'll ring you if there's any more news.'

Paige felt bad about lying to Tom but there was no point worrying him unnecessarily. She'd tell him about her visit to the surgery later.

That afternoon Angus brought Callum to the park. Burnaby Park was in an idyllic location at the bottom of Burnaby Hill, stretching down to the sea. The playground in the park was a credit to the community council who funded it, recognizing the need for such a facility in the child-packed constituency. There was a wooden adventure playground for older children, and a brightly painted metal climbing frame, a set of miniature swings and a snake-like curving slide for the younger ones. It was a fine, if cloudy day, and they'd brought marshmallows to roast over the campfire that Angus had promised to help Callum build on the shore.

While collecting driftwood to make their fire, Callum saw a boy sitting on the steep rocks down by the sea. Callum was most impressed, he wasn't allowed to climb on those rocks alone as Angus said they were too dangerous. The boy looked familiar – white blonde hair and little round glasses. I've seen him somewhere before, Callum thought.

'Hello,' he called over. 'Want to help me collect some wood? We're making a campfire.'

The boy stared at Callum for a few moments, then nodded and climbed carefully down the rocks towards him.

'Are you here on your own?' Callum asked as they gathered up driftwood in their arms.

The boy shrugged his shoulders.

'Are you here with your mum and dad?' Callum tried again, not one to be ignored.

He shrugged again and then shook his head.

'I'm here with my friend, Angus.' Callum pointed up the beach where Angus was putting the fire together. 'Well, he's my minder really but he's not bossy like normal minders. We do cool things together like bungee jumping and snorkelling.'

The boy stared at him. 'Bungee jumping?' he asked in a quiet voice. 'Really?'

'Yes.' Callum chatted away as they collected more wood, stopping every now and then to make sure the boy was listening. After their arms were full, he started walking towards Angus.

'Come on,' he said to the boy who seemed reluctant to follow him. 'Are you not hungry? We have marshmallows and sausages and bread for toasting.'

The boy's eyes lit up. He was rather hungry. He hadn't eaten since this morning and his stomach was starting to make strange gurgling noises. He nodded at Callum.

'Come on then!' Callum powered on ahead, dropping some of his wood as he ran.

The boy bent down, collected up the wood and walked slowly towards Angus.

'Hello,' Angus said, sitting up on his hunkers. 'What's your name?'

The boy said nothing.

'This is my friend,' Callum explained. 'He was on the rocks over there. All by himself too.'

'Really?' Angus asked. He looked at the boy carefully and

then looked around. There didn't seem to be anyone in the park except themselves. 'Are you on your own?'

The boy said nothing, nodding slightly and staring at Angus, his light blue eyes shining a little behind his rather severe glasses. Angus decided not to push it. Maybe the child was lost.

'Can he have some of our campfire food?' asked Callum.

'Of course,' Angus said. 'I've started building the fire, we just have to light it now.'

'Can I do it?' Callum asked hopefully, fearing the answer.

'Yes, if you're very careful with the matches,' Angus said. He knew Callum would want to impress the other boy and he wanted to build his self-confidence.

'Cool!' Callum grinned. 'I'll be real careful.'

Angus showed him how to strike the match safely away from his body and how to light the firelighters. He knew fire-lighters were cheating a bit, but the kindling he'd found was a little damp and he knew only too well how short Callum's attention span was. If the fire wasn't lit within minutes, Callum would lose interest.

When the fire was burning successfully, Angus turned his attention to Callum's new friend.

'Do you like this beach?' he asked the boy.

The boy looked at Angus, nodded and went back to staring at the fire.

'Are you lost?' Angus tried again.

He shook his head.

'Do you live near here?'

The boy thought for a moment. 'Daddy does. He lives near the other beach.'

'Sandybay beach?'

Another nod.

Callum was watching the boy with interest. 'I met you at the puppet show,' he said, suddenly remembering. 'You were there with your dad. Molly works with your dad, doesn't she?'

Another nod.

'Molly from the bookshop?' Angus asked Callum. 'Molly who lives with Kate?'

'Yes, silly.' Callum laughed. 'I don't know any other Mollys.' He knew he'd been a bit rude but luckily Angus didn't seem to notice.

Callum smiled. 'Hugh! Your name is Hugh. I remember now.'

'Is your name Hugh?' Angus asked gently.

Hugh nodded and stared at the fire.

Angus could sense that something was wrong. The boy was practically on the verge of tears. Had something happened to him? Why was he on his own – he couldn't be much older than Callum.

'Before I ring your dad,' Angus said gently, 'is there any-thing you'd like to talk about? Did someone upset you?'

Hugh scrunched up his eyes. He wouldn't cry, he wouldn't. But tears began to cloud his eyes and he pushed up his glasses and brushed them away.

Angus put his arm around the boy and gave him a gentle hug. 'It's OK,' he whispered. 'You're safe with us now. Let's have something to eat and then you can tell me what's wrong.'

Hugh looked at him gratefully. 'Do you have anything to drink?' he asked. It was a warm day and his throat was parched.

'We have fizzy orange,' Callum said, oblivious to the boy's tears. 'I'm not normally allowed it, Mum says it makes me hyper. But Angus said I could have it today as a special treat. I'll share my can with you if you like.'

'Thanks,' Hugh said quietly.

Angus smiled at Callum. 'Good lad. Let's start cooking the sausages. I think Hugh could do with something to eat.'

'Me too!' Callum grinned. 'I'm starving!'

Paige winced. Her right side was aching badly and she couldn't do a damn thing about it. That was one of the downsides about being pregnant. She normally relied on heavy doses of pain killers to see her through her aches and pains, but this time she could take nothing. Stress headaches were her body's speciality, those and an occasional searing pain in her right knee from an old soccer injury.

She put her head in her hands and tried deep breathing for a few minutes. It didn't help. She stood up, went into the kitchen and flicked on the kettle. Maybe a hot water bottle would help. She pulled it out of the cupboard under the sink and put it on the counter. Waiting for the kettle to boil, she bent over the kitchen counter and put her forehead on the cool surface, which gave her some relief.

'Paige? Are you all right?' Tom walked into the room and stared at her. 'What are you doing?'

She straightened up a little too quickly, causing blood to rush to her head, making her feel dizzy.

Tom looked at her in alarm. She was very pale and seemed wobbly on her feet. He put his arms out and guided her firmly into a chair.

'Sorry, I just feel a little faint,' she said, trying a smile. 'Nothing to worry about.'

'If that's the case,' he said, 'why did you just wince?'

'I didn't,' she lied.

'And why is your hot water bottle on the counter? Do you have a stomach ache?'

She shook her head. 'I'm fine, honestly.'

'I'm not convinced.' The kettle boiled and clicked itself off. 'Will I make you some tea?' he offered kindly.

She nodded. 'That would be nice, thanks.' The pain came again and she took a sharp intake of breath.

Tom looked at her in alarm. 'I'm not stupid, Paige! What is it? Please tell me.'

'It's nothing, just a little twinge. The doctor said . . .'

Tom stared at her. 'What doctor? Jilly?'

Paige sighed. 'I didn't want to worry you . . .'

'Well, now you are worrying me. When were you at the surgery?'

'This morning,' Paige admitted. 'I've been having this pain in my side off and on the past few days and I wanted to talk to Jilly about it.'

'And?' Tom asked impatiently.

'She said there was nothing to worry about, it's hormonal. My pelvic muscles are stretching apparently – it's quite normal in pregnancy.'

'What else did she say?'

'Nothing really.'

'Paige, you're keeping something from me, I know you are. If you don't tell me I'll just ring Jilly and ask her myself.'

Paige sighed. 'OK. She said to try and get more rest, that's all.'

'And?'

'To remember to take my iron tablets.'

'Anything else?'

'No, OK, that's it,' Paige snapped. 'Now could you please stop harassing me? I have enough on my plate without this.'

Tom raised his eyebrows but said nothing. He made her a mug of tea and put it down on the table in front of her. 'Drink this. Then I think you should lie down for an hour or two, Paige,' he said evenly. 'The dinner this evening will be easier to deal with if you get some rest beforehand. I can deal with Callum and Alfie when they get back.'

Paige glared at him. 'As I keep telling you, I'm fine. I don't need a rest. Just leave me alone.' She shoved the mug away from her and stood up, slopping some on the table in the process. 'Stop treating me like some sort of invalid. I'm not sick, I'm just pregnant.'

'I know that,' Tom said gently. 'Sit down, love, and drink your tea.'

'No! I'm going to the study and I don't want to be disturbed. OK?'

She strode out of the room leaving Tom staring at her back in disbelief. Paige was prone to the odd mood but she hadn't snapped at him like that since Alfie was a few weeks old and she was over-exhausted.

'Paige!' he said loudly but she ignored him. A few minutes later he decided to check that she was all right. As he opened the door to the study he heard a strange noise. He stepped in. Paige was collapsed over her desk, sobbing as if her heart had broken.

'Oh, Paige. What's wrong?' He walked towards her and began to stroke the back of her head.

She looked up, her eyes red, puffy and full of tears. 'I can't do this any more,' she wailed. 'I'm so bloody tired all the time. And I never see Callum or Alfie. I'm a bad mother.' She began to cry again, heavy tears falling down her cheeks.

'Don't be silly,' Tom said. 'You're a great mother. You're just under a lot of stress at the moment. Things will get better after next week, you'll see. You'll get elected and . . .'

'That's just it!' Paige interrupted. 'I don't know if I want to get elected. What about the boys? And the new baby? Maybe I'm not being fair to all of them. I'm a selfish person and I don't deserve children.'

Tom thought for a few moments before saying anything. 'Paige, I understand what you're saying, really I do. But you've worked so hard over the last few years to make this happen. Being a Deputy is all you've ever wanted. Burnaby needs you. Hell, the country needs you.'

Paige smiled at him through his tears. 'I know, Tom. But

Callum's been so happy over the last few weeks. Maybe all he needed was some one-on-one attention, like Angus said. I'm scared he'll go back to Little Orchard in the autumn and he'll regress.'

'That's not going to happen,' Tom put his hand on hers. 'Because we won't let it. Politics is part of who you are. You can't abandon it because you feel guilty. I'm sure a lot of working mothers feel just like you. Think about it. The kids will be fine.'

'I just don't know,' Paige said. 'I'll be working such long hours and it will put a real strain on our family life.'

Tom said nothing. He stared straight out the window, a strange look on his face. He had a habit of staring into space when he was thinking.

'Tom?' Paige asked gently. She wiped the tears from her eyes. 'What is it?'

'I was just thinking,' he said, then smiled at her. 'No, ignore me, it's nothing.'

'What?' she demanded.

'It doesn't have to be you,' he began tentatively. 'I have equal responsibility for this family. I could take leave of absence for a year – the building society are quite flexible that way. I've been thinking about it for a while now. I could look after the baby and Alfie, bring Callum to school . . . no, it's a stupid idea, forget it.'

'Why do you say it's stupid?'

'It would never work. We'd be completely broke for one thing.'

Paige shrugged her shoulders. 'Money isn't everything. Besides, Deputies get paid reasonably well.'

Tom smiled. 'So you've come around to the idea?'

She shrugged again. 'Maybe. If I do get in, would you really take a year off?'

Tom nodded. 'Yes. If we could afford it, I think I would. Do you think I'd be able for it? I've never really looked after a baby on my own before.'

'Of course you would. You're great with Alfie.' Paige smiled. She was beginning to feel a whole lot better. Her tears had stopped and the heaviness in her heart had started to lift. Maybe there was a way they could make things work. 'And you'd take over all the household jobs too?'

'Like what?' Tom asked.

'The washing, cleaning, cooking, gardening . . .'

He laughed. 'Paige, give me some credit. I already do a lot of those – the cooking and the gardening anyway.'

Paige considered for a moment. 'I suppose you do. Except cleaning the bathrooms of course.'

Tom grinned. 'I keep telling you, you're far better at that than I am.'

'Excuses, excuses.' She smiled back. 'Tom?'

'Yes?'

She threw her arms around him and gave him an almighty hug. 'I'm lucky to have you. You're a wonderful man.'

'Why thank you, Deputy.'

'I'm no Deputy yet.'

'You will be, Paige. Trust me.'

She smiled at him. Suddenly everything began to click into place.

'What do you think Callum will say?' Paige asked. 'About you staying at home.'

'I'm not sure. I hope he'll be pleased. Angus has news for him too. He rang me this afternoon as soon as he heard.'

'What news? Why didn't you tell me?'

Tom smiled. 'I didn't exactly get the chance.'

'Sorry,' she said, contrite.

'Not to worry. Angus has just been appointed as a teacher in Burnaby National School. And guess what class he'll be taking?'

'Not Junior Infants?' Paige asked in amazement.

Tom nodded. 'Callum's new class. Isn't that great?'

'It's bloody brilliant! The best news I've heard all day. And it's been quite a day. Callum will be over the moon. He adores Angus. We're blessed.' She looked up at the ceiling and put her hands together. Tears threatened her eyes again, this time tears of joy. 'Thank you, God. I don't know what we've done to deserve this, but thank you.'

Chapter 16

Molly

Molly looked up from her computer screen for the first time that morning. She wasn't due in to work until after lunch as she'd taken a half day to try and get some writing done. Luckily her phone had been quiet – up until now that was. She reached down, grabbed it from the floor beside her and answered it.

'Hi, Molly, it's Sam,' said the familiar voice.

She felt a warm glow in the pit of her stomach. 'Hi, Sam.'

'I'm not interrupting anything, am I?'

'No, not really. I'm writing but I should probably take a break.' She glanced at her watch. 'I've been at my desk for almost three hours.'

He whistled. 'That's impressive. It's only half nine. That means you must have got up at about six o'clock. There's dedication for you.'

'Don't remind me,' she groaned. 'It nearly killed me. But I was fine once I'd had some coffee and toast. How's the shop?'

'Grand. I was just ringing to say that a researcher from the Pat Bolan radio show rang to ask about the Book Festival. Her name's Julie. They want to interview some of the authors and talk about romance books in particular. She wants you to ring her back this morning. I hope you don't mind.'

'Not at all, that's great news. I'll ring her back right now. Do you have the number?'

He read it out to her and she jotted it down.

'I'll see you at one in Coffee Heaven,' Sam said. 'And Molly?'

'Yes?'

'Are you dressed yet?'

'Mind your own business,' she laughed. She was still in her pyjamas. 'See you later.'

After talking to Julie, a lovely woman and a huge Rose Lovett and Jennie Tracker fan, Molly went back to her short story. She found it difficult to concentrate after the interruptions, her mind was jumping all over the place. She read over what she'd written earlier that morning and noticed several spelling and grammar mistakes, highlighted on her screen by green and red squiggly lines. It was funny, she never noticed them when she was writing, only afterwards. She clicked on the spell check and began to correct them.

Her short story, which she'd given the working title of 'Concrete Pictures', was really coming along. Her two main characters – Lisa and Art – had started to take over, telling their own stories almost without her help. Most importantly of all, for the first time in a long while, she was really enjoying writing. Her fingers clicked over the keys as fast as they could to keep up with the pictures and images that swarmed into her head. She had no idea where the story or the characters had come from. Often, listening to writers talking about their work she scoffed when they said that the characters just took over and told their own story. But in 'Concrete Pictures' this seemed to be exactly what was happening. Maybe she was finally discovering the secret of writing. Maybe not. Maybe Sam was spurring her on to achieve greater things with his gentle encouragement and support. Whatever was happening, she thanked her lucky stars for it.

She read over the second section one more time. It wasn't bad at all – pretty readable Molly thought. Although she might need to pick the pace up a little, it was dragging a bit. Heaven knows what anyone else would think of it though. Then she had an idea.

'Have you seen Hugh, Molly?' Sam asked Molly later that day in Happily Ever After's office. His face looked pale and his wild eyes scanned hers hopefully.

'Hugh?' Molly was confused. Why would she have seen Hugh? 'No. Is something wrong?'

'Yes. Brona dropped him off half an hour ago. I've just got off the phone to her. She said she was in a hurry and dropped Hugh outside the door. There was a tall man with glasses at the front of the shop and she presumed he worked there. She told Hugh to go inside and ask the man where I was. I must have been in here with you at the time.'

'Glasses?' Molly asked. 'Felix doesn't wear glasses.'

'I know.' Sam clutched the back of her chair as if he was about to fall over.

Finally Molly clicked. She gasped. 'You don't think the man . . .'

'Don't,' Sam said. 'I'm already thinking the worst.'

'Maybe the man was a customer and Hugh just wandered off.'

'That's what the guards said. They're on their way. I've already tried Burnaby main street but there's no sign of Hugh. Can I take Felix and try the back streets?'

'Of course.' She stood up. 'I'm coming with you.'

'What about the shop?'

'I'll close it. This is far more important. Your dad will understand.'

Sam nodded curtly.

Molly grabbed her bag. 'Let's go.'

They walked out and Molly immediately spotted Denis loitering outside Coffee Heaven. As soon as she saw him a terrible thought crossed her mind. It was him – the tall man with glasses. What had he done with Hugh? She ran towards him. Sam and Felix followed her.

'Where's Hugh?' she asked angrily. She held both his arms and began to shake him. 'What have you done with him? It was you in the shop, wasn't it?'

Denis stared at her in alarm. 'What are you talking about, Molly?'

'Were you in the shop about half an hour ago?'

Denis said nothing and stared at the pavement in front of him.

'This is serious, Denis, were you?'

He nodded nervously. 'I just wanted to see you. I only stayed a . . .'

'Did you see a small blond boy with glasses?' Felix asked calmly.

Denis looked at Felix. 'Actually I did. He walked in and then . . .'

'You bastard!' Molly shrieked, thumping Denis on the chest. 'I knew it was you as soon as I saw you out here. Where is he? I can't believe you've stooped this low. You evil . . .'

Denis put his hands in the air. 'Hold on just a minute. What are you accusing me of? Child abduction? Molly, are you mad? Is that what you think of me?'

'Well, you've been stalking me for weeks now, you creepy shit,' Molly said angrily, unable to stop herself.

Denis looked at her in alarm. 'Stalking you? But . . .' He broke off and stared at the ground again. 'I've been out of order, haven't I?'

Yes!' Molly said. 'Way out of order.'

'Listen,' Sam interrupted. 'This isn't really helping us find Hugh, is it?'

'Sorry,' Molly said quickly. 'Of course, what am I thinking?' She turned towards Denis. 'You said you saw Hugh.'

'Hugh was the blond boy in the shop?' Denis asked.

'Yes! What happened exactly?'

Denis thought for a moment. 'He walked in the door, waited until the car outside had driven away and then walked straight out again. I thought it was a bit strange at the time so I watched him out the window.'

'And?' Sam asked impatiently.

'He started walking down the main street and off to the right, towards the sea.'

'Did you follow him?' Molly asked.

'No, of course not. Why would I follow him?'

'Thanks,' Sam said. He turned towards Molly and Felix. 'We'll try the Strand Road area.' They both nodded in agreement.

'I'll come with you,' Denis added.

Molly glared at him but said nothing. They could use all the help they could get. As they split up to search around Strand Road – Felix and Denis went to the left and Molly and Sam to the right. Molly was glad Denis hadn't insisted on going with her. She'd finally had enough of his erratic behaviour. It had to stop. He was lucky she hadn't shopped him to the guards yet. Speaking of which, a squad car pulled up alongside Molly and Sam.

'Are you Sam Devine?' the guard asked levelly.

Sam nodded.

'We haven't had any luck with your son yet but we'll keep looking.'

'Thanks. Someone saw him walk down this way,' Sam explained. 'Maybe he was headed towards the sea.'

'There's not much we can do at this stage, I'm afraid,' the

guard said, 'except keep looking. We'll keep you posted on your mobile. If you hear of any other sightings please ring us.'

'Of course,' Sam nodded.

As the squad car drove away Sam looked at Molly and ran his hands through his hair. 'This is hopeless,' he said. 'We'll never find him. And it's all my fault.'

'It's no one's fault,' Molly said. 'Things just happen sometimes. We'll find him, don't worry.'

'What if we don't? You hear such awful stories . . .'

'You've got to stop thinking the worst. He's a smart boy, he'll be OK. We'll find him, I know we will.'

They walked down the road, scanning every garden and every car that drove past. In less than five minutes they'd reached the sea, which stretched out in front of them, winking in the sun, as if mocking them with its beauty.

'I suppose we'd better try the beach,' Sam said, despair creeping into his voice. There were miles of it to comb – from Sandybay right down to Wicklow.

Molly didn't like to ask if Hugh could swim.

As they stepped onto the beach, Molly's phone rang in her bag. She was tempted to ignore it but something told her to answer it.

'Molly?'

'Yes?'

'It's Kate. Angus just rang me. He was looking for Sam's number. Do you have it? He's got Sam's son Hugh with him.'

Molly almost fainted with relief. 'Wait one second,' she said to Kate.

She turned to Sam. 'Hugh's with Angus, a friend of Kate's. He's safe.'

Sam began to cry. 'Thank God,' he whispered.

As Molly hugged him tightly, she could feel the tension melting away from his body.

'I'd better ring Brona,' he said, pulling away after a few

minutes. 'She's worried sick.' He looked at Molly before punching in Brona's number. 'Thanks,' he said, brushing away the last of his tears.

'For nothing,' she smiled at him. 'I'm just glad that Hugh's safe.'

They ran the whole way back to the bookshop where Angus had arranged to meet Sam. As soon as Sam saw Hugh he ran towards him and threw his arms around him.

'Where were you?' Sam asked, drawing back and looking at his son severely. 'We were so worried about you. Why did you go off on your own like that?'

Hugh looked up at Angus who was standing beside him. Angus nodded at him and smiled.

'Hugh asked me to talk to you on his behalf,' Angus said. 'But let's go into the coffee shop first and have something to eat. The boys ate all the sausages and marshmallows and I'm starving.'

'Good idea,' Molly said.

'But . . .' Sam began. Molly took his hand. 'The shop can wait. Everything can wait. Come on.' She led him inside.

A few minutes later Brona rang Sam. 'I'm outside the bookshop but it's closed. Where are you? Have you found him yet?'

Sam explained everything and a moment later Brona came bustling into Coffee Heaven.

'Hugh! You naughty boy!' she said walking towards him. 'How could you put your dad and me through this? Have you no sense? We were worried sick.'

Hugh looked at her nervously.

'Sit down, Brona,' Sam said levelly. 'Apparently Angus has something to tell us.'

Brona stared at Sam. 'Who's Angus?'

'I am.' Angus smiled at her. 'I found your son on the beach. Actually Callum did to be precise. To cut a long story short, he's a bit worried himself. Aren't you, Hugh?'

Hugh nodded solemnly.

'Would you like to tell your mum and dad what's worrying you?' Angus asked.

Hugh shook his head.

'Would you like me to tell them for you?'

Hugh nodded, staring at the table.

'Tell us what?' Brona asked.

'Why don't you go and play with Callum at the next table?' Angus suggested to Hugh. 'Look, he's making a pie with all the sugar sachets. That looks like fun.' Normally he'd stop Callum from making a mess on the tables, but today he was glad of the distraction.

'Callum? What are you building?' Angus asked.

'A sugar igloo,' Callum replied. 'But I need some more napkins.' Angus passed him some. 'I'm going to soak the napkins in milk and stick them on the top of the cup and cover it in sugar, like an igloo.'

Hugh looked on with interest and then got up and joined Callum at the adjoining table.

'Well?' Sam stared at Angus impatiently.

'To get straight to the point,' Angus said, 'Hugh is worried that he won't be able to see you any more, Sam, now that his mum's boyfriend has moved in. That's why he ran away.'

'Moved in where?' Sam asked Brona in confusion. 'What boyfriend?'

'Glen,' Brona said quietly. 'You met him a while ago, remember? He only moved in last week. I was going to tell you but . . .'

'But what?'

'Oh, I don't know. I thought you might be funny about it, that's all.'

'If it affects Hugh then you should have told me.'

'I know and I'm sorry. But nothing will change. You can still see Hugh whenever you like. He needs you around.'

'Have you told him that?' asked Sam.

'What?'

'That nothing will change.'

'Not exactly. I didn't think I needed to.'

'I see.' There was silence for a moment.

'And he's also worried about you and Molly,' Angus said to Sam. 'He thinks you like her more than you like him.'

'That's just ridiculous!' Sam said. 'I love Molly but he'll always come first. He knows that. Why would he think that?'

'He's young,' Angus said evenly. 'You both need to talk to him and tell him how much you love him. Reassure him that he's important in both your lives. He notices a lot more than you think and he's feeling a little left out at the moment. He needs more stability, I think.'

Brona nodded. 'You're right, Angus, you talk a lot of sense. Thank you. Are you a psychiatrist?'

Angus laughed. 'No, I'm a primary school teacher.'

'Thanks, mate,' Sam said. 'Now I think we have some talking to do with our son.'

Angus smiled. 'Why don't I take Callum home? I think he's caused enough mess for Alex to clean up already.'

'And I'd better reopen the bookshop,' Molly said glancing at her watch. 'Ring me later, Sam.'

'I will. And thanks, Molly. Thanks for being there.'

'Talk to you later.' As Molly walked out of the shop her mind was racing. Sam had said he loved her. He'd also said that Hugh was the most important person in his life, more important than her. She wasn't sure how to feel about that.

'Molly!' a familiar voice called her from outside the book shop. It was Denis. The last person she wanted to see right at this moment. She walked towards him.

'Hello, Denis,' she said, resigning herself to the fact that she'd have to talk to him sooner or later. 'I have to open up.' She put the key in the lock.

'I won't keep you,' he said following her inside.

'I'm not really in the mood for talking —' she began.

'I understand,' he interrupted. 'I just wanted to tell you that from today on you won't be hearing from me. I've decided to move on. I still love you, I probably always will, but it's time I found someone else. Sam seems like a decent man. I hope you'll be happy together.'

Molly stared at him in shock. 'Um, well, thanks Denis. I appreciate that.'

'I'm sorry I wasn't more helpful with finding Hugh. Maybe I should have followed him but I wasn't thinking.'

'You weren't to know,' she said kindly.

'Did you really think I'd abducted him?'

Molly shook her head. 'Not really. I was upset and worried. I shouldn't have said that.'

'It's OK. I've put you through a lot recently and I'm sorry.'

'That's all right, Denis.'

'Bye, Molly.' He leant over and kissed her on the cheek. 'Have a nice life.'

'You too,' she said as he walked away.

She sat down on the stool at the front desk, leant forward and put her head in her hands. All in all, it had been quite a day. And next weekend was the Burnaby Book Festival. She had so much to do it was scary. But right at that moment all she could think about was Sam.

Chapter 17

Molly

'Why do they have to make these book posters so damn big?' Molly complained to Anita as she fought to keep another Bonnie Evans poster on the wall of the Burnaby Arts Centre.

'Blu-tack won't hold it,' Anita said trying not to smile. 'Here, try these.' She handed Molly some drawing pins.

'Is it OK to use them? They'll make holes in the walls, Anita, maybe . . .'

'Stop fussing, I'm sure Tara won't mind.'

'Tara won't mind what?' Tara, the arts administrator of the centre asked as she walked in the door of the lecture room.

'Sticking drawing pins into your newly painted walls,' Anita explained.

Tara shrugged her shoulders. 'Go ahead. The walls are there to be used. I'd love to get notice boards put up eventually but money's quite tight at the moment. Is there anything I can help you with?'

'Yes,' Anita said. 'The PA system. You'd better show me how to use it in case it acts up. In my experience, microphones never work when you want them too. Especially those clip-on ones.'

'You shouldn't have any problems with ours,' Tara said. 'Touch wood.' She touched the back of a chair and smiled. 'They're all brand new.'

'Excellent!' Anita said. 'One less thing to worry about.'

As Tara showed Anita how to work the PA system, Molly finished putting up the posters and resting the show cards on the windowsills and on the long speaker's table which was on a raised platform at the top of the room. Tara had already put all the chairs out, facing the platform, and had decorated the table with elegant flower arrangements. With the posters and balloons, all provided by the various speakers' publishers, the room was starting to look pretty good.

Sam and Felix were setting up the mini bookshop in the smaller room next door. Down the corridor, a journalist from *Sunday Ireland* was waiting patiently to interview Bonnie Evans who was currently on the way back from the RTE radio studios where she'd caused quite a stir on one of the morning radio shows. Molly and Anita had listened to it while setting up, horrified yet delighted with the controversial things Burnaby's most famous daughter was saying.

In the space of twenty minutes Bonnie had managed to criticize just about everyone in Ireland – from crooked business men, to politicians, publicans, farmers, housewives, working mothers, students and rude children – the whole gauntlet of Irish society in fact. Not to mention other writers. She hadn't made herself popular on air, the average listeners ringing in to complain about her harsh views attested to that. But it was compulsive listening and great publicity for the Book Festival.

One besotted man had even rung in to ask Bonnie to marry him. He admired her fiery temper and her outspokenness, he said. Bonnie had thanked him but then gone into a tirade against marriage and why it was a raw deal for any woman. The man, give him his due, took it all in his stride and said he'd happily take her on if she changed her mind. It was quite a show!

As Molly placed the last show card on the table, her phone rang.

'Molly?'

She recognized the voice immediately. 'Paige, where are you?'

'Don't ask, I'm sorry but I'm running incredibly late and the battery's gone on my mobile. I'll be there in ten minutes.'

'Not to worry, we've done almost everything now, so don't rush.'

Paige sighed. 'I'm so sorry, I really did mean to be there to help . . .'

'Paige, get a grip. The election's in three days, you're not Superwoman. See you in ten minutes. I'll be in the cafe helping Alex set up the table for the literary lunch.'

'See you then.'

'Was that Paige?' Anita asked.

Molly nodded. 'She's on her way.'

'I'm now fully trained to work the PA,' Anita said. 'So what's left to do?' She glanced at her watch. 'Maybe I should get back to the shop. I'm sure Milo's fretting by now, stupid man.'

Molly stifled a smile. They'd bullied Milo into looking after the shop for the afternoon, well Anita had anyway. His soft spot for her hadn't abated, which was coming in quite useful.

'You do that,' Molly said. 'He's probably dying for some designer coffee at this stage. I'll stay here. If we need you I'll give you a ring.'

Anita kissed her on the cheek. 'I'll be back once we've closed up the shop. See you later.'

Molly walked her out, then strode into the Arts Centre cafe. It looked fantastic. Tara had hired tables, chairs and all the table settings from a local catering company, who had kindly given them everything free of charge. All they had to do was get the table linen laundered before they returned it. Harry was pottering amongst the tables, putting finishing touches to the simple yet stunning central arrangements.

He smiled at Molly as soon as he spotted her. 'What do you think?'

Each round table was covered with a simple white cloth and set with gleaming cutlery and starkly white plates. The glasses had been polished to perfection, and shone as if they'd been lit from inside. In the centre of each table was a glass bowl surrounded by brightly coloured exotic flowers in mini vases. As Molly looked closer at the bowl beside her, she realized that each bowl had a healthy looking goldfish in it, swimming away merrily in the clean water.

'Fantastic!' she beamed. 'Where did you get the goldfish?'

'From the pet shop in Sandybay. They're on loan. We have to take very good care of them, I gave my word.'

'Where's Alex?'

Harry smiled. 'Where do you think? In the kitchen. She's checking out the facilities for tomorrow.'

'What's on the menu?'

He thought for a second. 'Let me see – soup made by Matty, I'm not sure what kind, smoked salmon, salads, home-made bread and lots of delicious looking sweet things.'

'I can't wait,' Molly said feeling decidedly hungry. She'd brought a cheese sandwich for lunch but had forgotten to eat it in the end. It had been such a busy day. But everything was almost in place. 'Do you need any help?'

'No, I'm almost finished.'

'I really appreciate all your hard work. You and Alex have been fantastic.'

Harry shrugged his shoulders. 'Thank Alex. She bullied me into it. She's got a good heart and she likes helping people.'

'She's a great girl, isn't she?' Molly smiled. Kate had told her all about Harry and Alex's romance and she was delighted for both of them. Even though they were like chalk and cheese they seemed to get along famously and Harry had calmed down a lot since meeting Alex. She was obviously having quite an effect on him. Molly had always found him a little difficult to talk to, but he'd been positively charming all day. He'd even turned down a television appearance to help.

Molly stretched her arms over her head. 'I'll go into the hall and set up the registration table and the notice board then. Call me if you need me.'

'Will do.' Harry went back to his beloved flowers.

Molly met Tara in the corridor.

'There are masses of calls on the answering machine about the festival,' Tara said. 'I've checked some of them and they are all asking if the event's booked up. What will I tell them?'

'We have room for about twenty more at the talks but the lunch is completely full,' Molly said proudly. 'Would you like me to ring them back for you?'

'Not at all, I'll do it,' Tara said kindly. 'It's going to be some weekend, isn't it?'

'It sure is,' Molly agreed.

'There you are, Molly,' Paige interrupted them. 'Hi, Tara.'

'If it isn't the Councillor herself,' Tara said. 'How's tricks?'

'Good,' Paige said. 'Busy but good. Now put me to work.'

'Gladly,' Molly said. 'What are you like at photocopying? We need some more programmes.'

'A whiz.' Paige laughed. 'Lead on.'

'Who is that?' Anita asked Milo, gesturing towards a tall, blond man at the back of the shop. He was wearing black trousers, a black long-sleeved T-shirt and trendy steel-rimmed glasses and was talking notes on a palm pilot. 'He doesn't look like a customer.'

'Oh, pay no attention to him,' Milo said, drawing her attention away from the back shelves. 'He's from the council. Something about moving a water mains. Um, Anita, an order just arrived. It's waiting to be priced in goods-in. Would you like to see the new titles? There's a beautiful looking hardback Margaret Atwood.'

'I've been waiting for that.' Anita smiled. 'Thank you, Milo.'

He led her towards the goods-in area and followed her in. 'I'll see you in a few minutes,' he promised. 'I'll just finish with the council guy.' He went back out onto the shop floor and shut the door firmly behind him.

'Fine,' Anita said absently, her hands stroking the deliciously cool blood-red matt jacket of Atwood's new book. She couldn't wait to read it again. She'd been given a proof copy but it hadn't looked nearly as elegant as this finished product.

'Well?' Milo said, approaching the man, his voice low. 'What do you think?'

'It has possibilities,' the man replied. 'Distinct possibilities.'

'Any sign of Rose?' Molly asked Kate the following morning. Kate was manning the Book Festival registration desk, with the help of Cathy and Trina.

Kate shook her head. 'Nope. But Jennie's in the office with Tara and Anita.'

'Well, that's something I suppose.'

'Don't worry, she'll be here any minute,' Kate said. 'I'll come and get you as soon as she does.'

'Thanks.' As Molly walked back towards the lecture room, where Paige was waiting patiently to launch the event and introduce the speakers, she saw many familiar faces among the crowds and nodded and smiled at them in recognition – regular customers from the shop, two librarians from the local library, Connie Calloway and some of her cronies. As she made her way past the on-site bookshop she spotted Sam talking to Angus.

'Hi, Sam, hi, Angus.' She smiled at them both. 'I didn't take you for a romance fan,' she said to Angus.

'I'm not really. Lily mentioned it and I thought I'd come along just for the morning as it sounded interesting. She knows Bownie from way back.'

'Of course she does,' Molly said. 'Lily knows everyone.'

'How's everything going?' Sam asked. 'Will you be starting on time?'

'I hope so,' she said. 'We're still waiting for Rose to arrive from the airport.'

'I think she may just have arrived,' Sam said gesturing with his head to the doorway. Kate was standing there waving at them, the tall, red-headed Rose to her side.

'Thank goodness,' Molly said with relief. 'Let the show begin. See you both later.'

'Call into the shop when it's all over,' Sam said. 'I'll be there this afternoon to help Dad. Felix said he'd hold the fort here.'

'Great, see you later then.' She gave him a wide smile. He really was lovely. She walked towards the door.

'Rose, I'm Molly, one of the organizers, and you've already met Kate.' Molly held out her hand politely.

'And I'm Rose.' Rose smiled warmly at her and shook her hand firmly. 'And I met Anita and Tara in the office. And Jennie of course. I believe you're anxious to start. So lead on, I'm ready when you are.'

'Are you sure?'

'Absolutely.'

Molly felt a surge of adrenaline rush through her body. 'Right. Let's get started then.'

'That was brilliant!' a woman enthused to Molly after Rose and Jennie had received their second standing ovation. 'Such interesting women, and such accomplished speakers.' She touched

Molly gently on the arm. 'Thank you, my dear, for arranging this Festival. I'm having such a good time.'

'I'm glad. And are you staying for the lunch and the afternoon session?'

'Of course, my dear, I wouldn't miss it for the world.'

Molly looked around the lecture room and was delighted to see so many smiling faces.

'They were great,' Paige said, stepping down off the platform where she'd been sitting with Rose and Jennie. The two authors were surrounded by fans, signing books like there was no tomorrow.

'Weren't they?' Molly agreed.

'It seems to be going well so far. Who am I sitting with at lunch?' Paige asked.

'Millie from the *Burnaby News*,' Molly replied deadpan.

Paige groaned. 'You're not serious. I was hoping never to meet her again after all that photograph business.'

'I'm joking,' Molly replied. 'You're sitting with Connie Calloway.'

Paige stared at her. 'You're not funny, you know that?'

'Sorry, couldn't resist. You're at the top table with me and Anita.'

'Good.' Paige smiled and took Molly's arm. 'I'm starving.'

'How's the bump today?' Molly asked.

'Fine. I was feeling a little ropy yesterday but I cancelled a dinner last night and went to bed at eight.'

'Good woman, you have to take care of yourself, Paige.'

'Don't you start. You're as bad as Tom.'

'It's only because we love you.'

'I know, I know. Now where's the food?'

Molly led her to their table and they sat down. The room was already filling up with people, almost exclusively women, and there was a buzz of excitement in the air. A little while later, when Rose and Jennie walked into the crowded room, followed by RTE television news cameras, everyone stood up and clapped again.

'Hey, we might be on the telly.' Paige laughed and nudged Molly. 'Smile!'

Sure enough, the cameraman swung the camera around the room and rested the lens on Paige's smiling face. As an election candidate, with a fair chance of a seat, she was certainly worth capturing on film.

As everyone settled down into their seats, Anita stood up and addressed the room. 'Welcome to the first Burnaby Book Festival Literary Lunch,' she began. 'As you'll notice there is a vacant seat at every table. As the lunch progresses, you'll get the chance to meet different authors as they take that seat. The authors will move anti-clockwise around the room every fifteen minutes. At least that's the idea. Whether it works or not remains to be seen.' Everyone laughed politely. 'And now I'd like to introduce the authors and ask them to take a seat at a table. In no particular order – you've already met Rose Lovett and Jennie Tracker.' Another deafening round of applause and many cries of 'Sit here, Rose', 'Over here, Jennie'. 'And our very own Bonnie Evans.' More applause. 'All the three C's – Clare Connolly, Ciera Donald and Catriona Reilly.' Applause and whistles. 'Tina Laycock and Antonia Ash .' More applause. 'Cleo Holmes, Nancy Dealy and Peggy Walsh.' More applause. When Anita had finished her introductions she sat down again.

'Well done,' Molly said. 'Do we not get an author?'

'We already have one,' Anita replied. 'You.'

'I'm not an author,' Molly snapped.

'You will be,' Anita said, ignoring Molly's sharp tone. 'Now let's eat. Paige had already demolished all the bread rolls on the table. She must be famished.'

'Sorry,' said Paige, 'blame the baby.'

*

Molly sat between Paige and Kate for the afternoon session on 'Getting Published', with Anita to Paige's left, who was ignoring Milo Devine to a spectacular degree. Milo had arrived just in time for coffee and had found a spare chair and squeezed himself in beside Anita, much to her chagrin. He had then followed her like a puppy dog into the lecture room and sat down beside her.

'Who's on the panel?' asked Kate.

'You could read the beautifully and tirelessly photocopied programme,' Paige suggested.

'Or you could tell me and save me trouble. I'm feeling very lazy after that glass of wine at lunch.'

'Are you sure it was only one?' Molly smiled. 'I distinctly saw you order another bottle for your table.'

'Well, it might have been more like three,' Kate grinned back. 'But no more, mind.'

'Did you enjoy meeting the authors?' Molly asked her.

'Yes! Some of them were a riot. And others were really smart and well read. And so nice. You'd never think they were famous authors. Cleo Holmes has a real thing about shoes too, so I was talking to her for ages. In fact, I think she missed a table change because of me. It was a great success, well done to all of you. Now will you tell me who the speakers are or do I have to batter it out of you?'

'I think they're about to tell you themselves,' Anita said jumping to her feet. She was supposed to be introducing the speakers who were seated on the platform waiting patiently to begin.

'Welcome back, everyone,' Anita began. 'I hope you all enjoyed your lunch. Now I have the great privilege of introducing the panel who will talk to you this afternoon on the subject of "Getting Published – Tips from the Top". From Trinity Publishers in Dublin we have Maggie Stevens who is the Sales and Marketing Manager; next up is Bonnie Evans,

who I'm sure you all know is originally from Burnaby and now lives in the South of France and is one of the world's best selling romance novelists; Cleo Holmes, another highly successful writer from Dublin; and last, but certainly not least, the only man on the panel, Gerry Begley, from the highly respected Begley Literary Agency. And first up will be Cleo.'
Anita sat down as everyone applauded.

'Phew,' she whispered to Paige. 'I'm glad that's over.'

'You were great,' Paige whispered back as Cleo stood up and began to talk.

'Hello, everyone, I'm Cleo Holmes and I'm delighted to be here today with so many readers. I met some of you at lunch and it was lovely to talk to the people who appreciate my work. Writing is quite a solitary occupation and I don't get to meet many readers face to face. So I'd like to quickly thank the organizers here today for this fantastic Book Festival.' Everyone clapped enthusiastically. 'Now getting published can be a very frustrating business for new authors,' Cleo continued. 'Many of you here may be writers interested in seeing your own work in print, members of writers' groups or simply readers who are interested in the whole book world, including publishing. I hope you all find this session on getting published interesting and stimulating.' Cleo then went on to talk about her own experience – how she found an agent and got her first book published by Trinity Publishers in Ireland.

Paige turned to Molly. 'She's a good speaker isn't she?' she whispered. 'Very clear and easy to listen to.'

Molly nodded. From what Cleo was saying, having your first book published was pretty miraculous considering the competition. In fact, Cleo was making Molly feel downright despondent. What chance did she have if it was so difficult – less than none, she figured.

Cleo continued. 'You have to enjoy what you're writing and your heart must be in it 100 per cent.' She went on to explain the different genres and which genres were particularly popular at the moment.

'She's very thorough,' Kate whispered to Molly. 'I never knew there was so much to it.'

Molly nodded in agreement and went back to listening.

Anita was watching Molly with interest. Molly was totally focused on what Cleo was saying and was even jotting down some notes on her programme. Anita smiled to herself – maybe Molly was finally taking her talent seriously. Unbeknown to Molly, Anita had read several of Molly's short stories which had been stored on the computer at work. Molly's home printer was always playing up and she often saved and printed out her writing in the Happily Ever After office. Anita knew Molly had the potential to be a great writer, if she'd only believe in herself enough. But she knew Molly would have a fit if she thought Anita had betrayed her trust and read her stories, so Anita could say nothing.

'I wish all the writers in the audience the best of luck,' Cleo said, concluding her talk. 'And the best advice I can give you is don't give up. If you really want to be published you will. You just have to believe in yourself.'

'Hear, hear,' Anita murmured.

Everyone clapped enthusiastically. As the applause died out Maggie stood up.

'Hello, I'm Maggie Stevens, from Trinity Publishers, Cleo's Irish publishers. I'm going to explain what Trinity are looking for from new writers and how prospective writers should submit their book. Practical things like presentation of manuscript, how to send it in, how long you can expect to wait for a reply and so on.' Maggie was as good as her word and gave a slick, well-prepared talk.

Next up it was the agent, Gerry Begley. 'Most UK publishers expect writers to have an agent. In fact, the odds on getting published from what we call 'the slush pile' in the trade –

the unsolicited manuscripts sent in by authors directly to the editor of a publishing house – are tiny. So that's where I come in.' He explained his role in the whole publishing business.

'Seems like a nice man,' Paige said to Molly when Gerry had stopped talking. 'Maybe you should ask him to be your agent.'

'Get real!' Molly laughed. 'He wouldn't be interested in me.'

'You never know,' Paige replied mildly.

'Shush, it's Bonnie next,' said Molly.

Paige studied Burnaby's most famous daughter with interest. She was wearing a flamboyant wine-coloured cardigan, over a floor-sweeping black velvet dress. Her thick, rich dark red hair was piled on top of her head in an elaborate chignon.

'Attractive woman,' Kate whispered to Molly and Paige. 'Great cardigan.'

'Shush,' someone behind them muttered.

They grinned at each other and stifled the laughs.

'I'm Bonnie Evans,' she began, then snorted. 'As if you needed to be told. I am one of the world's best-selling authors and I think most of what is published today is unadulterated crap.' Several members of the audience gasped. The journalists at the back of the room began to scribble furiously. 'I think any writers out there who want to be published need to think long and hard.' She stared at the audience intensely, making eye contact with some, making them jump. 'Are *you* good enough? Is *your* work crap? Because if it is, don't bother trying to get published. And I think writers' groups are evil.' More gasps. 'Filling people's heads with silly notions of grandeur. Most people *can't* write. And you cannot be taught to write – I believe it's something you are born with. It's as simple as that. I have the gift, a very special gift. But most don't.'

A woman at the back of the room stood up, collected her things together and walked out, banging the door behind her.

'I've offended someone!' Bonnie clapped her hands together with glee. 'Excellent! Now what I have to say is very important so please listen carefully.' She looked around the room again. 'If you do have the gift, you must use it. Indeed, if you have any creative gift you must use it. If you can write you must put your whole being into your writing and produce the very best book that you can. I will now tell you how I discovered my own talent and how it has changed my life.'

'Powerful stuff,' Paige said after she'd finished and Bonnie had received a rapturous standing ovation. 'She's some woman.'

The three women watched as Anita stepped onto the platform and began to thank all the speakers, shaking their hands warmly. Within seconds the platform was surrounded by people, most wanting to meet Bonnie. She'd made quite an impression.

'No kidding.' Molly smiled at Paige.

'I found her quite inspirational,' Kate said thoughtfully. 'And she wasn't afraid of upsetting people, was she?'

'Quite the opposite,' said Molly. 'Most refreshing. And speaking of which, who's for a drink? There's a press reception in the cafe now to announce the winner of the writing competition and you're both invited of course. I'd better stay here and see if Anita needs anything done.'

'Is there food?' asked Paige.

'You've only just eaten,' Molly pointed out.

'It's not for me, it's for junior,' Paige said, rubbing her stomach gently.

Molly smiled. 'Good excuse. There's finger food and wine. Will that do you?'

'It will,' Paige replied.

'Excellent!' Kate stood up gingerly. 'My bum's killing me. These seats aren't exactly padded.'

'Maybe it's you who isn't exactly padded,' Paige pointed out with a smile. 'So quit complaining.'

An hour later, Anita stood in front of the crowd at the reception. She tapped the microphone head softly to check it was working and took a sip of water before starting. She stood up tall and addressed the crowd. 'I'd like to welcome you all to the prizegiving of the Burnaby Short Story Competition which has been run in association with the *Burnaby News*. Beside me are the two other judges, Millie O'Shea, the Editor of the *Burnaby News* and Bonnie Evans. The winner gets their story published in the newspaper as well as five hundred euro, kindly sponsored by Star Insurances in Burnaby, and just this very afternoon Gerry Begley has also kindly offered to represent the winning author. Quite a prize for a new writer. Judging this competition was very difficult. The standard of entries was very high.' She half-expected Bonnie to snort at this, but thankfully she didn't. Anita continued swiftly. 'But there was one story which really stood out from the rest. It was a story about starting again, about getting one's life back after a terrible tragedy – the death of a young child.'

Molly caught her breath. Did Anita just say the death of a child? Surely not? She listened to Anita carefully.

'The writer's prose style draws you into the story and the characters are extremely well rounded. I'd like to ask Bonnie to announce the winner.'

Bonnie cleared her throat theatrically. 'The winner is Mary Parker with her story "Concrete Pictures".' Everyone began to clap and looked around the room for Mary Parker.

'Could Mary Parker please come up and collect her prize,' Bonnie continued.

'What's wrong?' Paige asked Molly who had lurched sideways into her, spilling the last of her drink. Luckily Kate had

gone to the bar for more. Molly's face was as white as a sheet.
'Molly?'

Molly looked at her, a strange expression on her face.

Suddenly Paige clicked. 'It's you, isn't it? Mary Parker.
Molly, how exciting! Go up and collect your prize!'

'I can't,' Molly hissed. 'They've made some sort of mistake.
I can't have won.'

'Is your story called "Concrete Pictures"?'

Molly nodded.

'Well then, it's not a mistake. Go on.' She pushed her gently
towards the stage.

At that moment Kate came back, two glasses of red wine
and one of sparkling water balanced in her hands. 'Have I
missed anything?' she asked. Paige gestured towards the top
of the room.

'What's Molly doing up there with Bonnie and Anita?' Kate
asked in confusion.

'She only won the writing competition.'

'But they just said someone called . . . Oh, I see . . . Mary
Parker *is* Molly Harper. You think she could have made a bit
more of an effort with the pseudonym.'

Paige laughed. 'She never expected to win. I wonder what
she's saying to Anita.'

'Let's get closer and see,' Kate suggested.

They wound their way through the crowd, towards the top
of the room.

Molly was actually trying to persuade Anita to give the
prize to someone else. Anita was having none of it.

'You won it fair and square,' Anita said firmly to Molly's
protests. 'In fact, it was Bonnie who insisted that your story
won the prize. She said she'd leave the judging panel if you
didn't win.'

'But . . .' Molly protested.

'Is this Mary Parker?' Bonnie asked.

'Yes, and she won't accept the prize. She says she doesn't deserve it.'

'Don't be silly, girl. Some of the stories were rubbish. Yours wasn't. You have real potential. In fact, I think you may have the gift.'

Molly looked at Bonnie in surprise. 'Really?'

'I always tell the truth,' Bonnie said evenly. 'I'm renowned for it. Now stop being so stupid and accept what's your due.'

Whatever she felt about Anita, Molly was far too scared to say no to Bonnie.

'OK,' she said quietly.

'Excellent.' Bonnie stood beside her and faced the audience again. The room became quiet.

'And here is Mary Parker.' She handed her an envelope. 'Well done, Mary. Would you like to say a few words?'

'Um, no, thank you.' Molly's hands were shaking and she felt very faint. She hated public speaking and hated all those upturned faces watching her.

'Go on,' Paige encouraged from the floor.

'You can do it.' Kate smiled up at her.

Molly looked at them both and smiled back. She took a deep breath. Maybe she could.

'Um, I'd just like to say thanks to the judges for choosing my story. I've been writing for a few years now but I thought I was one of the crap ones, as Bonnie so succinctly calls them.' Everyone laughed. 'But I guess I'm not. And as some of you will know, my name is not Mary Parker, it's Molly Harper and I work in Happily Every After. I used another name because I didn't want anyone to know I'd entered the competition. I just wanted some feedback on my writing. But I never expected to win. But, um, thanks very much. I'm, um, delighted. And in complete shock to tell the truth. Thanks.' Everyone clapped warmly.

Anita stepped up to the microphone. 'Well, done, Molly.

It Had To Be You

And now I'd like to ask Councillor Paige Brady to close the Burnaby Book Festival for us.'

'Oh no!' Paige whispered to Kate under her breath and handed her her glass. 'I forgot I was doing this. I've nothing prepared.'

'Not you as well.' Kate laughed. 'You and Molly really are a right pair.'

Chapter 18

Kate

Kate gazed out the window at the fluffy, candyfloss clouds, illuminated by the blazing sun – the whole scene like something out of a Hollywood movie about heaven. The pilot had just announced that they were less than twenty minutes from Boston's Logan Airport and Kate could hardly contain herself. Her stomach was fluttering in anticipation at seeing Jay again. The fact that he didn't know she was coming only added to the drama. She rested the back of her head against the headrest and closed her eyes. In less than two hours, she'd be safely in his arms, cocooned by his love, basking in his admiration. She couldn't wait. She dozed off, into a deep dreamless slumber.

As the plane landed smoothly on the Boston tarmac, Kate let out a sigh – she'd never been the world's greatest flyer and was always relieved to be on solid ground once more. As soon as they'd pulled into the terminal, she gathered together her jacket, handbag and compact travel suitcase. As she was only flying over for a long weekend, she'd decided to travel light.

Walking smugly through the terminal with her hand luggage, past the poor souls in the huge, bustling baggage reclaim hall, and out through one of the entrance doors, she hopped straight onto one of the 'Massport Shuttles' like a real native. From here she was swiftly delivered to the Airport 'T', where she sat and waited for an underground train to take her safely to downtown Boston. As always she sent up a prayer for the efficient city transport network. It was one of the things she'd missed after moving back to Ireland.

It was Saturday afternoon and as she sat waiting for the train, she rang Jay's mobile. He tended to be busy at weekends – catching up with friends, shopping (unlike Irish men Jay liked to shop), and taking day trips out of the city. He was also a big Boston Red Sox fan and liked nothing better than to spend time in Boston's famous baseball park, Fenway Park, watching his favourite team compete. His mobile rang out. He probably can't hear it, Kate thought. Or maybe he's left it at home. His home number had changed recently and he hadn't remembered to give the new one to her yet, so she couldn't try there.

Kate tried to remember their exact conversation the previous evening. He'd said he had no definite plans but would probably meet a friend for lunch and go shopping for the afternoon. Then he might go out for dinner in the evening. It seemed a little strange to Kate who happened to know that his weekends were usually planned weeks in advance, but as he kept impressing on her, he'd changed. Maybe this weekend spontaneity was part of the new Jay. Perhaps she should have told him she was coming over, he could have met her at the airport, but, no, Kate thought, that would have spoiled the surprise.

A little later, after a pleasant enough 'T' ride and a ten-minute walk, Kate stood outside his apartment building. She rang his apartment on the huge brass intercom board beside the front door. There was no answer. Damn! She tried his mobile again – again no answer. Well, he's bound to be back at some stage, she reasoned, thinking again that surprising him might not have been the best idea in the world after all. What was she going to do now? She was overheated from walking in the early afternoon sun, and her hair had begun to stick to her forehead. In fact, she could do with a shower. Failing that, she needed to go somewhere cool and spacious, somewhere with a good air conditioning system, somewhere with a left luggage department so that she wouldn't have to drag around her wheelie suitcase all day. Not that it would be all day, she hoped.

She racked her brains for inspiration. She'd love to browse the clothes shops on Newbury Street or even visit Filene's Basement, but both would be incredibly hot and crowded on a Saturday afternoon. She could visit one of the huge bookstores – Barnes and Noble or Borders but that wouldn't keep her occupied for more than an hour or two. Then she had a thought. All the time she'd lived in the city she'd never visited the famous art gallery – the Boston Museum of Fine Arts. Well, she had no excuse this time – it was cool, spacious and air conditioned; they would look after her suitcase while she was there and it also had a cafe and toilets. Plus it was only two stops away on the 'T'.

Delighted with her decision she tried Jay's mobile one more time. Still no answer. Half an hour later, stepping through the doors of the rather grand museum building, she tried once more with the same result, then turned her own mobile off and plunged it into her handbag, determined not to try Jay again until later.

As she strolled through the huge exhibition rooms, unencumbered by her bags and jacket, she drank in the art and ancient objects surrounding her. Mummies, hieroglyphics and Old Kingdom sculptures in the Egyptian rooms, Buddhist sculptures, Chinese ceramics and the huge array of strikingly familiar Impressionist pictures from Monet to Renoir to Gauguin.

Several hours later, calmed and soothed by the art and the surroundings, and physically refreshed by a nice salad lunch and lots of chilled fruit juice, she collected her bags, promising herself that she'd visit again very soon. Maybe she'd even drag Jay along next time.

She walked out the door and tried his mobile again – still no answer. At this stage she was getting a little worried. Maybe he'd gone away for the weekend with friends unexpectedly. What would she do then? She rubbed her temples, feeling a tension headache coming on. I'll go back and wait for him outside his apartment, she decided. I don't have any other choice. He has to come back sooner or later.

Sitting on the steps of the apartment she felt a shiver of déjà vu which she tried to banish as soon as it wiggled its way into her head. This is just like last Christmas Eve, a voice said, waiting for Jay outside his apartment. Wondering where he was, what he was doing. Yes, but this time, she reasoned, it's totally different. Completely different. He's not married any more and he even offered to move back to Dublin to be with me. She took out the museum guide from her handbag and began to fan her face. She tried not to look at her watch but she couldn't help it. Almost six. He had to be home soon.

She heard voices behind her and swivelled around. A tall dark haired man was walking towards her. There he is! Kate grinned. That's Jay walking in front of that woman with the buggy. She felt a huge rush of relief spread through her body. Thank goodness! She jumped up and waved.

'Jay!' she shouted excitedly. 'Jay!'

He put his hand over his eyes to shield them from the sun. Then he stopped dead. He stared at Kate in amazement as if she was some sort of alien from another planet, complete with green skin and stun gun. The woman stopped beside him and said something. Kate couldn't hear the conversation as she wasn't close enough. He said something back to the woman. Kate began to walk towards them. Jay put up his hand as if to say 'stop', but Kate continued unabashed.

'Jay?' she said as she approached him. 'What's wrong?'

As soon as Kate looked at the woman's face she realized what was wrong. Because the woman pushing the buggy beside Jay was his ex-wife, Cindy. Kate recognized her immediately. And to top it all she looked at least four months pregnant, her rounded belly protruding proudly beneath a tight white T-shirt.

Kate stared at Jay in confusion.

'What's going on here?' Cindy asked. 'Who's this woman, Jay? She looks kinda familiar.'

'Just a friend from work,' Jay said, resting a reassuring hand in the small of his wife's back.

'Hi.' Cindy smiled at Kate uncertainly. 'I'm Cindy, and you are . . .?'

Kate looked at Jay. She felt her blood falling like a sheet from her face and upper body into her feet. Her palms began to sweat and she felt unable to say anything. 'Jay?' she managed finally in a weak, whispery voice before her body felt freezing cold and the whole world went blank.

'Granny, are you in?' asked Kate, gripping her mobile tightly. She'd turned it on as soon as the plane had landed on Irish soil.

'I am,' said Lily. 'And where have you been all weekend? I was looking for you yesterday but your mobile wasn't working.'

'Can I call over?'

'Of course, love. Is anything wrong? You sound a little strange. Where are you?'

'Dublin Airport.'

'The airport? But it's not even nine. What are you doing there?'

Kate gulped back the tears. 'I have to go, Gran. I'll see you in a while, OK?'

Lily sensed that this had to do with Jay but kept her thoughts to herself. What had the rat done now to upset her darling granddaughter? Had he stood her up?

'Take care of yourself, poppet. Granny Lily's here for you, understand?'

Kate clicked off her phone and immediately began to cry. It

was such a relief to talk to her granny. She felt such an almighty fool.

'Kate,' Lily said as she opened the door. 'Come here and give your old granny a hug.' Kate dropped her bags and lunged immediately forward, hugging Lily with all her might and breathing in the familiar scent of rose water.

Lily was shocked at Kate's appearance. She looked like she hadn't slept for days – her eyes were sunk into dark grey sockets and her face was red and blotchy as if she'd been crying for hours without stopping. Her breath was ragged and irregular and she was shaking.

'Come into the kitchen and we'll have a cup of tea. I'll put some brandy in it for you, pet, that'll help.' She led Kate towards the back of the house, sat her down at the kitchen, then went back into the hall, moved the bags and closed the hall door behind her firmly.

Back in the kitchen, Lily clicked on the kettle and stood waiting, leaning against the kitchen counter. She knew better than to ask too many questions. Kate would open up in her own good time. There was no hurry.

'He's still married, Gran,' Kate said immediately without prompting, unable to keep it in any longer. 'He's not separated at all. And they have a second child on the way.'

Lily stared at her in shock. After the episode last Christmas she'd thought she'd heard it all – but this was worse, much worse. How could a man behave in such a way?

'He lied to me, Gran. About his wife, his son . . . everything. He even told me that she'd lost the first baby – his son. How could he say such a thing?'

Lily stood behind Kate and put her arms around her and kissed the top of her head.

'It's all over now,' she crooned. 'You're safe with your Granny

Lily, now.' Kate gave a huge sob. 'That's it,' she continued. 'Let it all out, love.'

Kate cried for almost ten minutes without stopping, huge gut-wrenching sobs. Tears rained out of her eyes in a deluge, spilling onto the kitchen table in splashes. Lily rubbed her back, then held her firmly as she wept. 'It'll be all right,' she whispered to Kate. 'You're home now. Home with Granny Lily. Try to take deep breaths now, there's a girl.'

After a little while the sobs grew further and further apart and Kate's breathing began to go back to normal.

'I'm sorry,' said Kate, wiping her eyes and face with the large man's handkerchief Lily had given her.

'Sorry for what?' Lily asked gently. 'None of this is your fault. You've nothing to be sorry about.'

'But I feel such an idiot. How could I have let this happen? I should never have trusted Jay again. I'm so stupid.' She held her head in her hands and rocked backwards and forwards.

'Don't be too hard on yourself,' Lily said. 'It happens. Everyone makes mistakes, especially where love is concerned.'

'And she was so nice to me,' Kate said, starting to cry again. 'I feel so terrible.'

'Who was nice to you?' Lily asked gently. 'Maybe you should start at the beginning. Tell me everything.'

'I can't,' Kate whispered. 'I just can't.' Tears began to roll down her face again.

Lily patted her hand. 'Try. It will make you feel better. Then we never have to talk about it again.'

'Promise?'

'I promise.'

'OK.' Kate wiped her eyes and took a deep breath. 'I met him in the Killiney Arms the week before last,' she began slowly. 'He was over on business and he'd asked to see me. I should never have gone but I did.' She told Lily the whole sorry story – from that first heady evening with Jay, to fainting at his feet outside his Boston apartment block.

'Oh, Gran, I was mortified. I must have been out of it for several minutes. When I opened my eyes I found Jay standing over me and Cindy kneeling down beside me. She'd put the baby's blanket under my head and was wiping my forehead with a damp babywipe.' Kate cringed inwardly at the memory.

'What happened then?' Lily asked gently.

'They took me into their apartment. Once we were inside Cindy asked Jay to make some coffee. He seemed a bit reluctant to leave us alone together, but he wasn't really in a position to argue. When he was in the kitchen, she looked at me and asked me straight out was I having an affair with her husband. I nearly died. I didn't know what to say. I couldn't look her in the eye, I just nodded and stared at the carpet. I expected her to hit me or shout at me at the very least.'

'What did she do?' Lily asked.

'She started to cry. It was awful, Gran. She said she knew something was going on, that things hadn't been right between them for a long time – his mind seemed to be somewhere else. Cindy said he'd been carrying on with a girl from the office called Tammy for a few months but she'd confronted him about her and he'd stopped seeing her. She said she was sick of it and couldn't live with him any more. She'd stopped trusting him. I was so ashamed. I said I was sorry, that he'd told me he was separated. And then she said in this really sad voice, "They always say that, don't they?" Oh, Gran, I felt so bad. She was being so decent to me and then Jay . . .' She shuddered at the memory. 'He'd been standing at the door listening. He walked in and started telling Cindy how much he loved her right in front of me, how I didn't mean anything to him, how he couldn't live without her, how she had to give him one more chance. Cindy stood up and slapped him on the cheek. And then she told him to get out. At this stage the baby was crying in the buggy, I was crying,

Cindy was crying and all Jay could do was stare at me. "You've ruined my life," he said to me. "I'll never forgive you." Then Cindy said "Jay, you've no one to blame but yourself. This woman isn't to blame. You are. Now get out. You'll be hearing from my lawyers in the morning."'

'It's like something from a novel,' Lily said before she could stop herself.

Kate looked at her and then began to smile through the tears. 'Gran!'

'I'm sorry but you know what I mean,' Lily said. 'It's all very dramatic. What happened after he'd left?'

'Cindy made us some coffee and we talked while she fed the baby. She asked me what had happened with Jay and I told her everything. I reckoned I owed it to her to be honest. We got on pretty well, to tell the truth, in the circumstances. After we'd talked for a few hours she booked me on a late flight and I came home.'

'You must be wrecked,' Lily said. 'Would you like to lie down? The spare bed's all made up.'

Kate shook her head. 'I'm not tired. Maybe later. I slept a little on the plane. The air hostesses were so kind. I kept crying – I couldn't help myself. One of them sat with me for a little while to make sure I was all right.'

'The kindness of strangers,' Lily murmured.

'I really loved him, Gran,' Kate continued. 'He asked me to marry him only last week. He even said he'd move to Dublin to be with me but he was obviously lying the whole time. Just like he did before. I feel such a fool. How could I have trusted him?' She thought for a moment. 'But, you know, Gran, in a strange way, I don't feel as bad as I did the last time he crushed me. It's as if my heart will never hurt as much after that. Jay hardened it last Christmas.'

Lily smiled at her. 'Your heart isn't hard, Kate. Believe me, I know. But that Jay has a lot to answer for. At least you weren't married to him and suffering all those affairs. Poor Cindy. What's she going to do now?'

Kate shrugged her shoulders. 'She said she's going to divorce him. But who knows? They may be able to patch it up. There are children involved after all.'

'Sometimes it's not in the children's best interest for the parents to stay together,' Lily said thoughtfully.

'I guess not.' Kate yawned. 'Maybe I am a little tired. Can I take you up on the offer of a bed?'

'Of course. And when you've had some sleep I'll make us some lunch. How about that?'

Kate gave Lily a hug. 'Thanks. I don't know what I'd do without you.'

'Go and get some rest now,' said Lily. 'You've had a right old shock to your system.'

'Thanks, Gran.'

As Kate made her way upstairs, Lily drained her tea, by now a little cold. She put her elbow on the table and rested her head on her hand. For some reason she wasn't worried about Kate this time. Kate was right – she was in a far worse state last Christmas. She'd been so distraught then that she couldn't talk about what had happened for days. Kate was in a much better place now. If only she'd find a nice young man, someone who'd care for her and nurture her. Someone she could trust. Someone like Angus. Lily had done all she could to help things along. If it was meant to be they would find each other. But maybe they both needed just a little more assistance.

'Did you have a nice break?' Molly asked as soon as Kate walked in the door on Monday night.

'Yes, thanks.' Kate replied evenly, dumping her suitcase at the bottom of the stairs. She'd spent most of the previous two days wrapped in a duvet on her granny's sofa watching television and eating junk food. But considering everything that had happened she felt remarkably all right. Jay had rung her mobile countless times but she'd switched it off eventually. She had absolutely nothing to say to him. She'd listened to the first of his messages – saying how Cindy really was out of the picture now and how he and Kate could be together forever. Obviously Cindy really had given him the boot and he wasn't prepared to be alone for longer than a minute. Still there was always Tammy in the office, Kate thought wryly after she'd deleted the message. I'm sure she'll take you back you creep. It had hurt her to know that there had been other affairs, that hers wasn't 'special'. But however much it hurt her, she kept thinking about Cindy. It was a thousand times worse for her. Kate swore that she'd never so much as smile at a married man again, even if he had separation or divorce papers to prove that he was 'available'.

'You missed all the drama on Saturday,' Molly said as Kate flopped onto the sofa.

'Really? What happened?'

'Sam's little boy went missing. It was terrible. Sam was in bits.'

'I can imagine. With all the child abductions on the news, I'm not surprised. They found him though?'

'Yes, thank goodness. Your friend Angus found him on the beach and brought him back. The poor child had got it into his head to run away.'

'Angus?' Kate asked with surprise.

'Yes, he was quite the hero. Managed to convince the little lad to come back home of his own accord. Poor mite had it in his head that no one wanted him around.'

'I know the feeling,' Kate murmured.

'Sorry, I missed that,' said Molly. 'What did you say?'

'Nothing, don't mind me. It's good to be back. How was your weekend apart from the drama?'

'Good thanks. But you have to tell me all about your holiday.

I've never been to Boston. What was the weather like? Was it hot?'

Kate nodded. 'Yes, very. Makes a nice change. I wasn't out in the sun much though. I spent a lovely day in the museum and um, saw my friend.'

'How did that go? Was it fun?'

'Not exactly,' Kate admitted. 'It was a bit of a disaster to tell the truth.'

Molly sighed. 'I'm really sorry to hear that. I know you probably don't want to talk about it but I'm here if you need me.' She was quite used to Kate's obsession with privacy.

Kate thought for a second. She felt bad. Molly was a good person and seemed genuinely sorry for her troubles. It wouldn't hurt to tell her what had happened, in fact, it might be just what she needed. Granny Lily had been great and she'd made her realize that talking to a sympathetic ear really was the best therapy. 'You know, Molly, I do want to talk about it this time. I know I haven't always told you everything in the past.' Kate smiled gently. 'In fact, I'm sure I've been more than a little evasive. But if you have the time I'd like to tell you all about Jay.'

'Is Jay your American friend?'

'Yes. At least he was.'

Molly smiled back at her. 'Kate, I've all the time in the world. Why don't we open a bottle of wine and settle in for the night?'

'You know, I'd like that,' said Kate. 'I'd like that a lot.'

'Does this mean I can borrow your Jimmy Choo boots?' Molly tried her luck.

'Don't push it,' Kate laughed. 'Those boots are sacred. But we'll see.'

Chapter 19

Paige

Paige woke up. She felt terrible – her neck was stiff and her buttocks were numb. The inside of her mouth felt dry yet sticky and she had a desperate urge to clear the gunge by brushing her teeth. Her suit jacket had fallen off her while she slept, leaving her cold and shivery. She should never have taken Tom's advice to have a nap in the car. She wondered what was going on inside the polling station, the large town hall in Dublin city. When she'd left the election count it was two in the morning and it was now almost five. She stretched her arms over her head, as much as she could in the confined space and flexed her feet and buttocks. She'd better go back in. She flicked on the inside car light and studied her face in the rear-view mirror, wincing as she saw the pale, unkempt reflection. She licked her two index fingers and removed the black mascara stains from underneath her eyes, rubbing gently so as not to pull and redden the delicate paper-thin skin. She then pulled her bag from under the car seat and found her emergency make-up kit. A few minutes later she felt a little more presentable. She braced herself for the scramble through the crowds at the count. At least Tom and her supporters were easy to spot – to the very far left of the hall, against the wall and beside Jackie Pile's gang.

'How are you feeling, love?' Tom asked after he'd given her a huge smile and hug.

'Groggy,' she said truthfully. 'I'm sure I'll be fine in a few minutes though. What's been happening in my absence?'

'Mark's in and they're counting his second preferences as we speak.'

'How's it looking?'

'Hard to tell. Annette seems pretty confident – she's already given RTE an interview about what she'll do when she's in government.'

Paige bit her lip. 'Really?'

Tom smiled. 'Yes. But she'll look pretty stupid when you win the seat, won't she?' He squeezed Paige's hand.

'I can't bear all this tension,' Paige said. 'It's excruciating.'

'I know,' Tom said gently. 'But it'll be all over soon.'

'And we have a final count in Dublin North,' a voice boomed over the PA system.

Paige and Tom listened as the official read out the final results.

'In the Dun Laoghaire Rathdown constituency,' another official read a moment later, 'we have eliminated Hilda Murphy, Miles McGreinna and Rex Reximus.'

Tom nudged Paige. 'There's just you and Annette left.'

Paige's face was pale. She said nothing.

'I think you should sit down,' he said. 'I'll go and find you a chair. Back in a minute.'

'Thanks,' she said gratefully. She was feeling rather faint.

He pushed his way through the crowds.

Jackie Pile appeared beside Paige and touched her on the shoulder. 'How are you bearing up?' she asked Paige kindly.

Paige shrugged her shoulders. 'OK, in the circumstances. I'm delighted you got in again. Well done.'

'Thanks. And I look forward to working with you.'

'If I get in,' Paige sighed. 'It's going to be close.'

Jackie smiled. 'I have every confidence in you, Paige. You've worked hard and you deserve it. If there's any justice in the world, you'll be elected.'

'Thanks.'

'And we have a recount for the last seat in Dun Laoghaire Rathdown constituency.'

Jackie whistled. 'You were right about it being close, Paige. I hate recounts, I don't envy you.'

'You're an old hand at all this,' Tom said, overhearing Jackie's last comment. He opened the plastic folding chair he was holding and smiled at Jackie.

'It never gets any easier though,' Jackie said. 'Would you like some tea or coffee? We have some at our table. And some sandwiches I believe, although I can't vouch for their freshness.'

'That would be great, thanks,' Paige said gratefully. Although sitting down now, she still felt faint and something to eat might help her blood-sugar level.

An agonizing hour later, Tom put his hand on Paige's shoulder. She'd been dozing in the chair, leaning against his side.

'They're about to announce the result,' he said.

Paige raised her head, looked over to the right and tried to pick out Annette in the crowd. It wasn't hard. She was standing on a chair, craning to the see the stage, one steadying hand on her husband's shoulder. At that moment Annette looked over towards Paige, as if sensing Paige's gaze. She nodded in recognition, no emotion showing on her face, her eyes lingering on Paige for a few moments before swivelling back towards the stage.

'Annette looks very confident,' Paige said to Tom in a low voice.

'That means nothing,' Tom assured her, staring at the stage.

'There's our official. He's been handed the result sheet. Here we go.' The man walked towards the microphone. Paige took a deep breath and braced herself for bad news.

'And in the Dun Laoghaire Rathdown constituency on the second and final count, Councillor Paige Brady has one hundred thousand and fifty-six votes. On the second and final count Councillor Annette Higgins has one hundred thousand and forty-two votes. I hereby elect Councillor Paige Brady to the fourth and final seat.'

A roar of approval swept the hall and all around her people clapped and cheered.

'Well done, Paige.' Jackie kissed her warmly on both cheeks.

'Where's the new Deputy?' Paddy Burns boomed as he made his way towards her. 'Congratulations, my dear.' He gave her a huge bearhug.

Paige was overwhelmed. She clung to Tom's hand, the tears freely flowing down her cheeks.

'Have you anything to say to us, Deputy Brady?' An RTE radio journalist thrust a large grey woolly microphone in her face.

'Um, yes,' Paige said. 'I'm delighted and I'd like to thank everyone who voted for me.'

'Are you surprised that Councillor Higgins didn't get in?'

'Yes,' Paige said honestly. 'I suppose I am.'

'How do you feel about her comments about you this evening?'

Paige raised her eyebrows and looked at Tom. He smiled at her and shrugged his shoulders.

'I wasn't aware that she'd made any,' Paige replied evenly, refusing to be baited. 'And it's all a little irrelevant now, isn't it?'

'I suppose it is,' the journalist said reluctantly. 'But I think you should know that she called you . . .'

Paige put her hands in the air. 'I honestly don't want to hear,

311

thank you very much. I think Councillor Higgins has her own problems to be getting on with, don't you? And I'm sure what she told you was said in the heat of the moment. Now would you like to talk to Deputy Pile? She's right beside me.'

'Um, yes, sure,' the journalist said and left Paige alone.

'Well handled,' Tom said.

Paige smiled at him. 'Hey, I won. There's no point in rubbing her nose in it.' She yawned. 'Now, let's go home. I'm exhausted. We can celebrate tomorrow night. Right now, me and the baby need some sleep – in a bed!'

'Anything you say, Deputy.' Tom put his arm around her protectively. 'Home it is.'

The following morning Paige woke up and remembered instantly. A warm feeling flooded her whole body – she'd won the election and she was now a full-blown Deputy. The enormity of the situation began to sink in. She glanced at the clock radio beside the bed – almost eleven o'clock – she should have been up hours ago. It was all very quiet downstairs – maybe Tom had taken the boys out for a walk.

She pushed herself up in the bed. She was still exhausted, exhausted but elated. She wondered if everyone had heard the news yet. She'd texted Molly last night but she must ring her mum and Tom's mum this morning. Although by this stage they'd probably have heard on the news. She got out of bed, slipped her feet into her slippers and wrapped her towelling dressing gown around her. Her stomach was starting to round out now – soon she'd be in fully-fledged 'preggy' gear, but for now her looser clothes sufficed.

'Tom?' she called as she walked down the stairs. 'Hello? Anyone home?'

She heard a muffled giggle from the kitchen and smiled. Callum was probably in hiding – waiting to jump out at her from under the table or behind the curtains.

As she walked into the kitchen she was met by a host of smiling faces – Tom, Callum, Molly, Kate, Lily, Angus, Tom's mum and dad, and her own mum. And Alfie looked on with interest from his highchair in the corner.

'Surprise!' Callum said. 'We're having a party for you, Mum.'

Paige laughed and looked down. 'But I'm still in my pyjamas.'

'It's my fault,' Tom said. 'I invited everyone over. I thought we should celebrate now as I have a special surprise arranged for you this evening.'

'What sort of surprise?' Paige asked with interest.

'You'll have to wait and see.' He smiled.

'Have some cake, Mum,' Callum insisted, pulling her towards the kitchen table by her dressing gown tie. 'Come on. Granny made it this morning and it's still warm. It's chocolate!'

'Well in that case.' Paige looked at the large rectangular cake which was sitting on the table. 'Congratulations,' it read in white icing surrounded by little silver balls.

'Thanks, Mum.' Paige smiled at her mother.

'We're all very proud of you,' her mother said. 'I'm afraid the icing isn't quite set, but I'm sure it will taste fine.'

Tom handed Paige a knife. 'You do the honours,' he said. 'We're all dying for a slice.'

'I can't believe you're a Deputy now.' Molly grinned. 'Does this mean we have to watch what we say around you?'

'Not at all,' Paige said. 'It won't change me one little bit.'

'Will you be famous, Mum?' Callum asked.

She ruffled his hair. 'No, Callum.'

'But you'll be on the telly?' he asked hopefully. 'On *The Den* children's show?'

She smiled. 'Doubtful. Unless Dustin the Turkey invites me.'

'I'll write to him and tell him all about you,' Callum promised. 'I'll tell him what a good mummy you are and then he'll have you on.'

'You do that,' Paige said.

Everyone laughed.

Tom organized coffee and tea for everyone while Paige talked to Molly, Kate and Lily about the nerve-wracking night.

'How did you feel when they announced the final count?' Lily asked.

'I was in shock to be honest, I was convinced Annette had pipped me at the post. And it came as a huge relief I suppose, after all the hard work.'

'We all knew you could do it,' Lily said.

Paige smiled. 'Thanks.'

'Sure didn't Gran cajole all her friends to vote for you,' Kate quipped. 'Which must be practically half of Burnaby.'

Lily laughed. 'At least three quarters, please.'

Paige smiled. 'I couldn't have done it without all of you. And without Tom of course. And Angus.'

'I did nothing,' Angus insisted, handing Alfie back his soggy Liga biscuit.

'You kept Callum entertained,' Paige pointed out, 'and helped with Alfie. That's hardly nothing.'

Tom tapped his coffee mug with a tea spoon. 'I'd like to propose a toast. To Deputy Brady. May God protect her and all who sail in her.'

Everyone laughed.

'I think he's calling you a ship, Mummy!' Callum said delightedly.

'Tom!' Paige protested.

He grinned at her and winked.

'To Deputy Brady,' he repeated. They all raised their mugs and clunked them together. 'To Deputy Brady.'

*

That afternoon Tom met with his boss in the building society. He'd been working for Hannah Brookes for over five years now and they'd always got on well. She was a kind, if somewhat formidable woman who kept her staff firmly in line and had a habit of being a little more abrupt than most would like. Walking into her office, Tom felt a little nervous. He had no idea how she would react to his request.

'Hello, Tom.' She looked up from her computer screen and smiled. 'Please sit down.'

'Thanks.'

'How's Paige? I believe she's our new Deputy. Do congratulate her for me.'

'I will.'

'Now what can I do for you?'

'I'll come straight to the point, Hannah. Paige and I have been discussing the coming year and we feel that the children need one of us around. Callum will be starting school next year and we'd like to be able to collect him every day and do his homework with him – that sort of thing. And as you know, Paige is expecting again next year.'

'Go on,' Hannah said evenly.

'Well, um, I was hoping to take a year's unpaid leave to stay at home with the kids. Paige will be working all hours and um, we thought this might be a solution.'

'I see,' said Hannah. She said nothing for a moment. 'Have you taken parental leave before?'

Tom shook his head. 'No. If I've needed any extra days I've taken them out of my holidays.'

'You're a good manager, Tom. I'll be sorry to lose you.'

Tom caught his breath.

'I'll rephrase that,' Hannah said quickly. 'I'll be sorry to lose you for the year, but I understand completely. My own are all teenagers now, but it's still a struggle to keep the house running smoothly. I know how hard it is when they're younger, believe me. Besides, according to European Law you're entitled to several months unpaid parental leave if you have children under four or five. I can't quite remember the details but one of the women in the Bray branch has just started three months' parental leave.'

'Really?' Tom asked. 'And my job is safe even if I take as much as a year off?'

Hannah smiled. 'Of course, we'd hate to lose you permanently. And maybe you'd consider doing some consultancy work for us at home?'

'I'd be happy to,' Tom said eagerly.

'You're a good man, Tom,' Hannah said thoughtfully. 'There's not many husbands who would put their wives' careers before theirs. I admire you.'

Tom blushed. Hannah wasn't usually renowned for her compliments. 'Thanks,' he murmured.

That evening Tom arrived home early from work.

'Anybody home?' he shouted as he walked into the hall.

'Daddy!' Callum came careering towards him and threw his little arms around Tom's waist.

Tom picked him up and threw him in the air. 'How's my best boy?' He grinned. 'Have you been good for Angus today?'

'Yes! And he told me about being my teacher. Isn't it cool?'

'Very cool.' Tom smiled. 'But you'll have to be extra good for him in class.'

'I will,' Callum said solemnly. 'Angus has already told me that I have to be a good mample.'

'Mample?' Tom was confused.

'You know, show the others how to be good.'

Tom clicked. 'A good example.' He tried not to laugh.

'Yes,' Callum nodded solemnly. 'A good mample.'

They went into the kitchen where Angus was feeding Alfie some sort of mushy goo.

'Hi, Tom,' Angus said. 'Want to take over?'

'Sure.' Tom pulled off his jacket and hung it over the back of one of the kitchen chairs. Tom removed his tie and shoved it unceremoniously into a jacket pocket. Won't be needing one of those soon, he thought. He took the plastic bowl and spoon off Angus and sniffed the bowl's contents. 'Banana?'

Angus nodded. 'Banana and apple. Paige made it.'

'Where is Paige?'

'Upstairs having a rest. She was looking a little worn out so I took over Alfie's tea.'

'Thanks,' Tom said gratefully.

'No worries. So how was the office, dear?' Angus asked with a grin.

'Fine, thanks.' Tom laughed. 'Actually it was good. I asked my boss for a year's parental leave and she said yes.'

'That's great! Callum will be thrilled to have you around more. He's always saying how he'd love to do more things with you.'

'Really?' Tom asked. 'You never mentioned it before.'

Angus shrugged. 'You and Paige have been under a lot of pressure recently. You didn't need any extra guilt trips.'

'I suppose not. I look forward to spending more time with him. He's growing up so fast. And I believe you told him about being his teacher.'

'Is that OK? I hope you didn't want to tell him yourselves.'

'No, it's fine. And he's delighted.' They both looked at Callum who was colouring in a picture of Spiderman with chunky crayons.

'He's a good kid.' Angus smiled. 'I look forward to teaching him.'

Tom coughed. 'Um, I know we've never really said it to you before, not properly anyway,' he began, 'but we really appreciate all the time and effort you've put into his nibs this

317

summer.' Tom gestured towards Callum with his head. 'It's made all the difference. We really are very grateful.'

'I know you are.' Angus smiled at Tom. 'And it's been a pleasure, really. He's a real little charmer.'

'Well, thanks anyway.' Tom punched Angus gently on the shoulder. 'And are you sure you're OK to babysit this evening?'

'Yes, positive. I'm sure it'll be useful to the school to have Deputy Brady owing me a favour.'

Tom laughed. 'You're probably right!'

Later that evening Paige had her usual wardrobe dilemma, except this time it was worse. The dark brown suede trousers she'd intended to wear were far too tight around the waist. She'd tried leaving the button and zip undone and pulling a black jumper down over her stomach but that made her look bulgy and made the seat of the trousers bag unbecomingly. Besides, what if her trousers fell down during the night and she didn't notice? She sighed and put the outfit back in the wardrobe.

'What's up?' Tom was lounging fully dressed on their bed, watching her. He'd already changed out of his work gear, showered and shaved and was rearing to go. He hadn't had much for lunch and his stomach was starting to complain loudly.

'I can't find anything to wear,' she complained.

'Can I help?'

She smiled at him. 'I don't know, can you?' She put her hands on her hips provocatively and raised her eyebrows.

'I think you should go out just as you are,' he said. 'You look great.'

She smiled at him and looked down at her black lacy bra, matching G-string and hold-up stockings. 'I think I might get a little cold. Besides, unless we're going to a lap dancing club I don't think it's quite appropriate.'

Tom got up and walked towards her. He stood behind her, wrapping his arms around her waist.

She flinched. 'Your hands are freezing!'

'They'll soon warm up,' he promised. He moved them up her body, lingering over her breasts. He unhooked her bra and deftly removed it, throwing it onto the floor.

'Tom, we have to go,' Paige protested. 'We'll be late. Besides, Angus is downstairs.'

'There's no mad rush,' Tom said. 'And Angus has taken the kids out to the park, bless him.' His hands caressed her breasts and he began to kiss the nape of her neck gently. She turned around and smiled at him. She was actually feeling quite good all day and Tom seemed to be in flying form, it would be a shame to stifle him. Besides, they hadn't had sex for weeks as she hadn't been feeling up to it. And once the baby came . . . she shuddered to think how tired they'd both be. They should grab every opportunity they could, especially if Callum and Alfie were otherwise occupied. 'In that case . . .' She kissed him firmly on the lips, put her arms on his shoulders and pushed him backwards towards the bed.

'Deputy Brady.' He laughed, as they fell onto the bed. Paige silenced him with another kiss.

'I had an interesting meeting with Hannah today,' Tom said later that evening after they'd ordered their food. They were sitting at a secluded table in their favourite restaurant, Fallon's in Burnaby.

'Oh?' Paige took a sip of her wine and smiled at him. 'What about?'

'Things.' He smiled mysteriously.

'Go on,' she said impatiently. 'What things?'

'About taking a year off to look after the kids.'

'Really? What did she say?'

Tom smiled again. 'She said yes. She's going to promote Annie Jones on a temporary basis and take on a new trainee manager to replace her.'

Paige looked at him with a strange expression on her face.

'What?' he asked. 'Are you not happy? It's what we'd discussed, Paige, before the elections.'

'I know. But we didn't really go over the details – the financial end of things for example.'

'I've had a look at the figures and as long as we don't go wild we should be fine. It'll mean no foreign holidays for example, and we won't be changing the cars, but we'll manage.'

She was quiet for a moment, her fingers running up and down the stem of the wine glass, her eyes fixed on the dark red wine.

Tom allowed her time to collect her thoughts.

'I guess I haven't had time to take it all in,' she said finally. 'I didn't expect it all to happen so quickly I suppose.' She looked him straight in the eye. 'To tell the truth, it makes me feel a little inadequate as a mother. I feel like you'll be taking over and that I'll just be in the background, plodding away at work.' She sighed. 'I'm sorry, I'm not being fair. It's what we'd agreed, I know. I just didn't expect to feel like this.'

Tom put his hand on hers. 'Paige,' he said softly. 'You'll always be their mother. Nothing can change that. You'll always have a special relationship with them. I'll just be the one doing the school run and changing Alfie's nappies, that's all.'

Paige snorted. 'And you're more than welcome to Alfie's nappies. You're right, I know you're right. But I just feel kind of, oh, I don't know – left out, I suppose.'

Tom smiled at her warmly. 'Paige, you won't be left out of anything, I promise you that.'

'I'm sorry, I'm being really ungracious,' she said. 'Most women would be delighted to have such a supportive husband.'

'That's what Hannah said.' Tom smiled.

'I really am very lucky.' Paige leant over and kissed him on the cheek. 'And I do love you, Tom.'

He stroked her hand. 'And I love you too. More than ever.'

Paige felt a warm sensation in the pit of her stomach. She knew the next year was going to be hard for both of them, but as long as they were together they'd get through anything.

Chapter 20

Molly

'Before we get started I'd like to apologize,' Milo began as soon as the other Book Club members had settled into their seats and stopped discussing their favourite event at the book festival, which they'd unanimously declared a huge success.

'Why?' Paige asked.

'Yes, what have you done now?' Anita asked with a sigh.

Molly tried not to laugh. Anita was sitting beside Milo and from what she could see the cold war between them still hadn't thawed.

'I recommended *Bright Light of My Soul*,' he said picking up that's month's book choice and turning the elegant-looking matt grey paperback over in his hands. 'It got some great reviews in hardback and I thought it would be an interesting read.' He stopped for a moment.

'Milo, are you saying that you didn't like it?' Paige raised her eyebrows.

'No I didn't, not really,' Milo admitted. He put a finger under the collar of his trademark black polo neck, as if letting some air in. 'It wasn't the easiest read, was it?'

Anita snorted. 'But I thought you informed us at the last

meeting that we should all be reading more literary fiction, that our tastes were too, how did you put it, ah yes, "unformed" and "unrefined".'

'I didn't say that, did I?' Milo asked, getting a little red in the face.

'I'm afraid you did,' Harry said, smiling broadly at him.

'Dad!' Sam hissed at him. 'I must have come in after that,' he said to the table. 'It's not as if he's the world's greatest reader himself. In fact up until he bought this shop . . .'

Milo coughed loudly. 'Um, yes, well, I'm sorry if I caused any offence at the last meeting. I was wrong.'

'We won't be reading any more of your recommendations for a while anyway,' Cathy laughed. 'I hated *Bright Light of My Soul* – it was so depressing. I don't mind depressing as such, but there was absolutely no hope shining through at all. It was a weep fest from start to finish. Nothing of any interest happened to the main character, Hoppy. And what kind of name is "Hoppy" for a woman anyway?'

'I thought it was supposed to be a kind of twist on the word "happy" myself,' Trina said. 'But that's probably a bit too obvious. It's her first book though, isn't it? Una Franklin's. Maybe she'll cheer up a bit in the next one.'

'Let's hope so,' Anita nodded. 'She can't get any worse. And what about the men in the book? They were all totally nasty characters – from your man Frankie, her first husband, to that guy who killed her at the end, Joe. I know as a gender men are not perfect,' she looked pointedly at Milo, 'but they're not all bad.'

'I agree,' Sam said. 'It was a pretty bleak reflection on men. But some of the women weren't any better. Didn't her own mother practically sell her to Frankie for a piece of land?'

'That's right! She was horrible to Hoppy,' Molly agreed. 'And her so called "friend" Susan wasn't much better."

'The one who told the guards that Hoppy was a prostitute?' Kate asked.

'Yes.' Molly nodded. 'She was a nasty piece of work.'

'What are you doing after this?' Molly whispered to Paige an hour later. The debate on *Bright Light of My Soul* was beginning to wind down and the group were now discussing choices for next month's book. 'Going for lunch with you.' Paige smiled.

'Great!' Molly squeezed her friend's arm. 'I wasn't sure if you'd be free, Deputy.'

'What do you think, Molly?' Anita asked her, interrupting them.

'Sorry?' Molly replied. 'I missed that.'

'Cathy was asking if we could order copies of an American title in time for next month's meeting?'

'Depends on the book,' Molly said. 'But it shouldn't be a problem if the American wholesaler we use has it.'

'Well then, I vote we take a break from literary fiction,' Anita glanced at Milo and he winced.

'Hear, hear,' said Cathy.

'I agree.' Trina nodded. 'Let's have something with a real story this time. And a happy ending please, if it's not too much to ask. Optimistic at the very least.'

'Well then, I nominate Bonnie's new book,' Cathy said. 'It's only available in the States at the moment so we'll be the very first people to read it. It's based in Burnaby apparently and we might even recognize some of the characters. She told me about it at the festival.'

'Excellent!' Anita clapped her hands together. 'Any objections?'

Everyone shook their heads.

'Back to decent fiction then,' Anita said, her eyes lingering on Milo. 'And about time too.'

*

The following Monday, Molly lingered outside the Begley Literary Agency, her stomach twisted with nerves. She looked up at the imposing Georgian Merrion Square building and fished in the small pocket of her oversized red leather bag for her powder compact, flicked it open and checked her face. She hoped she was dressed appropriately. She'd spent ages last night deciding what to wear, with Kate and Paige's patient help, and had finally settled on a pair of old reliable black trousers, a white shirt (Kate's) and a dark red fitted cashmere cardigan (Paige's). She completed the outfit with a black beaded choker (Paige's), the red bag (hers) and killer Jimmy Choo black high-heeled boots, Kate's pride and joy, which she'd insisted on lending to Molly for good luck. She'd popped a pair of runners in the bag just in case her feet were crippled from the heels on the way home as she'd taken the Dart train to abate the extra stress of driving in the Dublin city traffic, not to mention finding an elusive parking space.

The three of them – Molly, Kate and Paige – had had a delightfully girly evening in the end and Kate, usually dismissive of 'girliness' had really got into the spirit of things. Kate had turned out to be a dab hand at making pink cocktails complete with authentic blender-produced slushy ice, slices of orange and lemon, and tiny multi-coloured paper cocktail umbrellas that she'd discovered in the cupboard under the sink, left over from some party or other. Molly and Paige had been most impressed. Molly regretted drinking quite so many of the 'Deputy Brady Delights', as Kate had christened one of her dark pink concoctions, not to mention the 'Milly Molly Mandys' which were blood red and full of vodka, or the baby pink 'Catikins' but it had been a great evening.

Molly glanced at her watch. It was just after ten and if she didn't go in now she'd be late. She smoothed her trousers down her legs, checked the eye and hook fastenings on her shirt, as Kate had warned her they had a habit of coming undone at inopportune moments, and walked up the steps towards the imposing red front door. She rang the intercom beside the discreet 'Begley Literary Agency' brass nameplate and waited. A moment later, a friendly woman's voice answered.

'Hello? Begley Agency. Can I help you?'

'Um, it's Molly Harper.'

'Hi, Molly, Gerry's expecting you. Push the door and go up the stairs. Our offices are at the back of the first floor, in the return.'

'Thanks.' Molly stepped inside and looked around. The hall was amazing – it had soaringly high ceilings, complete with what seemed to be original plasterwork. A large, ornate crystal chandelier hung from the middle of the space, dangling weightily from the most organic ceiling rose Molly had ever seen. It was made up of huge fronds of fern-like leafy foliage, all curving and twisting down from the horizontal plane as if growing towards the floor. The hall was painted creamy white and the black and white tiled floor set it off beautifully. As Molly walked up the stairs, she could feel the thick pile of the cream carpet under the thin soles of her boots. The Begley Agency was obviously a huge success judging by appearances and Molly was distinctly impressed and overawed.

'What would Mr Begley want with me?' she asked under her breath. 'He obviously has more than enough clients to be going on with.'

'Hello.' As Molly reached the top of the stairs she was greeted by a small, dark haired young woman. 'You must be Molly, nice to meet you.' She held out her hand and smiled.

'Hi,' Molly said, shaking her hand firmly. She followed the woman through a doorway and into a small, bright office, furnished with a simple mahogany desk, an armchair and an antique-looking coffee table stacked high with book trade magazines – *The Bookseller*, *Publishing Ireland*, *Inis*, and *Dublin Books*.

'Gerry will be ready for you in one minute. He's just on the phone to an editor at the moment. He spends most of his day on the phone – he gets hundreds of calls every day.' She gestured at the chair. 'Please, make yourself comfortable. Can I make you some tea or coffee?'

'No thanks, but I'd love a glass of water,' Molly said.

'No problem.' The woman came back a few minutes later with a tall glass and handed it to Molly. 'I'm Julie by the way, Gerry's assistant and general dogsbody.'

'Nice to meet you, Julie.' Molly smiled shyly. 'Quite some offices you have here.'

Julie laughed. 'Most of this building belongs to the accountancy firm Gerry used to work for. We just rent this bit off them. It's not as glam as the rest of the building but it's in a great location. We get to impress clients with the address,' she lowered her voice, 'and the accountants get to namedrop the literary agency to make themselves sound more interesting. Plus we recommend a lot of our clients to them. So, everyone wins.'

Molly smiled again.

Julie noticed how tightly Molly was clutching the bag on her knee. 'You're probably nervous, but don't be. Gerry's a lovely man and he's very easy to talk to.'

'What were you saying about me?' The door opposite Julie's desk opened and Gerry himself stepped out. He smiled at Molly. 'I hope it was nice.'

'Of course it was, Gerry.' Julie winked at Molly. 'Sure why wouldn't it be? Great man like yourself.'

'Indeed.' Gerry laughed. 'Sorry to keep you waiting, Molly. I'm sure Julie was keeping you entertained. Please come in.' He held the door for her and Molly stepped into his office. Julie was right – it wasn't as glam as the rest of the building but it was still an impressive room. The end wall was made up of richly coloured stained glass depicting a phoenix rising from vivid orange flames. In the centre of the room was another large mahogany desk and to the left and right there were filing cabinets and shelves and shelves crammed with books of all shapes and sizes.

'Do sit down,' Gerry said. 'Have you ever talked to an agent before, Molly?'

Molly was taken aback. 'Um, no,' she murmured. 'Never.'

He looked down at the sheets of paper in front of him. 'Am I the first person to read some of your stories?'

She nodded shyly. She hoped she wasn't blushing too noticeably, her cheeks felt decidedly pink.

'Your work has a lovely fresh feel,' Gerry said. 'I think you have real talent. Unfortunately there's no real market for short stories at the moment. And I think your *Price of Gold* saga is a little too ambitious for a first book.'

Molly's heart dropped. He didn't want her. Of course he didn't – a highly respected man like Gerry Begley. What was she . . .?

'How would you feel about that?' he asked. 'Could you try it?'

'Sorry?' she'd missed what he'd said.

'Writing a contemporary novel. What do you think?'

Molly looked at him in surprise. 'Um, I could give it a go.'

'Your short stories are excellent and I'm sure Julie could place them for you in magazines, say *Trend* for example and *Dublin Books*.'

'Really?' Molly asked with delight. 'That would be great.'

'I liked "Concrete Pictures" very much. How would you feel about expanding that story into a novel? The two main characters were very strong and I think there's a lot of meat to them.'

Molly smiled. Meat? She wasn't quite sure what to make of that but it sounded like a compliment.

'How about writing five or six chapters and a plot outline and then we could put a proposal together for a publisher? How does that sound?'

'Fine,' Molly said. 'Great, I mean. I think I could do that.'

'I'm sorry, I never asked if you wanted me to represent you. You may like to look around for someone else. There's Josie O'Hara of course, and Phelim . . .'

Molly didn't have to think. Gerry seemed like someone she could trust, plus he genuinely seemed to like her work. 'No, I'd like you if you'll have me.'

'Of course I'll have you, my dear.' Gerry's eyes twinkled. 'I'd be delighted to be your agent. I think we'll get along just swimmingly.'

'So do I.' Molly smiled back. 'And I'll get writing straight away.'

'That's what I like to hear,' Gerry said. 'Welcome to the family, Molly. I'll ask Julie to draw up the official papers allowing me to act as your agent. Maybe you could come in next week and sign them?'

'I'd be happy to.'

'Good, and you can tell me all about your progress on "Concrete Pictures".'

Molly skipped down the building's steps after the meeting, almost twisting her ankle in the process and causing her to lurch ungainly against the dark blue handrail. She straightened herself up, rubbed her side where she'd hit the solid metal and smiled. Nothing could dampen her mood at this moment, not even a large bruise

'So how did it go this morning?' Sam asked as soon as she'd stepped foot in the bookshop. He was sitting on the stool at the front till, keying some customer orders into the computer. There were a few customers browsing the shelves but all in all it was pretty quiet.

'Really well.' Molly smiled and dumped her bag on the counter to the relief of her poor shoulders – she always carried too much junk 'just in case'. She hadn't bothered changing into her runners either and was starting to regret it. Kate's boots were killers in more ways than one. She was dying to take them off and give her soles and insteps a rub. 'Gerry was nice, he wants to be my agent. He's going to place some of my stories with magazines, well, his assistant Julie is, and he asked me to try writing a book based on "Concrete Pictures".'

Sam laughed. 'Try stopping for breath, Molly!'

She smiled at him again. 'Sorry, was I gabbling? I'm just so excited about the whole thing. I can't believe it's all happening. First winning the short story competition, now this.'

He jumped off the stool, walked around the counter towards her and gave her a huge hug. 'If anyone deserves it, you do,' he kissed the top of her head. 'Well done, you.'

Molly felt on top of the world. Not only did Gerry want her, she had the kindest and nicest boyfriend in the world.

'Thanks,' she said.

'Ahem,' a customer coughed beside them. 'Can I pay for this?'

'Sure.' Sam grinned and winked at Molly. 'Why don't you go into the office and put your feet up for a few minutes. I'll deal with this.'

'That would be great if you don't mind. I'll be back out in a while.'

Once in the office Molly flopped down in a chair and rang Paige again. She'd tried her on the walk down to the train station, positively hopping to tell her the good news, but Paige's mobile had been turned off.

'Molly, I was just thinking about you. How did the meeting go?'

Molly told her all the details.

'Fantastic!' Paige said enthusiastically. 'He sounds like just the man you need. So, I guess you just have to get writing now.'

Molly bit her lip. The reality of the situation was only starting to kick in. 'What if I can't write a whole book? I've tried before and I've always come unstuck about halfway through. I've never finished a whole one before.'

'This time it's different,' Paige assured her. 'You've just won a prize for you work and you've got an agent. Everything's changed. You're a real writer now and it's your job to write. Just like it's my job to stop dog owners from allowing their dogs to poop on the beach. I know which job I'd rather do right at this minute.' Paige laughed. 'And I thought being a Deputy would be much more glamorous than being a Councillor. How wrong can you get?'

'Right now, alleviating dog poop sounds much easier to me.' Molly sniffed. 'Paige, what have I done? I can't write a book. Who am I kidding?'

'Listen to me, Molly.' Paige's voice sounded firm and unbending. 'You most certainly can and you most certainly will. I want you to go home this evening, have dinner, go for a walk and then sit down at your computer. Read "Concrete Pictures" again. Read it over and over as many time as you have to.'

'Why?'

'To get it into your thick skull that you can write, dummy,' Paige said. 'I know you have a book in you and I bet Sam thinks so too. And Anita. And Gerry has confidence in you, and he's a professional who doesn't know you from Adam. It's about time you had a little confidence in yourself, Molly. Do you hear me?'

Molly nodded.

'Molly?'

'I was nodding.'

'So you'll stop thinking negative thoughts?'

'Um, I suppose so.'

'And you'll sit down this evening and write?'

'I will,' Molly said.

'Promise?'

'Promise.'

'I'll ring you later. Now, smile, Molly. You *can* do it, don't forget that.'

'Thanks, Guru Brady.' Molly laughed. 'I feel much better now. Talk to you later.'

Molly smiled as she clicked off her phone. Just then Sam popped his head round the door.

'Dad's here for the meeting. Are you ready?'

'Damn, I'd forgotten all about it. Is Anita here yet?'

'Yes, she's talking to Dad. From what I managed to eavesdrop, they're going to the theatre together this evening.'

'Really?' Molly raised her eyebrows. 'I thought she couldn't stand him.'

'I know.' Sam smiled. 'Wonders will never cease.'

'Give me two minutes. I presume the meeting will be in here?'

Sam nodded. 'And Felix is covering the shop floor for an hour or so.'

'We'd better get going then I guess,' Molly sighed. 'Lambs to the slaughter and all that.' She looked at him carefully. 'What has your Dad said to you? What do you know? I know you know something.'

'As I keep telling you,' he put on a feeble Italian accent, 'I know nothing. Nothing I'm at liberty to tell you anyway. Trust me.' Sam looked down at his hands. Molly sensed there was something he wanted to tell her but for some reason he couldn't.

Molly sniffed. 'He's going to change the shop, I know he is. He's never liked the pink and purple shelves and quite frankly I think the whole "romance bookshop" thing is just an embarrassment to him. I can see it now – "Milo's Cool Literary Bookshop" – all black and grey shelves. Black leather sofas, jazz music, poetry readings . . .'

'Hello, are you ready for the meeting, Molly?' Anita walked into the office, interrupting Molly in mid-flow.

'Um, yes,' Molly said. She looked at Sam who was trying not to laugh. 'Ready, Sam?' she asked pointedly.

'Sure, whenever you are.'

They all sat down in the small office, Molly behind the desk, Anita and Sam on the sofa and Milo beside them on a fold-out chair. It was decidedly cramped.

'So, Milo,' Anita began, 'why are we all here?'

Milo cleared his throat theatrically. 'As you all know the bookshop figures haven't been the best in recent weeks. But I'm delighted to say that the festival was a huge hit and . . .'

Anita stared at him, her eyes narrowing. 'And what?'

'The figures in the last two weeks since the festival have been very strong. So, I've changed my mind. The bookshop can stay as it is for the moment.'

Sam looked at him in surprise. This wasn't what he was expecting.

'No jazz music?' Molly asked.

'Well, maybe a little jazz,' Milo said. 'But no black shelves and you can keep the name.'

'Thanks very much,' Anita muttered. 'Milo, what do you mean – "for the moment"?'

'For the foreseeable future, does that clarify it?' said Milo.

'No,' Anita said firmly. 'It does not. I want you to guarantee that you won't change the shop, not now, not ever. Like you promised me when you bought it.'

'But I can't do that!' Milo protested. 'Something might happen, romance might go out of fashion.'

'Romance will never go out of fashion.' Anita glared at him. 'Not that you've ever read any of it. So how would you know?'

He looked straight back at her. 'For your information, I read one of Bonnie's books only last week.'

'Really?' Anita was genuinely surprised.

'Yes, really. And I liked it. I'll be reading her next book, for the reading group. After that I thought I'd give Rose Lovett a go.'

Molly looked at Anita, who had a strange expression on her face, Molly couldn't quite read it.

Sam whistled. 'Three books in one month, Dad. You'd want to watch that. Reading's a dangerous thing. Addictive. So when are you going to tell them, Dad? Are you going to play at book-selling for another few weeks, another year, another two years? That wasn't exactly the plan now, was it? Your architect was on the phone yesterday. He asked for Mr Devine so I took the call. I can't believe you've been lying to me, your own son. How could you?'

Milo looked at Sam in shock, his face growing pale. 'I don't think this is the time or the place, Sam. Why don't we discuss this later. I think . . .'

'The plan?' Anita asked Sam, steel in her eyes. 'What do you mean?'

'Ask him,' Sam gestured at his dad. 'I had nothing to do with it, Anita, believe me.'

Milo looked sheepish. 'Ignore Sam,' he muttered. 'He doesn't know what he's talking about.'

'Milo,' Anita said firmly, her voice dangerously low. 'Go on.'

'If you won't, I will,' Sam said, a threatening edge to his own voice.

'But . . . ' Milo looked at Sam. There was a dangerous glint in his son's eyes.

'I mean it, Dad.'

Milo sighed. There was no way out, he'd have to come clean. 'I bought the bookshop to knock it down and build offices and apartments. The architect was ringing to discuss the planning application. He needs to make one or two small changes to the plan. So it'll take a while to get the application passed. But in the meantime the bookshop will stay as it is, of course. At least that was the plan. But now . . .'

Anita slapped him across the face. 'You nasty little man. How could you?'

Milo put his hands to his face. 'I'm sorry, Anita. But I'm a businessman. At least I was.'

'That's no excuse, Dad,' Sam said. 'Why didn't you tell me at the very beginning? You're unbelievable.'

'I knew you'd never manage to keep it a secret. You'd too damn nice for your own good, Sam, that's your problem.'

'And once the building started, you'd fire me, along with the rest of the staff, was that it?' Sam demanded.

'Of course not, I was hoping you'd manage the whole project. You did do two years of engineering, after all. I thought it would work out for the best. Your brother, Miles, is very happy working for me.'

'I'm nothing like Miles,' Sam said with icy calm. 'I was happy, am happy working in the bookshop. I don't need a high-powered job like you or Miles, working all hours, never seeing my family. I'm ashamed of you, Dad. How could you dupe Anita like that? You promised her that the bookshop wouldn't change.'

'And it won't,' Milo said.

'What?' Anita cried. 'Spit it out, man!'

'That's what I've been trying to tell you all,' Milo said. 'I've changed my mind. I'm not going to develop this site at all. It'll stay as a bookshop. I'm going to sign the deeds over to Sam. I want you to own it, son.'

'I don't want your charity,' Sam said angrily. 'How dare you?'

Milo smiled. 'I knew you'd say that. Which is why I'm going to take a good chunk of the profits for the next ten years until you pay back every penny.'

'Sounds reasonable,' Anita said. 'Don't be stubborn, Sam, take his offer. Stupid man's trying to make amends for what he's done. Idiot that he is.' She shot a withering glare at Milo. 'And don't think you'll be taking me anywhere this evening, you damn fool.'

'But Anita . . .'

'Don't but Anita me. You'll have to do a hell of a lot of grovelling to get out of this one, Milo Devine.'

Milo stifled a smile. 'Yes, Anita,' he said meekly.

'So you'll accept your dad's offer?' Anita asked.

'I'll think about it,' Sam said. 'I'll have to discuss it with Molly first. If she'll manage the shop with me I'll consider it. It would have to be what we both wanted.'

Molly's heart melted. 'Oh, Sam,' she said before she could stop herself. 'I'd love to.'

Anita looked at Molly and smiled warmly. 'Good, that's settled then.' She glared at Milo. 'Count yourself lucky Milo that you're still standing. Now let's get back to work. We have a bookshop to run after all.'

'I'm exhausted.' Molly flopped onto Sam's sofa that evening and kicked her runners off. Her feet were still hurting. 'What a day.'

Sam handed her a steaming mug of peppermint tea and sat down beside her.

'Thanks.' She smiled at him. 'But I still can't believe you didn't tell me about that architect.'

Sam shrugged. 'Sorry, I thought it was for the best. He only rang yesterday and I thought you had enough on your mind to be honest, what with meeting your agent and everything.'

'You're probably right, speaking of which,' she looked at her watch, 'I can't stay long, I have to go home and write. I promised Paige.'

'Not to worry.' Sam reached over, took the mug out of her hands and placed it on the floor. 'But you have to do it for yourself, not for anyone else.'

'I know.'

He smiled. 'But before you go there was something I wanted to ask you.'

'Yes?' she said immediately.

'Don't be so impatient, woman. Follow me.' He stood up and offered her his hand.

She took it and followed him out the door and down the corridor. He pushed open the door of the spare room.

'What do you think?'

Molly looked around. The late August sun shone through the windows, illuminating the new empty pine bookshelves and matching desk.

'Did you make all this?' she asked.

He nodded. 'What do you think?' he asked again.

She smiled. 'It's great. A home office. Now you can mull over all those exciting bookshop invoices from the comfort of your own home.'

He said nothing for a moment, looked at her and smiled broadly. 'It's not an office, it's a study. It's for you. To write your book in. I thought, um, in time, when things settle down with Hugh, that you might like to live here with me. So this will be *your* study, not mine. Well, say something.'

Molly could feel tears prick her eyes. She looked up at him. 'Are you sure?' she whispered.

'Yes, positive.'

'I'd love to live here with you. I understand about Hugh, so whenever you think he's ready that's OK with me. Until then, you might even let me use the study. I think I could write a book here, in fact, I'm sure of it.' She ran her hands over the smooth surface of the top of the desk.

'Of course, it's your room now.'

'And this is the nicest thing anyone's ever done for me.' She threw her arms around his neck. 'Thank you, Sam.'

'It's a pleasure,' he said as she covered his face with kisses.

Chapter 21

Kate

'What are you doing here?' Kate asked Angus suspiciously as she walked into her gran's living room.

He looked at her, red paintbrush in his hand. 'Same as you, I presume, painting – or are they your normal clothes?'

Kate looked down at her ancient navy tracksuit bottoms, complete with holes in the knees, paint-splattered runners and an inside out light grey sweatshirt.

'Of course not,' she replied archly. 'Won't you excuse me?' She flounced out of the room.

'Gran!' Kate said walking into the kitchen where Lily was having a cup of tea. 'What's Angus doing here?'

'I must have forgotten to tell you,' Lily said mildly. 'He offered to help paint today.'

Kate glared at her.

'Don't look at me like that,' Lily said. 'He's a nice lad and very easy to talk to.'

'I have no intention of talking to him,' Kate said sharply.

Lily tried not to smile. Her granddaughter really was very stubborn. But still, it was a good sign if she felt so strongly about Angus. Much better than apathy. 'Why ever not?' Lily asked.

'Just because.' Kate didn't feel like explaining right at this minute. Besides, she wasn't sure if she understood why Angus always managed to get under her skin – it didn't make sense. She'd had quite enough of men in the last while and however 'nice' Angus was she had no intention of becoming involved with anyone ever again. It was time to start concentrating on her career. She had a lot of dummy dates to catch up on – that would keep her busy. She was far too busy to think about anything else. And she'd had a couple of ideas for leather baby shoes – not that she intended to do anything about them of course – but it was nice to know that her talent hadn't completely deserted her as she'd feared. After breaking up with Jay the first time around, Kate thought she'd never design again. Maybe finally her heart was finally starting to heal.

Lily watched Kate's face. She seemed lost in thought. 'Would you like some tea?' Lily suggested. 'Or coffee? Sit down and have a break before you get started with the painting.'

Kate stared at her. 'I'm not painting with *him* in the same room.'

Lily laughed gaily. 'Listen to yourself. You sound like a petulant teenager, Kate. It'll take half the time with the two of you and you can keep each other company. Give it a go and if it's really awful you can leave after lunch, OK?'

Kate muttered something under her breath and walked out of the kitchen.

'I presume that's a no to tea, then,' Lily said to herself. She smiled and hummed softly as she washed down the sink and the kitchen counter tops. Some days she liked cleaning, she found it cathartic. As she wiped down the cooker, she thought about Kate and about Kate's parents. It was no wonder that Kate found it hard to talk intimately to people – her own parents had spent their early married life screaming and shouting at each other. Billy Bowan had never been a nice man. Luckily his fiery temper had abated with age and nowadays he and Cleo, Lily's daughter and Kate's mother, seemed to live a reasonably stable life all things considered. About time too. Lily sighed. It was all in the distant past but Lily feared it had all left an indelible mark on her only grandchild, one which she'd carry for life. It was no wonder she'd always been drawn to attractive, powerful, older and bullying men who ultimately always treated her badly in the end. Men like her own father.

'You're back,' Angus said looking up at Kate. He was kneeling down on the floor, painting carefully around one of the plug sockets with a small brush.

'Let's just get this done,' she said shortly, not wanting to encourage small talk. 'Where are the brushes or will I make a start with the roller?' She surveyed the walls. Angus had already painted the corners, edges and around the plug sockets of three out of the four walls.

'The roller, I think. I'll finish what I'm doing and then I'll join you. What do you think of the colour?'

Kate considered for a moment. Lily had chosen a rich, warm red, very different to the previous creamy white. 'I'm not sure, it's difficult to imagine the whole room red. Won't it make the space seem very small?'

'Maybe. But it's a decent-sized room so it shouldn't matter too much. And the light is very good.'

'I'll guess we'll have to wait and see.' Kate moved towards the paint tins which were resting on a large white dustsheet, aka one of Lily's old bed sheets, and crouched down. She levered the lid off one of the tins and moved the paint tray beside it.

'Let me help,' Angus said. 'Those tins can be a divil to pour.'

Kate was about to refuse his offer but he was beside her before she could open her mouth. He gently took the heavy tin out of her hands and poured a generous amount of the viscous liquid into the tray.

'Thanks,' she murmured grudgingly. She pushed back some stray hair behind her ears and stood up. Tray in one hand and roller in the other she began painting the opposite wall to Angus, as far away from him as she could get.

'How was Boston?' Angus asked after a few minutes. 'Paige told me you were over there for a holiday, lucky thing. I spent a summer working there in college on a J1 visa. I loved it.'

'Really?' Kate left it at that. She had no intention of discussing her trip to Boston with him but she didn't want to completely ignore him – she wasn't that rude.

'Lily told me you used to live in Boston,' he continued unabashed. 'How long were you there for?'

'A while.'

'I see.' Angus wasn't one to be put off easily. He soldiered on. 'I stayed in an apartment near Fenway Park. Mad place. Underneath the apartment block there was a pizza restaurant – very handy, and this second-hand shop which only opened when the owner felt like it. But it had amazing things for sale, dirt cheap too. Old clothes from the '40s and '50s, records and tapes of really bizarre bands and weird hats and shoes. Hundreds and hundreds of pairs.'

'I think I know the place,' Kate said before she could stop herself. 'I used to go there to buy shoes.'

'I forgot about your strange collection.' Angus laughed. 'You'll have to show me it one day.'

Kate went silent again. She hadn't meant to talk to Angus at all. She was letting her resolve slip. She loaded the roller with some more paint and concentrated on covering the wall.

'Little Callum will be in my class this year,' Angus said, still unwilling to give up. 'Did Paige tell you?'

'No.'

'He seems to be really looking forward to school. When I was there on Friday he dressed up in his uniform for me. He was dead funny, parading around the house like a male model. You should have seen him, Kate. His grey trousers were far too big for him – Paige hadn't had a chance to take them up yet. He was tripping over the ends.'

Kate smiled. Callum really was a hoot. 'I hear Tom's taking a year off to mind the kids,' she remarked.

'I know, isn't it great? I think more fathers should do it. It makes sense if their other half has a good job. What do you think?'

'I suppose you're right,' Kate said thoughtfully. 'Although Irish men aren't exactly known for their love of childcare and housework.'

'Hey, that's unfair!' Angus laughed. 'We're getting better. I'd have no problem minding my own kids. I'd love spending time with them. It would be a privilege.'

'You'd like your own then?'

'Of course, wouldn't you?'

'I'm not sure.'

Angus stopped painting and looked at Kate but her back was still towards him. 'Why ever not?' he asked gently.

'Not everyone wants them you know,' she said quietly. 'I suppose you had a happy childhood?'

'Yes. Most of the time. Didn't you?'

Kate said nothing. She continued to move the roller up and down the wall. Angus noticed that there was no longer any paint left on it. He walked over and lifted the tray off the floor for her.

'You might need some of this,' he suggested.

'Thanks,' she murmured, dipping the roller into the tray.

Angus noticed that her eyes were glittering. Surely he hadn't made her cry?

'Um, did you hear about Sam's boy, Hugh running away?' he said, changing the subject.

Kate nodded. 'Molly told me the story. Sam must have been in bits, poor man.'

'He was. But Hugh hadn't gone far, thank goodness. It all worked out all right in the end.'

'And you were great,' Molly said. 'Talking to the lad and making him feel better.'

Angus shrugged. 'Anyone would have done it.'

Kate considered this for a moment. 'No, I don't think they would have. They might have brought the boy back to his parents but they wouldn't have stuck around to help sort everything out.'

'Maybe not. But as I said, I like kids. I just wanted to help.'

'Here,' Kate thrust the roller into his hands, 'I'm just popping out to the loo. Be back in a minute.'

Sitting on the edge of Lily's bath and staring at the white tiled floor, Kate wondered why she was feeling so strange. Lily was right, Angus was a nice man. A very nice man. Not as charismatic as Jay maybe, or as good-looking as some of her previous boyfriends. But he had other qualities. Deeper qualities. Damn it, he was a kind man who cared about other people and he liked her. He'd as much as told her so, over and over again. So what was her problem? She put her head in her hands. Maybe it was finally time to break the habit of a lifetime. She took a few moments to collect herself and then walked back down the stairs to the living room.

'Angus, I've got something to say to you.'

Angus looked over at Kate who was still lingering in the doorway. 'Really?'

Kate smiled. He had red paint splattered in his hair and a large red stripe on his forehead where he must have brushed a painted hand. 'Yes. I'm sorry if I've been a bit . . . um, funny towards you. But you were one of my clients you see.' She stopped, feeling decidedly awkward. 'Anyway, I'm sorry. You're a nice guy.'

Angus sighed. 'I see.' He sounded disappointed. He began to paint the wall again.

'What?' Kate asked. 'What did I just say?'

He raised his eyebrows. 'Are you serious?'

She nodded.

'You called me "nice".'

'So?'

'Kiss of death. Believe me.'

'I really don't have a clue what you're talking about, Angus.'

He snorted. 'Yes you do. Let's just paint.'

'No, I'm trying to talk to you. But you're not making any sense.' She walked towards him. 'You have paint on your forehead.'

He reached his left hand up to touch it.

'It's worse now. Look at your hands.'

Both his hands were covered in red paint. 'What can I say, I'm a messy painter.' He wiped both his hands on his jeans, leaving dramatic red smears all down the denim.

She put her fingers in his paint tray and touched his forehead gently. 'You looked better with the red stripe.' She smiled, backing away from him.

He stared at her, grabbed her hand and forced it onto her own cheek, leaving a blob of red paint.

'Angus!' she shrieked loudly. 'What are you doing?'

'And you look better with red cheeks.' He laughed.

She looked up at him. His eyes twinkled back at her. He was smiling broadly and still holding both her hands, his grip firm. Her breath began to quicken. Was he going to pull her towards him and kiss her?

'What are you thinking about?' he asked. 'You have a funny look on your face.'

'Do I now?' she asked, cocking her head to one side.

'Are you flirting with me, Kate? Because if you are . . .'

'Of course not.' She shook her head. 'Sure, why would I do that? But come to think of it, I do owe you a date.'

'Really?'

'Yes. How about tonight?'

'Are you serious?'

She smiled at him.

Angus smiled back. 'I think that could be arranged.'

Lily backed away from the door. She'd been standing there listening since she'd heard Kate shrieking and had hurried up from the kitchen to check that they weren't killing each other. But from what she'd heard, killing each other was the last thing on their minds.

'So, how was your date with Angus?' Lily asked Kate on the phone the following evening.

'How did you know? Did he tell you, I'll murder him!'

Lily laughed. 'I'm psychic, you know that. And to tell the truth, I also have a bad habit of listening through doorways.'

'Gran!'

'Tush, child. Anyway, are you going to tell me about it or not?'

'I suppose so,' Kate said reluctantly. She knew what Lily was like – she'd go on and on at her if she didn't spill the beans so she might as well. Besides, part of her wanted to tell her gran everything. She'd already told Molly all about it after all. She felt she had to after she and Angus had woken Molly up at one in the morning with their tipsy giggling in the hall.

'It went really well, Gran. We went out for dinner in Cicero's and then went for a walk by the sea. And that's all I'm telling you.'

'Are you seeing him again?'

'Maybe.' Angus was calling over that very evening as Molly was going to the pub with Sam, but she was damned if she was going to tell Lily that.

'I'm glad, he's . . .'

'Nice. I know.' Kate laughed. 'Now I have to go, Gran. I've something in the oven.'

'Dinner for Angus?' Lily asked astutely.

'Gran! Goodbye.'

*

'You look great,' Angus said as Kate opened the door. 'New shoes?'

Kate looked down at her precariously high-heeled strappy silver sandals, peeping out from under her denims. 'Like them?' she asked. 'You don't think they're too much with the jeans?'

'Not at all, they're great.' He handed her a clinking bag.

She peered into it. 'Three bottles!' She laughed. 'Are you crazy? It's a Monday night.'

'We're celebrating.'

'Celebrating what?'

'The full moon.' He grinned.

'You're quite mad, you know that?'

'I'll take that as a compliment.' He looked through the open door into the sitting room. 'Is Molly here?'

'No, she's already left.'

'So just the two of us then?'

Kate smiled. 'Yes. But don't go getting any ideas, young man. Follow me.'

She led him towards the kitchen, plonked the bottles down on the counter, took two glasses off the already-set table and grabbed the corkscrew.

'Red or white?' she asked.

'Red please. Can I open the bottle for you?'

'No, I've got it, thanks.'

Angus sniffed the air. 'Something smells good.'

'It's pasta with meatballs. I hope you like it. I'm not much of a cook but it's fairly difficult to mess up pasta.' She pulled the cork out of the bottle with a resounding pop and poured out the dark red liquid.

'I love it,' said Angus.

'Sit down, it'll be a few more minutes.' She gestured towards the table.

'Thanks.' He looked at the dark pink tulips in the vase at the centre of the table and the candles in their tall silver candlesticks. 'You shouldn't have gone to so much trouble.'

Kate blushed a little. 'It was no trouble, really.' She handed him a glass of wine and tipped her own glass gently against it. 'Cheers! To the full moon.'

'To the full moon and to us,' he said.

After dinner, they slumped onto the sofa in the sitting room, bringing a fresh bottle of wine with them. They'd already shared one bottle and Kate was feeling comfortably relaxed. She'd kicked off her heels and was rubbing the ball of her foot with her fingers. She loved her new sandals but they weren't the kindest to her feet.

'Let me,' Angus offered, putting down his glass.

'No, honestly, I'm fine,' Kate began, but before she knew it he had her foot in his lap and had begun to massage it expertly.

'I used to give my mum foot rubs,' he said, working his thumbs into the ball of her foot and almost making her groan with relief. He really was very good at this, Kate thought. She lay back and closed her eyes. 'Tell me if I'm hurting you.'

'No, that's great.'

After a few minutes he moved onto the second foot. When he'd finished, Kate's feet felt wonderfully rejuvenated. She opened her eyes and smiled at him lazily. 'Thanks, you're a star.'

'No problem.' He brushed a piece of hair away from her face. 'You're beautiful, do you know that?'

Kate smiled. 'And you're very good for my ego. You're not so bad yourself.'

He leant towards her.

Kate's heart gave a tiny leap. He'd given her a gentle kiss on the lips last night while saying goodbye, but she wasn't sure how she'd feel about . . . He leant over again and gave her a firm yet tender kiss. She tried to block all her preconceptions out, and kissed him back, gently at first, then more strongly. To her surprise, he seemed to know exactly what he was doing. To be honest, she'd expected him to be an average kisser at most, but he was actually supremely talented. A little less forceful than Jay, which wasn't a bad thing. In fact, she thought, as he began to stroke her back through her cotton top, Angus was a bit of a natural.

'Are you OK?' he murmured into her neck. 'Should I stop?'

She pulled him closer towards her. 'Don't you dare!'

'You look very happy,' Molly said the following morning over breakfast, instantly noticing Kate's wide smile. 'Good night?'

'Very good thanks.'

'And was that Angus letting himself out earlier?'

'I'm sorry, did he wake you up?'

'It's fine, I was already awake. So he stayed the night then?'

'Might have.' Kate spooned a large amount of cereal into her mouth and crunched away.

'That's great.' Molly smiled. 'He's a lovely guy. Really cute too. Patricia will be livid. She's asked him out several times since the Booksellers' Ball but he's always said no.'

'Really?'

Molly nodded. 'Must have been saving himself for you.'

'Must have, poor man.'

Molly laughed. 'Listen, I bumped into Alex last night in the pub. She said to ask you to drop into the coffee shop first thing, she has news for you.'

Kate glanced at her watch. 'I have a meeting with a client there at nine, so I'll call in a little early to say hi. I wonder what's up.'

'Who knows? She was in flying form though. Harry was there too. They make such a darling couple, don't they?'

Kate nodded and stood up. 'I'd better get a move on then.' She rinsed her breakfast bowl in the sink and dumped it in the dishwasher. 'See you later.'

The coffee shop was quiet and Kate spotted Alex as soon as she walked in the door. She was making sandwiches behind the counter, her back to the room.

'Alex?' Kate said.

Alex turned around and beamed. 'Hi, Kate. Give me one second.' She rinsed her hands under the tap and dried them on her apron. 'Would you like a coffee?'

'Love one.'

'I'll join you if you don't mind. You sit down and I'll be over in a minute.'

Alex brought two large mugs of coffee over with her and sat down beside Kate. She placed her hands on the table in front of her.

'So how are things?' asked Kate. 'Molly told me you had news.'

'I sure do.' She picked up her mug and Kate suddenly noticed the large, sparkling ring on her ring finger.

'You're engaged!' Kate smiled. 'I don't believe it. When did this happen?'

'On Saturday night. We haven't really told everyone yet, so I'll have to take the ring off now, but I wanted you to be one of the first to know.'

Kate leaned over and kissed her warmly on the cheek. 'I'm delighted for you both.'

'And it's all thanks to you,' said Alex. 'I hope you'll come to the wedding.'

'I'd be honoured. But you know, it had very little to do with me, Alex, honestly.'

'But you gave me the confidence to talk to Harry. I would never have approached him without your help. I must recommend you to all my single friends.'

'But remember I don't normally do girls, so to speak.'

Alex laughed. 'That sounded bad, but I know what you mean.

But maybe you should. You have a gift for bringing people together, it's your duty to use it. Us Irish girls need you.'

'Maybe you're right,' Kate mused. 'It might be fun. I'll certainly think about it. Now I think my client has just walked in. If you'll excuse me . . .'

'Of course.' Alex stood up. 'And thanks again.'

A small, red-cheeked man with a receding hairline walked towards Kate. He was wearing a plain navy sweatshirt over what looked like billowing multi-coloured pyjama bottoms. She had her work cut out with this one. She smiled as he approached the table. 'Paddy, I presume?' She stood up and held out her hand.

He nodded shyly, blushed and took her hand in his. He had a surprisingly firm handshake and kind eyes. Maybe there was hope.

'Nice to meet you,' she said. 'I'm Kate.'

Kate swung open the door of Baroque and sauntered in. She'd had a very productive morning, managing to squeeze in three client meetings and a quick lunch with Molly. And Alex's news had put her in a great mood too.

'Hi, Cathy. How was your morning?'

'Fine, thanks. What has put you in such a good mood?'

'Just life in general,' said Kate, dumping her bag on the counter at the back of the shop. 'Beautiful day, isn't it?'

Just then Trina came bustling in the door. 'I have news!' she shrieked. 'I was just at the clinic and I'm pregnant. And the doctor says everything seems to be all right this time. I think I'm going to have a baby!'

Cathy shrieked with joy and immediately gave her a huge hug. 'I can't believe it, that's fantastic!'

Kate watched a little shyly before moving towards Trina and kissing her on the cheek. 'That's great. Well done. When are you due?'

'Around Valentine's Day – can you believe it? I'm so happy.'

'You deserve it after everything you've been through,' said Cathy.

'Thanks.' Trina wiped the tears from her face and sat down. 'Now you'll have to get on with those baby shoes,' she smiled at Kate. 'You have no excuse.'

'Actually I did come up with a few designs,' Kate said casually. 'Would you like to see them?'

'Of course!' Cathy said immediately. 'You're a dark horse, Kate.'

Kate pulled her sketch book out of her bag. She'd intended to work on them a little bit more before showing them to Trina and Cathy but it felt like the right time to share them. It was turning out to be quite a day.

Chapter 22

Epilogue – A Year Later

Paige

'How's my favourite god-daughter? Behaving yourself, Jess?' Angus rubbed the baby's cheek tenderly and gently with his fingers. 'How's she been?' he asked Tom.

'Pretty good, touch wood,' Tom said still standing in the doorway. 'Come in, Callum will be delighted to see you.'

'Mr Cawley!' Callum tore down the hall and threw himself at his favourite teacher.

'You can call me Angus now,' Angus laughed. 'Except in school, of course.'

'But you're not going to be my teacher in September, are you?' Callum asked dejectedly.

'No, you'll have Miss Peters. She's lovely. I hear she gives treats on Fridays to the best table.'

'Really?' Callum couldn't hide his interest. 'What kind of treats?'

'Special pencils, I think. And stickers.'

'And sweets?' Callum asked hopefully.

'I don't think so,' Angus said. 'But you never know.'

'Would you like a cup of tea?' Tom asked him.

'If you're not busy . . .'

'Not at all. It gives me a good excuse not to hang out the baby's washing.'

Angus followed Tom into the kitchen. 'Here, give me Jess while you put the kettle on.'

'Thanks.' Tom handed her over and began to rub his right shoulder. 'She's getting really heavy.'

'Where's Alfie?'

'At Granny's,' Callum interrupted. 'It's just me and Daddy today.'

'And Jess,' Tom reminded him.

'But she doesn't really count,' Callum said patiently. 'She doesn't do anything. Just eats and cries and poos.'

'Callum! He's very taken with his new baby sister as you can see.' Tom laughed.

'After I've had my tea, why don't I take you out for a while, Callum?' Angus suggested. 'Give your dad some peace. What do you think? If that's OK with you, Tom.'

Tom grinned and gave him a thumbs up. 'That would be great.'

'Cool!' Callum practically jumped up and down on the spot. 'Can we go to the zoo, Angus, please?'

Angus looked at his watch. 'Sorry, Callum, we'd never get across the traffic in time. But what about the pet farm in Bray?'

'Yes! I'll just go and get my wellies.' He dashed out of the room. 'And don't worry. I'll tidy up my toys before we go.'

'Hasn't lost any of his energy I see.' Angus smiled at Tom.

'No kidding.'

'So, how are things? Still enjoying being at home? I haven't seen you since the summer holidays kicked in. Sorry I haven't called in sooner.'

'Not to worry,' Tom said. 'Things have been busy but I'm enjoying being with the kids. Most of the time at least. Although I'm not sure about next year. We may need extra help then.'

'Really?' Angus was curious. 'Why so?'

Tom grinned and pushed his hair off his face. He really did need a haircut but with the three kids to keep under control it was hard to find a slot. 'We haven't told many people yet, but Paige is expecting again.'

'No! Are you serious?'

'Couldn't be more so. It's a little sooner than we might have liked, but hey, four is a good-sized family. And they're opening a crèche in the local government offices in Dun Laoghaire which will make life much easier. We've already put Jess and the baby down for it next year. I'm hoping to work in the mornings and look after the gang in the afternoons.'

Angus whistled. 'You'll be busy.'

Tom nodded in agreement, poured boiling water from the kettle into two large mugs and added tea bags. 'Milk and sugar?'

'Both. Two sugars.'

Tom put the steaming mug down on the table in front of Angus.

'Thanks.'

Just then Paige walked into the kitchen. 'Is there enough water for another mug, I'm dying for a cuppa?'

Tom smiled at her. 'Of course, Deputy.' He prepared her a mug, added a dash of milk and handed it to her.

She kissed him on the cheek. 'You're a honey. Hi, Angus. A natural with Jess as always. Would you like to keep her?'

Angus laughed. 'What would you do if I said yes?'

'The way she's been sleeping, I might take you up on the offer.'

'How's work?' Angus shifted Jess a little as his cradling arm was starting to go dead.

'Will I take her for you?' asked Paige, noticing his discomfort.

'Not at all, she's grand.'

'To answer your question, work's great. Busy, but great. I

have a meeting in Blackrock this evening so I'm only home for an hour or two.'

'Tom told me the good news,' said Angus. 'About the baby. Congratulations.'

Paige looked at Tom and back at Angus, grinning ruefully. 'In for a penny, in for a pound as they say. We must be mad.'

'Mad but happy.' Tom wrapped his arms around Paige's waist.

She turned a little and kissed him on the cheek. She felt truly blessed.

Kate

'Do you want them painted?' asked Angus, staring at the new shelves on Kate's living room wall.

Kate thought for a moment. Molly had recently moved in with Sam, leaving Kate with the lease, so she'd decided to live in the townhouse on her own for a while. Her new dating cum matchmaking service for men and women – 'If the Shoe Fits' was doing very well, her baby shoes for Baroque had been a great success and rent money wasn't a problem. Angus was angling to move in with her, but she was enjoying living alone and being self-sufficient. Still it might be nice having him to cuddle up to when the nights got longer. Maybe she'd ask him to move in at Christmas. A new beginning for them both and a good way to banish any lingering Christmas Eve skeletons.

'What about white?' he asked.

'Against the blue? Do you think?'

He nodded. 'Might be quite striking.'

'I think I'll leave them plain wood for the moment. I'll put the shoes out and then we can see.'

'So I'm finally going to see this famous shoe collection,' he said. 'I'm most privileged.'

'Better believe it, Buster.' She smiled. 'I might even let you see my own designs. I won an award for my green "Emerald City" trainers I'll have you know.'

'No!' he joked. 'Not the "Emerald City" trainers!'

She elbowed him in the side playfully. 'Stop slagging me.'

'Ow,' he protested, grabbing her around the waist and pulling her towards him. 'That's how you treat me, after my long weekend of hard work.'

'And Sam had nothing to do with it?' Kate laughed.

'Well, he might have helped a little,' Angus conceded.

'You couldn't have built the shelves without him,' she said. 'Admit it.'

'You're probably right. But I was the one running all the errands to the DIY store when we ran out of things.'

'You were, pet.' She patted his hand.

'I think we should christen the new shelves,' he said, kissing her firmly on the lips and pushing her towards the sofa.

'You don't christen shelves, that's beds.'

'Who says?'

'I suppose you could have a point.' She kissed him back enthusiastically. Angus Cawley had been a revelation to her. Not only was he kind and considerate, he was also passionate, spontaneous and fantastic in bed. To top it all he'd proposed marriage every day since last New Year's. One day in the not too distant future she could even see herself taking him up on the offer.

Molly

'And this is my office,' Molly said proudly to Paige. 'Sam built all the units for me, and the desk.'

'It's fantastic,' Paige said enthusiastically. 'What a lovely place to write. And what a view.'

They both stared out the window. The early evening sun was bouncing off the waves and the sky was still eggshell blue.

'Would you like a glass of wine?' asked Molly.

'Love one.' Paige followed her into the kitchen.

'Sam and Hugh won't be back for ages,' said Molly. 'They've taken Leon for a long walk on the beach to try and tire him out a little. Puppies are a lot of work. But Hugh adores him.'

Paige laughed. 'Wait till you have a baby to contend with.'

'At least babies don't chew the legs off your furniture,' Molly pointed out, 'and you can put them in nappies to avoid all those delightful "accidents".'

'True.' Paige laughed.

Molly handed her a large glass of red wine. 'Cheers!' she said lifting her glass to Paige's. They clinked glasses gently.

'Cheers,' Paige said. 'To you in your new house.'

'Thanks.' They sat down at the kitchen table.

'How's the book doing this week?' asked Paige.

Molly smiled. 'It's doing well from what I can gather. And there were nice reviews in *Dublin Books* and in *Taste*.' Molly's first book, the extended version of her 'Concrete Pictures' story had been published at the beginning of the month. Renamed *Just in Time*, with a show stopping red and white cover, it had already sneaked into the bestseller lists at number five and was the talk of Burnaby. It was hard to miss the dramatic window displays in Happily Ever After, Baroque, Slick Harry's and in Coffee Heaven. Alex and Harry were now married and living in domestic bliss in Wicklow with two black Labradors and a huge black Land Rover and were delighted to support their friend's book.

'And Anita loves it,' Paige reminded her. 'She told me yesterday – I saw her at that new Irish art exhibition in Halo.'

'Was Milo with her?' Molly asked with a smile.

'He most certainly was. Following behind her like a puppy dog, as per usual.'

Molly laughed. 'She still claims she can't stand him.'

'They're as bad as each other,' Paige said. 'And speaking of Milo, how's his son, your other half?'

'Don't call him that!' Molly protested. 'It sounds awful.'

'OK, then, how's your partner?' Paige said in a terrible fake American accent.

'Stop!' Molly giggled. 'Sam's just fine.'

'Good.' Paige smiled at Molly. 'I'm glad you found him. He's a lovely guy.'

'I know.' Molly smiled back. A moment later she gazed into her wine glass. Paige is right, she thought, I am lucky. I found Sam and somewhere along the way I also found myself. I'm Molly Harper, and I'm a writer.